The Burning Stone

JACK WHYTE

VIKING

VIKING

an imprint of Penguin Canada, a division of Penguin Random House Canada Limited

Canada • USA • UK • Ireland • Australia • New Zealand • India • South Africa • China

First published 2018

www.penguinrandomhouse.ca

*Publisher's note: This book is a work of fiction. Names, characters, places and incidents either
are the product of the author's imagination or are used fictitiously, and any resemblance
to actual persons living or dead, events, or locales is entirely coincidental.*

LIBRARY AND ARCHIVES CANADA CATALOGUING IN PUBLICATION

Whyte, Jack, 1940-, author
The burning stone / Jack Whyte.

Issued in print and electronic formats.
ISBN 978-0-670-07000-8 (hardcover).—ISBN 978-0-14-319696-9 (electronic)

I. Title.

PS8595.H947B87 2018   C813'.54   C2018-900626-9
C2018-900627-7

Jacket and interior design by Jennifer Lum
Jacket images: (illustration) Gillian Newland;
(pattern) Yulia Buchatskaya/Shutterstock.com

Printed and bound in the United States of America

10 9 8 7 6 5 4 3 2 1

Penguin
Random House
VIKING CANADA

To my beloved and greatly appreciated wife Beverley,
who seems no less mildly bewildered by this novel's publication
than she appeared to be at the unveiling of The Skystone *in 1992.*

And to two relative newcomers: my great-granddaughters
Reilly Burke, aged eight, and Melia (Millie) Strashuk, aged almost two . . .
the forerunners of an entirely new generation of descendants.

Author's Note

I'm starting to imagine how the late, great Yankee baseball player Yogi Berra must have felt when he was asked to describe what was going through his mind during his change of career from catcher to manager. He ended up, famously, saying that it was like *déjà vu* all over again.

I remember being involved in an almost identical struggle back in 1991/92, when we were preparing to publish my first novel, *The Skystone*.

My primary concern in my Author's Note back then was to give my readers some idea of the makeup and complexity of the Roman armies operating in the Province of Britain in the last few decades of the third century—their composition, their armour and weaponry, their strategies and techniques—and I was able to make a fair stab, I believed at the time, at describing the realities of third-century Roman military life to modern, North American readers.

This time around, though, my expectations have been different, yet oddly similar, grounded firmly in the needs of my twenty-first-century readers to be able to understand things that the common grunt soldier of Roman times understood instinctively, through example and experience. Soldiers used precisely the same kinds of everyday expressions that we still use two thousand years later; we just need to know where to look for them. Simple words such as the throwaway "thanks," ("*benigne*," pronounced with a hard "g" as in "ignore") or the names of the ingredients in a recipe for *garum*, a spicy fish sauce that was to the Roman legionary what tea was to the British Army's Tommy at the peak of the British Empire, seventeen centuries later.

As for pocket money, the largest coins that most legionaries would ever see would have been varieties of the almost pure copper coins known as *asses*, and when they saw those in anything resembling large numbers, they probably said "*benigne*" to the gods of wealth and property. *Braccae* were the leather trousers worn by the legions in winter, and they became the trousers of later years, the original "breeches."

The legionaries used almost the same system of weights and measures used in Britain today (known as the Imperial System), but a Roman pound weighed approximately twelve ounces, about three quarters of a modern, sixteen-ounce British pound, so three Roman pounds weighed close to a modern kilogram.

I went to great pains, in my Author's Note to *The Skystone*, to explain the workings of the various military formations that comprised the Roman Legion: ten cohorts to each legion originally, that number had later been revised to eight cohorts in most instances. I described the eight military centuries contained by each cohort, and the Centurions who commanded them. A full cohort numbered eight hundred men by then, rather than the thousand men of earlier times, so each legion, at full strength, contained a minimum of six thousand, four hundred soldiers, plus all the ancillary forces required—from medical personnel to kitchen staff, armourers, and an entire range of artisans—to keep them functioning. At no time, though, did I take the trouble to explain that, from the ordinary legionary's viewpoint, the most important building in a Roman camp—no matter the size, be it temporary marching camp or permanent legionary fortress—was his personal billet; the tent or barracks house that accommodated him personally, along with the intimately close, eight-man squad with whom he lived and fought. There were eight eight-man squads in each century, and they were quartered in the same position every night they were in camp, sharing everything the army could throw at them. Both squad and billet shared a common name; each was a *contubernium,* its members were called *contuberniales,* and the *contubernium* was the basic unit of a century of six hundred and forty men.

The daily military affairs of the cohorts were supervised by the legion's Centurions, but the legion itself was ruled by the nominal *Legatus Legionis*—the legionary Commander—with the assistance of a crew of staff officers comprising six Tribunes and the legion's senior Centurions. There were two distinct types of Tribune, each immediately identifiable to even the newest recruits. While most of the military Tribunes were ordinary, hard-working professional officers making their way steadily up through the ranks, that was far from being true of all Tribunes. The exception to the norm was the kind known as a *Tribunus Laticlavius,* a direct reference to the wide, highly visible stripe (the *laticlavus*) on his tunic. The *Tribunus Laticlavius* was an open and undisguised man to watch in the political arena, usually the younger son of a powerful senatorial family and almost always the second-in-command of his legion, there to be seen and admired as doing his public duty, no matter how mediocre a soldier he might actually be.

Most modern readers don't know that for several hundreds of years following the time of the first-century invasions under Claudius and the early emperors, there had been only three legions serving in Britain; these were widely and commonly known as the British Legions. I have opted to use the modern equivalent of the official titles of the British Legions in this book, since there were only three of them: Legio XX Valeria, the Twentieth Valeria, was based in Deva, which is now the city of Chester; Legio VI Victoria, the Sixth "Victorious," was based in Eboracum, modern York, though its major fame had been won in Iberia—modern Spain and Portugal—where it distinguished itself under the leadership of the Emperor Flavius; and Legio II Augusta, the legion known as the Second Augusta, which seems to have been headquartered in Isca on the Cornish Peninsula, in the modern town of Exeter in Devon, which was then called Isca

Dumnoniorum. For more than a hundred and fifty years prior to that, though, the Second Augusta was reputedly headquartered in another, more northerly Isca known as Isca Silurum, this one the modern town of Caerleon in south Wales.

And then, of course, there's the whole confusing question of why there were suddenly four emperors at the same time. That situation has perplexed more than a few people over the years, but the answer is really very simple. The period known as the "decline and fall" had its beginnings during the reign of the emperor Commodus, who was villainously played by the actor Joaquin Phoenix in the film *Gladiator*. For the next hundred and more years after his reign, the Empire began collapsing upon itself, and for the last seventy-odd of those years, a hodge-podge of ruinous so-called emperors, all bent upon enriching themselves, neglected the armies more and more outrageously at a time when the imperial borders themselves had never been more vulnerable. Soldiers went unpaid and unfed, and their weaponry and equipment were never renewed or upgraded, so that entire military units eventually began to disappear, drifting off to look after themselves in odd corners of the Imperial countryside, where they could maintain the remnants of their security and survive by their own skills.

That dissolution was stopped, for a hundred years or so, with the arrival of a new emperor called Diocletian, who had been a soldier all his life and knew precisely what was needed to reverse the damage.

He began by acknowledging that the Empire had grown too large for any one man to handle, and so he split it up into East and West, with an emperor and a deputy emperor for each region. The senior administrator was called the Augustus and held full Imperial power. His deputy, in both cases, was called the Caesar and was, *ipso facto*, the heir apparent to the Augustus's powers. It was a sensible system that should have worked perfectly, and it did at the outset until, of course, human nature began to assert itself and idealism once again became politics.

Hand in glove with those changes, Diocletian also moved to breathe new life and morale into the armies, by acknowledging what had gone wrong during the prior seven decades, and by putting an entirely new system of logistical supply and resupply into place, accompanied by a new recruitment campaign to guarantee that the needs of Rome's legions would be properly catered to thereafter.

Once the new system had been tested and proven reliable, though, it quickly became a rich target for organized thievery, perpetrated by the very people who had themselves been exploited by the former system and who now set out to grow rich by milking the new one, thereby drawing attention to the need for some kind of policing force.

It has always been the job of the military to police itself, of course. But how can Authority police itself when the police forces themselves prove unreliable? That matter was never explained or addressed directly during Diocletian's reign or during that of his successor, Constantine the Great, and so the details surrounding the resupply and refurbishment of the Imperial legions seventeen hundred years ago must, of necessity, contain much speculation. But speculation is the food of people who write historical fiction, and that is why this volume is a novel and not an academic treatise.

The Romans used the Julian calendar, whereas today we use the Gregorian calendar, introduced in 1582. There were ten months in the Julian year, and they varied in length from twenty-eight days (February) to thirty-one, with several being twenty-nine or thirty days long. January was the month of Janus, the two-headed god who saw both past and future simultaneously. March was the month of Mars and June the month of Juno, while the meanings of the two between are uncertain today. The next month, originally known as the fifth month, Quinctilis, was eventually renamed July, in honour of Julius Caesar, while Sextilis, the Sixth month, was renamed August, in honour of Caesar Augustus. The four remaining months, the seventh through the tenth, have remained unchanged ever since; September (from the Latin "septem"), October ("octo"), November ("novem"), and December ("decem").

Wednesdays, Thursdays, and Fridays did not exist in Romano-British times. Those names were coined later, to honour the Norse deities Woden, Thor, and Freya, and were added to the Anglo-Saxon language in the early Middle Ages. The soldiers of this tale would have spoken of Sunday as the Sun's Day, and Monday as the Moon's Day. Tuesday, though, was called Mars's Day and Wednesday was the day of Mercury—still called *mercredi* in modern French. Thursday was dedicated to Jupiter, Friday was the Day of Venus, and Saturday was the Day of Saturn. Saturn was also the god honoured at the celebration of Saturnalia, which ran from December 18th through December 23rd and was a season of gift-giving during which traditional familial roles were often reversed, with household slaves and retainers being served and catered to by their owners. It was the precursor of our modern Christmas traditions.

And so the traditional question of the Author's Note has been rephrased yet again: How much information is needed to make the modern reader feel at home in this fourth-century world? I hope this helps a little.

Jack Whyte
Kelowna, BC, Canada 2018

Place Names in the Book

Modern readers who try to identify the Roman towns of fourth-century Britain and France (which was known as Gaul at that time) can quickly become confused and disoriented because the tribal Frankish invasions that eventually changed the region's name from Gaul to France would not begin for at least another century. The reason for all the upheavals, puzzling though it may seem, is very simple: over the intervening centuries, great migrations moved people in unprecedented numbers. They invaded and settled and invariably brought their own languages, customs, and religions to their new homes. Thus, most of the names of the places in existence in Roman times have since changed radically.

Many small, unimportant Roman towns in Britain fell into disuse and disrepair during that time, while other, previously undistinguished outposts sprang into unexpected prominence under the pressures of history. One of the most startling results of all that movement of people, and the changes they brought with them, was frequent name changes for the larger, more permanent, and readily defensible population centres.

The Gallic port originally called Lutetia was home to the earliest Roman garrison fort established in northern Gaul to control the local Celtic tribes of the region. By the time the Romans withdrew their armies back to Italia in 401 A.D., though, its name had changed, and more than a hundred years after that, because of its strategic importance in controlling a key river crossing, the Frankish king Clovis, who founded the Merovingian dynasty, decided to make the former garrison town his new capital, calling it simply Paris.

The modern Turkish city of Istanbul had been a small but strategic port known as Byzantium for centuries, but in 330 A.D. the emperor Constantine rebuilt it and renamed it in his own honour, calling it Constantinopolis, although he also referred to it at various times as New Rome or Second Rome. The Vikings of the ninth century called it Miklagard ("The Great City") and even the Arab world spoke of it with awe, but its name was changed to the much less exotic Istanbul in the early 1950s.

The list that follows here is not at all comprehensive. Most of these names will be alien to readers today, but the places are all still there, and they are, for the most part, still thriving, albeit under different names. Those modern equivalents are listed here, too.

Roman Name	Modern Name	History
Byzantium	Istanbul	Known as Constantinople from the third century onwards, and generally recognized as the most powerful city in the ancient world, after the decline of Rome.
The Hellespont	The Dardanelles	The narrow waterway dividing Europe, on its western side, from Asia, on its eastern one. It also separated the Aegean Sea from the Sea of Marmara and was therefore known as the Gateway to Byzantium.
Caledonia	Scotland	It was long believed that the Roman armies did not penetrate far into Scotland, because there were/are very few Roman roads. But modern aerial and satellite photography, showing the foundations and distinctive outlines of many unsuspected marching camps, has generated a wealth of incontrovertible proof that previous beliefs were wrong.
Cambria	Wales	Modern Wales was not a Roman province and the Welsh did not even exist as a people until after the Roman withdrawals of the early fifth century, at which time a swarm of local warlords sprang up and established themselves as Welsh Kings.

Roman-British Towns

Ancient Name	Modern Name	History
Aquae Sulis	Bath	The oldest urban spa in Britain, its name meant "the waters of Sulis," a British incarnation of Minerva. It became modern Bath because its hot springs and baths were still active and working during the Middle Ages, centuries after the Romans left.
Branodunum	Brancaster	A road stop on the northern coast of Norfolk, the Roman settlement was the site of one of the Forts of the Saxon Shore, a series of castles built to defend the country against the Anglo-Saxon invasions that were beginning to come from the Germanic territories.
Camulodunum	Colchester	Colchester was the oldest Roman settlement in Britain, and had been the administrative centre of the Catuvellauni Celts since long before the Romans first invaded Britain in 43 A.D. The Celtic queen Boudicca destroyed it in 60 or 61 A.D., and then Claudius rebuilt it. He called it Colonia Victricensis, but then renamed it Camulodunum, perhaps in honour of its original name. No one knows how its name came to be changed to Colchester, but the suffix "chester" means that the town was

Roman-British Towns

Ancient Name	Modern Name	History
		once a *castra*—a Roman camp— and the local river is called the Colne, derived from the Roman word *colonia*, so the connection there seems self-evident.
Eboracum	York	One of the three great legionary fortresses that housed the so-called "British Legions," Eboracum was home to the Sixth Victrix Legion, which I have dealt with in my Author's Note.
Glevum	Gloucester	One of the most important river ports in western Britain, it lay on the upper reaches of the Severn estuary. At the time of this novel, it was still an active and very important port.
Isca Silurum	Caerleon, South Wales	Isca Silurum and Isca Dumnoniorum were both, at different times, home to the headquarters of the Second Augusta Legion, which moved its base as the military and political realities of Britain changed.
Isca Dumnoniorum	Exeter, third-century Cornwall	By the time of this novel, Isca Silurum in Wales had long been relegated to a lower status, while Isca Dumnoniorum had gained importance as the primary military base in South Britain.

Roman-British Towns

Ancient Name	Modern Name	History
Lindinis	Ilchester	Never a very great town, Lindinis owes its inclusion here to the fact that it was the closest settlement to the *colonia* that the Varrus family would establish at the place they called Camulod, close to the great north-south road that divided Britain.
Londinium	London	I have included this not merely for its generally known history, but also because it is a shining example of just how many changes the name of any city might have gone through from Roman times to our own.

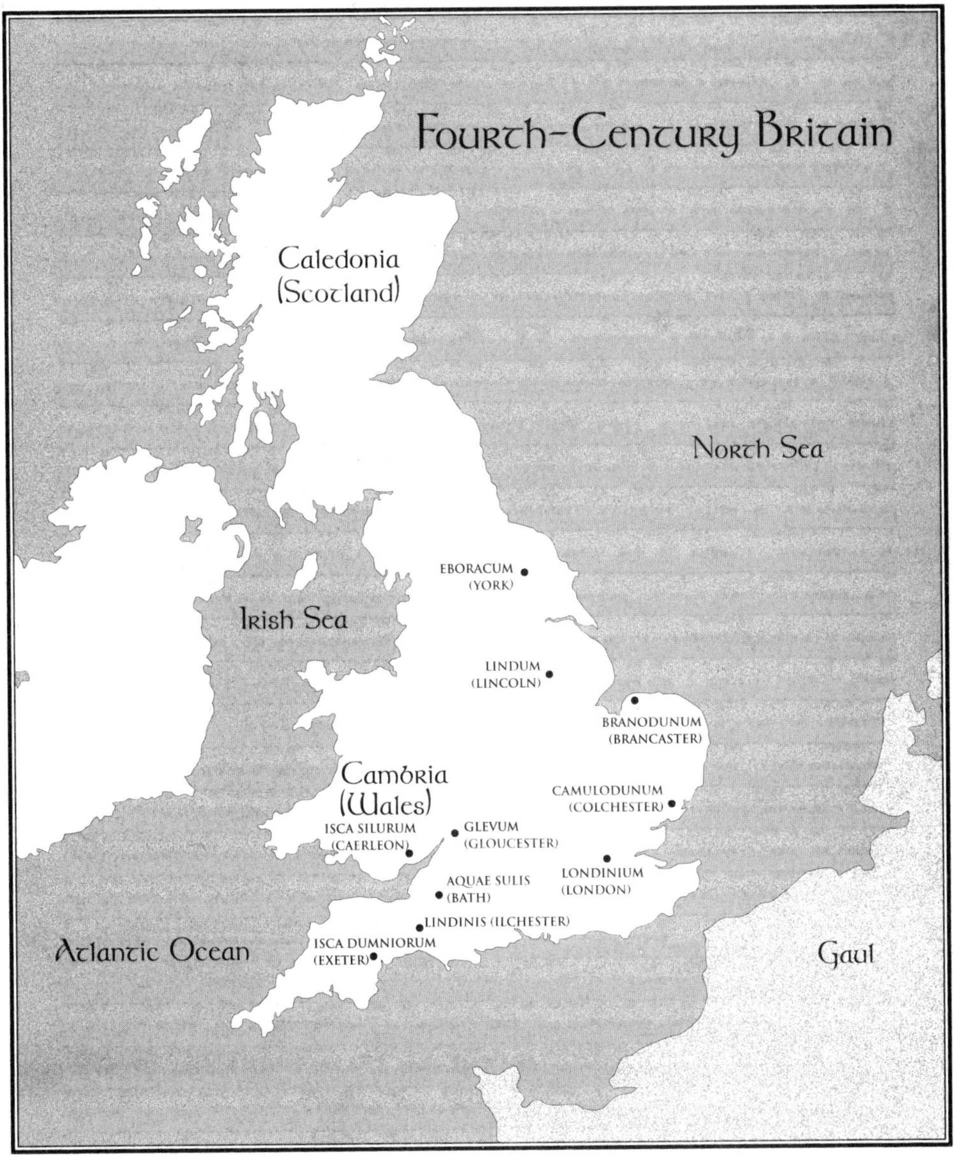

Fourth-Century Britain

Caledonia
(Scotland)

North Sea

Irish Sea

EBORACUM
(YORK)

LINDUM
(LINCOLN)

BRANODUNUM
(BRANCASTER)

Cambria
(Wales)

CAMULODUNUM
(COLCHESTER)

ISCA SILURUM
(CAERLEON)

GLEVUM
(GLOUCESTER)

AQUAE SULIS
(BATH)

LONDINIUM
(LONDON)

Atlantic Ocean

LINDINIS (ILCHESTER)

ISCA DUMNIORUM
(EXETER)

Gaul

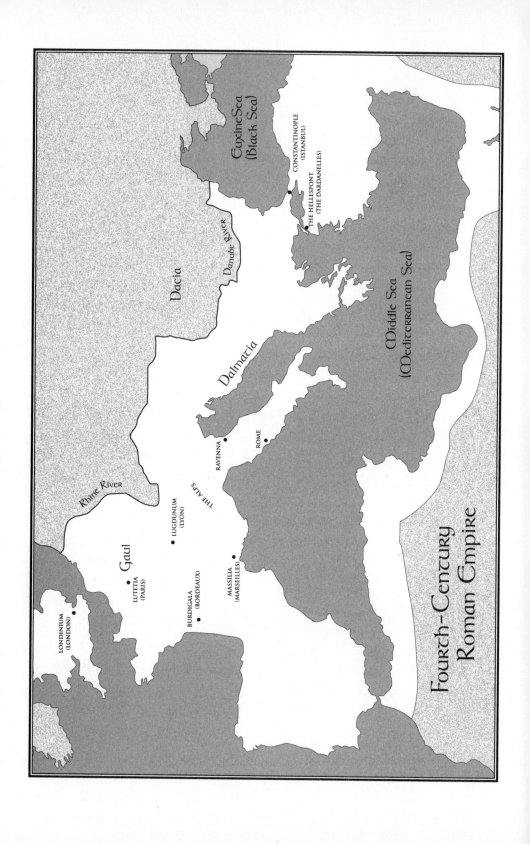

Fourth-Century
Roman Empire

PROLOGUE

Dalmatia, A.D. 310

"*S*wine shit!"

Young Quintus Varrus would never forget his grandfather's unexpected roar, for the oath was one the old man seldom used, saving it for special occasions.

Nor would he soon forget his father's reaction to it, for Marcus Varrus froze in mid-word, shocked into silence by the outrage in the old man's tone, and his eyes went wide in a way Quintus might have thought comical at any other time.

"*Listen* to yourself, man," his grandfather snarled. "You're puling like a baby, whining and whimpering like one of your Christian priests caught out in the streets alone, without an army of guttersnipes to back him up. Straighten up and behave like the man you should be. You're my *son*, by all the gods, a Roman legate, and I'll ask you to remember that—respect *my* dignity, at least, even if you show no consideration for your own."

Marcus Varrus drew his shoulders back, rigid with affront at his father's scorn, and watching him, Quintus knew instinctively that he was fighting not to answer too quickly. Quintus knew how much his father despised his tendency to stammer slightly when he grew upset, believing others would perceive it as a sign of weakness, and now the boy held his breath as he watched from his hiding place, seeing his grandfather's eyes narrow angrily in preparation for another outburst. Surprisingly, though, the old man waited, pointedly allowing his son the time to find the words he needed.

There were no servants in the dining room—his grandfather had banished them as soon as this latest argument began to show signs of boiling over—and none of the other three people sitting at the table even stirred. It seemed to Quintus that each of them was holding his or her breath too, eyes switching from one to the other of the two standing men.

Across from where his father and grandfather stood confronting each other as usual, his mother, Maris Antonina, appeared to be on the verge of tears, her nether lip quivering as she stared in wide-eyed supplication at her husband, willing him to keep quiet in the face of his father's growing wrath. Quintus's grandmother Alexia Seneca sat with her back to his hiding place, but he knew she would be wearing her usual ill-tempered glare of disapproval and he paid her no more attention, for among the multitude of the extensive Varrus family, she was the one he liked least. Quintus was far more interested in what his uncle Marius might be thinking of the current clash between the family's two dominant bulls.

Quintus was looking almost directly at him where he sat slouched with one elbow propped on the arm of his chair, his cheekbone resting on his knuckles as he watched the familiar, developing confrontation between his father and his brother. Marius had long since learned to watch, listen, and hold his opinions close during such arguments. Quintus knew that he was right to do so, for any attempt to intervene would instantly cause the other two to unite against him. Marius was Quintus's favourite among all his relatives, but to the rest of the family he was a disappointment and a black sheep.

Now his uncle stirred and turned slowly to look directly at Quintus's hiding place, one eyebrow rising high in an expression that was only slightly derisive while the lid of his other eye drooped slowly in a long, droll wink. They had shared such moments before, these two, and were veterans at surviving the constant squabbling that consumed the household by refusing to become involved. In fact it was his uncle who had shown him the hiding place behind a screen in the little-used side-board, having discovered it himself as a boy.

The two men had been arguing for some time, each as stubborn and unyielding as the other, their voices growing louder and more bel-ligerent, with neither man showing any sign of backing down, and now the moment had come when tempers would either boil over into fury or abate into sullen, simmering resentment. When Quintus's father finally spoke, however, his words were far less incendiary than anyone there expected.

"I was not *whining*, Father." Marcus spoke quietly, his voice almost calm, though his words emerged no less forcefully. "I merely said the way the negotiations between Constantine and the Christian leaders are developing would appear, according to the Christian pontifex, to be the will of god—"

"I heard what you said!" his father bellowed. "God's *will* was what you said, by all the gods at once. Or is it the *one* god's will, is that what you mean? The Christian god's? And if that *is* your meaning, tell me this: since when have you or I or any of us paid lip service to the god of the Christians or to his will? Since when have we abandoned our Roman gods? Did I not fight for years for my belief in them, spilling Christian blood under Diocletian's command in protection of our ancient deities? And since when has *any* man, priest or emperor, presumed to know the will of the gods? Is this Christian pontifex of yours more powerful than Rome's own Pontifex Maximus—or even more learned than Constantine and his advisors—that he dares to make such claims?"

"The Christian leader calls himself a bishop, not a pontifex," Marcus answered. "That error was mine. But yes, he believes he is all those things. He believes it because—"

"Hah! I *know* why he believes it. He believes it because he has no other choice, because his life and his livelihood depend upon it. He believes it because he *has* to. He believes it loudly and incessantly, day in and day out, because were he to stop proclaiming his belief from the rooftops, even for a day, he would be a dead man in very little time. He would starve, as men with nothing of value have always starved, or someone would kill him for lying to them for so long. He continues to live solely because most men are cowards and walk in fear of this god of his who might—just *might*—be able to strike them down from afar by some kind of sorcery or necromancy, though in truth he has no more physical substance than has Mars or Vulcan. What about you, Marcus Varrus? Do you believe this god of his has such power? What do you really know of this god, this Jesus that they worship? He's Jewish, is he not? A Hebrew from Judea?"

"He was. At least the man who reared him as his son was."

"Aha! The father of the god. Well, at least he's not so omnipotent that he can exist without a father. So, then, a Jewish, therefore an anti-Roman, god. Do you believe this Jewish Christian god has power over all the earth and skies?" He held up a warning hand. "You yourself, I mean. Not his followers—I don't care what *they* think. Do *you* believe he has such power?"

Marcus looked steadily back at his father. "I don't know, Father," he said finally. "If he is a god, as they say he is, then perhaps he has. But I'm not a Christian, as you are well aware. I merely work with them, as Constantine's envoy."

"But your wife is one of them." Grandfather Titanius turned his head to look at his daughter-in-law, Maris, for whom he had always shown great affection. "What think you, Daughter? Do you believe your Jesus god is all-powerful?"

Quintus's mother tilted her head high. "I do, Father," she said quietly.

The old man grunted. "I know you do, girl, and in a strange way I envy you your conviction, for I know it is real and deeply felt. But tell me this: do you believe this meek and humble Jesus god, whom your people call the Christus, would wantonly destroy a large group of men who offered him no offence? Could such a thing occur?"

Maris kept her chin held high, not haughty or defiant, but solemn and secure in her beliefs. Quintus saw that she was frowning slightly, however, as though troubled by her father-in-law's question, and he sensed that his mother was unwilling to respond too quickly to a query that might have hidden barbs. He himself had detected a strangeness in the deliberate way the question had been phrased. His father, too, was reacting to some sudden tension in the air, frowning in concern at his wife, then shifting his eyes suspiciously towards his father.

"Why would you ask Maris that, Father? She has no—"

"Be quiet and listen. This is important. Maris? Could that happen?"

"Could it—? Let me understand you clearly, Father Titanius. Wantonly, you said. Are you then asking me if my God would wantonly destroy anyone or anything without provocation?"

"I am."

She sat up straighter, turning the flap of her decorative stole back over her shoulder with one hand. "No, Father Titanius, my God would never do such a thing."

"And he is the one, true God, you believe? The only one?"

"That is what we believe."

"There are no others?"

Maris again shook her head. "Men speak of other gods, but they are all false. God is God. A single being, although with many names. The Creator of all life."

"And he is triune, is he not? Threefold? Father, son, and spirit, all in one?"

"So we believe."

"And what about the threefold deity of Egypt—Osiris, Horus, and Isis—that ruled before him? Does that not give you pause?"

"There was no God before Him, Father Titanius. God is God. It matters not what names men give to the Deity."

Titanius Varrus gave his son a sidelong glance before swinging back to address his daughter-in-law again. "Was your God omnipotent when Diocletian ruled the empire?"

Maris smiled gently, nodding her head as though humouring a child. "He was omnipotent before Rome began, Father, before the empire came to be. He made this world and all things in it."

"Of course. I merely wanted to be sure." He turned again to face his son, whose eyes flicked between his wife and his father. "So," the old man continued, "if this god will do no harm unprovoked and there is no other with his supernatural powers, how can we, or anyone, explain what happened to Petronius Provo's two cohorts in Dacia?"

For a space of heartbeats there was no response, and safe in his hiding place Quintus tensed and leaned forward, one hand cupping his ear towards the men so as not to miss a single syllable of what was to come. When his father did speak, though, he sounded mystified.

"Petronius Provo," his father said. "I know that name, or I used to . . . Is he not a friend of yours?"

His father grunted. "He's a dead man now. Long since gone. But he and I were close once. We grew up together. He and Diocles and I."

Marcus was frowning in concentration. "I remember that, too," he said. "At least I think I do. A long time ago, and there was something that happened in Dacia. I don't remember . . . What was it?"

The older man scowled, glowering from beneath his bushy eyebrows as he peered into nothingness. "No one was ever able to say what it was," he growled.

Quintus squirmed a little as he saw his father assume his affronted look again, peering about him theatrically as though to emphasize his disbelief. Even at the age of ten Quintus knew it was an affectation, but he suspected that his father was unaware of the mannerism, or that he used it so obviously.

"What?" Marcus Varrus said. "Do you mean that this event, involving damage or detriment to two prime cohorts in the field, went unreported?"

Titanius Varrus straightened up slightly, his eyes narrowing further as he contemplated his firstborn son with increasingly withering contempt. "Oh, you love the thought of that, don't you," he said, his voice barely audible. "An error of omission in the highest ranks, in the field. A missing tactical report, depriving the Emperor's busy little fact-finders of an opportunity to pry into places they should never be allowed to see. That sets your little martial heart to fluttering, does it not?" He grimaced, before squaring his shoulders and speaking again in his normal voice, the syllables emerging from his mouth crisply and in the tones of a military report. "If your question was intended to imply that someone present failed in his duty to record the magnitude of what took place that day, then my answer is that the sole failure of any person present at the events of that day was the failure to survive."

Quintus had heard every word, but he had no idea what his grandfather had actually said.

"What—?" Marcus swallowed. "I must have misheard. Did you say, a failure to *survive*?"

Titanius Varrus nodded. "That is precisely what I said. Whatever happened in Dacia that afternoon, not a single person lived to tell of it."

"But that's . . . that is clearly impossible, Father. Some must have survived, no matter how great the damage. There must have been at least two thousand men there."

"There would have been, normally," Titanius said, eyeing his son levelly. "I would even say perhaps three thousand, were one to include the usual adherents—families, retainers, camp followers, and the like. In this instance, though, all of those were marching with me in the main body, because Provo and his men were on high alert, carrying their own rations and moving too urgently and too quickly to wait for a baggage train and extra bodies. Also, we had been out there for a few months and had twice taken heavy casualties, so all told there were probably little more than a thousand men in his group. Eleven hundred at most. But every single one of them died."

His eyes went blank for a moment, but then he continued. "Until I saw the carnage with my own eyes, I was, like you, unable to believe such a thing could be possible. But it happened, and the carnage was absolute. Provo's cohorts weren't decimated—they were *annihilated*. When we reached the scene, four days later, we found no signs of life. There were no survivors, and hence, no written eye-witness reports. We also found no corpses."

"But—" Again Marcus Varrus had to stop, unable to find words to frame the questions he needed to ask. "So what *did* you find?" he finally blurted, all semblance of theatricality forgotten, though his disbelief was still clear in his voice. "*Some*one must have seen it, else how could you know what happened? It happened in the afternoon, you said, and four days before you arrived there. How could you possibly know that, if no one saw it and lived to tell of it?"

"I did not say no one saw it," Titanius Varrus said. "I said no one who was there when it happened survived. I saw it happen myself, with my own eyes, and heard it with my own ears."

"Then you *were* there . . ."

"So you might think, but no."

Marcus Varrus said, in a slow, placatory voice, "Father, believe me, I have no wish to quarrel with what you say, but that makes no sense."

"I agree. But I remind you that your objections are based upon human expectations. There was no human logic, and certainly no simple truth, in any of what happened that day. Forget simplicity," he said. "Attempting to attribute simplicity to any part of this renders you unable to imagine what I'm talking about. You fail to understand how I could see something without being there to witness it. *Think*! How could such a thing be possible?"

In the profound silence that followed, Quintus, in his hiding place, watched his grandfather look around him slowly, eyeing each of his listeners in turn.

"You need to pay heed to what I *said*," Titanius continued. "I told you I arrived at the place four days after the event took place, and yet I saw it happen. And how could that be, was all you asked. Well, it *could* be, and it *was*, because this incident took place on a more massive scale than anyone could comprehend.

"I saw it because I was looking up when it took place. In the space of an instant, and without warning of any kind, an enormous, indescribable noise filled our whole world, snatching the living breath from our chests and shaking the very air around us, and a gigantic ball of fire shut out the afternoon sky. It came from behind me, screaming across the firmament from east to west and turning the blue of the sky to smoke-roiled blackness in less than a blink. My horse spun around and instantly fell dead beneath me as the thing passed over us, and I ended up face down in the mud, grovelling like a terror-stricken slave and doubting my own sanity. Then all the world went white in one searing moment of . . . of what I can only think of as unnatural, even supernatural light, and there came a sound the like of which I have never heard again. Whatever it was that had passed above us, it deafened many of our men and blinded others, some of them for days, and others forever."

No one moved or breathed.

"One moment the day was tranquil and all was as it should be, and in the next instant the world was filled with noise and chaos, our army reduced to a state of gibbering, mindless terror. The western sky turned red, pulsing like a living heart before it quickly died away into roiling brown and black, smoky darkness, shot through with fire that engulfed the mountains beyond our horizon. But that face-down mud bath might have saved my life, or at least my vision, for it put my back towards the flash when it happened. All the men who were blinded that day had been facing west, looking towards the mountains when that blast of light occurred."

He moved to where Quintus's mother sat listening in open-mouthed horror and reached out to take her hand in both of his. "I swear to you, Daughter," he said, "on the honour of my name and that of your children, that every word of what I have said is true." He released her hand

and she sat frowning, her hand upraised still, her wide eyes fixed upon his face.

Marcus Varrus shook his head. "It was four days, you said, before you visited the spot where Provo and his men vanished, never to be found. Why did it take you so long?"

"Because we were that far away, with a range of mountains between us and where Provo and his people were supposed to be. The entire catastrophe—be it an explosion or an eruption—happened late in the afternoon, but it was almost as disastrous for us as it was for those poor whoresons who took the brunt of it. I know that sounds bizarre, but it is no exaggeration. What happened that afternoon came close to destroying not merely my command but my career as a soldier, and to this day I have never told anyone about it in detail."

"Never?" Marcus asked.

His father looked at him, and in his hiding place young Quintus was astonished to realize that there was no anger in the old man's face, and there had been no goading challenge in his father's question. He could not remember when he had last heard the two men speak to each other with genuine civility.

"Never," Titanius Varrus said. "Your mother has heard the tale before, many years ago, soon after the events took place, but I have never spoken of it to another living soul. What would there have been to discuss, with someone who had not been there? Judge from your own reaction to what you have just heard, and believe me when I tell you that no one who had not been there and witnessed the aftermath could ever begin to imagine the scope of it. And as for trying to describe it . . ." He grunted a sound that might have been a dismissive laugh. "There are no words powerful enough. Not in my mind, and not in all the books ever written. There are no words . . ."

He walked to the head of the table and resumed his seat, waving Quintus's father to his own chair as he did so. "Sit down," he said. "I don't know if I can talk much more about this, after so many years, but now I am willing to try, at least, and it will take time. We might as well be comfortable."

He turned then to his wife. "Alexia, you might not wish to hear this, so if you prefer to leave I will not be offended."

The old lady stirred slightly and turned to face her husband. Quintus wondered how she would respond, for she was notoriously sharp-tongued, but all she did was shrug.

Her husband nodded. "As you wish," he said, then drew a deep breath.

"I always detested Dacia," he said. "It's a foul, unfriendly place, unfit for human habitation, and we were deep in the heart of it, in the region the locals call Carpathia. We had been there for more than two months, a half-strength legionary force of five cohorts. The high command didn't think the opposition we were facing merited the attention of a full legion, and so we were detached as a special task force. Each of our cohorts had a full complement of six hundred fighting men—ten sixty-man maniples—with appropriate support staff and a full century of auxiliary forces, specially trained locals recruited from the surrounding region and thoroughly familiar with fighting in that kind of terrain. We numbered more than six thousand personnel, and I was the commanding legate.

"It had been a brutal campaign, against a force made up of Visigoths and Vandals—that's what we believed, at any rate, for we never came close enough to them to discover whether it was true or not. They were mountain fighters, though, and they were on their home ground, hitting us hard and withdrawing before we could react. They had started raiding south into our jurisdiction from the Danube territories towards the end of May, and they had been leading us on a chase ever since, using hit-and-run tactics that we were almost powerless to fight.

"They would hide from our sight for several weeks—an easy thing to do in those endless, forested hills—and then they would hit us from all sides at once, striking hard and inflicting heavy casualties, then disappearing like smoke before we could form our battle lines. We were practically helpless among those trees, as you can imagine. Our auxiliaries were a godsend, but there were only a hundred of them to begin with, and we had no replacements for them as they fell.

"Eventually we grew familiar with the terrain, and we worked out a plan to bring the bastards to bay. We would split our force in two, to catch them between a hammer and an anvil at the southern end of a chain of mountains high enough to stop them running away. I took three cohorts along the main road on the eastern flank of the mountains—though 'main road' is too generous for what was little more than a goat track—while Provo took his force down along the western flank, on the other side of the range. Theirs was the more difficult route, for they had no road at all and had to traverse cliffs and slopes that were sometimes close to vertical, but they were able to make better progress because we had their baggage with us.

"But less than a week after we had set out, some kind of pestilence broke out among Provo's legionaries, and it decimated them in a matter of days, according to his scouts, who had finally caught up to us after days of searching.

"My force was close to the south end of the mountain range by that time, about five miles from our goal and about fifteen miles south of where Provo had been forced to make camp and allow his men to rest. He sent word with the scouts that he would come to me in person to report his situation, because he was afraid his men were unfit to fight and he wanted to talk to me. He said that after his scouts got back and told him where to find us, he'd come directly across the mountain separating us."

"And did he?"

Titanius shrugged. "I never heard from him again. He must have died with his men."

A brief silence settled over the group, until Marcus Varrus said, musingly, "No one ever speaks of Dacia nowadays. I don't even know where it is."

"And that is as it should be," his father said. "It's an abominable place, mostly untracked forests and unclimbable mountains. The Black Sea is its eastern border, and its southern one is the north bank of the Danube. And in the north and west, it's shut in by the mountains. The entire country is covered in impenetrable forests, with scarcely a usable road in the whole godforsaken place. Those of us who were tasked with holding and maintaining it were glad when we abandoned it to the Goths, back in the thousand and twenty-fifth year of Rome—what the Christians now call the year 272."

"That was three years before I was born," Marcus said.

His father quirked one eyebrow upwards. "Aye," he growled. "I suppose it was . . . Anyway, we were there two years before that—were there for five years, in fact, before they called us home—but it would have been late in 270 when the thunderbolt fell."

Another pause ensued, and Quintus tried vainly to hitch himself closer to the partition between himself and the speakers, but his face was already pressed against the fretted carving of the screen that concealed him. He heard his father say, "The thunderbolt. Is that what you call it?"

Titanius nodded, his expression sober.

"A thunderbolt the likes of which the gods would hurl in ancient times? Is that what you mean?"

Another nod and no change in the older man's expression. "Precisely the same. Had you seen what I saw that afternoon, you would have no thought of questioning the name."

"It . . . fell, you said. Did you see it fall?"

"No. I saw it pass above my head, but I didn't see it strike with my own eyes."

Everyone at the table sat silent after that, and to Quintus it seemed as though they had all been stricken mute, incapable of asking what he himself was on the point of crying out to know: what was a thunderbolt, and where had this one come from?

"So what did you do then?" his father asked eventually. "After the thing had fallen, I mean."

Titanius shook his head. "I have no idea. I can't remember . . ." He looked around at his family. "I know that must sound like dereliction of my duty, but I swear it was no such thing. I've tried ever since that day to recall what happened afterwards, but I have no memories at all. I suspect, though, that the truest answer would be *nothing*. For it had seemed to all of us when the thunderbolt came down on us that the world was ending. We did nothing for the longest time, and I have no idea how much time went by before we began to gather ourselves together and regain our wits. We had been plunged into chaos in a single heartbeat, our formations destroyed and our military readiness wiped out as though it had never been. Our pack animals all ran amok, screaming and bawling in terror, and most of the wagons they had been pulling were overturned and shattered beyond repair."

He paused. "It was the screams of the men that frightened me most, though. I must have been deafened at first, for I remember my hearing came back to me very gradually. When first I looked up from the mud, the whole world was silent. There were empty-faced men walking and staggering everywhere I looked, most of them in armour and none of them in control of themselves or anything else. They all looked demented. And though I could hear nothing, I could see they were all screaming, as mindlessly terrified as the beasts, and I was no exception. Seeing my own soldiers all around me, lost and witless, appalled me to the depths of my being. Officers and men alike, uncomprehending and bereft of hope . . .

"And then my hearing started to return and all the horror of the screaming settled over me—the screams of maimed and mutilated men and animals and the unhinged, mindless screams of men demented by fright they were ill equipped to handle." He stopped again, staring into nothingness, then added, "And yet, terrified and demoralized as we were in the chaos that now surrounded us, we were days away from where the thunderbolt landed."

Titanius looked over at his son, his head tilted slightly to one side. "And so, perhaps you can understand why I chose never to speak of it with anyone. What could I have said? How could I explain it? There had never been anything like it. Our chief surgeon was a Greek. He came up with a Greek word for it. Called it *cataclusmos*, a kind of unimaginable disaster."

"So you made no move to look for Provo at that time?"

"*Look* for him?" It seemed for a moment that Titanius might smile. "Nobody even thought of him. We had enough troubles of our own to keep us all hard at work that night. It was only after our recovery efforts started that we began to discover we had more than a hundred men who had been maimed—blinded and deafened. How were we to deal with that? Our surgeons were trained to deal with battle wounds. They were ignorant of what to do to help those men. And that is just one minor example of what we confronted.

"No, we didn't think about Provo and his men until the afternoon of the following day, once we were satisfied we had returned everything in our camp to some kind of order. It never occurred to any of us that any harm might have come to them. We knew they were more than fifteen miles away, and on the other side of the mountain range, so it would not have seemed possible that Provo's people might have experienced anything similar to our own upheaval, let alone worse. But then two of our scouts came in from the west side, bringing stories that would have been unbelievable the day before. The news they brought back of the things they'd seen, distant scenes of raging fires and roiling chaos, was dire enough to start us moving quickly.

"I decided to go looking for Provo myself and ordered a full century, a hundred men, to march with me, each man with rations for a week. We left at dawn the next day, in pouring rain that lasted the entire day and made every step a misery."

"And it took you two more days to find Provo?"

"No, it took us two days to find the place where he might once have been." Titanius cocked his head again the way he had earlier, as though trying to hear something just beyond the range of his ears. "We never did find Provo, or any of his men," he said. "We never even discovered where they had been when the thunderbolt fell. We never went to look for them. It would have been pointless.

"We had been fighting against rain and mud and slippery slopes all day long, clambering hand over fist every step of the way up ever-increasing inclines as we fought to reach the crest of that damned mountain. The sky ahead of us was dark—black dark, the air filled with foul smoke. It stank abominably. There was no sign of flames or living fires, just that wretched, all-consuming stench of burning filth.

"The first of our men reached the top of the ridge eventually, a cause for celebration at any other time. I was in the second wave of climbers, and I remember thinking it strange that the men above us were as quiet as they were. Strange and ominous. When I made it to the crest they were all standing with their backs to me, staring into the distance ahead, and something inside me died when I saw what they were looking at."

He fell silent and everyone waited for him to resume, but it became clear that he had become lost again in his own memories.

Marius cleared his throat. "What did you see, Father?"

"A wasteland," Titanius said quietly, his eyes focused on some inner vista that no one there could share with him. "A wasted land unlike anything I have ever witnessed."

"Well, you've already said the place was unfit for human habitation." Quintus noted that his father's tone was decidedly less contentious than before.

"That was how it was in the normal run of things—a pigsty of a place. What I saw from that mountaintop, though . . . that was completely different, something stunning to contemplate." He frowned. "Have you ever seen grass bend?" The old man did not wait for an answer. "What I saw reminded me of a thing I had seen with the Emperor as a boy, but had forgotten for thirty years. That was near the town of Salona, in

Dalmatia, where Diocles and I grew up. We couldn't have been more than eight or nine years old, and it was near harvest time. We had been playing wolves with old Ankora's sheep, chasing them and frightening them half to death, when the old man himself caught us in the act. We knew we were in for a flogging if he came close enough to recognize us, but we knew, too, that he was more than half-blind, so we ran to hide among his standing crop. It had been a perfect year for growing grain and the crop was perfectly ripe, golden and heavy and thick, and we dived into it. Diocles landed beside me, giggling with that kind of insane glee that boys sometimes use to mask the terror of being caught and punished.

"He had been bending sideways as he ran, and as he fell flat, sliding along the ground, I was astonished to see what happened to the stalks of grain around him. They flattened and radiated outwards ahead of him in a wave, a wall of straws flattened, creating a circular pattern like those you sometimes see when a gust of wind strikes a field of grain. I saw exactly the same pattern on the day I stood on that mountaintop in Dacia and looked down on the devastation in the valley below."

"Waves of grain?"

Quintus could hear that mixture of not quite sneering contempt and patronizing condescension his father used when questioning Quintus about his sins. But if his grandfather noticed it, he ignored it.

"No, not exactly," Titanius Varrus murmured. "I was looking down on what had been a thick evergreen forest, undisturbed since time began. Yet each full-grown, straight-boled tree, four or five times the height of a mounted man, had been flattened like a stalk of straw. The valley below us was vast, wide enough for the far side to be invisible through the smoke in the distance and long enough, following the swell of the mountain chain, to suggest it might be ten miles or more in extent, north to south. At the centre of it all, perhaps a mile and a half from where I stood, was a black abyss, and from it the destruction stretched outwards as far as I could see on every side."

Quintus struggled to imagine the sheer, awe-inspiring scope of what his grandfather was describing. He could see part of it, each straw a tree, an entire forest levelled by the fury of whatever had happened, but his mind was incapable of envisioning the scale of such destruction, let alone the force that would be required to generate such havoc. When he looked out again into the dining room, he was astonished to see that the adults were no less incredulous than he was. They stared at the old man, uncomprehending.

It was Marius who asked the obvious question. "What was the black abyss, Father?"

Titanius Varrus looked again into the distance. "It was an enormous hole, obviously—incredibly long and wide and seemingly bottomless, and it had swallowed Provo's cohorts."

"All of them, a thousand fighting men? Surely not."

Quintus waited for his grandfather to respond angrily, as he invariably did upon having his words questioned, but the paterfamilias merely shook his head. "None survived that I ever saw. They were swallowed up and lost. We thought to go and look for them, but it was impossible even to approach the area."

"So you merely left them there, abandoned them?" Quintus's father asked, and the boy saw confusion stamped clearly on his face.

Once again the old man showed no sign of resentment at being questioned. He merely straightened up slightly and turned to look directly at his eldest son. "Have you ever seen a forest of evergreens?" he asked.

"Yes, in Germania, along the Rhine. They stretch for hundreds of miles."

"Good. And have you ever seen the snow cascades that fall from the mountainsides in northern countries during the winter months?"

"Yes, I've seen those, too, also in Germania."

"And have you ever stopped at the base of one of those cascades the following spring or summer, to take note of what is left behind after the snow has melted?"

Marcus shook his head.

"Not surprising. But I have. We lost an entire maniple of infantry one year, a hundred and twenty men plus their officers, during a storm in an Alpine pass in Cisalpine Gaul, and we went looking for their corpses when the snow melted that summer. We found some of their remains, including their broken unit standard, under a steep, overhanging slope. They had been wiped out by one of those cascades." He looked around at the others. "People think snow is harmless—they think of it as lethally cold, but not lethally heavy. When one of those snow slides comes down a mountainside, though, it brings everything with it. It strips the mountain face of trees and soil and loose boulders, mixing them all together so that anything in front of the falling mass is instantly destroyed. And when the snow melts away, what remains behind is a solid mass of shattered, tangled trees—hundreds, sometimes thousands, of trees, every tree that had been in the path of that cascade."

He turned again to his son Marcus. "I have one more question about forests. Have you ever seen an entire forest of evergreens—an entire forest, miles in extent in all directions—picked up bodily, torn out of the ground that had nurtured it, and then mixed—earth and trees and water and bedrock all churned together like the makings of a dried fruit cake— and thrown back down into the hole that had been scooped beneath it by the force that tore it apart?"

"Of course not." This time Marcus's words were barely audible as he began to grasp what his father was describing.

"No, of course not," Titanius said. "Well, again, I have. I'm sure you've watched our brick makers at work, mixing straw with mud and pebbles? Try, then, if you will, to imagine the same mixture made with mud and fully grown trees and boulders. Then try further to imagine how you would approach the edges of such a morass when the entire area for miles around the hole is ringed with flattened trees, all pointing away from the central hole with their tops towards you, but flat on the ground. Fallen in rows and layered waves like wheat stalks severed by a reaper's scythe, so that they form a solid, endless, impenetrable wall of compressed branches. You cannot walk between them or among them but must fight your way for every foot of headway you achieve."

"I—" But Marcus Varrus could say no more. His father's graphic description had brought home the enormity of the cataclysm that had engulfed the men in Dacia.

Marius spoke into the silence. "The thunderbolt, Father. Was it a fireball?"

Every head in the room swivelled from him to his father.

"A ball of fire. That's what I saw. A ball of fire big enough to destroy the world. It set the earth on fire when it landed—that's what the stink was. It was the stench of burning trees and mud and molten rock."

"I think I might have heard of such a thing." Marius sat up a little straighter. "I remember hearing rumours soon after I joined up, about a sighting that had happened years earlier, in the Pontus Euxinus—the Black Sea, as the people up there call it."

Uncle Marius was a naval officer, the first of the Varrus name to serve in such a capacity, and Quintus was proud of him for having achieved the rank of navarch, commander of a ten-ship squadron. The Varrus clan, though, was a military one, with a distinguished record of service that stretched unbroken all the way back to the days of Octavian, the first Caesar Augustus. No Varrus before Marius had ever served at sea, and the other men in the family looked down on him, considering the navy a poor choice. This made Quintus love him even more, perhaps in part because he himself had an infirmity in his leg which, although it did not much trouble him, would forever rule out a glorious military career.

"According to the tale, one of our squadrons had been on patrol in the waters off Moesia—not far from Dacia, now I think on it—and witnessed a thing similar to what you describe: a massive ball of fire that roared across the sky with a great, soul-shaking noise and fell into the sea, below the horizon, west of where they were."

Titanius was wide-eyed. "And did they report it to the authorities in the region?"

Marius shrugged, smiling. "What authorities, Father? From what I heard, this must have been at the time you yourself were in Dacia, around 270. The ships there *were* the only authority in the region."

Grandfather Titanius's face filled with wonder. "That must . . . it must have been the same thunderbolt. It *must* have been. Such things are unheard of. And they made no report of it at all?" He frowned. "I find that difficult to credit."

"Why so? There was nothing to report, other than the fact that the event occurred, and even then, few people who had not seen it would have believed it, as you have said yourself. The fireball supposedly landed in the sea, where it exploded, sending up vast clouds of smoke and steam, and vanished. The only sign remaining of the impact after that was a succession of enormous, swift-moving waves that almost capsized our ships. And so the story died away to live on as mere rumour—another old sailors' tale of strange doings upon the face of the deep. But all those witnesses were aboard a ship, and not anywhere near being close to where it landed. The impact occurred beyond the horizon, so they would naturally have assumed it landed in the sea." He paused. "Hearing what you are saying now, though, it occurs to me that if this thing, this fireball, was as huge as you say it was, it could have landed countless miles away inland, far beyond the sea. What they believed to be steam might well have been smoke. And so I believe you are correct. That event and your friend Provo's disaster must have been one and the same . . . But what about your incident? Did you report it?"

Titanius shook his head. "No. I did not. Or, not really. A thunderbolt fell from the heavens and landed on a military camp, destroying a thousand men? No one would believe that. And we would probably have been charged with dereliction of duty for losing a full thousand men in an unrecorded battle. I did submit a report that we experienced a volcanic eruption among the Carpathian mountains, with heavy loss of men. As far as I know, nothing ever came of it. We finished our campaign, inauspiciously with such heavy losses, and were eventually withdrawn when the Empire abandoned Dacia."

"But what about your blind and deafened men?" Marcus asked him. "Did no one in authority ever wonder about the sheer number of those unusual casualties?"

His father nodded. "Few of those survivors ever made it out of Dacia. The place was treacherous enough for normal, healthy legionaries. For maimed and disabled men the difficulties were far greater, and the mortality rate among the blind and deaf men was staggering. More than two years passed before we won home to civilization, and by that time those who survived believed they had been caught up in a violent volcanic eruption. To us all, it was the only credible reason for what had happened."

Titanius Varrus looked down at his hands, then up at his son. "I have talked more about it here at this table than I have in all the years since it occurred."

Marcus nodded. "Well, it makes a fascinating story, Father, but what does it have to do with Maris, or with the Christian god? I don't want to belabour this, but this would all have happened years before she was even born."

Titanius smiled at his son, a genuine smile that astonished his grandson watching from across the room. "You missed what I was trying to tell you, then," the old man said. "The tale has nothing to do with Maris. Yet it has everything to do with what people think and believe, and with how they behave because of that. And it has much to do with what makes me so angry about these Christians and their ways."

Marcus glanced from his father to his wife and back again. "I don't know what you mean."

The older man sighed. "I know you don't. You never have. But then, you have never been required to understand, have you? Your duties and your loyalties all lie with Constantine, and on his behalf you are much involved with the Christian leadership. I've been where you are now, serving my own emperor in my own day, but I confess I am unaware of what, precisely, you do on Constantine's behalf when you meet with these Christian leaders—which you seem to do far too often for my liking. So tell me, if you can, what *do* you do—what do you *discuss*—when you sit down with those people?"

"We talk," Marcus Varrus said. "That's all we do. I explain the Emperor's requirements to them, and then they discuss those among themselves and put forward suggestions of their own, which I, in turn, deliver back to Constantine."

"Does Constantine ever meet with them himself?"

"Occasionally. He prefers to have them aware that as Emperor he has more emphatic priorities." He paused, then added, "The Emperor has an agenda for dealing with the Christians, to which he adheres rigidly. He has no desire to be perceived either as being overeager to placate them or too easily accessible to them. As well, he must bear in mind at all times the jaundiced eyes of the College of Pontiffs constantly overlooking everything he does, and the jealous and zealous glares of the imperial ministers, who perceive their own first duty to be the preservation of the empire and the status quo. So he proceeds with great caution in all his dealings with Christians, never forgetting that their very existence threatens the empire."

"Aha! So he is aware of the danger they present. That, at least, is encouraging."

"Father Titanius, forgive me, but I really must protest." Quintus's mother sounded timid. "In what way could the Christian Church possibly threaten the empire?"

The old man smiled indulgently. "By overthrowing it, child." He paused for a beat, waiting for that to register. "I am not saying that your fellow Jesus-worshippers will physically pull the empire down in ruins. What I mean is that their creed itself undermines, and will eventually destroy, the very fabric of our imperial society. I can see you think the idea mad. Think about it, Maris. Christians believe there is but one all-powerful, all-knowing god and that all other gods are false, created by man for man's own ends. They believe they have personal, inner access to their god, and that their god is the ultimate supreme being, outranking—and therefore invalidating—any earthly emperor. There is an insidious revolutionary aspect to the Christian way of life that is unconscionable to those of us who take pride in our history and in our civilized, Roman way of doing things. They believe that the sole reason for their existence here is to prepare to be resurrected into the next life in an idyllic place called Heaven. So if the state decides to kill them as a punishment, they will be eternally grateful. Christians are impossible to punish, and therefore ungovernable. If they ever become strong enough to enforce that belief, they will destroy Rome's pantheon in the blink of an eye, and with it all the priests and priestesses who serve its gods. That, in itself, is cause for bloody, violent revolution, because the priests will not go quietly into oblivion."

He dipped his head to one side and spread his arms, shrugging his shoulders expressively. "No matter how you examine it, my dear Maris—if, that is, you look at it with any logic at all—the Roman state and the Christians' church cannot long coexist."

He turned back to address his elder son again. "I have no doubt this is familiar to you. It probably guides your deliberations with these bishops, and that must give you a degree of familiarity with their beliefs. So you must know that all those beliefs are predicated upon their single god being a god of mercy and goodwill, of humility and simple fellowship, undying forgiveness and infinite tolerance. I find that impossible to stomach. To me, and to people like me, the mere notion of such syrupy, limitless, mind-numbing benevolence is inconceivable. It flies in the face of the nature of humanity. Constant cloying, incessant, unrelieved sweetness of the kind those people preach has to become toxic at some point."

He saw that his son and his daughter-in-law were both preparing to rebut what he had said and he forestalled them with a swift slash of his hand. "Wait! Allow me to finish, if you will." He continued, speaking directly to Marcus. "Your duty to Constantine led to your dealings with these Christian priests. You had no choice in the matter, and that is important to bear in mind. But priests are priests, Marcus, whether they profess to serve the ancient Roman gods or those of Greece, or even Baal of Babylon. And they all live with their hands extended, expecting the world to keep them in food and comfort in return for little in the way of work and less in the matter of substance.

"When I was your age, my duty and my loyalty were owned by Diocletian and I served him willingly—as loyally and faithfully as you do Constantine. He was a fine man, my friend Diocles—one of the finest men I ever knew, though I fear history will not be kind to him. The Christian priests condemn him now as a persecutor and blame him for the deaths of thousands of their followers during the purges that led to his abdication. But that abdication was voluntary, and the worst excesses of the anti-Christian campaign continued for seven years after Diocletian stepped down from the imperial throne. Galerius and Maximinus, lesser emperors in every sense, were the perpetrators there, and it was Galerius, damn his black heart, who first talked Diocletian into launching a campaign to protect the ancient gods of Rome and the civil order they represented. Diocletian allowed himself to be persuaded to take a stand in defence of the state religions, and from that point on Galerius took over, because Diocletian, as always, was too busy tending to the empire and its affairs to have time to be distracted by the self-serving squabblings of a petty religious sect. It was Galerius who pressed the persecutions, but since Diocletian was emperor of Rome, they laid the blame for everything squarely on his head." Quintus could hear the disgust in his voice. "That is all I want to say," he said. "On that topic, at least."

"I still don't see what you are driving at," Marcus Varrus said.

"Fundamentals," Titanius replied, rising from his chair. "I'm talking about fundamentals. The fundamental teachings of the Christians are based upon the belief that their god—the sole and only god—is a being of infinite goodwill, incapable of pettiness or violence, intolerance or injustice. If that is incontrovertibly so, as they insist, then which god hurled down the thunderbolt that destroyed Provo's cohorts and ravaged an entire countryside for miles around? Answer me that!"

BOOK ONE

Cornwall, A.D. 312

ONE

The third and last wagon lumbered by slowly, the noise of its iron-clad wheels lost in the fury of the downpour, swallowed by the hissing roar of rushing, falling, wind-blown water. As it passed him, the man crouching in the brush-filled roadside ditch straightened up slowly, bracing himself with one bent leg against the force of the torrent that battered at his legs. He watched until the wagon passed out of sight downhill and around the bend to his right, following the cobbled road that hugged the steep hillside, and then he pulled the sodden hood of his cloak more firmly over his head and moved quickly, making his way down the treacherous slope to his left, to where five other men waited for him.

The three wagons, confined by near-vertical slopes on either side, would follow a long, downwards loop to reach the same point, and when they reached it, every one of the six men aboard them would die, killed before they were even aware that they were being attacked.

The heavy rain would help in that, the watcher thought as he swung himself down the breakneck hillside, lurching from tree to tree and grabbing at low-hanging branches to stop himself from falling. He could not remember ever having seen a storm as savagely violent as the one raging now, and though it was damnably inconvenient, it also gave him and his men an advantage over the poor fools stuck in the wagons. They, because of the darkness of the tree-shrouded road, the late-afternoon storm, and the overwhelming roar of the pounding rain, could neither see nor hear

what was happening beyond the ends of their noses. When they reached
the end of the steep downslope they would find a fallen tree blocking the
road, and when they climbed down to move it aside they would die,
probably without ever seeing the men who would cut them down with
javelins from among the trees. It would be quick, and he and his people
would be miles away long before anyone found the bodies.

There had only been two wagons when he and his men had stopped
to water their horses around noon, at the mansio roadhouse near the
junction of the roads leading from Lindinis in the north and Durnovaria
in the east. He had noticed them when he arrived and sent one of his
men to walk by casually and try to see what was in them. The only thing
visible had been a heavy, iron-bound chest, carelessly concealed beneath
a heavy, pitch-covered cloth, but that had been enough. The wagoners,
oblivious to any danger, had been sitting at a table in front of the main
entrance to the mansio, feeding on whatever the place offered for sale.
There were four of them, dressed in plain, homespun cloth tunics and
hooded cloaks; ordinary, unimpressive men who looked as though they
would not know one end of a sword from the other. The watchers took
note and smiled knowingly at one another. They waited until they saw
the wagons take the south road, and once they were sure of their prey's
destination there was no question about where they would lie in wait
for them. The town of Isca, the sole place where the wagoners and their
cargo could be headed, lay slightly more than thirty miles to the southwest, and the watchers knew the exact spot on that road most suited for
robberies and assaults on unsuspecting passersby.

The heavy rain that started soon after the wagons left the hostelry,
and the happenstance of the two wagons being joined during the storm
by a third, also driven by two men, were merely unexpected bonuses. No
one knew what the new wagon contained and no one cared. Whatever
its cargo, it would have new owners before it came close to Isca.

Isca was the most southwesterly garrisoned town in Britain, at the
end of what was notoriously the worst stretch of road in the province,

on the peninsula known as Cornua, the Horn, which the locals mispronounced as Cornwall. The terrain there had defied the finest of Rome's road-building engineers at the very start of the conquest of the island hundreds of years earlier, before Rome, in its imperial wisdom, decided that the peninsula was too isolated and too savage to be worth the effort and expense of a pacification campaign. Cornua, they had decided, held nothing that Rome needed, and so the road had remained unfinished, and Cornwall itself had lain virtually undisturbed for two hundred years, since the time of the emperor Claudius.

Legend said that the five-mile stretch of road to Isca had been near impossible to build because of the terrain. The land through which it ran was ludicrously fractured—so broken and riven and shattered that it was close to impassable in places, criss-crossed with fast-flowing streams and rivers, bizarrely interspersed with bogs and lakes. The very bedrock in the region, it was said, had been impossible to build on, brittle and untrustworthy, incapable of underpinning viaducts or permanent structures of any kind. The road the Roman engineers had built there had been forced to follow the dictates of the land's contours rather than adopt the arrow-straight, tightly engineered thrusts of the typical Roman *iter*.

About three-quarters of a mile from the end of the rough section, at the bottom of a steeply winding descent through a tunnel of ancient trees that had overarched the roadway for more than a hundred years, there was a clearing containing a cavern that had been used for centuries as a sheltering point by travellers and as a rallying point by thieves and brigands. For more than a decade now the clearing had been policed by patrols from the garrison at Isca. There had been no robberies there for three years, though, and the patrols had recently been withdrawn.

That was where the watcher from the ditch was headed.

Far above him, on a tightly curving downhill bend of the looping road, a man called Marcus Licinius Cato sat on the passenger's side of the driver's bench on the third wagon and watched through narrowed eyes the edge of the cobblestoned roadway on his left as it seemed to disappear beneath the rim of the wheel below him. The cart's rear wheels lurched sideways across the wet stones, threatening to slide off the other side of the narrow road. The sideways movement forced the horses to brace themselves awkwardly against the yawing, dragging weight at their backs.

The downslope here was more severe than any Cato could remember seeing anywhere, even among the mountains in the north, and he was thankful that the road was as serpentine as it was. With fewer twists and turns and with longer, straighter descents, it might have been impossible to control the wagon. In the current deluge, the road was lethally difficult.

Watching the edge of the roadbed as it vanished beneath him, Cato could see this passage would be dangerous even in dry weather. He glanced up, searching the sky for lightness, but even as he looked he knew he was being foolish. The rain had been lashing down for more than an hour already, and each time he thought it could not sustain itself in such volume for much longer, it seemed to grow heavier. And on this particular stretch of road, the noise was deafening. The broad-leaved trees on either side, plane and elm and chestnut and oak, were enormous, their tops arching above the roadway to form a tunnel, and the falling rain hammered relentlessly against the canopy, from where it poured down onto the arched, tightly stretched leather covering of the wagon, creating a noise like the thunder of a thousand demented drummers.

From the corner of his eye he saw his companion Ludo turn slightly towards him, craning his neck in preparation to shout, and he leaned quickly sideways, cupping a hand over his ear to listen.

"This is . . . shit!"

It was impossible to hear everything, even with the words shouted right into his ear. "What is?" he yelled back at the top of his lungs, afraid for a moment that he might have missed seeing something, but the other man merely flapped a hand upwards at the storm before grasping the reins again.

"This whole . . . I'm starting to . . . gods are pissed . . . The old gods, not the new one."

"You need help? The brake?"

"Brake's useless . . . tits on a bull! *Watch out!*"

Cato flinched sideways, away from the sudden splintering noise as a heavy branch ripped away from a treetop and came sweeping towards him. Just before it struck him, it stopped short and whipped down and back, lashing the wooden side of the wagon beneath the driver's bench, and he saw that it had not completely broken free of the tree but was still anchored to the bole by a strip of bark that had undoubtedly saved his life. And at that instant, as though some god had clapped his hands, the rain stopped and the wind died. It was a stupefying moment because of its completeness. The rain and the wind simply stopped, instantly, so that even the sound of the still-falling cascades from the trees overhead seemed part of the enormous silence that ensued.

The horses stopped moving, the wagon stopped moving, and the men on the driver's bench stopped breathing. So profound and sudden was the stillness that Cato realized he could hear the rain receding through the forest on his left.

"By the Christ," Ludo said quietly. "I've never seen anything the like of that before."

"Nor have I," Cato said, paying no heed to the Christian reference. Ludo said whatever came into his head and held no reverence for any god, ancient or new. "That's the kind of suddenness that makes grown men afraid."

"Aye, men like me," the other growled. "I just about shit myself there. But it looks like I'm not the only one. Them other fellows have stopped, too."

At the end of the vicious downhill twist they had been negotiating, just before the roadbed swung into another turn, the wagon ahead of them had stopped in the middle of the road. The one ahead of it was already out of sight around the bend.

All around them, the sound of dripping water faded as the last droplets fell from the surrounding trees, and the silence seemed to spread.

"He's getting out," Ludo growled as the driver of the cart ahead climbed down to the ground and spread his arms, arching his back to relieve the kinks. Then he turned to look back and up to where they sat watching him.

"Quiet, suddenly, isn't it?"

The other driver clearly understood the tone, if not the words, of Cato's shouted question, for he answered it fluently and cheerfully in a language of which Cato understood no single word. Whereupon the man spun around and hoisted himself back up onto his bench, talking in the same outlandish tongue to his companion. Moments later, the wagon started moving again with a clatter of hooves and iron tires. Cato turned to look wide-eyed at Ludo, who was rubbing rain from his nose with the back of his hand.

"Did you understand any of that?"

Ludo sniffed. "No, not much more 'n you. But it was British."

"Didn't sound like any British I ever heard."

"Yup." There was no doubt in Ludo's voice. "That was Cornish. That's the way they talk down here in the Cornua. Like they're chewing every word and sucking on the vowels. So what d'you want to do now?"

"What do you mean?"

"Well, it looks like the rain might be finished, so do we drive on, or d'you want to dry off a bit? There's towels in the big chest at your back there, and we could wait for Leon and the others to catch up." He looked behind him and shook his head. "Wonder where they are, anyway."

Cato looked back at him, grinning and shaking his own head. "They won't be far away, if they haven't drowned already. You'd really stop right here and try to dry off, even though we're being dripped on from a thousand trees and our wagon's perched on a slope that would terrify most people we know?"

Ludo shrugged. "Your choice. Make up your mind."

"Let's get to the bottom of the hill and out of this damned tunnel before we do anything else. If the rain stays away, we can decide what we want to do next. Leon and the others aren't going to overtake us on this slope. They'd have to be mad even to think of it. If they have any sense at all, they'll have ridden around and be waiting for us wherever this damned chute levels off."

Ludo raised an open palm in what might have been a salute. "You're the magister, Magister. That's why I'm the driver."

"Then drive, and let's get out of this nightmare and back onto a decent flat road."

With a nod, Ludo released the brake, then geed the horses gently forward down the hill again.

When they rounded the next bend, they saw an open, almost level stretch of road several hundred paces long ahead of them, but the other wagons had already vanished. Neither man said anything, but Cato glanced sideways at Ludo a few times, waiting for him to push the horses to go faster. Ludo, though, was in no hurry. "The beasts are tired," he growled. "No point in whipping them into a sweat after what they've been through. We're not in any great hurry, are we?"

"No," Cato agreed. "We're not. Let them amble while they can." He swung himself around on the bench, grasped an iron stanchion at his back, rose to a crouch, then stepped back into the covered bed of the wagon.

Six chests and cases there took up most of the floor space, forcing him to move cautiously, but he sat on the one nearest the tailgate and rummaged in the box of outer clothing until he found his sword. It was a spatha, the long-bladed broadsword that many of Rome's fighting formations had adopted in recent years from their Germanic allies. He unsheathed it now and held it up in the dim light to inspect it briefly before setting it down and pulling his whetstone out of the scrip at his waist. Two hours a day he spent sharpening his blades, usually in four half-hour sessions. It was a discipline, and a healthy, necessary one, for the keenness of his sword blade, more often than not, was the edge between life and death for a fighting man, and Cato had been a fighting man his whole life.

The leather covering the back of the wagon had been drawn tight against the rain, but now he loosened the rope bindings and pushed the edges apart, creating an opening that allowed him to look out at the road behind him as he settled into the routine of honing the spatha's long blade.

It was a fine weapon with magnificent and durable cutting edges, made almost a half century earlier by a gifted slave who had lived in the Cato family's household, and as he began to sweep the palm-held whetstone along the blade's edges in the susurrant rhythm that had long since become a part of his daily life, as natural to him as breathing, he enjoyed the familiar shape of the hilt in his fist and imagined, not for the first time, that his father and grandfather would both have taken pleasure in the same sensation.

As he sat there stroking the blade, enjoying the hypnotic keenness of the sound, he quickly lost awareness of the passage of time, but he had been counting unconsciously, and when he came to the end of his pattern he knew, and he tested the edge of the blade with his thumb before replacing the sword in its sheath and reaching for his other weapon, the gladius he wore at his right side.

Most men, if they fought at all, used a sword and a dagger in tandem. Cato, like a few of his long-serving military friends, had come to prefer the sword-sword combination, spatha and gladius, the old and the new combined. For hundreds of years the gladius had been the sword of the Roman legionary, a short-bladed, heavy weapon designed for stabbing and chopping in close-formation, hand-to-hand combat. In the hands of Rome's heavily trained legions, it had been the most feared and fearsome weapon in the world. In recent years, though, partly the result of changes in legionary tactics and partly through necessity, the longer-bladed spatha favoured by certain barbarians outside the imperial borders had been adopted by some Roman military units, and because of its increased length and stabbing power, it had become the preferred sword of the heavy infantry units of some legions. Cato, who had trained in the use of both, now used both, the long spatha in his right hand and the gladius in his left.

Just as he began to sharpen the gladius blade, he heard a sharp, hissing intake of breath from Ludo. The two men had spent years living closely together, and he recognized it as an alarm. He was already twisting around as the wagon lurched to a stop.

"What?"

"Shit. We've got shit."

"Where?" He was straining forward, peering to see what Ludo had seen, but there was nothing visible except trees and clumps of undergrowth.

"Ahead and to the right. Up there by the big tree. Two men with javelins. See them?"

Cato had been scanning the bushes surrounding them for a threat, but now he looked in the direction of Ludo's pointing finger. About a hundred and fifty paces beyond, the tail end of the wagon that had been ahead of them was now visible. It, too, had stopped, and almost without surprise he watched one of the men Ludo had seen by the tree straighten up and throw his javelin towards the distant wagon. His eye followed the flight of the missile and he saw it hit a man who had leapt down from the tailgate and turned to run. The spear struck him in the middle of his back and punched him forward and off his feet to sprawl on the road, and then four, no, five men were converging on the wagons ahead.

"Shit," Ludo said again. "What now? We can't go anywhere, can't outrun them. Can't turn back—the road's too narrow. Where in the name of Nero's nipples are Leon and Stratus and the Twins? Lazy bastards are probably— Uh-oh. They've seen us."

The group in the distance huddled together briefly, then they turned as one to look back at the solitary wagon remaining to be taken. They stood looking for a space of heartbeats during which they might have been talking, and then, though Cato saw no signal, they began moving in unison towards the wagon. They showed no evidence of haste or of excitement; they merely walked forward stolidly, spreading slightly apart until they formed a front that filled the lower breadth of the road.

"You have your sword?" Seeing Ludo's affirmative nod, Cato clipped his own sheathed gladius into the ring at his right side and watched the strangers coming until they had covered about a third of the distance separating them from him and Ludo, and then he inhaled deeply and blew the breath out forcibly. "So be it," he said quietly. "Out of the wagon. Pull your cloak up over your shoulders and cover your blade. Don't let them suspect we're armed until they're close enough for us to reach them. I need to get my other sword so I'll get out through the back, as though I'm running. I'll keep the wagon between me and them. As soon as I move, stand up and raise your arms and try to look scared, and then climb down and move away from the wagon. Move slowly and try to look afraid . . . or bewildered. That shouldn't be too difficult for a man of your skills."

"It won't be," Ludo growled. "But I can't handle more than four of the whoresons. What're you going to do with the fifth one, all on your own?"

Cato grinned. "I'll manage it somehow. Once you're down and clear of the wagon, break to the rear and join me. We'll run up the road as far as the first bend and hope they'll come after us. And when they do, we'll hit them as they come around the bend." He sucked air thoughtfully through his teeth before adding, "But for now there's no need to hurry. We have a little time and they're expecting an easy kill. So let them come on, and wait for me to make the first move."

"What if they try to take us down with the javelins, from a distance?"

"Then you had better grow nimbler and faster than you've ever been in your life, and do it quickly. If they start throwing, I can't help you or myself. So let's hope they'll want to take us alive."

"Who d'you think they are?"

Cato was watching the men up ahead, cataloguing their appearance, and he shook his head. "I've no idea. Could be deserters. Two of them look military, and those two with the javelins look legion trained. Could be plain bandits, though, local clansmen out looking for plunder."

Ludo grunted. "Well," he said, "if they open those two chests we're carrying, they'll see plunder they could never have imagined. They'll be able to buy villas on the Palatine Mount with it."

"Right, they're close enough."

Cato stood up suddenly, turning as he moved, and flung himself into the covered back of the wagon, where he snatched up his spatha and hooked the metal clip on its sheath into its carrying ring on the belt beneath his cloak. He used his shorter gladius to slash the ropes securing the leather opening at the rear and leapt out. He landed easily, shook out his cloak to conceal his weapons, then swung around and to one side to look back at the approaching thieves, who were now running towards them. When he was sure they had seen him again, he spun back and sprinted for the tree-lined tunnel at his back, as if he were escaping back up the hill. It was less than fifty paces before the road started to curve, and he kept going until he rounded the sharp bend. As soon as he was sure he couldn't be seen from below, he dived to the left and hid behind the first good-sized tree among the bushes lining the roadside to wait for Ludo.

Sure enough, Ludo came hammering up the road after him, and as he rounded the bend Cato leaned out and waved him towards the other side of the road, to where there was an even thicker tree.

And then they drew steel and waited for their pursuers.

Who did not come.

Eventually Ludo stepped out of hiding and onto the road, where he stood looking at Cato. "They found the chests," he said. "So they won't be coming. Why should they? They're alive, they found our gold, and we ran away. So now we have to go back. Shit!"

Moving very slowly, Cato stepped back onto the surface of the road to join him, sliding the gladius into its sheath on his right hip, then using his left hand to steady the longer sheath of the spatha on his left side. Before he could slide the long blade home, however, they both heard the sharp, hard-pounding rhythm of iron-nailed boots running on the road below, approaching the bend, and they crouched as one, turning towards the sounds with their blades raised. There was only one person running down there, though, only one pair of boots. Moments later they could hear hard, heavy breathing and the footsteps slowed. Then there came a stumbling noise and the sound of a body falling, accompanied by a whuffing grunt and the unmistakable sound of a dropped sword clattering on cobblestones. That galvanized both of them and they went running, to find a single man lying face down in the middle of the road, the shaft of a short, heavy arrow sticking up from behind his right shoulder.

"Shit," said Ludo. "They're here."

Cato was already down on one knee, feeling for a pulse in the wounded man's neck.

"Well, we have a prisoner," he said slowly. "This one will live, and with any kind of luck we'll be able to coax him to tell us who he is and what he and his crew were up to."

"I say leave the whoreson here to die and rot. We've got enough grief with these other four riding our arses. And here they come." He turned away and spoke to the quartet now walking up the hill towards them, his voice reeking with disgust. "What took you people so long to get here?"

The man leading the approaching quartet stopped. His companions stopped at the same time, staring up at Ludo and Cato in silence as their leader grimaced, pinching the corners of his mouth slowly and deliberately with his thumb and index finger before he spoke.

"We were here ahead of you," he said, "waiting for you. But you were absent on parade. We waited for three wagons and there were only two. And then when you finally did show up, you jumped down and ran away, leaving the gold for the thieves. We would have come looking for you sooner, but we didn't know how far you might have run. And besides, I couldn't get these idiots to stand up and stop laughing long enough to tell them where you disappeared to."

Cato stepped forward to stand beside Ludo, his mouth twisted into a wry half grin. "Blame my cowardice, Leon," he said, and jabbed a thumb towards Ludo. "He told me I was being a weakling and my cowardice was showing, but I really thought they'd come after us for fear we might turn witness against them. We didn't expect you to be here. As far as we knew, you were behind us. When did you pick us up? And how did you get ahead of us on this awful road?"

Leon jerked his head backwards, indicating the trio behind him. "Thomas saw you from a field when you left the dirt road and turned onto the paved one behind the other two wagons. He was talking to a farmer, and wondered why the fellow was shaking his head as he watched the three of you head south. The old man gave him a tale about how the road was twisty and steep and how so many wagons and travellers had been robbed over the years on the straight stretch at the bottom of the last slope. Tom asked him the best way to get here on horseback, then came to get the rest of us. We swung east and rode down along the edge of the broken area, on decent ground. Got here about an hour ago and went into hiding. We were on the lookout, but this lot were really good. They were here before we arrived and we didn't even know it until their scout came down the hill and they started moving. After that they went back into hiding, and we stayed where we were. When they came out, we moved against them."

"Hmm. What about the people on the other two wagons?"

"All dead. Those lance throwers knew their trade."

"Knew? They're dead?"

Leon shrugged. "Aye. Tom and Dido took them out with their bows."

"Lances and bows . . . Long-distance warfare." Cato nodded to the taciturn man called Stratus, who responded in kind, and then he looked at the Twins, Tom and Dido. "So, you two again," he said. "Still haven't drawn your blades?"

The one called Dido grinned back at him. "I did. One of them was gut shot. His own fault. Saw me aiming at him and tried to jump aside, but jumped into the shot instead. He'd never have lived and wouldn't have wanted to. So I finished him with my blade."

"Then you honoured him. He should have thanked you."

Dido looked surprised. "He did, when he saw I meant to. But how could you know that?"

Cato dipped his head to the other Twin, Tom, who returned the salutation gravely. "That's why I'm the magister, Dido. I know things like that. Come on now. We'd better get down there and make sure there's no more ravens lurking around the wagons. You two carry our prisoner between you—and try not to kill him. We'll carry your crossbows for you. If he lives, we'll take him to Strabo in Isca. He'll know what to do with him."

Retracing his steps downhill behind the others, Cato thought, for possibly the hundredth time since he had met them, that the Twins were remarkably well named, considering their origins. Their real names, Thomas and Didymus, both meant, literally, "the twin," one in Greek and the other in Aramaic. But the two men, though they resembled each other so closely, were not even brothers. They had merely been paired together on joining the legions because of their marked resemblance to each other and they had remained together ever since, sharing most of their astonishing abilities, including their instinctive mastery of the rarely used crossbow, a miniature, hand-held adaptation of the great Roman artillery catapults used in siege warfare.

"Looks like they never reached our chests," Ludo said as they approached their abandoned wagon.

"They didn't," Leon answered. "As he said, Dido shot one before he could climb aboard the wagon. The other saw him fall and kept on running, until Tom shot him just up the road."

Cato passed their wagon without stopping, though Tom and Dido paused to lower their unconscious prisoner to the ground beside it, and he continued walking until he reached the rearmost of the other two. He had counted six more bodies by then, tallying eight in all. Four of those were obviously the wagoners, for they were all unarmed and sprawled around the carts they had been riding in. The remaining two corpses, both wearing scuffed black leather military armour, were the lance throwers he had seen earlier. As he started to move again, though, he saw the arm of another man, draped over a fallen log that otherwise concealed him from view.

"So," he said, "how many of these animals were there?"

"Five," Leon told him. "That one behind the log seems to have been in charge. He'd been acting as spotter at the top of the hill, and when he came down, it was clear he was giving the orders."

"And what's in the wagons? Did you check?"

This time it was the taciturn Stratus who shook his head. "No," he said, then placed a foot on the hub of the rear wheel of the wagon closest to him and sprang up effortlessly into the bed. The cargo lay covered with a heavy, waterproofed sheet of tar- or bitumen-covered leather. He seized one thick corner and wrested it aside, uncovering a layer of three long wooden cases banded with iron straps.

"Shit," Ludo said. "More gold?"

Stratus scanned the floor around him, then stooped and picked up a long pry bar. He inserted it between the lid of the chest and its wall, then threw his weight on it, ripping the nails out until he could hook his fingers under the lid and wrench it open. He straightened up to look down into the chest.

"What is it, Strat?"

Stratus crouched down again and reached into the chest. Then he braced himself and thrust himself up, straightening his legs with an enormous heave. He turned to let them all see what he had—he was clutching a large, rusted mass of solid metal—then swung away again and dropped it back into the chest, where it landed massively on top of others like it, shaking the whole wagon.

"Loaf ingots," Cato said quietly. "Big ones, too. Fifty pounds each, at least, maybe sixty. Solid iron. Probably worth its weight in gold to some people, Ludo, so you were almost right. How many in the crate, Stratus?"

"Let's see. Six in each layer . . . Twelve."

"And three crates? That's thirty-six ingots. If the other wagon has the same load, this is a rich haul on its own."

Dido ran ahead to check the other wagon.

"Headed for Isca, you think?" This was Leon again.

"Where else? It's a garrisoned fort. Garrisons need new weapons all the time. I think my friend Strabo might be glad to see this."

"Three crates in this one, too," Dido shouted. "Seem to be the same size."

"So be it, then," Cato said. "Let's get moving. Tom, Dido, bring in the horses and tether them to the wagons, then take this one. Leon and Stratus, you take the other, and Ludo and I will keep the one we came in. We can't be much more than ten miles from Isca, so we should get there before dark. Let's just hope the rain doesn't come back."

"I hope the hypocausts are working when we get there," Leon drawled, flicking off a bead of water that had trickled down from his matted hair to the tip of his nose. "Otherwise I might never get warm again. A hot bath and a hard rubdown work wonders on a day like this, so let's get there quickly."

"Let's get there *safely*," Cato said. "We don't know this country, so we can't afford to be careless, not this close to the end of the road. Besides, the hypocausts will be working. When did you ever hear of a garrison town without hot baths?" He looked around at all of them. "Right, then. Let's move out. Ludo and I will take the lead from here on."

TWO

Two hours later, when the rain returned, they were still on the road, in the middle of nowhere but on high, open ground on a fairly level surface. The rain, nowhere near as heavy as it had been earlier, was nonetheless heavy enough to soak them again and chill them to their bones, so that when Cato shouted the word back, just on the edge of nightfall, that he could see beacon lights in the distance, the entire group offered thanks to the gods.

The town gates were closed by the time they reached them, but Cato had no intention of sleeping outside in the rain until morning, and had taken steps to ensure they would be admitted. On the approach to the town he'd climbed into the back of his covered wagon to towel himself dry and change quickly into his best uniform. He stayed there, out of the rain, until the wagons stopped in front of the gates, then blew a long, clear, sustained blast on the metal trumpet he kept among his general kit.

Moments later he saw movement on top of the overhanging gate tower and jumped down from the wagon, throwing his cloak back over his shoulder to show not merely an elaborate officer's cuirass but also, and unmistakably, the thin stripe of senatorial purple that bordered his tunic and defined him as a *tribunus laticlavius*, a high-born political functionary with powerful connections who was using the command structure of the imperial armies to enhance his own career. Without having to pause for effect, since he knew that everyone there knew instantly who and what he represented, he removed his ornate helmet with its distinctive bright green Legio VI Victrix crest and shouted up at the guards.

"I am Marcus Licinius Cato, tribune of the Sixth Legion in Eboracum, here with imperial dispatches and supplies for your commanding legate. Open up."

Two bowmen stepped forward on either side of the tower and aimed their weapons down at him as shouts and the sounds of bustling activity broke out on the other side of the wall, where the guard was being reassembled hastily to reopen the enormous gates. When they did, Cato replaced his helmet and saluted the centurion who stepped out to greet him as officer of the day in command of the town guard, then handed over the pouch containing his credentials.

The officer, clearly a long-serving garrison subaltern, checked Cato's documents cursorily, raising one eyebrow as he recognized the seal on one particular piece, then returned them.

"Welcome to Isca, Tribune," he said. "If you'll follow me, I'll arrange an escort for you to the camp."

"I'll be obliged to you, Commander. Please lead on."

He waited stoically, showing no signs of impatience as a junior officer, with the rank of decanus, was delegated to form an eight-man squad to escort his party through the town and to the main gates of the garrison headquarters, and he gritted his teeth in silence as he watched the hastily summoned unfortunates emerge confused from the guardhouse to form the detail. He was the latecomer, after all, arriving well after the appointed curfew, and any inconvenience was purely of his doing. These men had completed their shift and were entitled to their rest. They should not have been required to accommodate the whim of some unknown, arrogant bastard of a visiting officer who wanted to show how important he was. Finally, when the decurion in charge announced that his squad was fully prepared and ready to march, Cato thanked the officer of the day with a courteous nod and gave the signal for his wagons to fall into line behind their escort.

The town was settling into its end-of-day routine. It was almost full night by now, and lights glowed in many of the households that lined the main streets, though those lights that beckoned from the taverns appeared to shine more brightly and to be more welcoming. The main route through the vicus, the town that had grown up around the original encampment, ran a haphazard course because that was how it had evolved over hundreds of years. Behind the camp walls where the garrison lived, everything was laid out in straight, rigid lines.

The south wall of the legionary fortress of Legio II Augusta formed fully half of the northern end of the town, and their escort led them around in a half loop to approach the principal, eastern gates. The procedure of gaining entrance was repeated: the guard officer of the day, this time a young man barely out of boyhood, followed by a groom leading a cavalry mount, approached and saluted crisply. He welcomed Cato and his party formally to Isca Fortress on behalf of Legio II and its legate, then offered to escort them directly to the praesidium, the headquarters building.

"I will be grateful, Commander," Cato said, forestalling the young man as he was about to swing away to mount his horse. "But first we should attend to a formality." He turned slightly to indicate the wagon behind him. "And not one, I think, that you would wish to take directly to the praesidium."

As the officer turned back, looking at him curiously, he continued. "We have a prisoner in our wagon—a thief, probably a deserter, captured in the act of robbing and murdering the four men who owned two of these three wagons. We caught him in the middle of it. Him and some others, but the others died there. He's badly wounded and in need of medical attention. Can you take him off our hands?"

"Of course, Tribune." The young man turned to his lieutenant, an older man stamped with a senior ranker's look of long, hard service.

"Decanus, four of your men to carry the prisoner to the cells. Send another to summon the medical orderly on duty."

As the sergeant moved to obey, though, the watch commander changed his mind. "No, wait. Do it the other way around. Take him straight to the infirmary and hold him there under guard. If the medics release him, then they can take him to the cells. But keep track of what's happening and report to me at end of shift." He looked back at Cato. "Anything more, Tribune?"

Cato shook his head, and the young officer said, "Right, we'll go in now. This way, Tribune."

He turned smoothly and stepped up into the cupped hands of the waiting groom, who hoisted him easily up and onto the horse's back as Cato swung himself up equally smoothly to the driver's bench beside Ludo. As soon as he was seated, the horses leaned forward and pulled the wagon into motion.

The young subaltern ignored them from then on as they did him, all of them knowing that there was no need for anyone to escort them, other than to satisfy the tokenism of official security. No one who was not a bona fide member of the local garrison was ever permitted to go anywhere unescorted within the confines of a Roman camp. It was a rule of such long standing and so universally acknowledged that it went without having to be said, by anyone. The fact that Cato was a visiting tribune of senatorial rank merely made it a matter of courtesy that he should be escorted by an officer rather than an enlisted man.

Beyond the fortified passage inside the tower protecting the main gates, the Isca installation was laid out in a rectangle, with the exact precision of every other military establishment that had been built in the millennium since Rome's expansion began. The main gates themselves faced east, as they had since Rome's earliest days, and the central road, the Via Praetoria that bisected the camp, led directly westward from the gates to the praetorium itself. This building housed the unit commander, who might rank from a senior centurion to an imperial

legate or even an imperial prefect or full consul, depending upon the
size and importance of the garrison.

In the original marching camps of the early legions—overnight,
bare-ground accommodations furnished with leather tents and protected on all four sides by guarded earthen walls thrown up each day
from the ditch the men dug to front them—the praetorium had been
small but functional, the commander's tent the largest in the enclosure
and measuring no more than ten by twenty feet.

As those camps had grown over the years, though, becoming permanent settlements with huts and roofed buildings, then growing into
forts, then fortresses and garrisoned towns, the original encampments
had been rebuilt and greatly expanded, many of them multiple times, as
decades turned into centuries. The basic rectangular plan had been
retained, but the earthen walls and wooden buildings had gradually
been replaced by stone, and the principal interior accommodations had
become far more spacious and more imposing, with the praesidium now
occupying as much space as was required for the garrison's headquarters,
and the quartermaster's department, the quaestorium, located directly
to the rear of that and always securely guarded and heavily protected.

The contents of the three wagons Cato's men had brought would
go directly to the quartermaster's, but not before Cato had received an
itemized notification of receipt from the senior duty cleric in the
headquarters building. Another receipt would be issued by the quartermaster's people in due course, once the delivery had been taken into
inventory, but to Cato that was incidental. The cargo he had delivered
was too important, and too valuable, to be entrusted to unqualified
personnel, and Cato had no intention of consigning any of it into the
hands of minor functionaries until he had in his possession a formal
acknowledgment of delivery and receipt, signed and sealed by the
praesidium secretariat.

The guards on duty in front of the headquarters building snapped to
attention as the trio of wagons approached with their escort, and the

mounted officer, his duty done, did not even bother to dismount as he waved to Cato, inviting him to climb down and present himself to the lead guardsman, who had already stepped forward, his hand extended to accept the documents Cato held ready to pass to him. Before Cato could complete the step towards the man, though, a different voice intervened.

"I'll take that, since I'm here," the darkly mellow voice announced. The speaker stepped forward into the light from a deeply shadowed area beside the main praesidium doorway. He glanced at the mounted officer. "You can leave this with me, Commander Tesla."

The young guard commander straightened immediately—almost guiltily, Cato thought—then nodded abruptly and even seemed to come close to saluting nervously before he caught himself. He pulled his horse into a rearing turn, then trotted away in a clatter of iron-shod hooves on cobblestones.

Cato ruefully remembered the tongue-tied awe that every young officer trainee experienced at least once in his career when faced with the unexpected, overwhelming presence of a legendary veteran, and so there was no doubt in his mind about the watcher's identity. He knew he was now in the presence of Regulus Culver, the primus pilus, or senior soldier, of the Second Legion.

There was only one primus pilus, one "first spear," in each legion, and only three legions in all of Britain: the Twentieth, Legio XX Valeria, was based in Deva, in north Cambria; the Sixth, Legio VI Victrix, was based in Eboracum, in northeast Britain; and the Second, Legio II Augusta, formerly of Isca Silurum, in south Cambria, was now established at this more southern Isca, in the Cornua.

"Pilus Culver," Cato said, turning towards the man and nodding courteously. "An honour to meet you in person."

The great man showed no reaction that this unknown officer should know his name. As one of only three men of his rank in all of Britain, he expected it. He gazed at Cato indirectly, almost from the side of his eyes, his face expressionless, his lips slightly pursed, then nodded his head, the slightest fraction of an acknowledgment, and held out his hand for the documents Cato was holding.

Cato relinquished them immediately and stood watching as the pilus scanned them, wondering which aspect of Culver's personality had been most responsible for the man's elevation to the rank he now held.

It would never have occurred to him to doubt that Regulus Culver had earned every scintilla of the distinction he now bore, but he was sufficient of a realist to know that all men are not born equal, and that even among a far-flung field of equals there will always emerge one dominant character to stand *primus inter pares*, first among equals. Every group threw up an alpha leader, and invariably the difference between that leader and the others of the pack devolved upon character and personality. Above all other things, soldiers put their faith in the men they chose to lead them.

Nowhere was that more true than in the selection process that resulted in the creation of a primus pilus. In theory, every recruit held the potential to become the First Spear of a legion someday. Promotion through the ranks was a constant of military life, and each promotion in Rome's armies was earned by merit. Ideally, therefore, the highest rankings should be achieved by those outstanding performers who worked hardest and longest in the quest for consistent, meritorious advancement in every aspect of soldiering. The process had been going on for more than a millennium, and it never seemed to fail, with the overall winner's laurels going to the man who proved himself, over the years, to be the single most proficient soldier in his legion. He was the man who became First Spear, nominally the second but in many ways the primary, most powerful man in the entire legion.

Such was the man Cato stood before now, and he was mentally cataloguing all he'd ever heard about this paragon. Regulus Culver had become a legend not merely among the ranks of his own legion but throughout the armies of Britain, and he had done so long before he became First Spear. He had done it, in fact, before he became first anything, at the age of eighteen when he was a peach-faced acting squad commander, temporarily in charge of an eight-man contubernium. Young, ignorant, and still wet behind the ears, he had rallied his squad behind him and led them into battle, distinguishing himself against all odds, and he had done it so well, and so convincingly, that now young soldiers looked at him with starry eyes as the living embodiment of everything they might hope to achieve.

And yet looking at him now for the first time, Cato was aware that no matter how much power he wielded nominally, Regulus Culver represented only the rank and file of the empire's legions. And that, in essence, meant the lower levels of the Roman populace. The legionary ranks were filled with conscripts, auxiliaries, and mercenaries, and many of those—the great majority, in fact—were not even Roman citizens.

Roman law demanded that every able-bodied man serve at least two decades in the legions, but since the earliest days of the Republic there had been those, particularly among the patrician class, who were entitled, through birth and privilege, to serve the state better and more efficiently—or at the very least more comfortably—in a role above that of simple-minded infantry recruit. Cato himself was dressed as one of those, aware, even as he looked at Culver's polished splendour, that his own purple-edged tunic defined him as a man of senatorial rank and therefore head and shoulders above the common ruck of ordinary folk, even one who had achieved the pinnacle of First Spear status.

That Culver's rank was real while his own was a mere sham failed to register with Cato, because the truth was that, as a policeman investigating military corruption, he lived so steeped in deception and subterfuge that he had lost almost all awareness of who he really was. For now, he was Marcus Licinius Cato, senatorial tribune of Legio VI Victrix, of Eboracum, and that was all he needed to be. He stood patiently, therefore, as the famous soldier's eyes flicked over the documents.

As the senior soldier of his legion, Regulus Culver had full responsibility for its training and combat readiness, and he determined his legion's field tactics in time of war. As well, he was responsible for the welfare—in every sense of that word—of all the soldiers in his care. His responsibilities covered the arming, provisioning, and supply of all legionary adherents and extended to their creature comforts, their financial and banking arrangements, their payment for services, their personal health and that of their extended families, and the provision of clean laundry and adequate sanitation facilities for all of them. He was also responsible for the maintenance and provisioning of all the legion's departments, ranging from barrel making to the daily purchase and preparation of fresh produce, the stockpiling of fermented fish sauce—the garum that supposedly kept the legions in the field—the endless manufacture of sandalled boots, and the fabrication of nails with which to sole them. In addition to all of that, he functioned as the eyes and ears of the legionary legate, exercising virtually absolute power as the legate's deputy, notwithstanding that commissioned officers of the legion's general staff were officially designated second-, third-, and fourth-in-command. None of those men would ever dare challenge the First Spear's de facto power.

Culver finished his meticulous examination of the documents and stood up straighter, still without having looked directly at Cato. He was a big man, taller and burlier than Cato, and his breadth and solidity were emphasized by the polished bulk of his glossy cuirass of embossed leather embellished with the symbols of his rank and prowess; medallions and insignia, row upon row, attesting to his worth. He sniffed and looked down one last time at the documents before turning to cast his eyes over each of the three wagons in turn. He shrugged, raised a hand to his waiting decanus, and waved in the direction of the quartermaster's buildings farther along the street. "Take 'em over there, Thorvil," he said. "Stores will see to them. And take our guests to processing." He turned to his guards. "Canis, go with 'em."

"Not yet, Magister Culver," Cato said, punctiliously correct in using the correct form of address. "I can't permit these wagons to leave my possession until I have spoken to your legate."

He watched the barely perceptible stiffening, admiring the fellow's coolness as he incorporated all the lessons of his military life into not yielding an inch while he scrupulously avoided saying, doing, or even intimating anything that might be construed as insolence to an imperial, political officer. They both knew better, after all, than to imagine that a strict observance of propriety would offer a defence against political influence. The pilus merely squared his shoulders, pulled himself a little more severely erect, and tucked his elbows in close to his sides, a burnished model of military correctness and precise decorum.

"Certainly, Tribune," he said tonelessly. "If you will wait here for me, I'll try to find the adjutant. I'll inform him that an officer from— where was it? Eboracum? Yes, that's it. A tribune with three wagons from Eboracum is asking to speak to the imperial legate. Please wait here. I'll be right back." He started to swing away, full of purpose, but hesitated. "I ought to warn you, Tribune, it might take some time. Legates can be . . . difficult. You know how it is. I've seen men grow long beards waiting out here."

"I'm sure you must have," Cato replied, trying not to smile. The adjutant Culver had mentioned would almost certainly be a *tribunus laticlavius*, a senatorial tribune, and probably second in overall command to Strabo, the legion's legate. And his purple-edged tunic would be appropriately wide-striped, outranking Cato's thin-striped one.

"Ludo," he said. "Go with Decanus Thorvil and Trooper Canis. Unload my personal effects and your own kit bags, then see to the delivery and documentation of the wagons and their cargo, but don't let anyone unload anything until you receive clearance from me. When I send word, you can finish the delivery and then have the horses cared for. I'll send for you once I know where you're to be fed and billeted."

He turned back to face the stone-faced primus pilus, acutely aware that no single person nearby had moved, let alone blinked an eye, since he had contradicted Regulus Culver.

"I promise you, Magister Culver," he said quietly, allowing his voice to soften to confidentiality, "your legate will see me. He's married to my sister. Just let him know that Rufus Cato's at his door, cold and wet and hungry."

The other man's eyes went wide with surprise, and then all the hostility vanished from them and he raised his clenched right fist to his left breast in salute. "Rufus? *That* Cato? Come with me, sir. You should have told me who you are."

THREE

Despite the brightness of the headquarters reception area, there were few people in there at that time of night, and fewer still paid any attention as Culver guided Cato to a spot by a long, low counter. He signed to Cato to wait while he raised a hinged flap and passed through to vanish behind the maze of screens masking the activities at the rear from public view.

Moments later, a set of high, ornate doors swung slowly open and a tall, aristocratic-looking man stepped into view and looked across the reception area. He was fully but informally armoured, in the style that denoted working headquarters staff—more for effect than for efficiency—and his eyes crinkled into an incredulous smile. He swept out, arms stretching in welcome, and enfolded Cato in a bear hug.

"Rufus," he said, squeezing almost hard enough to buckle Cato's armour. "I can't believe it. I thought Regulus must be mistaken. What in the name of the new god are you doing here? Are you alone? Come in, come in, man."

He stepped back and ushered Cato into the room beyond the ornate doors, and as Cato entered his noble brother-in-law's formal quarters, his command centre, he stopped on the threshold, abashed, as his eyes scanned the trappings of imperial power and wealth that awed him even though he had known he would find them there. This was the first time he had seen his sister's husband in his official capacity, and the initial impressions that threatened to overwhelm him sat ill with his memories of this man whom he had known for years but saw now in a new light. Cato had been in garrison headquarters buildings before, on many occasions, but he had never seen anything on a scale like this. This was one of the great permanent garrisons of imperial Britain, and it took his breath away for a spell. The furnishings were opulent, the floors of priceless mosaic, and the marble-panelled walls were hung with enormous draperies and formally set displays of pageantry. The legate's desk, a massive thing of richly polished wood, was at least three full paces wide, he saw, and two-thirds as deep, and the curule chair behind it was flanked at the rear on either side by busts representing the ruling masters of the western empire, Maxentius, the Augustus or supreme ruler, on the right, and Constantine, his Caesar or deputy ruler, on the left.

Behind both of those, centred upon the rose-coloured marble panel directly behind the legate's chair, a white marble bust of Diocletian, the former emperor during whose reign Strabo had joined the legions, took pride of place despite being smaller and less imposing than the two newer busts.

There were three men in the large room when Cato entered, one of them being Regulus Culver. The other two were looking at Cato with curiosity, and Cato correctly identified one of them as the adjutant before Strabo spoke, recognizing the wide-striped toga of a senior senatorial tribune.

"Gentlemen," Strabo said. "Say hello to my wife's brother and a former close colleague, Marcus Licinius Cato, known to all his friends— and he has no shortage of them—as Rufus. I'm sure you will have heard me speak of him in the past, but here he is now, and no doubt bringing urgent matters to our attention." He smiled at Cato and waved towards the others. "These are my stalwarts. Regulus Culver, our First Spear, you've met already. The dandyish fellow is my adjutant and deputy, Gaius Valerius, and the other there is my factotum and personal secretary, Thaddeus Galban, the man who keeps me organized and isolated, thereby earning the gratitude and admiration of everyone else in Isca."

Cato cradled his helmet in the crook of his left elbow and exchanged greetings cordially with all of them, and when he was finished he stood at ease, one thumb hooked behind the hilt of the gladius at his right side as he waited for Strabo, who was already ticking items off on his fingers and detailing them to Galban. "The tribune will stay here, in my quarters, and he'll need lodgings for his men." He glanced at Cato. "How many with you?"

"Five."

Strabo's eyebrow rose slightly. "Five! You came all the way from Eboracum at this time of the year with only five men?"

Cato shrugged. "More would have been too many. Is the road different at other times of the year?"

Strabo grinned, a brief flash of white teeth. "In the snow, sometimes. Where are they now, these five?"

"At your quartermaster's stores, waiting with the wagons we brought." Cato suddenly felt the ache in his cold, wet legs and unobtrusively leaned his backside against the edge of Strabo's huge desk, then bent to place his helmet on the rug at his feet. "I told them to stay there until I sent for them," he continued as he straightened up again, glancing at Regulus Culver and raising a hand as though in apology. "And I told them not to allow anything to be unloaded until I sent them clearance to do so."

He looked back towards the First Spear. "That was before you knew who I was, Magister Culver, seeing me purely as an upstart nuisance. But please believe me when I say I had very good reasons for what must have seemed an insulting disregard for protocol." He folded his arms across his breast, then spoke again to his brother-in-law. "Two of the wagons with us were the pre-chosen target of robbers. We had joined them by chance when we encountered them on the road to Isca, looking for mutual support as we travelled through the worst storm I've encountered in years. The robbers thought there were only two of us— my other four men were serving as outriders, shadowing us. When my outriders saw what was happening, they moved in against the thieves and killed them—or all but one of them—but not before the thieves had killed the crews of the other two wagons. As it transpired, their cargo proved to be very valuable. Each wagon carried thirty-six loaf ingots of solid iron weighing fifty to sixty pounds apiece. We knew no more than that they had been bound for Isca, so when we saw the ingots it seemed safe to assume they would have been bound for your stores. Our own wagon, though, has a very different kind of cargo, and I didn't want anyone knowing what it was before I had a chance to talk to you."

"I see. So what would you have me do with it, exactly?"

"Send someone trustworthy to bring it here and place it under guard until its contents can be checked and a receipt issued to me for delivery in full. It contains four cases. They are for you, dispatched from Eboracum two weeks ago. There were two other cases. They contain my personal kit, including my dress armour, but my men will already have taken care of those along with their own kit."

A slow smile was flickering on Strabo's face as he listened, and when Cato fell silent he nodded encouragement. "Go on, then," he said. "Don't stop there, now that you have us all wondering about it. What's in the four cases for me?"

Cato was silent for a moment, enjoying their suspense. Then he said, "Money to pay your troops for the next half year."

The stillness that settled on the room was sudden, so he knew he had stunned them, but it lasted no more than a few heartbeats before everyone started to speak at the same time.

"Gentlemen!" Strabo's raised voice quelled the others instantly. "Forgive us all," he said to Cato. "That might have been the very last thing we expected to hear. How, and why, would you bring us such a large volume of money all the way from Eboracum?"

"Because three of the last five shipments of that kind, from two paymasters' offices—one in Londinium and one in Eboracum—have been intercepted and stolen, on the road and under heavy escort. The three garrison posts they were destined for were Lindum in the north, Camulodunum, and Aquae Sulis." He looked from one to the other of the watching officers, all of whom were eyeing him in astonishment. "We arrived here safely," he said. "Whether or not the official pay-master's train will do the same remains to be seen. It was dispatched five days ago, I believe. But there's an official investigation under way and I'm a part of it, and I'll be happy to tell you all I know after I've washed and had a glass of wine." He looked at Strabo again. "Can you wait that long? *Will* you?"

"Of course we will. There is no hardship involved in waiting for the rules of hospitality to be satisfied before we question you further. Absolutely none." Strabo almost seemed to shake himself and then started rattling off instructions again. "Thaddeus, delegate a junior duty centurion to collect Cato's men and look after them. Tell him to have two of his men bring the tribune's baggage here, directly to my atten-tion, and instruct him to personally billet the tribune's men in the prime barracks space closest to the kitchens. And tell him to make sure they have extra bedding. But first have him take them to the bathhouse. I've little doubt they'll appreciate some hot steam and a good rubdown, too, after what has evidently been a long, tense journey. And tell Yarro I'll have need of him immediately." He cocked his head. "Is there anything else you need, Rufus?"

Cato smiled. "Nothing I can think of, other than to see my sister."

Thaddeus Galban cleared his throat. "Done, sir," he said. "I'll send Yarro to wait on you before I do anything else."

"Now that I think of it," Strabo said to his officers, "we all might benefit from a change of clothes and some time to let the day wind down, and I want all three of you to hear what Rufus has to say. So we'll meet again in an hour from now, in my personal quarters."

The primus pilus smiled slowly. "My tongue's already tasting the wine."

"Good man," Strabo said. "An hour, then. Valerius, did we finish off that last amphora of Falernian, or is there enough left for us to enjoy?"

"Oh, there's no shortage," the adjutant drawled in the manner of an aristocratic Roman aesthete. "That was far from being the last amphora." He bowed ironically, but winked at Cato as he did so. "Never let it be said that Alexander Strabo's friends went thirsting for nectar while a Valerius was within call. I'll be there in under an hour."

As he strutted grandly away, Strabo grinned at Cato. "That was for your benefit. He doesn't really talk that way and he's a staunch friend. Maria dotes on him. But his family estates lie on the Faustian slopes of Mount Falernus, where the very finest wines are made, and his four younger brothers keep him well supplied with their best product. Which means that we, his brother officers in Isca, benefit from being his friends.

"As for seeing your sister," he added, as though it were an afterthought, "well, that's another matter altogether. Maria's not here, and she is not going to be happy when she returns to find you came to visit while she was gone . . . I don't suppose you could stay until she gets back?"

Cato grimaced. "Unlikely. Unless you're talking of a few days. Where is she?"

"Not close by." Strabo waved a hand vaguely. "By this time, she should be somewhere between Italy and Illyricum, probably crossing the Adriatic with my parents now, headed for Salona in Dalmatia. I'll tell you all about it later." He turned away and scanned his desk, taking in the piles of tightly rolled and sealed cylinders, and grimaced. "This can all wait until later. In the meantime, let's go to my quarters and get rid of some of this armour." He hesitated. "That's right. You've never been here before, have you?"

"Not *here* here, no. I've been in Isca, but never in the legate's private quarters."

"Aye, well, don't let it awe you. It's quite a lot like other officers' quarters—only bigger and far more luxurious." He laughed. "I mean it. Once you stop gawping around and your eyes return to their normal size, you'll see it's just a place like any other. Besides, there's a large fire burning in the grate and I think you, at least, might be glad of it. Bring your helmet with you. Yarro can look after both of us, and my robes will fit you. You'll feel much better once you're dry and warm again. But I don't want you falling asleep before you finish telling us all you have to say. Come."

A man was waiting for them in the sumptuous dressing room, and Strabo introduced him as his steward, Yarro, and informed him that their visitor would need to borrow some clothing temporarily.

"Of course, sir," Yarro murmured to Cato, his eyes flickering over him, measuring him for height and bulk. "You and the legate are of a size, so I can see no difficulty." He turned then to help the legate shed his light garrison armour, and it was clear that their routine was long established. Strabo held himself erect and extended his arms, allowing the steward to unbuckle and unclip his harness with the minimum effort. Then, while Yarro was hanging the armour on its pegs on the wooden stand in the corner, Strabo crossed to the floor-length closets that lined one wall. He selected a long, white robe of snowy cotton and threw it to Cato, then chose another for himself.

"Magister Cato will bathe, Yarro," he said to the steward. "He has been on the road from the north for weeks and is in need of some pampering. So take him to the steam room and show him where everything is, and he can have a cold plunge and a hard rubdown. Then visit the cooks and arrange a small dinner for five in my private quarters. Nothing too elaborate, perhaps something left from last night. You know what will serve best. Then you can collect Magister Cato and bring him to my study. We'll dress again then." He turned to Cato. "In the meantime, I can finish some of the work on my desk. Don't take too long in the steam room. A quarter of an hour in my masseur's hands should bring you back to life. He can undo knots you weren't aware of, in muscles you never knew you had."

———

When Yarro led a renewed and refreshed Cato back into Strabo's personal quarters, he found the legate deeply absorbed in work, the desk in front of him still piled high with cylinders and the air heavy with the distinctive, slightly acrid smell of atramentum, the dense black ink used on official documents, overlaid with the warmer, more mellowing aroma of the melted wax used to seal those documents. Strabo held up one hand, stopping their approach. "Your timing's perfect," he said. He signed the piece of correspondence in front of him, sprinkled sand on it to dry the ink, and rolled it expertly into another cylinder that he held tightly in one hand while he melted the end of a stick of reddish wax in the candle burning in front of him. He dripped hot wax onto the seam of the cylinder, then pressed the small metal die that registered his insignia on the rapidly hardening wax, before blowing on it to set the wax and seal.

He pushed away from the desk, spreading his hands to indicate the documents piled in front of him. "That is a week's paperwork, right there, right now. And I'm so glad it's done. I think I deserve a cup of wine to celebrate." He stood up and reached out to grasp Cato's shoulder. "Valerius should be here directly with a fresh amphora of Falernian, and the others should be arriving any moment."

He led Cato from his office into another, much larger room, and through that into a far less formal and more comfortably furnished chamber. "This is Maria's favourite room," he said, beckoning him towards the fire in the large iron grate in the centre of one wall. "That's her chair on the left of the fireplace. Mine's on the right. Sit down, sit down."

Cato sat, and stretched out his hands to the leaping flames. Strabo then launched straight into a description of the three men they were waiting for—everything he thought Cato might need to know, and how and why they had become the most important and highly trusted men in his command.

Gaius Valerius's claim to his position, he explained, had been staked since boyhood. The two boys had been bosom friends since early childhood, their families closely related on several levels of blood and kinship. Although Gaius's family home was in Italy, he and Strabo had spent much of their boyhood close by each other in the densely developed villa area around the spa town of Aquae Sulis, just south of the Sabrina Estuary, where the Britannic elements of the influential Valerian family's business empire were centred. The Valerians were immensely wealthy, their influence potent and far-reaching. The two boys had joined the legions in Britain together on the same day, and though they were posted to different stations to complete their training as staff officers, they had been reunited when Strabo took command of Legio II in Isca and asked for Valerius specifically as his adjutant.

Regulus Culver, on the other hand, had never known Alexander Strabo before Isca, but he and Strabo had developed an immediate liking for each other on first meeting, and that had soon blossomed into a deep and committed friendship based on shared values, deep mutual respect, and a wholehearted commitment to the welfare of every aspect of the legion they served.

Thaddeus Galban—and Strabo was grinning as he spoke of it—might have appeared to be the odd man out among the trio, because he was very young, much younger than any of the others, and his position within the legion's hierarchy was that of a very junior, inexperienced underling. But no matter how it might appear to be, Strabo said, that was emphatically not the case. Galban had earned Strabo's highest regard within the first six weeks of taking up his new position as the legate's senior clerk. The young newcomer had gone straight to the heart of every assignment, assembled and examined whatever evidence he found available, and delivered his conclusions clearly, concisely, and fearlessly to his legate. In every instance his findings had been meticulously researched and were accurate and unbiased, and Thaddeus Galban had soon become one of Alexander Strabo's most trusted subordinates.

When he had finished talking about Galban, Strabo shifted in his chair. "I'm glad you came today, Rufus, because I had decided to speak to these fellows tonight. We need them, urgently. I think you should know, before we go in, that we'll be speaking of the brotherhood tonight. But don't be surprised when I tell them that we haven't got time to prepare them as we normally would."

Cato's face showed his surprise. "Why not? That's highly unorthodox, is it not? I don't think I've ever heard of anyone going through the raising unprepared."

"You haven't, but there's little I can do to change anything. The main thing is, they're good men and I've had them vetted. Exhaustively. Now I need to raise them and put them to work, and quickly. You'll understand why once you've heard what I have to say."

Cato nodded. "So be it, then. I won't argue or even look surprised. Thank you for the warning." They sat in unhurried silence staring into the leaping flames, and Cato decided that he might not find a better time to ask the question on his mind. "So," he said. "Why is my sister in Italy, and with your parents? Did you two quarrel?"

Strabo glanced sideways at him, a tiny frown between his brows. "No," he said seriously. "It might be easier if we had—quarrelled, I mean—but we haven't really had a fight since we were wed, and that's the truth. No harsh words and no injured feelings. And we've been wed for almost four years, so that's something of an achievement." He hesitated. "But we—Maria—lost another child last year. Eight months ago. That was her third time in less than three years, and it . . . it affected her badly. We had both been ridiculously careful in our behaviour from the first moment of knowing she was with child again, because we were painfully aware of the danger of losing it. But it happened anyway. Five months into her term."

He shifted his weight and rubbed his eyes, and Cato watched him in silence, deeply troubled by his evident grief. "It was no one's fault," he continued. "Least of all Maria's. But she believed she must have done something wrong to cause it, and she simply . . . stopped. Stopped everything, as though she had given up all interest in continuing—in living. And I believe she had. I thought I was going to lose her. She wouldn't get out of bed, wouldn't eat, wouldn't talk, and wanted nothing to do with me." He sucked in a great, shuddering breath. "I was at my wits' end, and so I wrote to my mother—she was my last resort. As soon as she read my letter, she travelled down here with the old man in tow, at forced march speed, and took over Maria's care. It took them more than a month, but eventually they brought her back to living, and after that they convinced her to go home with them to Aquae Sulis, to the baths there." He paused, gazing into the fire. "Of course, I couldn't go with them. But several weeks after they left, a letter came from Maria, telling me she was feeling better, and I could see it was true, simply from reading the letter. And from then on we wrote to each other regularly." Again he stopped.

"Then, three months ago, my father was summoned to Dalmatia, to a meeting in Salona, with you-know-who. The call was unexpected, and clearly urgent, but the invitation included my mother and my sister Clara, which was surprisingly gracious. Clara's married now, though, and no longer living in Aquae, so the mater and pater thought it would be good for Maria to go in her place. And so they wrote, informing me—there was no time to ask my permission, since they had to set sail immediately from Glevum—and promised to take care of her and bring her back safely in a few months' time." He shrugged. "So here I am, wifeless, and lacking even a mistress to console me."

"I'm sorry to hear that, Alex. I didn't know."

"How could you? I meant to write and tell you at the time, or soon after, but as matters went from bad to worse, I lost track of things . . ."

Cato leaned forward and squeezed his forearm. "Don't even think about that. It's water under the bridge. And there was nothing I could have done, other than fret, so you did me a service. But I'm glad you haven't taken a mistress to console you." He grinned. "I had a friend who did that, and soon he had to take a mistress to help him forget he had a mistress. Believe me, no matter how lonely you might be, a mistress is the last thing you need. A whore, perhaps, once in a while. But a mistress? Far too much trouble and responsibility." He changed topics seamlessly. "You say they sailed from Glevum. They went by sea all the way?"

"Gods, no, that would take forever. No, they sailed directly south to the tip of Gaul, then down the western coast to land at Burdigala. From there they were to travel overland to Masilia on the eastern coast, and then sail from there to Corsica, Ostia, and Rome. About four weeks, perhaps five in all, in good weather."

"And the weather was good, I take it?"

"Good enough. We have heard nothing to the contrary. But that took them only as far as Rome. I don't know what my father might have had to do there, but I suspect he'd have avoided the city if he could have and gone directly east to the Adriatic coast, where he could buy passage on a ship to Salona. And if my calculations are correct, they should be crossing the sea about now, if they're not already in Salona."

"Hmm." Cato knew that the best thing he could do now was to mind his own business and say nothing more on the topic of his sister, and just then he heard Yarro announcing the arrival of Strabo's three guests.

"Wait," Strabo said, raising a hand to detain Cato as he started to stand up. "We haven't finished here, so let those three wait a little. Show them into the dining room, Yarro, and tell them we'll join them in a moment. Is the fire lit?"

Yarro bowed slightly from the waist, his pained expression suggesting that the legate should know better than to ask such a patently insulting question.

Strabo watched Yarro depart, then turned back to Cato.

"How are *you*, Rufus, and I mean how are you, really? I've just realized that you haven't said a word about Rhea or Nicodemo since you arrived, and that's not like you—although the way I've been going on, you haven't had much chance. They are both well, I hope?"

Cato looked away. "Aye," he said softly. "I hope so, too."

"What? What are you saying? What am I supposed to make of that comment?"

"She left me, Alex. Months ago." Cato's voice was barely audible, and he stared into some private distance, avoiding his brother-in-law's eye. "Took the boy and vanished one day while I was away from home."

"No!"

Cato, not watching him directly, was aware that Strabo's mouth was opening and closing and that his fingers were clenching and unclenching spasmodically. Finally, Strabo dropped his hands to his sides and asked, quietly, "Where is she now?"

"I have no idea. She simply vanished, leaving no trace of herself or the boy."

"That's ridiculous. Did you try to find her?"

"Of course I did, at first. But when it became clear that she had no wish to be found, that she had gone to great lengths to be unfindable, I . . . stopped."

"She *hid* from you? That is iniquitous."

"No, Alex, it's not," Cato said. "The fault was mine. Rhea might have been a good military wife, had she had a man who cherished her and stayed in one place, but she was ill suited to sharing the kind of life I live. She couldn't handle the not-knowing that surrounds me and everything I do, all the secrecy and the clandestine shuffling and the constant mystery and absences and silences and lack of explanation. I had seen the warning signs and I should have heeded them, but I ignored them until it was too late."

"What warning signs?"

"All of them. And though it seems the height of blind stupidity to me now, I ignored them because I didn't know what they were. I was too deeply mired in the shit of my own life to be able to see the misery in hers. Rhea was deeply unhappy with our life, and afraid for mine all the time. Because of who we are and what we do, I was constantly away from home, always on duty, and always available to everyone for everything—except where those things applied to my family. And then I rode into a trap one day last August, chasing deserters up by the Northern Wall, and got myself skewered by a rusted spear. I should have died there, but Ludo and some others got me out and drove me to one of the mile castles on the Wall. Against all odds, they found a military surgeon there who knew what to do with me."

"He saved you, obviously."

"Aye, he did, but more by good fortune than good judgment, according to his own testimony. I lost consciousness for more than three weeks, stone dead to all appearances, and he fed me through tubes of sheep intestines—don't ask me how. He told me afterwards how he did it, but I hardly understood a word he said. Anyway, by the time I got back to Eboracum to complete my recovery, I had lost about a quarter of my body weight and Rhea had been mourning me for nigh on two months.

"When I arrived home she became hysterical, stunned that I was still alive in the first place and horrified at the condition I was in. She made me promise I would stay in garrison after that, and I half believed I would. But then I got fit again, and inevitably another crisis came up, and I went out to deal with it. And when I returned, she was gone, and had been gone for more than a week. I can't blame her. Knowing what I did to her and the boy, for so long, I can't find it in me to be angry with her. I truly hope they're happier now, wherever they are."

"You've no idea at all?"

"None."

"Your son, how old is he now?"

"He was five in March."

"Nicodemo . . . An unusual name. One of your family names?"

"No. It's just pulled from the air. Rhea liked it. I don't know where she heard it. It's Nicodemus in Latin, but she preferred Nicodemo."

"And you haven't tried to find them recently?"

Cato shook his head. "Not really. I've put out word among some of the people I know that if anyone sees them they should let me know when and where, but I haven't tried to hunt them down. And I'm at the stage now where it doesn't hurt too badly if I don't think about it too deeply." He stood. "Can we go and join the others now?"

Strabo nodded. "Of course. Forgive me if you think I pried too much."

"Nonsense. I thought no such thing. It's simply—not easy to talk about. Let's join the others and have that drink you earned with all the paperwork you finished."

FOUR

"**W**ell, gentlemen, if you are all agreed that we can do no
more damage to this food, we can attack the business
of the evening. What say you?"

When no one objected, Strabo nodded to Yarro, and within moments
an entire cadre of serving staff moved into the dining room and began
to clear away the remains of the meal. The servants were all men, and no
one there would have expected anything else, since this was a legionary
headquarters. Some were permanently attached to headquarters staff as
stewards in the quartermaster's division; the others, all in light garrison
uniform, were ordinary legionaries assigned to temporary kitchen duties.
After they were gone, Yarro checked that the fire in the brazier was
freshly fed, then bowed to the legate before leaving, closing the doors
securely behind him.

"What was that wine we drank with dinner?"

It was Valerius who asked, and Strabo looked at him with his
eyebrows arched high. "It was the same one we always drink with
venison, as you know perfectly well," he said. "One of the new reds,
from southwestern Gaul. And I know that what you really wanted to
ask was why didn't we drink the wine you brought. And the answer
to that, as you know equally well, is that your Falernian is simply too
precious to waste with venison. So we will enjoy it all the more
now." He stood up and addressed the others. "While we are preparing the drinks, gentlemen, you may group the chairs around the fire.

A semicircle, if you will, and not too close to the brazier. Leave room in front of all of us."

As the other three rose from the table and began to pull their heavy, high-backed table chairs into place in front of the leaping fire, Strabo and Valerius crossed to a tall cupboard against the wall, where Strabo retrieved a serving tray that held five large stemmed drinking cups of clear, precious, and practically flawless glass, while Valerius pulled out a rectangular tub of polished silver filled with fragments of chipped ice in which sat a tall silver ewer whose sides ran with condensation. Valerius set the ice-filled chest on the low sideboard beside the fire, while Strabo distributed the cups.

Cato, settling into his chair in front of the fireplace, cleared his throat in anticipation, for this was something new to him. He had tasted Falernian wine from time to time, but never the very best of them. Falernian wines came exclusively from the slopes of Mount Falernus, in the district known as the Campania, surrounding Napoli, midway up the Italian boot. He knew now, thanks to Strabo, that the wines produced by the house of Valerius ranked among the finest of the Faustians, those superb wines grown in the prime vineyards that had once belonged to Faustus, the son of the dictator Sulla, who had been a contemporary of Julius Caesar. He knew, too, that the best vintages of all came from late-harvested grapes gathered—still frozen—after early frosts. The succulent wines that resulted were then cellared in clay amphorae for as long as twenty years, and commanded prices that none but the wealthiest could afford.

Now Gaius Valerius bent towards him, extending a brimming cup of liquid the colour of dark honey. "Your health, Magister Cato," the adjutant drawled, smiling. "But be careful. It can be lethal, and this is a fresh amphora, so none of us knows how potent it might be."

There was silence then for quite some time as all five men sipped appreciatively at what they all agreed to be the most wonderful wine they had ever tasted.

Strabo eventually broke the mood. "So, gentlemen," he said, "we've matters to discuss, the first of them being Cato's tidings and the delivery he made to us tonight." He turned to Cato. "It must be close to three hundred miles from Eboracum to here. You came all that way with a wagon full of coinage and no more than five men. I find my eyebrows twitching when I think of the dangers of such a long haul, with a such a valuable cargo. Those five men of yours must be highly qualified."

"They are. The best at what they do and the best of what I might expect of anyone who ever joined the legions. You know one of them, in fact. Ludo. You met him in Deva, when you first met Maria."

"Aye, mayhap I did, but as you say, that was the first time I ever laid eyes upon my wife. After that, my mind is blank. Awareness of your sister eclipsed all possibility of my noticing anything else, let alone remembering another man. So I'll greet your man Ludo as an utter stranger, I'm afraid. Who are the others?"

"Four friends of long standing—to one another as well as to me. Their names are Didymus and Thomas, and Stratus and Leon—"

"Didymus *and* Thomas? That's the same name, in different languages."

"Yes, Greek and Aramaic." Cato turned his head slightly, to include the other three men. "Both names mean 'twin,' so that's what we call them—the Twins. It helps that they're practically identical. Stratus and Leon, on the other hand, couldn't be less alike. Stratus is enormous, strong as a bear, and Leon is our thinker, as clever and intelligent as Stratus is strong. All four are very close-knit, and they are all lethally effective in everything they do."

"And what do they do? Normally, I mean."

That question came from Thaddeus Galban, and Cato looked at him, smiling very slightly. "They work for me," he said, and young Galban blinked once and said nothing more.

"They belong, then," Strabo said, in a tone that was not quite a question.

"Yes, they belong." Cato kept his eyes on Galban and saw the brief confusion in the younger man's eyes as he tried to understand what had been said. And that confusion showed him that the youthful secretary had not yet learned all of his legate's secrets. A glance at Regulus Culver and Gaius Valerius confirmed what he had suspected there, too: Valerius also belonged. Culver, judging by his frown, did not.

"Three shipments stolen, you said, from Londinium and Eboracum." There was no doubt in anyone's mind that Alexander Strabo had absorbed everything Cato had said when he arrived, and had no need to hear it all again. "I presume the missing shipment destined for Lindum was the one from Eboracum. The two for Camulodunum and Aquae would have originated in Londinium. Do we have any idea who was behind the thefts?"

"We know exactly who it was." The statement was blunt. "It was the same crew of thieves we stopped last year, when they were raiding the grain trains south of Lindum. They're still out there, but they've upgraded their operations—and their depredations. Last year the harvest was bad, so they stole grain. We intercepted them, killed some of them in skirmishes, hanged half a score of others, and thought we had put them out of operation. But we hadn't. They simply refilled their ranks and changed direction. Now they're stealing the coinage we use to pay our troops—gold, silver, and copper. One successful raid on a paymaster's train might have been random chance. Two of them, though? And three stretches belief. We checked the chain of command in all three jurisdictions affected by the raids, and we're confident we know who two of the three informants were—or are. Those two are from Camulodunum and Lindum, and in the time I've been on the road, we've probably identified the third source, in Londinium. All are senior officers, highly placed and privy to confidential information, including delivery schedules and routing plans for the paymasters' shipments. And all of them, believe me, are destined for courts martial as soon as we have gathered sufficient proof to nail them to the crosses they deserve to hang on. We also recognized the style of the raids. These attacks were planned in detail."

"Planned by whom?" Regulus Culver was leaning forward, tensed like a hound on a leash.

"We know the name of the principal operative, the man who organized and led the raids. His name is Appius Endor, but behind his back people call him the Basilisk. Have you heard of him?"

"No," Culver said.

"I've never heard of him, either," Galban said, "but I know what a basilisk is, I think. Isn't it mythical? Some kind of reptile so hideous that its gaze can kill?"

Cato nodded. "Something of that kind. Its stare is supposed to be lethal, even its breath. Not a pleasant creature to encounter in a dark place. But an appropriate name for a man like Endor. We are familiar with how he operates, and from that, and what we learned from the three raids, we were able to infer that he still works for the same people who employed him last year and the year before. We still don't know who those people are, though, and that's the sticking point. We could take him into custody at any time, depriving them of their main field commander, but that would only give us a short breathing space before they replaced him with someone new, someone unknown to us. We chose to retain the basilisk we know over the chimera we wouldn't. So rather than arrest him, we watch him closely and constantly. The hope is that sooner or later he will lead us to his employers, or at least into some situation from which we'll be able to learn, or to deduce, who is behind the whole thing."

"Pardon me," Thaddeus Galban interjected, "but who are *we*? Do you mean the authorities? And when you say your men *belong*, what do they belong to? The imperial army?" His earnest young face was wrinkled from the intensity of his focus.

Cato grinned at him and confused him further. "No," he said. "And yes." He then looked directly to Strabo. "I am presuming you've decided to raise these two. Otherwise they wouldn't be here. So now would be an appropriate time to do it, to put the pilus's mind at ease and save young Galban from an apoplexy." He saw his brother-in-law smile and nod, and he turned back to Galban, who had subsided into his chair, open-mouthed and wide-eyed. "Prepare for the next step in your progress, then," he said. "You, too, Magister Culver. You should both refill your cups before anything else is said. And if Gaius Valerius has no objection, I will, too."

"Permit me," the lanky adjutant said, rising lithely and bringing the ice-filled chest from the sideboard to place it on the floor between them and the fire. He then refilled their cups from the chilled ewer while the two outsiders sat looking from one to the other of their three companions in bewilderment.

When they were settled again, Strabo rose to his feet. "A libation, my friends, to the Unconquered Sun." He waited while the others rose to join him, their cup-bearing arms extended, and then they all bent forward slightly in unison and tipped their cups to allow a little of their wine to spill into the melting ice, in tribute to their military god, Mithras Sol Invictus, Mithras the Unconquered Sun. The salutary ritual completed, they resumed their seats, and Strabo took a token sip before starting to speak.

"When we say we *belong*," he began, "it means that we have advanced to the fourth level of initiation into the sacred mysteries of Mithras, an estate about which you two know nothing. You are both initiates of the third level, and until this moment you have supposed that there was no further to advance. Am I correct, or have you heard whispers to the contrary?"

He scanned their faces as they gaped at him, and then he nodded in satisfaction. "Good. But there is life beyond the third level, and your oath of silence extends to embrace that knowledge henceforth. It is now time for you to advance to the fourth and join the fraternity we call the syndexioi—the brethren united by the handshake."

Strabo pointed his index finger at the space above the heads of the two initiates. "From the moment you enter that status," he continued, "your lives will be forever altered, for the simple act of shaking hands with any man will enable you to know, merely from the grip exchanged, who belongs to our fraternity, who does not, and which level of initiation each man has attained. The lowest level will be the fourth, the highest the seventh, and each of those men will be bound under sacred oath to stand as your brother in time of greatest need."

He looked from one to the other of the two initiates. "Before I continue I must formally ask, as you are all aware from your previous initiations: is either one of you unable or unwilling to commit to proceeding from this point onward?"

Culver moved his head briefly in a tight little shaking motion, frowning ferociously. Galban sat rapt and motionless.

"So be it," Strabo said. "I will decree the killing of a white bull within the week, and we will proceed with the ritual ceremonial meal one month from tonight." He glanced sideways at Cato. "Unfortunately, Brother, you may not be here to attend our celebrations, but we have sufficient brethren in Isca to complete the consecration with ease."

Cato nodded in acknowledgment, and Strabo, once more the imperial legate rather than the friend, again addressed the two supplicants.

"You have both eaten meals of the bull four times, beginning with the least attractive part, the tail, which some initiates consider the tastiest and most delicious part of all—when properly prepared." One corner of his mouth flickered. "And of course it is always most properly prepared for our first-level initiation, as spicy, thickened soup and succulent meat stew.

"When you rose to the second level, you ate bull ribs, roasted over air-blown coals with thickened garum, onions, garlic, and salt. The third level, your finest thus far, brought you to a meal of the tenderest loin, to mark your graduation from the ranks of novices and signify your status as an entitled soldier and servant of the Unconquered Sun." He sniffed.

"For most men, that is enough. A man may live a long and honourable life of service, with distinction, as a third-level brother."

He sipped at his cup of Falernian and savoured it before he resumed. "For others, though," he said, "and by that I mean for those qualified and prepared to work and sacrifice to earn the privilege, the third level is merely a beginning, and the sole way forward thereafter is by invitation."

He regarded the two initiates, whose eyes were locked on his, and sipped again from his cup, managing to appear both relaxed and magisterial at the same time. "That invitation, when it comes, is not extended lightly, nor is it tendered, ever, at the whim of one particular person. Each prospective candidate, without exception, is proposed and sponsored by a trio of current brethren, men who have observed him closely for a long time and who must concur upon nine out of ten points of referral. And then, after that proposal has been accepted, each candidate is watched even more carefully, in absolute secrecy, by other brethren for a probationary period of two years. The objective of that surveillance is, of course, to ensure that the nine points of assurance agreed upon by the nominating trio, which included fundamental attributes like honesty, loyalty, sincerity, probity, and truthfulness, were accurate and dependable. You two have now been under scrutiny for the requisite two years, and I am privileged to tell you that your elevation to the fourth level has been approved. I had intended to tell you so tonight anyway, but Brother Cato's fortuitous arrival has made the occasion even more appropriate. You will have to undergo initiation, of course, but at this stage that is a formality. For all intents and purposes, you are now syndexioi, brethren of the handshake. And the fourth-level version of that handshake I will now teach to you."

Culver and Galban rose to stand with him as he carefully taught the supplicants how to extend the proper grip and how to respond to it when they encountered it from someone else.

Cato and Valerius watched critically, and when they were satisfied that the ritual had been properly learned, Cato proposed a toast to the two new members of their brotherhood. Afterwards, he looked again to Strabo, who said, "So be it. We have much yet to do tonight and I think that, for convenience and ease of conversation, we should move back to the table." He set his cup down on the dining table and pulled his own chair back to where he had sat at dinner.

When everyone was seated again around the table, Alexander Strabo held up his drinking cup. "My friends, we should give thanks, yet again, to Gaius Valerius for this excellent wine, but we have formal matters to attend to now, so I suggest we drink no more of it until we are done— other than what is already in our cups, I mean. Regulus, Thaddeus, we can talk openly now. Ask us anything you wish."

There was a pause before Galban raised a hand slightly and said, "I have a question." He turned to Cato, who was sitting next to him. "*Us*, you said when you first spoke of belonging. I *think* I know what you meant now, but I'm not entirely sure. I suspect there is more than you were admitting. Am I correct?"

Cato grinned at Strabo, who was sitting at the head of the table. "You're right," he said. "This lad cuts right to the centre of things. And yes, Thaddeus, you are correct. There is more, more than you can begin to imagine, and you're going to have to absorb most of it quickly— abnormally quickly, I regret to say, because of circumstances. I'll leave it to your legate to explain."

"From now on," Strabo said, "you are going to be asked to accept many things on trust, with no more to rely on for backup than our assurances as your new brothers. We're going to ask you to change your minds, sometimes even to change your thinking, radically, even to deny much that you have been taught to believe until now. It might shock you deeply at first. As Cato said, we would normally take the time to introduce you gradually to new ways of thinking and of perceiving things, but in this case we have no time. You have both known me and worked with me for years now, and you know Gaius Valerius as well as you do me. With him as my witness, then, I can do no more than ask you, as brothers in the Unconquered Sun, to trust me. Can you accept that?"

Regulus Culver grinned. "Of course we accept it. Don't we, Thaddeus? After all, what option do we have? If we don't, you'll kill us." No one else smiled, and his face sobered instantly. "Pardon me," he said. "Ill-timed humour. On my oath to Mithras, I swear loyalty."

"And I do, too," Galban added.

"So be it, then. Let's get to work. Think about this, both of you: what would you identify as the single most important thing that Diocletian did during his reign? I need each of you to decide on one event, or one decision, that set him apart as an emperor."

Galban ventured, "His persecution of the Christians?" The very tone of his voice, though, tentative and timid, betrayed his lack of confidence, and no one chose to comment on his suggestion.

Regulus Culver was much more positive. "Diocletian saved the god-forsaken empire," he said. "Couldn't do anything more impressive than that."

"How so?" Strabo's question was unemphatic.

"How *so*?" Culver looked astonished, but then he frowned and looked about him, scowling. "Are you asking me that as a brother or as an imperial legate?"

"A brother. Pretend I've no idea what you're talking about. How did Diocletian save the empire? Convince me."

The primus pilus looked down at his own knees, his brow creased deeply. He sat motionless, and no one made any sound that might distract him. Eventually, he cleared his throat and sat up straight.

"Well, he saved the armies, for one thing. When Diocletian came to power, the legions were on their last legs, because for years they hadn't been supplied as they should have been. Whether that was through incompetent government or stupidity within the administration doesn't matter. The only thing that mattered was what wasn't happening, and what *was* happening was destroying the legions. Some units—hundreds of them, truth be told—had been left in the field, unsupported for years, abandoned to live or die on their own initiative. So they had taken to living off the land around them, plundering local farms and businesses to maintain some semblance of readiness. They had lived for too long with no regular supplies—no weapons, no food, and no pay—and many of them had disintegrated completely. Those still intact, and there were too few of those, couldn't have lasted much longer without help." He paused.

"But it wasn't that alone," he continued. "It wasn't just the military situation, though all the gods know there would be no Rome without the legions. When Diocletian seized the reins, the whole empire was tottering like a chariot on the edge of one wheel. It was a shit-clogged mess from end to end, a brimming latrine set to swallow up the whole world. And it had been that way, growing worse all the time, ever since Severus Alexander was murdered. That was seventy years ago. After that, everything went downhill like a runaway wagon. The power blocs in Rome, who really ran the empire, panicked after the murder and started raising taxes, pretending that there still was an emperor. But there wasn't. The Praetorian Guard had made sure of that when they killed Alexander. He was the last of the Severans. Anyone with a brain in his head knew there was no heir."

Strabo was frowning, and he held up a hand. "I think I might have misunderstood you there. I thought I heard you speak of power blocs in Rome, who really ran the empire. Was that correct?"

Culver gazed back at him and nodded slowly. "That's what I said. Factions, organized clusters of self-fattening maggots, all serving the imperial court in one way or another, all advising the imperial deity, and all looking after their own interests, manipulating everything from behind the scenes. Court eunuchs, members of the imperial council, members of the imperial family, relatives of the imperial family, friends of relatives of the imperial family, army generals—too damn many of those—and entire legions of arrogant priests, smug, smirking clerks, and self-important underlings. They call themselves assemblies and councils and caucuses and guilds and colleges and they're everywhere, and they all have their own agendas. And yet nothing in any of those agendas has much to do with anything beyond their own self-interest. Certainly it has nothing to do with the welfare of the empire or any of the common people in it."

"You astound me, Regulus." Strabo was wide-eyed with admiration. "I had no idea you cared so deeply, or at all, about such matters."

"Don't know as I care that deeply," Culver said with a shrug. "It interests me, that's all—the corruption of it all. I know about it mainly because my brother Faro loves to write about things like that. He's a scholar and a scribe who has lived in Rome all his life, attached to the imperial staff, and he has always been intrigued by ambitious and ruthless people, ever since he was a lad and saw the mayor of our local town commit a murder and walk away unscathed simply because he *was* the mayor. From then on Faro was fascinated by the things people are willing to do in order to gain power, the things they'll do to feed it and maintain it and hang on to it once they have achieved it. Most of all, though, he watches how they use their power. And every now and then he writes to me, telling me of his findings." He shrugged again. "Over the years I've come to enjoy his musings, and even to think for myself, trying to see beyond the obvious things surrounding me. And when I do, I tend to get angry."

"Fascinating," Strabo murmured. "Tell us more, if you will, about what Diocletian inherited."

Regulus Culver sniffed deeply, now at his ease. "Well, for one thing, the armies—those that remained operational, I mean—had gone mad. There was no line of succession after Severus. The dynasty was done, and there was no legitimate claimant to the throne. And the Praetorians had finally destroyed themselves in killing Severus. They had been loathed and distrusted for decades, but that crime wiped out the last vestiges of belief anyone might have had in their integrity.

"In the old days, when a situation like that arose, a victorious army would propose one of its own as emperor, an *imperator* triumphant on the battlefield. But before Diocletian, with no successor in sight, every unit in the empire seemed to elect one of its own. Faro told me—and believe me, he knows—we had near fifty emperors proclaimed in different places throughout the empire in forty years, and fewer than ten of those survived for more than two years. It was insane."

"They weren't all bad, those men," Cato demurred.

"No, they weren't. A couple of decent men rose up during that time. Claudius the Second was the best of them. He might have made a real difference if he had lived, but the plague got him before he was two years in power, so we'll never know. The truth, though, is that no one, anywhere, trusted anything anymore. People had lost faith. The government had devalued the coinage, almost completely cutting down the amounts of gold and silver in coins, so traders stopped trading because they couldn't rely on being paid full value for their goods. When a merchant can't trust that there's gold in a gold coin, he can't trust anything. That was an absolute catastrophe, and one we still haven't heard the last of, you mark my words."

He turned to Thaddeus Galban, clearly believing that the secretary was too young to understand the gravity of what he was being told. "Before all that trouble started," he explained, "a single gold aureus weighed one fiftieth of a gold pound—a solid, measurable truth against which all the lesser coins, from a silver denarius to a copper as, were valued. And there were supposedly a hundred denarii to the aureus. Supposedly, I say, because five hundred to one wasn't uncommon in areas where the market demanded that. As for sesterces, at supposedly one hundred to the denarius, the response to that would have been a loud laugh, because they were really trading at something like three hundred to the denarius, so the real value was close to nil. Before Diocletian came along, there was barely any silver at all in a denarius, and people refused to use them, so some dimwit in Rome came up with the idea of a double denarius, and they made it out of some new amalgam of rubbish that was supposed to be a new and precious metal, half silver and half gold. What was it called?" He looked at Cato but provided his own answer. "Antoninianus, that was it. A very fine-sounding name for shit. Cities all over the empire were setting up their own mints and stamping out their own coins and they were all rubbish, so thoroughly debased and devalued that no one knew what anything was worth in real terms, so no one would touch money. People started bartering again, staying close to home and trading locally with people they knew. They stopped travelling because it wasn't worth the time and effort when all they were likely to find on their journeys was grief."

"Diocletian did stop the damage, though." This was Valerius. "He issued the new gold coin, the solidus, to regain that lost confidence."

"Regain, my arse," Culver said scathingly. "There was nothing left to regain by then, even at one thousand denarii to the new solidus, and it wasn't Diocletian's fault. Introducing the solidus was a fine effort, but it was much too little, far too late. There are folk out there today who have never heard of a gold solidus, let alone seen one, and the things have been in existence for more than ten years by now. But they were minted in *Rome*. And for the most part, they're still in Rome. Do you believe there is a single farmer in Gaul who is going to feel better about feeding his family because he knows gold coins are being used in Rome?" He shook his head. "That is never going to affect anything in his life, and your Gaulish farmer was well aware of that long before Diocletian ever thought about being emperor."

He stopped, scowling angrily, then shook his head for emphasis. "No, by the time Diocletian came along the empire was a mess from one end to the other, and barbarian invaders were howling on all sides— prancing, godless creatures from the farthest depths of the world outside the empire's borders, cursed Persians in the east, slant-eyed Huns on the northern banks of the Danube, and whole federations of bare-arsed barbarian tribes in the northwest, along the Rhine." He shook his head again. "I'm amazed that he took on the job at all. I wouldn't have, I know that. Not for *five* imperial crowns. But he could see what the problem was, and he moved to solve it instantly." He stopped abruptly. "Do any of you know what that problem really was?"

"Of course," Strabo said. "The empire was too big for any man to rule alone."

"Absolutely correct. Too big and too deeply damned by uncaring gods. And why? Because for ages the emperors hadn't really been emperors at all. They'd abdicated their power soon after the rule of the original Caesars, ages earlier, handing the running of the entire thing over to councils and caucuses and bureaucrats in return for the privilege of being left alone to live a quiet life in privacy. And that's what I was talking about when I spoke of power blocs. It's hard to accept, but until Diocletian started kicking arses, there hadn't been a real emperor since before Septimius Severus founded his dynasty more than a hundred years earlier. In all that time the empire had been run by functionaries, all of them hiding behind the image of whatever 'divine' emperor was in power." He stopped suddenly, as if aware that he had been speaking treason. "Well, you asked me what I thought, and I told you."

Strabo was looking from one to the other of the men sitting with him, his eyebrow quirked high. He looked at Thaddeus Galban last. "Interesting viewpoint, don't you think? Do you agree with it?"

"I do." There was no hesitation. "I agree with the primus completely. I had not thought about it until he spoke of it, but as soon as he did, I knew he was right. And the more he said, the more I agreed with him." He sipped at his wine, then asked Strabo, "What answer were you hoping for?"

"Oh, the first part, about saving the armies. But Regulus kicked that aside as being unimportant in the greater scheme of things."

Galban's eyes narrowed. "No, sir," he said slowly. "The primus said nothing about its being unimportant. He merely defined it as one of a mixture of ills. But I suspect that until he did so, you thought that saving the armies was the most important part of all. Why?"

"Why?" Strabo rested his chin on the ends of his steepled fingers. "I suppose because I saw it as the reason we five are here together." He hesitated. "The 'us' you asked about earlier."

"Forgive me, sir," Galban said, frowning, "but I don't follow you."

"Nor should you, because I'm making no sense—at least not yet. Diocletian did save the legions, because from the moment he assumed power he made it his priority to see that they were all supplied. He tolerated no sloth. He insisted that records be kept to ensure that materials were delivered on time and as ordered, and he would accept no excuses for poor performance. Diocletian had absolutely no patience for half measures. As emperor, he was commander-in-chief, and as commander-in-chief he made sure that every man under his command had appropriate clothing, armour, weapons, food, and everything else required to do what was demanded of him—which was to protect the empire.

"That was an enormous undertaking, and it was not achieved overnight, but it was achieved. From among the legions under his own direct command he conscripted a corps of loyal, trusted young officers—young and loyal being the important words there—and charged them with the duty of making his vision a reality. He gave them the power and authority to ensure that whatever needed to be done was done properly, and that people at every level of responsibility were held accountable for the performance of their duties."

Regulus spoke up then. "I remember that. It was just before I joined the ranks myself. I've been in for twenty-five years now, and he'd been emperor for about three years before I joined up." He grunted a sound that might have been a stifled laugh. "I remember how excited everyone was in my first camp, because they had just been paid—really paid, I mean, with hard money in their hands—for the first time in ages. And a new train of wagons had come in with weaponry only the month before—new spears and swords and factory-made shields blazoned with the legion's crests and colours. You're right, Legate. It gave all the legions a new grasp on life and gave us back our pride. In those days we thought him a miracle worker."

"He was," Strabo said. "Diocletian had a miraculous ability to pick men for their talents, to set them challenging tasks, and then to leave them to get on with what he asked of them. Very few men have that kind of ability, that kind of confidence. But it inspires insane levels of loyalty and encourages ordinary men to perform extraordinary feats that they wouldn't normally think of tackling. Those young officers he charged with supplying the legions—and my own father was one of them—performed prodigiously, and the most amazing aspect of their achievements was that few of them had any experience doing the kinds of things he asked of them. But they learned how to do them better, and how to speed things up, and they perfected a system of logistics, a method of connecting all the armies throughout the whole empire, that hadn't existed ten or twenty years earlier.

"And then they learned something else. About something that, perhaps foolishly, they hadn't expected to find. Human nature at work."

Galban absently picked up his glass cup and had raised it to his lips before he saw that it was empty. He set it down distractedly and said, "Forgive me for being dense, sir, but I still don't know what you are talking about."

"You're not being dense, Thaddeus," Strabo said straightforwardly. "You're being young. And you are thirsty. I think we're far enough along now to be able to have some more wine." He looked at Valerius. "Gaius, would you?"

Valerius rose immediately and crossed to the table that held the chilled wine.

"Regulus," Strabo said, "can you help Thaddeus?"

"Aye," the primus pilus growled, almost to himself. "Mayhap I can . . . Human nature at work, you said. Seems to me, after spending all my life in this empire's army, that every time I dream up a system to ensure that everything runs smoothly for a time, in whatever billet I'm posted to, there's always some know-it-all who'll spend whatever time is needed to figure out a way to outwit me and my system and to profit from it. And every other officer I know, in every other unit, says the same thing. There's always a rodent in there who'd rather steal than work. It seems to be a part of human nature, if you can call Rome's legionary grunts human. Am I right?"

Strabo smiled. "Go on," he said.

Culver turned his head slightly to watch as Gaius Valerius filled his cup with more of the rich, amber wine. "But that was only in the confines of my own camp," he continued. "You were talking about a system that was empire-wide. A system that *delivered* empire-wide. And so I'd guess that somebody had devised a way to get around the system and get rich by infiltrating it and robbing it without being caught."

Strabo clapped his hands together. "Bravo, Brother Culver. I couldn't have described it better myself. Diocletian's new system of logistics was being pillaged by a highly organized group of criminals who had at their disposal what seemed like limitless funds for criminal activities throughout the empire. They were operating far and wide, intercepting shipments and stealing entire trains of wagons filled with military supplies, which they then sold in nearby markets. It was outrageous. It was successful. It was highly secretive. And it soon gave birth to the 'us' you were curious about earlier, Thaddeus. The 'us' that started all this."

Thaddeus Galban picked up his cup and held it out straight-armed to Regulus Culver, who touched it with the rim of his own, and then he said to Strabo, "Fine. Now tell us who we are and what you'll be expecting of us."

Alexander Strabo laughed, a brief burst of sound that reflected the amusement and pleasure in his eyes. "We'll expect everything from both of you as new recruits, and then we'll demand more. That should be no surprise to either one of you. You've both been in the legions long enough to know how all the scut jobs go to the newest recruits. It's an article of legionary faith."

Galban twisted his mouth wryly in agreement, but as the others laughed at his discomfiture, the humour leached from Strabo's face, replaced by a blank, solemn mask. The others fell silent and turned as one man to face their commander.

"As for who we are," Strabo resumed, "that's another matter entirely. We are the syndexioi, brethren of the fourth level of the sacred mysteries of Mithras. And in the eyes of the world, we do not exist."

"But we do exist," Galban said. "That's why we are here."

"Correct, Brother. We do exist, and we are here."

Galban's brows wrinkled. "Correct," he repeated. "We do exist, even though the rest of the world doesn't know it . . . I know that, for I had never heard of the syndexioi until tonight. So how does this connect to the breakdown of Diocletian's system?"

"I was beginning to think you might never ask me that. If you really think about what we have been discussing here tonight, the connection might come to you."

He waited, watching the younger man's face, then prompted him. "Corruption," he said. "Corruption and secrecy. Each one makes the other necessary." His eyes flicked sideways. "Can you see that, Regulus?"

The primus nodded. "Yes, sir," he said. "It's understandable. Corruption can't survive after being exposed, and that means it needs secrecy."

"Exactly." Strabo looked again at Thaddeus Galban. "Listen closely, both of you," he said. "Diocletian was a fine emperor. But he was an emperor, and for that very reason he had many enemies. But one thing no one could say about him, whether friend or enemy, was that he was stupid. Nor was he indecisive. This was the man who rejuvenated the legions with nothing more than his own integrity and his own will.

"As soon as they brought him proof that his system had been penetrated and that thieves were undermining his work, he arrived at two conclusions. First, the rot was thriving. He had to find it and destroy it. Second, in order to succeed, he would need help—help from large numbers of loyal, experienced, dedicated, dependable, and trustworthy people.

"And at that point, Gaius Aurelius Valerius Diocletianus, emperor of Rome, reached what any sane man would have considered a dead end. The empire was filled with men who would rush to do his bidding, but finding men who could meet *all* his criteria—loyalty, experience, dedication, dependability, *and* trustworthiness—well, that was another matter entirely."

"Aye." The assent emerged as a bass rumble from the primus pilus, who was unaware that he had even uttered it.

Strabo continued. "He had a solid corps of veterans with whom he could start—those very officers who had designed his system in the first place. But right at the outset, he couldn't use them, because he was faced with the simplest problem facing anyone who ever attempts to stamp out corruption. Can either of you tell me what that is?"

Galban nodded. "He didn't know who to trust."

"Precisely. How could he even begin to *guess* who was trustworthy? Where was he to start, knowing that a single word in the wrong ear could result in the enemy finding out that he was now aware of them and preparing to move against them? Bear in mind that the problem was deeply rooted by that time, and he had to assume that those wrong ears could be anywhere, and listening."

"That must have cut the heart from him," the primus pilus said, "if he was as proud as you say he was of what those men had achieved. But he must have found *some*one to trust, otherwise we wouldn't be talking about this. Where did he start looking?"

"He started," Strabo said, "the same place you did."

The primus blinked slowly. "I don't follow," he said.

"You do. We all follow. Think, Regulus!"

Culver's frown slowly gave way to amazement and he said, in awe, "The brotherhood! Diocletian was one of *us*? One of the syndexioi?"

"He was. And why should that surprise you? He started out as a common grunt like every other conscript. He fought his way up through the ranks the same way all of us did. He became a member of the brotherhood as soon as he was fit to qualify, and went through the three levels of the Mithraic mysteries when all his friends did. But Diocles had always been exceptional in everything he did, and because of that he was soon invited to join the fourth level, the brethren of the handshake. He had been a brother for years, but he had never made much use of his entitlement. At that critical time, though, he recognized that all the virtues that he needed most—all the attributes he required in those who would undertake this task with him—were already there, in place among his own brotherhood.

"At a plenary session of the syndexioi, he laid out to his brothers the difficulties facing the empire and its armies. He pointed out how immensely well organized the thieves were, and made it clear that they could not operate without help from people within the armies, people who knew the details of the shipments being raided and were no doubt profiting enormously from feeding off their own."

"I'd crucify all of them," Culver muttered, but Strabo ignored him.

"He then requested permission to proceed against this criminal organization under the auspices of the Mithraic brotherhood, and with the full benediction of the syndexioi, stressing the need for absolute secrecy and trust."

"And?" Galban jumped in. "What happened?"

"The brotherhood gave him its blessing. How could it not? It is the brotherhood of the mysteries of Mithras the Unconquered Sun, and Mithras is the god of soldiers. Diocletian was calling for Mithras's divine aid directly, asking for his assistance to defend Rome's soldiers against iniquity. And so we were born when Diocletian created a new entity, the like of which has never existed in Rome's history—a specialized secret force within the military, dedicated to eradicating corruption within the legions. And to ensure its absolute security, its membership would be drawn solely from the ranks of the syndexioi, bound by the sacred oaths they have sworn to Mithras Himself."

Culver shook his head in ungrudging admiration. "Forming a new group like that would have posed no difficulty for the emperor. He already knew how to do it."

"Did he?" Culver's comment was clearly unexpected, and Strabo frowned. "How?"

"From his early days." The primus pilus appeared surprised that Strabo would have to ask him that. "He was in the prefecture of Illyricum—in Lesser Moesia, in fact—when he was young. Didn't you know that? That's where he first made his name, fighting under Probus when *he* was emperor. It's where he was invited to join the Invincibles."

"The Invincibles." Strabo sounded nonplussed. "Who are they?"

Culver frowned. "You don't know? Hmm . . . I *think* that's their name. In fact I'm sure it is. They're some kind of elite group within the old Illyrican army—which is now, be it said, a very large part of the Roman army. They've been around for something like eight hundred years, and they're very jealous of their history and traditions. They run their own operations and in military matters they're apparently a law unto themselves in Moesia. They're something like us, now that I come to think of it—very private, highly self-sufficient, and they take themselves very seriously. The story I heard is that Diocles was invited to join them while he was in Moesia with Probus—one of the few Romans ever to be invited directly."

"I see," Strabo said. "And did you wish to make a point from that?"

"No," Culver said. "I simply thought that if all I've heard about Diocles is true, he would have studied what set these Invincibles apart, the things they had and did that marked them as elite. He would have taken it all in and stored it away in his head for some future time of need."

"I see what you mean," Strabo said. "And you might very well be right, but the emperor's been dead for nearly a year, so we'll never know, will we? All we can be sure of is that he established our force."

"So did he preside over this new force in person?" This was Galban again, and Strabo grimaced ruefully.

"No, how could he? He had an empire to govern and protect. He set the force up strongly, though. Arranged its funding so that it would operate as an autonomous entity funded by the imperial treasury—an obscure and appropriately opaque entity, mind you. He also ensured that its commander would be equally autonomous, free of restrictions and answerable only to the emperor himself. He then placed complete authority for the whole thing in the hands of one of his oldest and most trusted associates, Titanius Varrus, who had been born in the same town, perhaps in the same villa, as the emperor himself."

"Titanius Varrus," Galban said. "I've never heard of him."

"I have, but I never met him, though he's far from dead, apparently. He's quite the ancient Roman, I've been told. Noble, upright, virtuous, the very embodiment of *dignitas*. Among his own circle, he's generally known as Tertius, and he was Diocletian's closest friend, perhaps his only one. The two grew up as close as brothers—closer, in fact, since they chose each other as friends—and they joined the legions together in Italy when they came of age. I've heard that Varrus had the higher rank at first—Diocles's father was apparently Varrus's father's chief clerk—but he chose to follow Diocles once they joined the legions and his friend's inborn abilities began to show themselves, and he served him faithfully thereafter, throughout his life. A fine, upstanding man who proved worthy of the trust placed in him."

"I'm sure he was," Galban said. "I merely wondered that I have never heard of him."

Strabo turned his head slightly to address his young subaltern more directly. "He rose through the ranks, serving with distinction alongside Diocletian," he said mildly. "But then he moved deliberately into obscurity, and from there, for three decades starting before you were born, he ran an organization that is not supposed to exist, Thaddeus. Where *would* you have heard of him?" Galban looked suitably chagrined, and

Strabo continued. "No matter. So Varrus, once given control, organized the new force as he would have organized a newly commissioned legion, save that it had no name and no official existence in the eyes of anyone outside the fraternity, and fro—"

"Wait, how could that—?" Galban subsided immediately, grinning sheepishly. "Of course," he said. "Pardon me. The paymasters would all be brethren, too."

"They are now," Strabo said gently. "It took a few months, but it was achieved. Now, after decades in place, the officials necessary to the procurement of funding and facilities are all brethren. My own father ranks among the most senior of them."

Regulus Culver flicked a hand and asked, "Who took over when this Varrus fellow died?"

"No one," Cato answered. "Didn't you hear what I said? He is still alive and well and as efficient as he ever was. He runs the organization from his home base in Dalmatia. He's probably close to seventy by now, but he hasn't lost one whit of his ability to do his job. My father is over there with him now, on our official behalf, accompanied by my wife and my mother."

"Another question, if I may," Culver said. "What are we called? We must have a name."

"Why?" Strabo was smiling. "We don't *need* a name, Regulus. We all know who we are and what we do. Having a name creates a danger that someone might drop it carelessly somewhere, creating difficulties for everyone. So we decided long ago not to have a name. We never talk about ourselves with anyone but our brothers anyway. And now that you have joined us, you'll find out that while we communicate nothing of ourselves or our activities to the outside world, our internal communications are excellent—thorough and very precise." He turned his head and spoke to Galban. "You've been handling them ever since you started working for me, Thaddeus. Do you think there's anything obscure or inadequate about them?"

"No, sir," Galban answered, looking slightly bewildered. "But I don't know what you're talking about."

"Precisely. So bear that in mind and don't fret. It all seems over-whelming now, I imagine, but once you've had a few days to absorb what we've told you here, and you settle into the newness of it all, you'll feel much better, I promise you."

He sat back, bracing his shoulders against his chair, then stood up, clapping his hands together. "In the meantime, though—and I'm speak-ing to you two newcomers—we have arrived at the reason for your sudden advancement to the syndexioi, and it fits neatly into Cato's unexpected delivery tonight of paymaster's supplies to pay our troops. These people—thieves, brigands, pirates, call them what you will—are stealing more and more audaciously all the time, and they're making us look foolish. They have to be stopped, and we are the ones who have to stop them."

He glanced at each of the new initiates in turn. "So we are putting two new investigative procedures into place here in Britain immedi-ately, and each of you will be responsible for one of them. Those of us assigned to watch you more than two years ago are convinced that you are both capable of doing what is required. We've been doing advance planning on your behalf ever since"—he smiled broadly—"and holding our collective breath fearfully in case you failed to qualify for raising."

Strabo held aloft a long, narrow piece of scrolled parchment. "Regulus," he said, reading from what he had written earlier, "as primus pilus of the Second Legion, you are required, on my authority as impe-rial legate, to launch a thorough investigation into logistical irregulari-ties, including thefts and disappearances, that have been brought to your attention by sources inside your legionary quartermaster's divi-sion. You will announce that investigation formally within the next few days, and issue written orders demanding the surrender and delivery to you of all records pertaining to the ordering, delivery, and distribution of all supplies assigned to, and shipped from, legionary premises and installations in the past five years—" He broke off and looked at the adjutant, wrinkling his nose. "Should that be three years, Gaius, or would that be too short a span?" He blinked, and answered his own question. "No, let's make it the last *four* years. That should go far enough back to ensure that people see the seriousness of this, and it should be far enough back, too, to uncover any patterns that might emerge. We can dig back further after that, if necessary."

Regulus Culver was about to speak, but Strabo cut him off with a raised hand. "Wait, if you will. Let me finish. Clearly you're going to need an army of clerics, to examine everything that comes back to you." He began to pace the floor, his hands clasped at his back, one of them still holding his notes. "They're going to have to examine all of it meticulously, too. Meticulously . . . No stone left unturned." He reached the end of the line he was pacing and turned back. "That means they're going to have to know what to look for, where to begin—and that means, in turn, that you're going to need some highly specialized help to put all that together, organize a training schedule, and then instruct your people on how to go about what we require of them."

He reached the table again and stopped, unclasping his hands and reaching down to run his thumb over the flawless surface of the polished citrus wood. "Even were we to start tonight," he said, looking at none of them, "that would still take at least a month, and probably closer to two, to put into place. Add another month to that, to train your new auditors, and we'll be looking at starting the investigation three months from now."

He turned quickly to Galban. "Don't be tempted to laugh at Regulus's workload, Thaddeus. Your turn is coming."

He looked back to where Culver sat watching him warily. "So," he said, "you will have three months. Can you be ready? It will probably take that long for you to organize the information flow. Make it clear to all your subordinates throughout the legion that no delinquencies will be tolerated. Every item of record relating to every transaction or ship-ment over the past four years must be submitted. Records of all that kind of thing must be kept for ten years anyway, so there's no acceptable excuse for not providing them. Don't hesitate to demand immediate surrender of everything."

He smiled, though it was more with apology than humour. "And in the meantime, you will coordinate similar efforts by your counterparts in the Sixth and Twentieth Legions in Deva and Eboracum. They will undertake precisely the same procedures within their jurisdictions, save that they will submit everything they collect to your own auditors. You will have full authority to demand that because you'll be acting upon the written orders of our western Caesar, Constantine, who is currently governor of Britannia in addition to his other imperial responsibilities. So you will have no problem with the other primuses, apart from their inevitable gripes about being hard done by.

"That's about all of it, as far as your responsibilities go. We will discuss it all in greater detail in the days ahead, but have you any ques-tions now?"

"One thing," Culver said. "What's happening with Constantine, does anyone know? Last I heard, he was somewhere in Gaul, moping because Maxentius had accused him of murdering his father, Maximian. We know that's nonsense, for Maximian was always a backstabbing, treacherous whoreson and his son's no better, but what is Constantine up to now? Did he go back up the Rhine frontier to fight the Franks? He's supposed to be our emperor here, but how can he expect loyalty from anyone if no one knows where he is, or even if he's still alive? We have more emperors nowadays than hippodromes have horses, and I, for one, have no idea who's claiming power where these days. Between Maximian and Galerius, Maxentius and Maximinus Daia, Licinius and Eusebius and Constantine, I don't know who's who anymore."

"Who in Hades is Eusebius?"

Thaddeus asked the question, and Strabo answered it without

looking at him. "He's a Christian bishop—the leader of the underground resistance in Rome. Maximian afforded him a degree of recognition two years ago, hoping to win some time for other things. But he's not a politician."

"Did I hear that correctly?" This was the adjutant. "Did you say he is not a politician? This bishop, Eusebius—have you ever known a priest of *any* stripe who was not a politician? I warn you, if you ever meet one face to face and believe what he tells you, you will be wise to buy nothing from him."

"I can add a little bit to what you know, Regulus," Cato said, cutting through the banter. "We had a fellow arrive with dispatches from the Rhine frontier a few days before we left to come here. He told us that the two eastern emperors, Licinius and Maximinus Daia, each of whom called himself Augustus, cancelled each other out last year. Apparently they had half a war and then both resigned and signed a truce, so they're both effectively out of the struggle that's still going on among the others—most notably between Constantine and Maxentius. Constantine marched south from the Rhine in the late autumn last year, against the advice of all his advisors, to invade northern Italy and challenge Maxentius face to face. He's there now, as far as we know, and at last report he was alive and well and angry."

"Our thanks, Brother Cato, for your information," Strabo said. "But we are not yet finished with these plans, so let us return to them." He pulled his scroll between his fingers so that the part he had read hung down from the back of his hand. "You, young Thaddeus," he said, picking up his glass cup with his free hand to sip the last of what was left in it. "I can promise you with confidence that you will not be complaining of having too much idle time on your hands in the foreseeable future. You will have the same kind of tasks laid at your door that Regulus will, but the scope of yours will be far wider than the primus pilus's." He set down his empty cup, shaking his head when Gaius Valerius moved to pour him more.

"Regulus will deal with the military end of things. You, on the other hand, will be dealing with the suppliers who equip and feed the armies, with the sole exception of the minting authorities who make the coins the paymasters use. We already know how those are processed, and each shipment from our paymasters is counted by hand before being dispatched, so there is no need to investigate any of that. Everything else, though, including complete information about every single individual who knows anything about or is involved in the transfer of bullion from the paymasters' depots to its final destination, has to be intensely scrutinized, because someone among those people—at least one person and almost certainly more than one—is feeding information to the thieves. We will expect you or your people to discover who that is.

"You will have noticed, I hope, that I spoke of *your people*. No one expects you to do all of this alone. Like Regulus, you will have a team to assist you. Your primary task, beginning tomorrow, will be to establish a new corps of auditors. And before you say it, I know there is already such a corps in existence. But clearly, judging by the widespread evidence of its incompetence, it is untrustworthy and will be disbanded. It will be replaced by your new corps, and no one who served in any capacity in the old body will be permitted to join the new one. You will build your new organization with no other restrictions. As with the primus pilus's task, you will have a three-month preparation period, and beginning tomorrow, you will have access to all the information we have on the best people at our disposal. Anyone you want, you may take."

"Question," said Culver. "Will all these people be brethren?"

"No. That simply would not be possible. But at the supervisory levels and above, yes, the personnel will all be brethren."

"Records collection," Galban added. "How will that be handled? It's not inconceivable that I might end up with ten times the volume of material the primus receives."

"No doubt," Strabo agreed. "Probably fifty times as much. Bear in mind that you won't be bothering with local requisitions, however. The expenditures and purchases would be too small to provide evidence of theft on an Olympian scale. And as I said, you will not lack either help or resources. The word has already gone out to a number of our brethren who will be glad to work with you on organizing this. The men I've summoned should start to arrive in the next week or so."

Galban frowned, instantly cautious. "Won't people take note of a new influx of men? How will we explain them?"

"Thaddeus," Strabo said, grinning because he had known the question would be asked. "On any single day in Isca, there are more than six thousand men, sometimes ten thousand during summer training exercises, and they come and go all the time. You think a mere hundred more officers will draw any attention? Besides, there's nothing secret about what we'll be doing. We'll be establishing another system of auditors—more regulatory horseshit. That's the extent of what people will think, if they think anything at all."

He drew himself erect and looked around the table. "I believe we're finished now, my friends. For tonight, at least. I suggest another glass of Gaius's magnificent wine, and then lights out. We have busy days ahead of us, starting tomorrow. Except for Cato here, of course, and his friends. They are officially on furlough, having delivered their cargo safely."

Gaius Valerius stood up and began to replenish their wine glasses, and Strabo turned to Cato. "I haven't even asked. How long will you be staying? Not that I want you to go, mind you," he added, laughing.

Cato shrugged, watching idly as Valerius filled his glass. "I don't really know, Alex," he said, nodding his thanks to the adjutant as he picked up his cup and swirled the wine under his nose, savouring its aroma. "I haven't really thought about it. We'll stay for a day or two at least, give my lads some time to rest and recuperate. They've earned some time off and we've no immediate urgencies clamouring at us, so we'll wait and see what happens when the paymaster's wagon train arrives from Londinium."

Valerius returned to the table and settled in to listen, as did the others, all of them waiting to hear what Cato would say next about the paymaster's wagon train.

He looked around the table and smiled. "No point in looking at me," he said to all of them. "Whether the contents of the train are intact or not will be your problem to deal with, my friends. I'll simply want the information for the sake of curiosity, and to update our records in Eboracum. By the time we get back home I have no doubt someone will have found plenty for us to do."

"On that topic of things to do," Strabo said, "what can you tell us about this Basilisk fellow? I think Regulus and Thaddeus will find it useful to know whatever is known. Endor was his name, was it not? Appius Endor?"

Cato studied his brother-in-law from beneath a cocked eyebrow as he savoured a mouthful of wine. "That is his name," he said eventually. "He came to our attention about five years ago, appearing from nowhere, it seemed. He's an obscure creature, tends to shun the light. We've had some of our best people watching out for him for more than three years now, but he has been remarkably difficult to pin down. So we don't know much about him, but I'll tell you what I can. We know he's a peasant from northern Gaul, a Belgian, a kinsman to Carausius, the upstart emperor. He's well up in middle age, and stronger than most men half his age.

"We know little more about him, and much is pure hearsay. The gist of it, though, is that he's a bad man to antagonize—ruthless, merciless, savage, all the usual frown-inducing words come to mind, but none of them are adequate. The truth is that this swine is inhuman in his dealings with people. He lacks any of the normal restraints and moral limitations that govern people. He is a butcher, unbelievably brutal, and defiantly, deliberately appalling in the atrocities he inflicts upon anyone unfortunate enough to come between him and what he wants. And what he wants is total dominion—over everyone and everything within the scope of his influence. His own people live in fear of him, for when they displease him he's likely to disembowel them or hack off their heads. He is dangerous, unpredictable, and completely savage. And evil. That is a word I seldom use, though in his case it might be appropriate. The sole sin I have *not* heard attributed to him is that he eats the flesh of those he kills. Apparently he has not sunk that low . . . or not yet."

"Sol Invictus!" Strabo mouthed the words reverently, as a prayer rather than an expletive. "Do you know where he is based?"

"No. He moves around frequently, roaming far and wide, so we never know where he will appear next. For all I know he could be here in your area now." Cato grimaced. "We suspect he is dealing nowadays with the local warlords down here in the far southwest, many of whom have galleys. Have you heard anything like that?"

The legate shook his head slowly. "No," he said quietly. "Not a thing. We find the occasional bandit around here, but it's far quieter than it was ten years ago. I know most of the Celtic chiefs in the region, and none of them has given me any reason for concern—and I think they would if there was any danger of something serious happening. They remember too well what happened last time they singed the Eagle's wings, about fifty years ago."

"We've heard rumours," Cato continued, "that large amounts of stolen goods are being shipped from local ports along the coastline here across the sea to Gaul. We have naval vessels out there watching, but nowhere near enough of them, and our information is not reliable enough to justify our asking the fleet for more." His eyes sharpened, and he leaned in closer to speak urgently to his brother-in-law. "But hear me clearly, Alex, and mind what I'm telling you. If the son of a whore does turn up in your jurisdiction, treat him as you would a venomous snake. Or even more aptly, treat him as you would his namesake, a basilisk. Kill the creature as soon as you see it, before it can kill you or anyone close to you. Don't try to reason with him, don't try to negotiate, don't try to come to terms with him on any grounds. Kill him."

"You make him sound immortal."

"Then I'm misrepresenting him. He is as mortal as death and pestilence, and there's nothing even remotely godlike about him. Here are a few more things we know about him. We know he spent his early years in the legions, and he served well, too, it seems, because to this day he wears a medallion presented to him by Carausius himself. He wears that medallion all the time—he's never been seen without it. And he has been said to wear a necklace of human ears, too. From what I know about the man, I wouldn't be surprised if that were true, though I suspect that might have been something he did one time only, for effect. Anyway, he went to sea when Maximian gave Carausius command of the British fleet and ordered him to destroy the Frankish and Saxon pirates in the seas around Britain. And we all know how that turned out."

"I don't," Galban said.

Cato grinned savagely. "It must be wonderful to be as young as you are, Thad," he drawled. "I'm talking about something that happened twenty years ago."

"Twenty years ago I was three years old, playing in the streets of Deva. What did Carausius do to the pirates he was sent to destroy?"

Cato, still grinning, continued. "It wasn't what he did *to them* that scandalized the world. It was the fact that he himself became a bigger pirate than all of them combined. He didn't waste a moment before he started to line his own pockets. From the day of his appointment as high admiral of the British fleet, Carausius skimmed every treasure hoard he recaptured. It was blatant, and yet no one could gainsay him. He would take a pirate ship at sea, slaughter its crew, and confiscate its cargo. But who was then to say how large, or how rich, that cargo had been? No one could tell, except his own men, and he paid them well to keep silent.

"But he hanged himself with his own greed. Easy success bred laziness, and greed and laziness led to overconfidence. He took to following pirate ships at a distance, allowing them to carry out their raids while he anchored offshore from the targeted towns and ports, waiting for the thieves to sail back out. He would then capture them, slay their crews, take the booty, and sink the ships. People everywhere complained bitterly, for he didn't even have the decency to hide what he was doing, and Maximian condemned him to death, at which point Carausius defied the whole world and proclaimed himself emperor of Britain and northern Gaul. He almost made it work, too. He ruled for seven whole years—longer than most of his contemporary usurpers—before one of his own commanders assassinated him."

"Allectus," Galban said. "I remember hearing about him."

Cato nodded. "That's the man. He didn't last long, either. Three years was all he had before they killed him in Britain. I was in the legions by then. That was only sixteen years ago." He swept the backs of his fingers along the underside of his chin. "Endor stayed with Carausius to the end, they say, but he wasn't there when Allectus killed him, and he certainly didn't give the new emperor any opportunity to do the same to him. He disappeared, for years, and only resurfaced after Allectus himself was dead—" He broke off, then shook his head, smiling wryly.

"Something amusing?" Strabo prompted.

"Nah," came the reply. "Typical, though. I've heard the same story three different times from three separate sources." He looked around at the others. "The story is that when Constantius's army finally hammered Allectus's rabble, wiping them out north of the place they call Stonehenge, Allectus stripped off his armour and every vestige of anything that might identify him, and fled on foot, fulfilling everyone's expectations of what he might do in a crisis. But as he was scampering bare-arsed across the battlefield, he heard his name being called and turned to find himself face to face with one of Carausius's avenging kinsmen, who had ample cause to recognize his cousin's murderer, be he naked or fully clothed. The fellow apparently gutted Allectus on the spot, then beheaded him and left his head jammed onto the end of a spear stuck in the ground." He cocked his head. "Now, we know Allectus shed his armour, because the armour was found afterwards. We know, too, that someone killed him before he could escape. But can we believe that he was killed by a vengeful kinsman of Carausius? Could that be true? We have no way of knowing yea or nay. But as I said, I've heard three different versions of the tale and all of them named Appius Endor as Allectus's executioner."

He took a swig of his wine. "Speaking for myself, I would be surprised if it were not true, knowing what I know now about Endor. I find it totally credible that he might have been stalking Allectus from afar, waiting for a chance to avenge his adored leader. True or not, though, the mere fact that people can imagine that offers an insight into what kind of man the fellow is—a veteran soldier and a wily, world-wise survivor, trusted and trained by one of the greatest, most rapacious, and successful thieves of recent years. He wastes no time on petty things, he has no hesitation in killing wantonly, and if he is to steal, he will steal on an epic scale." He paused again, then added, "I firmly believe he has the intellect, and the vision, to dream up thievery on the scale we are dealing with here, but I cannot believe he has the kind of wealth or the connections he would need to finance such a huge enterprise. No, no matter how brilliant the man may be, he has hidden, powerful allies at his back, funding him. And they trust him because they know he will go to any extremes to protect himself, and them, and their joint enterprise."

He looked directly at Strabo. "Make no mistake, Alex," he said, then turned his head to include the other three men at the table. "And I'm including all of you, because this affects our brotherhood and everything we do. We are contemplating a conspiracy that might be unequalled in the empire's history—a criminal organization on a scale to daunt the gods themselves, and led by a formidable and unpredictable warrior."

The silence that ensued was ended by one question from Strabo: "So how should we deal with it?"

"Carefully." Cato raised his cup and gazed into the wine before draining it and setting it down. "Never lose sight of that need for caution, in everything you do concerning Appius Endor." He looked around the table again, meeting each man's eye. "You might think I have exaggerated, but I have waded through blood collecting the severed limbs of people he chopped to pieces. You need to deal with this man with all-encompassing caution. All of you. Because none of you can imagine the depths of his depravity."

After a brief, uncomfortable silence, Valerius spoke up. "You mentioned his backers and the funding they supply to him. How much money is involved?"

"We have no idea, but we do know the total is probably incalculable. The numbers, the amounts of goods and shipments, and the value in trade and bullion are far too big for people like us to comprehend. And that means the associated risks are equally immense, not only for us as syndexioi committed to stamping this thing out, but for the criminals. In plain language, it means that those most deeply concerned—the conspirators, our enemies—will not tolerate any threat to their activities. They will kill anyone—absolutely anyone, without hesitation—if they so much as suspect that he is aware of the existence of their organization. They demand complete secrecy and silence—deathly silence—in order to conduct their affairs."

He allowed them a few moments to dwell on that, then added, "And now we have no other option than to do the same, according to the same criteria. We have secrecy and silence on our side equal to theirs, protecting our existence and our identity. And we are about to go to war with them, toe to toe."

"You make it sound more frightening than field fighting," Galban said.

"It is," Cato answered him. "One error here, one slip dealing with these people, one lapse of discretion will bring swift and certain exposure and death. So please, raise your cups and we'll wish the Basilisk a well-earned death elsewhere, before any of us ever meet him."

BOOK TWO

Londuin, A.D. 317

FIVE

er foot landed painfully on the chipped edge of a badly
seated cobblestone and she lurched sideways, too quickly to
stop herself, and smashed her right shoulder into the sharp
corner of a brick wall. The sudden, flaring pain of it made her gasp, but
she was already staggering onwards, driven by terror. Her left hand
instinctively grasped the injury as she pitched forward, leaning into her
run again, her eyes swivelling, looking for a way out, and with her other
hand she reached down to claw at the hem of her *tunica interior*, the
tubelike underskirt that seemed to be growing ever tighter, constricting her legs and stopping her from running as fast as she wanted to. All
around her people were going about their affairs, paying no attention
to her, but Lydia forced herself to keep moving, willing herself to even
greater efforts.

Behind her, very close, she could hear the men cursing and shouting
as they came after her, and she could tell by the sounds of colliding
bodies and startled cries that they were knocking people aside as they
fought to catch her, struggling uphill against the flow of the crowd that
surged about them on its way down towards the market stalls along
the riverbank. A sudden gap, barely wider than she was, came into view
between two houses, and she threw herself into the tight space, bracing
herself against the glancing impact with the wall ahead of her and then
half spinning to run on along the narrow passageway, no time even to
glance back, all the while bending forward, trying to pull the hem of her

undergown up above her knees. Another solid tug, she thought, would set her free and she could quickly outstrip her pursuers.

Behind her, amplified by the confined space, she heard pounding feet gaining on her, and then a heavy, grasping hand clutched at her shoulder. Frantically, gasping for breath, she wrenched herself away, dipping forward without slowing, aware even as she did so that the ancient walls on either side of her were bulging in towards her, pinching the space ahead and threatening to trap her. But with that thought came a ragged, dragging sound and a grunt as the man behind her came into contact with the rough sides of the passageway and wedged there, his fingers losing their grip on her shoulder. She kept going, not daring to try to look back, but she knew she could not go much farther before they caught her.

She reached the end of the passage and burst into sunlight again. On her right, the street ended against a brick wall, high and blank with but a single, closed door, and she swung hard left, the sudden change of direction cutting off the oaths and curses from the passageway at her back, where the men were struggling to squeeze between the bulging walls. The warmth of the sunlight on her face felt like a blessing and gave her a surge of renewed strength, and she took a moment to stand still and pull the underskirt's edges up her thighs, and then she ran again, hard and fast, holding her skirts wide in both hands until she reached another, wider lane that ran back towards the marketplace.

Without thought, hearing again the running feet at her back, she took it and ran. There was safety there, she knew, among the crowds, if she could only make them aware of what was happening to her. Even as her stride lengthened, though, she saw the fourth and last of her hunters coming directly towards her, and she realized that he must have run past the passageway she had ducked into and continued to the next corner. He saw her just as she saw him, and she saw his sudden grin, could almost hear his grunt of triumph. A narrow archway loomed on her right and she dashed through it with a half sob of relief that turned into a moan of panic as she smelled the place and realized she had trapped herself.

She was in what might once have been part of a house but was now a roofless, walled-in pen for animals. The space contained a few goats, and scattered piles of straw and hay, and the acrid stink of dung- and urine-fouled straw made her breath catch in her throat. The rear wall had long since collapsed, and the litter of broken bricks and masonry there offered her no hope of easy passage, dressed as she was in her long stola, with flimsy thin-soled shoes that were little more than slippers. The archway at her back was the sole entrance to the place, and she heard the rushing feet skidding to a halt behind her.

Before she could even turn to face them, she was hit heavily from behind, thrown forward and pulled violently sideways at the same time. She spun around, off balance, as her fast-moving attacker barged past her and threw his arms around her from behind, pinning her arms and pulling her back against him, digging the fingers of one hand brutally into her breast. A second man, now facing her within arm's reach and grinning with anticipation, was the demented-looking wretch who had leered at her in the market as he stepped towards her with a crazed, lust-filled look on his face that left her in no doubt about what he was thinking. Seeing him there between the market stalls, she had thought he was alone, and in spite of all the lessons she had been painstakingly taught throughout her life by her four brothers, she had turned to flee, believing she could outrun him. Too late, she had seen that he had three others with him, and suddenly they were all coming after her.

Barking a sound that might have been a laugh, the lout dropped to his knees in front of her and clawed with both hands at her stola, grasping at it with clawing fingers and then jerking his arms apart, attempting to split the fabric. The material was stronger than he expected, though, and he grunted, gripped the cloth more firmly, and braced himself to pull again, his face dark with anger. Before he could do anything, though, Lydia let her whole weight drop into the arms of the man holding her, trusting that he would support her instinctively, too surprised to let her fall. He did, clutching her more tightly, and she snapped her left foot upwards, high, driving at the kneeling man's shoulder. He shied away, releasing his grip to brush her kick aside with his arm, and immediately she brought her right knee up, almost to her shoulder, and drove her heel straight into his face, sending him flying backwards. The man holding her recovered his wits and heaved her around and away, throwing her to land on her side on the rubble of the fallen rear wall. She fell hard, biting her tongue painfully and feeling the stones digging against her body.

She pushed herself sideways, scrabbling and kicking against the loose masonry, fighting to find a purchase for her feet and thrusting herself up on her arms just in time to see both assailants coming for her again while the other two hung back to give them room. Forcing herself up, she was aware of the inner sheath of her clothing slipping down around her legs again just as two pairs of groping hands took hold of her. But they were not groping with any kind of sexual intent.

The man who had thrown her down grasped her again, his fingers digging into her shoulder and his other hand clamping around her neck, and she shut her eyes and opened her mouth to scream and something hammered fiercely into the side of her face. A wave of blackness burst over her and she fell, sprawling, and then rough hands were pulling at her, trying to wrench her legs apart and being frustrated by the binding tightness of her underskirt. A hand thrust against her chest, pinning her, and then came a suddenly loosening tension, the sound of ripping fabric, the slightest touch of smooth iron against her inner thigh. As her belly spasmed in terror, she felt a thigh being thrust between her own as rasping, rancid breath gusted into her face. Her stomach heaving at the stench, she opened her eyes and saw a strange thing happening.

It was the wild man with the crazed eyes who was tearing at her, but his eyes moved now sideways, as though distracted by something, and then they widened, and she saw a hand with widespread fingers reach for him. It grasped the hair that fell over his forehead and wrenched him violently away from her. He released her and clutched frantically at the hand. Through a sudden blur of movement a black-clad form filled her vision, and she saw a heavy blade sweep up briefly, then plunge down, its arc ending in a meaty-sounding chop.

All movement stopped.

The black-clad figure above her remained motionless, and she blinked, trying to understand. Then to her left, the man who had thrown her onto the stones leaned stiffly sideways, tilting over the ramshackle fence of the pen towards the animals. He, too, was staring wide-eyed, but his gaze was directionless, and his right hand fell limply from where it had been trying to hold his severed throat together. He toppled slowly sideways, smashing the fragile fence as he fell, and lay motionless, bleeding sluggishly into the straw.

The silence was broken only by the chewing of one of the goats.

"Are you badly hurt?"

She stared up at him. Apart from a wide, deeply dimpled chin and the tip of his nose, she could see nothing of his face. It was lost in the depths of a large, hooded cowl of the kind worn by priests and wanderers. He must be a priest and a Christian, she thought. But he had just killed two men, so she knew that could not be right.

She answered his question in a ragged whisper that hurt her throat. "No."

He pointed down, indicating her nether parts but staring steadily into her eyes, and she remembered the sound of ripping cloth and looked down to where her skirts had been torn apart across her hips, exposing her legs and belly to the navel. She reached down quickly, fumbling to pull the tattered edges together as she struggled to sit up.

"Here," he said, reaching a hand down to her.

His voice was deep, but not rumbling-deep like her father's, and he sounded young, she thought, with a strangely detached part of her mind that ignored the scandalous condition of her clothing. She gripped his hand and pulled herself to her feet, trying to hold her torn skirts together with her free hand, and as soon as she was standing she used both hands to cover herself, clutching the edges of the fabric tightly in her fist. There was blood everywhere; more blood than she had ever seen; more blood than she could ever have imagined. It covered the floor and lay pooled in the straw of the beasts' pen; it even oozed in sluggish rivulets down the wall.

Life blood, she thought, though she could not have said why. Blood was blood and all of it was life blood, until it was spilt. At her feet, the man who had held her arms sprawled awkwardly where he had toppled over the fence. Beyond him, closer to the door, the reeking man lay dead, too, twisted unnaturally, his head attached to the bloodied ruin of his neck by a mere hinge of flesh. He had fallen across the legs of the third man, who lay beneath him with his spine arched backwards and his face wedged into the corner of the wall by the entrance arch. And beyond the arch itself, flat on his back on the stones of the lane outside, lay the last of them: the fat one who had cut off her escape earlier. She knew he was dead, though she could see no signs of blood on him. He would have been the first to die, she knew, because he must have been standing at the doorway when the black-clad man arrived.

She looked back at her supposed rescuer. Whoever he was, he stood motionless, watching her intently, and she sensed, even though she could see nothing in the depths of his cowl, that he held his head cocked to one side. The thought came to her that there was nothing menacing about a man who cocked his head out of curiosity.

"Who are you?" she asked eventually. "Where did you come from?"

"My name is Varrus," he said, in a voice that was both quiet and deep. "Quintus Varrus. I followed you when I saw these scoundrels run after you from the marketplace."

"You were there?"

She saw a movement inside the hood, as though he had nodded. "I was. I regret not having reached here sooner, in time to stop them."

"You did stop them. You killed them all." She was surprised to hear how calm she sounded, her voice level and matter-of-fact, betraying none of the hysteria that had been roiling in her mind since she ran from the marketplace.

"I know, but I meant in time to stop them before they caught you. As for killing them, I had no choice. They would certainly have killed me had I not . . . and you, too, when they were done. But don't waste time fretting over them. They were animals and they deserved what happened to them."

She snorted derisively. "Fretting over them? I would have killed all four of them myself if I could have. And no animal, no matter how savage, would ever sink to that level of baseness, so don't demean the beasts by naming those *things* animals."

The man raised one hand and tugged the hood of his cowl further forward over his brows, hiding his face more completely. "I know a few young men from the marketplace who would be most impressed to hear such words from you, Lady," he said in a voice that, while not mocking, nevertheless contained a note of gentle raillery. "For none of them, awe-stricken by your beauty, would believe you capable of saying a thing like that." He ignored the way her mouth had dropped open in outrage. "Mind you, I agree with you entirely, and I doubt if your father, or any of your brothers, would question the rightness of what you say, in light of what happened."

She opened her mouth again, but when her voice came back to her she sounded chastened, the outrage she had felt moments earlier now forgotten. "You know who I am?"

"I know your name, but little more than that. I saw you in the market a week and more ago, and then again a few days ago, and I asked who you were. They told me your name is Lydia Mcuil."

"But you know my father and my brothers?"

"No. I know who they are, and I have seen two of your brothers, pointed out to me in the marketplace, but I know no more than that."

She frowned at him. "But how would you know even that much about us?"

"I asked, as I said, one day last week when you passed by in the marketplace. I am a partly trained student smith, and your family is well known among the smiths in Londinium. A father and four sons, all of them smiths from Hibernia, respected and renowned, with but a single female—the beautiful red-haired Lydia—in their tribe."

"Wait, stop! I need to think." She looked around again at the bodies strewn about. There were already flies crawling on their dead faces and in their open wounds, and now that her anger and fear were subsiding, she found herself seeing things differently. Regret welled up inside her like a bitter brew, souring the back of her throat. She had known she was being foolish before she first set foot in the marketplace that morning, that she should not have gone there alone and unprotected. Her father and her brothers had warned her a hundred times about the dangers involved in simply being an attractive young woman in such an open, lawless, unprotected public place. She had protested that the military fortress was a mere two-minute walk from the marketplace and that there were army patrols everywhere, upholding the law and protecting the public, but they had scoffed at her, telling her anyone with a brain knew how corrupt and incompetent the army was. She had known she was being wilful even as she set out from home, but she had been determined to prove them all wrong, clinging blindly to the pig-headed, arrogant belief that she knew what was good for her, knew it more clearly and far better than everyone else, and knew, too, that she, Lydia Mcuil, was invulnerable—old enough, clever enough, and bold enough to risk any danger and to escape unscathed. Now, looking at the four corpses, she knew how different was the raw truth; knew how fortunate she had been that this unknown, black-robed man had taken note of what was happening and had followed her in time enough to rescue her from certain death.

Without warning, her stomach heaved, and she fell to her knees, then to all fours, and vomited. The stranger stood waiting patiently, looking away, until she had spat the last bitter traces from her mouth. Then, as she wiped her lips with the back of her wrist, he bent forward again and silently offered her his hand. She reached out and grasped it and pulled herself to her feet. Without another word being said, he took her by the wrist, tugging gently for her to follow him, and led her out of the goat pen and into the lane. There, he removed his black cloak and offered it to her, holding it out at arm's length.

She saw now that the cloak had concealed a heavy, sleeveless, ankle-length robe of the same hard-wearing black cloth, belted loosely at the waist; no more than a long strip of coarsely woven woollen cloth with buckle fasteners down both sides, at front and back, and a hole in the neck. The straps of a large, blackened leather bag crossed his chest from his shoulder to his waist, where they were secured by his belt, preventing the bag from moving too far. The large, deep cowl appeared to be separate from the rest of the garment, for its ends were tucked down inside the neck hole, and so it concealed his face still.

"There's blood on it," she said, pointing to where a patch of the cloak had been saturated by gouting blood, glistening like oil in the slanting light of the lane. He glanced down, then straightened up to his full height.

"Damn! I hadn't seen that. Is there any more?" He shook out the folds of the heavy garment and held it up towards the sun, and she stepped forward to help him, spreading one side wide with both hands as they scanned the piece together, but there was only the one bloodied patch.

"There's a drinking trough inside for the beasts. I'll wash this off before we go. It's too noticeable to leave the way it is. What about the rest of me? Can you see any more?"

"Turn around, slowly."

He turned compliantly, holding his hands away from his sides, but she could see no more blood.

"That's really surprising, you know," he said. "There's none on you, either, and yet it's thick everywhere else. I've never seen so much gore. You'd think it would be black, coming from such creatures, but it's red like everyone else's. Stay here, I'll be right back."

She heard water splashing inside the pen, and then he came back to her, wringing the last drops of water from the cloak. He draped it over her, holding it judiciously until she could settle it without chilling her shoulders, then left her to conceal the bareness beneath her torn skirts as well as she could.

She watched him curiously while her hands were busy with the adjustments to her clothing, restoring herself to a semblance of modest decency. His now-bare arms were heavily muscled, and as he crouched to grasp the dead man by the armpits, she saw that his thighs were solid, too, layered with muscle to match his arms. As she watched him drag the dead man into the animal pen without noticeable effort, she took note of the breadth of his shoulders and found herself wondering at having suspected, even briefly, that he might be a renegade priest. She had never seen such musculature on any priest.

He returned and, placing a guiding hand on her shoulder, gently steered her back, by the shortest route and without uttering a word, to the crowded marketplace at the foot of the hill by the riverside.

SIX

Lydia was surprised that the marketplace looked much as it had earlier, when she had fled from it ahead of the four men who had hounded her. There were more people than before, and there was more noise and bustle, but she was vaguely disappointed to see no indication, anywhere, that anything untoward had taken place there that day. Then she saw one fat-bellied man ogling her, his pendulous lower lip quivering as he stared down at her legs, and she pulled the black cloak tighter around herself and moved closer to Varrus, not daring to glance down to see what had drawn the fat man's gaze. From then on, very much aware of the condition of her clothing and her own vulnerability to prying eyes, she stayed close behind her rescuer, keeping within arm's reach of him, her eyes downcast as she tried to move without rolling her hips, willing herself to walk like a sexless doll, her arms motionless at her sides, her fingers clutching the black folds of the man's cloak so that it enveloped her completely, and walking wherever he led her.

He stopped without warning, so that she bumped into him. "Are you thirsty?" he asked, and she nodded, immediately aware that she was, though until he asked she had not thought of it.

"Good. We'll sit here. It's central and I know the owner." He took her by the elbow and guided her towards a rough table at one corner of the junction of the two main roads dividing the marketplace. It was a busy and popular spot, offering access to all four quadrants of the market, and all four corners of the intersection were crowded with chairs and tables to attract customers to the vendors of food and drink whose stalls dominated the meeting place. The south corner, where Varrus had chosen to sit, was shared by the stalls of two vendors, though only one of them sold food and ale. The other sold brightly coloured shawls and clothes for women. Varrus held Lydia's chair and stood over her until she was comfortably seated and had rearranged his cloak about her, then he went to where the two vendors stood talking to each other and watching him as he approached.

He spoke to both men, clasping hands with each of them. They were both looking at her now, their curiosity stamped clearly on their faces, and she turned her face away, determined not to look back at them. But every instinct made her want to see their expressions and judge what they might be saying about her. She bit down on her lips and forced herself to take note of the scene about her.

She had not been to many other towns since moving to Londinium from her home in Eire, but from those she had seen, she knew that the marketplace in Londinium was large and prosperous, drawing vendors, traders, and merchants from far and wide, many even from beyond the seas, in the Gaulish lands to the south and east. Most market towns, she knew, held their largest gatherings once a week, but Londinium's market was open twice weekly, on the third and sixth days of the week, and on both days the vast space of the open market was completely filled. The site was perfect, laid out in the meadows along the riverfront beside the walls of the fort, with the buildings of the town sprawling outwards from the walled fort to cover the higher ground above and behind the teeming market stalls.

The two main roads by which she now sat divided the market into four quadrants: the northern quadrant, the oldest of the four, was given over to fresh produce from the farms of the fertile river valley; the eastern quadrant featured livestock and meats from the same farms, offering swine, kine, and fowl of all conceivable kinds for sale and trade, together with the entire range of butchered and prepared meats. The southern quadrant, closest to the riverbank, offered all the goods brought in from the sea and from the rivers and surrounding marshlands. The edges of the south quadrant were lined with wharves and docks, and lading space was hard to come by, so thick was the press of vessels arriving and leaving.

The western quadrant was Lydia's favourite, and she was far from being the only woman in Londinium who thought so. Known simply as "the market" to all women, it was the treasure trove for those who took pride in their homes and their persons. This was the place where wonders of all kinds could be found by anyone with the patience to look closely and a discerning eye for the rare and incomparable: bolts and rolls and spools and reels of lush, brightly coloured, and exquisitely woven and wound fabrics and cloth and cords and ribbons, and all the thousand and one things that craftsmen and artisans, painters and dyers and artists of all kinds, could provide to highlight that wealth. And one of the finest suppliers of such goods, one of the most highly regarded, she knew, kept his stall right here, at this junction, outside the bounds of "the market" itself. He called himself by a single name, Dylan, and he was one of the pair with whom her black-clad rescuer had gone to talk.

Varrus returned now, clutching a tankard of ale in each hand, a large one for himself and a smaller one for her, a thick, woven, bright green garment of some kind folded over one arm. It was clearly a cloak or a cape, rather than a simple shawl, for it was bulky, though beautiful and obviously wondrously thick and soft. It was a beautiful colour, too, a rich and lustrous green, a full shade darker than the torn gown she was wearing beneath his cloak.

"Here," he said, offering her the bundle and ignoring the way her mouth had fallen open in surprise. "Try this. If the colour is wrong, or you don't like it for any reason, you can go and choose another one. The man already has his money."

"I can't take this," she protested, grasping the thing with both hands
and kneading the rich softness of the material. "It's much too much,
too—" She stopped, fighting down a ludicrous sense of panic, then
glanced wildly towards the stall at her back, where Dylan was watching.
"I can't accept this. I— It humbles me that you would even think of
such a thing. And I thank you most earnestly for the thought, Master—"
She hesitated. "Varrus? Is that your name?" He nodded, and she continued, realizing she was gabbling. "Truly, I cannot, could not, accept such
a gift. I know that merchant and his goods. His name is Dylan and his
clothing ranks among the most costly in all Londinium."

"I know him, too," he said, his mouth—all she could see of his
face—quirked in a half smile. "His brother Rhys was my closest friend
for years. He's dead now, but Dylan and I became friends by association
with him. And it's true that his goods are costly. But that's because they
are the best in all Britain." He shrugged, looking down at her. He had
made no attempt to sit. "I believe in purchasing the best. Always have."
He blew air out through pursed lips and bent to pick up the garment.
"I'll take it back to him if you truly wish me to," he said. "But I fear I'm
going to need my own cloak back soon." The corner of his mouth
twitched, barely perceptibly. "I've seen but the merest glimpse of what
your gown concealed before it was torn apart and ruined, but if you care
to continue displaying it once you have returned my cloak, I'll be happy
to look, along with everyone else."

She opened her mouth at the sheer effrontery of what he had said,
but before she could say a word he tossed the green robe back into her
hands.

"On the other hand, should you prefer to remain covered, I can tell
you truthfully that the cost of that thing will cause me not the slightest twinge of discomfort. Money does not concern me, Lydia Mcuil. I
could buy you his entire stock without a thought." Again a tiny hesitation before he added, "The decision is yours."

She wondered if he was laughing at her, but she could see nothing but good-humoured concern behind his gentle smile. And besides, another question—and its own answer—had already formed in her mind: *What decision? There* is *no decision to be made.* Refusal of his kindness, for whatever reason, be it pride or stubbornness, would condemn her to the indignities of walking practically naked through the streets to her home, clutching her rags in both hands while vainly trying to protect her most intimate parts from the leering, prying eyes of men like those who had attacked her.

She nodded demurely and draped the soft green robe over the edge of the table in front of her, spreading its lower half so that it covered her from the waist down. Then she removed his black cloak and held it out to him wordlessly, and as he took it from her she had already begun adjusting the new garment, which looked magnificent on her. He watched, standing hipshot and holding his cup of ale, as she arranged the folds of the new garment to hang exactly as she wished them to, and then he moved to sit in the chair facing hers, where he stretched out his legs and sat back comfortably, sipping pensively at his ale and continuing to watch her, but making no attempt to interfere with her thoughts.

She was grateful for that, though she would not have said so, for she had much to think about, all of it focused upon this stranger—this apparently wealthy stranger—who had quickly placed her heavily in his debt. But what she returned to over and over, with a rapidly increasing feeling of annoyance, was that she had no idea what the fellow looked like. In the face of all that had happened in the past little while it was a petty concern, she knew, but she was finding it to be intolerably frustrating, and she was on the point of asking him to take off his hood when they both became aware of the approaching tread of marching feet, and they turned together to look in the direction it was coming from.

"Aha," he said quietly. "The vigilant protectors of the public peace."

A squad of legionaries was marching towards them from the east, where the praesidium, the garrison fort of Londinium that was built on the riverbank, lay. They were the regular street patrol, a ten-man squad, two of them holding long, lethal-looking spears. The remaining eight carried lightweight skirmishing shields slung over their arms and held cudgels rather than the brutally heavy rectangular scuta and short swords carried by regular infantry. Their leader was a bored-looking corporal, and he was followed by a unit standard bearer and a stroke drummer, a boy of about twelve whose rhythmic drumbeat served as an advance warning to everyone that the watch was coming.

Varrus murmured, "They don't look very victorious, do they?"

"I know the one in front, the decanus," Lydia responded, sounding worried.

"You know him? Personally?"

"No, but I recognize him. His name is Nerva. My brother Shamus locked horns with him a month ago, over a girl in a tavern. They fought, and Shamus left that fellow bleeding in the street."

"You were there?"

There was a rising inflection in his voice, betraying his surprise, and she flashed him a scandalized look. "In a tavern? No, of course I wasn't there. Shamus told me about it later, when I was attending to his cuts."

"But if you didn't see the actual incident, how do you know that's the same man?"

"Because we saw him again the next day, in uniform this time, at the gates of the fort. Shamus pointed him out to me. Until then he didn't know he had hit a soldier. The decanus had been off duty and out of uniform when they fought."

"Hmm. And did they speak again, fight again?"

"No. He didn't see us, and we moved away."

"So he would not recognize you, were he to see you?"

"Me?" She shook her head emphatically. "No. Not at all. He's never laid eyes on me."

The soldiers were about thirty paces away when the corporal shouted a command and they swung left, marching northeast as though they had some firm destination in mind.

As they passed out of view, Lydia turned back to Varrus. "Why should they look victorious?"

He smiled. "It was a joke, nothing more. The garrison here in Londinium belongs to an auxiliary unit of the Sixth Legion, based at Eboracum, nowhere near here. Don't ask me why. That's military thinking at its finest. Anyway, their legionary designation is the Victorious Sixth. Do you know Eboracum?"

She shook her head. "I've heard of it, but I know nothing of it, other than that it's north of here."

"It is. It's in the far northeast, more than a hundred miles from here. One of the oldest Roman-built towns in Britain, and the fortress there was established by the emperor Hadrian to house the Sixth Legion, which he brought here from Iberia when he started building his wall. They were already called the Victorious Sixth, having won the distinction years earlier in Hispania, and they've been serving here ever since—more than two hundred years now—along with the Twentieth Legion, the Victorious Valerians, and the Second Legion in Isca. Together, they're called Britain's legions. The Twentieth has been based in Deva, or Chester, for almost as long as the Sixth has been in Eboracum. It was always Deva to the Romans, but the local Celts have been calling the place Chester since soon after the original fort, the castra, was built there, about three hundred years ago . . ." He checked himself suddenly. "You haven't heard a word I've said, have you?"

She answered with an impatient shake of her head. "I was thinking about those four dead men. Will they be found soon?"

He shrugged. "Probably, as soon as whoever owns that pen goes to visit his goats."

"And what will happen then?"

"They'll be disposed of, like other refuse," he said, his tone dismissing the entire matter as unimportant. "Whoever finds them will call the local watch, and they'll summon the garrison unit that patrols that district. And whoever turns up to look at the scene will probably arrange to have the corpses carted away and buried."

"But won't anyone come looking for us?"

He smiled. "Why would anyone come looking for us? They'll find four dead men and they'll have little difficulty seeing them for what they were. They might even recognize them, for I would be much surprised if this was the first time those four ever tried anything like that. And as for you and me, no one saw us, as far as I could tell."

"How can you say that? You weren't there until the very end, but I was running through crowds of people most of the time they were chasing me. Hundreds of people must have seen me."

His smile did not falter as he shrugged one shoulder. "Aye, perhaps, but how many paid any attention? People seldom pay attention to what goes on around them. And what would they have seen, even had they looked? A young woman running, perhaps even a terrified woman being chased by four ruffians and running for her life—but in that case, fearful for their own lives, they would have wanted no part of what was happening to her.

"Even fewer people would have noticed me, because I look like a beggar, and who looks closely at a beggar? They're afraid they'll be asked for money." He shook his head again. "Besides, even if they attracted any notice, neither of those people, young woman or beggar, would appear likely to be the killer of four men. And believe me, no one is likely to step forward to say they witnessed what happened yet made no effort to intervene. That would put the onus on the army to find the killer or killers, and while the garrison patrols might be corrupt and incompetent, they are lazy and vindictive, too. They will have no wish to waste time searching for what they will believe to be a dangerous band of killers, long since vanished. So if anyone *were* to step forward with a tale of having seen what happened, that person would probably be silenced. Ergo, no one will come looking for us."

Lydia believed him, for everyone knew the street patrols—ordinary legionaries from the garrison seconded for policing duties to the office of the aedile, the local magistrate—had no interest in doing anything beyond the minimum required of them. They would never volunteer to hunt for a criminal whose crime had been killing other criminals.

She continued to stare at him, a strange look on her face, until he asked, "What? What is it?"

"Nothing," she said. "I was thinking, that's all."

"Thinking about what?"

"About you. If you set out after us from the moment we left the marketplace, what took you so long to catch up to us? I am very glad you arrived when you did, more grateful than I can say, so please don't think otherwise, but I am curious." Her tone sharpened noticeably. "And why do you wear that silly hood?"

In response, he sat up straighter and pulled his legs in, then raised both hands to push the hood back from his head, letting it fall down over his shoulders, and the breath caught in her chest.

The first word that came to her as she saw him smiling at her, his wide mouth filled with bright white, even teeth, was *beautiful*; the man was beautiful, and much younger than she had imagined, with startling dark blue eyes that gleamed at her from a face framed with rich, blond, curling hair and deeply tanned by the kind of sunshine seldom seen in Britain. She was vaguely aware that she was gawking.

"To cover my head," he was saying, apparently oblivious to the effect the sight of his face had had on her. "That's what hoods are for. And it took me some time to catch you because you left me so far behind at the start. By the time I made my way through the stalls to follow you, you had disappeared. Fortunately, I was in time to see the last of the men running after you, the fat one, so I followed him. But you must have been moving really fast." He shrugged. "I chased the fat fellow as quickly as I could. But I can't run, though I have learned to walk more quickly than most men."

She frowned at him. "What do you mean, you can't run?" She stopped, suddenly afraid that she might have offended him, but his eyes crinkled with amusement and his teeth flashed again.

"If you were Roman you would know exactly why," he said. "But of course you're not Roman. Obviously, because we're using it right now, you speak Britannic street Latin sufficiently well to deal with the locals, and even with the Romans. But your natural tongue is Eirish. Is that what you call it, or should I say Erse?"

She nodded, her gaze narrow and intent, but apparently he didn't care that she had not confirmed a pronunciation because he continued. "You are Hibernian by birth and upbringing, I know, so you can't be expected to know what I'm talking about, but in the Roman tongue— as it is spoken in Rome, I mean—my family name, Varrus, would tell you why I can't run."

She was still frowning at him, shaking her head. "Explain it to me, then."

"In Roman society," he said quietly, "the name Varrus is what we call a *cognomen*, or a nickname. It used to be spelled with one 'r,' not two, and no one remembers how or why it was changed, but someone once told me it had something to do with wanting to dissociate our-selves from an ancestor called Publius Quinctilius Varus, who was disgraced when he lost an entire army of four legions—that was a consular army, more than twenty-five thousand men—in Germania. Whether that is true or not, I neither know nor care." He paused, looking at her good-humouredly. "You'd be surprised how many ancient and now honourable Roman names started out as nicknames describing some family characteristic. Caesar means hairy in Latin, did you know that?"

She shook her head.

"Well, it does. Strabo, another famous family name, means cock-eyed, and Balbus means stutterer. And the fact is that Varrus, whichever way it's spelled, means knock-kneed. You see, in our family the males are sometimes cursed with malformed legs. It's not often a major impediment, but it's sufficiently common to have won the family the name. Most Varrus men, if they're affected by the family curse, are no more than mildly handicapped. Knock knees are common among us, but otherwise we are mainly unremarkable." He hesitated. "I'm one of the more irregular ones. My right leg was twisted when I was born—twisted in my mother's womb, not after I emerged—and as a result, I was never able to run like others. It's a thing I've learned to live with, but it kept me out of the armies."

"You sound as though you resent that."

"I do," he said mildly. "I have always resented it. Bitterly. The Varri have always been a military family, and my ancestors have served with distinction in the legions since the days of the first emperor. The one and only thing I always wanted to do, more than anything else, was to follow in the family tradition and join the legions when I was sixteen. But I had this." He sat back on his chair and thrust his right leg out in front of him again, and this time, even though the limb was covered by the thick black robe he wore, she could see that it was splayed unnaturally to one side, and her heart swelled up with emotion for his misfortune.

He noticed her look. "I hope you don't think I'm feeling sorry for myself, because really I'm not. I've lived with this all my life and I accepted it years ago. But it still has the ability to catch me off guard whenever I see someone take notice of it."

She sensed that he would be offended if he knew how deeply the sight of his twisted limb had affected her, and so she changed the topic.

"You're *not* a Christian priest, are you?"

He barked a laugh of pure delight. "A priest? Me? Absolutely not. How could you even think such a thing, and me with blood on my hands?"

"Then why do you clothe yourself like that? Does it please you to be taken for a priest?"

He sobered slightly, shaking his head. "No, it does not. But until you said that, I had no idea that anyone might think it. I dress this way so that I might be overlooked. I suppose I have always thought of Christian priests as being unimposing and generally anonymous, and now that you mention it, that has obviously influenced the way I've opted to dress and behave. The real truth is that I wear these clothes to hide my limp, and I wear the cowl to hide my hair."

"Why would you want to hide your hair? It's beautiful."

He smiled. "That's much more a woman's word than a man's. I can't think of a single man I know who would ever consider his own hair beautiful. But if you mean it to signify that my hair is distinctively different from most men's, I would agree with you. But the hair's not so important, now that I'm no longer in Italy. Fair hair is not uncommon here, as well you know. It's disguising the limp that is my main concern nowadays."

"Why should your limp concern you? It's hardly even noticeable—well, I didn't notice it. And limps are everywhere."

"I don't need to hide my *limp*, Lydia Mcuil. It's *me* I need to hide, and this leg, and the limp that goes with it, is too distinctive—too noticeable. It would identify me very quickly to anyone seeking me."

"But who would be seeking you? You said the patrols won't bother looking for us."

"Nor will they, I promise you."

"Then I'm thoroughly confused. Who else would be looking for you?"

"I don't know." He saw her look of exasperation and held up both hands quickly, his grin widening. "Truthfully, I'm not trying to be difficult. I really don't know. In fact," he added, speaking slowly and with great exaggeration, "I am not even sure anyone *is* looking for me. It might be all in my imagination." His grin vanished and his voice went flat. "But until I know beyond dispute that no one is looking for me, I need to conceal who I am."

Lydia tilted her head to one side, considering the man in front of her. "Why?" she asked after a short silence. "Why would you even think such a thing, let alone say it out loud? Have you any idea how ridiculous it sounds? Some people might think you mad for saying a thing like that. Or think you were trying to make yourself sound important and mysterious."

He sat watching her, nothing more than a suggestion of wry amusement on his face. "Is that what you think?" he asked eventually. "That I'm trying to make myself seem important?"

In spite of her annoyance, she found it easy to smile at him. "No. But you make that need for secrecy sound very ominous."

"Not ominous," he said quietly. "That is not the word for what I'm talking about. Ominous means threatening, but at the same time it offers at least a glimmer of hope. The intent of an omen is to warn of something to come, something that might yet be avoided, and that's not what I'm talking about at all." He paused—for dramatic effect, was her first thought—but then he continued, keeping his eyes fixed on her. "Two years ago—two years and three months ago, to be precise—with no warning and for no discernible reason, on a day when my uncle Marius and I were away from home, our entire family was killed when our ancestral home in Dalmatia burned down around them. No one survived. Every person present, family, guests, and servants, died in the flames and was burned beyond recognition. I lost my paternal grandparents, my father and mother and three widowed aunts, my older sister and four brothers, and two cousins. Fourteen dead . . . murdered, it became clear afterwards."

"Murdered?" Her face had drained of colour and her voice was almost inaudible. "Why? Who would—?"

He shrugged his broad shoulders. "No one has ever discovered why, and no one has ever admitted any knowledge or suspicion of who might have been behind the assassinations. But by the following day no one was in any doubt that someone, somewhere, had ordered a massacre. I should have been there, too, among the slain. And with the help of my uncle Marius, I have been in hiding ever since, trusting no one."

"God have mercy on us all." She blessed herself with the sign of the cross. "Fourteen people?"

"Fourteen *Varruses*. Sixteen other corpses were found in the shell of the villa—servants and retainers. So thirty people died that night."

For a long time Lydia sat frowning, gazing into nowhere, but then she sat straighter and squared her shoulders. "Two years and three months ago, you say?"

"Yes. Why?"

"No matter. But it is long enough to have blunted the first sharp edges of your pain, for the which, thanks be to God." She hesitated. "It's no wonder you trust no one."

That earned her another flashing grin, the more captivating because it was so unexpected where she had expected pain and outrage. "I trust you," he said.

She smiled back at him, unable to prevent herself. "And why would you do that, Master Varrus?"

"Why would I not? A man should be able to trust his wife, should he not?"

"His—?" When she spoke again, her tone had hardened. "That is a foolish thing to say."

"How is it foolish?" He was sublimely untouched by her frost-edged comment. "It's the truth. I intend to make you my wife and to keep you well fed, well housed, and content with your life from the moment you agree. I may dress like a pauper, but I assure you I am capable of supporting a wife." He flashed his wide, white-toothed grin again. "But we don't need to talk about it here and now. I'll speak to your father when the time is right."

"And what makes you think my father would even bother to

acknowledge you?" She had wanted to keep her voice icy, but her question lacked the edge she had tried to give it.

"Because you are his only daughter and I saved your life. And he will have no doubt that my wish to have you as my wife is genuine, because I will offer him an ample bride price." He hesitated. "You do have that custom in Hibernia, do you not?"

She was flabbergasted and flustered by his audacity and irreverence, though the stirrings in her breast told her she was far from being displeased by them, but she did not know how to respond to such a frontal assault from a man she had known for barely a single hour. And so she changed the subject.

She forced herself to frown. "You used the word 'assassination' speaking of your family . . ."

"Go on, lovely Lydia Mcuil," he said, not quite teasingly. "What is it you want to say?"

She nibbled at her lower lip for a moment, frowning and pretending to be displeased with what he had called her, but then she said, "It's clear your family must have been wealthy, to have a villa and so many servants, but I've always thought only important and powerful people were assassinated. Isn't that true?"

"Normally, yes," he said quietly. "Otherwise it's simple murder. Dead people are left strewn around in both cases, but assassinated people normally have more elaborate funerals."

She stared at him, thinking he was being flippant, but she realized his comment had sprung from some inner well of resigned fatalism. He gazed back at her and she grew flustered, blurting out a question that sounded banal even as the words left her mouth.

"So your family was not normal, in that sense?"

"Hah!" he barked, sounding almost amused. "My family? Normal? My grandfather and my father would have had you thrown into a prison cell for even voicing that thought. And my grandmother Alexia Seneca would have had you chained there naked for her guards to use. And that

should tell you how far removed from your idea of normal my family
is—or was."

"Alexia Seneca? You mean the Roman banking family? Those
Senecas?"

He nodded. "Those Senecas."

"Your grandmother is a Seneca?" Her eyes had grown round with
wonder, for even in Eire the wealth of the Seneca family had been legendary.

"She was," he said quietly, "though it gives me no pleasure to admit
it. Her father was among the richest of the clan in his day. Owned more
than half of Rome, they used to say, and three-quarters of the people in
it. And my grandmother considered all of them to be beneath her, even
the most ancient and powerful patrician clans.

"Children are supposed to love their grandmothers, I know, but
from the moment I grew old enough to form my own judgments I
detested Alexia—still do, even though she's been dead these two years.
She was a nasty, self-absorbed, and cynically evil woman. Evil is an
attribute that very few people can truly merit, you know, but my grandmother earned every vestige of the designation. She was a wholehearted,
dyed-in-the-wool sow, though to say that maligns those simple brutes.
My grandfather Titanius, who for many years had the misfortune of
being wed to her, was a close friend of the emperor Diocletian for most
of his life, because he and the emperor grew up together in the same
small town in Dalmatia, across the Adriatic Sea from Italy. When
Diocletian was emperor he loved to claim that he was the son of a
simple scribe. In fact, his father was chief scribe to my great-grandsire,
Gaius Varrus—Grandfather Titanius's father."

"Your grandfather must have been a remarkable man," Lydia said
quietly.

His right cheek twitched in what might have been the beginnings
of a rueful smile. "I never really knew him as a man. He was my grandfather, a presence in my life, but not an influence. I doubt he ever said

more than a hundred words to me in fifteen years. But according to what I have heard, he was remarkable in his youth, and he survived the reign of Diocletian and outlived the man himself. A generation later, my own father, until his death, was an intimate and trusted friend of Constantine, representing the Emperor's interests in long, involved dealings with the leaders of the Christians in Rome."

"Dear God in Heaven," she whispered, awed in spite of herself. "So who could have wanted to kill both of them?"

He grinned. "Practically anyone who ever met them, I've been told, but as I grow older I increasingly suspect that that might have been less than true." He shook his head slowly. "Who can tell, though, really? I've racked my brains for years now, trying to arrive at some understanding of what my grandfather or my father might have done—either one of them or both together—to draw down the fate that befell them and everyone around them. All I can say with certainty is that they were both men of power with powerful connections. And yet at the end of everything, all their power was useless in protecting them or their loved ones." His eyes sharpened suddenly. "You haven't touched your drink," he said, eyeing her tankard. "Do you not like it? Can I bring you something else?"

"No, no," she protested. "I've been listening too closely, that is all. My drink is fine. See?" She raised her cup and drank deeply, emptying the cup and setting it back down on the table, then covering a polite belch with her hand.

"I know now," he continued, "though I never thought about it while they were alive, that both Grandfather Titanius and my father had no shortage of powerful enemies, because each of them was headstrong and powerful in his own right, and power such as they had and exercised breeds both rivals and enemies. But even today I could not begin to guess where to start looking for their killers. Before it happened, my life—thanks to my physical deformity—had been such that no one ever planned for me to follow in the footsteps of either one of them. Unfit from birth to join the legions, I was consequently deemed unfit for anything else, and so I learned nothing of politics and I have never experienced the intrigue of the imperial court. My father had four other sons, all grown men by the time I was born and more suited for their plans, so when I was a child no one really cared what I did, so be it I stayed out of everyone's way and found my own ways to amuse myself." He shrugged, his lips turning downwards in self-deprecation. "They provided me with tutors, and my mother saw that I learned the things a boy of my station ought to learn, but there was little more to my family life than that. And now that they're all dead, except for my uncle Marius, I'm merely continuing to do what I did before. I keep myself out of sight and unremarkable, and hope to be spared to live my own life."

When Lydia spoke again, her voice was quiet. "So how did you . . . ?" She paused, then collected her thoughts and began again. "What did you do when you discovered what had happened, that everyone had been murdered? How did you even *know* what to do?"

"I didn't," Varrus said, and she took note of the quiet acceptance and the lack of bitterness in his voice. "I knew nothing about it until I reached home again, three days after it all happened, and by then everything that had to be done had already been done. My uncle Marius was on furlough and had arrived for a visit the morning after the massacre, and as the sole surviving member of the family—or so everyone thought—he had had to see to all the funeral arrangements. He was standing in front of the ruins of the villa when I showed up. Like everyone else, he thought I had died in the fire as well, and as soon as he saw me he knew my life would be in danger if the killers discovered I had survived. So he hurried me away into hiding in Italy before anyone could recognize me, and he kept me hidden in his home in Capua, near the Bay of Naples, for the next year and a half. You know the Bay of Naples? No, I suppose you wouldn't, but it's an intensely beautiful area. It was there I learned how to survive in what had become a new and hostile world."

He looked at her through narrowed eyes, then continued soberly. "That's when I learned to stop dressing like a rich, spoiled brat and make myself inconspicuous. That's when I learned to keep my mouth shut and to stifle the arrogant, spoiled-rich-brat pronouncements I'd been spouting since I was born. And I didn't learn any of those lessons easily. I didn't want to believe that my family had all been murdered. I tried to convince myself it had all been an awful accident. But that was folly. Anyway, Marius brought in tutors—special tutors, highly knowledgeable in their particular areas—who taught me how to live like prey, with one eye diligently on the watch for predators at all times. He most certainly saved my life. And eventually, when he had to return to his command, he had me brought here to Britain, because he thought no one would think to look for me here, so far away from home."

Lydia sat frowning. There were so many questions she wanted to ask.

"Where had you been when your family . . . died? It sounds as though you had been away from home for a long time."

"I had been. I was visiting Florentia, a town in the north of Italy. I had gone there with Rhys Twohands on an expedition—it was a long journey, two weeks each way—to examine a new kind of iron plough-share he had heard about."

"Who is this Rhys Twohands?"

"He's . . . he *was* my father's head smith and my closest friend. He taught me all I know about smithing."

"Where is he now, your closest friend? Oh, I forgot—"

"We buried him last week, here in Londinium." He saw that the information had left her wondering at her own clumsiness, so he held up one hand. "Be at peace," he said quietly. "You asked a perfectly innocent question. He died of injuries that he received weeks earlier, when we first landed in Britain."

"What happened to him?" Her question was barely audible.

"An accident, a silly, pointless accident that should never have happened. We had reached port early that morning, after eight days

of bad weather at sea that had damaged our ship. We had been travelling from Brigantium—that's a seaport in northern Iberia. While
we were waiting for our goods to be offloaded, Rhys decided to go
looking for a market where he could find out the going price for his
sucinum."

"Sucinum?"

That won her a grin. "You would call it amber, I believe. That's what
Grandmother Alexia called it, and she had large quantities—necklaces,
bracelets, beads, and brooches made from the stuff. It is precious and
greatly sought after as jewellery by those who can afford such things.
If it contains preserved insects, it's even more valuable. Rhys had taken
a substantial hoard of it in payment for a job of work he'd done while
we were in Florentia. He discovered that the best place to sell his amber
was probably Londinium, which pleased him immensely because that's
where we were heading. I remember how round our ship's captain's eyes
grew when he saw how much of it Rhys had.

"Anyway, he found a market as soon as we got here—probably this
very one, now that I think of it—and sold about half of his bag of amber
for more gold than he'd ever dreamed about. He arrived back at the ship
just as the crew were unloading the heaviest of the cargo from the
hold—ingots of iron that they had used for ballast. A pulley block
snagged and a rope snapped and the whole pole derrick collapsed over
the side. A flailing rope caught Rhys going up the gangplank. Whipped
him off and threw him into the side of the ship, where he fell between
it and the wharf, one arm hanging by a flap of skin. We pulled him out
and bound up his wound and sent for his brother Dylan, who we knew
lived nearby. Dylan took us back to his house, and I've been there ever
since, but Rhys never recovered . . . Never showed any signs of wanting
to. He was a smith, and he had lost an arm. So he simply . . . faded, day
after day until he died, early last week."

Lydia reached out and laid her hand on his. "Forgive me," she said.
"I had no wish to bring you painful memories. I had no idea . . ."

"How could you have? You didn't know me until this morning." He stopped, his brow wrinkling. "What's wrong? You look troubled."

"No, merely curious. Why did Rhys come with you all the way to Britain? I know he was your friend, but he was much older than you are and you said—or you implied—that he had lived most of his life in Damatia, did you not?"

"Aye, but Britain was his birthplace and he still had contact with his brother here, so when he heard I was coming he decided to come with me. His father had served with the Twentieth Legion at Deva, in Cambria, and he wed one of the local Cambrian women. Rhys learned the art of smithing as a boy in the military fortress at Deva, and he was an accomplished smith by the age of sixteen, when he joined the legions himself and was transferred to Londinium. He ended up in my father's command sometime after that, as a smith. Years later, when my father was transferred back to Rome, he took Rhys with him, and he's been with our family ever since. It was he who taught me how to light a charcoal fire and swing a hammer."

"I'm sure my father would understand why that would make you grateful," she said. "I— I'm sorry to keep returning to what is surely a painful subject, but . . . Why did anyone suspect that murder had been done in so many deaths? It was a fire—did it not seem like a tragic accident?"

"It did, at first," he said. "But something seemed amiss from the start. For example, neither Marius nor I could remember a single occasion, be it on feast days or other special occasions, when every single person on that estate—family, household servitors and tenants, freedmen and slaves—had been inside the villa at the same time. It was a thing that simply never happened. That was nowhere near our largest estate, but it was large enough that there was always work of some description—great or small, but always urgent and pressing—being done somewhere."

"Nowhere near your largest estate? Your family owned others?"

He gave a sheepish smile. "Several others. The grandest of them, on the Palatine Hill in Rome, was the ancestral family residence, but it was seldom used since my great-grandsire died. There was another on the island of Capri, and yet another in Egypt, on the banks of the Nile near the Pyramids. The villa where the deaths occurred was just a small place on the Adriatic shore, little more than a summer house, really. And yet we were expected to believe that on this single occasion, every single person on the estate had found reason to gather inside the villa at the same time. All their blackened bones were there, in the ashes of the fire . . ."

"All of them? That seems unbeliev . . ." Her lips continued to move soundlessly.

"It *was* unbelievable. And it still is. For another thing, there were too many ashes. Far too many for a villa built mostly from local stone. Stone doesn't burn—or at least it doesn't produce ashes. And yet the gutted walls were drifted with wood ashes. Marius decided—and I now agree with him—that everyone must have been killed wherever they were found on the estate, and their bodies taken to the villa afterwards and burned together in an enormous funereal pyre. It was an organized slaughter, we became convinced, carried out by a determined group sent to make sure no one escaped."

"I see . . . So how long have you been here?"

"In Britain or in Londinium?" He tilted his head very slightly to one side. "Same answer, either way. We arrived by ship, four weeks ago this very day."

He smiled at her again, but there was a different glint in his eye this time, and he was shaking his head.

"What are you smiling at?" she asked, curious to know how he could find a smile within him after what they had talked about.

"At you," he said.

"And why? Do you find me amusing, Master Varrus?"

"Not at all," he protested. "I find you intriguing, and very enjoyably so."

"How, intriguing?"

"Well, for one thing, no more than an hour ago you were fighting for your life, and mere moments later all the men who had hunted you were dead. You only met me today, and you are wearing a new garment to hide the fact that your own clothes were forcibly torn from you, and yet here we are sitting together drinking ale and telling each other stories. You amaze me, Lydia. I only wonder what you will do now."

She blinked at him. "What do you mean, what will I do?"

"Next, I meant. What will you do now you're no longer in danger?" He cocked an eye at her. "Don't you want to go home?"

"I do," she said, surprising herself with how oddly submissive she sounded. "I want to, but I'm afraid to face my father and brothers. They'll be angry at me, and rightly so, for being stubborn and stupid and ignoring their warnings."

"About being alone in the marketplace." It was not a question. "Many warnings?"

His tone was sympathetic, and she nodded. "Incessant."

"But you'll pay heed to them in future, will you not?"

She nodded again.

"Then they won't stay angry for long," he said gently. "They'll be too grateful that you lived and learned a valuable lesson. I think I had better take you there. Is it far?"

"No, it's very close. It will take us less than a quarter of an hour."

"And how long has it been since you left?"

"I don't know. I can't remember."

"Did you go anywhere else between home and the marketplace after you left this morning?"

"No. I came straight here."

"Then you probably haven't been absent for overlong. Your family might not even have noticed that you're missing yet. I watched you arrive and you weren't here for long at all before—"

She silenced him with an open hand as she sat up straighter and peered over his right shoulder, her eyes fixed on something behind him.

"What is it?" He kept his eyes on her. "What are you looking at?"

She gave a sharp, dismissive shake of her head, and he carefully turned around to scan the scene at his back. Lydia was vaguely aware that he was looking in the wrong place, searching for something much closer than the activity that had attracted her own eyes, but she was too caught up in the apprehension of what she was seeing to explain it to him.

The watch patrol had come back into view, their circuit of the far side of the marketplace complete, and she had watched idly as their corporal, Nerva, flanked by his drummer and standard bearer, extended his arm in the signal to wheel right, then began to lead them up the gentle slope towards where she and Quintus Varrus were sitting, about sixty paces away.

That much she had watched without interest. But then other movements had caught her eye, some distance along the intersecting road. In an instant she was on her feet, her heart racing as she rose on her toes, straining to see over the people in between, and knowing she was powerless to prevent what was about to happen.

SEVEN

Five men—four of them Lydia's brothers, and she didn't know the fifth—were running towards the marketplace junction, looking urgently around them in all directions as they approached. They were soot-grimed and wearing work clothes, and it was obvious that they had dropped everything they were doing and come running, and Lydia knew with a chill that they had come looking for her. Shamus, her youngest brother, was in the lead, closely followed by Callum, Declan, and Aidan. They were running directly towards the centre of the marketplace, threading their way impatiently between the stalls and around the growing knots of people ahead of them as they went, and already she could hear the sounds of consternation from the crowd at being jostled by the running men. She took a few steps forward and started to wave, opening her mouth to shout to them, but before she could, she saw Nerva throw up his arm in an abrupt signal to halt his men, and she knew he had recognized Shamus.

"That man there, in front," Nerva shouted. "Take him."

The ten men at his back changed formation quickly, the two spearmen moving immediately to either side to flank their eight club-carrying comrades, and their corporal drew his short sword, extending it towards the four Eirishmen. The dull, foot-and-a-half-long blade of his gladius glinted in the sunlight, and Lydia looked past it in horror at the deliberate way the soldiers were advancing to confront her brothers, how fluidly they moved forward, spreading apart and doubling their speed to attack gait as they went. Appalled by what she knew was about to happen, she bit down on her knuckle, too terrified even to try to scream a warning, though she knew she was too far away for her brothers to hear.

She half-turned to look behind her, wildly hoping the man Varrus would assist, and she blinked in disbelief, for he was nowhere to be seen. In panic, she spun back towards her brothers.

The soldiers were still trotting forward, their shields raised, and for a few agonized moments she was afraid that none of her brothers would even see the danger they were in, too caught up in their own activities. But then Aidan saw the patrolmen running to intercept them and he shouted a warning. She saw Shamus, still in the lead, recognize Nerva instantly.

In one glance, it seemed to Lydia, Shamus understood what was happening. He stopped running immediately and spread his arms to stop his brothers, too, roaring at them in their native Eirish as he spun to face them.

"Lads, for the love o' God, wait! Wait!" Even from as far away as she was, his words came to her clearly. "This is the pig I told you about, the one I thrashed for hitting the lass in the tavern. It's me he's after, but they'll kill us all if we try to fight them now, so leave me here, in God's name, and go and find Lydia. I'll be fine. I'll give him no reason to harm me."

Declan snapped something in response, and though she could hear nothing of what he said, Lydia knew he was pointing out that Nerva had no need of any reason, for she would have argued the same.

Shamus turned back towards the Romans, and all four brothers now stood silent and motionless, facing the men of the watch warily. They offered no provocation at all because they were fully aware that the soldiers were looking for any excuse to start swinging their clubs. Lydia perceived, on some level, that the fifth man who had been running with her brothers had vanished just as effectively as the Roman

Varrus had, and the realization jarred her from her trance-like shock and sent her running towards the confrontation.

"I told you to take him!" Nerva shouted. "The one in front. He's the ringleader."

The two spearmen stepped forward, crouching low and extending the long, tapering points of their weapons to within inches of Shamus's throat while two of their fellows slung their shields over their shoulders and advanced to seize his arms.

She saw Aidan, beside Shamus, snarl and start to lunge forward, but he froze as the two spearmen instantly thrust the points of their long weapons at his brother's neck. A bright splash of blood welled up under Shamus's chin and spilled down his bare chest. It was little more than an emphatic threat, but she almost choked with fright as Shamus threw back his head and bent sharply backwards, freeing the point from his flesh but causing a much greater flow of blood.

"No!"

Her scream caught everyone's attention, drawing not only her brothers' eyes but Nerva's, too. The corporal turned slowly to where she now stood less than twenty paces away. "I'm here. I'm safe," she said in her own language, though none of the men could hear her choked whisper.

"You! Woman! Come here. Who are you?" When Lydia ignored him, Nerva clicked his fingers and waved one of his men forward. "Bring her to me. Move!"

He spoke to one of the others, half-turning his head. "And you, Tullus, get that red-headed whoreson on his knees, and if any of the others moves to stop you, kill them all."

The man called Tullus, standing behind and slightly to one side of the soldier holding Shamus's left arm, stooped and swung his cudgel lengthwise, hard across the back of Shamus's legs, expertly dropping him like a felled ox. Now Declan lunged forward, but he ran into a hard-swung club and was knocked sprawling, while the other two brothers, threatened by the ready spear points, were quickly pinioned and forced to their knees. As soon as all four were immobilized, the soldiers bound their arms and hands tightly with leather thongs, then shackled their ankles with longer ties that would allow them to hobble but not to run. They were far from gentle with their prisoners, but none of them made any attempt to obey the order to kill them.

"Now bring the woman here," Nerva snarled, and when no one moved quickly enough his snarl turned into a bark. "Now, I said!"

Lydia watched the soldier come to take her. She felt paralyzed and impotent, disabled by the plight that had so suddenly overtaken her brothers, for she could neither help them nor save herself. The man took hold of her by the arm, firmly but not unnecessarily so, then guided her to stand in front of Nerva. The look in his eyes as he scanned her from head to foot made her feel soiled and tawdry. She knew that the very richness of the magnificent green cloak that the young Roman had bought for her would normally have been sufficient to impress and abash the lout in front of her, but that effect had been nullified by her scream. Now she suspected the fellow thought she might have stolen the garment, or earned the price of it lying on her back. She straightened her spine and looked at him defiantly, expecting him to belittle her for the amusement of his men. All he did, though, was point with his thumb to the huddled prisoners.

"These men are dead meat," he said. "Thieves and troublemakers. But who are you?"

She hesitated, though she could not have explained why.

"You know them, don't you? Who are they, and why do you care what happens to them?"

Still she said nothing, and his eyes narrowed to slits.

"You screamed. You screamed when you saw them. We all heard you. So speak up. We know you're not mute." He laughed at his own wit, and she gazed at him with loathing, conscious of the crowd of slack-mouthed onlookers who had gathered to gawk at the spectacle.

Knowing somehow that the worst thing she could do now was to show fear, she drew herself up to her full height and put all the contempt and disdain she could muster into her voice.

"They are not thieves. And they are not troublemakers."

He sneered at her. "Oh! Then I must beg your forgiveness for having made an error. Here I was, policing the common marketplace with my patrol party as is my appointed duty, and when I saw these four half-naked, armed, and angry men burst into the forum area and start running, clearly bent on mischief of one kind or another, I assumed, evidently wrongly, that they were a threat to the common good. So I arrested them. And you now wish me to release them." He nodded to himself. "Well, I'll be glad to do so . . . as soon as you tell me who they are, how you know who they are, and why you screamed when my men took them."

"They are my brothers and they came looking for me."

He said nothing for a space of heartbeats, the sneer fixed, then nodded again. "I see. Your brothers, coming to look for you. Well now I must ask you, why? Were you in some kind of danger?" He waited, and when she failed to answer him, he continued. "D'you take me for a fool, woman? Why would four grown men come running through a public marketplace looking for their equally grown sister? Or is the truth that you are really their whore, and they your pimps? That must be it. They put you here to work for them, right? Else how would they have known where to find you?"

The fifth man she had seen running with her brothers must have summoned them. She knew that had to be true, for otherwise there was no sensible explanation for her brothers to be looking for her. He must have seen her running through the marketplace from the four men now lying dead in the goat pen. He had run to find her brothers, certainly, in hopes of saving her. But the other man, the Roman, Quintus Varrus, had run to find *her*. He had run after her and he had killed four men to save her life, and if she said anything at all about that to this bullying lout of a soldier she knew she would be condemning a young man who had done nothing worthy of punishment. Worse than that—and the sudden awareness of this settled upon her like a crushing weight—she would be denouncing a man already running in fear of his life from unknown and powerful enemies who might be hiding anywhere in plain sight.

And so she stood mute while Nerva gaped at her in mock astonishment, as though he could not believe she was making him wait for her response. She stared back at him, expecting him at any moment to order his men to seize her.

But then she saw his expression change as his focus shifted to something behind her. A tiny frown appeared between his eyebrows, a sudden flicker of alarm, perhaps confusion, in his eyes. And then a cold, disdainful voice spoke from directly at her back.

"Decanus," it said, addressing him by his rank. "Are you blind as well as stupid?"

Nerva's mouth opened as though to speak, but the reaction was one of shock rather than outrage, and the unknown voice pressed on, flat and hard-edged and uncompromising.

"Yes, you heard me correctly. I called you stupid and you are probably too stupid to know why." The voice paused, as though waiting for an answer, and then continued in a tone of command that left no room for hesitation or doubt. "State your name and rank."

"Nerva," the bully said, swallowing with visible difficulty. "Decanus, Fourth Garrison Cohort."

"Well, Decanus Nerva, look closely at this woman you have insulted, and then call her a whore again if you dare. Look at her! Does she resemble any of the drabs you see in the pigsties you frequent? This woman has both a respectable name and a station, neither of which is any concern of yours but both of which you have maligned. And her brothers came running here because I summoned them to assist me in matters that are equally of no concern to you."

The speaker paused, as though to allow the venom in his words to register completely, and then he ended the confrontation flatly and with authority. "Do yourself a service while yet you can, Decanus Nerva, and oblige me by taking yourself and your associates out of my sight."

Lydia found herself transfixed by the look that had come over Nerva's face, for even as he glared at the man behind her she could see he plainly knew he was faced with something beyond his capacity as a squad commander, and yet he was stubborn enough to show his resentment of the situation, and angry enough to be defiant.

Stupid is the right word, she thought. *The fool is too stupid to see anything he has no wish to see, and lacks the wit to know when to be quiet and walk away.*

She had no doubt that the man who now stood behind her was the stranger she had seen with her brothers. She was frowning fiercely as she tried to recall what she had noted of him before he vanished, but there was no face in her mind.

Nerva, though, was looking directly at the fellow as though he might spit at him. His eyes flickered sideways, checking to see that his own men were watching and would assist him if needed, and then he spoke out.

"I don't know who you are, citizen, for all your noble clothes, your Roman looks, and fancy talk, but I know who I am and I do not have to suffer this kind of abuse from you. I am a squad commander of the City Guard of Londinium going about my lawful duties, maintaining public order as required of me, and no one other than my own superior can exercise authority over me when I am on duty. And that means I can arrest you, if I think fit, and haul you in to face the man I answer to."

"And who is that man?" The voice at Lydia's back was implacable. "What is his name?"

Nerva's right eyebrow twitched up a little, but he answered without hesitating. "Reno Cocles, pilus prior, Third Cohort—"

"Legio VI Victrix," the man behind Lydia concluded in the same flat voice. "And who is *his* superior nowadays—the legion's legate, I mean?"

"You should know that, friend, since you know so much else, so don't you try to bully me. What's *your* name?"

For a moment she thought the unknown man might not answer, but then he said, "My name would mean nothing to you now, were I to say it aloud. But it will in future, I promise you. This might mean something, though, without a name being spoken. But I caution you to be wary of what you say next."

The speaker had moved closer to her, his voice coming from right behind her head, but as she started to turn to look at him, she felt fingertips against her shoulder, pushing firmly to stop her from turning. Then his other arm came into view from her right side, holding out an embossed cylindrical container of highly polished boiled bull's hide. Lydia barely noticed the cylinder, though, because the sight of the arm holding it out had shown her that she was wrong. This was not the man she had seen with her brothers. That man had been dressed in a plain brown tunic, unadorned and ordinary. The arm from behind her was clad in a toga-like garment of sumptuous white wool, lined with a thin, delicately woven border of imperial purple, and the mere sight of it had reminded her, not at all incongruously, of Quintus Varrus's claim that he was being sought by powerful men. Few men wore anything resembling a toga nowadays, and fewer still wore the imperial purple, especially in Britain. No wonder, she thought, that Nerva had hesitated to assert himself at first.

The decanus, in the meantime, had reached out tentatively to take the proffered cylinder, touching it hesitantly as though he feared it might turn into a writhing serpent and bite him. When its owner relinquished it, Nerva stood holding it, hefting it foolishly at arm's length and obviously not knowing what to do with it.

"Open it," the voice said, and Nerva obeyed. The tube was less than a foot long and about the width of his palm. He removed the cap on one end and fished inside with his finger before upending the thing to allow a tightly bound scroll to slide out into his waiting hand. He held out the leather case to Tullus, who took it from him, then slid a slender ivory binding ring along the scroll until it came off and dropped into his palm as the scroll sprang open. As he grasped the document more securely, spreading it with both hands and holding it high to peer at it, Lydia looked past him and saw perplexed frowns on the faces of those craning to see what it was. But then, because of the way Nerva was holding the scroll up in front of him, between her and the bright sun, she saw a flash of colour and looked at the document itself, seeing the reverse of a garish design on the translucent vellum sheet. With a sense of wonder approaching awe, she recognized what it was, for she had seen its like drawn on her father's work table by a visiting bishop the previous year: a cross surmounted by a Greek *X*, with the Greek letter *R*—which looked like a Roman *P*—superimposed upon it. Together, the two symbols—pronounced, she was told, as *chi* and *rho*—formed the first two letters of the name christos, or saviour.

It was obvious, though, that Nerva had never seen such a thing before and had no idea what he was looking at. He peered at it for long moments, clearly suspecting, from its elaborate appearance, that it must have some kind of importance. Eventually his lips curled into the semblance of a sneer and he released one end of the scroll, allowing it to snap back into its cylindrical shape.

"Very pretty," he drawled, affecting disdain. "Does it mean something?"

"Read it."

Nerva's eyebrow twitched. "It is a picture. There are no words."

"There are words. Potent words. Look again, along the bottom, beside the seal. One line of words."

Nerva looked at the scroll again, knitting his brows, clearly unable to read what was there.

"It says," the man at her back said softly but distinctly, "'This man acts in my name.' And it bears the initials C. A." The voice paused for a count of three heartbeats. "C. A. Does that mean anything to you?"

When Nerva eventually shook his head, frowning, the man behind her sighed. "C. A., written like that, Decanus, is the signature of the Emperor himself. Constantinus Augustus. Do you understand now why you should have said nothing, or do you have a particular wish to be thrown into prison today, to die for interference in matters that are none of your concern?"

The colour drained from Nerva's face but then, belatedly, he stood to attention with his eyes fixed on a point somewhere above his interrogator's head. He swallowed hard, then started to say something.

"No!" Lydia jumped, the voice was so close to her ear. "As I said, you are both blind and stupid. You have said more than enough here to condemn you for causing a public spectacle over imperial affairs. Take me to your commanding legate, now."

Lydia almost felt pity for the wretch. He was staring in panic now, his eyes darting around as though looking for salvation of any kind. He finally gathered his wits and straightened up to his full height, attempting to pull the remnants of his shredded self-respect about him.

"No need for that, Senator," he rasped, his voice barely audible. "I can see I made a mistake. I'll leave you to go about your business." He snapped to attention, clicking his heels and bringing his clenched right fist to his left breast in a salute. Lydia waited for the other man to respond, but no answer materialized, and she saw a tiny tic of fear flicker between the corporal's brows.

"You made several mistakes," the man behind her finally said, his voice clipped and hard-edged. "And that was another one. I have no need of your permission to go about my business here. Now get you gone about your own duties, and be thankful if you end this day with your rank intact. Your name is? Tell me again."

"Nerva, Senator."

"Be on your way, then, Decanus Nerva. But before you go, release those men and have your people break up this crowd and send them about their business. Quickly now."

The decanus managed to keep his face utterly expressionless as he stepped forward and held out the cylinder for the man behind Lydia to take. Then he slapped his open palm against his cuirass and spun on his heel, rattling out orders to the men in his squad, who had been standing open-mouthed like the crowd around them. They immediately started liberating their four prisoners and dispersing the onlookers,. Lydia thought the probability was high that no one there, soldier or gawker, had understood one whit of what had just happened.

Nor, she realized, had she. She was very much aware of the man yet standing at her back, a man whom she had never seen and did not know, but who had nonetheless emerged from nowhere to exert enormous influence upon her life within a matter of moments. All her instincts were warning her that she might be in danger, but even as she had that thought, she recognized the inanity of it. To the best of her knowledge, she had never set eyes upon this man. How then, she reasoned, could she possibly be a danger to, or in danger from, someone utterly unknown to her?

But then, Quintus Varrus had been in very clear and deadly danger from someone completely unknown to him, someone whose identity he could not even begin to guess, someone who had slaughtered his entire family for no known reason. And to escape the threat of death by unknown hands, Varrus had fled from his homeland to start life over in the farthest place from there he could imagine. And so, she realized, she might well be in danger from the unknown presence at her back, and she felt a chill when she wondered whether, whoever he was, he had seen her earlier with Quintus Varrus.

In a kind of daze, she was aware that her brothers were collecting themselves and making themselves presentable, looking decidedly sheepish. She watched Callum rise to his feet, grinning shamefacedly at her and chafing his wrists where the leather bindings had dug deep. And as he started to move towards her she hardened her resolve and turned swiftly to face the man at her back.

Her unknown rescuer had stepped away and was watching her, and when her eyes met his, she froze.

His upper lip quirked upwards on one side. "I thought you might react like that. That's why I stopped you from turning around earlier. That decanus, idiot though he was, might have been most interested in your reaction to the sight of me."

In the months and years that were to follow, Lydia would try vainly to remember what went through her mind in the few moments before she regained the use of her tongue and her powers of reasoning, but she would never be able to recapture the sensation of having her perceptions turned upside down, forcing her to reassess everything she had believed she knew about the young Roman called Quintus Varrus. For of course it had been he who stood behind her and faced down the bully, Nerva. Nothing in the haughty demeanour of the unseen man at her back was even faintly similar to the self-effacing, laughing-eyed young man with whom she had been bantering moments before.

Three times she attempted to speak, and three times she was unable to articulate a sound. She stood gaping at him, her eyes moving up and down the length of him. Where she had formerly seen a starkly clad young man in a coarse, black, homespun scapular, she now saw a shining symbol of imperial Rome, draped from shoulder to ankles in a snowy-white woollen robe reminiscent of the classical toga of the pre-imperial Roman republic and even bordered with purple needlework resembling the *toga praetexta*, the toga of the ancient Senate. His long golden hair, which had been tousled and untidy earlier, was now carefully combed to frame his high forehead and deeply tanned face.

"Your brothers are wondering what's wrong, Mcuil," he said gently. "You should talk to them."

"How—? Where did—?"

"I'll explain everything later, but there is no great mystery, I swear to you. But first, talk to your brothers."

Some remote part of her mind registered that he was telling her to do the right thing, and she willed herself to turn and face them. As she did so, he spoke to them himself.

"Good day to you all. My name is Varrus, Quintus Varrus, and I am a friend of your sister's." He cocked his head, eyeing Lydia again, and added, "At least, I hope she considers me a friend."

"Why don't we know you, then?" It was the eldest of the four, Aidan, who asked the question, his voice suspicious but not quite truculent, and Lydia was grateful, for she knew how easily truculence could come to him.

He turned his head to look at his sister. "You were being chased, we were told. Someone frightened you in the marketplace and you ran away, and he followed you. Is this him?"

"No! This man saved me."

"Saved you from who?"

"I don't know. I didn't know any of them."

"*Them*? There was more than one?"

"Aye," she said. "There were four of them."

"*Four* of them? Then where are they?" Aidan's frown was thunderous now, and all four brothers glowered around them, as though expecting to find the guilty parties cowering in plain sight.

"They're not here, Aidan," she said, her raised voice demanding his attention. "They chased me, yes, but they're not here now. Master Varrus—saved me from them." She had been on the point of saying "killed them," but she managed to stop herself.

Aidan caught the hesitation and peered at her intently. He turned again to Varrus, speaking sideways to Lydia but watching the other man's face. "And how did he do that, I wonder, and him with not even a knife to wave at them? Did he run through the city streets wearing that too-clean robe?"

"No, I did not," Varrus said quietly, but the tone of his voice, the authority it contained, silenced Aidan Mcuil as though he had been shouted at. "I have changed my clothes since then. Your sister is safe and unharmed, as you see. And the men who frightened her will bother her no more."

Declan began to speak, but Aidan stopped him with a sidewise chop of one hand, pursing his lips and narrowing his eyes to slits. "And how might I be expected to know that's true," he asked in a voice even quieter than Varrus's. "Am I supposed to take your word for it? A *Roman's* word?"

Lydia wanted to tell Aidan to be quiet, wanted to warn him not to insult the man he was challenging, but before she could speak Varrus laughed, shaking his head as though in appreciation of some jest. "No," he said. "I would not ask you to do anything so foolish. But you could ask your sister if it's true. She saw me kill them."

The silence that followed that utterance was profound. For long moments it lingered, those final five syllables seeming to hang in the air. Somewhere within that strangely artificial silence, Lydia found herself understanding the true enormity of what her rescuer had said. For the first time, she fully understood that four men who had been alive that morning were now forever dead, and that Quintus Varrus had killed all of them. And in a flash of memory she recalled her father, who had been a soldier in his youth, telling one of his friends earnestly that he had never taken a man's life and doubted that he ever could, no matter what the provocation.

And she knew, with an absolute certainty that came from beyond her own knowledge, that the single most important man in all Londinium at that moment was the young Roman, Quintus Varrus.

"You killed them?" Aidan said. "By yourself? Four men?"

"Of course he did, you idiot!" she snarled, suddenly furious with her eldest brother, to whom she had never before said an angry word. "Had he not, none of us would be here now. He and I would both be lying dead in a dung-stinking goat pen, and you four would be running around bleating like lost lambs, trying to find me."

She found a fleeting satisfaction in seeing the stupefaction on the faces of her brothers, none of whom had ever heard her sound so scathing. "You doubt my word, or his? D'you think I would lie about a thing like this? Yes, he killed them. Four of them. One at a time. All by himself. With a sword. And now they're all dead, and we are alive."

She swung to face Varrus now, who was looking at her with a peculiar, musing expression on his face. "Well?" she demanded. "What have *you* to say? What do we do now?"

He raised his eyebrows at that, and then shrugged. "I would suggest you all go home. All except you, Shamus. I'll need you to come with me."

"And where are *you* going?" She knew even as she asked that the question was impertinent, but it was out and she could not retract it.

He looked at her and his mouth quirked into an almost-smile. "I am going walking, with your brother Shamus, who is well known to Nerva. We are going to walk briskly in the direction of the praesidium in the garrison headquarters, and we are going to make sure that we pass close by the decanus and his patrol on our way there. Needless to say, we won't be going into the fortress, but Nerva will have no way of knowing that and I hope to convince him that we might be going to visit his commanding legate, to complain about his conduct. That should keep him concerned enough to be very careful about how he behaves and what he says for the remainder of the day. And when we have finished, Shamus will bring me back to join the rest of you at your father's smithy."

Lydia was almost squinting at him, so intently was she trying to see through what she thought to be his false equanimity.

"Do you *know* where my father's smithy is?"

His smile grew slightly wider, infuriating her even as she accepted that she had no reason to be angry with him. "No," he drawled, "but I'm sure Shamus does."

He was mocking her, she knew, though he was being gentle and her brothers had no inkling of his raillery, and suddenly all the fight went out of her. "So be it," she said, sounding thoroughly subdued. "I'll warn my father that you're coming and tell him what you did for us this morning. And you will dine with us tonight, so make no other plans." She turned to Shamus, who had been looking from one to the other of them. "You look after him, for we are all in his debt—not just me—and bring him home with you as soon as you can."

EIGHT

Shamus fell into step beside the strange fellow. He was curious about him, and eager to question him, but his more taciturn elder brothers had taught him long since that betraying ignorance was a sign of weakness, be it in trading, in dealing with strangers, or in life generally, and so he strode beside the Roman in silence. He felt abashed—and he could feel the truth of this in the speed of his heartbeat—to be walking as an apparent equal with such a well-dressed and obviously important personage, when it must be obvious to anyone who looked at them that they were far from being equals.

On the other hand, his stubborn Celtic pride would not permit him to yield place to the other man by as much as a single step. And he remembered his father saying, years earlier, that no one could gauge the true worth of a man by the quality of his clothes. And so he matched the Roman stride for stride, noticing the man's limp.

They reached the bottom of the hill where the road split to enter the marketplace in two different directions, and the Roman stopped at the fork and looked to the right. "What's up there?"

"Women's market," Shamus said. "Fresh farm stuff mainly, then women's stuff beyond that."

"Then we go the other way. Vegetables and women's clothes don't need patrols to safeguard them. We'll go to the left. That's where the garrison headquarters is. We want to have that idiot Nerva see us passing by together, heading for the praesidium. Nothing like the fear of being noticed by his legate to put a guilty-minded decanus off his food."

Shamus could only nod his head, finding nothing to say that would make sense, since he knew nothing of armies or military custom.

"Good," Varrus said, though Shamus had no idea what he meant. "Then give me a little time to buy one of those cloaks over there, and we'll go and find him." He had pointed to a nearby booth selling used clothing, and when he saw the blank look of surprise on Shamus's face he swept his hand downwards, indicating his startlingly white robe. "Don't you think I look slightly unfitted to pass unnoticed through a crowd? Give me a moment, that's all I'll need."

Shamus watched him sort quickly through a rack of garments until he found a dark, nondescript ankle-length cloak of heavy, waxed wool, made in the style of the ancient military cloak called the sagum. Varrus threw it over his shoulders to check it for length, and once sure that it reached his ankles, he paid the merchant his asking price without demur, leaving the fellow standing open-mouthed as he covered his magnificent white robe with the plain, well-worn woollen garment.

A short time later, having overtaken the patrol without being noticed, the two young men stood side by side, looking for a suitable spot where they could allow themselves to be seen by Nerva.

"Why don't we wait outside the fort?" Shamus was working hard to appear unconcerned as he stood watching the approaching soldiers, and Varrus glanced at him sideways.

"Where outside the fort?" he asked.

"By the gates. Then we can be sure they'll see us going in as they arrive."

Varrus cocked his head. "That's exactly why we can't do it," he said, and Shamus blinked at him. "We can't do that because then we would be inside," Varrus said. "And I have no intention of entering that place."

"Why not? You're a Roman citizen."

"Aye, I am. A Roman citizen who long ago lost any false notions he might have had about the probity and *dignitas* of official, imperial Rome.

I want Nerva to see us going in that direction and to draw his own conclusions from that, but I have no wish to go in there. We'll need to intercept him sooner, and some distance from here, so let's be about it."

Not long after that, from a window in a street-side tavern, they watched Nerva's patrol approach, then break into a double-paced trot and change smoothly into confrontation mode when a street brawl suddenly broke out among a gang of half a dozen ruffians some distance ahead of them. There was little chance that the disturbance would result in arrest or incarceration, for Nerva's squad was too close to the end of its tour to want to incur extra duty time or inconvenience through arresting mere nuisances. They would dispense rough punishment in situ. At any rate, the size of the purse Varrus had handed to the leader of the brawlers was large enough to compensate them for their time and trouble.

As the squad members set about breaking up the squabble, restraining the participants and restoring order, Varrus removed his drab cloak and handed it to Shamus.

"Carry that over your arm, will you? If I pass by him carrying it, he'll wonder why I have it. Now, move when I do, and once we've started walking keep moving and don't even glance in his direction. Let's go."

He stepped out boldly, almost swaggering as he went, and together they passed within paces of Nerva and his guards, paying little attention to the scene other than a casual glance, and passing Nerva himself without a flicker of recognition. Shamus was watching for Nerva's reaction and saw the decanus freeze the moment he set eyes on the white-clad apparition with the golden hair passing almost within arm's reach of him. Shamus kept pace beside Varrus, knowing that Nerva's hands were full and he could do nothing to deter the pair of them from heading resolutely in the direction of the garrison commander's quarters.

They walked straight into the open, cobbled space in front of the fort's main entranceway, and when they knew Nerva could no longer see them, veered left until they reached the high city wall that continued directly from the fort's southwestern corner. It was pierced there by an open postern gate. The entry was broad, perhaps three strides in width, and the approximate height of a man standing on the platform of a heavy dray. Varrus noticed that it was unguarded, enabling traffic to pass freely into and out of the town.

"What's through there?" he asked, pointing at the postern with his thumb.

Shamus looked at him sharply. "Don't you know?" His suspicions about this fellow and his sister instantly renewed, his voice emerged heavy with distrust and dislike, but the other did not appear to notice.

"How would I know?" he said reasonably. "I don't even know where we are now. Well, I do, I suppose, since we're outside the fort, but I've never been up here before. My lodgings are down by the riverside, and until today I've had no cause to venture beyond there and the marketplace."

"And how long have you known our Lydia?"

The Roman seemed oblivious to the menacing tone of the question, for he did no more than shrug one shoulder. "Since this morning," he said. "I'd seen her before, several times, and I knew who she was, but we had never met and I doubt that she had ever noticed me. I saw her again in the market this morning, and then I saw her start to run, and saw the men who started after her. I didn't like the look of them and so I followed. Caught up with them eventually, and stopped them before they could harm her. When it was all over, I brought her back to the market, where you found her."

"Did you hurt yourself in that chase?"

"No. Why?"

"You're limping. You try to hide it, but you're injured."

Now the Roman's obviously genuine smile made Shamus frown again, though this time in confusion. "Ah," Varrus said. "No, I'm perfectly well. I was born with a twisted leg, that's all." He shrugged. "So, where's your smithy from here?"

"You really don't know?"

"I really don't know," Varrus said.

"Through there," Shamus said, pointing at the postern gate. "On the other side."

"Outside the city, you mean?"

"Aye, but not far. Just on the other side, almost against the walls of the fort."

"That close? Why didn't you say so before?"

Shamus looked at him wide-eyed. "I thought you knew where you were going."

"No, Shamus, I thought you were leading me home to your father's smithy. That's what Lydia told you to do."

"And that's what I've done, isn't it?"

The Roman paused for a moment. "I suppose it is. But you made it look difficult and it seems to me I did most of the leading," he added with a grin. "Let's go, then."

They passed through the gate side by side, and as soon as they emerged from the shadowed gateway, Varrus stopped to look around. The great wall at their backs now towered above them like a mountain cliff. A two-cart road ran along the foot of it, weeds thrusting up between the cobblestones. In both directions, he saw a number of stone buildings parallel to the wall, some of them appearing abandoned and two that had collapsed completely. Several others, though, looked substantial and strong, well kept and evidently lived in. His gaze was drawn towards the middle distance where a large body of water reflected the light of the afternoon sun into his eyes.

"Is that a river? I thought the Thamis was Londinium's only river."

"It is," Shamus said. "That one's more like a broad stream. It's called the Fleyt and it runs into the Thamis on the far side of the walls."

Varrus angled his body to look back to his right again. "And who lives over there, in the big place beside the wall?"

"We do. The long brick wall there is the left side of our smithy. The other part, stretching off towards the town wall, that's the wall of our house."

Varrus was frowning. "Why would your father build there, outside the town walls?"

"It's safer, for one thing," Shamus said. "When there's trouble inside the gates and they turn out the garrison, you'd rather be out here than in there, believe me. It doesn't often happen, but when it does, it's usually bad. Besides, it's less crowded this side of the wall, and we're close to our most reliable customers—the quartermaster's office is just the other side of the wall, and the farmers who supply the city market are mostly along the Fleyt. But my father didn't build the place, he bought it, because it had belonged to a cooper and already had a forge of sorts."

"And when was that?"

"Oh, it was a long time ago—sixteen or seventeen years. I was too little to remember."

"And your family was living in Britain before then?"

"Aye."

"Here, in Londinium?"

"Aye."

"So you've lived here all your life."

"Aye, but not a-purpose. We're Eirish. Father came here to work, is all."

"And someday you'll go home to Eire. Is that what you mean?"

"Aye. Someday."

"And will your father be at the smithy now?"

"He would be, on a normal day," Shamus answered, "but today's not normal, is it? He's probably at the house, waiting for us to get back."

"Then let's go and join him."

The younger Mcuil almost grinned. "Are you sure you want to do that? The old man can be wicked when he's angered."

Varrus looked again at the smith's premises and then turned back. "And you think he'll be angry at me?"

The other shrugged.

"Really?" Varrus persisted. "For saving his daughter's life?"

The Eirishman's eyes flickered up and down the Roman's white-clad frame. "You don't look like the kind of man he likes to see around his daughter," he said quietly.

Quintus Varrus dipped his right shoulder in a gesture with which Shamus Mcuil was already becoming familiar. "That might have been true before this day," he said. "Now, though, I think things might be different. Let's find out."

The Mcuil family's premises turned out to be far larger than Quintus Varrus had thought at first glance, for that first glance had been from the rear, and from behind one corner of the buildings, at a distance upwards of a hundred paces. He began to walk along the lane beside the high, blank, windowless wall Shamus had said was the side of the house, and he counted ninety paces before he reached the end of the lane where it met the street that fronted the buildings. Seeing now the spotless whitewashed wall that separated the house from the street, he felt a twinge of guilt for having expected less than he found. In truth, the Mcuil place was more of a villa than a mere house.

The front wall, he judged, was some seventy paces in length and almost twice his own height, and had a decorative arched and roofed gate set into it that would be, he thought, sufficient to accommodate any vehicle that might seek entry. Twin buildings flanked this ornate gate tower, each single-storeyed and with peaked, red-tiled roofs. The gates themselves hung from massive iron hinges and were made of hand-span-thick balks of solid, blackened oak and topped with a row of sharpened iron spikes. The Mcuil smithy, a lean-to structure at one end of this front wall, was freshly whitewashed, a dazzling, almost bluish white, with one large, shuttered window high up. Its roof too was red-tiled, and at the end of the wall with the window was a working gate, also whitewashed, giving access to the smithy yard. It was unadorned and wide enough to admit a large wagon drawn by a team of horses.

What attracted his attention most, though, was the roar of fast-flowing water, and he moved forward to where he could see down into a stone-walled channel at the end of the Mcuil property. Varrus gauged its width as perhaps six paces at the top, and its sides were lined with the same stone that had been used to build the fortress. The water that it channelled roared down at a prodigious rate, spuming high where it dashed against a rounded corner and was flung sideways, disappearing to the right some fifty paces from where he stood. Quintus pointed. "Farther down there, just around that corner, this drives your father's waterwheel. Am I correct?"

"How did you know that?" Shamus made no attempt to hide his surprise.

"Because your father is a smith and has four sons who work with him. That means a big smithy, and that would need at least one large bellows. And the best and biggest bellows are always water-driven. I know because my best friend was an apprentice smith, almost fully trained, and he had a water-driven bellows where he worked. That's probably why your father bought this place."

"That's right," Shamus said. "Our Aidan says Da nearly choked when he saw what was here." He nodded towards where the churning mill race vanished around the corner. "That ditch runs all the way round three sides of the place before it runs off to the Fleyt River. So by the time the water hits the waterwheel it's strong enough to spin the thing without effort. Nobody's ever been able to beat that rushing water. Not even us lads, and many's the time we near died tryin'."

The two men retraced their steps until they reached the entrance, where the Roman stopped and stepped back, tilting his head up towards the tiled roof of the gate tower. As he did so a gust of wind tugged at his hair and brought a familiar and welcome odour to his nostrils. "Charcoal smoke," he said. "The hot-iron smell of a working smithy. Not another smell like it in the world."

Shamus had turned to look at him. "You know it?"

"I ought to—I've lived with it for long enough. How old are you?"

"Almost seventeen."

"And I'm almost eighteen, so I probably know it better than you do."

Shamus sniffed. "Nah," he said. "I was born smelling it."

Varrus grinned and dipped his head. "I can't argue with that," he said.

He looked up again at the roofed tower in front of him, then glanced the length of it from side to side. "Courtyard house," he said. "Roman built, by the looks of it. But it's different. The house is on one side instead of in the middle."

"I don't know nothin' about that," Shamus said. "Before my time. But there is a courtyard, though it's more storage and work space now."

Varrus realized that the hostility and suspicion had vanished from the young smith's voice, and in consequence his speech sounded more fluid, more musical. Varrus assumed that the lilting cadence he heard now must be the natural rhythm and sound of Shamus's Eirish parentage.

Shamus glanced sideways at Varrus. "You still sure you want to go in?"

"Isn't that why we're here?"

Shamus shrugged. "It's what Lydia wanted, aye. I just wondered about you. But come, if you want."

Shamus stepped forward and leaned against the heavy gate, and stepped through as the massive thing swung open easily. "Don't often see these gates shut during the day," he said, waving Varrus through, then putting his shoulder to the back of the door to close it again. "Matter of fact, I don't think I've ever seen 'em shut when it wasn't a festival day of some kind."

Varrus stopped a few paces inside the gates, his eyes scanning the cluttered-looking yard only briefly before he recognized a well-organized absence of clutter. He took in the house—huge but elegant, occupying an entire corner of the enclosure—some kind of storage room, and a stable with open double doors and stalls for four horses. Along the bottom of the high perimeter wall adjacent to the smithy was a row of ten rust-dusted pyramids of iron loaf ingots, aptly named, he knew, for the way they resembled loaves of bread, and his eyes narrowed in appreciation of the care with which they had been laid out on a raised wooden platform that was slatted for ventilation. The ground under the platform was a gravel bed, he noted with approval, and the area surrounding it was clean and dry, with no weeds to be seen.

"Not even on Sundays?" He drawled the question casually, to deflect Shamus's attention from what he felt must be his all-too-obvious curiosity. "You don't observe Sundays as a day of rest?"

"Nah." The younger man shook his head. "We work on Sundays, us. Always 'ave, 'cause we've no other choice. Most of the folk we work for need work done on Sundays, seems to me. We'd go hungry if we didn't work Sundays. That's Christian, that day-of-rest rubbish—as if ordinary folk can even think to do that. Lydia's Christian. You knew that, didn't you? Mam was, too, and so's the other women. Da sometimes goes to services wi' Lydia, but no more'n once or twice a year, mostly at Easter. But the rest of us, my brothers an' me, we don't bother much wi' stuff like that." His voice suddenly dropped to a near whisper. "Ho, boyo, watch you, now."

Ahead of them, a man had emerged from the house and now stood watching them from the darkness beneath the overhanging, pillared roof of the colonnade that fronted it. His shoulders and head were hidden in deep shadow, but it was plain that he was a big man, tall and broad.

"Your father?" Varrus asked, barely moving his lips.

"Himself, it is." Shamus's voice was equally quiet.

Varrus felt the other's fingertips between his shoulder blades, pushing him forward, and he stepped towards the watching figure, halting just short of the first step up to the portico, where he stood looking up at the man above him. For long moments neither man moved, but then the senior Mcuil stepped fully into the light of the afternoon sun and squinted appraisingly at the white-clad Roman facing him. His gaze swept down the length of the toga-like robe Varrus was wearing and then snapped back to engage the eyes that looked steadfastly back at him.

Varrus could see that Lydia's father was enormous in every respect, dwarfing any other man he had ever known. And yet there was none of the gross bulk about him that was usually associated with the term "big man." With four adult sons and a grown daughter, he must have been close to fifty years old, yet he had the physique of a man decades younger, with no swelling to his belly and no pendulous flesh visible on his bare, heavily muscled arms.

He wore a heavy leather apron over a plain, knee-length tunic of coarse-woven, undyed wool, and the thick leather hide of the apron was softened and glazed to supple blackness from years of use. It had leather shoulder coverings attached to it, made in overlapping layers like the armoured epaulets Rome's legionaries wore and clearly designed to protect its wearer's shoulders from fiery flying embers. It was for the same reason that the smith was close shaven. His hair was so tightly cropped that it, too, appeared shaven, his scalp bright beneath a thin but dense cap of iron-grey hair. To protect his feet and legs, he wore thick, knitted woollen stockings, their tops folded down over thick-soled, hobnailed boots that were scarred and even deeply pitted in spots with the residue of burning embers from Mcuil's forge.

"Callum's in the smithy," the smith said. "He'll have need of you."

Shamus moved away immediately, and Varrus knew that he and Lydia's father were now the only two in the yard—not Mcuil the smith, but Lydia Mcuil's father. Her enormously large father, he thought rue-fully, resisting the urge to grimace. Far too large a man to have disliking you. He would be a formidable opponent in a fight, an enemy to be reckoned with under any circumstances.

The big man grunted, looking directly at him. "My daughter tells me you're a Roman," he said, and Varrus merely looked back at him, unsure of how he should respond. "She also tells me that you killed men to save her life."

Still Varrus made no response, held motionless by something in the older man's expression.

"Four men, she says." He paused. "Four dead men."

Varrus decided he was being goaded and had already had enough. "Correct, Master Mcuil," he said. "Four men who are now dead. You might think I murdered them, but I believe they earned their deaths. They were four unwholesome creatures who could be relied upon to debase everyone with whom they came in contact. Would you rather I had spared them? That way your daughter would be dead, and I would, too, but neither of us would have murdered anyone. Would that have pleased you more?"

The big man's eyes did not waver. "No," he said, "it would not. And yourself must surely know that. I was but wondering where you found the courage to kill four men, for I know you must have needed courage."

The words, and the tone in which they were spoken, were so different from what Varrus had expected in reaction to his anger that he stood open-mouthed, his resentment forgotten.

Mcuil continued philosophically, "Men don't die easily—or so I'm told. Of course I've no experience—I've never killed a man. Truth be told, I've seldom fought one, even without weapons, because I've never needed to, being the size I am. But I've been told that killing a living man is never easy, and no blade is ever sharp enough to guarantee a quick, clean ending to any such act. Even when taken unsuspecting, an ordinary man will fight like a demon to stay alive, and those four you faced today must have been both aware and desperate. They must have fought hard to live, and you . . . If I may say so, you lack the look of a desperate fighter. Yet you took all four of them. I doubt I could have done that, provoked beyond bearing though I would have been."

Quintus Varrus shrugged, but kept silent.

"Have you killed men before?" Mcuil must have thought the question intrusive even as he asked it, because he raised a hand quickly. "That's no affair of mine, I know, but you . . . you look too young to have done such things, and yet Lydia says you didn't get sick and you didn't seem disturbed by what you had done. And she told me you have never been a soldier."

"I'm nearly eighteen, Master Mcuil. At eighteen, Alexander of Macedon—the one they call Alexander the Great—had conquered the whole world. And he had the falling sickness. Julius Caesar had it, too. I'm no Alexander, nor even a Caesar, but I am who and what I am. I was born with a slightly twisted leg, sufficient to keep me out of the legions, but it did not prevent me from learning how to use weapons.

"My family was murdered when I was fifteen—all of them—and I have killed three men since then. Before the four I killed this morning, I mean. I had also killed a man—my first one—mere days before my family were all killed. I was travelling with my friend Rhys Twohands and we were attacked by bandits on our way home to Dalmatia. There were five of them, and I killed one of them, more by sheer good fortune than through any skill. I did vomit, that first time. I had never felt anything more loathsome than that man's warm blood on my hands. But Rhys made it clear to me that, had I not killed that man, he would certainly have killed me." He smiled, wryly. "When you believe, deep inside you, that there are people looking to kill you and complete the extermination of your family, you find yourself quick to assess threats and even quicker in eliminating them. Does that answer your concerns?"

Mcuil gazed at his Roman guest through slitted eyes, then waved him forward. "Come inside. I owe you my daughter's life and that is a debt indeed, so my house is yours for as long as you wish to stay."

NINE

"**S**o why were you following my daughter this morning in the first place?"

The two men were seated in the dining room, where Dominic Mcuil had been questioning Varrus closely, all with a view, Varrus knew, to verifying what Lydia had told him about her earlier misadventures. The Eirish smith had shown no rancour or discourtesy. His manner had been brusque but forthright from the start, befitting a concerned father looking out for the welfare of his only daughter. Varrus quickly determined that Lydia had told her father about almost everything he and she had discussed, though it was plain from the older man's lack of fatherly outrage that she had made no mention of his declared intent to wed her. Lydia herself had appeared only once, when she had served her father and him with jugs of ale drawn from a wooden keg that sat on a table against the end wall of the dining room. Her sole comment, accompanied by a tiny smile, had been, "Five men, all ale drinkers. No wine in this household." And then she had vanished into the interior of the house.

"I wasn't following her," Varrus answered. "At least not at first. I was merely looking at her, from a distance."

"So you simply chanced to see her."

"Not simply," he said. "In truth, I was looking for her. I had seen your daughter twice before and I was hoping I might see her again on this occasion."

A frown flickered between the smith's brows. "Twice before? Where?"

"Right there in the marketplace, a few days apart. She was with another woman, an older woman with dark hair, streaked through with silver. A servant, I thought."

"Companion, not servant. That was Camilla, she was a close friend of my wife's. She's like a mother to my girl. How did you come to notice them two, out of all the people in a crowded market?"

Quintus Varrus's upper lip quirked as though he were about to break into a grin. "I didn't notice *them* at all, Master Mcuil. I saw Lydia first, and after that I was blind to all else. It was impossible not to notice her because she shone like the morning sun, brightening the entire world around her. Your daughter is a marvel. You must surely be aware of that?"

"Oh, I'm aware of it, Master Varrus." The smith's growl was sardonic. "Believe you me, I am aware of it. You are not the first wide-eyed young man to tell me that . . . So you weren't following her?"

"No, not until she started to run. She looked afraid, I thought, and then I saw those men going after her, and that's when I followed."

"Thanks be to all the gods you did. What did they look like?"

Varrus hitched his shoulders and shook his head. "I don't know—dirty, and threatening, I suppose. Definitely out of place anywhere near your daughter. From first look, I knew nothing good could come from them."

"Was there anything similar about them? Anything they had in common? Think, Master Varrus. It could be important."

"No . . ."

"What?" The smith leapt on the slight hesitation. "Something came to you. What?"

The young Roman frowned. "I don't think it means anything, not really, and I'm not really sure even now that I even saw it . . . but it seems to me that two of them might have had similar wristbands. Of braided leather—"

"With blue stones in them."

"How—?" Varrus's eyes went wide with surprise.

"They were Blues," Mcuil said, his face twisted in a grimace.

"What does that mean?" Varrus asked.

"The Blues are a clan of criminals—a kind of brotherhood—the worst in Londuin, which means they are the worst in all Britain."

"You mean the Roman Blues, the charioteers? That's impossible. The Roman Blues don't wear blue stones or bracelets."

"No, they wear blue headcloths and blue belts. But that's in Rome. Here in Britain they wear bright blue pebbles entwined in leather thongs, and it's far from impossible that you might have killed four of them. They don't race anymore, 'cause there's no hippodromes in Britain today—none since they shut down the last big one up there in the north decades ago—and so the gangs have turned to other means of sport. The Blues are professional thieves, with ways of distributing their wares that would leave most people gape-mouthed with wonder. They're almost as well organized as lawyers are, and they are merciless. They'll be looking for the killer now, I expect. Did you see anyone else there? Or did anyone else see you?"

"I—I don't know. I chased those men for a mile, and almost everyone else was coming towards me. A hundred might have seen me. But none of them followed me, I am confident of that, and I saw no one afterwards. The place where I killed them was narrow, and hidden among high buildings. It was shut in, enclosed on all sides except for the access lane. There were no vantage points at all. And I dragged the bodies out of sight to give us time to get away before anyone discovered what had happened."

He paused, frowning as though reviewing what he had just said. "Your daughter's clothes were torn, so I gave her my cloak to cover herself with until we were safe in the market again. Someone might have noticed her before that . . . I don't know . . . She was distraught, as you would expect, but she coped well with it. I was able to arrange for a decent wrap large enough to conceal the damage to her clothing. That's when I told her who I am, and that I knew her name."

"And how did you know her name?"

"Because I had asked about her, the first time I saw her. Everyone knew her, it seemed to me, and I was impressed by the high regard folk had for her, and the way she seemed unaware of it."

"And what about this Nerva fellow? Where did you go with Shamus, once that drama was over and the others came back here?"

"Up to the garrison fort. Nerva's a bully—but that makes him easy to deal with, once he sees you know him for what he is. I wanted him to think we were going to report him to his commanding legate, so we made sure he saw us passing by in that direction while he was yet on patrol."

"And *did* you report him?"

"No. I never intended to. But I wanted him to think I would. That should convince him to keep his head down and safely out of sight at least until he realizes that nothing more has come of what happened."

"Hmm. And what *did* happen?"

Varrus blinked. "What d'you mean?"

Mcuil leaned forward and placed his elbow on the table, holding his jug of ale up at eye level and peering past it to where Varrus watched him. "The Emperor's licence," he said in a lower tone. "The labarum that you carry. That's what I mean."

"You know its name. That surprises me. What do you want to know about it?"

"Lydia told me you showed it to this Nerva fellow—though the fool didn't know what it was. But she knew what it was, my Lydia. She recognized it because she'd seen one like it, or a drawing of one, right here in her own home."

"That sounds . . . interesting." Varrus cocked his head. "Can I ask how that happened?"

"You can. It's no secret. An old friend I hadn't seen for thirty years came by to visit us one day, a year and more ago. He's a Christian bishop now, and he knew somehow that we was living in Londuin, so when his work brought him here he came to call, to see if my wife had yet succeeded in converting me to their faith. He didn't know she was dead, you see—my wife. But while he was here he told us the story of how in a dream the Emperor Constantine saw that symbol in the sky, the cross with the Greek letters *chi* and *rho*, for the christos. He drew a picture of it for me, right then and there on the table in my smithy, and Lydia was there. He said Constantine saw a message in his dream—a sign saying, '*In hoc signo vinces*,' meaning 'In this sign, conquer.'

"The very next day after that dream, he told us, Constantine won a great battle, the battle of the Milvian Bridge, and he became Emperor, and soon after that he became a Christian and took God's sign as his personal standard. His *personal* standard, his vexillum. The labarum . . ." He tilted his head to one side, staring quizzically at Varrus. "Now there might be a handful of good reasons for you to be carrying the Emperor's personal insignia with you, but if any of them is valid, then I'm left with one more concern. My daughter told me about what happened to your family, and about your fears for your own safety now. She told me you're in hiding, but you don't know who you're hiding from, and that's why you came to Britain. You think there's little chance of your being recognized here, she said, by any who might wish you ill. Is that right?"

Varrus nodded. "It is."

"Hmm. Then I'm surprised you would ever lose sight of that, even for a moment. So would you tell me, if it pleases you, how a bright young fellow like yourself would hope to keep himself unnoticed in a place like this—a provincial capital that's swarming with Roman officers and magistrates—by declaring himself to be about the personal affairs of the Emperor?"

Varrus stared unblinkingly at the older man, then dipped his head infinitesimally to one side in a tiny gesture that managed to convey self-disparagement. "It doesn't appear to have been too clever, does it? But it was the best course of action I could think of at the time—part spur-of-the-moment impulse, part calculated risk."

"That makes no sense."

"It makes sense to me."

"Then explain it to me."

Quintus Varrus took a long, slow pull of the fine dark ale. He swallowed, then smacked his lips. "Are none of your sons married, sir?"

The big man frowned, perplexed. "Why would you ask such a thing? What has it—?" He calmed himself. "They're all wed, save for Shamus—wed and bred," he said, and then his brow cleared and he beamed good-naturedly. "Ah! I see now why you'd ask. Yes, the house is usually full of wee folk—grandsons and granddaughters and the like—but they're all away, today, with Aidan. He's gone to deliver a new plow, and since he had to take Declan in the big wagon, to help him carry it, Declan's wife opted to go along, too, and take all the little ones with her, to pick blackberries along the riverside, and once *her* mind was made up, the other two wives decided to go, too, with their littluns. It's only a short ride, so they'll be home by nightfall . . . But you're right, the place is quiet today."

Varrus nodded, then eyed the jug of ale on the table in front of him, turning it slowly with one fingertip. "About what I did in the market," he said. "With the labarum. Everything happened quickly, so I did the only thing I could think of."

"Lydia said you disappeared. One moment you were there beside her, and the next time she looked, there was no sign of you. Where did you go?"

"To my friend Dylan's place of business, no more than a few paces from where we were sitting. Dylan's a cloth merchant, and he had been storing my belongings for me, so I ran to change my clothes. I knew, dressed as I was as a nonentity, I could do nothing to alter what was going to happen, but were I to appear as a wealthy Roman, I might be able to intimidate Nerva."

"You said you had no time," the smith said. "But that thing you're wearing is a rich man's garment—costly and complicated. It must have taken you a long time to strip off what you were wearing and then change into that."

"Not at all," Varrus said. "I had no need to undress first."

He stood up and spread his arms dramatically so that his sumptuous garment fell into its fully draped proportions, dropping into scalloped, sculpted folds of snow-white woollen perfection. Then he took a long, exaggerated step away from the table and spun slowly in a stately pivot, ignoring the astonished expression on the smith's face. That done, he reached up and shook out the drapes from his shoulders before flipping their ends backwards to hang down behind him like a cloak. He then undid two cunningly concealed fabric-covered clasps at his left shoulder, loosened the slipknot that bound a belt of white cloth around his waist, opened the garment down the front and shrugged out of it. He dropped it across the back of his chair.

He stood there in the same clothes he had been wearing when Lydia first saw him.

"As you can see, the robe is an artifice," Varrus said, grinning at the effect his transformation had had on the smith. He picked up the robe. "But it's a clever one, heh? I bought it in Napoli." While he talked he folded it lengthwise once and then again, then shaped it carefully into a neat bundle, which he tied into a parcel with the white belt. "From a distance, it looks ancient and cumbersome, like a formal toga from the time of the Caesars, but it's really nothing of the kind, and it's much more modern in design. It's what all the richest people in Italy are wearing nowadays."

He placed the bundle on the table in front of him, picked up his ale again, and took a healthy swig. "At that moment, though, in the marketplace," he said as he sat again, "the thought of it came to me in a flash, like an inspiration from the gods themselves. I rushed into the tent in Dylan's stall, and he brought hot water to wash my face and hands and insisted I brush my hair properly, to look the part I was about to play. I remembered the cylinder containing the labarum among my things and snatched it up because it looked—" He paused. "It looked official. It struck me as the sort of thing a man of affairs might carry, so I slung it over my shoulder and ran back out into the street."

"And this labarum. Where did it come from in the first place—after the Emperor signed it, I mean? How did you lay hands on it?"

"It was given to me . . . By my uncle Marius."

"And how did *he* come to have it?"

Varrus hesitated. "He had it from a dead man."

"A dead man." The Eirishman smiled, the corners of his eyes wrinkling. "Now that's an answer sure to provoke more questions, and I think you will not argue."

Varrus smiled back at him. "No, I won't argue. It was provocative."

"Aye, and I am provoked. Can you tell me whence came this dead man?"

"I can. He was found aboard a drifting boat in the Euxine Sea, which you might know better, if you have heard of it all, as the Black Sea."

"I've never heard of it. Is it black, then? A black-watered sea?"

"No, not even slightly. I've never seen it, but my uncle knows it well. He was stationed there, for three tours of duty with the Moesian fleet that operates against the barbarian invaders from north of the Danube River."

"I've never heard of that either."

"It's very famous. And huge. It makes the Thamis look like a trout stream, I've been told. It forms the entire northern border of the empire, from east to west. And to reach it, you have to sail to the farthest northeastern reaches of the Aegean Sea and traverse the narrow seaway there, the Hellespont, that separates Greece from Asia. That takes you to a little neck of land straddling the trading routes of the world, that holds the city of Byzantium—the one Constantine wants to call Constantinopolis. And behind Constantinopolis, stretching northward, is the Euxine Sea.

Its northern shores are peopled by savages, and the Moesian fleet has been winning fame up there for decades now. Anyway, Marius tells me the waters are crystal clear, not black at all, though they appear grey under leaden skies most of the time."

"And your dead man was found there. Was he drowned?"

"No, he had died of exposure, a long, slow death from being adrift too long without food or water. There were four others with him, all of them long dead and dried up by the summer sun. No one knew how they had come to such an end. Pirates would have killed them outright, thrown them into the sea, and kept the little boat, which had a mast and spars. The best anyone could suggest was that they had been aboard a larger vessel that was caught in a storm and wrecked, and they had managed to scramble aboard their little boat, only to perish from lack of food and water."

"And what about the labarum?"

"It was in the tube it occupies today, tied to the waist of the best-dressed corpse in the boat, and it was taken to my uncle with the remainder of what was found on board. Marius knew what the labarum was, having seen copies of it before, so he knew the fellow had been an imperial envoy. But precisely who he was, or what his business might have been, was beyond divination. And so, as navarch and senior officer in the area, Marius took possession of the document, intending to deliver it to his commanding admiral when he returned to his base.

"In the event, though, Admiral Niger, whom my uncle trusted implicitly, had set out to sea mere days before Marius's squadron reached port, and in his absence his duties had been assumed by a deputy whom my uncle detested for being a corrupt, politically appointed lickspittle, a puppet to a conspiracy of imperial courtiers rumoured to be enriching themselves, at every opportunity, at the expense of the navy and its personnel."

"So he did not leave the document with the deputy."

"He did not. As he told me later, the labarum was indisputably genuine, signed by the Emperor's own hand. But even more significantly, it had no history. There was no record of when it had been issued or to whom. Yet simple possession of the document endowed its bearer with all the personal power of the Emperor Constantine himself. And as such its potential for abuse was frightening."

Mcuil sniffed. "And your uncle never handed the thing over to his admiral?"

"He did not, because he never saw him again. Admiral Niger died at sea on that voyage. Discovered among the last orders the admiral left behind before he set sail was a signed commission promoting my uncle to Italy, in recognition of twelve years of outstanding service to the empire. It was well timed, for my uncle was sick and tired of the northern frontiers and besides, he would have hated serving under the new admiral—the deputy he so despised. Marius simply kept the labarum because no one knew he had it and he knew no one he could trust to return it safely to where it had been issued.

"That was the summer our family was murdered. Later, when Marius and I arrived back at his quarters in Napoli, he insisted I take the labarum. He thought it might someday be advantageous for me to have some such safeguard—something I could produce in time of dire need. Though frankly I had little faith in what it might do for me."

"And you believe that what took place this morning was such a time?"

Varrus picked up his mug and sipped at it, finding, to his mild surprise, that the ale had grown noticeably warmer since he had tasted it last. "Near enough," he said. "Besides, it worked, didn't it? Nerva went away and no one is any the wiser."

"Don't be too sure of that," the smith said. "This is a small place, for all they call it a provincial capital, and not much gets by folk. What are we, thirty thousand people? And most folk in Londuin knows most everybody else, at least to see 'em, if not to talk to 'em. And people do love to talk, especially about the likes of rich young fellows who turn up out of nowhere carrying credentials out of Rome that are signed by the Emperor's own hand. That's worth talking about, by my reckoning, so I would say you'd best take note and plan accordingly."

The smith rose to his feet, tilting his jug to show that it was empty and asking mutely, one eyebrow raised in question, if Varrus, too, would like some more. When the younger man declined, he moved to the keg on the table and poured himself another, speaking over his shoulder as he watched the rising level in his jug. "Lydia said you've been here a month. Tell me how you learned to speak our tongue so well in such a short time. It seems impossible."

"And it would be, had I begun a month ago," Varrus said, shifting in his seat and flexing his leg under the table. "But I've been speaking it for most of my life. We spoke Latin in my father's household in Dalmatia, but my old teacher came from here, was born right here in Londinium— Londuin you call it, is that right?"

"Aye, that's what we call it, some of us at least, but we're not Roman. The Romans call it what you did."

Varrus nodded. "Anyway, Rhys was born here and he taught me to speak the language when I was young enough not to ask him why." He shrugged. "Which meant I was young enough to learn it quickly."

"And why do you think he would take the time to do that?" the smith asked as he moved back to his seat at the table.

"Loneliness, probably. I've wondered about that, too, from time to time, and loneliness or homesickness seem to be the two most likely reasons. He had been away from Britannia for a very long time, and not a single person could speak to him in his native tongue. And there was I, young and eager to please, so he began to teach me the occasional word or two in his own language. And once begun, it became a source of pleasure to both of us, as a means to pass the time—and to communicate with each other when we had no wish to be understood by others."

"And your parents did not mind?"

"My mother didn't mind. She thought it wonderful that I should want to learn another tongue. My father, though?" The corners of his mouth turned down. "He didn't know about it and wouldn't have cared anyway. He was barely aware of my existence."

"Hmm . . . This teacher, was he the smith Lydia told me about?"

"He was. Rhys Twohands, so named because he was equally skilful with either one, no matter what he was doing."

The big smith shook his head in wonder. "That would be a powerful advantage at a forge."

"And at an anvil," Varrus said. "Holding tongs in either hand with equal ease and wielding a hammer skilfully with both . . . He always made me feel inadequate."

"Aye . . . Lydia said you were a smith." The pause that followed, emphasized by his eyeing of the bundled white robe, was eloquent, so that he barely had to ask, "Is it true?"

Varrus sat back and crossed his arms. "I would like to think so. But you might think otherwise. I spent most of my boyhood in Rhys's forge, and for more than five years before we left home he trained me seriously, every day, to be a smith. But I never thought to ask him if he considered me an able apprentice, or even a satisfactory student. I did it for the pleasure of it. I never thought to work at it as a livelihood. And I never thought that he might die before I could find out."

"Aye," Mcuil said again. "I understand." He took a swig of his ale. "So what will you do now?"

"What, about being a smith?"

"No, I mean in the aftermath of today's events. Where will you go? You obviously can't stay in Londuin."

Varrus frowned. "Why not?"

"Why not?" Mcuil's eyes widened. "Because you're a marked man!" he said. "You've made the provincial authorities aware of you, and now they'll come looking for you. They have no choice. You've provoked their interest, and almost certainly their fear, by appearing unexpectedly

and waving your labarum around under their noses! They'll be scram-
bling to find out who you are and where you came from and who sent
you, because until they discover all there is to know about you, they'll
see you as a threat."

"A threat to what? I don't even know who we're talking about."

"Nor do they! But you can be sure that, as men of power in a Roman
provincial capital, every one of them will have something they want
to hide from prying eyes in Rome. That's the disadvantage of being
involved in politics—no one holds his secrets more closely than a guilty
politician, whether that be in Eire, in Londuin, or in Rome itself. None
of them can afford to trust anyone but himself, and so none of them
trusts anyone . . . and they'll all be trying to find you because each one
will see you as a threat to whatever it is he is up to." He hesitated, reading the disbelief in Varrus's eyes, and then charged on. "And don't delude
yourself that they won't know where to look, because they'll look everywhere. This isn't Rome, with its teeming mobs and anthills of people.
This is Londuin. It's small, and they have an entire bored garrison that
they can muster to hunt you. They'll turn this whole town upside down
trying to find the wealthy, well-dressed young man from Rome who
was waving the Emperor's insignia about in an open marketplace.
They'll roust out every roadhouse in and around the city, and when they
don't find him there they'll ransack every lodging house and drinking
den in this entire region. And when they've done all that, they'll start
going from house to house."

He stopped, cocking his head. "Do you really think no one took
note of what you did? Do you believe for one moment that the people
who deal in such things, in court politics and mysteries, might not hear
about a thing like that?"

He shook his head emphatically and pointed a finger towards the
white bundle on the tabletop. "That robe, that thing you wore today,
might be the most dangerous thing you own now—apart from the
Emperor's labarum, of course."

Varrus sat silent, his face betraying nothing of his thoughts, but then he inhaled sharply and straightened in his chair. "You're right," he said. "I'd thought of none of that . . . Stupid of me, and unforgivable to have brought danger into your house. Forgive me. I'll leave immediately."

"No, you won't. Stay where you are and finish your ale. I wasn't telling you to go. I was pointing out a truth I thought you might have missed. And I was right. But you're safer here, for now at least, than you would be anywhere else. If anyone took note of you when you left the marketplace, they would have seen you heading towards the garrison headquarters, just as Nerva did, and they'd have assumed you was going there on official business to do with the Emperor. It's unlikely anyone saw you come here afterwards, because not too many folk live in this area, and none of them's the kind who'd ever dream about going to talk to anyone in a uniform. So you'll stay here safe for now, and there's an end of it."

Varrus nodded. "Thank you, then," he said. "I don't know what else to say."

"You saved my daughter's life today, so there's no need to say anything." The smith rose to his feet and placed his mug carefully on the serving table at his back. "Come with me into the smithy, and let's find out how much you know."

TEN

It did not take long for the smith to satisfy himself that his guest, despite all appearances, was familiar with working smithies, for he watched him closely from the moment they stepped through the doors, noting how Varrus stopped on the threshold to take a sweeping inventory of the interior. The young man took particular interest in the enormous bellows against the farthest wall and the way the jointed wooden arms that powered the device were driven in turn by the massive, revolving waterwheel just on the other side of that wall. He also saw the precise moment the Roman's eyes took note of the system of perfectly inclined stone sluices that brought a steady, gentle stream of water gliding almost silently from the top of the wall down to the quenching pits beside the forge that dominated the room.

Mcuil was immensely proud of his forge, the working centre of his universe, for there was not another to match it in all of Londuin. It was built entirely of a substance Varrus did not recognize, though logic told him it must be clay of some description. It was startlingly white under its much-stained coating of smoky yellows and sooty black, the white underneath standing out in unexpected brilliance where it had been worn away or chipped by one workplace vagary or another. It was easily three, perhaps even four times larger than would be found in any normal smithy, and the young Roman nodded in admiration at the clean, spacious extent of it, easily large enough for several men to work at it together, as was evidenced by the three separate fire baskets on the bed of the huge hearth.

"A beautiful forge," Varrus said. "Did you build it yourself?"

"Every bit of it," the big man said. "This used to be a cooperage, so it had a forge of sorts when I bought it, used for making and shaping the iron hoops for the barrels they made, but it was a lightweight thing, nothing like the kind of forge I needed, so I ripped it out and started again from nothing, designing what I wanted. It turned out as close to perfect for me as it could have been, and I'm more than simply proud of my water system. There's nothing to compare to it in all Londuin." He smiled. "Besides, I happen to believe that if a smith can't build his own workplace, he has no right to call himself a smith."

Still smiling, he stepped over to a workspace fronting the forge. It contained a heavy, flat-topped anvil and was lined on one side with a solid oaken bench from which hung hammers, mauls, tongs, and pincers of all shapes and sizes. "Hand me that bit of iron, would you?"

It was obvious which piece of iron he was referring to—it was the only piece on the top of the anvil—and Varrus smiled, too. Then, without saying a word, he stepped to the rack of tools and chose a pair of tongs about the length of his forearm. Manipulating the tool easily with one hand, he picked up the metal scrap Mcuil had indicated, hefted it effortlessly, and flipped it in the air, end over end, catching it smoothly and flipping it again before setting it down gently within easy reach of Mcuil's hand.

The big smith smiled ruefully. "Well, I had to try."

"I would have been disappointed if you hadn't," Varrus said, grinning back at him. "It's the oldest lesson in the trade, but no apprentice ever learns it until he picks up a piece of metal with his bare fingers and learns that it had been red hot moments earlier. He'll never make the same mistake again. *Beware black iron.*"

He nodded then towards the complex apparatus against the wall by the forge. "Those bellows are magnificent. We had a set at home in Dalmatia, but not that big. And your forge is spectacular. What did you use to build it? It looks like white clay."

"And it is. Pure, white clay. I brought it here from Eire, from near where my mother's people lived, in the heart of the mainland. There are great pits of it there, and the local people are all potters. They make their pots and decorate them wondrously, and then Roman merchants buy them up and ship them off to Gaul and other places. The clay is superb, smooth and easy to work, and the pots made from it are iron-hard, baked for days in kilns that are old beyond counting. So when I came to build this place I sent my brother Liam home to bring me back enough clay to build this forge and the ovens attached to it, *and* the chimney to vent all the smoke well away from where we work."

"You sent him all the way to Hibernia for clay? That must have been cripplingly expensive."

"And why not? It was the only kind of clay I had ever found that would allow me to do what I needed to do with it. I'd worked in other people's forges until then, forges made from brick and other kinds of stone, and even concrete, but none of them suited the demands of the work I was doing. Sometimes you have to spend gold to make silver, but if you do it right, the silver you haul in can soon outshine the gold you laid out. Once I built the forge, I earned more for my work than I ever had before."

Varrus again studied the bellows apparatus and the way its outlet pipe tapered into the forge at the very base of the fire bed, and now he noticed a junction point, from which another pipe led off and vanished through a vent in the smithy's wall, a brick wall that he now saw curved inwards in a quarter circle. He squinted, trying to see better in the gloom of that corner, and saw the outline of a door.

"What's out there, beyond the wall there?" he asked, pointing.

Dominic glanced idly towards the door. "Oven," he said. "For smelting ore."

Varrus stared at him. "You smelt your own ore?"

"Sometimes, but it's not exactly mine. Good ore's not easy to find around here."

"So you bring it in?"

Mcuil flashed a grin. "You might say that. You know about smelting?"

"A little. I've worked with it. Where do you get your ore from?"

"Rome."

"*Where?*" Varrus heard the shock in his own voice and stopped short, thinking he was being teased, but Dominic Mcuil was no longer smiling.

"Rome," he said, straight-faced. "But really from Camulodunum. The armourers up there like my iron ingots, so we have an arrangement. They send me ore, and I smelt it into ingots for them. They pay us for our work and everyone is happy."

Varrus was frowning slightly. "But that makes no sense. Why would they send ore all the way here? Have they no furnaces in the garrison fort at Camulodunum?"

"They have, but it seems our kilns make better iron. Come and look."

He led the way through the door in the brick wall, and there, surrounded by high stone walls on every side, stood two brick-built, cylindrical furnace ovens, each one fed by a narrow pipe from the smithy's enormous bellows.

"They're huge!" Varrus said. "Higher than I've ever seen before, I think. Why is that?"

"It seems to be the reason for our smelted iron being so"—Mcuil hesitated—"desirable, I suppose." He paused again. "You know how a smelting oven works, in principle, don't you?"

"Yes, I do. Are you telling me your ovens are this tall because you want to pile more fuel under them, so the ore benefits from the full force of the fire beneath?"

The smith twisted his mouth, considering that, then nodded. "I am, I suppose, but I should say both yes and no. My brother and I were taught by the same master smith, in Gaul." He saw Varrus's eyebrows twitch in surprise. "Aye, Gaul. Our father was a smith when we were all small, but after he lost an arm at the forge he became a trader in metal goods, including weapons, and he moved us all to Gaul, where we lived very well in a town near the city of Lugdunum. He apprenticed us both to a wonderful smith called Oskar of Lugdunum, a ferocious taskmaster and an unforgiving teacher whom we both came to love outside of the smithy.

"Now, every blade maker worth his salt understands the importance of charcoal in hardening iron. They may not know precisely how the process works—no one really does—but they know that ordinary, malleable iron, cooked in charcoal, takes on, to widely varying degrees, an extra amount of hardness, and that can result in extraordinary blades. It's an uncertain process, and it can never be successfully predicted, but when it works well, the results can be astonishing.

"Well, Oskar had a theory of his own, and though it sounded mad, his process worked remarkably well most of the time. He was very secretive about it, though. He was convinced that if his theory were proved true, everyone would start using it and he would lose the competitive advantage that kept his family fed and made his blades famous. I don't mind talking to you about it, though, since you are not likely to be keeping company with any soldiers in the days ahead. In essence Oskar believed that the difference was achieved, not in the cooking of the metal—in creating the bloom, as he called it—but in the direct aftermath of the melting of the ore, when the molten iron fell through the charcoal ashes to the collection pan at the bottom of the oven. He came to believe that something, some magical, unknown component in those coating ashes, penetrated and hardened the iron as the molten metal fell through them."

"That does sound mad," Varrus murmured.

"I told you it did. So Oskar built his ovens taller than anyone else's and kept them hidden. And his iron grew harder than ever, able to be worked and reworked as often as it needed to be and to hold an edge that came close to defying belief." His face quirked into an off-centre smile. "Best of all, though, no one paid attention to his ovens because he built himself a magnificent new forge of shining white clay that he shipped in from Belgium. And years later, obviously, I built my own for exactly the same reason. And my white clay forge is the envy of every smith in Londuin."

"I don't doubt that," Varrus said, stretching out his hand towards the nearest oven's wall. It was cold.

"And does Oskar's process still work, here in Britain?"

"It would work anywhere. I don't know why, but it works every time, and the sole reason for it has to be that extra distance the molten iron falls through burning ashes. And so, twice a year, Liam sends down a train of wagons filled with prime ore that's brought in to Camulodunum by water, and I send him back loaf ingots of fine iron. He then uses that metal to make superior weapons for garrison and legionary officers—blades far more than a simple cut above the kind of swords churned out in the state factories. Our customers are more than happy with our goods and they pass the word to others, so we do well."

"So the ingots in your yard—I noticed they're all stamped with the same die. Are they yours, from these ovens?"

"From these ovens, yes, but they are not all mine. Most of them—a hundred and thirty, to be exact—will be shipped to Liam when the next load of ore comes in. That will be some time next month or in the first half of the one after that."

"You said the ore is shipped in to Camulodunum. Do you know from where?"

Dominic shook his head. "I have no idea. It could come from anywhere in the empire. I know it arrives on enormous freight carriers that sit at anchor offshore, before it's unloaded into smaller craft to be shipped upriver to forts and garrisons with smelting capabilities." He reached out a hand, looking down at it as raindrops began to fall around them. "I thought I felt rain a moment ago," he said. "Let's go in."

"My thanks, sir, for entrusting me with the knowledge of your ovens," Varrus said, and followed the older man back through the smithy. But on the way he stopped, his attention caught by something propped up, as though on display, on a long, narrow shelf on the wall. Mcuil watched as the younger man moved towards the shelf and stopped to stare intently at the device before picking it up with both hands.

"What is this?" He didn't even look at Mcuil as he asked the question.

"It's an iron faceplate for a horse."

Varrus held the piece up higher, looking at it with slitted eyes. "Of course it is. With that length and shape and those flared eye protectors it couldn't be anything else, could it? It's not Roman, though. Where did you find it?"

Mcuil's mouth twitched into a half smile. "Why would you say it's not Roman? What else could it be?"

"I don't know," Varrus said quietly, still peering at the thing, turning it from side to side as he studied it, searching for some clue to its identity. "It might be any of several things. But none of them is Roman. It's ancient—older than anything I've ever seen made for a horse. And this iron's black, blacker than any made today." He hefted the faceplate with both hands, feeling the weight of it. "It's heavy and it's thick, probably case-hardened when it was forged, and it's deeply pitted, so it was badly rusted at some point, though it's been well looked after since then. I'd guess this was made no sooner than a hundred years ago, and it's probably far older."

He finally looked at his host. "And it's not Roman because Romans have never used armoured horses. Legionary cavalry is light and nimble. It has to be. Its sole purpose is to provide a fast-moving shield to protect the legions while they're regrouping into battle formation." He hefted the piece again. "Armour like this would slow them down too much."

Mcuil was still smiling. "Now it's my turn to be impressed," he said.

"No one else has ever been that definite about that piece before. And you're right. It isn't Roman."

"What is it, then?"

"It's Macedonian."

Varrus stared at him. "The Macedonia that Alexander ruled?"

"Aye, and his father Philip before him." He pointed to the faceplate. "But that, I think, is from Alexander's time."

Varrus tilted his head very slightly to one side, narrowing his eyes. "You mean this thing I'm holding has a connection to the man who conquered the world of his day? To Alexander?"

The smith nodded. "To his cavalry. I do."

"How could you possibly know that? Alexander died six hundred years ago."

"Closer to seven hundred, if I remember what my old teacher hammered into me. But that, I am assured, belonged to one of his cavalrymen. Do you read Greek?"

"I do."

"Then look at the markings there, between the eyeholes. The writing's hard to see, but it's visible."

Varrus stepped sideways and held the metal up in a beam of light from a high opening. He stood peering at it for long moments, then lowered it and turned back to Mcuil.

"Hetairoi," he said. "It's hard to read, with all the rust pitting. I've heard the word before, but I can't remember what it means. Do you know?"

Mcuil ignored the question. "What about the drawing?"

"What drawing? You mean these scratches above the word?"

"Look closer. Someone took great pains to scratch metal on metal right there, in that particular spot. And you're right, the rust pits don't help. But look again, and try to make sense of it."

"Well . . . it could be a stick man, I suppose. And if it is, he's carrying something over his shoulder. A long pole of some kind, with a . . . with a crossbar on the end of it."

"Pointing downwards."

"Aye."

"It's a sarissa."

Varrus's eyebrows twitched upwards. "Is it," he said. "Well, you'll get no argument from me. But what's a sarissa?"

"A spear with a really long shaft, perhaps four or even five paces long. It was carried over the shoulder, pointed downwards, by a mounted man. The men who carried them were called the hetairoi, the companions of the king, and they were supposedly the finest cavalry of ancient times."

"The Companions. Of course. I remember hearing about them when I was little. But I never believed they were real."

"Oh, they were real. There's not the slightest doubt of that. They were all from the nobility, because they had to provide their own mounts and weaponry and only the wealthiest of men could do that, and they were all volunteers, riding as friends of the king rather than as soldiers or conscripts. Philip of Macedon started it, inviting his young nobles to ride with him, and they became known simply as the Companions. It was Alexander, though, who really made the rank a great honour. He inherited a following of about six hundred men when his father died, but over the next ten years he built the Companions up to a strength of five or six thousand."

Varrus was staring at him in amazement. "How do you know all this?" He instantly realized his question could have been offensive and made to apologize, but the big man cut him off.

"Nah, I learned it all from my old teacher. His name was Father Domnuil and he was my mother's oldest brother. Before he came home to die with us in Lugdunum and ended up teaching me and my brothers for five years instead, he spent more than thirty years in Egypt, in a place called Alexandria. Do you know of it?"

"Of course. It's one of the world's great cities."

"Aye. Well, Domnuil worked as a scribe in one of the libraries there. He spent a lot of time digging into everything he could find about the Ancients and their world, and he was fascinated by every-thing about Alexander the Great." He hunched his shoulder briefly in a fatalistic shrug. "I suppose he passed that on to me, though I was no scholar." Again he pointed at the faceplate Varrus was still holding. "He taught me enough, though, that I knew what I was seeing when I first came across that thing. And it was that crossbar you noticed that convinced me that what I was seeing was real and that it came from the time of Alexander."

"The crossbar? How so?"

"Because Domnuil had taught me that in Philip's day the sarissa was a long, plain spear. A rider used it against the first enemy soldier he met—skewered him with it like a spitted rabbit. But then he had to leave it behind because the spear shaft went right through and the dead man's weight would rip it from the rider's grasp. But Alexander's armourers added the crossbar just below the spearhead. That stopped the shaft from going in too far and offered at least a chance that the rider could pull it free of the corpse as he rode past and then use it again. It may not sound like much, but it doubled the killing potential of a charging horseman."

Varrus was nodding. "Aye, it would have . . . So where did you find this?"

"In the marketplace. The huckster selling it told me it was from Alexander's cavalry, but even I could see he didn't know what he was talking about. There was something about it, though, something that made me look more closely at it, and that's when I saw the drawing and realized that he was right, even though he thought he was lying. So I bought it—though not for the price he was asking."

"Then who might have done the drawing, do you think? The man who owned it originally?"

"Nah. He would have known who he was. It was probably drawn by someone who found it later and knew what it was, but the gods alone know why anyone would have gone to that much trouble for what must have been a useless article by then. Nonetheless, though, you are holding a piece of solid history in your hands there."

Varrus stared solemnly at the artifact for long moments, then replaced it on the shelf.

"My sons think I'm mad to keep the thing, but I think it's the craftsman in me that tells me to do it," Mcuil said. "I believe that creators like us—smiths and artisans—have special gifts. Some men are passionate about their craft, whatever it might be, and when they are, when they care that much about what they do, they produce fine work." He tucked his hands into his armpits, almost shyly, Varrus thought. "You probably think me daft, too, but I admire things like this. The man who made that is long dead and forgotten, but that piece he made so carefully and well is still here, after hundreds of years, and it could still be used for its intended purpose. That, to me, is a kind of immortality."

He stopped short, having seen the quick look of surprise on his young listener's face. "Oh, I don't mean *that* kind of immortality. I'm not talking about living gods. Men can't be immortal, but their exploits can. Their achievements can bring them a measure of immortality." He stopped again. "What?" he asked. "What did I say?" And then he laughed. "No need to blush, Master Varrus," he said, waving an open hand. "You're wondering how a know-nothing Eirish smith can talk about degrees of immortality. I'd wonder the same thing myself if I were you and heard me. But it's all due to Christian priests—or to one Christian priest, Domnuil. Us Eirish are great Christians when we're not being pagans, you know. But the godly uncle who was my teacher taught me how to think of things beyond the immediate."

"Beyond the immediate." Varrus smiled. "That sounds momentous. What does it mean?"

"It means what it says. Most men concern themselves only with what is going on about them, here and now. Which really means they scarcely think at all. Domnuil taught me to recognize things of import and take note of them beyond their present needs. Things like what we're going to do now with you, for example. Between the men you killed and the men you challenged, you've put yourself in danger for as long as you stay in Londuin."

"And I came here thinking I was avoiding people who want to kill me," Varrus said. "I suppose I really haven't handled this well."

"I think we need to make you disappear. To Camulodunum."

Varrus frowned. "And why would I go there?"

"Well, it's a hundred miles from here, for a start. And my brother Liam lives there now. And I've had a problem, see. Liam had an accident in the forge a few months ago, and now he can't work as well as he did. He has no sons, and so I've been thinking about sending Shamus and Callum to help him out." He picked up the tongs Varrus had used earlier, examining them as he continued. "Trouble is, I can't afford to lose Callum right now—we've too much work in hand. And Shamus needs watching. He's wrong-headed, sometimes, as you have discovered." He paused. "For the past year and more he and I have been coming closer and closer to open warfare. He says he doesn't want to be tied to a forge all his life, and I have to admit he's not the dedicated smith his brothers are." He moved forward to replace the tongs in their place on the rack by the workbench, then turned and leaned back against the bench itself, looking Varrus straight in the eye.

"My daughter tells me you might be looking for work as a smith. Are you? Because if you are, we might be able to help each other out, you and me. I could arrange for you to vanish into a smithy in Camulodunum for a year or so until whoever might be looking for you forgets that you were here." He smiled at the expression on Varrus's face. "Think about that before you say no. It would be a perfect hiding place. No sane person would expect to find either an aristocrat or a wandering priest in a blacksmith's shop in a small provincial town."

"Or a member of the Varrus family, for that matter. I agree, Master Mcuil, and my first question should be why you would do such a thing for me, but I think you've given me the answer to that already."

"I have. You would be doing me a great service in three areas, in addition to the one for which I already owe you—saving my daughter's life. You would be helping my brother, helping me to meet my obligations by keeping Callum here where I need him, and relieving me of the need to fret constantly over my youngest son."

Varrus stood frowning slightly, nibbling at the skin inside the corner of his mouth. "It seems like an easy choice," he said, "but it contains far more substance than I had thought about until now." He looked into the smith's eyes. "Do you need me to agree now?"

"Not at all. Take all the time you need. In the meantime, though, we have other things to attend to."

He crossed to the door of the smithy, where he leaned out and shouted for his daughter, and when she came in a short time later, rubbing absently at a smudge of dust or flour on her nose and smiling cheerfully at him, Varrus felt his insides thrill at how lovely she was. Then his stomach swooped in panic as it occurred to him that he had given her father no indication of what he thought of his daughter, or what he hoped to do about it. That omission, he knew, could cause him much grief if he did not address it soon.

"Lydia," her father said, "Master Varrus will be staying with us for a while, but he can't go outside these doors again until we find him some new clothes that are neither black nor white. You can go back to the market and see to that. And this time you will oblige me by taking Callum with you—and no arguments, Missy. You should have no difficulty finding clothing for a working smith, and he's about the same size as Shamus."

Lydia was eyeing Varrus up and down, grinning saucily. "He is," she said. "But bigger through the shoulders. I'll find something suitable."

Varrus smiled back at her. "Dylan will have everything you need. No need to look farther."

"Ah, but you're wrong there, Master Varrus. Dylan the cloth merchant will have nothing among all his goods that a working smith might wear. He is a rich man's supplier."

Varrus wrinkled his nose, aware that she was laughing at him. "You're right, of course. That was silly of me. But go to his stall and talk to him anyway, if you will. Explain what has happened and he'll use his connections to provide you with everything. I left a few things with him, so please ask him for them, and warn him, if you will, to say nothing about knowing me if anyone asks about me. Be sure to tell him we need to deflect attention, not attract it. And tell him, too, that I'll come by and settle with him later."

She had listened with pursed mouth. "And do you really think I hadn't thought of all that?"

He quickly held up his hands in surrender. "Of course not," he said. "Pardon me. I spoke without thinking. Do as you think best."

"She'll do that anyway," Dominic Mcuil said, reclaiming his daughter's attention and then addressing her directly. "But do it quickly and come back here quickly. I doubt anyone will be looking for either of you yet, but there's no point in taking foolish risks. And while you're away, I'll see our guest to his sleeping quarters."

Within moments, she was gone and Varrus, deeply thrilled and flustered by the knowledge that he was now to live under the same roof as Lydia Mcuil, and bemused by the breathtaking unexpectedness of the change in his life, followed her father into the darkness of the rearmost part of the house towards the sleeping accommodations. He noted that they appeared to be typical of their kind while resembling in no slightest way the kind he had used in his former life. At home in his parents' villa in Dalmatia, his bedchamber had been spacious, built on an upper floor and open to the light and the night sky. That, though, had been luxury, a rich man's indulgence. Here in Britain, as in most other Roman-occupied territories, sleeping quarters were precisely that: small, dark chambers containing little more than a cot bed and intended primarily for rest. They might, like the one to which Mcuil now led him, have a degree of brightness provided by a small, narrow window mounted high in one wall that allowed daylight to filter in, but for the most part they were permanently dark and completely unused during daylight hours.

Dominic pulled back the curtain separating the cubicle from the narrow passageway that fronted it, serving five other identical niches. There was still enough light filtering through the reed curtain covering the window to enable them to see the furnishings. With a glance Varrus took in a narrow cot with a thin mattress and blanket, a small, square-topped table, and a long shelf mounted on the wall above the bed. There was a bronze oil lamp on the table, and Dominic moved in to light it from the one he carried with him.

"You'll sleep here now," he said. "Shamus is next to you on the right and Marco, my steward, is on your left. The door at the far end of the passage leads out into a small courtyard, where you'll find another door that lets you into the bath house. It's nothing great as baths go, but it works and the water is hot, so if you want to use it, scrub away. Now, can you find your own way back to the smithy?" Varrus nodded. "Good. Come and find me when you're ready."

Varrus began to empty his knapsack and to stack its few contents neatly on the narrow ledge above the cot while he wrestled with his conscience as to what he must do next. He had comported himself well since coming here, Varrus thought, except for the single critical omission of not telling Dominic Mcuil that he wanted to marry his daughter. That, he knew, could cause him much grief if he did not address it soon.

Less than half an hour later, he and Dominic Mcuil were seated once again across from each other at the dining table with drinks in front of them. Varrus had decided that the time had come to declare his intentions regarding the big Eirishman's daughter, but he was only beginning to appreciate, with no small degree of fear, just how much grief that decision might cause him.

Then suddenly and without warning, as though he had divined what was in Varrus's mind, the big smith thrust himself up from the table and stood glowering down at him, flexing the fingers of both hands and looking as though he might erupt into bone-crushing anger. He started to turn away, seemingly overcome by fury, but then he hesitated and swung back to face

"You're not the first young stallion to come in here looking to wed my daughter, you know. Not by long odds." The Eirish lilt in his voice was clearer now than it had been earlier, conveying no hint of anger despite his lingering scowl. "Did you say anything about this to her? This tomfoolery talk of marriage?"

"Yes, I did."

"Did you, by God? And what did she have to say?"

"She said you would run me off."

"*I* would run you off? And what about her?"

Varrus frowned. "If you're asking me if she also threatened to run me off, then no, she didn't. She gave me no reason to think she was displeased."

"No reason to think she was displeased . . ." The smith's voice was soft as he repeated the words, but then it hardened instantly. "And the two of you never set eyes on one another, never even spoke, until today? You still say that?"

"It is the truth."

Mcuil made a popping, sucking sound with his lips and sat again at the table. He gazed at Varrus through slitted eyelids. "My daughter, Master Varrus, has a mind of her own. It's a well-known source of scandal around these parts. Not that she ever did anything scandalous," he added quickly. "I didn't mean it quite that way. The scandal I meant lies in the pleasure the old biddies around here all get from whispering about how she's unbiddable. She will not be told what to do or how to behave in certain things . . . like taking a husband, or even tolerating visits from those who might think to wed her. God knows I've tried to find her a suitable man, several times, but she would have none of them, and so I stopped trying. She had convinced me to believe that when she takes a man it will be one of her own choosing and I'll have nothing to do with it, other than being present for the rites and welcoming the fellow into my home thereafter. And now you come along, from beyond the seas, and in mere hours you tell me she has given you no reason *to think she was displeased*."

Varrus did not know how to respond to that and so he said nothing. Mcuil shifted in his seat and sank lower, squaring his shoulders against the back of his chair and staring back at him mutely.

"So," Varrus said eventually, unable to sit quiet any longer. "What are you saying?"

Mcuil pushed himself upright, then looked down at his hands, meshing his fingers and pressing his thumbs point to point. "What I am saying—and earlier today I would not have believed it possible that I might ever say such a thing—is that if Lydia decides to take you you'll hear no complaints from me. You saved her life today, and probably the lives of her brothers, too. I have no doubt of that, and you should have no doubt of my gratitude." He spread his hands wide and smiled. "She is my daughter and she is the light of my life, the image of her mother, may God rest her soul. She herself will decide who is to be the man in her life and none of us can influence that choice. You might be the one. We'll see. But as her father, I have the duty of ensuring that she goes through this life without being hurt in any way that I can prevent. And that, as I'm sure you will understand, dictates that I need to do everything I can to satisfy myself that the man she chooses will be worthy of her."

He paused, looking Varrus squarely in the eye. "I like you, Master Varrus. Considering how little I know of you, I like you surprisingly well. So let us talk, you and I, about realities, and then about possibilities."

Quintus Varrus smiled, suddenly feeling much better. "I'm listening," he said.

"Good. First, then, as Lydia's father, I am not happy about the speed with which this . . . this situation has sprung up." He held up both hands, palms outwards. "Come now, let's be honest. A proposal of marriage within hours of a first meeting, with no time for a knowledge or understanding of each other? And then the additional complication that the man involved, the man to whom my beloved daughter is attracted, might have little time to live? Lydia's future happiness is all I currently live for, so I find the possibility of early widowhood for her to be unsettling, to say the least, and I hope you can see why I might think so." His Celtic lilt became even more pronounced so that his voice was almost liquid in its gentle sibilance. "It is, I am sure you will agree, unusual, to express it mildly. Time can and will, of course, change everything you believe today. You may grow to love and admire each other deeply. Or you might grow to loathe each other. Either outcome, though, will take time, and if it takes you five times as long as you have known each other to this point for each of you to discover that the other is not quite perfect, then less than a single week will have passed. Do you see what I am saying?"

"I do, and I agree. But I will not change my mind yet."

"Nor should you, so be it you bind yourself to respect my place as head of this house while you are living here."

"Agreed again," Varrus said. "But what, then?"

"Solutions. I will give you my blessing to approach Lydia openly. After that, depending upon how she receives what you say to her, we can decide how to proceed. For your own safety we're getting you away from here. Once you're installed in Camulodunum, you will be close to our family, involved in our affairs and, given Lydia's willingness, open to planning a life together with her later, when it is safe for you to emerge from hiding. We visit Liam frequently, so you two should not lack for opportunities to come to know each other. Does that seem reasonable?"

"Extremely reasonable. And I am extremely grateful."

"Then why are you looking so sombre?"

The young man's face broke into a nervous grin. "Because I think you've frightened me out of approaching your daughter," he said.

The big man's eyes went wide with surprise. "Why would you say that? Didn't you hear what I said a moment ago? I said you will have no opposition from me, so be it you treat my daughter with respect while you are under my roof."

"With respect," Varrus said, still wearing that same grin, "I heard you clearly. It's not you I'm afraid of now."

"Aha!" Mcuil outmatched the younger man's grin and slapped the tabletop. "Well, that's another matter altogether, that one, and I'm glad I will have nothing to do with it. When Lydia comes home, I'll make sure you have an hour together. You can tell me later what plans, if any, you will be considering."

Quintus Varrus had fallen asleep in the sun on the courtyard steps of the Mcuil house, and the late-afternoon shadows had chopped across the enclosed space by the time he heard the muted squeal of hinges that announced the opening of the outer gates. He sat up hastily, rubbing his eyes as the excited sound of children's happy voices made him aware of what was happening: the Mcuil clan had come home, riding in a large, four-wheeled wagon pulled by a mismatched pair of heavy work horses, one black, the other dun.

His own childhood, most of it spent at one or another of his grandfather Titanius's villas, had been privileged but lonely, so Varrus had seldom heard the kind of cacophony that can be produced by an excited brood of closely related, similarly aged cousins, and this was a lively, active, noisy brood. A round dozen boys and girls spilled out of the great wagon down onto the ground, shepherded by the three women who had mothered them, and he found himself smiling at the sights and sounds of their eagerness and their berry-stained enthusiasm. They appeared to range in age from about ten down to the youngest, a green-eyed, fiery-haired two- or three-year-old imp called Devlin—his name seemed to be loud on everyone's lips at once—who was already more than capable, as his grandfather would assure Varrus later, of causing a disturbance in an empty house. From that moment, Varrus's experience of the Mcuil household changed completely, and the quiet solitude that had seduced him into sleeping in the afternoon sunlight was banished, seldom to be experienced again. There were children everywhere after that, and with them, hand in hand, went noise and boisterous upheaval.

The two men on the cart's bench had seen him earlier in the day and now eyed him with a noncommittal curiosity. The three wives might have guessed at who he was, but if they did they showed no sign of it. They averted their eyes decorously after their first quick glances at him and moved quickly to keep the inquisitive children away from him.

Aidan Mcuil swung down and nodded to him warily, taking note of the change in his clothing, the elaborate, snowy-white wool having been replaced with stark, unadorned, black worsted cloth. "Master Varrus," he said quietly, nodding in greeting. "Are you waiting for someone?"

Declan had climbed down from the other side of the bench and now came around to stand behind his brother, nodding but saying nothing to the Roman, who shook his head and smiled.

"No," he said. "Your father is inside, working, and I didn't want to distract him, so I came outside to sit in the sun. And I nodded off."

"And there's no one else here?"

"Shamus is doing something in the workroom, and Callum went with your sister to find me some new clothes, an hour or two ago. They haven't come back yet. Let me help you unload the wagon."

Declan spoke then, suddenly smiling widely. "Nothing to unload," he said. "Went out loaded, came back empty—'cept for the women and little ones and their berries." He turned and walked to the lead horse, taking it by the bridle. "Come on, then," he said to the animal. "Let's get you out of that harness." He led the team away in a tight turn, and the three men soon had both horses uncoupled and rubbed down, groomed, and fed.

The brothers then took Varrus with them into the main family room in the house and chased the children out of the way while they poured themselves, and him, a mug of ale. They had obviously decided that he was trustworthy, and within the next short while he was introduced to Declan's wife Nella, Aidan's wife Mhairidh, and Regan, who was married to Callum. All three greeted him with warmth and genuine smiles, making him welcome, and before he became too tongue-tied in the face of so much attention, he was saved by the arrival of Lydia and Callum, both of them laden with armloads of packages. Since none of the others had been there when Dominic sent the pair out to find clothes for Varrus, the sight of their purchases triggered a storm of speculation on where the two had been and what they were carrying.

It was then that Dominic entered through the door from the smithy, followed by Shamus, who was drying his hands on a clean piece of towelling. The big smith stopped short on the threshold, looked around him with mock surprise, then called for silence in his great voice. Everyone hushed obediently, and he cocked one eyebrow at his guest.

"You thought the place was quiet when first you came, did you not, Master Varrus? Don't you wish now it could be as it was earlier? And these ones here are all grown up." He glanced around the room. "Where are the babbies?"

"They're in the other room, Da, where they always are at this time of day," said one of the women—Mhairidh, Varrus thought. "We saw Lydia and Callum come home with all that clothing, and we were wondering why, and what it was for."

"I'll tell you—as soon as I have something in my hand that's drinkable," Dominic Mcuil said.

Aidan quickly handed his father a mug of ale, and after a long pull at it Dominic wiped some foam off his upper lip with the back of his hand and swept straight into the story of everything that had happened that afternoon, and what he had decided to do in the face of the difficulties arising from the incident with the Roman decanus. He made no mention of his suggestion to Varrus regarding the smithy in Camulodunum, instead explaining why their guest needed to be differently dressed than he had been, and how important it was that none of them should say a word to anyone outside the house about his presence there. His family listened, glancing at Varrus from time to time, and when he had finished they nodded obediently and without demur.

Any hopes Varrus might have had of speaking with Lydia were quickly dashed when she approached him directly, smiling and leaning in close to him as though to whisper something confidential into his ear. He bent to meet her, feeling his heart rate increase as the sweet smell of her enveloped him, but all she said was, "Dinner for twenty. It doesn't cook itself, and tonight it's my turn, with Nella." She pulled her head back, grinning at him. "I'm at the wee table, too, tonight, so we might not be able to talk until later."

She reached out and squeezed his hand briefly, and he watched her move away in the direction of the kitchen, enjoying the pressures the mere sight of her retreating back excited in him and wondering, too, what she had meant by the "wee" table. As she disappeared through the door, closely followed by Nella, he turned reluctantly to the other men, meaning to ask for enlightenment, but he was immediately gripped by what Callum was saying to Aidan.

"You saw him this afternoon?" he interrupted. "When? And who was he with?"

Both brothers faced him squarely, though neither one gave any sign of being troubled by the interruption, and Callum said, "He wasn't with anyone. And I suppose that's why I noticed him. You don't often see soldiers in that area, and even less often do you see one on his own. And even so, all I really saw at first was that little vertical crest on his helmet, his decanus's insignia, and so I took a closer look, and it was him, Nerva."

"And where was this? Which part of the market?"

"The west quadrant, where all the clothes and fabrics are on sale. Lyddie and I were there searching for clothes for you, remember? He wasn't difficult to spot. It's all women down there, except for the stall-holders. There's hardly ever any kind of trouble in that quadrant."

"Which is why you seldom see soldiers there, is that what you mean?"

"Aye."

"So what was he doing?"

Callum made a wry face. "He wasn't *doing* anything, really—just walking about with a face like thunder, as though he might be looking for someone and there would be trouble if he found him."

"And do you think he was? Looking for someone, I mean?"

Callum shrugged. "How was I to tell? Short of walking up to him and asking him."

"Did he see you?"

Callum shook his head. "I saw him look my way once, but he looked straight through me without a flicker of recognition. I kept watching him and even followed him for a few paces, to be sure he had gone, because Lyddie was in one of the enclosed stalls and if she had come out he would have been sure to see her." He saw the question in Varrus's eyes and shook his head. "No, I didn't tell her I'd seen him. 'Twould only have upset her needlessly. Whatever he was there for, whatever he was looking for, it seemed to me he hadn't found it yet and he didn't know where to look next. It crossed my mind, though, that he might have been hoping to run into you."

That made Varrus blink. "In the women's market?"

"Why not?" Callum nodded his head downwards, towards the

Roman's feet. "From what he saw of you, that white Roman robe you were wearing, it wouldn't be too far a stretch to imagine you visiting there. Not much chance of finding the kind of clothes you were wearing in the leatherworkers' or the cobblers' streets or the used garment bins, for that matter." He hitched one shoulder in a shrug.

"That's fair," Varrus said. "Did you see him again after that?"

"No. Not a glimpse of him. He had moved on by the time we were done there."

"I'm empty," Aidan said, looking down into his cup. "Thirsty work, this listening."

They moved over to the ale cask by the wall, where Dominic joined them, and from then on they spoke of many things, waiting for their evening meal to be ready.

By the time they were ready to sit down and eat, Varrus no longer had any questions about the wee table. Dinner was a communal event in the Mcuil household, and the adults sat together at the main table while the children sat at the wee table, which was in fact only slightly smaller, supervised each night by a pair of adults—except for Dominic, who as paterfamilias was exempt. The duty that night had fallen to Lydia and Shamus.

The conversation at the adults' table was lively, most of it centred inevitably upon the various family units and the miniature dramas being enacted daily. And Varrus delighted in watching and unabashedly admiring the ease and skill with which Lydia handled her young charges, charming and entertaining them with smiles and laughter and sly humour, making them love her while she worked effortlessly on defusing emergent conflicts and dissolving juvenile jealousies and resentments. He watched her indulgently, loving everything about the way she looked, the way she spoke, the way she behaved.

The sole discordant moment came without warning when Shamus took exception to something his father had said or done and turned in an instant from being affable and relaxed to explosive anger. Varrus had seen or heard nothing that might have provoked the young man, but it quickly became clear, from the expressions on their faces and the rolling of their eyes, that the others around the table were used to such outbursts and had long since learned to ignore them completely. The adults continued to banter and the children continued to laugh and Shamus's interruption was quickly forgotten.

Eventually someone—Varrus could not have said who it was—began to clear away the debris of the meal unobtrusively and return the main room to its normal condition. The women and older children removed the remaining food and dishes, and Declan and Callum broke the wee table into its separate parts while Aidan and the two eldest boys returned the chairs to their places around the walls. As the guest, Varrus remained seated along with his host while all this was happening, and Dominic leaned over to tell him that he would now go, in person, and send his daughter back to talk with Quintus Varrus. And on that note, he wished the young man well in his venture, then rose and left him alone at the table.

After he had been sitting there alone for quite some time, he detected a stir of movement and looked up to see Lydia standing hip-shot in the doorway, leaning against one side of the door's frame and watching him with an inscrutable look on her face.

"Oh, there you are," he said, starting to rise to his feet.

She approached the table now, frowning slightly and waving him back into his seat, barely even meeting his eye as her own eyes swept around the room. Puzzled, and perched awkwardly on the edge of his chair, neither standing nor sitting, Varrus, too, looked around as though he might be able to identify whatever she was looking for. But her gaze settled on nothing, and she turned to look back at him with that same small frown still between her eyes.

She grew very still, and he sank back into his seat.

"What is going on here?" she asked.

Her voice was quiet, but it sounded constrained, so instead of answering, Varrus looked around the room again, searching for whatever might have upset or confused her. But there was nothing to see, and so he looked back at her.

"What d'you mean? There's nothing going on."

"Oh, but there is. There's something going on. I can almost smell it."

"There is nothing going on, Lydia," he said, in a more measured tone, "whatever 'going on' means. What can you smell?"

She peered more intently at him then, almost leaning towards him, her mouth pouting and her enormous eyes narrowed. "You told him, didn't you?"

"Told who what?" He asked the question blank-faced, but he knew what she meant and he said the words solely because he had no others with which to respond at that moment.

"You told my father you wish to wed me."

"Oh . . . Yes, I did."

"You did." And then a note of disbelief came into her voice. "You did? You really *told* him? Why would you *do* that?"

"I told you I was going to."

"I know you did, but I didn't *believe* you. I thought you were flirting with me, flattering me. I thought that was the way those things are done in Rome."

"Why would you think such a thing? I'm not from Rome and I never said I was. So how would I know what Romans do in these things? I don't know how people *anywhere* do that kind of thing. All I know is that I, Quintus Varrus, have never done that before and I don't even know if there's a way you're supposed to do it. But I meant every word of what I said. And I told you openly, at the first chance I had."

"Openly, yes. But not sincerely, surely? That would be madness . . . Insanity, Quintus Varrus. An hour or two before you spoke those words this morning, you did not even know me."

"Not true. I knew exactly who you were and had been looking at you hungrily for a week. I simply had not met you until this morning."

"Oh, please! There's barely a word of truth in that and you know it. We were thrown together by accident—a happy accident, for which I give thanks to God, but an accident nonetheless. Had you not been looking at me at that moment when I started to run away, you would have seen nothing at all and we would not be here. Before that, all you had done was to ask some questions about a girl who caught your eye in passing. Be reasonable, Quintus Varrus. You knew my name and you knew a little bit about my family—that they were smiths—which you found appealing for your own reasons. But you knew nothing about me, nothing about Lydia Mcuil, about who she is and what she likes and dislikes or what she loves and hates. And as for being hungry when you look at me, you will go hungry for a long time if you allow your tongue to outrun your good manners the way it seems to want to." She stopped and inhaled sharply. "I can't believe you talked to my father about that, after barely having met me."

"By then I had already killed men to save your life."

She took a half step back from him, looking him straight in the eye. "That is true," she said calmly. "You had. But to speak to my father about marrying me . . . To even mention such a thing at all, let alone discuss it with him . . . I can scarce believe the sheer *foolishness* of that."

"What foolishness?" he snapped back, stung. "There was nothing foolish about anything I said or did!" He stopped, knowing he could ill afford to grow angry, then exhaled deeply and willed his shoulders to slump down before he continued, softly. "It was frightening, though. I'll admit that. I was afraid of how he might react, and so I almost said nothing, but once he had invited me to stay under his roof, and had explained the dangers facing me out there from people I don't know and have no wish to meet, I could not accept his hospitality without telling him about us."

"Tell him *what* about us, Master Varrus?"

He could see from her creased forehead that she was exasperated but not yet really angry, though he suspected that might change quickly unless he could placate her.

"This 'us' you speak of does not exist," she continued. "How could it?" Her voice was clipped, which made her sound unsure and aggressive in a way that was new to him, and her face looked set and cold. "*Us*, the way you say it, makes you and me sound like a pair—two people who have known each other for a long time and who have decided to share each other's lives. And that is not even close to being believable. You know that. You are not a stupid man. So what were you hoping to achieve here?"

He rose to his feet and stood looking down at her, his own face now marked by a deep-graven frown, and he started to raise his hands as though to emphasize what he would say next, but then he simply stood there, motionless, looking at her and saying nothing at all for a long time before his brow cleared and he shook his head ruefully. He shrugged his wide shoulders and spread his hands, looking sheepish.

"You are right," he said finally. "I *was* hoping. But not anymore. I was hoping to fulfill a wish . . . a dream would probably be more accurate, though it sounds more foolish. But that's what I was hoping to achieve. A vision that has been real to me since I first saw you in the market with your friend Camilla, a week ago. I saw you that day and my life changed completely. I know—" He held up a palm to silence any protest she might make. "I know how foolish that sounds to you, but it's the truth. My life changed. Completely. Because my awareness of you—that you were alive, here in the same town with me, and that I had seen you almost within my reach—affected everything I did from then on.

"It changed the way I thought and behaved, and even the way I saw other people. Before I set eyes on you, other people—all other people— were a threat to me. I had no way of knowing who might or might not recognize me and sell my secret to someone who might want me dead. I had no close friends to turn to or to confide in."

His jaw twitched in what might have been the stillborn start of a smile. "From the moment I lost sight of you that first day, though, all the people there in that marketplace became possible sources of information about you, and I spoke to everyone, asking if they knew you, who you were and where you lived. In that way, I learned your name and I learned about your family being smiths, and then I found out that you came to the market, or to some part of it, at least once each week. And in trying to find out about you, without realizing it, I completely lost my fear of strangers. All the threats to my own safety that I had believed or imagined faded to nothingness once I accepted the need to find out as much as I could about you."

He saw her draw a breath, preparing to speak, but he forestalled her again. "No, if it please you, permit me to finish. I have a little more to add, and then I'll say no more."

She paused, head high, but merely nodded.

"I found out what I could about you, and I watched for you. Not because I ever really hoped or intended to meet you. I had no reason ever to suppose that you might notice me. I was content to look—and to pine achingly. And then, this morning, I saw you startle and turn to run away. You moved too quickly when you should not have, and because of that I saw the man who went after you. And the rest you know . . . And yes, it was fortunate that I noticed. But I have a need to confess to you, to purge myself of this, so bear with me."

He lowered his head, then turned on his heel and moved to stand behind his solid, high-backed chair, where he gripped the decorative acorn tops of the wooden uprights tightly. He was aware that he was using the chair as a shield, a barrier between himself and her, and he wondered if she sensed that too. He thought perhaps she did, because she neither moved nor spoke, leaving him to continue at his own pace.

He spoke, but it must have come out as little more than a mumble, because the next thing Lydia said was, "I can't hear you."

"Ah." He looked down again, at the backs of his hands clutching the chair, and spoke in a slightly louder voice. "I said I could not believe what I was thinking, or that I was saying it to you."

Another silence ensued until she prompted him. "You might have thought anything, but you said nothing. What were you thinking about? Is that what you need to confess?"

"Aye, it is." He raised his head and looked her square in the eye. "I gave chase, and followed you up the hill, trying to keep up with the man pursuing you. And all the way up there, fighting against the fear that I might be too late, I tried to imagine what would happen if I caught up to you. But all that time I was thinking only of saving you, protecting you, shielding your beauty and your innocence from the kind of filth that man would subject you to. I was thinking of you as an ethereal, unworldly beauty, some kind of impossible goddess, not a flesh-and-blood woman.

"And then I saw that the man chasing you was not alone. There were others, one of them a fat-bellied one who was even slower than I was. And I grew angrier than I have ever been, I think. Four slovenly pigs chasing one lone woman. So when I caught up with you I had no thought of offering them anything but what I dealt them. I knew what would happen if they had their way, and it was me against them. But I had surprise on my side, and I was fortunate."

He looked at her, and his eyes moved downwards to her skirts. "It was after the killing, when I looked down and saw what they had done to your clothing, exposing your nakedness, that I saw you as a living, breathing woman. And it was like being kicked into awareness. I saw your thighs, how soft they were, so smooth and vulnerable, and I tried to cover you up."

"You did cover me up," she said, her voice betraying no emotion.

"I did, but too late. The damage was done. I can still see what I saw then, and when I looked away, back into your face, I saw the size and the colour of your eyes and the shape and softness of your mouth, and the thought came to me that I would die happy if only I could take you back to safety and kiss your lips just once. We walked away and spoke afterwards as though we were old friends and nothing unusual had taken place between us. And then your brothers came running and I seemed to lose control of everything, including my memories of how you looked, so close to me and so beautiful. But I had told you by then that I wanted you to be my wife, and I meant it. And that vision of you has been in my mind all day, despite my efforts not to see it."

He took his hands off the acorn chair knobs and ground his palms together, inhaling deeply. "It's plain to me now, though, that I was deluding myself. And you are correct. I should have held my tongue. But when I spoke to your father I yet believed you would come to accept me. That's why I did it. I knew he would soon detect the desire I have for you, and I wanted to make him aware of my regard for you before I slept beneath his roof." He drew another deep breath before bowing to her from the waist. "I hope you will not think too badly of me. I'll be gone tomorrow."

She stared back at him expressionlessly without speaking for what seemed to him a long time, then quirked her lips. "And he did not object," she said.

"No, he did not."

"He did not tell you to leave his house . . . my father. Nor did he make any mention of this to any member of the family at dinner. I would have expected that, at least, had I known—that he would at least mock you a little, for your youth and inexperience if for nothing else. But he came to me in the kitchens instead and told me to come and talk to you." She watched Varrus closely as he took in each word she uttered. "It needed to be seen to now, he said."

Listening to her speak, it seemed to him that her voice, the very tone of it, sounded different, and it was a difference in attitude rather than anything else. Her brilliant and spontaneous self-assertiveness was somehow less sharp-edged now, eclipsed, he thought, by a diffidence that had not been present earlier, and the result was the merest suggestion of uncertainty in the cadence and delivery of what she said.

He leaned slightly forward to look directly into her eyes, drinking in his last view of the width and shape of them, the brilliant, blue-tinged clarity of the whites and the magnificent beauty of her green, gold-flecked irises. Expecting her to turn away and leave, he remained motionless, simply staring back at her and waiting for whatever she might say or do next.

Eventually she moved to the nearest chair and lowered herself into it, her eyes, still narrow and speculative, fixed upon his. "What did he say? What did he say to you when you asked him if he would consider your offer to marry me? Was he angry? Did he call you a fool?"

"No, not at all. He said that would be up to you, and that he had decided long ago that his opinion would be inconsequential in the matter of your choosing a husband. Very much like your mother, I think he said. The choice would be yours, to accept or to refuse. But there is little point in speaking of that now, is there? As I said, I'll be gone soon enough."

He told her then about her father's plan to send him to Camulodunum, for his own safety and to help her uncle Liam in the smithy there. Shamus would go with him, he explained, to put some helpful distance between father and son.

He fell silent then, and Lydia sat staring at him with the same frustrating, unreadable expression she had shown before.

There came a tap at the door and Dominic Mcuil pushed his head in. "Am I intruding?"

"Of course you are, Da," his daughter said. "But it's your house. Come in, come in. I want to tell you something."

The smith stepped forward almost timidly, Varrus thought, and looked from one to the other of them with his eyebrows raised. "Is everything as it should be?" he asked. "Do you two need more time?"

Lydia rose quickly to her feet, her voice tight and crisp again. "No, Da," she said. "We need no more time. Come here and look at this man."

"What about him?"

She continued speaking to her father but she never took her eyes off Quintus Varrus's face. "Look at him, closely. He is . . . unusual. We both know that to be true. But I have decided that I like him anyway, despite not knowing him well. I'm not saying I will be his wife. But neither am I saying I won't have him. If he and I can take the time to come to know each other, and if he is truly the man I think he might be, then I think we might be well together, the two of us." She spoke directly then to Varrus. "Well, Master Varrus, have you anything to say to that?"

Stunned, Varrus could only smile, tentatively, at first, but then he turned to her father. "I'm well content with that, Master Mcuil, and I thank you for the opportunity to speak my mind and make my case." His smile widened. "And as for you, my lady Lydia, I will bend my entire mind and heart towards making you believe I am the sole man with whom you could wish to spend your life. How often will you be able to come and visit us?"

Her father intervened before Lydia could respond, and left her smiling a tiny, secretive smile. "You keep your end of the bargain up there in Liam's smithy, Master Roman, and I'll see to it that you meet each other often enough in future—with suitable supervision, of course—for the two of you to be able to decide whether you wish to share your lives or not. It's less than three days' travel in good weather, and we usually get up and down at least once every few months."

He paused, grinning at some passing thought. "Tomorrow we can put you to work helping Callum and Shamus with a shipment of farm tools that he's readying for market. Callum told me they found you some suitable work clothes and some other gear."

"The hair," Lydia said. "We'll have to change that, too. It's like a golden fire on his head, drawing attention to him. So we'll cut most of it off and darken the rest of it."

"Darken it?" Her father sounded mystified. "How will you do that?"

She tossed her head, scorning the question. "As easily as you make a shoe for a horse," she said, speaking to Dominic but looking at Varrus, her head to one side, her eyes calculating. "Women do it all the time. How we do it is not important." She tapped Varrus on the shoulder. "You already have the dark complexion, so between one hour and the next, tomorrow, we'll change the look of you completely. Between that and the new clothes we bought, the men hunting you will have to look very carefully to recognize you."

"Other than my limp."

"Ach, that's nothing. They'll be looking for long golden hair and different kinds of clothing. You'll pass all but the closest examination."

Her father spoke up then. "Just the same, though, for all our sakes, you should be away from here and on the road the day after tomorrow, before the initial search for you turns up nothing and your hunters grow more determined. And if that fellow Nerva has any intellect at all, he will ask around the market and come here looking for you. So you had best be clear of this town by Saturday, for the odds are high that by Sunday you'll be too late."

He was interrupted by a sudden clamour of young voices in the kitchen at his back, and he cocked his head for a moment, listening.

"Bedtime," he said. "You had better go and help the others, Lydia. They'll be wondering where you are, so bid Master Varrus a good night and then get about your duties."

He nodded to Varrus, then turned and went out of the room, closing the door behind him and leaving them alone together.

"Sit down, Master Varrus, and tell me what you think of that."

He sat down slowly, barely even aware of what he was doing, and simply gazed at her, searching for the words to say that he thought her the most beautiful thing he had ever seen, and to swear to her that he would spend his entire life, from that day forward, seeking only to make her happy. But she gave him no time to speak. She stepped close quickly, reaching out to take him by the chin, then stooped towards him. For a brief moment, she hovered so close that he felt her breath on his skin and saw nothing but her mouth, the width and softness of it, a flash of white teeth behind her perfect lips, and then she kissed him, slowly, exploring him.

Then she straightened up again and stood looking at him.

"That was . . . pleasant," she said. "Sleep well, Quintus Varrus. Tomorrow we will coat you in new colours."

BOOK THREE

Colcaster, A.D. 317-318

ELEVEN

The sun's day, the first of the new week, had started well, the sun itself shining from a brilliant blue sky that was streaked in places with skeins of high, teased-out, insubstantial cloud, and Quintus Varrus felt sublimely happy: happy to be alive, happy to be in love, happy with the prospects that lay ahead of him, and happy to have succeeded in getting out of Londinium the previous day without being detected.

Now, a day and a half later and almost thirty miles farther north, he was lounging comfortably under a huge old elm tree that marked the end of a long, straggling line of hawthorns along the edge of a broad, slow-flowing stream. They had been walking for more than seven hours by then, pulling their cart doggedly by the shoulder straps attached to the wide central T-bar, paying no attention to the few travellers who passed them in either direction on the wide, paved road, and when the huge, solitary tree came into view as they breasted a slight rise, it had seemed to beckon them to the bright green sward of the riverbank. They had decided to camp there for the night and had quit the road gratefully. Now Varrus lay at ease beside a small fire in a much-used stone-lined pit, watching Shamus Mcuil wading silently and slowly through knee-deep water, his head bent, intently focused upon catching fish for their evening meal.

Their departure from Londinium had gone smoothly, though the day had been rainy and blustery. Dominic had been right about the need to leave quickly and exercise caution, for at the northeastern gate, the city guards were out in force, and a quartet of garrison officers in crested helmets had been vigilant, making sure that everyone passing through the gates was checked. One had glanced directly at Varrus and Shamus, but he paid them no more attention. Two drab, rain-drenched farm workers pulling a cart through the downpour on their way to wherever they were going plainly held no interest for him. A mile after that, safely outside the walls, they had passed by the city's easternmost gate, from which another main road led directly northeastward towards Camulodunum, a hundred miles away. There, too, guards had been stopping everyone on the way out, studying faces, examining every cart and wagon, and checking cargoes and passengers under the narrow-eyed scrutiny of another quartet of officers.

After five more hours on the road, they had found the burnt-out shell of a cottage and rested for half an hour, huddled together under the sagging remnants of a roof in one corner of the ruin while they each ate a handful of road rations—chopped dried fruit with roasted grain and nuts—from the bags they carried at their waists and washed it down with water from their goatskins. They'd dozed against the sheltering walls, content to be out of the worst of the weather for a time, and then set out again, heading doggedly through the pouring rain for five more hours. They spent the night in a tent in a sheltered spot in a grove of enormous beech trees close to the road. Sometime during the night the rain stopped, and they were back on the road by dawn, having exchanged their wet clothes for dry. As the new day, the sun's day, opened bright and clear, they'd broken their fast as they walked, chewing the sweet mixture from their ration bags and feeling increasingly better as the air about them brightened and grew warm.

A cry and loud splashes interrupted Varrus's reverie, and he looked up to see Shamus leaping about in the water, trying to keep his balance while grappling with a magnificent, brilliantly coloured fish. The creature was clearly determined to escape from its tormentor, but just when

Varrus thought it would succeed, Shamus managed to grasp it firmly for long enough to heave it high and far, sending it flying to land on the grass near Varrus's feet. Moments later, he had followed it to the bank, picked it up, and threaded a length of strong twine through its gills. He looped the twine securely over a stake that he had sunk into the ground by the waterside earlier, and lowered the captive fish back into the river.

"There," he said, unaware of Varrus's admiration. "That'll hold him fresh. He can keep himself alive until we've caught some company for him."

"Company? You mean there are more like that?"

"Hundreds more." The Eirishman spoke with the authority of experience. "This is perfect trout water. They're not all as big as this fellow, but there's enough his size to feed us well this night."

"What kind of fish is it?"

"Did ye not hear me? It's a trout."

"A trout? I see. And is trout good to eat?"

Shamus raised his eyebrows. "Is it—? Have ye never tasted trout? It's the best fish in the world, so it is. Wait till ye taste it. We have salt in the cart, do we not, and butter?"

"Aye, I think so," Varrus said, trying to recall what Lydia had said about the basket she had packed for them. "Salt, I know. And there's a covered clay pot. I think Lydia said it was fresh butter."

"Good, then dig them out, and some bread, while I catch us a couple more o' them fellows. You're not going to believe how good fish can taste."

As Shamus waded back out into the stream, Varrus made his way to the cart, where he untied the lashings at the tailgate and leaned in to pull out the basket of provisions. It was a large, rectangular basket made from woven willow twigs, cumbersome rather than heavy, its lid hinged with leather at the back and secured at the front with thick, buckled straps. Varrus hoisted it chest high and carried it back to the fire. Most of the things inside were meticulously wrapped in cloths of varying

weights and thickness, and the remainder were in clay pots of various
sizes. One of the larger pots, he knew, contained fresh salted butter,
made by Callum Mcuil's wife, Regan, the day before they left. A tiny
pot, covered tightly with a piece of fine cloth and tied around the neck
with a slip knot, contained a generous amount of precious and expensive
salt, painstakingly garnered from evaporated sea water out on the coast.

He set both of those pots carefully on the open lid without unwrapping them, then stood up and drew the gladius from the sheath at his
right side. He held it out in front of him and turned towards the closest
of the hawthorn trees on the far side of the big elm.

"Two ways to go from here," he called out in a voice loud enough to
carry clearly but not enough to intimidate. "You can step out and declare
yourself openly, or you and I can talk face to face with swords. Your
choice, but make it quick."

He heard a curse from behind him as Shamus realized what he was
hearing, and immediately after that came the sounds of splashing as the
younger man started to make his way towards land, but Varrus held up
his left hand to stay him.

For long moments nothing more happened, and Varrus was just
beginning to wonder what his next move should be when he saw a stir
of movement in the hawthorn grove and a man stepped into view, his
arms extended at his sides to show he held no weapons.

"Come nearer," Varrus said.

The man walked closer and stopped about ten paces away, eyeing
Varrus through narrowed lids.

"Why are you here?" Varrus asked next.

The stranger shrugged, his face unreadable. "I stopped here on my
way south, three weeks ago. Ate well, and slept well afterwards. So I
thought I would do the same again, coming back. Came through the
woods back there, along the riverbank, and almost walked right into
you. Must have been daydreaming. I'll move on, find someplace else."

Varrus had been weighing the look of him and listening carefully to what he said and how, and now he sheathed his gladius. "No need," he said. "There's ample room for three and we have a fire already lit. So far, though, we've caught but one fish."

The other flashed a grin, the merest hint of healthy white teeth. "I can fish. And I have fresh bread, hot from the oven this morning."

"Good. I can't fish . . . Never learned. See what you can do about fish, then. I'll mind the fire."

The newcomer scooped up a fine fish less than a quarter of an hour after that. It was easily as large as the first one, and moments later, a hundred paces downstream from him, Shamus caught a third, almost exactly the same size, just as Quintus Varrus finished assembling the set of iron roasting spits that Lydia had stowed in the bed of the cart.

With little talk on anyone's part, the three fish had been broiled over the fire and eaten off slabs of buttered bread with more than occasional sounds of appreciation and pleasure. The few remnants, fins, skin, and bones, had been burned in the pit before the fire itself was built up against the slowly gathering darkness.

"That was enjoyable," the stranger said, looking from one to the other of his hosts. "I'm grateful for the hospitality and I'm glad to be able to prove it." He sat up straight, crossed his legs, and swayed easily to his feet without putting his hands to the ground, then bent to open his pack, which he had been using as a back rest.

Varrus took stock of him as he moved. He saw a strong, agile man whom he judged to be at least a decade older than himself, broad shouldered and deep chested and with red-tinged brown hair that he wore long—not unusually so but unmilitarily so. That, in itself, told Varrus that he had been a soldier, because the man was unmistakably military in bearing and his hair would look completely natural in a soldier's crop. That impression was enhanced by the fact that he wore a legionary cintus around his waist—a thick leather belt with heavy armour-plated straps hanging from it to protect the crotch area—and from that hung a well-used regulation legionary short sword with the kind of polished hilt that only years of handling could impart. It was the same style that hung from Varrus's own belt, the so-called Hispanic gladius, with its two-foot-long razor-sharp blade. The tunic the fellow wore was brown, though; knee-length, plain and serviceable, edged with a dark green key design and definitely not military. Varrus had seen military tunics in all kinds of colours in Italy and Dalmatia, from black through a rainbow of shades to snowy white, but he knew that here in Britain, since the days of Claudius Caesar, the colonial legionaries had worn either Roman red or plain, off-white woollen tunics, with no variation.

He suddenly became aware that the stranger had stopped moving and was looking at him inquisitively. He glanced down at himself. "Is something wrong?"

"No," Varrus said hastily. "Not at all. I simply noticed that your sword is much like my own, almost identical in fact, and then I saw your cintus. I've been thinking about buying a better belt, and I like the thought of wearing a cintus, even though I might never need one."

"Pray you don't," the other man said, reaching deep into his pack and beginning to grope around. "I believe in being prepared, though. A groin wound isn't the kind of thing you want to be too late worrying about. Better to be ready for the unexpected. That's never a bad thing. Aha! Here it is." He drew out a plump wineskin. "You usually carry these things slung over your shoulder, I know. That's too risky for the likes of this, though. The very thought of brushing against something sharp with this under my arm makes me feel sick."

"Must be special, then," Varrus said. "What is it, Falernian?"

The stranger's eyebrows shot up. "It is. How did you guess?"

Varrus hitched his shoulders. "It was the unlikeliest thing I could imagine. Is it really Falernian?"

"Better. It's the very best of the best. It's Faustian."

Varrus opened his mouth to respond, but stopped himself and sat open-mouthed instead, knowing he must look idiotic but thankful that he had caught himself before admitting a familiarity with Faustian Falernian. Ill-dressed labourers in work-worn tunics would drink sour, barely palatable vinum if they ever drank wine at all. Not one in a hundred thousand would have even the vaguest awareness of what Falernian wine was. And so he forced himself to blink uncomprehendingly. "What's Faustian? I have never heard of it."

The stranger grinned. "Nor had I until about five years ago. And even then, I only discovered it by accident, by being in the right place at the right time. But they tell me it costs so much that only the richest of the very rich can afford to drink it."

"Did you steal it, then?"

The stranger's grin grew wider. "From the looks of me, I know, that would be a fair question. But no. I have a friend who feeds it to me once in a while." He pulled the stopper open and raised the wineskin, expertly squirting a quick jet of amber liquid into his open mouth. He lowered the skin and stood with his head tilted back and his eyes closed, rolling the wine around his mouth for a long time before finally swallowing. He opened his eyes and held the wineskin out to Varrus.

"Taste that," he said quietly, "and pass it to your friend. You may never taste the like of it again."

Remembering that moment later, Quintus Varrus would often think that even had his life depended on it, he could not have found the words to describe the sensations that filled him as that first jet of Faustian wine filled his mouth. It was as though all the colours of the rainbow combined in a single instant with the flavours of all the fruits he had ever eaten, to flood him with sensations of wonder and disbelief. It filled his mind with notions of ripe, succulent fruit and warm, flowing honey, yet it was light and airy, almost effervescent in its tingling freshness. He was unaware his eyes had closed until he swallowed, finally, and opened them to see the stranger watching him.

He raised one hand and pointed to his mouth. "That was Faustian?" he croaked. "It is . . . It's . . . A friend gave it to you, you said?" He passed the skin to Shamus.

"Aye, I did. I know you'll believe me, now that you've tasted it, but not many other people would. He's the eldest son of the family that makes this wine. He is a soldier here in Britain, and his brothers run the business together and send him wine by the shipload just to encourage him to stay away. I met him several years ago and we became friends."

Varrus could feel Shamus's eyes on him and turned to see the young Eirishman gazing at him glassy-eyed from beneath arched brows, licking his lips as though he could still taste nectar on them. "Did you like that, Shamus?" he asked. The boy merely nodded, apparently incapable of speech, and Varrus looked back at their visitor. "Can I ask you a question?"

"Ask away, but I might choose not to answer."

"This friend, the winemaker. How do you manage to stay in contact with him if he's in the legions? I'm a smith, so I know legionary troops move around more than ordinary people do, but even so, there's not much happens here in Britain between Romans and non-military folk. It's not encouraged—it never has been. Are you one of them, a soldier?" But if he was a soldier, Varrus thought, why was he pretending not to be? Had he been following them all this way?

The stranger sucked in a sharp breath and jerked his head in a nod. "Fair question, considering where we are," he said. "Before I answer, though, is there by chance a cup in that basket? There's something simply not right about drinking Faustian from a wineskin, so if you have a cup we can fill it and share."

"D'ye know, there's four cups in there," Shamus said eagerly. "Here, let me get them." He scuttled away, and Varrus stood up and threw a few fresh logs onto the fire, settling them down into the coals with the sole of his boot as Shamus passed around three horn cups. No one spoke as the stranger carefully poured a generous measure into each of them, then placed his own, with great care, on a flat stone by his feet. "If you'll pardon me," he said, eyeing the wineskin that was no longer so full and taut, "I'll put this away where it won't come to harm." He stowed it carefully in his pack before returning to the fireside, where he stooped to retrieve his cup. He then tipped a minuscule amount, barely more than a single drop, onto the ground.

"Wha—?"

"An offering," the stranger said, twisting his mouth wryly in response to their expressions of disbelief. "To honour the gods. It's the way Romans do things. The gods suck all the goodness from the offering before it hits the ground. Or so they say. I don't care how they take their share, though, provided they leave mine to me. They are the gods, after all, so they have more and better wines than we have, and I doubt they would begrudge us our little cups." He raised his cup. "So let us three drink to fine fish, good fellowship, and a sound night's sleep."

They drank in silent reverence, sipping and savouring the exquisite wine, taking great care to make it last for as long as possible, until eventually the stranger cradled his cup in steepled fingers and said, "Now I will answer your question, providing you will answer one of mine. My name is Cato, Marcus Licinius Cato, but my friends call me Rufus, for my red hair. I'm Roman, though I was born here in Britain like my father before me, and because of that I served my time with the legions along with every other citizen. I was a legionary staff officer for a time, and then I was wounded and rated unfit for active duty. Now I'm a courier. Not quite military but well connected and with some military privileges. I carry confidential communications between legionary commands, which keeps me well fed and active. The friend I spoke of is adjutant of the Second Legion, the Augusta, based in Isca, in the southwest." He scratched his nose. "Now let me ask you a question. Who are you, and why did you decide to let me stay instead of sending me on my way?"

Varrus hitched one shoulder, aware again of the need to be careful. "I'm Fingael Mcuil," he said. "And this is my brother Shamus. We were born in Eire, though now we live in Londuin, where our father has a smithy. We work for him, but right now we're going to Camulodunum, where our uncle has his own smithy and needs help . . . And I let you stay because I sensed no threat in you."

Cato shook his head. "Sensed?" he said, his voice heavy with disapproval. "You *sensed* no threat in me? Believe me, I am thankful, but what you said there is complete stupidity. We are miles from anywhere, here in this field, and you two have a cart that could be packed with treasures. The cart itself would be worth robbing you for, so it is foolhardy to put your faith in what you *sense* when you meet a stranger. You had no way of knowing whether I was a threat or not."

"Ah, but I did, for I had seen you earlier. When I first saw you, among the trees, you had a crossbow slung at your back, and I knew that if you had wanted us dead, we would be dead already, me while I was lying under the tree, and Shamus while he was balancing on one leg in the stream. When I saw you again a short time later, there was no crossbow. You must have laid it down when I called to you." He shrugged again, the same one-shouldered hitch. "So I decided to be hospitable. Where is your crossbow now, though? Shouldn't you retrieve it before it gets too dark to find it?"

Cato smiled. "It's already too dark, but I brought it with me earlier, when I brought in my pack. It's leaning against that tree there."

Muttering something unintelligible, young Shamus rose to his feet and moved to the other side of the fire, where he shook out his bedroll and lay down, wrapping his blanket around him. Within moments he began to snore softly.

"It's a wise man who knows when to go to bed," Cato murmured. "I should follow his lead." He glanced again at Varrus. "Is there anything else you would like to ask me?"

"There is. You say you came this way three weeks ago. Did you come from Camulodunum, and are you going back there now?"

"No to both questions. I came directly south from the fort at Branodunum on the coast. I passed by a good twenty miles west of

Camulodunum. And when I head back tomorrow I'll strike to the northwest to Durolipons, to visit the garrison prefect there. Why did you ask me about Camulodunum?"

"Because I've never been there, so I'm more or less lost out here. I was hoping you could tell us how far from the place we truly are."

"From Camulodunum? Three days at the most, in bad weather. The next few days should be fine, though, after the rain we've had. An early start in the morning and you should be warm in your uncle's smithy by nightfall the day after."

"That's what I thought, but it's reassuring to hear someone knowledgeable say it. I have another question, if I may. Isn't it dangerous to be carrying military communications around the country without an escort?"

The other barked out a laugh, the first Varrus had heard from him. "It is," he said. "And I have an escort. They're simply not with me now because the last visit I made was a personal one to Londinium, so they're waiting for me up ahead, in Durolipons, and they have the dispatches for the prefect there."

"What took you to Londinium?"

Cato cocked his head to one side. "You speak very well for a smith. Why is that?"

Varrus offered what he hoped was a disarming smile. "My father is Eirish," he said. "He was raised by Christians to believe in the power of literacy and education, so all our lives we have had tutors living with us."

The other nodded, musingly. "Would you be offended if I chose to say nothing of why I went to Londinium?"

Varrus raised one hand apologetically. "Not at all. I am often too curious, but with no wish to be inquisitive. Let me put another log or two on the fire, and I'll wish you a restful night."

"My thanks, then, Fingael Mcuil," the man called Rufus said. "This has been . . . interesting. I've never met an Eirish smith before."

Varrus smiled back at him and touched a finger to his forehead in salute. *And you haven't met one yet in me*, he thought.

TWELVE

"Uncle Liam? It's me, Shamus."

The man bent over the anvil paused, his downward stroke arrested, the two-pound hammer poised in his right hand, but he did not turn around. Instead, still looking forward, he straightened up and carefully set down the rapidly cooling blade he was holding, laying the hot iron gently on the flat surface of the anvil on his left. Then he placed both hammer and tongs on the flat brick surface of the workbench on his right. Only then did he slowly—and awkwardly, Varrus thought—turn to face the open doors to the street, pulling the covering off his head to reveal a mane of silver hair hidden beneath its long, leather flap.

"Shamus?" he said, squinting into the bright light from beyond the door. "Is that you?"

Shamus threw open his arms and stepped forward to hug his uncle.

Varrus knew that Liam Mcuil needed help. That was why Dominic had asked him to come here. He knew, too, that there had been an accident of some kind, right in the smithy, which was never good because smithy accidents, nine times out of ten, involved fire and serious burns, and the remaining one in ten had to do with heavy hammers, sharp edges, and powerful blows. But Dominic had told him nothing about the nature of the accident, or how severely Liam had been injured.

Yet what he saw now was encouraging. The smith had four limbs, all of which had appeared to function normally as he hammered the blade he had been working on and then moved to greet his nephew, and his long, lantern-jawed face was unscarred. There had been a hesitancy, though, in the way the smith turned around from his work, a hint of something less than fluid grace.

He became aware that Shamus was talking about him to his uncle, beckoning him forward to present him, and he approached the man, holding out his hand. "Master Liam," he said. "It's a pleasure to meet the man clever enough to ship the clay for Dominic Mcuil's white forge all the way from Eire."

Liam Mcuil stood with his head tilted gently to one side and a dimple showing in his right cheek, brought out by a well-used smile. "I can see how you and my brother would get on well," he said. "There's no mystery there, for I can tell that you're both talkers. And Shamus here tells me our Lydia looks kindly on you. That tells me right away you're an even better talker than Dominic. So why are you here?"

The question caught Varrus unprepared, and he half-turned to Shamus for help, but saw instantly that none would be forthcoming, for Shamus's face was as blank as a newly whitewashed board. "I'm here to help you out, if you'll have me," he said. "Your brother told me you've been short of help since your recent accident. He didn't say what had happened, but he'd been prepared to send Callum here for a few months to help you meet your obligations. In the end, though, Callum couldn't be spared, and so your brother asked me if I would consider coming in his place."

"So you're a smith?" He scanned Varrus slowly from head to foot, and then he sniffed. "You don't look much like one," he said, his face unreadable. "But Dominic seems to trust you. How long have you worked for him?"

Varrus drew a deep breath. "I haven't worked for him. But he tested me, and questioned me, and he appeared satisfied that I am qualified."

Liam Mcuil stood stock-still, one eyebrow raised in a manner that left no need for him to speak in order to express what he was thinking.

"He has never seen you work? And he sends you to help me? Is that not grand? And what, in Ler's name, am I supposed to do with you, and me not knowing if you can tell one end of a chisel from the other?"

Varrus held up his hand to stem the flow of words that he anticipated would grow stronger. "Permit me, Master Liam, if you please. I am familiar with all the tools in your smithy. I can use all of them. Your brother satisfied himself on that matter, and I would not be here if I were unsure of my own abilities."

"Then why has my brother never seen you work?"

Varrus had known that he would have to tell his story sooner or later, if he were to stay in Camulodunum and work in the smithy, but he had assumed that he would have time to settle in and come to know his employer a little before being required to reveal the details of his personal affairs.

He glanced again at Shamus, who was standing like a witless lump, then turned back to Liam. "There is a sound reason, but it's a long tale." He pointed with his thumb towards the open street at his back. "Have you another place where we can talk, some place that's not as public?"

Liam Mcuil was peering at him doubtfully, almost squinting with the effort of trying to read him. "Aye," he said, jabbing a finger towards a low, ill-fitting door in the wall. "In there." He moved towards the door immediately and Shamus started to follow him, but Varrus stretched out his arm and stopped the younger man in his tracks.

"Not you, Shamus," he said. "I need to talk to Liam privately . . . Alone, that means."

Shamus looked surprised, and then indignant, and for a moment it looked as though he might argue, but then he threw up his hands and walked away towards the rear of the smithy, saying he was going to see his aunt.

Varrus followed Liam into a tiny room that, from the piles and rolls of parchment and paper on every flat surface, he guessed served the smith as a records office. He asked Liam's permission to shut the door, then closed it as securely as it could be closed, aware of the smith's quizzical eyes on him, and leaned back against it as though to hold it in place. And for the next half-hour he told Liam Mcuil the story of his life, leaving out nothing that he thought might be necessary to the smith's understanding of why Quintus Publius Varrus, a Roman aristocrat, had come to Camulodunum to seek employment in his smithy.

The other man sat silent, listening closely and making no attempt to interrupt, and when Quintus eventually lapsed into silence, he sat there for moments longer. Finally, he straightened in his chair and nodded.

"That makes sense out of what you said before," he said mildly. "It took longer to tell than I thought it might, and I heard more in there than I ever heard before, or ever expected to hear, about things that folk the likes of me never get to hear about in the normal way of life." He gazed at Varrus with his head tilted to one side as though reassessing him carefully. "You're far less than half my age, I would say, and yet you've probably travelled ten times farther than I ever did and seen more things than I could ever dream about. I won't question anything of what you've told me, because was any word of it untrue my brother would never have sent you. But I still don't know if you've the skill or the strength to swing a heavy maul or shape a piece of iron." Again he scrutinized Varrus from head to toe. "Where did you get that sword you're wearing? I'm guessing it's the one you used to save Lydia."

Varrus dropped his hand automatically to the hilt. "It is," he said. "I found it in a town called Florentia, in Italy."

"Did you buy it? Personally, I mean?"

"I did."

"Who from?"

"From the man who made it. His name was Ichthus. I remember that because he was eating fish when we arrived."

"It's the Hispanic sword." Liam had no interest in the maker's name. "That's what they call it, a *gladius hispaniensis*. The heavy infantry legions brought it back with them from Iberia a hundred years ago, preferring it to their own. It's longer, heavier, and sharper than the old legionary short swords used to be."

"I know." Varrus was careful to show no hint of surprise that the Eirishman should know the weapon's Latin name. The man was a smith and therefore, he presumed, an armourer to some extent.

"Well then, you're not completely ignorant. Can I look at it?"

Varrus drew the sword from its sheath and passed it to him, hilt first, and the smith eyed it appraisingly, hefting it for balance.

"Hmm. How did you know it was worth buying?"

"I didn't know," Varrus said. "Rhys Twohands said so, and I trusted him, so I bought it."

"Twohands . . . That's the fellow who died in Londinium, the one who taught you smithing?"

"Yes."

"And why was he looking in that particular place, do you know? You were a long way from home and he could have found a sword anywhere else, in the hundred miles between where you were and where you lived."

"He could have. I had a serviceable sword and we were not looking to buy a new one. But we heard about this famous Florentine sword maker, Ichthus, who had been legion trained, and Rhys wanted to go and look at the fellow's wares. He picked out this sword, and I bought it."

"Well, he had a good eye." Liam Mcuil flipped the heavy sword vertically and caught it easily by the end of the blade, and returned it to him, hilt first. "It's a fine weapon. Let's hope you don't have any need to use it here in Colcaster."

Varrus raised his head, frowning slightly. "Colcaster?"

Mcuil grinned. "Aye, Colcaster. It's what the folk who live here call the place now, and of all the names it's had, it's the easiest one to say. Claudius named it Colonia Claudia Victricensis. Can you believe the stupidity of that, for the name of a town? I've heard tell he named it in honour of the Twentieth Legion, the Valeria Victrix—as well as himself, of course—but who knows? That was two hundred years ago and by that time the Victrix legion was long gone from here. Anyway, the folks around here paid no more attention to it then than they do now. They were content with Camulodunum, the name it's had since before the time of Boudicca, and even that's a jawbreaker. But the old ways are changing. There's new folk coming here all the time, and there's more retired veterans living here." He shrugged. "So now it's Colcaster—the walled fort on the River Colne, or something like that."

Varrus had been listening with a tiny, bemused smile on his face. "Forgive me," he said, "but it seems you have more than a passing knowledge of Britain."

"It's my *business*," the other said, sounding surprised that he should be asked such a question. "I need to know that kind of thing. I'm a smith, a master blade maker, and I rely on the Roman armies for my livelihood. So I pay attention to them. I know their history. The three legions in Britain, their cohorts and the territories they police and govern, along with names and ranks of commanding officers and armourers and quartermasters and junior officers and senior centurions, all provide me with my stock-in-trade and my family with its daily bread."

He stood up. "And speaking of bread, come and meet my wife, Shanna. She'll have drained Shamus dry of information by now and she'll know all she needs to know about you. If our Lydia's taken a liking to you, that'll be enough for her and she'll try to fatten you up like a prize pig. You probably think I'm gulling you, but wait you, now, and you'll see for yourself."

"I thank you for the warning," Varrus said. "But let me ask you one more question before we go."

The smith remained where he was, standing behind the table that served him as a desk. "What can I tell you?"

Varrus lifted one hand slightly, in a silent request for patience. "I know you asked your brother for help. I also know you have work that you're concerned about finishing on time, and I know, too, that you had an accident recently that has impaired you somehow. So if it pleases you, and if I am to work with you, tell me about those things. You don't appear to be seriously impaired in any way, though I noticed a slight hesitation in the way you move when you turn your body."

"You have keen eyes. Aye, I stumbled and fell at the forge, about four months ago, and set myself afire. Shanna seized the bucket and doused the flames before they reached me too badly. But the trouble was that I was forging a sword at the time and the blade, yellow hot, fell with me. There was nothing a single bucket of water could do against that. I burnt my belly and my left side, under the ribs—badly. Not an enjoyable thing, believe me. It's almost healed now, but it still pulls when I turn the wrong way, so I'm careful about how I move. What else?"

"The workload. What's involved, and why are you so concerned about meeting your commitment?"

"Armour. Ring-mail tunics—what they call lorica hamata. That's what has me concerned. I make them for the garrison officers, have done for years. It's slow, painstaking work, but it's profitable. I was managing well up to the time I fell, but I couldn't work for months after that and now I have three of them left to make, out of an order of six, and they have to be ready within six months, by the Ides of December, in time for the garrison festivities at the closing of Saturnalia."

"Three of them, in six months? That should not be too difficult, should it?"

Liam snorted. "No, not at all. Unless, that is, you want them to be well made. Have you ever *seen* how those things are made?"

"No, but I know they're heavy and worth their weight in gold to a legionary."

"They would be worth that to me, too, if I could get the whoresons finished. It's time that concerns me first and foremost, not the work itself. They are not that hard to make. Much of it is straightforward donkey work that any reasonably clever boy can do, once he's shown how, but it's mind-numbingly tedious."

"How so?"

"Because it never seems to end. There's no escaping it. Each full hamata tunic, complete with shoulder reinforcements, takes up to thirty thousand metal rings. Thirty *thousand*, all the same size and thickness, less than the width of the pad of your thumb. And they all have to be made by hand and then attached to one another, half of them solid rings, the others, alternating with them, made to be riveted shut once they're in place and threaded through the solid rings next to them on four sides, holding the entire fabric together."

He turned away cautiously and rummaged through a pile of papers behind him, withdrawing a hand-sized sample and tossing it to Varrus, who almost dropped it when the solid weight of it took him by surprise.

The smith nodded, clearly having expected that. "There are state-run manufactories that do nothing else but produce stuff like that, and that piece you're holding is made of plain *iron* rings. Even with trained people working full-time on them, year in and year out, each one of those iron shirts takes about two and a half months to assemble."

Varrus was peering at the individual rings around the edges of the sample because they were easier to see than those in the mass of the thing. "You have to make these? These rings?"

The smith made a huffing sound. "Not me, I promise. Slaves make them, one at a time, by hand, in the manufactories I mentioned. That's where the wire is made." He saw the lack of comprehension in Varrus's eyes. "Each ring is made from a piece of wire."

"I see. And where are these manufactories?"

"They're everywhere, throughout the empire, such a common sight that most people don't notice them. You've seen them yourself. There are some close to the edge of town here, outside the city walls, enormous enclosures, each of them containing a number of separate buildings where hundreds of slaves, perhaps even thousands of them, do nothing else but make wire, all day long, every day of every year."

"Thousands? I find that hard to credit."

Liam looked at him as if he were mad. "What is hard to credit is that it takes several people two and a half months, working together, to make a single shirt. *That* is hard to believe. And how many of those shirts do you think are being made? How many legionaries are there in all the empire's armies? There are probably close to thirty-five legions today. And there's at least five thousand men in each legion and sometimes twice that many in the frontier units, and probably half of all of them wear ring-mail tunics. So that's approaching a hundred thousand tunics, each of the whoresons taking two and a half months to make . . ." He seemed to have stunned even himself.

"The first thing you have to do, though, before you can start making the shirt, is to make the wire for the rings, and it has to be either iron or bronze because everything else is too soft to turn away a hard-swung blade. The ones I use are bronze."

"And why do you use bronze?"

"Because it was worth my while, until I fell. It's picky, fussy work, but highly profitable and it produces a much finer, luxurious-looking tunic. The three remaining shirts I have to make are for staff officers up at the fort on the hill, so they have to be of superior quality in every way—polished bronze with gilded buckles and brass embellishments. Nothing resembling the coarseness of the iron things the ordinary grunts wear. And so we have to make bronze rings—we being me and now you and young Shamus and any other willing bodies we can recruit. It's donkey work, as I said, and anyone can do it, and I have another building where we make rings and nothing else. Thousands of wire rings—tens of thousands of the things—and every one of them practically identical to all the others . . . Are you perhaps beginning to see why I might be concerned?"

"I think so. But you think it can be done in time?"

The smith shrugged. "Of course it can, provided nobody wants to sleep for the next six months."

"Well, I'm glad to hear that, at least. It can be done, so we'll do it."

THIRTEEN

By the time his first six months in Colcaster ended, Quintus Varrus's life was altogether different from anything he had ever imagined it might be, and he had no wish to change a single thing about it. He discovered very quickly that Liam had not been exaggerating when he predicted that his wife, Shanna, would take him to her heart and would thereafter try to fatten him up like a pig. She did, but all the men were working so hard for the duration of that six-month period that both he and Shamus ate everything she placed in front of them and neither one gained a smidgen of extra weight.

Lydia Mcuil had come up from Londinium during that period, too, accompanied by Dominic, and they had spent a week with the family. Among other things, Varrus had been glad to see that Shamus's hostility to his father appeared to have lessened, blunted, no doubt, by the time and distance of their separation, but assisted greatly by the visible emergence of self-confidence in the younger man, who had proved beyond dispute, in the gruelling, day-to-day grind of the previous months, assembling the endless tapestry of ring mail, that he was more than capable of applying himself to a monotonous and thankless task.

It also transpired at that visit, though Quintus himself would never have believed it earlier, that he was too busy and preoccupied, and too bone-tired, to do anything other than react with simple, genuine pleasure to Lydia's presence, spending hours talking quietly with her each evening before falling headlong into his bed and passing out immediately. More

than three months had gone by since he had last seen her, on the
morning he and Shamus left for Colcaster—he no longer thought of
it as Camulodunum, unless he was talking to someone from the garrison—and for the first few moments after her arrival he had worried
that they might no longer be able to talk with each other as openly and
easily as they had that first day they met. After exchanging shy, tentative smiles, though, they quickly fell into the easy, bantering compan-
ionship they had enjoyed at the outset. Then she mortified him by
taking mischievous delight in pointing out, one night at dinner, that
Varrus's hair was growing yellow again at the roots, and as soon as dinner was over she produced the hair potion she had brought with her
and made a great fuss about cutting it considerably and darkening it
again in the middle of Shanna's kitchen, to great hilarity from the others. Varrus took it in good spirit, and everyone enjoyed watching him
undergo his transformation. And from that point on, though he knew
the entire family was watching and paying eager heed to their behaviour, Varrus allowed himself to relax and enjoy the simple delight of
being near her.

He could not have been more aware of her sexually had they been
alone together constantly and free to explore each other as man and
woman, but they never were alone, and that made the tingling tension
between them even more pronounced and jealously guarded than it
might otherwise have been. He could feel his insides vibrating with
excitement each time she came into a room and each time she passed
close to him, or smiled at him, or touched him even by accident. But
the number of those brushing touches increased as time passed, and the
accidental element vanished quickly, and he learned to interpret her
expressions and to read what was in her eyes when she looked at him.
On three short-lived occasions, seizing precious moments when they
were unobserved, she had kissed him, tenderly and wistfully the first
time, but then with fast-mounting passion that left them both breathless and shuddering, and from the look in her eyes after the third time,

he knew that the same feelings that were threatening to rip him apart were affecting her equally.

The single great solace of that short visit, though, lay in the evident fact that the Mcuil family accepted their relationship and the mutual affection and attraction that was so obvious between them. It was clear to everyone that Lydia was looking on him with more than casual favour, and that he was besotted with her, and the warmth and atmosphere of an extended family gathering to celebrate grew more pronounced from day to day, so that on the day she and her father left to return home, no one seemed to think anything of the fact that the young couple's fourth kiss, chaste and slow, yet tender and clinging, took place in front of them all.

The following morning he was back at work, the drudgery of the meticulous, boring routine depriving him of everything but the need to concentrate on achieving absolute sameness in everything he did, and he swore an oath that he would never, ever again work with bronze wire or metal ring armour.

But then, less than six weeks later, the work was suddenly over, the last of the armoured shirts completed, its lustrously polished bronze perfection draped over a wooden life-sized figure with the five others, subtly reflecting the light from the glimmering sconces on the smithy walls. Varrus lifted a cup of wine in salute to it. *I hope you save lives*, he thought, *because I know the people who wear you, these next fifty years and more, will have no idea of what a monstrous bastard you were to make, ring by ring by gods-cursed ring.*

The smithy had been cleared out for almost two weeks, with not a single small bronze ring in sight, when Varrus walked in one morning from the street and turned to face the wall, then stopped short in the act of unwrapping the thick muffler from around his neck. It was the month of January, and the first fierce storm of the winter was raging outside.

The snow on the shoulders of his cloak was already melting quickly in the warmth of the smithy, but Varrus stood as though frozen in place, staring down at an object on a narrow table against the wall by the door, next to the rack of wooden pegs from which he was about to hang his wet clothes.

"Is this new?" he asked, speaking to no one in particular as he reached down to pick up the object. To his surprise, though, he failed to lift it, his clenching fingers slipping off its smooth surface, unprepared for its solid weight. He gripped it again, more firmly this time. It was metal, he knew that much, but he didn't know what kind. He held it up carefully, cradling it in both hands, and turned towards Liam, who was busy near the forge. "What is this? I've never seen it before."

"It's Ler's Skull." The smith's mouth quirked into what might have been either a wry grin or a distasteful grimace. "And it's been sitting there for years. The reason you've never seen it before is that until now you've never come in wearing a wet cloak and gone to hang it up on the pegs there. Some fisherman gave it to Rann, Shanna's first husband, to pay a debt, years ago. I kept it after he died, as a curio, for it's worth nothing."

Varrus lowered the object gently back onto the narrow table, and then removed his snow-wet cloak, but he continued to look at it all the while and as soon as he could he picked it up again, holding it up to his eyes in the light from the partially open door. "I can see why you call it a skull," he said. "It looks like one. But what's it made of, and who is Ler?"

"Ler is one of the old gods," Liam answered from just behind him, having crossed the smithy floor unnoticed. "The god of the sea, where I come from. As for what the thing is made of, your guess would be as good as mine. Not any metal I've ever seen. Not iron, I'll swear to that . . . Far too hard, for iron."

"You've tried melting it, then . . . Of course you have."

"Melting it, *and* smelting it. Rann put it in the blast furnace for days, forcing more air into the chamber than he ever had before, but without even the beginnings of a melt. Absolutely nothing. That thing came out of there as pristine pure as when it went in."

Varrus heaved the object gently into the air and caught it again. "It's hugely heavy," he said. "Like lead, or even gold. Do you know where it came from?"

"From the sea. That's why I called it Ler's Skull. Fisherman dredged it up in his net somewhere. Brought it to Rann, thinking it might be worth something because of its weight. Even he could see it was metal, from the way the light caught the dome of it. But we've never found out anything more about it. Don't know what it is or where it was made, or even if it was made at all. A curio, as I said. No more than that."

"Aye. So why d'you keep it here?"

The smith grinned. "Because it makes a grand doorstop, to hold the door open in fine weather. Besides, I don't want to throw it away. I've grown attached to it."

Varrus smiled. "You are not the only person in your family who keeps things like that. Dominic does the same."

"Ah, no, not so. Not quite." Liam wagged his finger from side to side. "Dominic's curios have purpose—or had purpose, at one time. He collects old weapons, and I do, too. It's a thing we learned from our father, who collected war clubs all his life. Some of those were elaborate and beautiful, and as boys we were taught repeatedly that some men have the gift of being able to infuse great beauty into what they make by hand. So as we grew to become smiths and craftsmen, we learned to respect the craftsmanship of smiths who went before us in the distant past. Would you like to see my own pieces?"

"I would," said Varrus, and he followed the smith back through the rear part of the smithy and into the house, where he used a large key from the bunch at his waist to open a door that the younger man had never known to be unlocked in the six months since his arrival. The small room beyond it was very obviously the smith's own private territory, because it was filled with a kind of organized chaos of old and exotic weapons, many of them arranged in displays while others were mounted in boxes and cases that had clearly been made specifically to house them. Liam crossed to the wall beneath a shuttered window, where he used a thin rope tethered to a cleat there to manipulate the slatted shutters, letting in more light.

Varrus stood in the small space in the middle of the floor and looked all around him in amazement. There were weapons everywhere: swords and daggers, axes and clubs of every conceivable shape and size. Some of them were ancient, showing clear signs of ages of neglect, many of the iron-bladed weapons among them almost entirely destroyed by rust. But there were other blades, and spearheads, some made of bronze and others of softer metals unknown to him, that showed no signs of aging at all. And there were heavy, primitive war clubs, many with heads made from smoothed stones or metal balls that had been bound with rawhide thongs to handles fashioned from long bones, some of which he thought appeared to be human. The rawhide bindings on those had dried into bonds that were as hard as iron, but he suspected that they must be brittle with age and that if anyone struck anything hard with one of them, the bindings would shatter like splintered bone. Every piece, he saw, had been carefully cleaned and treated with some kind of preservative, like a clear varnish. He saw what he estimated to be fifty or more exhibits before he lost track of what he had already seen and what he had not, and he turned to his host in wide-eyed astonishment.

"This is—" He stopped, shaking his head with a smile of disbelief. "I don't know what it is, Liam, to tell you the truth. I have never seen anything like it. Where did it all come from?"

The smith flapped a hand as though in dismissal of it all. "From everywhere and anywhere," he said, "over the course of years. I never set out to collect anything. Never even thought of such a thing. It simply happened. Some of these were my father's—the war clubs. That's how it started, I suppose. I always enjoyed looking at them, and sometimes I played with them when I was a tadpole, though the old man would have flayed me if he'd caught me. And when he died, I didn't want to part with them. And over the years I simply found the others, or bought them, or traded for them if I saw something that caught my fancy."

"And why do you keep them here, in this room?"

"To protect them." The smith spun slowly on his heel, an outflung hand indicating the profusion of his collection. "No one else cares about them, and the result of not caring is carelessness. Most people would think me mad for thinking so, and you might be one of them, but I believe these pieces deserve respect, if for no other reason than that they survived for so long when so little else from their times did. More than that, though, I think they deserve it for the craftsmanship that made each one stand out for me when I first found it. And so I keep them locked up because I don't want them mishandled or abused by people who have no interest in them." He looked around at the cases with fondness. "I enjoy the old clubs, but I love the blades even more . . . the way they were made."

Quintus Varrus bowed his head admiringly. "You are a philosopher, then," he said quietly. "And far from thinking you mad, I agree with you. These instruments deserve respect for what they are, and I admire you for providing it for them. Have you a favourite among them?"

"I do," Liam said, "but you'll be surprised to see what it is." He pointed over Varrus's shoulder. "Hand me down that box there. The small one. Lift it onto the table."

There were two tall wooden cases propped upright on a shelf against the wall at his back, and Varrus lifted down the smaller one, surprised by how light it was, for it looked strongly made and substantial. He placed it on the table that occupied most of the floor space, and the smith undid the simple hasp and threw open the lid.

"Do you know what that is?"

Quintus stared blankly at what lay revealed. He shook his head, then frowned and bent forward to look at the device more closely. It was an oddly shaped serpentine piece of wood, and the image that popped into his mind was one he had seen as a boy: a drawing of an African snake called a cobra, stretched out on the ground in a long, undulating series of sinuous curves. It was perhaps a hand's length longer than his own arm, and he saw that it had been cunningly and painstakingly crafted. When Liam told him he could pick it up, he did, and knew at once it was some kind of bow, but he could not identify the how or why of it. It was far lighter than he would have believed it could be, almost feather light, and he brought it closer to his eyes and turned it one way and then another as he tried to make sense of the strange, vertical striations in the wood.

"Is it a bow?"

"It is. A Scythian bow."

Varrus held it farther away, extending his arm and looking up at the weapon. "That's what I thought when I picked it up—that it was a bow, I mean. But it's shaped wrongly. I see notches for a bowstring, but look, they're on the wrong side of the shaft, and the curves in the stave make the thing useless—the string would touch those outer curves. How would you aim it, or even hold it?"

"I thought exactly the same thing when I first saw it," Liam said, smiling. "That it was backwards. But the man who gave it to me showed me how wrong I was. He was an armourer and had spent much of his life up on the empire's northeastern border, beyond the Euxine Sea. According to what he said, the lands up there grow nothing but grass—endless oceans of grass—and the people are all savages. He said they're all short and hairy, but they breed the fastest and hardiest horses in the world. And some of them are called Scythians—the people, I mean, not the horses. There are lots of others up there, too, all barbarians—Huns and Goths and others like them, and they all ride horses. Well, these Scythians were horse warriors—they probably still are, but they were famous because they used their bows from horseback, and this is one of those bows. That's why it's so short. They were made to be used by small men on horses, and the Scythians conquered their part of the world using them."

Varrus was unimpressed. "Doesn't look like much to me," he said. "Doesn't look strong enough. Too flat, and too thin."

"You're right," Liam said. "It doesn't. But that's because you're looking at it backwards. See those straight lines running up along the outside edge there? What d'you think those are?"

"They look like layers of some kind."

"That's what they are. Three flat layers, all bonded together. Woodworkers call that lamination, and each layer strengthens the others. The first layer, on the outside, is wood, though I don't know what kind. But it's backed on the inside by a layer of long, thin strips of bone, glued on for strength. And then behind that again, on the very inside of the bow, there's a third layer, this one of animal sinew, boiled and stretched and then moulded into place and trimmed to act as a pliable bonding layer on the inner surface. It's called a recurve bow, precisely because of the way it's made and curved. We're accustomed to seeing only arced bows here in Britain, but this kind has two curves, one of which looks awkward to us, but that awkward look makes the weapon ten times stronger than you think it could be. You string it exactly the opposite way from the way you would an ordinary bow. Look, I'll show you."

He reached into the bow's case and pulled out a rolled bowstring, quickly shaking it out and grasping the two ends to stretch it, twisting it and smoothing out the kinks. It resisted him strongly, and Varrus bent forward to look at it, finally deciding that it must be some kind of hard, twisted yarn, or perhaps even sinew, lightly oiled to keep it from drying out completely, and made with a loop at each end. Once he was satisfied that he had softened the string sufficiently to work with, Liam picked up the bow stave, slipped a loop over one end of it, then braced that end on the floor, against his foot. Then, holding the free end of the string in his right hand, and moving deftly and with the ease of long practice, he tucked the upright end against his shoulder with his left hand and leaned heavily on it, forcing it against what Varrus had assumed would be the natural direction of its flex. When he had forced

the top end down to the level of his chest, he quickly fastened the loop
he had been holding into the notch in the top of the stave and stood
erect, holding the suddenly transformed weapon out at arm's length,
and Varrus realized that the notches had not been on the wrong side of
the stave after all.

"Try it," the smith said. "I've no arrows, but you can test the pull."

Varrus did, and found it far more difficult to pull the bowstring
back to his shoulder than he would ever have imagined. He handed it
back, shaking his head ruefully. "I would never have believed that if
I hadn't watched you do it. That's the strongest bow I have ever pulled.
Mind you, I doubt I have held a bow more than six or seven times in my
life, and that was when I was a boy. But none of them were anywhere
near as powerful as that one . . . No wonder it's your favourite."

"It's not," Liam said. He pointed again. "That one is, but I can't string
it."

Varrus lifted down the other tall case. It was twice the height of the
first one, though not much wider, and it was heavier, though not by
much. He gasped when the lid was swung open to reveal another bow
stave, for this one was easily twice the length and thickness of the first,
and it had been fitted perfectly into a fabric-lined, lovingly shaped
niche that had been carved to hold it.

He stood stunned for long moments. "No," he said eventually. "I
don't believe it. I could barely pull the small one you showed me. And
I don't think I have ever met a man who could pull a bow as big as this.
It would take a giant. You said the Scythians were little people."

"And so they were. But this bow came from Africa, not from Scythia.
It's the same kind of bow, recurved, but it's not Scythian. Someone cop-
ied the design, and whoever he was, he was a master craftsman. Look at
the inlay work."

Varrus did look, and the workmanship was truly wonderful, with
sinuous strips of variously coloured woods inlaid in fanciful, interwoven
patterns in the glossy, lacquered frontal panels of the triply layered stave

above and below the thickness of the smoothly sculpted leather-covered grip.

"The leather's dried out," he said.

"So would you be after a few hundred years. It can be replaced if anyone ever needs to use it again."

"You said you can't string it. Why not?"

"Because I have nothing strong enough to string it with. Where would I start to look for such a thing?"

Varrus was surprised to hear that. "I would start by going to the man who made the bowstring for you for the smaller bow. There can't be much difference between making one for that and one for this, other than length and thickness."

"So you might think," came the reply. "But apparently that's not the case. I went to that man first. He told me it couldn't be done. He wouldn't even try. Said the idea was ridiculous."

"Did you show him the bow?"

"No, I told him about it. He didn't believe me."

"That's hardly surprising. I doubt if I would, either, without seeing it. It sounds like the kind of story fishermen tell—about those fish that no one ever sees but them. How did you obtain the thing, anyway?"

"From an old friend who knew I admired it—a man for whom I did a great amount of work. He spent the last years of his army career as a legate with the Second Trajan Legion in Egypt, in Alexandria, and picked it up there. When he died, he left the bow to me, naming the gift in his will." He smiled. "He never used it, of course. He was far too old to pull it, even when he first bought it. I'll never pull it, either, but we kept it safe, between us, and if there's life after this one, as the Christians say there is, then its maker and its owner will both be happy that it still exists, for it must be unique—"

He frowned suddenly and grimaced, sucking air sharply between his teeth, and he hunched forward, pressing the heel of his hand against his ribs above where he had burned himself.

"Liam, is it bad? I'll go and fetch Shanna." In the previous few weeks Varrus had noticed his employer doing the same thing more and more frequently, and he knew that their physician had left Shanna some kind of opiate for when the pain grew intense. But Liam shook his head and waved his free hand in a negative, then held it up, bidding Varrus be silent and wait.

Finally, he drew a deeper breath and began to straighten up slowly, and the colour returned to his face. "Right, then," he said. "We'll say nothing of that little incident to Shanna, right? It's over now, so not a word. You hear me?"

"I hear you," Varrus said.

"Good." He inhaled again, deeply, then released the air slowly through his pursed lips, testing himself for lingering pain, and then he straightened perceptibly and flexed his shoulders. "So," he said, "where was I? Yes, I remember. I was about to say that we have now established that you can make and assemble bronze rings. So it's about time now to find out if you can make a blade. Are you ready?"

Varrus nodded, resigned to accepting Liam's minor tyranny. "I am, whenever you are."

"Good, then let's find out. We can't afford to stand around here all day doing nothing."

FOURTEEN

The test this time was practical; no questions asked. Liam told him to sit down on a stool by a workbench, then went to a metal rack of heavy wooden shelves along one wall, where he selected a two-foot-long rectangular piece of iron a thumb's length wide on all four sides. He brought it back and dropped it on the bench. "Show me your sword," he said.

Varrus unclipped the weapon from his belt and handed it across, and the smith bared the blade and set the sheath aside. He laid the sword down next to the iron bar. "You have one week to turn this, into one of these," he said, touching the iron bar first and then the sword. "And even I would find that a difficult task to complete in time, though it is possible. You had best get started." He walked away without another word.

Varrus looked wryly at young Shamus, who was watching with his mouth hanging open. "Close your mouth before it fills with flies, Shay," he said, then stood up and crossed to the forge. He dropped the iron bar on the brick apron and reached for the rope that controlled the bellows.

And that was the start of what he would think of for the remainder of his life as his *real* life, because from that moment on he barely had time to think about the life he had lived before he arrived in Colcaster and first inhaled the atmosphere of Liam Mcuil's sooty, smoky smithy. From the moment he picked up that bar of iron, his whole existence became centred upon the art of working with glowing, fire-hot metals and the craft of learning how to use them and make them obey his will. He frequently forgot to eat that week, so deeply immersed in what he was doing that he might not have eaten anything at all had Shanna not brought him food and stood over him, silent and menacing, to make sure he took the time to eat it. But he made his first sword that week, and he was proud of it, despite his awareness of its every flaw. It was the first blade he had ever made entirely with his own hands, beginning with a piece of crude, barely refined iron and transforming it into a serviceable weapon entirely with his own skills, working on it alone and asking for neither help nor guidance.

Time and again, though, during that first, agonizing week, he took time to remember his friend Rhys Twohands and to thank him silently for all the lessons he had taught a small boy who had been hungry for knowledge of an adult craft. Where the majority of busy men would quickly have lost patience and shooed the child away, Twohands had welcomed young Quintus and praised his curiosity, encouraging the boy to seek out and discover the truth in metal. And so young Quintus Varrus had learned to handle and shape hot, softened metal while most other boys his age were playing at being soldiers. He was not jealous of their play, for he had learned early, and with finality, that he could never be a soldier, and so had set himself to mastering those things he *could* control. And as a child, watching his hero Rhys Twohands at the forge, he had learned that iron, the hardest metal known, could be controlled, could be shaped into things of worth and enduring beauty by men who were sufficiently strong-willed and determined to master its secrets.

On the day ordained for the sword to be finished, there was a full finger's depth of snow on the ground and the wind was bitterly cold. Familiar people on the streets were rendered unrecognizable, their shapes and features hidden under mountains of protective clothing. Liam was waiting outside the smithy when Varrus arrived, and the two men exchanged nods before Varrus pushed open the doors and hung his heavy cloak and scarf from a wooden peg.

He went directly to the hearth and stirred up the banked embers from the previous night, raking them thoroughly before blowing them into life again with a hand bellows and adding fresh fuel. Only when the coals were glowing healthily again did he cross to the quenching trough and pick up the weapon that lay on the ledge beside it. It had a hilt of sorts, no more than two simple shaped blocks of wood strapped on either side of the tang, since it was the blade's quality that was being judged, not a sword's appearance. He hefted the piece and swung it sharply, in a truncated chop, then flipped it lengthwise and extended it, hilt first, to his adjudicator, who took it and walked away to scrutinize it in the light from the open doors.

Once again Varrus was aware of Shamus lurking in the shadows at the rear of the smithy, but he paid the young smith no attention as he walked to the edge of the forge and leaned against the brickwork, fighting to keep his face expressionless while he waited for Liam's judgment. The younger man had been a constant presence, hovering at the edges of Varrus's vision ever since he had started working on the sword. To the young Eirishman's credit, he had kept himself well out of the way and had taken care not to interfere or interrupt. In fact he had barely spoken a word to Varrus in all that time, and Quintus had soon grown used to having his silent presence nearby.

At first, he had suspected that Shamus might be resentful of him, having taken umbrage at the way Varrus was welcomed by his uncle's family, but he quickly came to see that was untrue, that what he had taken to be resentment was nothing more than wonderment. The young smith, he realized eventually, was simply in awe of him, for reasons Varrus could not begin to fathom.

A flicker of movement snapped him out of his reverie, and he saw that Liam was coming back to him, gazing down at the sword, and when he arrived he looked up and met Varrus's eye, nodding. "Good," he said.

"No more doubting questions from me. It's not perfect, but you know that already. There's a few small bits and bumps, and the finish could be smoother in places, but I know older, more experienced men than you—working smiths, some of them—who could not have done this as well as you have managed to, in the short time I gave you. Here, hold this."

He handed the sword back and reached beneath his arm to pull a length of red cloth from a pocket inside his tunic. He spread the cloth on the bricks beside Varrus. "I didn't expect you to finish. I was prepared to judge you on the progress you had managed to make in the time you had." He reached out and wiggled his fingers, and Varrus passed the sword back to him, then watched as he wrapped it neatly and with great care in the folds of the cloth. "There," he said, and tucked the red-wrapped package beneath his arm. "Now come with me."

"Where to?"

"You'll see when we get there." He turned then to his nephew. "Shamus, Quintus and I are going out, on a matter of business. I want you to stay here and finish what you have to do today—it's not much, so you should be finished easily by the middle of the afternoon—then bank the fire really well and close up. You can take the remainder of the day off. And tell Shanna, if you will, that we'll see you all at dinner."

It looked colder than ever outside, especially when seen from the warmth and comfort of the smithy, but both men were wearing trousers—the heavy woollen braccae worn by the legions serving in cold climates—and thick, knitted woollen socks under heavy boots, and they took the time to wrap themselves up warmly, arranging their cloaks and scarves comfortably to muffle them before they ventured out into the snow and the biting wind.

As for where they were going, it turned out to resemble a victory tour of Liam's best customers. In each case, Liam behaved precisely the same way, introducing Varrus as his new assistant and producing the new sword, telling the tale of its creation out of a single bar of iron in a matter of mere days, and generally giving each customer the impression that their affairs would be in good hands whenever Quintus Varrus worked on their behalf. From its beginnings in the premises of the smallest customer, a well-fed barrel maker who ordered all his iron hoops from Liam, the presentation that day grew into a ritual and then matured into a ceremony as the smith grew more familiar with which words worked best and generated the most goodwill, and Varrus played to perfection the part of the obliging apprentice.

The last call of the afternoon was the most important and, for Varrus, the most significant, for it led to something more defining and more lasting than either he or Liam could have anticipated. He came close to missing it completely, though, for towards late afternoon they turned a corner and Varrus found himself directly in front of the main entrance to the fort that housed the Camulodunum garrison. The sight of the guarded gates stopped him dead in his tracks and he felt his throat close up with panic. Then Liam stopped, too. He looked back at Varrus in surprise, then looked towards the gates.

"What's wrong? You've turned pale."

No, Varrus thought. *I need not run. I am Fingael Mcuil and I no longer have golden hair. And no one knows me.*

He smiled and shook his head. "There's nothing wrong. I remembered something I meant to do today, that's all. It's nothing important. I'll do it tomorrow. Who do we have to see here?"

"A mad bastard called Ajax. Ignatius Ajax. A wild man. You'll like him." Liam walked up to the decanus in charge of the guard and told him who he was and that he was there to visit the garrison's master-at-arms. Without a word, a legionary ushered them into Ajax's cubiculum, waved them towards a pair of chairs fronting a writing table that was covered with weighted-down piles of documents, and left them there.

The armourer's office was comfortably furnished but not excessively so, with the handsome, finely made table taking up much of the floor space. A pair of sloping iron racks against the wall behind the chair held ten candles apiece, and the two chairs that Quintus and Liam now

occupied were placed directly in front of the desk, with a small table
between them that held a broad, circular lamp with multiple wicks.
None of the lights were burning now, because the office was bright with
sunlight that spilled in through the high windows in the room's eastern
and southern walls.

It was what hung on the walls in the crosshatched afternoon light
that took Varrus's breath away, because it was clear at a glance that the
armourer collected swords. Varrus had never seen so many of them in a
single room. They were hung in definite patterns, vertically and horizontally and in circular arrangements, on every available wall surface. From
what Varrus could see, the collection comprised every type of sword,
from old, battered legionary short swords that demonstrated the unifor-
mity of most Roman weapons, of different ages but identical in detail,
mass-produced for more than a millennium by slaves in state factories to
feed the insatiable need of the empire's legions, to blades that showed
individuality and even personality. There were few of the early Roman
legionary swords, he noted, for those had all been produced in bulk and
were largely unremarkable. But he saw many different versions of the
cavalry sword known as the spatha, a stabbing weapon with a thirty-inch
blade. Varrus had never used a spatha, even in training, because Rhys
Twohands had distrusted the reliability of the long blade. He was convinced, from some experience in his life with the legions, that a spatha
would bend under extreme pressure.

The majority of the swords in this collection were swords like Varrus's
own, the Hispanic gladius. They varied in shape and length and texture,
and even in weight and balance, rarely radically but unmistakably, and
the fact of so many of them being here in this one place, each of them
carefully hung outside and in front of its sheath, told Varrus that their
collector was a man of infinite patience and exhaustive knowledge of
the art of making blades.

One particular example drew his attention, seeming to shine like
silver where the afternoon light touched it. It hung low on the wall by

the door, and he stood up and went closer to it. As he crouched to examine it, the door swung open and a man strode in. He stopped abruptly and glared down at Varrus with a thunderous frown.

"What—?" he demanded. "Who in Hades are you? And what are you doing scuttling around on my floor?"

"He's with me, Ajax," Liam said hurriedly, rising to his feet. "A cousin from Eire. I brought him here for you to meet him."

Ajax made no move to acknowledge the smith, and Varrus gazed up at him, frozen. "You'd better teach him some manners, then, hadn't you?" He was speaking to Liam, but he kept his eyes on Varrus. "Or don't you believe in decorum or deportment?"

"You're a collector," Varrus said.

"That's observant of you," the armourer said back. "Should I be impressed? Stand up and look at me!"

Varrus rose slowly to his feet. "I'm an admirer."

"Are you, by all the gods at once? An admirer of what, boy? Fine women, other pretty boys, or men in armour?"

"An admirer of fine blades."

Ajax hesitated, the very briefest of pauses, before stabbing a finger sideways at Liam. "Sit down," he said, then looked back at Varrus. "You, too. I'm going to go out and tell myself this didn't happen. When I come back, I want to find two supplicants here, waiting to enlist my support for something they want to do."

As the door closed behind the armourer, Liam shook his head ruefully. "You startled him. Never a good thing to do with soldiers. I told you he was a mad bastard, did I not?"

"You did. But you also said I would like him."

"You will. I promise."

FIFTEEN

The two smiths did not have long to wait before the door swung open again and Ignatius Ajax stopped on the threshold, looking from one to the other of the two men. "Liam," he said cordially, without a glimmer of acknowledgment that he had seen them moments earlier. "What brings you here on such a bitter day?"

He reached up and removed his ornate parade helmet, a magnificent thing with a high, gilded crown beneath a shoulder-wide centurion's crest of soft-looking rich brown horsehair, and set it carefully down on the work table. He had not been wearing it when he first entered.

Liam stood up and held out his hand, and they greeted each other and exchanged pleasantries, but Varrus paid little attention to what was being said. He was too busy looking critically at Ajax this time, now that he had the opportunity to examine him.

The man was imposing, even intimidating, in his size and bulk, an impression heightened by the solid, heavy substance of his ornately gilded parade armour with its exaggerated, segmented shoulder plates and the profusion of medallions and awards that covered his breastplate and proclaimed his prowess and distinction in the legionary hierarchy. Ignatius Ajax, in the splendour of his brown and gold regalia, looked every man's vision of the perfectly endowed, upper-echelon legionary centurion. His arms and legs were strong and solid, the layered muscles in them visible each time he moved. His hair was cut in a military crop, and his face was broad and impassive, making him appear resolute, with

238

a square, stubborn-looking jaw and eyes that were wide and intelligent. He wore the off-white woollen tunic of the Sixth Legion, and it was hemmed to two fingers' width above his knees. On his feet he wore elaborately sandalled, highly polished boots over heavy knitted socks that were the same colour as his tunic and were folded down below his knees. His loins were guarded by an elaborate baltea, the traditional armoured kirtle of metal-embellished straps suspended from the waist belt. Embossed leather braces on his forearms and matching greaves on his legs completed the picture.

"You look very official for a midweek afternoon," Liam said, and Ajax looked down at himself.

"Aye. Once every sixth week these days. Full parade and inspection."

"Is that new? I've never been aware of midweek inspections before."

"Sub-legate's orders. Not everyone likes it, but I, for one, think it's a good thing. We've been at peace for too long and things have grown too lax around here. Everyone is growing more and more sloppy and careless, from month to month. Not just the grunts—some of the officers are almost as bad as the malcontents. That affects discipline and morale. So now there's a Legate's Parade every six weeks, and may the gods have mercy on anyone who doesn't measure up to expectations."

"What kind of expectations?"

Ajax grinned at him. "Any kind we decide to adopt at the time," he said. "Cleanliness, to start with—both personal and in weaponry and equipment. And general discipline, concentrating on obedience to orders and instructions, reaction times, visible attitudes to authority and responsibilities. There are no limits."

"That sounds . . . harsh," Liam said.

"Aye, you might call it that, I suppose. Some bleeding hearts do. But they're the kind of idiots who have never seen a wild man running at them waving a sword or an axe. You stop thinking that kind of shit very quickly once you realize your life depends on how well the men around you respond under unexpected attack. When the shit starts flying around your head, you either react instantly and instinctively, or you die. So if your aim is to run a successful army—and ask yourself why would anyone want to run an *un*successful one—you had better keep your standards high all the time, and your expectations higher." He turned his head slightly to include Varrus in his summation. "So we dress up in our finest finery and preen ourselves in public, making great show of punishing sloth, sloppiness, shoddiness, and lack of unit pride. Our aim with these new inspection parades is to re-establish proper values. All in the name of building up morale, which is really what an army needs in order to function well." He broke off and looked around him. "I think it's time now for a cup of wine."

He went to the corner and opened a small wooden cupboard mounted at waist level on the wall. He spoke over his shoulder as he reached inside. "We haven't even started yet. At the next parade, we'll announce a four-week schedule, and within the year we'll hold these things every second week." He came back to the table clutching three horn cups in the fingers of his left hand and a long-necked ewer in the other. "And by that time we'll be having inter-unit contests to tie in with the events, involving the presentation of awards." He set down his burden carefully on the edge of the table.

"Well," he said, "we're here, so let's drink. Parading is thirsty work. Which means you'll get no sympathy from me if you think it's piss. So drink with me, and then you can show me what you brought, Liam—apart from your young friend here."

They raised their cups and drank, and then Liam laid the wrapped sword silently on the table, pushing it gently in Ajax's direction with his fingertips. The armourer put down his cup and picked up the bundle, hefting it in his hand before unwrapping the sword and raising it to where he could examine it closely. He turned it over several times, tilting it one way and then another, brushing his fingers lightly over the blade's surface all the while. Then he pushed his chair back from the table, laid the weapon across his knee, and bent forward at the waist, pushing down hard on each end of it. The blade yielded visibly, then snapped back with a hum when he removed his hand from the end of the blade. Varrus was watching him closely, but Ajax's expression was unreadable as he raised the blade back close to his face again, then pursed his lips and tested the cutting edge with his thumb.

Finally, he looked back at Liam. "So let me guess," he said quietly. "This young fellow made this. In your forge. Am I correct?"

Liam nodded.

"Well, it has merit—more so than most of the attempts I've seen from apprentice smiths in recent years. But it's raw, Liam, so I don't understand. You know my standards, and my requirements, so why would you even think to bring me this?"

"It's his first," Liam replied, looking steadily at the armourer.

Ajax sat silent for the space of five heartbeats before he asked, "What does that mean, *his first?*"

"What I said," Liam said. "It's his first sword. His first attempt. Made it in six days, unsupervised and with no help. From an iron bar welded in my smithy. And no template other than another sword."

The big Roman sat without moving for some time, staring at the sword in his hands, but then he set it on the table in front of him, straightened his back against the chair, and pushed his hips forward, slouching in his seat and lowering his chin towards his breastplate. "His first," he said. "This was his *first* attempt at forging metal and he made a sword, is that what you are saying?"

"No," Liam said. "I said this was his first attempt at making a sword. He has been around smithies since he was a boy and so he knows the basics of smithing, taught by a former legionary smith. And he's been working for the last half year on completing those mail tunics we made for your junior officers." He shrugged. "I simply thought you should meet him, so you will know who he is in future, once he has perfected his craft."

"Hmm." The armourer drained his cup and looked at Varrus. "Your blade has a central spine, with blood channels on both sides. Where did you learn to do that?"

"My old master made all his sword blades that way: central spine, twin channels, straight, hardened edges, wide V point."

"All his swords. How many did he make?"

Varrus shrugged. "Scores," he said. "Perhaps hundreds." Only as the words left his lips did he realize how revealing they were, and Ajax pounced before he could recover.

"Hundreds? Of swords? In Eire? Was he equipping an army?"

Varrus recovered quickly, his mind racing. "We were not in Eire," he said, not daring to look at Liam. "I grew up in Dalmatia, across the Adriatic Sea from Italy, near the town of Salona."

"But you're from Hibernia."

"My family's from there—all smiths—but my father, a distant cousin to Liam, was attached to the Seventh Claudia Legion." He had a sudden mental flash of his father's villa, and the lie came to him easily, surprising him. "He was a wheelwright, based in Viminacium, in Moesia. I was born there, but we moved to Dalmatia when my father's employer, a successful military supplier, retired to his estates there. A year after that, my parents both fell sick and died, and I was raised by a friend of my father's, a smith called Rhys Twohands, who took pity on me. It was his wife, Anna, who took me in, really. They had no children of their own, and so they raised me as their son. Anna taught me to read, and to write and count and keep records—"

"Wait," Ajax interjected. "A village woman, the wife of a wheelwright, taught you all that?"

Varrus flapped a hand at him, frowning as though impatient at being doubted. "Anna was more than that," he snapped. "And she was not a village woman. She had been with the family for years when Rhys met her, a trusted, privileged member of the household staff, tutor to all the merchant's children. When she adopted me, I attended lessons with the other children in the household. And at the same time, Rhys started teaching me his craft. He taught me all I know, and then he died, with Anna, in a fire . . . I came back to Britain last year and found some of my father's family still living in Londinium."

Ajax went back to scrutinizing the sword in his hands before holding it up where Varrus could see it. "Do you believe you can do better than this?"

"I know I can. All I need is time to work at it."

Ajax sniffed loudly and rose to his feet. "I can give you that." He cocked his head to Liam. "Providing you have no objections, Liam?"

"To having him taught by you and Demetrius? You think me mad? How much time can you give him?"

"Half days, every day."

Ajax looked back to Varrus. "Mornings," he said. "You'll have to come here on your own." He stooped forward to pick up both horn cups. "What was your name again?"

"Fingael. Fingael Mcuil."

"So be it, Fingael Mcuil. We'll see you in the morning. The guard changes at dawn, so be here before the changeover and come directly to me. I'll be waiting for you." He held up the new sword and looked at Liam. "Would you object if I kept this tonight? I want to show it to someone." Liam shrugged and spread his open palms, and Ajax turned back to Varrus. "Be sure to get a good night's sleep, because tomorrow you'll be busy. And now I have to go and take off all this fancy clutter before I melt. *Vale!*"

Neither man spoke as they walked back through the complex that housed the garrison, and no one paid them the slightest attention. Only when they were outside the gates on the public street again did Varrus turn to Liam.

"Tell me what happened in there," he said, and the smith grinned and slapped him hard on the upper arm.

"What happened? You landed on your feet, my lad. You are now apprenticed to the foremost expert on sword blades in all of Britain."

SIXTEEN

And so Quintus Varrus entered the netherworld of the garrison armouries, to become quickly lost in a metal-smithing world the like of which he had never imagined. He had known three smithies in his life: his father's, run by Rhys Twohands, in Dalmatia, and the two Mcuil smithies in Britain. All three had been spacious, clean, and well maintained, brightly lit and airy even on the busiest of days when, at full capacity, they might have employed five or six men apiece. Nothing in any of them had prepared him for the noise-filled chaos of smoke and darkness, the clamour of ever-conflicting sounds, or the sooty, grit-filled, breath-catching air and seething activity he found in Ignatius Ajax's domain.

Of course, all his first impressions were wrong that first day, bred of his own apprehensions, the insecurities of any stranger in a strange realm, for as he stood hesitating on the threshold, peering into the murk ahead and wondering where he should go, a huge, burly man came striding out of the billowing smoke, much of which, Varrus realized later, must have been steam generated by hot water and the icy air.

"Mcuil?" The big man saw Varrus nod and turned away, beckoning him to follow, then led him through a bewildering series of twists and turns, between haphazard heaps and disciplined piles of metal, until he stopped in front of a high, narrow pair of doors with a small, shuttered opening on the wall on one side. He grasped a handle, pulled open one of the doors, and pointed inside with his thumb. "There y' go. Ask for

Decius." And before Varrus could thank him, he had vanished back into the maelstrom of noise that was the armoury.

Blinking his eyes against the irritation of the smoke-filled air, Varrus stepped through the door and found himself in a narrow, quiet passageway facing a battered wooden counter. It was a much-used place, he could see, with a scarred and scuffed wooden bench running almost the entire length of the wall on his left, presumably for people to sit on while waiting for whatever it was that people waited for in here, but it was vacant for the moment, and he pulled the door closed at his back and walked forward to the counter. A harassed-looking clerk saw him there and demanded to know his business. But as soon as he heard the name Decius, he opened a flap in the countertop.

"Through here," he said, not uncivilly, and led the way to a cubicle in which sat a very elderly and distinguished-looking man, who stood up to greet Fingael Mcuil by name and turned out, unsurprisingly, to be Decius. His full name, he explained, was Decius Decius, and he had been clerk of the armouries of the Sixth Legion in Camulodunum for close to thirty years, and senior clerk, with the honorary title and pay grade of advanced supernumerary, or presiding finance specialist, for seventeen of those years, the last fifteen spent serving under Ignatius Ajax.

He informed Varrus that he would take him to meet his initial supervisor shortly, but before he could do anything more, he had to register him as a bona fide serving member of the legionary auxiliary, and that on completion of the paperwork, Varrus would become a full apprentice, serving in the armouries and entitled to the wages of a serving recruit. That would change after six months of basic training, Decius said, whereupon Varrus would be paid as a qualified legionary, and a year after that, providing that he performed acceptably and lived up to his employer's expectations, he could expect to be paid a regular salaria, or stipend, the amount to be negotiated by his employer, in this instance, Ignatius Ajax.

Varrus said nothing, surprised that anyone—and most astonishingly, the Roman state—would consider paying him for learning what he wanted to know. He had talked to Liam at length the night before, and he had been surprised to discover that Ajax's brusque offer to train him had astounded the smith, too. The possibility had never entered Liam's mind. He had taken Varrus there, he said, simply to meet Ajax and to let the armourer know the Mcuil smithy now had a promising and amiable new associate, another Mcuil. The true reason for his visit, though, was that he knew and liked the armourer, who was one of his best customers, and knew, from past visits, that Ajax would offer him a warm chair and a welcome drink, perhaps a cup of hot, honeyed vinum, at the end of a long, hard, cold day spent trudging door to door, criss-crossing the city. Liam had expected nothing more.

Now, Varrus stood waiting, watching the clerk's bald head as the man finished writing down the information Varrus had given him, duly registering the new recruit, and sprinkled sand across the surface of his ledger to dry the ink.

"There. All done," Decius said, rubbing his hands together as though drying them. "Now come with me and we'll find Turco."

"Who is Turco?"

"Turco will be your temporary . . . guardian, I suppose, until we find the work to which you are best suited. Everyone is different, with differing abilities, and your next few days will be spent undergoing tests to—" At the sound of iron-studded boot soles he looked over Varrus's shoulder. "Ah! Magister Ajax! Good morning to you."

"*Ave*, and hail to you, my friend," Ajax answered. "I see you found Mcuil. Have you signed him up?"

"Yes, Magister, I have. I was just telling him how Turco will be test—"

"Testing him to see where he fits in. No, Decius, not this time. Tell Turco, if you will, that I already know where this one will fit best." He shrugged, to take any sting out of his comments, and beckoned with his fingers for Varrus to follow him as he swung away and strode

off again, talking loudly over his shoulder as he went, against the noise
of metal being moved and worked. Today Ajax was without the imposing trappings of the military, bare-headed and unarmoured, dressed in
a plain, belted woollen tunic, thick-soled, sandalled boots over bare feet,
and a short, shoulder-protecting kind of half cloak. The sole weapon he
wore was a gladius, the Hispanic type, hanging at his right hip, and
Varrus could not imagine him ever having to unsheathe it here, although
part of him knew that, should such a need ever arise, Ajax would not
hesitate to draw it.

"I've already spoken with one of my men about you," he shouted,
forcing Varrus to concentrate on listening to his words and to shut out
the distractions coming at him from every direction. "My best man, in
fact. He knows why you are here, what I saw in the blade you made. He
also knows what else I need to know about you, and what I want him
to discover about you." He vanished into a billowing cloud of vaporiz-
ing steam, and Varrus followed him steadfastly, only to find him waiting
three paces ahead, his arm thrust backwards to hold him in place.
"Careful." He stepped to the side, sucking in his belly.

A man emerged from the gloom ahead and eased past him, moving
backwards and pulling an unsteady, squeaky-wheeled cart filled with
round bars of rusted iron. Varrus drew aside, too, letting the fellow pass
him as Ajax relaxed and flicked some imaginary rust stains off his tunic.
Then, continuing to shout against the noise as though there had been
no interruption, he moved on.

"His name is Demetrius Hanno. Sounds like a Roman name, Hanno,
but it's not. He's from Macedonia—Northern Greece, he calls it." He
stopped again, this time in a short, narrow passageway between tall racks
holding long, cylindrical bars of rusted metal twice as tall as he himself
was, and laid a restraining hand on Varrus's arm to hold him there as
another large group of his people squeezed by them, manhandling a
number of open containers on tiny, squeaky wheels. He nodded to a few
of them as they passed by. "Do you know any Greeks?" he asked, and

seeing Varrus's headshake, he went on. "Well, Demetrius doesn't look like a Greek. And he certainly doesn't sound like one. To hear him speak, you would think he was tutored in the finest schools in Rome. Never at a loss for words and never a word out of place. Doesn't slur, doesn't mutter." He stepped right inside one of the racks holding the metal bars, and Varrus stepped in beside him, to let pass a container that was larger than the others.

"So where *was* he educated?"

"He was a slave. And a gladiator. And he taught himself everything he knows. The man is a prodigy. He'd make a damned fine emperor, and he'd do the job alone." The cart passed them and the two men moved on. "Don't expect him to welcome you, though. Not at first. He might not speak to you at all for a day or two. Demetrius is . . . different. He's intimidating—in his looks, I mean. You'll like him eventually. But don't let his appearance put you off. At what he really *does*, he's the very best. No one can come close to his abilities, and he will be the best teacher you will have ever known. I promise you that even if he dislikes you. If he does like you, though, you'll *never* find a better teacher or a more loyal friend."

Once again he whipped up an arm, interrupting their passage and peering at something ahead of them that Varrus couldn't see. "Saros!" he shouted. "If that's what I think it is, it shouldn't be on this side of the building. And if someone told you to bring it over here, I want to know who that someone is, and when he was appointed to overrule me. Have your people turn it around right now and take it back to where it was, and ask Centurion Pella to come and talk to me when he has time, would you?"

He turned his attention quickly back to Varrus and smiled, the first smile Varrus had seen from him. "We have close to four hundred men working here every day," he said. "Sometimes even the best of them get things wrong. And one more word on Hanno." He actually winked. "Don't work hard to make him like you. He'll see through that and resent it. Just be yourself, and he will either like you or he won't. Nothing you can do—nothing either one of us can do—will alter that. Mind your feet here now. It's treacherous."

Ahead of them, the floor appeared to be of concrete, covered in standing water that glistened dully, reflecting light from what Varrus could only surmise must be oven furnaces and open fires. Thick wooden planks had been laid down end to end to serve as pathways between the work areas with heaviest foot traffic, and Varrus stepped firmly onto the wooden path selected by Ignatius Ajax.

When they came to the end of the wooden pathway, they stopped at a place that resembled Liam's smithy, save that it was more than ten times larger and housed upwards of twenty men, all of them hammering iron bars in all hues of heatedness.

"Demetrius!"

At the sound of Ajax's voice, one of the labouring men straightened and turned around, and Varrus felt his jaw drop. He snapped it shut immediately, fairly sure no one had noticed.

Demetrius Hanno was not merely huge. He was a giant, head and shoulders taller than the next-tallest man there, and with the slab-like facial features common to all giants. Varrus had first seen one—a real giant—when he was ten years old, but that had been a shambling, piteous, almost witless creature whose life had been shamelessly twisted to provide a source of endless, mindless awe and laughter to others, whether he performed feats of superhuman strength or capered pathetically in shackles, chained to an equally malformed dwarf.

This giant, Varrus could see, was no halfwit. He had the massive, distinctive face, the heavy, hanging brows and jutting jaws, and the flattened cheekbones and pendulous lips of the other giants Varrus had seen, but the deep-set eyes that peered out from under the shaggy, undivided brow were bright with light and intellect. Varrus saw the way they scanned him, head to toe, cataloguing everything about him, from the way he stood to the angle of his head as he gazed back directly into them.

"This is Mcuil," Ajax said. "I'll leave him with you. I have to go and talk to Pella. That idiot Saros was over here, moving the stock into precisely the wrong place after I told him specifically where it ought to go." He turned to Varrus. "Fingael Mcuil, this is Demetrius Hanno. He'll see to you from here. I'll speak with both of you again later." He combined a clenched-fist military salute with a good-natured nod, then turned and walked away.

"Come," Demetrius Hanno said, and Varrus followed him into an interior room at the back of the smithy. It was obviously Hanno's personal domain, for the furnishings were made to fit his enormous size. "No one disturbs me here," the giant said. "I call it my sanctum, and no one ever enters it other than by my leave. Sit." He indicated a pair of normally sized chairs that looked like children's seats beside the other furniture in the room, and lowered himself into the cushioned wooden armchair behind the huge work table. He reached down to the floor and brought up Varrus's blade. He looked at it expressionlessly, then laid it flat on the table and pushed it across towards Varrus with one finger, spinning it slightly as it went.

"Ajax saw something in this," he said, and his voice suited his appearance, emerging as a long, deeply resonant series of rumbling sounds, although every word, every individual syllable, was clearly articulated. "What it was, I do not know, but whatever it was, it caught his attention instantly. In truth, I do not know if I would have seen it, or paid attention to it. But that is your good fortune, and now you have the opportunity to benefit by it. Ajax is master here in the armouries, not I, but it is my good fortune to be able to assist him."

The giant leaned forward and picked up the blade again, then held it up in front of him and pinged the nail of his middle finger against the slight but prominent ridge of metal that ran along the centre of the blade, from the boss to within a finger's breadth of the point. "Tell me about this ridge," he said. "This . . . spine."

"Spine is correct," Varrus said. "That's what Rhys Twohands called it."

"Who is Rhys Twohands?"

"He is— He was my teacher. My boyhood teacher. He's dead now. But he it was who taught me how to make a blade. No, that's not true, either. He *tried* to teach me how to make a blade, but I was too young to learn at first, and there was never enough time afterwards. And where we lived then, he could never find the kind of fuel he needed for the forge."

"He had no fuel for his forge, a smith?"

"No, there was plenty of fuel. We used the same charcoal as all the other smiths. But for the work Rhys wished to do—the crafts he had been taught over years by an exiled Persian smith, the knowledge he wanted to pass on to me, in turn—that fuel was not good enough, he said. Time after time, for years, I heard him say that, and he was always working to prove himself wrong. He never did, though. The charcoal we had would not burn hot enough, and he could never build a bellows big enough to do what he wanted most to do. His employer—"

He stopped, having almost blurted out that Rhys's employer had been his own father, Marcus Varrus. He drew a deep breath, composing himself. "His master had no interest in the things Rhys dreamed about. He wanted only implements his slaves could use to till the ground and harvest the crops, and he would not waste money on a furnace he believed he didn't need. So Rhys swallowed his dreams and taught me simpler things. But he always said that someday he would teach me how the ancient Persians made their blades—the blades that could bend double and spring back into shape, their edges unharmed and so keen that men could sometimes make them sing."

"But he did not."

"No. He died before he could."

"So he taught you nothing."

"It was what he taught me that Ajax saw in my blade there. The spine, as you called it. Rhys was never able to make his ancient sword, but he never stopped trying, even though the tools he had were inadequate.

And I paid attention to everything he did and listened to everything he said, even when he knew he would not succeed. I could see what he was trying to achieve, and I understood why he could not achieve it."

"And why was that?"

"Because his tools were what they were and his fire was—"

"No. I meant, why could you see what he was trying to achieve?"

Varrus blinked, as if unable to believe that Hanno had failed to grasp what he had said. "Because I had been *listening*," he said. "Because he was my *teacher*. I understood everything he told me. I knew how the process was supposed to unfold, how it would have unfolded had he been able to create a fire hot enough to do what needed to be done. But he couldn't . . ."

They sat in silence for long moments, interrupted only by occasional ear-shattering bursts of noise from the work outside, and then Hanno rose abruptly to his feet, his movements precise and deliberate.

"Come," he said, and once again Varrus followed him meekly until he heard a deep-throated roaring noise somewhere ahead of him and turned around the corner of a sooty brick wall to see a sight that made him forget everything else he had seen and heard that morning.

He was standing in one corner of a huge, rectangular, brick-paved open-air space enclosed on three sides by high, windowless brick-walled buildings, and in the exact centre of the space, isolated from everything around it by an encircling walkway five or more paces wide, stood a single but complex structure: the tallest, largest brick-clad furnace he had ever seen. It looked as though it incorporated two separate, over-sized ovens, but otherwise it was comparable in every detail to every other furnace he had seen, yet as different to all of them as Demetrius Hanno was to other men. Most of all, though, it made him think immediately of Dominic Mcuil's tall oven, and he resolved to find some way of discovering, discreetly, if there was more of a connection between Dominic Mcuil and these men here than he had suspected.

The air between him and the outer wall of the kiln shimmered from the heat being thrown out, and he noted now each feature of the thing, including a long, glazed earthen pipe, as wide as the chest of a large man, that emerged from the ground close to the base of the furnace wall and tapered to less than a quarter of its size before it disappeared into the brickwork. He turned to the giant, who was eyeing him.

"Bellows?" he asked, and went on without waiting for an answer. "Tubular air chutes, piston driven, powered by a waterwheel on the far side of that wall. Am I correct?"

Hanno inclined his head. "Correct," he said. "You have seen such a device before now?"

"Aye, very similar but much smaller, in my uncle Dominic's forge."

The giant indicated the high furnace. "Would this have pleased your friend Rhys Twohands, think you?"

"I believe the very sight of it would have gladdened him. Does it burn hotter than other furnaces?"

"It does, as I differ from dwarves."

"Hmm. And what are those?" He nodded towards a wide rectangular board equipped with long carrying handles and shoulder straps and loaded with thick, empty earthen bowls, some of them nested inside one another and all of them heavy looking. They were made from a material he did not recognize.

"Those are crucibles," Hanno said. "They probably mean nothing to you now, but you will come to know them well."

Varrus nodded, and looked around him one more time. "Rhys would have loved this," he said, "and I will hope to earn the privilege of working here."

Hanno nodded his huge head impassively. "I believe you might," he said.

SEVENTEEN

Throughout the month that followed, Varrus spent most of his time head to head or side by side with Demetrius Hanno, bent over an anvil as the big man hammer-welded metal strips or gazing down with him at drawings on a workbench as Hanno sought to perfect the tapered outline of a cutting edge or an emerging sword blade. Varrus seldom spoke, but by that time, whenever he did say something, his words were heeded, and though his opinions might later be dismissed, Hanno always discussed their dismissal with him, analyzing their weaknesses so that his student was constantly learning.

The true beginnings of his comprehension of where his studies might be going, though, came on a morning when he had been watching his mentor finishing a blade, shaping it effortlessly into a long, slender, flawless weapon with a barely discernible leaf-waisted flair in the first third of its length. Varrus had been watching the birth of this particular piece, admiring the care and attention with which Hanno had used a round-nosed chisel to fashion the delicately graduated twin channels flanking the central spine, and he was now anticipating the pleasure of watching the giant start smoothing and burnishing the lovely blade and adding a hilt. He was astounded, then, when Hanno hoisted it up to eye level with the tongs, studied it for several moments, hefted it speculatively, and then turned away to bury it in the coals of the forge again.

"What are you doing?" Varrus made no attempt to mask the horror in his voice, and Hanno glanced sideways at him.

The giant selected a long, slender rod from the pile beside him and thrust it, too, into the forge beside the blade. "It needs to be a little heavier," he said.

"But it was perfect!"

Again came that sideways glance. "No. Had it been perfect there would be no need to add more weight. It was flawed—too light. What frightens you?"

"Frightens me? Nothing frightens me. It simply seems like a waste—a waste of time, more than anything else."

The giant turned down his lips and tilted his head sideways. "Time well spent is never wasted. This will be a better blade next time. Are you afraid the metal will grow soft, with too much forging?"

"No! That's nonsense. You know that's not why I objected."

"Then why *did* you object?"

"Because it was done! It was beautiful and you threw it back into the fire. Some soldier might have taken great pleasure in owning that sword."

To Varrus's astonishment, Demetrius Hanno began to smile, and his gigantic features were transformed. He stood up and flexed his enormous shoulders, then bent his elbows and clenched his fists, twisting slowly from the waist, first left, then right. When he was done, he picked up his tongs again and removed the barely heated sword blade and the fresh metal rod from the charcoal, setting them side by side on the brickwork edge of the firepit. "We can reheat these later," he said. "For now, walk with me."

He crossed directly to a wall cabinet that contained finished samples of some of the work his people had produced in the armouries. He picked out two Hispanic swords and hefted them, one in each hand, before replacing one and closing the cabinet. He tested the edge of the sword he had chosen with his thumb, then made his way outside, into the vastness of the high-roofed, clamorous armouries, carrying the naked blade. There, to Varrus's surprise, the giant ambled about aimlessly, looking all about him as he weaved his way around and between obstacles until he reached a junction of two wide pathways, where he stopped, staring off to his right before he straightened up to his full height and headed off in that direction. Varrus followed him, but saw no attraction there, other than a pair of legionaries in the distance, talking with one of the armoury's staff, recognizable by his dark grey tunic.

That, though, was indeed what had attracted Demetrius Hanno, for he made directly towards the distant trio, shouting to them to wait. They stopped talking, watching curiously as he and Varrus approached. Hanno flipped the sword he had been carrying and held it out, hilt first, to the decanus, who took it hesitantly, his eyes shifting nervously from Hanno to Varrus and back, wondering what was happening here.

"Swing it, try it," Hanno ordered, and the fellow did so, tentatively at first, and then more boldly as he began to appreciate the weight and balance of the weapon in his hand. "You like it?"

The man's eyes widened and he nodded.

"It's yours, then," came the growling rumble. "Take it and look after it well. But give me yours, the one in your belt."

Mystified, but agreeably, the decanus did as he was bidden, and Hanno thanked him with a nod that included the other two men, then strode away again, retracing his route until he and Varrus were back at the smithy.

"Now," the smith said. "Watch this."

He went straight to a heavy vise bolted to one of the wooden workbenches and spun its screw open far enough to let him insert the first six inches of the decanus's blade vertically between the jaws. "Six *unciae*," he growled. "Far enough to clear the point and isolate the blade." He took hold of the sword's upright hilt, the heel of his hand down so that the boss of the hilt showed above his thumb. "This is a standard, state-issued

Hispanic sword, selected at random, as you witnessed, from the equipment of a serving soldier of decanus rank. This is the weapon that ensured Rome's conquests and carved out its empire. Now watch."

He flexed his fingers and then gripped the sword tightly, and Varrus watched in awe as the enormous muscles in the giant's arm twisted into corded knots from the pressure he was exerting. And then, slowly, the blade began to bend and buckle, yielding with a stressful groaning sound until it was barely recognizable as having been a sword at all.

"The noise came from the friction between the blade and the jaws of the vise," Hanno said. "Swords do not scream as they bend. That is reserved for people to do."

Varrus had been watching grimly as the sword blade twisted and bent. "Tell me, then," he said. "What did all that achieve?"

"To this point? Nothing at all, except to demonstrate that the blade was of inferior quality. But if the demonstration of that inferiority enables you to see from now on that we, as weapons smiths and sword makers, have responsibilities, then it will have served its purpose. Our sole purpose as makers of blades should be to ensure that those blades are as close to indestructible as we can make them. The moment you accept that as the truth that governs your life as a smith, your life itself will change." He loosened the jaws of the vise, pulled out the ruined weapon, and tossed it casually on top of a pile of scraps waiting to be melted down and reused. "You cannot degrade a blade by reforging it, unless you are unforgivably careless. Reforging enhances the best features of your metal—makes it more malleable, more ductile, more willing to be shaped and handled. Do you remember asking me about the crucibles?"

"I do. By the furnace oven."

"It is time now for you to learn what we use them for. Or do you know already?"

Varrus shook his head slowly. "I know nothing about them, save that they looked heavy and I didn't recognize the material they were made from."

Hanno nodded gravely. "Many smiths are strange people," he said quietly, without making any effort to explain his change of topic. "Taciturn, moody, often solitary and secretive by nature. Jealous of their knowledge and unwilling to share it."

"Cooks are the same way," Varrus said, smiling.

Hanno looked down at him sharply. "What did you say?"

"I said cooks are the same, the same as smiths, solitary and secretive, afraid of having people steal their most precious secrets."

"That is absolutely true," the giant said, his face awash with astonishment. "I had never thought of it before. What made you think of it?"

"I knew a cook like that once, in Dalmatia. He ran a large kitchen and could feed more than a hundred people at a time, and his food was famous. There were things that he alone knew how to do, dishes and intricate blends of tastes and flavours that he alone could make. But even though I was a young boy, I could see he lived in fear of someone stealing his secrets, for they were what kept him separate from other, lesser cooks."

Hanno was nodding. "And so he kept them to himself, safe in his head. That surpasses simple selfishness or foolishness, for when such people die, whatever special knowledge they have dies with them and is lost forever. That is why those of us who are glad to share our knowledge are grateful to be able to do so. Your friend Rhys Twohands was one of those, the enlightened kind. I fear, though, that he never even knew what he was lacking—" He held up a hand to forestall Varrus's protest. "It is true," he insisted. "You told me so yourself, by your failure to recognize those crucibles. Time now to learn," he said. "But notice I do not say to understand, for no one seems to really understand what I will tell you now. It is all mystery and sorcery."

He looked around to see what everyone else was doing, and apparently seeing nothing to cause him concern, he beckoned with his head and led Varrus again into his sanctum, where he waved him to a chair and sat at his table, thinking and frowning for a few moments before he began to speak.

"You know that we smelt iron and then work it to remove impurities, and you know the metal thus made is called wrought iron. Beyond that point, though, no one knows anything with certainty. Clear understanding stops and the mysterious ways of the gods assume control. The deities inform us what we ought to do."

"Do you mean Vulcan?"

Hanno shrugged massively. "We assume that Vulcan's is the loudest voice in this arena, but who can say with certainty? The gods are gods. We are but men. The gods permit us to achieve the things they wish us to achieve, but at the same time, they defy us to understand why we should achieve what we then do. And that is more true with iron than with any other thing I know. We, being mere men, fail to understand what we are doing, even while achieving the results the gods decreed. Are you understanding me thus far?"

"I believe so. You are saying we do what we do in ignorance of how we do it."

"Not quite. We do what we do in ignorance of *why* we do it. The how is straightforward. We follow the rules we were taught by our own teachers. In time, if you follow faithfully the rules I will teach you, you will be able to do everything I do, and if I have taught you well, you should be able to surpass me in skill one day. That is simple truth, dictated by logic. But in the making of strong blades, logic has no validity. And so at times we must rely on simple faith, and place our trust in matters that appear to be sorcerous. Tell me about the Persian smith who taught your friend Rhys."

The shift left Varrus blinking. "I— I don't know much at all," he said, looking bewildered. "I never asked about him. Rhys spoke of him from time to time, and always with affection, but I didn't know the man. He died years before I was born."

Hanno nodded his great head slowly. "That is reasonable, but think hard, for it could be important, and I believe you may find you know more about the man than you believe you do. Take as much

time as you need. When you are ready to tell me what you can, I will
be outside."

Perhaps half an hour had elapsed when Varrus opened the door again
and joined Hanno, and the two went back into the sanctum. Hanno
was carrying two steaming drinks, one of them in a pot that must have
held five or six times as much as the mug he passed to Varrus, who
raised it to his face and sniffed the fragrant steam deeply.

"That smells wonderful," he said. "What is it?"

"The juice of crushed apples," the big man said. "Heated and sweetened with honey and cinnamon. Do you know cinnamon?"

Varrus nodded. "From when I was a boy, in Dalmatia. It brings back
memories."

Hanno smiled. "And speaking of that, what have you remembered
about your friend's Persian?"

Varrus wrapped both hands around the barrel of his mug and sipped
from it cautiously, reluctant to consume it too quickly. "His name was
Agaton—there was more to it than that, but that's what Rhys called
him. Rhys's people were fisher folk who lived on the northern coast of
Eire, and they took in Agaton when he was washed up from the sea after
a storm. That was before Rhys was born.

"He had worked as a smith in Persia, and his skills were highly
valued by Rhys's people, for they had no other smith. They built him a
smithy, but the tools Agaton made for them were poor things, because
he could never make his fires burn at the kind of heat he spoke of having used in Persia, so he was never able to create the kind of metal that
he needed to make swords like the one he'd made for himself. Rhys
spoke often of that sword, of how fine and how sharp it was. He told
me it could cut a falling feather in half, and that its blade could not be
blunted by other blades, for it would cut them in half as easily as it
would the feather. That sounded incredible to me—it still does—but

Rhys swore he had seen it do so with his own eyes." He sighed. "I believed him then, and I believe him still. I believe that sword existed."

"I do, too," the giant said, in what was, for him, a very quiet murmur. "I have seen such swords. Very few, but they were truly wondrous, so flexible and finely made that they could bend in half and immediately spring back into perfect shape. So tell me more about this Agaton, and how he taught your friend."

"He taught him all he could, according to the materials he had at hand. He smelted iron from red ore he found in the neighbouring hills, but he had to be content to work with all its imperfections. It was fortunate that what the village needed most were simple iron tools and utensils, for the smith had no way of hardening or tempering the iron he produced, other than case-hardening a few chopping tools. But yet he taught young Rhys the elements of forging and annealing metal, and taught him how to weld and shape a spined blade in the style, if not the substance, of the Persian sword, which was curved, Rhys said."

"So your friend taught you the art of case-hardening?"

"He taught me how to case-harden a blade, if that's what you mean, but he never spoke of it as being an art."

"Oh, it is, when done properly, and it produces wondrous results for certain tasks, like putting a hard edge on a wrought iron blade. How did your man do it?"

Varrus hitched one shoulder. "Is there more than one way?"

"Of course there is, just as there is in doing most things. How did he teach you to do it?"

"By making a soft blade, then packing it in a tight-bound and clamped mixture of ground bones and charcoal and reforging it. The outer surface hardens and will hold an edge, but the inner core remains wrought-iron soft, strong and resilient."

The giant nodded. "That is the common method. Another is to pack the blade in a mixture of ground hooves, salt, and shredded leather mixed with urine and then reforge it. The sealing of the box containing the mixture apparently has great importance, in both instances, to the success of the procedure, but no one can say why." He flexed his shoulders again. "I know there is no resemblance between the two methods, and no defensible reason why either one should work, but both of them do, so who are we to quibble?" He paused. "So where did your friend Rhys end up?"

Varrus grinned. "The same place we have ended up. Searching for the secrets of forging stronger metals. He spent years in the army, as an armourer, then worked for a wealthy merchant, delivering military supplies to the legions. When the merchant retired, he took Rhys to live with him on his estate, as his smith. I met him there, for my father worked in that villa, too."

"And the Persian. What became of him?"

"He died, a long time ago, but that's all I know." He stopped and his eyes narrowed. "What? There's something in your eyes. Some doubt. I can see it."

The big man nodded. "I doubt he was a smith at all. Your friend's tutor, the Persian. He had worked in a smithy, that's clear, perhaps as an apprentice or trainee—he might even have been a slave—but he could not have been a smith. And he most certainly did not make that wondrous sword himself."

Varrus was frowning now. "How could he not have been a smith? What are you saying?"

The big man grimaced. He picked up his cider pot, peered down into it, then set it down again. "Empty," he said regretfully. "I don't remember drinking all that . . . I am saying that this man had rudimentary knowledge of the craft he claimed. He had sufficient knowledge to build a smelting oven and produce wrought iron, and he had the basic skills to fashion tools from that and do some primitive metal crafting. Fortunately for him, he needed no more than that, working with iron among your friend's fisher folk people. Bear in mind what the ancients said about people who have such good fortune. In the land of the blind, the one-eyed man is king."

Varrus shook his head. "No. I told you, he was hampered by the fuel he had to use, the peat. He could not generate or sustain high heat."

Every aspect of Hanno's giant face showed his scorn. "Am I then to believe that in all of Eire there are no smiths to make weapons for the throngs of warriors described by every soldier who has landed there since the time of Claudius? That no one, in all that land, understands the making of strong fighting blades? And so there was no one, anywhere, to whom this man could turn for assistance, in desperation?"

He shook his head with finality. "Had your Persian really been a smith, Mcuil, he would have known about the second stage of making superior iron, and clearly he did not. And there can be only one reason for that. He had not been taught." He crinkled his eyes at Varrus. "I said that smiths are secretive by nature, jealous of their knowledge and unwilling to share any of it with people they consider undeserving. That, I have been told, is especially true of the Persian smiths, where their lore is considered precious beyond price, to be safeguarded at all costs."

"From slaves, you mean."

"No. I mean from everyone who is not among the elect, the sacred smiths. Even here, in the army of our state, we grade our students with great care. Not one of them can ever advance in his training without having proved beyond a doubt that he has earned the right to learn more. That is all part and parcel of craftsmanship, of establishing and maintaining standards by which we can abide and prosper. And the truth of that enables me to look at any smith and know, within moments, how far his training has advanced." The great head cocked to one side as the deep basso voice growled, "You are aware of that, I hope."

"I am. What you say is true."

"That rule is strict here, but it is far more so among the smiths of Persia, I have been told. No ill-trained pretender would ever be permitted access to the secrets of their guilds. Had your Persian been a smith, he would have known, and understood beyond doubt, the second step to making better iron. He would have learned the secrets of the oven and the crucible. And despite all the difficulties he encountered later, had he even known of those secrets, or heard about them and their uses, he would have—must have—spoken of them to your friend. But Rhys Twohands never spoke to you of crucibles."

Varrus shook his head in reluctant agreement, but then added, as an afterthought, "But could Rhys not have learned about them otherwise, in his time with the legions?"

"He might have," the giant said quietly, "if he had worked in places where the crude metal was prepared. But there are few of those. For the most part, those few places—armouries like this one, all of them near the sea or on navigable rivers—have an area specially made for that kind of work, because it is incessant, and the furnaces are never cold. They make iron constantly, with shifts of slaves labouring day and night to keep the process flowing smoothly. And then they ship the finished goods in trains of wagons, in bars and rods and ingots, to the docks, where they are loaded onto ships and distributed throughout the empire."

"Would it not be easier to—?"

"To have every garrison produce its own? No, it would not, and if you but think about it you will soon see the chaos that would result from such laxity. Production on the scale required to supply the legions is an enormous task, and it demands highly disciplined maintenance and meticulous controls. The individual crucibles yield very small amounts of metal, and they have to be small in size, though please do not ask me why that should be so, because that falls within the realm of mystery. So the oven racks are built to hold as many as they can. But that capacity, too, depends upon the size of the oven and the bellows."

"And so places like this contain many furnaces and ovens," Varrus concluded.

"Correct."

"And like me, most people never suspect that such places exist."

"Also correct, although no one tries to conceal them. People simply do not care. They have other matters to concern them, and though iron

governs their lives in many ways, the matter of making it has no importance to them."

Varrus sat silent for a while, mulling over what he had been told
before he asked his next question.

"These crucibles," he said. "What do they do? What is this second
step you spoke of?"

"It is the next step into the mysteries the gods keep hidden from us.
The crucible is a key to understanding their will, but it is an imperfect
key. It works as they intended it to work, but it does not permit us to see
how it works, because it works within the furnace. Come with me now.
I'll show you."

EIGHTEEN

Ignatius Ajax arrived as they were leaving, meeting them at the door of Hanno's sanctum. He said nothing of why he had come. He simply looked at both of them with a raised eyebrow, stepped aside with a sweep of one arm to allow them to pass him, then fell into step behind them. The armourer was wearing armour again, but it was a simple leather harness, scuffed in places where he had bruised it in the course of his work, and his wearing of it indicated he had been conducting business in the headquarters building that day.

Hanno spoke over his shoulder to Ajax. "It has come time for Mcuil to learn about the second step," he said.

"That was quick," Ajax responded, sounding not at all surprised and speaking as if Varrus were nowhere near. "I thought he'd take another month, at least. That's what we talked about, you and I, not ten days ago. What happened to make you change your mind?"

Hanno stopped so abruptly that Varrus, directly at his back, walked right into him and had to step back hastily as the giant turned around to face the armourer.

"He told me about cooks," he said.

"Cooks." Ajax looked from Hanno to Varrus. "You talked about cooks. That's very . . . profound. Is it not?"

"Not profound," came the reply. "But relevant. And you have never thought of it before, any more than I had."

"You might well be correct, because I have no idea what you're talking about."

The giant swung away, walking again until he reached the yard with the tall furnace, then went through a door that Varrus had not noticed before. Inside, the walls were lined with sturdy, waist-high workbenches, some with low shelves mounted above them, and all with much-used storage space beneath. Varrus saw metal bins and large wooden barrels, and in one corner, a low-sided wooden box full of high-grade, glossy charcoal. The room was bright and airy, thanks to the rows of narrow windows lining two exterior walls. The three men working in there had all stopped what they were doing when the door opened, and the giant dismissed them with a wordless grunt and an unmistakable jerk of his head. They left immediately, without so much as a glance at either Ajax or Varrus.

As soon as the door closed behind them, Hanno spread his arms dramatically, indicating the room and all its contents.

"I'm waiting," Ajax said, after an uncomprehending look around. "Enlighten me, O Wise One."

"Mcuil observed that cooks are like smiths. Both are secretive, jealous of what they know, afraid of being robbed of their ideas, their knowledge, their hard-won experience and expertise."

"No one can steal experience."

"No, but they can steal secrets, which in turn may enable a clever thief to claim expertise . . . The expertise of processing iron blades, for one thing."

"And how is that like cooking? Because the cook and the smith both wear aprons?"

Hanno gave Ajax a pitying look. "A cook fears to lose his secrets of preparing food. A smith fears losing his secrets of preparing metal. And in a parallel unseen before today, a smith cooks his creations with great similarity to how a cook prepares his finest meals. Wait! Before you say more, look."

He stepped to the workbench running along the wall beside the door and gently folded back the long white cloth that covered the items laid out on it. One of them was a heavy bowl with thumb-thick sides, and he picked it up and threw it casually to Varrus, who caught it easily but came close to falling backwards with the unexpected weight of it.

"That is a crucible," Hanno said. "You already know that."

"What's it made of?" Varrus tried not to gasp with the effort of holding it motionless.

"Fire clay."

"Fire clay." He grappled with the rough-surfaced thing until he had it firmly grasped in both hands, then braced himself and held it up and out as though to weigh it. He could not decide whether it had been thrown on a wheel or made by hand.

"And where would a man find fire clay?"

"Here?" Hanno pointed with his chin. "In one of those barrels beneath the bench over there. Look for yourself."

Varrus set down the crucible, then lifted a loose lid on one of the barrels and saw bricks of greyish clay, immersed in water. He hesitated, then answered his own unvoiced question. "Of course. To stop the clay from drying out." He looked to Ajax, whose lips were pursed and whose eyes looked speculative, then at Demetrius Hanno. "This must have something to do with the second step you spoke of."

"Everything. And everything to do with those unknown ways of gods that I spoke of. And now it has also to do with the secret formulas of cooks." He stepped over to where a number of long cloth aprons hung from a row of pegs along the wall. "Mcuil," he said, taking an apron from the end peg and slipping it over his huge head before tying it around his waist, "I know you have been in a crowded kitchen before now, when you lived in your villa in Dalmatia, but, Ajax, tell me, have you ever been in one?"

"In a kitchen?" Ajax looked amused. "What kind of question is that? Of course I have."

"Ah, I know you have, Natius, but what I really meant was, have you ever looked at what is there, at the heart of a large kitchen, where the senior cooks prepare their finest, most jealously guarded dishes?" He paused, looking expectant, then said, "No? I thought not. Well, look now, because it differs little from this."

Ajax cocked his head, not quite smiling. "Demetrius, my friend, should I be concerned about you? Are you feeling unwell?"

"No, Natius, my friend, you should not. I am merely amazed by how unobservant I have been. You know my friend Claudius Casper, do you not? His rank is yours."

Ajax jerked his head in acknowledgment. "Quartermaster's centuriate, both of us. I run the armouries, he runs the caterers."

"No, he has responsibility for the catering division, but he actually *runs* the kitchens. And he permits me to stand beside him, talking with him while he works, even while he is preparing banquets."

"So?"

"He has no fear I might steal his secrets, because he knows I have no slightest knowledge of what he does. He has no fear of me, no jealousy. Because I offer him no threat. And yet we both go about our work in exactly the same way." He waved his hand again towards the bench, including Varrus in his invitation to look. "For you were right, we both wear aprons to protect our clothing. We both assemble, measure, and prepare our ingredients in advance, with great care, and then we mix and blend them, with great care, in order to achieve a desired effect. We cook them in an oven, with great care, paying attention to the cooking time and to the way we remove them afterwards, with greater care than ever, from the heat . . . And I cannot believe that has escaped my notice until now."

"Ingredients," Varrus said, looking at the contents of the tabletop.

"Precisely." Hanno reached into a large, deep, wide-mouthed jar and pulled out a fistful of whatever was in there, then opened his fingers to let it fall onto the workbench with a sound like falling gravel. "What is it?" he asked Varrus.

Varrus picked up a few pea-sized pieces and examined them. They were tiny drops of solid metal, heavy, dark grey and flecked with black. "Iron?" he asked. "Bits of iron?"

"Bits of wrought iron. Yes. But specially prepared for this process. Smelted and hammered to remove most of the slag, though not all of it. That remaining slag is of great importance to us, but we do not know why. And so, for this procedure, we do not hammer the entire mass until we drive out all the slag, as we do in creating cleanly wrought iron. We work it slowly instead, until the iron, which is porous and sponge-like at this stage, falls apart in tiny pieces. When that happens, we stop and gather the pieces and the slag that still pollutes them, and we wash them carefully, taking care not to dislodge the slag that still adheres to them."

He swept the spilled handful of iron bits into his other palm, dropped them into the crucible, and added the same amount again.

"So. There is our main ingredient. To that we add the enhancers, the additives that will impart the magic and add allure to the final product, thus."

He bent beneath the tabletop, reaching for the box of charcoal. He gathered up a large handful, then began to break the individual lengths of brittle, black, powdery fuel into pieces smaller than a thumb pad, placing them in the crucible. When he was done, he mixed them with his fingers, grinding them against the iron beads. That done to his satisfaction, he dusted his hands off over the bowl and reached for another wide-mouthed jar, this one capped with a disk of dried cork. He removed the cap and pulled out a few dull but still green leaves, then placed them, one at a time, over the mixture he had prepared.

"For succulence," he said, but offered no other words to explain either what they were or what purpose they served. Finally, after a glance around the tabletop, he reached into a large, pot-bellied clay vessel against the wall, more like an urn than a jar, and scooped out first one handful, then another, of a dull greyish-white powder, which he shaped into a conical pile on the table's surface.

"What's that?" Varrus asked him.

"Crushed seashells. Limpets and oysters. We add them thus." He scooped up a handful and poured it gently over the mixture in the crucible, directing the falling powder towards the most obvious holes between pieces, and continuing, adding more of the powder from the urn, until there was nothing visible in the crucible beneath the even surface of the powdered shells. When he was satisfied, he smoothed the surface gently, leaving a space of about half a thumbnail's length between it and the upper rim of the crucible.

"Is that it?" Varrus was not even sure what his question meant, but he felt disappointed, cheated almost, though he could not have explained why, and from the way the giant looked at him, he could see that Hanno had noticed.

"No," Hanno said. "That is the mixture of ingredients. It remains now to place the crust on the pie." He reached out his giant, questing hand yet again.

Varrus had seen the disk of damp clay leaning against the wall at the back of the table. Now, Hanno picked it up gently by its edges, then flipped it over and held it on the extended fingers of his huge left hand, exposing an inset flange around the rim of the disk. Without removing his eyes from the lid, he groped with his right hand for another jar, this one with its sides slick and coated with wet clay, and Varrus slid it closer to him. The smith grunted in thanks, then reached in and scooped up a handful of wet clay, transferring it to the outer edge of the flange and spreading it liberally, one-handed, smearing it thickly until the entire flange was covered. He then scooped up more of the clay mixture, squeezed it between his fingers over the neck of the jar to make its consistency thinner and more pliable, and applied a generous coating of it to the top of the crucible itself. Then he used both hands to settle the sealing lid atop the crucible, pressing it firmly into place.

"There," he said, giving the lid a last downwards push. "That is it, for the time being, at least. Now it simply has to be cooked."

"Why must it be sealed so tightly?"

"Another mystery. But all of us who use this method know that if it is not sealed perfectly, the process will fail. The same applies to the powdered seashells. No one knows their purpose, but none of us doubts that they have one. Prepare the crucible perfectly in every way, take fullest care with every aspect, then omit the seashells, or substitute some other compound in their place, and your process will fail. The metal obtained from it will be inferior. No one knows why, but that has been proved, time and again, ad nauseam."

Ignatius Ajax watched Varrus keenly as he asked his next question. "What about the cooking? Which oven do you use? The big one outside?"

"Why would you think that?" Hanno replied.

Varrus sucked on something in his teeth, then looked from one to the other of the two men. "Because it is big, because it is right outside, and because it's the only one out there. There are fifteen smelting furnaces and ovens in this armoury—I've gone around and counted them—but none of them comes close to the one outside this room, either in volume or capacity."

Hanno looked over at Ajax, who looked straight back at him in silence, and then his mouth twisted into a lopsided smile. "And what do you construe from that?"

Varrus hesitated, aware that he was on the point of saying something he might later regret. Now he thrust his thumbs down into his belt, beneath his apron, his eyes going to Ignatius Ajax first, then to Demetrius Hanno. "May I speak my mind, without fear of being punished?"

The giant shrugged. "So be you say nothing punishable, yes."

Varrus caught his breath, then plunged. "I think there is more here than people know."

The other two men looked at each other blankly, and then Ajax asked, "Which people are you talking about?"

"The people with the power to stop whatever is happening here. The legate, I presume. The high command."

Hanno made to speak, but Ajax stopped him with an upraised hand. "Go on. What else do you think?"

"Well, I know you are the garrison armourer, a commissary centurion, as you say. But I don't think you are a smith. Demetrius Hanno is certainly a smith, but you seem not to be. And yet you two are friends and you spend more time daily in the smithy here, talking to Demetrius Hanno, than you do anywhere else. It's almost as if you two were conspirators or secret collaborators. But in what? I have been asking myself for some time now, what could you two be sharing that the authorities might want to terminate?"

Ignatius Ajax smiled with half his face, the right side of his mouth curving upwards to expose a gleam of teeth. "And have you found an answer to give yourself?" The smile widened, barely perceptibly. "I warn you, you should think before you say more, because I'm remembering stories I was told as a child, about Julius Caesar at the Rubicon River."

Varrus shook his head. He was committed to his course now. "The legate here, Lucius Placidus Pompey, is not respected. He has authority, but despite his august name, he lacks credibility, and his behaviour is scandalous by any measure. Even the merchants and street vendors in the town know that. The man is venal and grasping, vain and petty. But as legate he is protected by the full, majestic force of imperial law against anything that might resemble mutiny. The single man in all of Britain who could demote or remove him is the colonial governor, and he is overseas with the Emperor." He stopped, slightly out of breath, looking again from one to the other of his listeners. "Have I yet crossed the Rubicon?"

Ajax made a face. "Well, you have certainly earned a charge of mutiny and sedition. But you have said nothing of this alleged conspiracy between myself and Demetrius Hanno. What is it that we are, allegedly, conspiring to protect or conceal?"

The silence now was deafening. Varrus glanced quickly sideways at Ajax, but the armourer was bending forward with his arms crossed, his backside against the edge of a workbench and his helmeted head down, concealing his face. He looked back at Hanno defiantly.

"Testing new metals. Forging new kinds of weapons. You, Magister Hanno, are a smith. A very fine one. That is evident. But all you want to do is what you do. You want to make better swords and you have little patience for anything that interferes with that—including officious busybodies and incompetent superiors."

He turned to Ajax, who kept his head lowered, refusing to look up as Varrus spoke to the crest of his helmet. "You, Magister Ajax, are an armourer and a collector of fine blades. Far more important than all that, though, you are a leader and an organizer. You understand what the management of a complex manufactory entails, and even more, you understand the ways and means of avoiding official interference and circumventing unnecessary procedures. Most important of all, you understand the methods by which a legion and a garrison function effectively—this garrison, most particularly. You appreciate that once a garrison is deemed ineffectual or moribund, its days are numbered. So you work very hard to keep this one functioning smoothly and efficiently by presenting flawless, unfailing results from your armouries. By processing a seemingly inexhaustible supply of weapons and iron bars. And thanks to that, Legate Pompey smiles on everything you do. He depends upon you to keep his career presentable, and you work hard to do that—not because you want to, but because you know that by doing it, you can keep him blind to what is happening beneath his nose, in his armouries.

"What do I think you two are conspiring over? I believe you are conducting experiments that no one in authority has authorized— building furnaces and ovens unlike any others, and working on new ways of hardening metal. For that, you have built the high ovens by the smithy, but even so, you cannot produce all the high-quality metal you need, and so you have an arrangement with my uncle in Londinium, Dominic Mcuil, whereby he sends you the output from his special oven to augment your own production. And in return, you send him illicit supplies of iron ore from all over the empire, materials intended for the military, not a civilian contractor like himself. So there is the partnership. Demetrius Hanno handles the unseen experiments and in turn you keep him safe from the attentions of the praetorium and the legate."

He stopped, having finally run out of words, and for long moments no one moved and his heart sank as he recognized, too late, the enormity of what he had said. He kept his eyes focused straight ahead, staring at the large jar of powdered seashells on the workbench and hearing his own inner voice raging at him for being such an idiot, for condemning himself so damningly that nothing he could do or say thereafter could ever change anything he had said.

And then Ignatius Ajax, who was still slouching against the bench with his head down and his arms crossed, sniffed loudly and lifted his head, turning to Demetrius Hanno.

"Moribund, he said. And ineffectual. Have you ever heard an Eirish barbarian speak like that before? That fluently and with so much conviction? I told you he was one to watch, did I not?" He turned back to Varrus. "I came here today to talk to you about something that came to me almost by accident, in that I was there when it arrived and someone recognized your name and knew you worked for me."

Varrus was left open-mouthed by the change of topic, and several moments passed before he was able to ask, "What about it?"

"Your name? It's Mcuil. You should know that better than I do."

"No, I mean, what about everything I've been saying here?"

"What about it? You had most of it right. All of it, in fact. So are you in or out?" He saw the look of utter confusion on Varrus's face and added, "The *alleged* conspiracy, I mean. Are you in or not?"

"I don't believe I have any option, do I?"

"Of course you have options. You simply have to pick one. If you choose to join us, we'll tell you a little of what's happening—enough to keep you curious but happily ignorant—and life will continue as before. If you opt *not* to join us, we'll kill you and throw your corpse into the river. It's not a difficult choice—you simply say yes or no. So choose."

It finally sank home to Varrus that the armourer was teasing him, straight-faced and solemn, and he began to relax. "So if I come in, you'll tell me what's going on?"

"No. I said we'll tell you a little bit. No more than that."

"So be it, then. I'm in."

"Good, then we're almost done here, so you can stop looking so unhappy. The most important thing Hanno had left to tell you, before you turned into the Golden Orator there, was that your parallel was sound—cooks and smiths are much alike, and the cooking is the most important step in either process. That's why we had to build a higher, bigger, better furnace with a giant bellows—to control the cooking. Dominic Mcuil built the first one, several years ago. We improved upon his creation here, enlarging and refining it, with his cooperation. He and I have known each other for years. What we do here is, we fire the furnace at ferociously high heat for days—higher heat than any I've ever heard of, or Hanno either—and then we let it cool at its own speed until the oven is cold to the touch. That long cool-down is the wondrous part—the mystery. Again, no one knows why, but once that's done—fierce, air-blown heat for days and then a long cooling down—then everything afterwards can be done at normal smithy temperatures, so be it that you handle it gently at the very outset. That's the dangerous time, right after the metal leaves the crucible, for when it's new, fresh from the oven, the metal can be brittle if you overheat it again and you can shatter it and ruin it.

"So we heat it slowly at first, and hammer-work it gently until the impurities all fall out, and as we reheat it and rework it, time after time, that brittleness fades and the iron grows more malleable and easier to handle all the time. And then we hammer it flat and stretch it, and fold it and flatten it and stretch it again, and we keep doing that until we can form it into strong, thick bars. And eventually, from each of those bars, we make a weapon. The finest weapons ever made by Roman smiths. And sometimes we mix our metal with the metal from Dominic's oven, which is damn near as good as ours. And beginning tomorrow, Demetrius will show you how to do it."

He looked sideways towards Hanno. "Right now, though, I need him. He and I have matters to discuss. May I take him away?"

"Aye, there's nothing to be done now, anyway. His time is up."

"Excellent." Ajax stood straight and adjusted his clothing. "Follow me, Recruit Mcuil. For you, this day is not yet done, and all we can do is hope that it will continue to unfold as smoothly as it has until now."

"No, wait! A moment more. A single question on a matter that disturbs me . . ."

He waited as the two senior men exchanged glances, and then Ajax nodded. "One question, then. Ask it."

"Will anyone ever do anything about this legate? I realize that might not be good for you and what you do here—your conspiracy, as you call it. His removal could potentially expose your activities, but the man is thoroughly corrupt."

"He is. And his corruption has not gone unnoticed, believe me. But Lucius Placidus Pompey is no concern of ours. What befalls him in the future will create its own upheavals, but they should not affect us here. Is that what you wanted to ask?"

"Yes."

"Then we are finished here. But I promise you, Pompey will fall."

NINETEEN

Ajax struck out for the main door of the praesidium building across from them without speaking, walking quickly and holding his head high so that the protective guard of his helmet deflected the rain down onto his back rather than into the neck opening of his body armour. The guards saw them coming and stood at attention, prepared to greet the centurion, but apart from a casual nod and an informal salute to both of them, Ajax strode on through the doors and into the main hallway. There he stopped instantly and stretched his arm backwards to stop Varrus, too. The place was alive with movement, with people bustling in every direction everywhere Varrus looked. Ajax stood with a perplexed look on his face, staring across the open floor, with all its quickly moving bodies, to where his own official cubiculum sat empty, its open front looking out onto all the activity. Three men sat facing it, their backs towards Ajax and Varrus as they stared straight ahead, obviously waiting.

"What's wrong?" Varrus asked quietly. "Are those men waiting for you?"

"I don't know, and I don't care. They're not important and I have no time for them. But I had forgotten about *this*." His terse nod indicated the chaos all around them. "It was madness to come here. Let's go back to the armouries. We can talk there." He moved back the way they had come, and Varrus kept pace with him all the way, without another word.

Ajax's work office in the armouries bore no resemblance to the

official one he used in the headquarters building, with its collection of
swords: it was a tiny place, dowdy and utilitarian, with stools instead
of high-backed chairs, and a scarred old trestle table for a work surface,
but it was warm, and it was dry, and it was well lit and quiet—insofar as
its occupants had long since been inured to the incessant noises of the
workplace and were now unaware of them. The armourer took off his
helmet and set it on the floor inside the door, then swung his sodden
cape over his head, leaned out into the workplace, and shouted for
an assistant, beckoning for Varrus to hand over his cloak, too. When an
eager young apprentice came running to the door, Ajax handed him
both cloaks and told the boy to spread them near the forge to dry and
then to run to Demetrius Hanno's forge, apologize for disturbing him,
and ask the smith if he would consider blessing his centurion with a hot
jug of his spiced apple drink.

"I had some of his drink earlier," Varrus said. "It's really good."

"Aye. He loves it. Keeps a pot of it simmering by the forge all day
long in weather like this." He waved a hand towards one of the three
stools against the wall. "Sit." He then moved to the trestle table and
picked up a tube that lay there. It was a typical military dispatch case:
a cylinder of hardened leather, capped with sealable covers at both
ends and equipped with a leather strap that allowed it to be slung over
a shoulder. He set it upright on one end, then turned back to Varrus,
perching himself on another of the stools.

"So," he said. "Here is where you and I will begin all over again."
He narrowed his eyes to mere slits and pursed his lips, then stared at
Varrus for a long, discomforting space of ten heartbeats before he continued. "I knew from the outset, when our paths first crossed, that you
were different. I didn't know why, but I sensed something unusual about
you. I thought at first it might have been a talent for working metal, and
in recent weeks I had begun to believe that's what it was. But I never
would have suspected you of sorcery, or of having supernatural powers.
Until these past few days."

"What . . . ?" Varrus stared blankly. "I don't . . . I don't understand," he managed to say.

"Smelters and smiths change red earth into iron," Ajax said. "And in Egypt, I have heard, there are sorcerers who claim the ability to change lead into gold. But when I look at you I see, right before my eyes, some-one who changes charcoal into gold, and I know something is wrong."

Varrus felt the abyss yawn open at his feet. "You know," he said in a dead, hopeless voice.

"I know many things. It's my responsibility to know things. That's why I'm the armourer here. I know, for example, that you came to me some months ago as an eager young Hibernian tyro, Fingael Mcuil, with a hunger to learn about making blades. I believed you must be Eirish, because had you been otherwise, you would be in the legions, not merely working for them. But I did not know then that you have a physical flaw that would bar you from legionary service no matter who you were. I know, too, that since then you have set me on my arse, time after time, with the way you speak and the things you know, things that you could never have learned in Eire, or even in your father's smithy in Dalmatia, or wherever you grew up. You use words no Eirish smith should ever know—and 'moribund' is only one of them. And in the past few days the hair close to your scalp has turned to gold—not just to early grey, which is what I thought was happening when I first noticed it, but to bright, yellow gold.

"I know you're an impostor, too. I was sure of it from the outset, but since then I've been asking around, and no one I've spoken to has ever met or heard of a living Eirishman calling himself Fingael Mcuil. That would be like me calling myself Romulus of Rome and expecting to be taken seriously. Fingael Mcuil is one of the legendary giants of your people—a myth, like Hercules or Priam, King of Troy. The state of Rome is paying you a salaria, believing you to be who you said you are, and you are manifestly not who you said you are. That alone is grounds for a court martial with an outcome of execution . . . So, as I said, here is where you and I will begin all over again, and where we go from here will rest with you. For the time being, at least. Who are you?"

Varrus had listened to Ajax's accusation with mounting dismay, and his thoughts had been racing along with the armourer's words, so when the armourer finished with his final question, he answered without hesitation.

"My name is Varrus. Quintus Publius Varrus. I—"

The speed with which Ajax's hand flashed out to silence him startled him into freezing mid-word, and only then did he realize that the young apprentice had returned, bearing a steaming kettle of spiced apple juice. Ajax rose and thanked the lad, then closed the door behind him. That done, he poured two horn cups of the hot drink and set one down by Varrus before returning to his seat.

"Roman," he said. "And patrician, I suppose. Varrus is an ancient name. I suspected you might be Roman, but the patrician part makes no sense. A smith *and* an aristocrat? I smell a tale of dire, uncommon import . . ." He made no attempt to cover up the skepticism in his voice. "Do you want to tell me about it? About how you came here, and why and from where?"

"Yes. I do."

Ajax wrinkled his nose and sniffed, but then he sipped at his drink and made himself as comfortable as he could in such spartan surroundings. "You have my attention," he said.

No one disturbed them as Varrus told his tale, and by the time he had finished it his hot drink was cold and untouched.

Ajax had listened closely to the entire story, making no attempt to interrupt with questions, and when Varrus finally fell silent, the armourer sat staring into emptiness. Finally, he straightened his spine and stretched, then raised his cup and drank what remained in it. "You really believe the Roman authorities in Londinium were searching for you?"

"They were searching for someone that morning," Varrus replied, "and they were being thorough. I was glad to be safe outside the city gates at the time. I do believe they were looking for me, most likely because of the Emperor's labarum. It was foolish of me to wave that around the way I did."

"Hmm . . . Had you not waved it around, though, things might have quickly gone from bad to much worse in that marketplace, so don't be too regretful. You might have saved lives, but you will never know, one way or the other. Do you still have it?"

"I do."

"Then bury it. It's probably the most dangerous thing you'll ever have in your possession. Believe me."

"I do. I learned the truth of that when I fled Londinium."

"And the Blues—that's the part that made me raise my eyebrows. You killed four Blues, all by yourself?"

Varrus grimaced dubiously. "Dominic thought I had. I killed four gutter creatures, I know that. But as to whether they were Blues or not, I simply do not know. I had been in Londinium for no more than a few weeks, and I moved on within days. I didn't know what a Blue was, and I still don't."

"If I were you, I wouldn't lose much sleep in mourning them, whether they were Blues or not. But I'm glad you've told me everything, finally."

He reached to pick up the dispatch cylinder on the table at his back, and as he did, Varrus asked, "So when do you want me out of here? Or do you prefer I leave right now?"

Ajax looked at him with raised eyebrows. "I don't want you out of here. All I wanted was to know who you really are. I already knew *what* you are. You're a willing worker who knows how to smile and when to laugh, and has the makings of a damned fine smith, and that's all I really care about—I didn't want to lose a good smith simply because he felt he couldn't trust me. That's why I'm glad you told me. Now we can trust each other. You might want to start wearing a smith's hood, though, to cover your hair, like most of the others who work with sparks flying around them. And once you start working on the new swords with Demetrius, you won't have time to scratch your head between now and next Saturnalia."

He held up the cylinder. "This came today, addressed to Fingael Mcuil in care of Liam Mcuil, smith, in Colonia Claudia Victricensis. I have no idea what's in it, but it's official, dispatched from colonial headquarters in Londinium." He passed the cylinder over to Varrus. "I'll leave you alone to read it."

"No," Varrus said, looking at the cylinder and seeing his name on a scrap of parchment melted into the red wax seal. "You don't need to leave. I don't know what's in here, but I doubt my life will be threatened by it. What about my name, though? What will I do about that?"

"Keep it to yourself and guard it jealously. The crew here knows you as Fingael Mcuil, so it might be best to keep it for now. People don't really care what you call yourself in here, as long as you can do what you're supposed to do, and do it competently. Later, if you ever go back out into daylight wearing decent clothes, you can use your Roman name and no one will be any the wiser. Now, will you open that damn cylinder?"

Varrus broke the seal and shook out the contents, catching them in his free hand: two letters rolled lengthwise in the manner of scrolls, but with separate pages. One was much more substantial than the other, and each was held closed by a thin, flat ring of bone or ivory. The smaller of the two had been inserted into the centre of the larger one, and so he unrolled it first, scanning to discover that it had been written three weeks earlier by Rhys's brother Dylan, on the first day, the Kalends, of March. It was written in Latin, and intrigued, he began to read it, whispering the words for his own ears.

Ajax stood up and collected Varrus's untouched cup. He emptied it back into the kettle, then turned away. "I'll heat this up again," he said, and left Varrus to his reading.

Londinium. The Kalends of March
To Fingael Mcuil

That opening, alone, stopped Varrus and made him smile, for the name
it used told him that Dylan had been in touch with the Mcuils in
Londinium, which meant he had been talking to Lydia, and a sudden
surge of longing for her almost overcame him. He thrust it aside, however, refusing to be diverted, and noting, as he continued reading, that
Dylan knew precisely where he was and what he had been doing.

> Greetings, my friend:
> My neighbour Malachai, who has the market stall next to
> mine and is a Christian, informs me that this is the 318th year
> in the Christian calendar or, as they phrase it, the year 318 in
> the time of our Lord. Whichever way one counts the years,
> though, be it in the old Roman fashion or the new, there can
> be little doubt that our world is changing rapidly.
> A week ago, I received a summons to attend the office of
> the quaestor in the fortress here, and when I presented myself
> I was informed that a package had been delivered in trust to
> the garrison commander for my attention. I was told that it was
> a military communication from the headquarters of the Italian
> fleet at Classis, near Ravenna, and that it had been sent to me
> in person by Vice-Admiral Marius Varrus, the sub-prefect of
> the Ravenna fleet.

Varrus scanned what he had read for a second time, wondering what
on earth his friend was talking about. It was one thing to pretend that
Quintus himself was called Mcuil—arguably a necessary subterfuge—
but it was another altogether to designate an inaccurate rank to Marius,
whom Dylan had never met or, to the best of Varrus's knowledge,

even heard of. Beginning to feel the slightest niggling of concern, he read on.

> On hearing that name I remembered that my dear brother Rhys had been an associate of a naval officer called Varrus who served on the northern frontiers years ago, and so I accepted the package gratefully and with great curiosity, assuming it held tidings of my brother.

Varrus sat frowning now, his brows drawn together ferociously. Rhys had died in Dylan's own home, less than a year ago, so what Dylan had written here was absolute nonsense. But then the tension inside him began to abate rapidly, because Dylan must have known that Quintus would recognize it as nonsense. Which meant that Dylan had written the letter anticipating that it might be read by eyes other than Quintus's own. Feeling much better, he returned to the letter, scanning it now with an eye for what was really being said rather than what was written.

> The package contained a letter, addressed to me, from the admiral himself, telling me who he is and explaining that several years ago he had persuaded his close friend, my brother Rhys, to undertake an urgent and clandestine mission on the admiral's behalf and, incidentally, on behalf of the Empire. Admiral Varrus had asked him to travel north, into the area of the city of Aquileia on the upper shores of the Adriatic Sea, there to observe and report upon activities among the local tribes who were reportedly harbouring and assisting Gothic invaders from the Rhine frontier. Rhys had apparently carried out similar missions in the past, the admiral told me, and had been well rewarded, but the work was secretive and dangerous. Rhys had vanished into the northern territories soon after that, and had not been heard from since. After waiting for

more than a year, the admiral had presumed Rhys dead, killed while in the field.

Again Varrus paused, but no longer in puzzlement, and went back to reread the passage, smiling this time in admiration of the elaboration of the lie he was supposedly being told.

Several months earlier, however, shortly after the feast of Saturnalia the previous year, after having heard nothing of Rhys for several years, the admiral had heard a report of a man purporting to have escaped from captivity among the Goths on the Rhine, in company with two other men, both of them metal smiths from Hibernia. This man in the report had won home to Italia, but his two companions had chosen to steal home to Britain. The admiral had tried immediately to find out more, for the report he had heard had been specific, even naming the other man's name, and stating that he was a smith like Rhys himself.

The search had been fruitless, though, because the man who had claimed to have escaped with Rhys could not be found, making the story appear to be no more than a baseless rumour. Admiral Varrus, however, remains convinced that what he heard was true, and that my brother is still alive somewhere. He also remembered that Rhys had given him my name and details of my occupation in Londinium before he left to travel to Aquileia, and so he resolved to send me my brother's remaining personal effects, which Rhys had left in his care. He told me he would ship them by sea from Ravenna, consigning them directly to the garrison in Londinium, in the hope of finding me, but that he was sending the letter directly overland to Gaul by military courier, in the hope that I might receive it in advance of the arrival of my brother's personal effects.

I have no doubt that you are now wondering why I should write to you of this, but the answer is simple: the man with whom my brother supposedly escaped from captivity has the same name as you—Mcuil. Is there the merest possibility that you might have encountered, or even heard of one of your name, a man called Mcuil, who has recently returned to Britain from the Rhine frontiers of Roman territory? If there is, and if you know of such a man, I beg you to inform me. You may find me as I found you, through the good offices of Rome's garrisons.

Dylan Dempster

Varrus had been so engrossed in reading that he had failed to notice Ajax coming back into the small room and setting a freshly heated drink within reach of his hand, but when he looked up, there it was, and behind it was Ajax himself, eyeing him.

Varrus picked up the drink and sipped it, feeling its biting, sharp tang flooding his mouth with tingling sensations. "*Benigne*," he said, raising the cup to Ajax.

The armourer nodded back, then inclined his head towards the letter in Varrus's hand. "Does that bring ill tidings?"

"I don't know what it brings," Varrus said. "I've read it through three times and I'm still not sure I understand it. Here, see what you can make of it." He held the letter out and Ajax looked at it askance, as though it might be dangerous.

"Are you sure you want me to do that?"

"Yes, I am, because I want to know what it means, and you might be able to understand it better than I can."

Ajax read it the entire thing through, twice, and then lowered it and looked at Varrus.

"So what do you not understand?"

"Well, the major part of it is nonsense. Rhys is dead. He died in Londinium, in Dylan's arms, not long ago. And he was never on the Rhine frontier. He was in Dalmatia, with me. He never knew my uncle Marius, either, beyond seeing him in the villa on occasion, and that was seldom twice in any year. Marius was always at sea. And Marius is a navarch, not a vice-admiral. Sub-prefect of the Italian fleet! Nonsense!"

"No," Ajax demurred. "You can't be sure of that. Good officers do win promotion, and you said earlier your uncle was a good officer. And it's been what, two years since you last saw him?"

"More . . . But you're right. He could be an admiral by now. The rest is shit, though."

Ajax looked down at the letter again. "Perhaps not. Has it occurred to you that this was deliberately written to confuse? Not to confuse *you*, necessarily, but perhaps to mislead anyone who might intercept it, or read it for the wrong reasons."

"Yes, I saw that eventually. Still, why would he worry about anyone else reading it? Who would even know he'd written it? And who could access it between there and here, especially since he was sending it through official military channels?"

Ajax looked genuinely regretful. "Mcuil, Mcuil, Mcuil," he said. "Bear in mind why you ran away from Londinium in the first place. You thought the authorities were hunting you. The *authorities*—nameless, faceless, and all-powerful. Don't you think there's a danger they might still be looking for you, interested in anything to do with the Mcuil family?" He ignored Varrus's crestfallen look. "What about the other letter?"

"Gods, I didn't even remember it."

Ajax's grin flickered at the corner of his mouth. "No wonder you get confused," he said. "Your mind's like a cloud of midges, buzzing everywhere in tiny circles, getting nothing done. Read it now, then. See what it says."

Varrus picked up the second, larger scroll, and removed the ivory retaining ring. He cleared a spot among the clutter of documents on the table, then unrolled the new letter and laid the sheets of parchment face downwards, pressing them flat and holding them against their tendency to curl up again, finally laying a broad metal file across them to keep them flat. He wiped both hands on the front of his tunic beneath his apron, then grasped the edges of the flattened pages and rolled them up tightly again, this time in the opposite direction, holding the finished roll tightly for a count of twenty. When he released his grip this time, the pages sprang open and remained open. Handling them more gently now, he spread them apart, revealing that they were six identically sized vellum pages, carefully cut and shaped with a sharp-edged instrument. He turned them over and scanned the first page, and instantly grinned.

"What?" Ajax asked.

"This is from Marius. Six pages of it. And anyone but me would go mad trying to read it."

"How so?"

"Because it's not a language that can be written. It's gibberish."

"Let me see."

For a while Ajax peered at the pages, frowning at the close-set lines of black writing that covered them, words that were completely unintelligible. "That is . . . It's insane," he said eventually. "It looks like writing, but it makes no sense. What's the point?"

Varrus laughed, feeling completely at ease with the centurion for the first time, and enjoying it. "The point is, Magister Ajax, that there's nothing insane about this, and you were absolutely correct about the purpose of the other letter being to confuse. Let me explain.

"There is not much for normal, healthy, intelligent young people to do on the coastlands of Dalmatia in the heat of summer. It can be a lonely, desolate place, despite the perfect weather every day. I had few friends as a boy, but my uncle Marius was my closest friend, and in the summer of my twelfth birthday, my uncle and I amused ourselves—he was on leave from the Moesian fleet at the time—by inventing our own written language that no one else could understand."

He saw Ajax starting to raise a hand to interject. "Wait. You'll see in a moment. There was an island a mile off the coast from where we lived—a tiny place, peopled by fishing folk. They had nothing to offer anyone and nothing worth stealing and they wished for nothing more than they already had, and so they never left their island, not even to visit a neighbouring one. Marius and I went there to visit many times over the years—my grandfather was the nominal owner of their island—and we came to know them well. They were a primitive people, and they had their own language, as simple as their lives. We learned to speak their tongue, but it had never been written. So we wrote it, purely for the pleasure of it. Once we worked out how, it was easy."

"Easy? It must have been hugely difficult."

"No, we wrote it in Latin, simply writing down the sounds as they were spoken. When we read it aloud, it was their language, but no one who did not know it would ever have guessed that." He nodded towards the letter in his hand. "No one but Marius wrote that letter, and no one but I, in all the world, would ever understand it."

"You said it was a simple language, spoken by simple people. What happened when you wanted to write a word that didn't exist in their language?"

Varrus handed him the letter. "Find me a word in there that you can understand."

Ajax scanned an entire page and then a second one before he said, "I can't."

"I know. And yet they are all there, straight, sophisticated Latin words like 'moribund.' It's a simple trick. When we had to use a Latin word, we simply transposed letters. We would write the word out, then write it out again, but this time using the preceding letter, with the sole exception of the very first letter of the alphabet, which we wrote as the

Greek kappa. So to translate this, I will need sufficient time and some paper to write on."

"How much time?" Ajax had already risen to his feet.

Varrus fanned the pages. "Six pages . . . An hour?"

"Do it, then," Ajax said. "I'll bring you some paper and a pen and some ink, and then I'll come back in an hour."

An hour, per se, was an indeterminate amount of time, an approximation, but when Ajax returned to his cubiculum, Varrus was reading his letter, smiling to himself. He waited for Ajax to sit down, and then began to read.

Hail, Nephew!

I trust this will find you alive and well wherever you are. I have no way of knowing where that might be, but I know it must be far removed from our old spying spot in the sideboard in Salona. The world has greatly changed since both of us used that haven to lurk at anchor, years apart, on the edges of our family's adult world.

I am now an admiral, and I hope that will make you smile, remembering how the men of our clan looked down their patrician noses at the navy. I even have an imperial rank and title: Vice-Admiral Marius Sulpicius Varrus, Sub-Prefect of the Ravenna Fleet, the second most senior imperial fleet, based in the port of Classis.

Unfortunately, great though the honour is, and it truly is close to being the highest rank in our navy, I now command a praesidium in the city and spend my days behind a desk, my nostrils clogged with the acrid smell of ink as I attempt to keep our navy afloat in the face of determined undermining of everything we try to achieve. But that is my misfortune, not yours.

If all went well, this should have reached you through your friend's brother Dylan, to whom I wrote in Londinium. Rhys had spoken of him not long before you and I last parted company, and noting that this Dylan had achieved a reputation for integrity, I persuaded Rhys to provide me with information on how I might find his brother, should a need arise.

That, in turn, should ensure that if you are reading this, you must be completely confused by now, because I gave specific instructions to Dylan on what to put in the letter I asked him to write to you, the sole purpose of which was to mislead anyone seeking to pry. I know that original letter will be delivered to the quaestorium in Londinium, because I am sending it by military courier, but I have no control over what happens beyond that delivery. We are still Varruses, you and I, and I know beyond doubt that I am being closely watched, though I do not know by whom.

So, to business. I am under constant watch, but I am truly convinced that I am not in any present danger of being killed. Whoever the people were who murdered our family, they seem content to believe I have no interest in pursuing or exposing them, and that is partly true, since I do not know where I might even begin to look, or whom I might trust in any aspect of my concerns, and the very act of inquiring, by itself, would condemn me. I received a letter two years ago, soon after I assumed this posting. It was from an unknown source. It congratulated me on attaining my new rank and said bluntly that I would not be molested were I to continue to attend to my duties and make no effort to investigate the tragic accident that befell my family. The letter disappeared from my personal quarters soon after I received it, so I know there are those close to me whose task it is to watch me. Apart from that single incident, though, I have been left alone.

Forgive the digression. I hope you are safe-hidden by now, secure in a new life. Pass my good wishes to Rhys Twohands, if you will.

As for his brother Dylan's letter, you may disregard that completely. If you received it, then you are reading this, and I swear to you that had I known how tedious it would prove to be to write a lengthy epistle using this method, I would never have worked so hard with you to create it.

The chest of which I wrote to Dylan, containing his brother's personal effects, will never arrive, for it never existed. I referred to it in my letter solely to provide me with a reason for contacting him in the first place, should anyone prove curious, and to alert you to the fact that I am now in contact with him, assuming that, through his brother, he will know how and where to find you.

You will, however, receive a chest one of these days. It is coming to you under the auspices of the imperial navy, accompanied by a naval military escort. What point in holding admiral's rank and failing to exploit its privileges? I have used mine ruthlessly and shamelessly in this endeavour. When it arrives in Londinium, the chest will be delivered to a prominent and highly regarded lawyer who is in my debt, and upon receiving it, the lawyer will inform Dylan, who will arrange to forward it to you. The chest is wooden, bound with hammer-welded iron straps, then wrapped in heavy sackcloth and coated with several layers of size to seal it tight, with a final covering of clear, heavy wax. It comes without keys, for reasons that should be self-evident. To open it, you will have to destroy it, but it was made to be destroyed. You will not harm its contents in breaking it apart, and with your natural eye for the correct way of doing things, I suspect you will have no problems opening it.

The contents belong to you alone. I have no need of them. Use them well and live long and peacefully.

Marius

For long moments, the two men sat in silence, and it was Ajax, unsurprisingly, who broke it. "So. You're to be rich."

"I think not," Varrus said. "The chest might never come. There is a vast distance between Ravenna and Londinium by land, and the route would be dangerous in places. By now that chest could be lying lost and shattered somewhere high in the Alps, or stolen by pirates, or intercepted by the people watching Marius. Any of a thousand things could have happened to it. And even if it does arrive someday, we have no means of knowing what's inside it."

"Think about that," Ajax demurred. "A big chest like the one he describes, shipped all the way from Italy under military escort. It must be worth more than you and I would ever see in a lifetime." He stopped, frowning. "Why are you smiling?"

"I've just remembered. Earlier you spoke of trust and said we could now trust each other. You had no idea how quickly that would be put to the test, did you?"

"No. Did you? And do you trust me with this?"

"The secret of my wealth? Of course I do. And in return for your silence I'll share it with you. I must warn you, though, all the wealthy estates have long since gone, the monies for their sales vanished into the coffers of the bankers. Those that were left were plainly unworthy of the effort that would have been required to steal them . . . No, whatever is in that box, it's more than money and probably far less valuable. Nevertheless, I'll share it with you gladly."

"No, you will not. I'll have no part of that. I wouldn't know what to do with even a little wealth, other than to get drunk and waste my life. But in truth, though, if this thing comes, what will you do with it?"

"I don't know . . . Keep it hidden, I suppose, whatever it turns out to be, and hope to find a decent use for it someday."

"You could buy an estate, live like a senator."

Varrus shook his head, but he was grinning again. "No, not with the kind of money likely to be there. But I might buy a smithy of my own. That would be good to have."

"And you could marry that young woman from Londinium. That would be good to have."

"Aye," Varrus said. "It surely would."

TWENTY

A full month later, on the first really warm, sunny day of the new spring, Lydia Mcuil found herself pacing back and forth in a mood that she herself would have called a snit had she been watching anyone else doing it. But of course she was not watching. She was venting her frustration, striding up and down the length of the stables that flanked Liam's smithy, carrying forkfuls of new fodder to the cribs fronting the stalls of the eight horses quartered there, working with far more energy and pent-up tension than the task required. She was waiting for Quintus Varrus to arrive, nervously aware that he had no idea she was there waiting for him. It was less than an hour after noon, and if he were coming, she knew, he would be arriving soon; but he was already late, delayed, no doubt, at the armoury by one imaginary crisis or another, and she was growing increasingly afraid that he might not come at all. He worked every morning in the armoury, she knew, and his pattern had been to finish there at noon and then return to the smithy to work with Liam in the afternoon. But he had not come the day before, Liam said, nor the one before that.

Lydia had listened in mild disbelief as Liam told her how well Shamus had adapted to his new life, how he was now working steadily and showing signs of taking pride in the work he was doing. And so there was less need for Quintus to be around in the afternoons, he said, since between them, Liam and Shamus were easily capable of running the smithy.

Liam told Lydia that Quintus Varrus and the giant smith Demetrius Hanno would work far into the night in the forges, sometimes neglecting even to eat until, stupefied with the heat of the furnaces and the efforts of plying iron hammers and glowing metal, they would fall into cots in the armoury and sleep like dead men for seven or eight hours before rising and throwing themselves into their work again.

It was only once every two weeks, during the two- to three-day periods when the main smelting furnace was burning and there was little to do other than tend to the firing, that Varrus would take time to come home to the smithy to change and launder his clothing. He had told Liam on his last visit, three days earlier, that they were preparing to load the ovens again the following day, and so Liam had assured her that he would return today, at noon.

Lydia and her father had arrived the night before, after a long, difficult haul with three wagons from Londinium in poor weather. She had intended to send Quintus word that she was here, confident that he would be more than happy to know it, but something in the way Liam talked about the passion with which Varrus had thrown himself into whatever it was he and the giant were working on had made her reluctant to disturb him. So, hesitant in spite of all logic to impose herself on him, she had decided to wait in patience, bolstered by Liam's assurance that Quintus would come home that day.

She heard a loud clatter outside the open door and turned quickly to see what had caused it, but was disappointed to see her brother, wrestling with a heavy, moss-coated old barrel, manhandling it noisily to bring it directly beneath the new downspout he had installed the day before. She felt a swelling surge of irritation at him, and realized at once that she was being unreasonable. Shamus did not even know she was there watching him, and her bad temper would have no effect on whether or not Quintus came back to the smithy today.

Biting down on her impatience, she stood quietly and watched Shamus as he finished hauling the water barrel into place and then adjusted the downspout, positioning it precisely where he wanted it to be. When he was done, he stood back from it, drying the palms of his damp hands on his hips, then wiped some moisture off his forehead with the back of his wrist, and she recognized the unhurried satisfaction on his face that came with finishing a job well done. It seemed to her then that her vision shifted somehow—she almost experienced the change physically—and she saw her brother through fresh eyes, eyes that now held no trace of the impatient scowl that would have darkened her face automatically when he lived at home, when the ill feelings he had harboured for their father had poisoned the air.

At dinner the night before, she had been dreading a renewal of the sullen hostility that had existed between her brother and her father, and she had prepared herself mentally to ignore it and to concentrate on keeping the first shared meal of their visit pleasant and enjoyable. Yet Shamus was clearly no longer the sullen boy who had slouched away from Londuin with Quintus Varrus that rainy morning nearly a year earlier. He had grown up, in the space of mere months, and while he and Dominic were ill at ease with each other initially, there had been no overt signs of lingering hostility on either of their parts, and she had watched a gradual but discernible thaw taking place between them as the meal progressed.

She had been painfully aware of Quintus's absence, though, despite her best intentions, and had surprised herself with the depth of her unexpectedly bitter anger that they should be in the same town at the same time and not be with each other, and that the fault was hers alone, because she had been unwilling to let him know of her arrival. She was wishing, too, that he could be there with her to share her amazement at the transformation of her prickly-tempered brother, because she needed someone to reassure her that she was not imagining the lessening of tensions at the table. But she had received that reassurance nonetheless. Surprised at hearing a note of jocularity in a brief exchange between Shamus and their father, she had looked up and found her uncle Liam watching her from beneath slightly raised eyebrows, and when she widened her eyes at him, mutely questioning what she had heard, he had given her a long, knowing wink.

She watched Shamus stoop to pick up a fallen pickaxe from the ground near his feet and rest the shaft on his shoulder as he slowly scanned the surrounding yard, checking to see that all was as it should. Then he started to walk towards the stables.

"Lydia? Is that you?" He had stopped on the threshold, peering into the dark shadows. "What are you doing in there?"

"I'm feeding the horses. I'll be done in a moment."

He came inside slowly, and then stood there, watching her as she piled hay into the crib in front of the last of the stalls.

"We never see more than two horses at a time in here," he said quietly, setting the pickaxe down by the side of the door. "Except when you and Father come up from Londuin, and then we hire a stableboy. And yet here you are doing his work for him. Why?"

She leaned her hay fork against the front of a stall and pushed a strand of hair away from her eyes. "Because I needed to do something," she said. "I was tired of being bored." She looked at him in the doorway. "You seem very happy here in Camulodunum. Is that because of Uncle Liam's happy outlook on life, or is there some other reason I don't know about?"

He looked at her shrewdly, tipping his head slightly to one side. "Now why would you ask me that, dear sister?"

She picked up her fork again and moved to a pile of clean straw in a corner beside the door. "Because I've seen you smile more times since we arrived yesterday than I did in all the years before you came here, and I'm curious about why that should be so. Does Quintus Varrus have anything to do with it?"

"Quintus? No, not at all. Why would you think that?"

She shrugged in the act of scooping up a forkful of straw. "Because he is the only thing I can think of that might account for such a great change in you—he's the only new element in the picture. It can't be Uncle Liam. You've been around him forever and it never made you light-hearted before." She hesitated, gazing at the straw. "You haven't fallen in love with someone, have you?"

The moment she saw the shock on his face she knew she was right. "Dia!" she said, covering her mouth with her hand. "You have! You've met a girl! Who is she? Tell me, tell me."

He flapped his hands at her, urging her to lower her voice, while he glowered around him, his face filled with utter panic, and she began to giggle, even though she knew it was not the wisest thing to do.

"Don't laugh at me," he hissed, glaring at her.

"I'm not, Shamus," she gasped, trying to compose herself. "I'm not. I swear I'm not laughing at you. I'm laughing because I'm giddy with gladness for you." She reached out impulsively and grasped him by the wrist, pulling him with her as she moved to perch on the outer edge of one of the forage cribs, where two of the draft animals were munching softly behind her. He allowed himself to be pulled to stand beside her, his expression sullen.

"Don't be angry with me, Shamus," she said. "I'm really truly glad for you. But why are you so upset? Does no one know about it?"

"Of course no one knows about it." He sounded anything but care-free. "How could anyone know about it? I scarcely know the girl myself. I've hardly even spoken with her. Met her three weeks ago and didn't say a word to her until ten days ago."

Lydia looked at him in genuine astonishment. "Why on earth not?"

"Because I couldn't. Never had the chance. So I just stood and looked at her, for days."

"Stood where? Did she know you were watching her?"

"She knew. She'd smile at me from time to time. Watched me as I watched her."

"So why didn't you speak to her?"

"Because she's foreign. Doesn't speak our language. Not yet. She knows a little bit, but not much at all. And she has brothers and a father, and none of them likes the idea of letting local men anywhere near her. She told me that, after we started talking."

"I thought you said she doesn't speak our tongue. Where is she from?"

"Somewhere in the west. Cornwall? Have you heard of it?"

Lydia shook her head. "No, I don't think so. How long have they been here?"

"A year, I think. Perhaps two. I asked her that, but I'm not sure she knew what I was asking. It's not easy, talking to someone when you don't both speak the same language. But it turns out we can understand each other's home language, if we take time and speak slowly enough. They're different tongues, but there's room to talk together in them. Anyway, her father and brothers are leather workers, and they have a stall by the marketplace—a shop, I suppose, for it's open every day. And that's where she works."

"So what is her name?"

"They call her Eylin."

"Eylin. That's a pretty name. So how did you manage to start talking to her, with all those frowning brothers watching her all the time?"

"She makes deliveries sometimes, to some of the bigger houses. I followed her one day and she stopped and waited for me to catch up, and we liked each other. I was afraid her brothers might see us at first, but they didn't. I knew for the first time, though, how you must have felt with us all looming over you and protecting you before you met Quintus."

Lydia thought about that for a moment. "I'm glad you realize how I must have felt. It's not pleasant, being watched suspiciously by everyone, is it? So how often do you see your Eylin now?"

"Every day, for half an hour, if she has deliveries to make. For shorter than that, without talking, if she doesn't. It's growing easier to talk to her all the time, though. When we do talk."

"And does she feel the same way about you that you feel about her?"

Her brother shrugged his broad shoulders. "I don't know," he said. "I know she likes me. She always smiles at me as soon as she sees me, and I sometimes think she watches for me."

"Good for you, then," Lydia said. "For both of you. I promise I won't say a word, until you're ready to tell everyone yourself."

They heard the sound of Liam's voice shouting Shamus's name, and he stood up quickly. "I'd better go," he said. "Why did you come in here, though? Did Liam ask you to tend the horses?"

She smiled. "No," she said. "I was hoping that Quintus might be coming back today . . ."

Shamus grinned at her. "Then stay here and wait for him. He'll be here soon, I know, because they're firing the ovens up at the armouries. He's probably finishing up whatever he was doing, and if he doesn't know you're here he'll have no reason to come running back in a lather, will he? I promise you, he'll be here."

She watched him go, then walked forward to the doorway and looked across the outer yard to the smithy's entrance from the street, and felt her heart leap in her breast as she saw Quintus Varrus striding towards her in the distance. Though he was wearing a smith's hood of black leather that she had never seen before, he was instantly recognizable, even from more than a hundred paces, by his upright bearing and his slight but unmistakable limp, and she felt gladness flare up in her. She could even tell, from the way his mouth was pursed, that he was whistling to himself as he walked.

She had decided to have him months before, the second time she had come north with her father, but it had not been a flighty or unconsidered opinion, even then. She had liked and enjoyed the man she had come to know, admiring what she had learned about his character, temperament, and personality. She had kissed him once on the lips, very briefly, and very chastely, on the night before he left Londinium with Shamus. That had been at her own instigation, simply to satisfy her curiosity about whether she would enjoy the sensation of kissing him. She had been pleased to discover how pleasant it had felt.

Unfortunately, nearly four months had elapsed before she had the opportunity to test the experience again, but on her first visit to Camulodunum she quickly found it to be habit forming, as well as physically demanding, in the sense that her body had demanded more than she was prepared to permit it at that time. She had spent more than a few sleepless nights since then, regretting that she had not pursued things further. At no time, though, had Quintus Varrus sought to press her, and she had been grateful to him afterwards, suspecting that had he pushed her hard enough, she would have yielded.

The months since then had passed quickly, endless as some of them had seemed at times, and she had long since decided, firmly, that Quintus Varrus was the man she wanted. She knew beyond a doubt that she would be a good wife for him, and to him, and she knew with equal conviction that he would love and protect her and the children they would have. And yet . . .

She was a Christian and she suspected that Quintus Varrus was not. They had not discussed it at any time, and indeed Lydia had been at pains to fend off any suggestion, in any conversation, that might give rise to the matter of religion. She had no doubt that Quintus Varrus was a fine, upstanding man, but her father was what she considered a "sometimes" Christian, and though it made her feel guilty to behave as she had, she had avoided the topic scrupulously for fear of causing any conflict.

Now, watching her man draw close, she knew the time had come to face it head on.

Lydia watched avidly as Quintus Varrus stepped in through the street gate, and she saw the precise moment when he noticed the three empty wagons and realized that she must be there. He stopped abruptly and straightened to his full height, reaching up to pull the greasy black leather hood from his head, exposing the clean, short-cropped golden hair that had almost completely grown back. An explosion of laughter from the open door of the smithy drew his attention and he turned towards it. Lydia stepped into the stable doorway before he could move towards the smithy, though, and he hesitated, his eye attracted by her movement at the edge of his sight. He turned again, looking in her direction, and she thrilled to see how his face lit up with joy, seeing her there. He started to reach out, taking an instinctive step towards her, and then froze almost in mid-step, suddenly awkward and unsure of himself. Seeing that, his sudden vulnerability and hesitancy, her heart went out to him, and she reached out her hands, smiling and saying his name.

He was beside her in a single stride, towering over her, and she reached up and pulled his head down slowly to where she could kiss him, a demure, chaste, fond, tentative greeting that quickly transformed itself into a blazing fire that neither one of them felt inclined to interrupt until Lydia felt the hardness of his arousal pressing against her and pulled away quickly. He raised his hands chest high, letting her go, and they stood staring at each other, breathing erratically and shuddering with awareness.

Finally, though, Lydia reached out and seized his hands. "I told you your hair would grow back quickly, did I not?"

"You did," he said, smiling. "And it has. Almost."

"You can throw that ugly cap away now. It makes you look ordinary. Much better to go bare-headed."

"Aye, I would, except that I still need it to cover my yellow hair, since you don't visit me often enough to keep it dyed for my disguise."

"Yes, but that was almost a year ago and no one has come looking for you, so you should be safe enough now, here in Camulodunum."

"You mean Colcaster, do you not?" He grinned in his pleasure at her unmistakable and unconcealable distaste.

"You, too?" she said. "Such an ugly name. It is Camulodunum—a Celtic town, for all its Roman-sounding name." She tightened her grip on his hands. "Now come with me, before anyone sees you." She backed away, pulling him with her into the darkness of the stables and the warm, rich smell of horses. "No one knows you are here yet," she said, "so we can hide from them for a while, because you and I need to talk together with no other ears listening."

She looked around her then, noticing that four of the horses were watching her from their stalls, their ears pricked forward as though to listen to anything she might have to say. "There is nowhere to sit," she said, looking around as though hoping to prove herself wrong before she added, "Though perhaps it might be better that what we have to discuss be conducted standing up." She glanced at him keenly, gauging his reaction, but he simply continued to smile gently and enigmatically, his eyes slightly crinkled.

"Standing upright, you mean, as opposed to lying with each other in the straw?"

She opened her mouth to speak, but no words were in there to emerge, and she realized he had shocked her and began to laugh. "Exactly," she said. "That is exactly what I mean." She hesitated, then plunged ahead. "The first day we met, you told my father you intended to marry me. Have you changed your mind since then?"

"Not a bit, Lydia Mcuil," he said, his smile unchanged. "Not even a whit. I've simply been biding my time, and trying to use it productively while I waited for you to see how right I was."

She tipped her head a little to one side, then nodded, though he could not tell whether the nod was for herself or for him. "It is time to end this time-biding, then. I will have you gladly, Quintus Varrus, if you will still have me— Wait!" She had thrown up her hand to stop him from reaching out for her, and he stopped, holding his head back, one eyebrow quirked. "Wait, Quintus, if you please," she said again. "I have to say this now, before things go any further." She looked around again nervously, as though searching for inspiration. "I have one main concern, and it has nothing to do with our being able to live together amicably and contentedly as man and wife, or to have children, or any of those things that most people fret over."

"Then if it's none of those things," he said gently, "what is it? You can spit it straight out into the open, Lydia, no matter what it is. I have no secrets from you, and I intend to have none. Tell me what is worrying you."

"I am Christian," she said quietly. "And you are not. You are a Roman citizen. And I am not." She paused, gazing into nothingness with a tiny crease of worry between her flawless brows. "I have a fear—and it may seem irrational, but it is real to me nonetheless—that those two simple facts might create difficulties for us in the years ahead."

"Religious difficulties?" He laughed aloud. "I think you can dismiss that from your mind, my love. It has been several years now since Constantine recognized Christianity formally at Milan—"

That brought Lydia's head up quickly. "Aye," she snapped. "Five years. And only a few years earlier than that—what, seven in all?—Diocletian and his cronies were bringing the entire power of Rome's armies against what they called the Armies of Christianity.... That was less than a decade ago, Quintus, but too long ago for you to remember. You were still a boy, not even grown, and I was even younger, but I remember because they murdered my mother, supposedly for treason, when she was no more guilty of treason or sedition than I am. They murdered her for being a Christian, in a dispute over what you now laugh at as *religious difficulties*."

"Oh, Lydia, forgive me." Varrus straightened up as though he had been slapped, and spun away from her, turning completely around, looking up into the rafters before coming to rest facing her again. "I had no idea. How can I alter what I said? Forgive me. I had no wish—" He stopped, and tried again. "It never entered my mind that I could hurt you by what I was saying. Especially with such silly, thoughtless words. What came out of my mouth—what you obviously thought you heard me say—was not what I meant to say at all."

He raised his hand to point at the bright sunlight beyond the doors. "Look," he said. "It's a beautiful spring day outside, the first truly fine day this year, and the first day of our new life together, so why are we standing here in a dark stable?" He reached out his hand to her and she took it hesitantly, peering up at him. "I promise you," he told her, "I can resolve your difficulty and answer all your questions, even those you have not yet voiced. Come outside with me and I'll hoist you up onto the bed of one of the wagons and we can talk in the sunlight." He grinned, tentatively, seeing the doubt in her eyes and guessing accurately at its source. "And no one will disturb us, I promise you. We have waited long enough for privacy, the two of us, and now that you have said you'll have me, by all the gods, including your Christian one, we will *have* privacy, if I have to chase all your relatives off these premises."

He checked himself again. "Lydia, my love, I knew your mother died when you were very young. Several people told me that, including Liam, and I understood her death was tragic and unnecessary. But no one ever actually said she had been killed during the persecutions. I didn't know. I suppose I might have guessed, given the timing, but at the time I was a child in Dalmatia. I had never heard of Britain and knew nothing of Galerius and his bloodthirsty ways. And I agree with how you have defined your mother's death. She was murdered, for her beliefs. But think of this. I might not be Christian—in fact I'm nothing, really, when it comes to having faith in gods of any stripe—but my mother was Christian, so I am not unfamiliar with what your religion entails. Believe me, my love, we can take care of your concerns."

He led her to the open tailgate of one of the wagons and checked that it was recently swept before he turned her to face him, with her back to the cart. He took her by the waist in both hands, exulting at the soft, yielding pliancy of her body, then bent his knees slightly, hoisted her high in the air and held her there, smiling up at her, his smith's muscles making light of her weight.

"By all the gods at once," he said. "I love the feel of you. And the look of you and the scent of you and the beauty of you all in one wondrous, breathtaking reality." And he lowered her slowly and gently to sit on the wagon bed. "Now sit there and talk to me. Marriage," he said. "Talk to me about that. What would be your expectations of me, as a husband?"

"The same virtues I have been seeing in you since we first met," she said, smiling now. "Nothing to strain your principles or bend you away from being the man you are. I would expect your love as a spouse, your respect as a partner, and your admiration would be a welcome addition to both of those, though I know it will be my responsibility to earn and maintain all three. I would expect you to provide a home for us and for our children, and to do all in your power to hold them safe against the world and its excesses. And I would expect you to allow me to pursue my own beliefs in my own way, without interference, so long as I do nothing to disgrace you or shame you openly. That would be my entire list. Does anything about it seem unreasonable?"

"No, not a thing."

"So be it," she said. "So now it is your turn. What would you expect of me, as your wife?"

He shrugged his wide shoulders. "That you be yourself, for that is what I fell in love with—the wonder of what you achieve in simply being yourself. Give me that, and pass it to our children, and you will hear no complaints or other demands from me. Now tell me about ceremonials."

She blinked at him. "I don't know that word. What are ceremonials?"

"Rites, religious rituals . . . ceremonies to mark important events like marriages. I know you disapprove of Roman gods—my mother did, too, Roman gods and their priestly servants. She regarded them as little better than augurs and sorcerers, though she refrained from saying so aloud. But if you wish to have a Christian priest attend your marriage service, I would have no objection."

She gazed down from her seat at him, wide-eyed and blinking slowly. "I have never given any thought to that," she said quietly. "I have heard of people doing it, though, having priests witness their declarations and ask God to bless their wedded lives, but in all those cases the people were both Christians, man and wife."

"Then what would you do, normally? You must have thought about how you would mark the day of your marriage. It could hardly be no more than another ordinary day, surely."

She pursed her lips and looked up to the sky. "No, it should be the best, most memorable day of my life until that time, and it will be. I will see to that. It will be a day of celebration for everyone we know." She looked down again. "But as to how we go about the actual rite, the making of our compact . . . Well, there I am uncertain and will be glad to take advice from you on any details you might think of. By and large, though, I would do as my brothers did, I suppose, and my father before them. None of them are really Christians, not in the way so many of our neighbours are, but they believe in holding to the traditions of our people."

"And what are those traditions?"

"One man, one wife—a common pledge to honour each other and to stand together in the rearing of children. That's the most important part, I think. The two people stand up freely, in front of family and friends, and declare their intent to live thereafter as man and wife, and they join hands as a symbol of their voluntary union. Sometimes their hands are tied with coloured ribbons, and sometimes they exchange rings or other tokens, but I think those details differ from place to place and clan to clan and even family to family. The man and woman exchange gifts, too, usually possessions rather than money, where I came from, as a sign of their joining together and sharing their worldly goods. And then there's a public declaration that the couple has made a new family, branching off from the families of their birth. I think that's part of the ritual, too."

"Really? You include all of that? That surprises me."

Her eyes widened and she bridled. "Why would my people's customs surprise you?"

"Because they're so close to the way my own people used to do things in Dalmatia. There's almost no difference. Do you have the *aquae et ignis* rite, too?"

She looked at him blankly. "The what?"

"*Aquae et ig—*"

He was interrupted by a raucous shout from the door of the smithy, for Dominic had looked out and seen them together. "Quintus," the smith roared. "Come inside! We've been wondering where you were."

"Give me a moment," Varrus said to Lydia. "I'll come right back."

He walked briskly over to the smithy and embraced the big man, and as they hugged each other tightly, he spoke into Dominic's ear.

"You told me a long time ago that if your daughter would have me you would raise no objection. Well, she has just told me she will, and the last thing I need here and now is to be interrupted before we can finish what needs to be said. Can you keep the others away from us until we're done?"

Dominic Mcuil thrust him away violently, holding him out at arm's length and grinning at him ferociously before he tugged him back into his huge arms and tried to crush his ribs in a giant hug. "Go then, lad," he said, in what for him was a whisper. "I'll see to it you're not disturbed."

Varrus went directly back to Lydia, and stood again at the wagon's tailgate. "What I was speaking about is a Roman marriage rite," he said. "They call it *aquae et ignis*, which means 'water and fire,' and it's the ritual presentation, husband to wife, of those two necessities of life. It is based on the knowledge that a man can survive for a long time without food, but will die quickly without water, and without fire he will freeze to death in darkness. It's symbolic of the husband's contract to care for his wife throughout their lives together."

Lydia shook her head. "I don't think I've ever heard of anything like that. But did you tell my da?"

Varrus nodded, grinning.

"What did he say?"

"Not much. I asked him to leave us alone to talk and he said he would make sure we are not disturbed."

"Dia! Did he, by God?" She cocked her head again in the endearing manner that he loved. "You have never had a moment's doubt that he would accept you, have you?"

"No. He told me so when first we met, and I believed him. He couldn't wait to get you off his hands, and I took him at his word." He laughed and cringed away as she swung her fist at his head. "Besides, I had enough to worry about, wondering if *you* would accept me. I didn't have time to fret over what your da would think." He moved towards her, placing a hand on either side of her on the wagon's edge and leaning in until their faces were inches apart. "But you did accept me," he murmured, and she leaned towards him and kissed his mouth, a long, delicious kiss with no other contact between them.

When they eventually pulled apart, looking into each other's eyes, he murmured, "So then, no priest. The next question, then, is when to do it. Have you any wishes on that matter?"

"I might wish to change my mind about the priest, once I have thought about it. Would that displease you?"

"No. I told you that already."

She smiled, wrinkling her nose. "As for when, I would happily do it now, but that would be inconsiderate of us." She saw his eyebrows go up. "No, really it would, Quintus. We have to think about where we will live, where our home will be. Normally we would live at home with Da and the boys until we can afford to build a house. Have you considered that?"

"No, not really. Not at all, in fact." He paused, then blurted, "Haven't even thought of it. That's the real truth." He stopped again, looking bewildered. "I suppose . . . I suppose that, inside my head, I've been building a life for you and me here in Colcaster, and now I'm suddenly hoping that won't horrify you. I like this town. And I love my work at the armouries. But I hadn't even thought about what would happen were you to decide you can't live outside your Londuin."

She leaned forward and laid her hand on his arm. "Be at peace, Quintus. Be at peace. I like this town, too. I always have. It's the closest thing to home I can imagine. And you are safer here than you would be in Londuin, so that decision is easily made. We will live here, in Camulodunum."

"It's Colcaster."

"No, my dear, it is Camulodunum."

"I could argue, if I didn't love you," he said, almost in a whisper. "Camulodunum is no less Colcaster than Londinium is your Londuin."

"Perhaps, in your mind," she murmured back. "But Camulodunum is where we two will live," and she quieted him by laying her fingers on his lips.

"That decision brings problems in its train, though." She smiled at him and moved closer. "We have to consider the nuptials themselves, the wedding feast—for with my family taking part it will be a feast, you may depend upon that. Where will that be held? It should be here, since this will be our home, but most of the people I would like to attend will have to travel the hundred miles between Londuin and then find lodgings. That in itself will be a costly and complicated undertaking. And where will we live, you and I, once we are wed? We can't stay with Liam and Shanna for long, not with Shamus there already. Their house is half the size of Da's—far too small for five adults to live in all at once. Besides, we will need a place of our own—*I* will need a place of my own."

"You will. And you will have one."

"How?" The look she gave him had no doubt in it, but neither did it lack surprise.

"I'll build you one."

Her smile lit up her face like an inner light. "You are a smith, Quintus Varrus, and I'm sure you are the best at what you do, but you are not a builder."

"That's true, but I am a gifted and charming smith and I have friends who have many friends. The man who hired me, Ajax the armourer—"

"I know Ajax."

"Ah! Of course you do, through your father. Well, Ajax knows everyone in this town and most of them are indebted to him one way or another. When I tell him I need to build a house for us to live in, he will have a crew of builders working on it within hours, I promise you. I told you I was rich when we first met, but you never asked how rich I was. Had you asked, the answer would have been, 'Not very,' but that leaves me rich enough, nevertheless, to build us a decent house." He frowned a little. "I see what you meant about not rushing into this. It could grow complicated."

She tapped the end of his nose with her fingertip. "It will, I promise you. And at the very moment when you think you have it under control, it will sprout new complications like green shoots of grass. Believe me. I have been involved in planning five marriages among my friends, and no two are alike."

"Then I'll be glad to leave all that to you," he continued, in the quiet, intimate voice he had been using earlier. "Except for when you need me to contribute."

She was about to speak but broke off, hearing hooves clattering on the cobblestones at the gate, and she looked over Varrus's shoulder in astonishment.

"That's Callum's horse," she said. "I'd know him anywhere."

TWENTY-ONE

"It *is* Callum," Lydia said. "Callum! What are you doing here? You're supposed to be at home, running the smithy."

He reached up and pulled off his hood, then scratched his head, grinning widely. "Aidan and Declan can take care of that easy enough without me," he said, then nodded a greeting to Varrus and pointed over his shoulder with his thumb, to the high-sided, two-wheeled cart at his back. "Quintus, come and see this."

He led them both to the rear of his cart, where he removed the pins holding the tailgate in place and lowered the heavy flap, exposing the sole item in the cargo compartment. "This thing here arrived for Da soon after he and Lydia left to come here, but we all knew it was meant for you. We knew, too, that nobody wouldn't be coming back this way again much afore year's end, so then and there, soon as it arrived, we flung it onto the cart and I set out to catch up with Da and the wagons. I couldn't, though. The weather was ungodly wicked for a long time, slowing everything down an' just not shown' any signs of blowin' over, and then I ran into some trouble further up the road."

"On the main road? What kind of trouble?" Varrus was frowning, for he had heard tales of mayhem and confusion on the roads, a state of affairs that would have been unprecedented a mere ten years earlier. Rome's imperial roads carried the life's blood of the empire, so they had been regularly patrolled for as long as anyone could remember. But a decade or so earlier, some budget-conscious imperial functionary had noticed that road traffic had declined drastically, and in his money-grubbing wisdom—and under pressure from the imperial treasury to cut down on expenses everywhere—he had deemed the roads to be no longer worth the expense of guarding. The regular patrols had been discontinued, and lawlessness had moved onto the main roads and worsened rapidly until people's fear of being robbed on the open road had effectively put an end to inter-city travel throughout Britain.

"Bad trouble," Callum said, shaking his head. "A band of outlaws robbed and burned a hamlet at a crossroads 'bout 'alfway between here and Londuin. They fair ruined the place. It seemed like every single person in that village 'ad been killed, and their 'ouses burnt down over their heads. It was really awful." He stopped, remembering, then shook his head again. "I thought about turning 'round and goin' 'ome, since I could see by then I wasn't going to catch up to Da an' the others. But I was 'alfway 'ere by that time, and so I decided to keep comin'. And 'ere I am. Da in the smithy?"

Varrus nodded. "With Liam and Shamus and some others. They'll be surprised to see you."

Lydia nodded towards the cart. "You say that's for Quintus?"

"Aye, but it's got Da's name on it. Some rich feller brought it by the smithy and asked after Da, and when I said 'e warn't there, 'e asked if Da could read and write. 'Course 'e can, I says, so then 'e sits down and pulls a pen, paper, and a horn of ink out of a wooden case 'e's car-ryin', and writes a letter to Da saying 'ow important it is that 'e reads this and sends the box on." He shrugged. "Aidan read it to us as soon as 'e 'ad gone, an' we all knew where it 'ad to go." He looked at Quintus. "It was to come to you, but under the name we gave you, Fingael Mcuil."

"How did you know that?"

"Because that cloth feller, Dylan, told us what would happen—that there was a box comin' to Da that should be sent on to you."

"What's in it?" Lydia asked Callum. "Do you know?"

"No idea."

"I know what it is," Varrus said.

"Then what is it?"

"It's a large box," he said, smiling at her. "Would you agree with that, Callum?"

"Aye," Callum said, "that's right. It's big, and solid, but most of all it's awkward. An' it's heavy, right enough, but not as heavy as it might be. So what's in it, Quint?"

Varrus shook his head. "You tell me," he said quietly. And then to Lydia: "It's some sort of family inheritance, from my uncle Marius. It is every bit as much a mystery to me as it is to either one of you two. Marius sent a letter to tell me it would be coming, but not exactly what would be in it. It's had a long journey—the truth is, I was sure it would be lost or stolen somewhere along the thousand or so miles between Italy and here."

Lydia had been peering at the thing and now she turned to look at him in mystification. "How will you open it? There's no way at all that I can see."

"I'll have to break it apart, Marius said. But I'm far from sure if I want to."

"Why not? If I were you, I wouldn't be able to wait to open it."

Varrus stood staring at the thing. "I think I might be a little bit afraid of knowing what's inside. Something is telling me nothing good can come of it." He paused. "My family died violently, remember. They were slaughtered, and their house burned down around them, consuming everything. There was nothing left but charred bones." He looked at her, and she saw the uncertainty in his eyes. "What, then, could be in here that I might want to have?"

Lydia laid her hand on his arm while Callum stood frowning, staying resolutely out of this. "But your uncle surely would not send anything to cause you pain, would he?"

"No, not deliberately. But who can tell what might or might not cause another person pain? I hurt you, in all innocence and ignorance, not an hour ago."

"That was different, Quintus. And it's already forgotten . . . Did your uncle really offer you no clue about the contents?"

"Not really. But I read enough to know that he really wants me to have whatever is in there, so all I can think of is that it's something that has to do with the family."

"Perhaps . . . Could it then have something to do with your parents, something that might have belonged to them, but would mean more to you than it ever could to him?"

"It might. It might be something of my mother's, but what? The simple act of looking at it would remind me painfully that she was lost—murdered, like your own mother, but for reasons completely unknown. And as for my father, well, I meant nothing to him, so why should I feel privileged to own anything that was his?" He drew a deep breath. "And that said, I have decided that I have no wish to open it. Or not yet. And perhaps not for a very long time." He looked at Lydia and smiled, relieved, she could see, to have made his decision. "You and I have far more important matters to concern us, and not enough time, I suspect, to attend to all of them sufficiently."

Callum had been watching and listening closely, his head moving from one to the other of them as they spoke, and now he deemed it safe to become involved again. "What's you two up to, then?"

"We're to be married, Callum," Varrus said. "And you're among the first to know."

Callum's face was transfigured by a shining grin that spread from ear to ear. "By Gor!" he exclaimed. "That's grand. Our da will be right glad. C'n I go tell 'im?"

"He already knows, but you can come with us and we'll all make it official."

"What about the box, then?"

"If you'll help me unload it, we'll stow it in the stables until I decide what to do with it."

Between them they manhandled the bulky case until they could lift it down from the cart, and then they carried it over and laid it against a wall in the stables, close by the storage area where they kept the stooks of straw for spreading on the floor. The crate was much lighter than it appeared to be, and in spite of himself Varrus began to wonder again what it could possibly contain, but he threw an old horse blanket over it and left it there, then went to join the others.

There was a festive atmosphere around the dining table that night, and the celebration lasted long after the dinner was finished, fuelled by the dark ale Shanna brewed herself according to an ancient formula that her people had used forever. Candles and lamps were relit when they burned out, and the large fire in the iron basket in the hearth was regularly replenished with fresh logs. The matter of inviting a Christian priest to the wedding festivities came up and was eventually rejected as being irrelevant, since no one there knew a local priest well enough to consider one worth inviting. Varrus watched Lydia carefully during that discussion, and she appeared to accept everything that was said, so he accepted that she had no objections to her pagan loved ones dismissing her religious wishes on grounds of practicality.

Varrus was nursing his fourth jug of ale and feeling at peace with the world when he heard Callum say something about heading back home the following day, and it shook him out of his lethargy.

"Why would you even think of going home tomorrow?" he asked, leaning forward between Callum and Liam to join the conversation. "That's insane. You've only just arrived, so stay and rest for a while, where it's safe. The roads are too damned dangerous these days for you to go traipsing off on your own. You would be asking to be robbed, being all by yourself, a single traveller."

Callum laughed. "Robbed of what? I've nothing worth stealing. The cart'll be empty."

Varrus looked at him in disbelief. "Think of that hamlet you told us about earlier." He did not attempt to be dramatic in any way, merely keeping his voice natural and therefore more emphatic purely through the contrast between his gentle tone and the words he was speaking. "The people slaughtered and their houses burnt on top of them. Do you believe those people were killed for their wealth? Butchered for the luxuries they owned? Look at yourself, Callum. You're wearing sturdy leather boots and a good, hard-wearing tunic. And when you're on the road you'll be wearing a warm cloak. And riding in a fine, strong cart, empty though it be. A valuable cart drawn by a heavy, strong, well-fed, and obviously healthy horse. Don't you think those would be worth killing you for? There are people on those roads today, desperate men, whose livelihood is based upon robbing, despoiling, and murdering whoever they encounter. They rob and kill them for the few things they possess. And there are more and more of those predators out there every day, because they know there's no one to stop them. In the old days, they didn't dare. They'd have had the army out looking for them before they even had the chance to plan another robbery."

"You sound very sure of your facts there, Quintus," Dominic Mcuil said. "Have you been talking about this recently with someone else?"

"I have. And often. Bear in mind my friends in the garrison armouries are mostly centurions of varying ranks. They talk about things like that all the time—about how unsafe the roads have become and about how the empire is falling apart because of the tight-fistedness of the imperial auditors and accounts keepers who are always cutting budgets. They never seem to have much difficulty finding funds for games and holidays and senatorial necessities, but when it comes to the armies, and I mean the domestic legions not involved in the frontier wars along the borders, they do nothing but whine and complain and plead poverty and cut funding. So we have no patrols now policing the roads, and soon we will have no roads because people will stop using them altogether and the money-grubbers will stop maintaining them."

"So what are you sayin', Quint? Should I not go 'ome?" Callum sounded genuinely perplexed.

Varrus knew Callum was not the cleverest of the four sons. "Of course you should go home, Callum. But you should leave here with some real hope of reaching there alive. Wait for a few days and go home with the rest of the family. That way there will be more of you, and by then we should be able to make the group bigger, for safety's sake. There are always people eager to combine with other folk to travel to Londuin in safety."

"Err . . . All righty, then, I'll go back with Da and our Lyddie. Say, when's you two gettin' wed, then?"

"I can't answer that question," Varrus said, and turned to Lydia beside him. "Can you?"

"Of course I can, my love." She smiled sweetly and leaned forward to talk to her brother. "We will be wed the very moment we are ready, Callum, and we will let you know well in advance, so you'll know it's coming." She then looked back at Varrus, batted her eyelashes at him demurely, and returned to her conversation with Shanna.

TWENTY-TWO

Mid-morning the following day, Varrus was interrupted while talking to Demetrius Hanno about the blade they were currently working on. Annoyed as he always was at being distracted from his work, he changed his attitude instantly when he looked up and recognized the insignia of a guardsman on the cuirass of the man who had spoken to him. The fellow saluted, then announced that there was a messenger at the main gates, asking for him.

It was Shamus, and Varrus felt his chest fill with dread when he saw the look on the young man's face.

"What's wrong?" he demanded as soon as he was close enough for Shamus to hear him. "Who's sick?"

"It's Liam," Shamus said, whey-faced, and in spite of himself Varrus felt a great surge of relief sweep over him. Liam had been sick before, from his injuries. He would recover. Varrus had no doubt of that.

"What happened?"

"He fell. Hit his head on the smithy floor. The concrete."

Varrus grimaced. "How bad is it, do you know?"

"Bad. I was there, behind him. I couldn't reach him in time to catch him."

"Is he bleeding?"

Shamus shook his head. "He was. Not so much now. Split the back of his skull open. He hasn't woken up since he fell. Da tried to stop the bleedin' but 'e couldn't, not for a while."

"How long ago did this happen?"

"This morning, early. Mayhap three hours ago."

"Damnation! Stay here. Right here. Don't move before I come back." He spun away towards the guardsmen. "I have to get to the infirmary. What's the quickest way?"

The guard decanus pointed into the main body of the fort and shouted instructions as Quintus took off at a run—past the quaestorium, and then the second building on the left.

Moments later he found the building and ran inside, shouting for help, to find himself in a small atrium surrounded by open-ended rooms, each containing a bed and nothing else. None of the beds were occupied, but a man appeared from another door.

"Hey, hey, hey! What's all the shouting about?"

Varrus went right to him. "What are you, a magus or an orderly?"

"I'm a physician. Who are you?"

"Can you treat head wounds?"

The other man pursed his lips. "Of course I can. That's why I'm in the army. What's wrong?"

"A friend of mine, an elderly man, has fallen and cracked his head. He is unconscious. My name is Mcuil and I work in the armouries. Can you come with me?"

"Yes," the other said, turning away. "I'll fetch my instruments." A moment later he returned, carrying a leather satchel. "Where is this man?"

"Not far from here, outside the fort. I'll show you. Come." He led the way, and they collected Shamus as they passed the gates on their way out.

Liam's smithy lay five minutes away at a brisk walk, and they covered it in less, going directly to Liam's bedchamber. The room was large and spacious and it was well lit and comfortable because Liam had built it to be so. It was also far more crowded than Varrus had expected, mostly with neighbours and friends, and for the first time since he had arrived in Colcaster he realized how many Eirish people there were in the narrow district housing the smithy. It was no more than two, perhaps three streets in extent, and it had no name, but everyone who lived there was Celtic, and most of them, like the Mcuils, were Eirish. The women were clustered around Shanna, whose face was dominated by her wide, uncomprehending stare.

Varrus called everyone to listen to him, and when the noise continued he raised his voice to a bellow, commanding instant silence. Raising his arms for attention, he indicated his companion and said loudly, "This is Gnaeus Aurelius. He is a physician attached to the garrison infirmary and he knows about injuries like this." He spoke directly to Aurelius. "Is there anything you need, Magister Aurelius?"

"Hot water, as hot as it can be," the physician said, gazing at the still form on the bed. "And cold water. More of the hot than the cold, though, and a constant supply." He continued to stare at the unconscious man, squinting through narrowed eyes. "Those bandages look clean—as clean as they can be with blood on them, I mean. I would like more of those. The same width, and in strips as long as you can provide." He glanced around the room. "Apart from that, I need room to move freely, and I need quiet, so everyone go away now, if it please you, and find other places to wait. And go even if it does not please you. Liam will thank you for that later."

Varrus took it upon himself to clear the room, approaching each family member and friend individually, and within a very short time the room was empty save for himself, the physician, and the immobile Liam.

Aurelius nodded tersely. "*Benigne*," he said. "My gratitude. Now that everyone has gone, though, I am going to need an assistant. Someone sufficiently calm and cool-headed to work around an injured, bleeding man, attending to his needs. That might be the man's wife, but then again it might not, depending on her temperament. I know none of these people, so I must rely on you to pick one of them to assist me."

"Am I acceptable? I know the man—I respect and admire him— but I won't swoon at the sight of fresh blood and I can help you move him around, if need be, better than any woman could."

"Excellent," Aurelius said. "So be it. Come over here and help me remove these bloodied dressings. I need to see what damage has been done."

That was the start of a long stint of hard, exhausting work that Varrus remembered little about afterwards. He recalled feeling vaguely relieved that the back of Liam's head was merely cut and not completely crushed, as he had feared it might be; remembered, too, that Gnaeus Aurelius frowned and made impatient tutting noises as he checked Liam's pulse from time to time. Most clearly, though, he remembered the physician's sharp intake of breath after he had cut away Liam's tunic.

"God's blood," he muttered. "No wonder you fell down. You wouldn't have noticed the bang on your head at all beside the pain of this thing. I'm surprised you could even get out of bed, let alone go to work."

Varrus remembered wincing at the sight of it, but afterwards he had only vague images of livid red and purple discoloration, deep folds of fatty-yellow, unnatural-looking skin, and black-scabbed areas of healing flesh.

He also remembered going to the chamber door at times and bringing in pails of hot, steaming water and armfuls of neatly rolled white cloth bandages, and he remembered flexing his legs and lifting Liam up in both arms at one point, then turning away from the bed while Aurelius rearranged the bedsheets before calling for him to set his burden down again. And he remembered, very clearly, washing his hands and forearms thoroughly with some kind of pungent, foaming soap that Aurelius gave him.

Afterwards, when they went back into the main part of the house and sat by the fire, Lydia came to meet them, bringing each of them a mug of Shanna's ale and asking them for information on Liam's condition. Aurelius explained that he had given Liam a sleeping potion that should keep him sound asleep for at least eight more hours, and that when he returned to his infirmary he would prepare some other medications and bring them back with him in the morning, when he would explain what they did and how they should be administered. He was also adamant that no visitors should be allowed into the sickroom other than Liam's wife, Lydia, and Varrus himself.

When Lydia left to spread the word of what she had learned, the physician raised his mug to Varrus and then sipped at his drink, staring into the fire.

One of the logs in the brazier gave way, and Varrus watched a whirl of sparks rise into the chimney. "The bang on his head is the least of his troubles, isn't it?" he said.

Aurelius shook his head and exhaled loudly through his nostrils. "Not the half of them," he said. "I've seen severe battle wounds that were nowhere near as bad as that. What in God's name happened to him?"

"An accident. In the forge. He fell while he was carrying a white-hot blade. It burnt him to the bone."

"It did far worse than that. When did this happen?"

"I don't really know. He won't talk about it. It was more than a year ago, though. I've been here for almost a year and he was over it by the time I got here."

Gnaeus Aurelius threw Varrus an unfathomable look. "You speak very well, and conduct yourself very well, for an Eirishman. How good a smith are you?"

"I know my craft."

"Aye, I'm sure you do. You have that air of competence about you that commands respect. How do men call you? Your friends, I mean."

Varrus cocked his head. "Fingael," he said, "or Finn."

"Then I shall call you Magister Fingael. So listen, Magister. I assume this man is your uncle, am I correct?" Varrus nodded, and the physician continued. "Well, I have no hesitation in saying that I have probably never met a more stoic or courageous man in my entire life. He should have died months ago. I am a Christian, and I am now speaking as a Christian. The fact that this man has actually been working in a smithy, in the condition I found him in today, is close to being miraculous. That he has remained alive for as long as he has with such wounds is a miracle in itself."

There was a long silence until Varrus said, quietly, "So there is nothing you can do to save him?"

"The Lord God Himself would be taxed to save this man, especially with the wounds he sustained today." He shook his head. "No, Magister Fingael. There is nothing I can do, save make him comfortable for as long as he continues to live." He held up a hand to stop Varrus before he could say another word. "You are going to ask me how long that might be, but let me ask this of you instead: how am I to know that? The infection and corruption in his wounds is rife—beyond salvage. I have never seen the like of it. The man should not be alive. And yet he is. Would you have me attempt to read God's mind? Well, forgive me then, because I cannot do that. All I can do is respect His dictates."

He raised his mug and drained it. "I have to get back to my infirmary. Fortunately, as you saw, we have no residents at the moment, so my temporary desertion might have gone unnoticed. I'm grateful to you for your assistance today. You were of great help. When I get back, I'll prepare those medications I mentioned. But I warn you, they are painkillers and sedatives, so expect no miraculous resurrections."

"What should I tell the family?"

"That he is gravely hurt and it is highly likely he will not recover. No need to tell them more. His wife, at least, has lived with his infirmity for a long time now, so she must believe it to be non-fatal, and that speaks even more directly to her husband's determination and stoicism. No need to disillusion her on that. It would only make her feel guilt she does not deserve. The blow to Liam's head was severe—ample reason to expect a tragic outcome, and I suspect the entire family already thinks that to be true." He stood up, setting his empty mug on the table.

"Between you and me, though, I'll be surprised if he survives the night. Farewell, Magister Fingael."

Varrus escorted Aurelius to the outer gate and saw him on his way, and as he turned back towards the house he saw Lydia waiting for him in the courtyard, her arms crossed on her breast. He hugged her in silence, kissing the crown of her head, and when she leaned back in his arms to look up at him, he asked, "How is Shanna?"

She looked away, over his shoulder. "How should she be?" she said. "Frightened, lost. What will she do now? She can't run the smithy by herself, without a smith."

"She has a smith. Shamus will do the work."

"Shamus doesn't want to be a smith forever."

It became his turn to lean back and look at her. "What is that supposed to mean? Shamus *is* a smith. That's what he does to earn his livelihood. If he has no desire to be a smith, then it's a secret of which I knew nothing."

"No one knows," she whispered. "No one but me. He's not even sure of it himself."

Varrus cupped her face in both his palms, peering into her eyes. "Lydia, my love," he said, "I treasure you more than anything in life, but this has been a long, frustrating day and I have no idea what you are talking about. Will you please explain this to me?"

She pulled herself erect and sniffed, dabbing at her eyes with a tiny piece of cloth she had been holding in her hand, and then she took him by the wrist and led him to where they had talked the previous afternoon, against the wagon by the wall. "Lift me up," she said, spreading her arms. When she was seated, looking down at him slightly, she drew a deep breath.

"Shamus thinks he is in love," she began, and then told Varrus all that she had discovered about Shamus and his love interest. "He told me this yesterday and made me swear to tell no one else. But that was yesterday, and none of us would have believed what today would bring. And besides, what he told me this afternoon changed everything. I could not have remained silent, knowing what I know now."

"Today? What more did you learn today?"

"The poor lad was distraught, blaming himself for not having caught Liam before his head could hit the ground. That is nonsense, of course, but not to him. He was inconsolable, and so I took him aside to see if I could comfort him. I thought it might take his mind off things if we spoke of his girl again today. But once he started talking this time, he could not stop and everything came out . . . how much he hated smithing, how he'd never wanted to be a smith but had been forced into it, as though it were a kind of slavery. And he went on and on about how he was going to marry his Eylin and steal her away to where he could build a business of his own, doing what he wants to do."

"Gods!" Varrus stood silent for a moment. "And what was that? What does he want to do? Did he say?"

"He wants to be cooper."

"A what?"

"A cooper. A barrel maker."

"In know what a cooper is, my love, but where did he conceive of *that* idea?"

"At home," she answered, unfazed. "In Londuin. Our smithy used to be a cooperage before Da bought it."

His eyes widened. "Well, yes, of course, but did Shamus ever *work* as a cooper? Or has he merely been dreaming of it?"

"He worked at it. When he was still a boy, too young to be trusted around the smithy and the forge, he worked outside for two summers, helping a friend of Da's who was a barrel maker. I remember how much he enjoyed it, but he never spoke of it again after Da let him go into the smithy . . ." She watched him intently. "So what will you do now, now that I've broken my promise to him not to tell anyone?"

"I don't know," Varrus said quietly, "but I'll keep your secret for as long as I can, because he's not likely to walk out of here tomorrow and set himself up as a cooper. He probably doesn't know how to make a barrel. Or he might know how to, but he couldn't do it himself."

"Would he need to?"

He cocked an eyebrow at her. "What d'you mean?"

She shrugged, prettily, and made a little pout. "Does a barrel maker have to be able to make barrels himself, if he employs others who can do it for him? Your Ajax is a garrison armourer and a collector of fine swords, you say, and yet he can't make a sword himself."

He stared at her and his lips began curling into a smile. "You are a devious woman," he said in tones of open admiration. "Admittedly he has no money, or any strong likelihood of earning it, but all he would really need is a willing investor to help him get set up and hire his own coopers. So his dream need not be impossible. Difficult to realize, certainly, but not impossible. Your vision would give him leave to dream, at least, and dreams come true, I'm told, from time to time."

"Even if they do not, they can fend off despair," she said. "And if Shamus even thinks he could learn the trade, working with a real cooper, it might give him hope for the future."

"Perhaps so. But it would do nothing for Shanna's need to have a smith around to run the smithy."

"There will be no need for that if Liam recovers. For as long as he remains alive, Shamus will not feel threatened in the matter of his freedom to move on." She hesitated, frowning at him. "What is it?"

"Gnaeus Aurelius thinks Liam might not live. The damage to his head is severe."

Lydia was silent for a moment, then asked, "How likely does he think Liam is to die of it?"

"He has no way of knowing. But he said he will be surprised if Liam survives the night."

"Dear God," she whispered. "I must pray for Liam's soul. Help me down, Quintus, quickly."

He lifted her from the wagon and watched her hurry away towards the house and her own room, where he knew she would close herself in and pray.

In the depths of the night, in the darkest hours before dawn, a keening wail woke Varrus, and he knew that Liam Mcuil was gone.

TWENTY-THREE

The day that followed Liam's death was leaden, in every sense—leaden clouds and ugly, sullen weather obscured the skies; leaden, surly, stolid drops of rain cast sluggish ripples into dull-looking puddles; and as the long hours shuffled by on leaden, weary feet, Varrus felt a lethargic, hope-sapping awareness of the finality of his friend's death, for it had been long months since last he thought of Liam as either master or mentor, although in truth he had been both. The whole house echoed eerily all that day from the absence of its normal bustle, with no more than the occasional shuffle of passing feet as folk moved listlessly from room to room, whispering if they had to speak, as if they felt it would be sacrilege to raise their voices. The neighbour women had come back again—for which Quintus was grateful—and had taken it upon themselves to console the widow and keep her simultaneously occupied and insulated while they prepared the bedroom for the rites to follow.

In the meantime, Quintus himself had much to think about. Liam's death had disrupted the affairs of the entire family, and what Lydia had told him about Shamus's discontentment had grown enormously in significance in the short time since he had heard it, so that now it flickered and leapt high in his awareness like a dancing flame, demanding his full attention. Knowing Shamus as he now did, it seemed to him that the young smith, with his ability to translate the workings of the world into antagonism against himself, was likely now to follow his own instincts, without thought of how his actions might affect others. And those instincts, according to his sister, were advising him to run, far and fast, before he could be trapped into a life he did not want.

Varrus could see where Shamus's departure might be a blessing in disguise for the unfortunate young woman Eylin. Unless her father and brothers revised their opinions of her would-be suitor—an eventuality that Quintus considered highly unlikely—Eylin would soon find herself facing a world filled with grief and regrets. It was ironic that Shamus's threatened disappearance would offer the young woman the real advantage of a brief period of heartache in return for a greater chance of happiness later. He thought, too, about the ways in which Shamus's absence might also benefit him and Lydia: with the younger man gone, there would be more space in the Mcuil house for the pair of them when they were married. He would not have to build himself a house. The corollary, though, was that he would have to undertake the running of Shanna's smithy, in essence taking over Liam Mcuil's livelihood, with responsibility for his aging widow. That would be a full-time commitment, he realized. It meant that he, not Shamus, would be tied to a life he did not want, unable to continue working in the armouries with Demetrius Hanno, developing new and better blades . . . And so the trap that threatened Shamus now stretched open its jaws for Quintus Varrus, who, until that very moment, had been blissfully ignorant of its existence.

Lost in his thoughts, he had drifted over to the street entrance to the smithy yard and was leaning against the end of the open gate, gazing into nothingness and unaware of his surroundings until the heavens opened without warning and vertical sheets of rain obscured everything, veiling the entire street ahead of him in a grey haze as the torrential downpour rebounded fiercely from the cobblestoned surface. He started to run back to the house, but knowing he would be drenched by the time he got there, he dashed into the stable on his right. He stood inside the door, shaking the wet from his head and slicking his short hair down over his forehead with the flat of his hand. The horse closest to him was chewing contentedly and watching him from little more than an arm's length away, and it chuffed gently as he smiled back at it, admiring the amazing beauty and delicacy of its long black eyelashes.

"Hello, Horse," he said, recognizing the beast as Callum's and reaching out to lay his hand on the blaze on its forehead. "You won't be going back to Londinium for a few more days, I fear. We have to take care of poor old Liam first."

The horse chuffed again, then tore off another mouthful of hay from the pile in the crib, and Varrus moved along the row, checking on each of the animals, a rare full complement of eight, and listening for the roaring of the downpour on the roof to abate. At the end of the row, as he was about to turn away, he heard a different noise from all the others, coming from the space beyond the stall. It was the sound of falling water, but this was a hard tapping rather than a liquid plashing. He peeked around the end of the stall and saw the box that Callum had brought earlier. The sight of it made him frown, though in a perverse kind of way he was glad to see it, for the events of the past two days had driven it from his mind, and now it gave him something else to think about, something far removed from funerals.

He crossed his arms on his chest and covered his mouth with two fingers, staring at the box with narrowed eyes, in no hurry to decide anything, but more curious about what it might contain than he had been since first he heard that it was coming to him, and he recalled what Marius had written: *It was made to be destroyed.*

TWENTY-FOUR

Less than half an hour later, having commandeered the assistance of the part-time stableboy to move it, Varrus was still debating whether he wished to open the box, and how he might go about it if he did decide to proceed. Between the two of them, he and the boy had managed to carry it without too much difficulty from the stables to the smithy, once the rain abated sufficiently to let them do it without being completely drenched.

Now, Varrus's inspection of the box confirmed what Marius had written a couple of months earlier. It was solid and seamless, coated with sized sackcloth that had formed a thick, durable, impenetrable shell, and then coated again with a clear, thick, hardened wax, and the more he looked at it, the more it was clear to him that the only way to open it was to break it apart. But with what kind of tools? Despite Marius's written assurance that he could not harm the chest's contents in breaking it apart, the prospect of assaulting the container with a heavy, iron-headed hammer was a daunting one. It would be time-consuming, for one thing, and notwithstanding his uncle's emphatic opinion, an errant blow might easily damage or even destroy whatever the case contained. Similarly, a sharp-pointed pickaxe was unsuitable, because while that would undoubtedly penetrate the box's hard shell, it might also mar or mutilate whatever was inside.

He turned away and moved to look at the racks and racks of tools Liam had collected over a lifetime of smithing. Most of them were fashioned for the handling of iron, but the craftsman in Liam had drawn him to well-made implements from disciplines other than his own, and he had amassed a fine collection of carpentry tools, which he kept separate from his ironworking tools. Varrus now looked more closely at the selection of drills, wood augers, and handsaws of varying sizes, together with some amazingly sharp-edged chisels and needle-pointed gouges, and it was the sight of one of those gouges, little more than an oversized awl, that supplied him with a sudden idea.

Within a very short time, using a long, thin, but very strong chisel with a narrow, razor-sharp blade, and driving it with a heavy carpenter's maul, he had chipped through the brittle outer covering of the box and was cutting into the wood beneath, quickly carving inwards and down until his chisel's point broke through completely and he felt no resistance. He had made a hole slightly less than the size of his thumbnail, and he went immediately to work on a second one to match it, perhaps three inches along. In no time at all, it seemed, he had finished that one and two more, visualizing them as four corners of a rectangle, and he could tell that he was going to have to sharpen his blade if he needed it for any more cutting. For the time being, though, he had no need to cut further. Instead, he took a short-shafted iron hammer and a metalworking chisel and quickly punched out the wood between the four holes. Into this longer hole he inserted the end of a pickaxe, then braced himself with one leg against the upper edge of the box and hauled backwards with all his strength, trying to pry the lid apart. That was wasted effort, for the constricting sackcloth with its thick and seamless coatings of hardened size quickly proved impossible to breach by brute force.

Undismayed, he reverted to using the wooden maul, though this time with a broader-bladed chisel, chipping away patiently at the sides of the hole he had made, widening it and lengthening it until it was big enough to admit the blade of a small handsaw. After that the work became much easier, because once he had penetrated the carapace of hardened glue, it became friable, breaking into small fragments under the saw's sharp teeth. He had thought at first that the layered sackcloth might be a nuisance, but in fact the overcoating of wax contained the splintered fragments, and the tension of the glue held it sufficiently rigid for the saw's blade to cut through it, at a shallow angle, almost like wood, save that he had to stop after every few strokes to remove loose fibres from the saw's teeth.

In little more than half an hour, working slowly and with extreme care, he had cut his way around the inner edges of the lid, save for where he had encountered two iron straps that ran from the back of the chest to the front. He had almost destroyed his saw blade the first time he hit one of those, not understanding what it had encountered, but then he had remembered Marius telling him that the box was iron-bound. From there, he had worked out precisely where he would find the remaining iron edges—one on either side of each of two straps, at the front and back of the lid—and then he sawed until he reached each one of them, by which time the muscles of his forearm were aching with the unaccustomed effort of sawing rather than hammering. Then, when only the coverings over the metal straps remained, he chipped away the glue that covered them and used a narrow metal file to cut quickly through the soft iron straps themselves, which yielded easily.

When he had finished filing through the last of the metal straps, the lid fell down inside. But it did not fall far, landing on top of something mere inches from the top, and now he used a pair of angled iron tongs to lift one side of the fallen lid, allowing him to grasp the other end and lift the lid out. And there he remained for long moments, gazing down into the box in astonishment.

It contained nothing but what appeared to be wooden scaffolding: horizontal struts of beautifully planed and squared wood, all apparently assembled haphazardly, yet with perplexingly great care, to do no more than support the sides of the box they filled.

It was made to be destroyed.

Baffled, he bent lower and examined the strut closest to him. It ran laterally from one side of the box to the other, a single, straight, square-edged piece of pale yellow wood, no more than two *unciae* in cross-section and showing no signs of brads or nails or any other kind of fastening where its ends abutted the sides of the box. It touched no other strut but the two laterals directly beneath it, in places that looked like uneven distances from either side. No brads. No fasteners. He bent closer still, frowning in concentration, and peered at the other pieces he could see, and they were all the same—uniform in cross-section and in length, depending upon whether they ran from side to side or from front to rear, and all beautifully made, crafted, in fact, by a master carpenter. Which made no sense at all.

Curious, he picked up the carpenter's maul and tapped the first crosspiece on the very top level, and when it did not move, he hit it again, harder. This time it did move, and he hit it a third time, hard and sharp, and it fell clattering onto the struts beneath it. He pulled it out and examined it closely, then set it carefully aside and went to work loosening the other three pieces on the top level. It was only when he was four layers down that he discerned what had been invisible until then. There was a solid object at the very centre of the space—another box, lodged firmly into place by the intricate framework of the surrounding struts and made of the same pale yellow wood as the struts themselves.

As soon as he saw what was there, he stopped being so meticulously careful in the way he removed the wood, and the process accelerated, though he was still forced to deal with each individual piece separately because of the way they were interconnected. Eventually, however, he had stripped out everything down to the beautifully engineered platform on which the box itself sat, held firmly in place by braces above, beneath, and on each side of it. He carefully removed a flat covering that was essentially another lid, then stood looking down at the box itself. It was planed and shaved to perfection, then polished to bring out the natural beauty of the grain, and it was rectangular and not overly large; his spread hands, held thumb tip to thumb tip, covered it nicely.

He stooped to lift it out of its cradle with both hands—and nothing happened. He grunted, adjusted his grip, and tried again, lifting much more strongly this time, and still it did not move, and he began to feel foolish. To lift it now, he knew, he would have to climb inside the box and squat, then lift it with his thighs, and that was plainly ludicrous, if only because the outer container was not big enough to permit him to do that.

He stood back and considered, then moved to swing Liam's pulley hoist around and position it above the box. And not too many moments later, the yellow box was sitting open on the apron of the forge while he gaped down at it, holding the letter that had been folded flat on top of the gleaming golden rows of coins the box contained: twenty columns of coins. He realized now why the packing crate had been so large. It had been designed to disguise the weight of its cargo. That much weight in a smaller box would have endangered everyone who handled it, but the same amount of weight in a container thirty times as large would draw no undue attention. He shook his head in admiration at his uncle's ingenuity.

Varrus closed the yellow box, cutting off the sight of the golden coins, then looked at the thick, many-paged epistle in his hand, fully aware that he ought to do something about concealing the treasure before he took the time to read his uncle's words. And so he set the letter down where it would be safe, then swung the pulley hoist back over the forge apron and used it to move the box into a shadowy corner by the flue, where he covered it with a nondescript cloth before replacing the hoist. That done, he went into the house to find a place to sit and read Marius Varrus's letter, which was written in straightforward Latin.

———

So, Nephew, if you are reading this then I know you must be reeling mentally and physically at what you found in the middle of that ludicrous box I sent you.

Let me put your mind at ease at once. The coins belonged to your grandfather, Titanius Varrus, and since I consider it unlikely that I will father sons of my own at this late date, and you are his last surviving relative in your own generation, the coins are yours by moral and by legal right.

Although my relationship with him was more than slightly constrained, as you know, I believe your grandfather to have been an astonishing and highly talented, sublimely gifted man. You know, of course, that the Emperor Diocletian and he were lifelong friends. In an age when Emperors rose and fell like porridge bubbling in a pot and no one, anywhere, dared put his trust in anyone; when "loyalty" and "integrity" were words laughed at by cynics everywhere, and fidelity to ideals and to principles was as alien a concept as the notion of chastity in a whorehouse; when the very gods themselves appeared to have turned their backs on Rome, ignoring the weltering, noxious stew of would-be Emperors and spurning the venality of a corrupt and thoroughly rotted system, the virtue that men once thought of as honour did not exist.

How, then, at such a time, could anyone have imagined the likelihood of an Emperor rising from the depths of nowhere to become the leader who would rebuild the armies and consolidate the Empire? Even more so, how could anyone, surrounded with the detritus of nigh on a century of imperial decay and self-centred imperatorial neglect, have been induced to believe that such an Emperor might flourish with the unswerving support of a single staunch, unflinching friend whose loyalty and commitment were never once questioned throughout his lifetime? Such tales are the stuff of legend, Quintus, but that is what your grandsire represented: he dedicated his entire life to the support and welfare of his friend and leader, Diocles. Titanius Varrus chose to follow Diocles, the son of a household slave on your great-grandfather's estate. That single fact says much about the character of both boys, long before they grew to manhood.

To this day, no one really knows the extent of what Titanius Varrus was called to do in the service of his Emperor, for much of what he did was sub-rosa. To say he was privy to imperial secrets at the highest level is merely to state what is obvious to anyone who looks. Yet I believe it was something to do with his earlier clandestine activities on behalf of his late friend and Emperor that brought about his eventual assassination and the deaths of all but two of our family.

Let me make it clear now that I have never voiced those suspicions to anyone, nor would I ever consider doing so. Suspicions are no more than opinions, and opinions such as those can trigger sudden deaths. I hope you see the sense of that and conduct yourself in similar silence.

In many ways, your grandfather was born out of his time, for he subscribed to beliefs that had fallen from favour long before he was born. He believed in the ancient Republican values that had predated Octavius Augustus and all the other Caesars who came trotting after him. Titanius Varrus believed in stern-faced, uncompromising honesty, in both speech and behaviour. His heroes included giants like Cincinnatus and Cato the Elder, both revered for their unswerving loyalty, integrity, and civic duty. More humorously, and with genuine irony, he distrusted banks and bankers—unsurprising, perhaps, given that he wed into the wealthiest banking family in Rome. I once heard him remark—while I was in hiding in our shared eavesdropping spot—that he had given the Senecas a slice of his soul already, in marrying their daughter, so why should he give them the remainder of it by being fool enough to trust them with his hard-earned wealth?

In keeping with that distrust, he was assiduous in hoarding his money, keeping its whereabouts unknown to anyone but himself and—albeit inadvertently—to me. Because once again, from inside our sideboard, I discovered his secret.

It was common knowledge that he was considered eccentric because he kept a leather bag on the table by his bed and would throw all his small coinage into it as it accumulated in his scrip. When he had accumulated sufficient asses for them to become a nuisance, he would convert them into silver sesterces, and when he had enough of those, into gold coins which would then vanish, never to be seen again.

I discovered where they vanished to.

It was high summer and I was eight years old, and we were visiting the villa in Salona. On that particular day I thought I had the house to myself, for I had watched my mother leave in the travel wagon, with my brother Marcus in tow, to visit the market in town, and I was glad to have escaped being dragged along. So there I was, looking for something to do in the magnificent formal dining room, when I suddenly heard my father's voice approaching. I barely had time to scamper into hiding in the sideboard before he threw open the door, shouting back over his shoulder to his steward that he did not want to be disturbed, under any circumstances. He closed the door firmly, and then began behaving very strangely.

He walked all around the room, opening each of the other two doors as he came to them, leaning out and peering right and left each time, clearly checking to be sure that he was, and would remain, unobserved, and I have thanked the gods ever since that it never occurred to him to look inside the sideboard!

Once he was satisfied that he was alone, he hauled aside the
main table, grunting with the effort. He groped under it and
pulled out a long T-shaped wooden rod. You will recall that
room had a magnificently intricate, tessellated floor of black,
white, and green marble tiles. He went to a specific spot on
the floor and positioned the end of the rod very carefully upon
it, then leaned on the rod's crossbar with all his weight, and I
was astonished to see what I later found to be a pair of handles
pop up from the marble pattern by his feet. He crouched down
to grasp the handles, then lifted off the covering of a cunningly
designed hole in the middle of the floor. You can imagine how
surprised I was by all of that!

From the hole he pulled out a tin or pewter jug, then
pulled a small leather bag from inside his tunic and poured the
contents into the jug—a long stream of falling golden coins.
I cannot say how many there might have been—a score, at
least, and perhaps more. I could tell by the way he braced himself as he hoisted up the jug that it was heavy, and I watched
him lower it back into the hole, replace the covering slab, and
step on the two handles to press them back into place. He then
replaced the rod under the table and slid the table itself back
into place before striding to the door and disappearing.

I dared to leave our hiding place eventually, but I did not
dare to go and look more closely to see if I could find the edges
of the hole or the spot on which my father had placed the tip
of the rod. I found it eventually, though not until much later,
when I was a grown man. And when the house burned down,
years later, I knew the hoard would still be there, securely hidden under the ruins.

It occurred to me, after the fire and the murders, that there
might be similar deposits in other places. My father did not lack
for property, as well you know. He had eleven villas altogether

when he died. Besides the main family residence on the Palatine Hill, he had major estates in Capri, Padua, Malta, and Sicilia. But those were all in urban centres, and I decided that it was highly unlikely he would conceal hard bullion in any of them, there being no security in public places or overtly desirable estates. Far more likely, I thought, that he would use his smaller, less ostentatious residences to conceal anything he wanted to keep safe. And of course, of the eleven properties, the last three remaining unsold were the smallest and least attractive. One of them had been taken over by a neighbouring landholder, and the other two simply sat empty and decaying.

I enlisted the help of a number of trusted friends in a diligent search of those properties, and we found identical repositories in all three villas, all similarly situated in the main dining room. None were anywhere near as rich as the trove we recovered in Salona, but the sum of them all should serve to keep you safely out of want for as long as you live.

As I have already said, I have no need of the coins. I have my imperial stipend, plus prestige and what passes now for power, and I need no more than I have. You, on the other hand, are somewhere Out There, alone and unknown as far as I can tell, but I have no doubt you will use this resource wisely. There are five thousand gold aurei in the box, the oldest of them dating from the time of Octavian, Caesar Augustus, and the newest of them, in the fourth level down, minted during the reign of Marcus Aurelius. After that time the value of the aureus declined from year to year as the intrinsic value was degraded by unscrupulous speculators, so your grandfather refused to deal in anything more recent than the mintings of Marcus Aurelius.

The bottom layer of coins, though, contains nothing but golden solidi, minted during the lifetime of Diocletian. There can be no deception there. The solidus is minted of pure gold, and though few of them were issued, there can be no doubt of their validity in real terms, and my father valued them highly. That layer contains one thousand Diocletian solidi. There is no more valuable coin in existence, and I know of no one other than yourself, among all the people I know, who can claim to have a thousand genuine Diocletian solidi in their possession. And any one of the other coins in the box could fetch ten times their nominal value from a sharp-eyed trader.

So there it lies, Nephew. You are rich. Wealthy beyond your former dreams. I reckon your personal worth now ranks anywhere between one hundred times and ten thousand times higher than that of the wealthiest person you know today. So be careful. Split up this hoard and hide it with greater care than you have ever given to anything in your life. Hide it and be jealous of it, for it could cause your death instantly were word of its existence to be whispered to the wrong person. This is your future life—your task is to ensure it will not be your death. Be sure, though, to keep the citrus wood box, for it was made, at my request, by the master carpenter of the Ravenna fleet and has a value all its own.

My love is yours, Nephew Quintus, and may your life be as fruitful and rewarding as I could hope for you.

Your appreciative uncle,
Marius

TWENTY-FIVE

In many ways, Quintus Varrus would think afterwards, it was fortunate that he had Liam's funeral to distract him from the implications of his sudden wealth, for he had no time in the ensuing days to think much about what had happened, let alone to grapple with the possibilities entailed.

He did give some thought to where might be a safer, more secure hiding place, but sitting where it was, in plain sight, covered by a simple piece of discarded cloth, the box was less than remarkable, and so he decided to leave it in the forge for the time being, knowing no one was likely to go near it until after the funeral, at least.

The cemetery in Colcaster lay along the roadside about half a mile beyond the city gates, and on the morning of the funeral the family was gratified to see how many of the townspeople had turned out to walk in the procession and pay their final respects to the self-effacing Eirish smith who had served their needs so diligently for close to twenty years. Varrus judged there to be more than a hundred people in the throng, among them several local merchants, prominent citizens, and even a few off-duty personnel whom he recognized from the garrison. He was not too surprised to discover that both the Romans and the Celts, despite their religious differences, followed similar procedures in honouring their dead before burial. It occurred to him that, irrespective of their origins or even of their individual status, people were not so very different in their feelings and their needs when it came down to the essentials of life's beginnings and its ending.

They were about halfway to the cemetery when Varrus noticed mounted soldiers ahead of them. Mounted men were an uncommon sight in Colcaster at any time, because the garrison contained no cavalry. In fact there were relatively few cavalry in all of Britain, he knew, for most of the urgent need for mounted warriors was concentrated in the border regions of the empire, where horse-borne hordes from beyond the northern and eastern frontiers were fighting grimly to break in.

He knew most of the garrison officers by sight now, and as they drew closer he could see nothing familiar about any of the mounted men. He was surprised to see that the troopers were neatly drawn up, patiently waiting for the procession to pass instead of coming ahead, as was their military right, uncaring of the effect upon the funeral and its mourners. It was clear that the formations were there in attendance upon a trio of very senior officers, their splendid armour distinguishing them as legates, the highest purely military rank an officer could achieve.

The senior man among them, on a stunningly beautiful black horse, was dressed in black armour. Beside him sat a pair of slightly less flamboyant aristocrats, and behind those was a massed phalanx of lesser luminaries and centurions, two of whom, from their trappings, were clearly cavalry decurions, each the commander of a thirty-two-man squadron. Two of them in attendance upon the senior general meant that his escort was two squadrons—sixty-four mounted men, all of them wearing heavy shirts of bronze ring mail of the kind Varrus had worked on in his early days in Colcaster.

As the funeral procession drew abreast of the commanding general, the officer drew himself up into a formal seated salute, followed by his entire command, a signal gesture of respect beyond anything that Varrus would ever have expected.

He retained few clear memories of the remainder of that day, and had no memory of even going to bed. Late that night, though, long after the household had settled down to sleep, Lydia came to his bed, laying her fingers over his mouth to warn him against making any sounds, and they made love, wonderfully and wildly and in total silence, all night long.

When he awoke in the morning she was gone. He knew that she had been there, though, knew that his memories of her were not the product of nocturnal dreams, for her scent was everywhere, clinging to his skin and hair and permeating the blankets that had caressed her and now urged him to stay where he was, enveloped in their warmth with his eyes closed, remembering the wonders of what they had experienced. As that smiling thought sank home into his drowsy self-awareness, though, he jerked upright instead, his eyes opening wide as he realized the full extent of what had happened. Lydia had come to his bed, not merely willingly but when he had least expected it. And his life had changed completely.

Lydia was going about her daily affairs with a contented smile upon her lips, bubbling with energy and anticipation as she waited for Quintus to emerge from the sleeping area and show his face. She had been bold, she knew that—bolder than she might have believed she could be. And she had no doubt at all that Quintus would have been deeply shocked at her directness and determination, had he not been sound asleep when she eased herself into his bed.

Her decision to claim Quintus—and that was how she thought of it, that she had claimed her man—had been spontaneous, arrived at in less than the blink of an eye after leaving Shanna sobbing quietly into her pillow. They had been talking, or Shanna had—Lydia had done nothing more than listen and murmur comforting sounds from time to time—about how quickly time sneaks by without our noticing, and how brief a time the gods allot us in this world to share with loved ones and to enjoy loving and being loved by them. And recalling those words on her way to her own bed, Lydia had turned around immediately and gone directly to cherish Quintus Varrus.

She heard a sound behind her and found him standing looking at her from the doorway.

"Hello, Quintus," she greeted him. "Did you sleep well?"

And suddenly he smiled, flashing radiant white teeth. "I'm not really sure if I slept at all, or simply dreamt the night away, but whichever of them is true, I would go back to bed right now if I could sleep and dream such dreams again."

"Well that sounds wonderful," she said, grinning back at him. "But it can't be. Too much to do here today."

He nodded, looking around. "It's quiet. Where is everyone?"

"Father and Callum are up at the fort, visiting Ajax. They haven't been gone long. Some neighbours came to take Shanna to the market. She didn't want to go, but they took her anyway. And I haven't seen Shamus at all this morning, so he must still be asleep. Are you hungry?"

"Starved," he said. "But Shamus isn't in bed. I looked. His cot's made up, so either he was out all night or he was up and out early this morning. Why did you ask if I'm hungry?"

"Because I made you a breakfast."

"A breakfast? Really? Do you mean a real breakfast, to be eaten at a table? I can barely remember when I last sat down to one of those. Not since I was a boy, I think. What have you made?"

"It's a little late for a daybreak breakfast, so let's call this a prandium, a mid-morning breakfast. I made puls—" She saw his puzzled look. "Boiled porridge of crushed grain with warm milk, sweetened with honey and dried apricots. There's also fresh wheat bread made overnight, drizzled with olive oil and toasted in the oven. I could add eggs, if you wish—and pork sausage."

"And I could die a happy man. Will you feed me like this every day, once we are wed?"

"Certainly not. Would you make a household slave out of me? But

I will hire a cook to feed you better than I ever could. My cooking skills are few."

"You'll hire a cook?"

"I will, the moment you begin to earn sufficient money to support one."

"Agreed," he said, reminded suddenly of the yellow box in the forge. His gaze lingered on the bare table. "Where is this wondrous breakfast?"

"It's ready," she said. "Keeping warm. Would you like me to prepare the eggs and sausage, too?"

"I would." He hesitated. "So be it you are willing, and not merely testing me for early signs of dictatorship."

"No, not at all. Sit, then. I'll bring it out to you." She disappeared in the direction of the kitchen, and as soon as she was out of sight he spun on his heel and trotted out to the smithy.

It was deserted, and he went directly to the chimney corner and pinched four or five coins out of the first densely packed row of fifty, closed the box, and covered it again.

When Lydia returned a few moments later, carrying a steaming bowl of porridge, he was in his seat. "That looks wonderful. Are you not joining me?"

"No, I had mine earlier, when I first made the puls, because I didn't know how long you might lie abed this morning. Besides, I have to cook your eggs and sausage."

"But you will sit and talk with me when you are done?"

She smiled again at him, widely this time. "Rely upon it, Quintus Varrus. It has been far too long since we did that. The last time we did, Liam was alive, but everything in our world has changed within the past five days, and we need to discuss how we are to deal with that. So eat your porridge. I'll be back."

The porridge was delicious, with exactly the right amount of honey and dried apricots to sweeten it perfectly, and as he set down his spoon and pushed the empty bowl away, Lydia returned with a wooden platter on which rested a round of heavy, crisped wheaten bread topped with a pair of eggs and several sausage links fried in pork fat.

"Eat," she said, setting it down in front of him and placing a knife beside it. "And listen. I'll do the talking while you chew, and when you're finished, we'll talk together."

He carefully cut a piece of the crisp bread, pushed a morsel of egg onto it, and raised it to his mouth.

She held up a hand and began to mark points off by touching her fingers. "One: Shanna is not a smith but she now owns a smithy. She has but two options. She must either find a qualified helper to run the smithy, or she will have to sell it, if she can find a buyer. Now, that first option was wiped out when Shamus told me he no longer wants to be a smith."

"I doubt that's true. Shamus likes to complain, and when he does, he always harps on that. But surely he would rise to meet this responsibility of helping his aunt?"

"No, I heard too much conviction in his voice to ignore what he said. He left me in no doubt, too, that nothing anyone in the family might say would sway him to do otherwise. My brother has had enough of smithing, Quintus. And that leaves Shanna with no option but to sell her smithy and move out, to live alone thereafter on whatever proceeds she can wring from the sale."

"She could always remain here and hire a smith to run the smithy for her, as she did with Liam." He speared one of the sausages on his knife point and bit off the end.

"That's true, I suppose. But she's twenty years older now than she was then and she might not be so fortunate in who she finds this time around. Think of the difference in size between a healthy smith and an old woman. Were she to pick the wrong man, she could condemn herself to a life of misery."

He made no attempt to reply to that, and she continued. "And then, of course, there is the matter of you and me and our marriage. When last we spoke of that, you talked about building us a house. Is that still in your mind?"

He shrugged, schooling his face to betray nothing. "Of course," he said. "Why would you even ask? Had it not been for what happened, I would already have spoken to Ajax about it and he would be hiring a builder and workers."

"But he is not, is he?"

"No, not yet. Why? Do you have something else in mind?"

She started to respond, then hesitated, looking at him strangely. And then she started to smile. "You already know what I'm thinking, don't you?"

"I'm not sure," he said quietly, swallowing his final mouthful and pushing his empty platter away. "That was a truly fine breakfast, my love," he said, wiping the edges of his mouth with finger and thumb. "But tell me what you are thinking, and then I'll tell you if it's what I thought it might be."

She sat straighter in her chair. "We could live here. Move in, I mean, once we are married, and then you could run the smithy." She squirmed in her seat as she waited for him to respond, and when he said nothing, she prompted, "Is that what you expected me to say?"

"It is," he said. "But as a workable suggestion it has one inherent weakness." He watched her as she frowned gently. "For that to work, I would have to give up my position at the armouries—my smith's training, for I am not yet qualified to join the smiths guild. I have two more years of training before I may legitimately claim to be a smith."

"But—"

"Yes, but . . . I know what you are going to say, my love. As long as I am in my own smithy, it would make little difference whether I am qualified or not. No one could challenge me at my own forge."

"Exactly."

"Not so. Believe me, love, I would enjoy believing that, if it were true. But the truth is that many people would refuse to use my services, rightfully claiming that I am unqualified. I am a student at this stage. A gifted one, I believe, but nonetheless an apprentice, learning how to be a master craftsman in the not-distant future. Demetrius Hanno and I are exploring better ways of making blades and treating iron—there's a new word he has taught me: *steel*. Steel is iron, hardened more strongly and more purely than any iron ever has ever been. It is utterly unlike any other form of iron, and I am learning how to make it consistently and predictably. When I have learned how, and can make sword and other blades with it, then I will be a smith—in fact a specialist smith, a blade maker. But that will take two more years, and there are no shortcuts."

She sat silent, her eyes lowered, but then she looked up and met his eyes and nodded gently. "You're right," she said. "I was wishing for the moon. You can't walk away from what you have, Quintus. It's an opportunity you will never have again. We'll find another way."

"We will, my love. In fact we have one now."

Her brows came together immediately. "Now?"

He smiled broadly at her, and his white teeth flashed in that sparkling grin that never failed to make her smile in return. "You have lost sight, my love, of the fact that I am Quintus Varrus, not Shanna Mcuil. I am not a frail old woman. I can hire a fully qualified smith without any fears that he might bully me. He'll handle the morning shifts, as Liam and Shamus did, while I train at the armouries, and I'll come back here in the afternoons. So you see, your plan will work very well, despite all your misgivings."

"My misgivings?" Lydia pretended to be angry, but her eyes were dancing and she could not conceal her excitement. "You beast," she hissed, swinging an open-handed slap far short of him. "You were the one who said it couldn't work!"

"No, and you need to control your temper, my lady. *And* to start listening more attentively. I said your suggestion had an inherent weakness. I did *not* say it was a fatal weakness, for I had already seen a way

around it. And anyway, I didn't want you to think yourself too clev—"
He stared at her.

"What? What are you thinking?"

"I'll tell you that if you will answer me one question."

"Ask me."

"Last night, in my bed, in the dark. How many times did we . . . do it?"

A flush of colour stained her cheeks. "I can't remember," she said eventually, her voice soft and breathy. "I stopped counting after the third time . . . Or perhaps it was the fourth."

"I counted six," he said, his voice as soft as hers. "Six times I poured myself into you, and every time I thought what I am thinking now: that I wanted to do the same thing in daylight, to be able to see your face and look into your eyes as I let go and lost myself in you. I want to look at you and see you looking back at me as I fill you."

The very air between them seemed to vibrate with tension, and then someone, somewhere outside, dropped something or knocked it over, reminding them that there were other people close by, and they both sagged, returning to the moment.

"Later," she breathed, almost inaudibly. "This afternoon. In my room. Wait for me to go and give me time to prepare, then follow me."

He nodded. "Done." Then he stretched out his hand. "Look at this," he said, and dropped the little wedge of coins he had been holding, so that they hit the tabletop and broke apart, rolling in several directions.

She watched them scatter, her eyes growing round, then reached out slowly and picked one up, examining it so closely that she was almost squinting in concentration. "Gold," she breathed. "Caesar Augustus." She picked up another and did the same. "Marcus Brutus."

Lydia weighed the three remaining coins in her hand reflectively.

"The box," she said quietly. "You opened your uncle's box. When?"

"Three days ago."

"And you said nothing? Not a word to anyone?"

He shook his head. "Too many other more important things to see to."

"What else did it contain? Can you tell me?"

"I can show you, if you'd like."

"I would." But she made no move to stand up, instead staring at the five gold coins in her hand, tossing them gently into the air from time to time as though trying to gauge the weight of them. "I've never handled a gold coin before," she said. "Never even seen one. Are these what they call aurei? Gold pieces? What are they worth?"

"They are aurei," Varrus said. "As to what they are worth, I'm not sure. I haven't seen too many of them myself, even where I came from. But I know those in your hand are ancient, stamped from pure, unadulterated gold. In all likelihood, according to my uncle, these are worth ten times as much in sesterces as a modern equivalent containing one tenth of the gold—if you could find such a thing. But that would only be if you could find the right buyer to sell them to. I'm going to have to approach that matter carefully. Which reminds me to ask you, if you will, not to mention these to anyone yet."

"I wouldn't dare," she said, still hefting them in her hand. "This is far too much money to discuss casually. Even at five times their face value in sesterces, I have more money in one hand than my father and my brothers could earn in a year."

"What you have there," he said, "should be about two years' revenue for Dominic's smithy."

"That is difficult to believe," she murmured, opening her fingers to stare at the coins in her palm. "Were there any more of them?"

"Five thousand of them."

He watched her freeze, gazing down at her palm for what seemed like an age before her head rose with comedic slowness and she met his eyes. "What did you say?" Her voice was barely audible.

"I said five thousand. Five thousand gold aurei."

"Five . . . thousand." She closed her eyes and spoke slowly, her voice holding no inflection. "Five thousand solid gold coins, each worth five hundred sesterces . . ." She looked at him again then, continuing to speak in the same flat tone, her slow pronunciation stressing each word as she uttered it. "That is five hundred thousand sesterces."

"At least," Varrus said. "The true value should be double that. You are marrying a wealthy man, Lydia Mcuil."

"I'm marrying a dead man if word of this gets out," she said. "What are we going to do, Quintus? We can't live with *this*."

He saw the panic in her eyes and stood up, moving to her quickly, and pulled her gently to her feet, gathering her into his arms and stooping to kiss the top of her head as he hugged her close. "Of course we can," he whispered. "Come, love, sit down again and I'll tell you how we'll do it, and you'll see the truth of it."

He seated her again, then took her hand in both of his, looking directly into her eyes and speaking softly but with authority.

"Listen now," he said. "We can live with this new wealth just as surely as we can live in a world without Liam Mcuil in it. It will be alien in some ways, and at first it will be difficult, but it will gradually become bearable as life goes on and we adjust. And you and I simply have to grit our teeth and adjust quickly. We have to plan our future carefully and concern ourselves, above all else, with concealing how much we truly have. We could never use so much wealth in our lifetime, but no one says we have to. Do you hear me, Lydia? No one is saying we have to use it all, or put it on display, or let the world know what we truly have."

She looked down when he said that, as though unwilling or unable to believe what he was saying, and he moved his hand to tilt her chin up until she was looking right at him again. "Hear me, my love," he continued, keeping his voice low and calm. "We will split it into tiny portions—into far smaller amounts, each of perhaps one hundred coins—and we'll bury it all, carefully, in secret, well-hidden places. As the need arises to trade them for silver, I will make arrangements to exchange them at fair prices. There will be no difficulty there. I have legitimacy, in that I can prove I, Fingael Mcuil, received a legacy, shipped to Britain through the good offices of the colonial military headquarters in Londinium, and dispatched from Italy by Sub-Prefect Marius Varrus, vice-admiral of the Ravenna fleet. The shipment contained the personal possessions and accumulated savings of my friend Rhys Twohands, who vanished in Upper Moesia while on a clandestine mission for the admiral several years earlier. That has all been legally established by letter, so the legitimacy of my sudden possession of gold coins will never be in question. Do you hear me, my love? Do you believe what I have said?"

She nodded, hesitantly, and he stooped to kiss her.

She was unresponsive at first—not unwilling but simply not participating for the first few moments, but then, gradually, she came to life, her mouth softening and warming, yielding to his growing urgency, then matching and outdoing it with her own until he lifted her and carried her to where he could brace his back against a wall and hold her high while she struggled to rid them of the barriers of clothing between their bodies and to share with him the need that had closed their minds to any possibility of being interrupted.

Afterwards, when he had lowered her, shaking and laughing, to huddle against him again, he hugged her tenderly and whispered in her ear.

"A lifetime of this ahead of us, my love."

She nodded, her head moving against his breast, and then leaned back and looked up at him. "That's true, my love, I know. But we have a lifetime of plain life to live, too, and much to be done before we can start to enjoy it."

He raised an eyebrow. "Such as?"

"Well, there's a wedding, for one thing."

"Aye, but—"

"No, my love, no buts. I am accepting your word on what will happen with the money— Where is it, by the way?"

"It's in the smithy. No one will see it before I move it."

"You have to hide it for a while. Have you somewhere safe?"

"I do." He had suddenly remembered a good hiding place—an old rusted, unused oven at the back of the forge, in an awkward little corner. "I'll hide them later this afternoon, while no one is around."

"Do that. But here's what I was saying. If I can accept your say-so on the matter of the coins, then you must accept mine on the matter of the wedding."

He blinked. "I will. But what does that mean?"

"It means that we are already married." She nodded towards the corner where they had so recently enjoyed each other. "That, what we just did there, was a wedding in every sense of the word, save that no one was here to witness it." She glanced around, wide-eyed, and laughed. "At least, my modesty hopes no one witnessed it."

She sobered again instantly. "But make no mistake, my love. That is what it was, in my eyes and in my heart. I could commit no more sincerely than that we were in a Christian ecclesia, swearing an oath in front of the assembled citizens of this town."

"I'm not doubting you, Lydia. I feel the same way. But I still don't understand what you are really saying."

"I'm saying kiss me."

So he did, at great length, then pulled away and leaned back again while he yet could. She broke free of his arms and took him by the hand, swinging him back towards the table, where she waited for him to sit, then sat beside him.

"Liam is newly dead," she said, "and most of my family is here. I set the rules to govern our wooing almost a year ago. I said I needed time to come to know you, and everyone else agreed, including you, even though it was not your wish. Well, that time is now in the past. I know you now, and I have come to love you and I have no slightest doubt that you love me. We want to be man and wife, and the time has come for us to be so. But the time is also ill suited to a wedding celebration, with the shadow of death still hovering around us.

"It is equally inconvenient because of the number of friends and relatives who would be forced to travel here in dangerous times and unpredictable weather. That would take months to arrange, and I do not want to waste those months. I want to share every day of them with you and no one else. So my proposal is this. We will stand up together here in this house, in the presence of those family and friends who are here, and we will exchange our commitments to each other and pledge to be man and wife henceforth, and then I will remain here as your wife while my father and brother return to Londuin."

"But . . . I think that is a wonderful idea, my love, but what about all your friends down there?"

"What about them? They are my friends, but they are down there, as you say. They may be disappointed to have missed my wedding, but they will all soon realize their good fortune in not having to travel all the way from there and back for what is really little more than a cele-bration dinner. They will recover from the shock, and they'll remain my friends."

"Well I would hope so. But I doubt your father would ever agree to that suggestion. And I doubt if I could blame him. You are his only daughter and he loves you dearly. But his pride in you is even greater than his love, and I suspect he would—and will—have difficulty in letting go of you so easily. You wait and see if I am not right. Dominic will want to part with you far more ceremoniously than this suggestion of yours permits. He'll want his entire family—all your brothers and their wives and children—and all his friends and neighbours, and yours, too, to be there to see you wed. Dominic Mcuil will want to launch his daughter into marriage in the grand style. You wait and see."

"We'll see about that. You leave my father to me."

"Happily, my love. I pledge that I will leave your father to you as long as I know that *you* will leave your father for me . . . Now, what will we do about Shamus?"

"What *should* we do about him? He's a grown man now, and much of that is thanks to you. He won't go back to Londuin, not as long as he has hopes for a life as a barrel maker with his Eylin."

"No, I agree. But he might stay here, with us, as a smith. For a short time, I mean, once we are married. Providing he knows that at the end of it—say in two years' time—I would help him to purchase a cooperage of his own."

"He would be a fool—and a very selfish one—to balk at such an offer!"

"And I could arrange to have him work in the afternoons, under supervision, as a trainee barrel maker at the fort. That would give him an understanding of the basics of the craft—sufficient to know, after two years, how to hire and supervise an employee of his own."

She blinked at him. "Could you do that?"

"Of course. And we both know the money is less than troublesome. This could work, if Shamus really wants to try it."

"And why would you want to help him to that extent? Out of charity? That would be his first question, because deep down he's proud, despite appearances. Do you have an answer he could live with?"

"Absolutely. I *need* him, Lydia. I need him here in the mornings for the next two years. And if he will oblige me in that, then I'll reciprocate and help him gain what he wants. We will be family to each other, brothers-in-law. Is that not reason enough? Besides, if I set him up in business I would expect a share of the profits, as a partner. Shamus would have no problem with that."

She sat silent for long moments, looking at him, then shook her head slowly and smiled at him. "You see?" she said. "That's the kind of thinking that makes me love you, Quintus Varrus."

He grinned back at her. "I'm happy to hear that, then, for that's the kind of thing I do with my eyes closed. Being clever takes far more effort. And so, barring your father's refusal to grant us his blessing, we are cancelling the wedding plans for your friends and family from Londinium, we are seducing Shamus into staying as a smith for a while longer, we are moving into this house instead of building one of our own, and we are going to live our lives in a way that conceals the fact that we have suddenly become immensely rich. Have I forgotten anything?"

"You have." She leaned in and kissed him. "What will become of Shanna, when this is no longer her household?"

"Why must we discuss that? Nothing will change for Shanna, apart from our living with her for a short time, in addition to Shamus, at least until our new house is built. The smithy will still be hers and I will run it, with Shamus's help, in return for living in her house. You're the one who will have to decide if we need to rearrange the rooms. We should have a bedroom of our own. I would insist on that, and I think we could easily enlarge the space in the north end of the house—it's mostly used for storage anyway. That's no more than a suggestion, but I think you could make it a reality, so let me know what you decide . . . Anything else?"

Neither of them could think of another thing, and there were still no signs of life elsewhere in the house, so Lydia went away humming towards her bedchamber, and Varrus split the boxed coins into four large nail bags of sturdy, hand-sewn leather and stowed them in the rusted oven in the corner of the forge, then followed her into her room, unaware that he, too, was humming under his breath.

TWENTY-SIX

Varrus was up and out of the house by dawn the next morning, feeling youthfully fresh and buoyant despite his nocturnal activities with Lydia Mcuil. Lydia, too, had survived the night in exceptional spirits and had been singing quietly to herself as she prepared another bowl of oaten porridge for him before sending him off to the armouries with a kiss. There appeared to be no one astir yet in the house when he left, and it crossed his mind that he'd heard nothing at all the night before to indicate that anyone had come home. They must have, he concluded. He simply had not heard them, having other, more pleasurable matters to engage his attention.

The gate guards at the fort greeted him as they usually did, and the decanus in charge of the detachment offered his condolences over Liam's death, but as he made his way across the parade ground towards Demetrius Hanno's domain, Varrus saw a body of legionaries, perhaps a full century of men, being drilled by a grim-faced junior centurion he had never seen before. He had the impression that the legionaries appeared to be far more focused than he was accustomed to seeing, though it occurred to him that he, too, might be on his best behaviour were he trying to impress such a hawk-faced taskmaster.

Hanno was bent over a workbench studying a drawing and he looked up and grunted a welcoming sound when Varrus walked in. "I'm glad you're back," he said. "Ajax asked to see you when you came in, before you start on anything serious. He is in his office—here, though, not over in the praesidium. Everything is well at home, I trust? How is Shanna holding up?"

"She seems to be handling it well," he said. "Lydia's with her this morning, just to keep her mind as far away as possible from thoughts of Liam. I'll go to Ajax now, then. Do you know what he wants, by any chance?"

Hanno was back over his drawing and answered without looking up again. "No, but he will tell you when you get there, I have no doubt."

"I ought not to be too long." He stopped in the doorway. "There is something going on, though, isn't there? There's a new drill instructor outside this morning, grinding the men as though they were raw recruits, and I saw at least two squadrons of cavalry coming in the other day, escorting some very fancy-looking top rankers, legates, at least. Cavalry, in Camulodunum? What's going on, Demetrius?"

"Not my business," the smith responded, not looking up. "Ask Natius."

Varrus was smiling as he walked away, thinking about how even Hanno, who never spoke in abbreviations, had shortened Ignatius Ajax's name. No one who knew Ajax well enough to speak to him ever called him by his full name, or even by his proper first name. He had simply always been Natius to his friends. He was still smiling when, as he approached Ajax's workspace, the door was pushed open and four men came out. They were all strangers to Varrus, and all were armoured but bare-headed, talking quietly among themselves. He drew aside against a wall to let them file by, and one of them looked at him in passing and nodded civilly.

Varrus returned the nod, and he had half-turned towards Ajax's door again when he became aware of one of the young apprentices from Demetrius Hanno's area sitting to the left of the door. The lad was staring down at his feet, which were well shod in a pair of legionary boots that were only slightly too large for him. He looked to be about fourteen, still a few years short of enlisting, and something about him, it might have been no more than his air of dejection, prompted Varrus to speak to him.

"Hey," he said, and the boy looked up. "You look as though you're waiting to be thrown into the cells. What did you do?"

The boy shook his head, his eyes big and round at being spoken to by one of Hanno's smiths.

"Come on, speak up," Varrus pressed him gently. "Did you steal something? Kill someone?"

"I didn't do anything."

The voice was calm, quiet, and somehow bigger than Varrus had expected from a boy that young, and he narrowed his eyes. "How old are you?"

The boy frowned for a moment, then said, "Ten, I think. But I might be twelve."

"You think you're ten? Don't you know? Big fellow your size, you ought to know your own age. Why are you here, then, if you didn't kill anyone?"

"Magister Ajax sent for me, for fighting."

"Fighting? You won, I hope. Did you?"

"I didn't lose."

"Good man," Varrus said, grinning. "What's your name?"

"Simeon, of Aquino."

"Aquino, in Italy?"

"Yes. My dad was born there."

"Good for him—and for you, I suppose. I've been in Aquino. I liked it, too. I'll leave you to it, then." Varrus turned away and was still smiling as he knocked on Ajax's door and went inside.

"Ah! You're here," Ajax said. "I was hoping you'd be back today. How are things at the smithy?"

"Quiet for the moment. We haven't relit the fires yet. I imagine Dominic will do that this morning."

"I'm sure he will. In the meantime, Demetrius has been waiting patiently for you. He's been working the last batch of metal we took from the oven, working your supply and his own, and I swear he must have welded each of those pieces twenty times in the past four or five days, heating and hammering and flattening and stretching them and folding and beating them again and again. He hasn't complained, but I know he's impatient to get you back to work again. Nobody else will do, none but you, and he wouldn't let any of the other trainees touch your iron. I've never known it to happen before in all the time I've been working with him. Anyway, he says he has the metal ready for shaping, so as soon as you're ready, he'll be chafing to get started."

"Good, then I'll get down there and waste no more of his time. By the way, who's the young lad outside? He looks like he's waiting to be marched away and crucified, and yet he seems like a nice young fellow. I've seen him around in the forge rooms, and I've never noticed him doing anything wrong—but he clearly thinks he's in trouble."

Ajax shrugged. "I know, and I don't know what to do about him."

"You mean he's a troublemaker?

"Gods, no! The very opposite, in fact, but I can't protect him."

"From what?"

"He's an orphan. I knew his father, a good man but killed in a skir-mish against some bandits. I found the boy a place here, about nine months ago when his mother died. He was fine for a while, but then some of the locals started picking on him and he fought back . . . very well. The kids he's up against—two brothers—are rotten little bastards, but their father's one of my most valuable armourers and I can't afford to lose him." He stopped, and an odd look formed on his face. "I don't suppose you might have a place for an apprentice and general dogsbody, would you? The boy's a delight, and he'll tackle anything. Just point him to it and tell him to go. He wouldn't cost anything, beyond his feed, and I'd pay for that happily. You wouldn't regret taking him, I swear . . ."

He fell silent, and Varrus found himself thinking that he could, in fact, use an extra pair of hands around the smithy. He decided quickly. "Why not? I can offer him a three-month trial, anyway, and if he works out, we'll see what comes of it. I'll have to talk to Lydia about it. That won't be a problem, though, I'm sure. I liked him on sight, so I'm sure she will. What did he say his name was?"

"Simeon," Ajax said.

"Simeon. Of Aquino in Italy. That is an unlovely, ungainly name. I'll take him home with me when I go, let Lydia have a look at him, and if she says so, he can pick up his belongings tomorrow. How does that sound?"

"Better than I could have wished for, my friend."

"I'm glad. Now, Demetrius said you wanted to talk to me."

Ajax smiled, rather ruefully, Varrus thought, and said, "We had visitors while you were away. Unexpected company."

"The newcomers? The cavalry escort and the party of gilded helmets and impressive plumes who came the other day? They pulled off the road and waited, to permit the funeral procession to pass. That was an unexpected and impressive courtesy, and it did not go unnoticed. Who were they?"

"Who *are* they, you mean. You recall that we spoke about Pompey and his behaviour? Well, they are now the new powers in charge here."

"What? Here in the garrison? What about Pompey, then?"

"Pompey is gone, and he will not be coming back." Ajax paused, enjoying the stunned look on Varrus's face. "D'you remember me telling you, that day we talked about him, that his corruption had not gone unnoticed? Well, the new legate arrived two days ago and Lucius Placidus Pompey was arrested, stripped of his command and his rank, and shipped out of here in chains within the hour."

"By the gods. Talk about Draconian measures! What brought him down? I mean, it's no small matter to strip a serving legate of his name and fame. There must be a heavy volume of condemnation and proof involved."

"He was found guilty of sedition and conspiracy to undermine the state and to impoverish the imperial treasury."

"Ah! Is that so? I would condemn him for that, too, in all likelihood, if I knew what it meant."

One corner of Ajax's mouth quirked into a tiny smile. "He was selling secret information—times and dates and other specific information, including bills of lading and delivery schedules on shipments of logistical supplies to legions and garrisons throughout Britain. Charges established and proved beyond any shade of doubt."

"Well, that would do it. And to whom was he supplying it? They'd have to know that to be able to convict him."

Ajax's smile widened. "Oh, that was known. He was selling directly to a very highly organized army of thieves, operating almost as efficiently as specialized military units. Specialized units dealing in theft, stealing food out of the mouths of our fighting soldiers throughout the empire."

Varrus's eyes had narrowed, listening to this, and now he asked, "Who are these people, this organization? If it's so highly organized, and operating empire-wide, people must have heard of it long before now."

"People *had* heard of it. We've known about it for years. We never really gave it a name, though, because we weren't supposed to know it was out there. So we had to keep our knowledge of it hidden."

"How could you do that, in the armies?"

"Sound question, young Mcuil. How, indeed?" He glanced away, as though debating with himself, then sniffed. "Don't suppose it makes much difference, now we've broken it, but I'm still telling you more than I ought to. We referred to it simply as the Ring, and we dealt with it in utter secrecy, for what should be obvious reasons."

"Who are *we*?"

"*We* are military personnel, not civilians. That's all you need to know and more than you should know. But we've been working to infiltrate the Ring and destroy it for as long as we have known about it."

Varrus nodded. "Accepted," he said. "I appreciate I don't need to know the details, as a civilian. But I have to ask how that kind of secrecy could even be possible. I know there are circles within circles and wheels within wheels in the army structures, because my family have all been military officers forever, but no secret can long survive being shared by more than two people, and even that is too many. Yet you are talking, potentially, about secrets among hundreds of people, for years."

"Decades. True," Ajax said. "But among those circles within circles are circles that are tightly self-contained and self-governing. We belong to one such circle, an ancient one, established in the earliest days of Rome, when all soldiers served a god of light. We call ourselves a fraternity—a brotherhood—and our internal bounds are constant and far-reaching."

"The Mithraic Order, you mean." He grinned, seeing the hint of dismay on Ajax's face, and added, shrugging his shoulders, "Military family. What can I say?"

"Right," Ajax said. "Well, when Diocletian was emperor, as a living member of our brotherhood he enlisted the support of our order to deal with these thieves—very well-connected and well-financed thieves— who had devised a means of exploiting his newly perfected system of logistics and supply." He paused, and looked shrewdly at Varrus. "You did know about his system, I presume?"

"To feed the armies again, while they still existed."

"Exactly. Because over the previous fifty to seventy-five years, when it seemed there were new emperors being vomited up by the armies every day, the entire system of procurement and supply had broken down and the legions were disintegrating, especially on the borders and the frontiers where the worst of the fighting was taking place against the incoming barbarians. In far too many areas—rapidly grow- ing and critical areas—food trains, munitions, supplies, and weaponry simply were not reaching the legions and garrisons, and the armies were falling apart. Literally disintegrating. Entire units, cohorts, and even smaller legions were disbanding and disappearing between one day and the next. And who could blame them? You can starve quickly when yours is but one hungry mouth among five or six thousand—and die even more quickly when your armour and weapons break or are lost on campaign and you have nothing to replace them with. It was the worst time in Rome's history."

"Were you serving then?"

That earned him a haughty look. "Fifty years ago? No, I can say with certainty that I was not. But then Diocletian came along, an army man himself, having come up the hard way, through the ranks. He knew exactly what needed to be done, and he did it. First among equals, he put together a team of the finest minds in the empire to rebuild the entire supply chain from top to bottom and from end to end—provisions, personnel, munitions and livestock, training and disciplinary standards, and vehicle acquisition programs to ensure prompt and efficient delivery throughout the imperial territories."

"Hmm. That was a major undertaking, when you hear it summed up like that."

"It was gigantic. And it was more than three years before the first stirrings of results began to appear. By the end of the first decade, though, the new system was operating smoothly. And no sooner was it running smoothly than these thieving bastards started milking it. Dribs and drabs at first, and then more all the time as some genuinely wealthy and unscrupulous people recognized the potential it offered— to grow fabulously rich off what was essentially an unending supply of plunder for those who knew where, when, and how to collect it. And that's when they started buying people like Placidus Pompey, seducing them with funds that were insignificant to the financiers of the Ring, but were irresistible to self-serving, dissatisfied senior officers.

"That's what our brotherhood swore to eradicate. That Ring. Diocletian himself charged us to stamp out corruption within the armies wherever we found it, and he gave us the wherewithal to do it in secrecy."

"A secret policing force? Is that what you are telling me?"

"I am not telling you anything, Mcuil. And if you think you heard anything, you must have been temporarily impaired."

"And so no details?"

Ajax smiled. "All kinds of details. And I'll be happy to explain them all to you in detail, should you ever join our fraternity."

"I see . . . But now your task is done?"

Ajax made a harrumphing sound. "The Ring is broken. We are quite sure of that. At least, we are confident we took the ringleaders. Scores of arrests, apparently, in the past month. Scores of dismissals and investigative tribunals everywhere. And many, many silent, unacknowledged executions. As for stamping out corruption in the legions, though?" He shook his head. "I doubt if anyone, or any organization, will ever be able to achieve that. Corruption is too deeply stained into human nature, I'm afraid, ever to be wiped out. But our brotherhood will keep working towards that end, so long as the legions themselves exist."

"What was your role in all of this? Personally, I mean."

"For the past six years here, under Pompey, I've been acting as a central clearance point for exchanging information between our operatives and investigators all over Britain."

"And Pompey knew that?"

"Pompey knew nothing. He was the reason I was assigned here in the first place. We needed someone to keep close watch on his activities without being under his nose every hour of the day. I had orders to win his confidence by making him appear to be a fine producer and therefore a fine officer."

"And it worked perfectly. So who has replaced him?"

"The new legate. The one you saw on the road."

"The fellow in the black armour?"

"That's the man. His name's Gaius Cornelius Britannicus. He was born and bred here in Britain, but he's been serving on the northern frontiers, along the Rhine, for the past ten years. He was given command of this garrison as a well-earned reward for outstanding service. He's a good man. You'll meet him one of these days, and you'll like him. He comes across as a bit standoffish at first, but he's the kind of officer his men look up to—the kind of man who'll draw his people off the road to avoid disrupting a funeral."

"Hmm. You knew him from before?"

"He was my first squadron commander, before I fell off my horse and joined the infantry. That was a while ago."

"Does he know your true function here? Is he a member of this brotherhood of yours?"

"That, Mcuil, is none of your business."

"Of course not. Pardon me for asking. So, what will you do now, with your primary task completed?"

"I'll stay here as armourer until further notice. We still need the clearing house."

Varrus nodded, then said, "I passed four officers as I came in. Brothers of yours, I assume. Who were they? Or am I not allowed to ask?"

Ajax laughed. "You can ask," he said, "and I can even answer. They are four of my oldest and best friends—all of my rank, centurion. We go back years, to my start as an infantry grunt in Eboracum. There used to be seven of us, and once we became brethren we worked together for years, trying to break the Ring. Then I was pulled out of the group for other work, oh, about ten years back, I would say, and finally posted here, nearly six years ago. Hadn't seen those fellows in that time, until they turned up with Britannicus two days ago."

"You said you were seven. What happened to the other two?"

The centurion heaved an enormous sigh. "One of them was killed, and not too long ago. His name was Ludo. The seventh one was Rufus. They cut the heart out of him, but they didn't kill him. They used him, then they threw him away—a casualty of war. Rufe was our leader, really, if anyone was . . ." He subsided for a moment. "Yes, he was, although I've never thought of him that way before. He was definitely the man we would all turn to in a crisis. But they made him absorb one blow too many and it sickened him. By *they*, of course, I mean the army—not the brotherhood and not the fighting army. I really mean the faceless, nameless, pissant pen-pushers, the ferret-faced, heartless clerks and gutless functionaries who really believe they are the ones who keep the empire safe. I doubt if any of those bastards has ever met a fighting soldier in the flesh. They certainly don't treat soldiers in the field like living, feeling beings. And they gutted poor Rufus. He resigned early last year, the fellows told me. I didn't even know until now."

He stood with his head down, gazing sightlessly at the surface of the table in front of him, and then he sucked in his breath and stood erect. "He did the job he was supposed to do," he said. "He warned them precisely what could go wrong, and they went right ahead and behaved exactly the way he had warned them not to, and the result was a bloodbath." Varrus had the distinct impression his friend was speaking to someone far beyond the room in which he stood. Perhaps even to the absent man Rufus himself. "And when Rufus went in again and cleaned out the rats' nest, those same useless incompetents arrested him for insubordination and court-martialled him for mutiny. Or they tried to. The brotherhood intervened, the court martial was quashed, and Rufus was exonerated. But the damage had been done and he decided he had had enough. I'm told he requested his release, his honourable discharge, and he walked away without a backward look, after twenty years."

His shoulders slumped and he turned his head slightly towards Varrus. "Poor bastard. Of all the people I've ever known in the armies, I would never have imagined that could happen to Marcus Licinius Cato."

He sighed again. "Listen, I have to go and talk with the new legate. But those fellows you saw—Leon and Stratus and the Twins—they'll be back here later this afternoon, around the fourth hour, for a cup of wine. So if you're free, why don't you come by and join us. I have no doubt you'll find out much more about the Ring, if you do, because these are the fellows who shattered it."

Varrus was already wide-eyed with anticipation. "I'll be there," he said, "but if I don't get some work done right now, Demetrius will be terminating my employment."

TWENTY-SEVEN

"Quintus! Where have you been? I've been waiting for ages! What took you so long?"

Varrus had not even known he was later than usual until Lydia came running to him the moment he entered the house. She was laughing almost giddily as she seized both his hands in hers.

"We can do it," she whispered, almost breathless in her excitement. "We can be married—tomorrow—or today!"

"Wha—?" It was the thing he had least expected to hear and he had to sit down, quite suddenly. "But what about Dominic? I told you, he'll never agree to that." He was shocked to discover that, faced with the imminent curtailment of all the freedom he had known, and the immediate assumption of a lifetime of responsibilities, a part of his mind was quite violently unwilling to come to terms with his becoming a married man within days.

"No, not at all, Quintus!" Lydia was saying. "Da says it's a grand idea and we should do it before he goes back to Londuin! He says the best thing for everyone is if we do what we decided to and just go ahead with a quiet family marriage with no one outside the family ever the wiser. For now, at least."

She paused, but only to draw breath before continuing. "But come the half year, we'll be able to take our friends from here with us and travel down to Londuin with the next load of iron ore, and he'll put on

373

an enormous celebration there that all our friends in Londuin can attend. Isn't that wonderful? And in the meantime, you and I will be man and wife here in our own home."

Looking at the dancing excitement sparkling in her eyes, he felt his heart swell up with love for her and he laughed out loud, forgetting all his misgivings. His dearest wish had been granted—merely a little more quickly than he had anticipated.

He pulled her close to whisper into her ear. "Forgive me, my love," he breathed, feeling her shiver with delight as his breath tickled her ear. "But I would never have thought any woman, even as small and perfect a being as you, could take the legs from me, let alone the breath. Your father actually agreed with us. That is—" He stopped and shook his head. "That is truly surprising. I can scarce believe I heard you say it." He tipped her head up to kiss her. "So be it," he said. "I love you with my whole being and your tidings make me very happy. Now, I had come in to tell you something, but then you surprised me with your news and drove everything else out of my mind."

She laughed. "Then speak up, Master Roman, for you may not have another opportunity."

"Hmm. That sounded alarmingly truthful," he said. "So be it, then. There's someone I want you to meet. I left him outside."

She cocked her head to one side. "That sounds very mysterious. Who is it?"

"A boy. His name is Simeon. I told Ajax I'd bring him to meet you, to see if you'd like him. He's in the yard."

"Why would you think I would want to—? You left him outside?" She threw up her hands. "You had best tell me what this is all about, and quickly."

He did so, and when he had finished she looked at him, frowning slightly. "So. You brought home a boy, an orphan, Simeon of Somewhere, to be an apprentice or a stableboy, and if I like him, he will stay with us. Is that correct?"

"I suppose it is, though it sounds like an ultimatum when you say it like that."

"What else could it be but an ultimatum, my love? You made an important decision and you made it without asking me for my opinion. What kind of boy are we talking about here? How will he affect our lives together? How old is he, and am I likely to like him, a complete stranger?"

Quintus shrugged, his expression slightly mystified. "He's a boy, my love. An orphan. He thinks he might be ten years old but could be twelve. And if there were any doubt in my mind about your liking him, he wouldn't be here, because I would not have brought him. Arbitrary as my decision might seem to you, I thought about it carefully today before I decided to do anything we might not be able to live with, and I brought him here for you to form your own opinion."

"Where will he stay, if I accept him?"

"Anywhere you want to put him. I'm sure he won't care. It won't matter to him where he sleeps, in the stable or in the smithy, as long as he has a roof over his head and food in his belly."

"Well, then, take me to him. Let's see what he looks like. But what will you do with him if I detest him on sight?"

"I'll take him back to the armouries. He doesn't know why he's here. He thinks I might need him to take back a message for me."

"Why would you need to send back a message?"

"Ajax has some old friends coming to his quarters later for a cup of wine, and he invited me to join them. But I think I'll send a message to say they can carry on without me. You and I have far more important things to talk about than whatever those fellows will be discussing."

"No, Quintus. If Ajax invited you, he wants you there for some purpose."

"No, my dear, I don't think so. Believe me, it was a spontaneous invitation."

"Nonsense. Ignatius Ajax doesn't understand what spontaneous means. He *always* has a purpose. You should go, Quintus, and meet Ajax's friends. Invite him to the wedding. Tell him to bring Demetrius Hanno and to come here at mid-morning on Saturn Day. Now, take me to this boy."

Varrus found Ajax at Demetrius Hanno's side in the armoury, and he told them both about Lydia's approval of taking on the boy as an apprentice, and then about the upcoming, unplanned wedding. The first thing they both asked him was what they could present to the bride as wedding gifts. The question surprised him, and Ajax was more than happy to point out to him that here in Britain, the ancient Celtic traditions of giving household gifts to the newly married couple applied even in Roman-British families. Varrus had decided months earlier what he himself would present to his wife as a wedding gift, as part of the Roman ceremony of spouses trading possessions in acknowledgment of their mutual interdependence from that moment on. Dylan had told him that his wealthy and discriminating clients would frequently purchase bolts of precious and exotic fabrics as gifts for just this purpose, and he had decided to surprise Lydia with precisely such a gift when she eventually consented to marry him.

Hanno had been busy at the forge when Quintus came in, and seeing begetting action as it so often did in his business, the younger man quickly became involved in hammer-welding the smith's newest blade, helping in the necessary but never tedious business of flattening and stretching the malleable metal, then folding it back on itself. This particular blade had been worked and reworked thirty-two times by then, and it would undergo the procedure at least ten more times before being judged worthy or unworthy of being accepted for the next step of the blade-making process.

It was only when a boy came looking for him, to summon him to

Ajax's quarters, that Varrus became aware of his surroundings again. He set the blade back in the coals, calling to Hanno that he was doing so, then set his tools back into place on their respective racks before removing his leather apron and heading off to join the armourer and his friends.

He knocked on Ajax's door and stepped right in to find everyone silent and looking at him in that unmistakable, slightly awkward way of people interrupted in mid-speech. He stopped at once, one foot still on the threshold.

"Ah, finally, there you are," Ajax said. "I was beginning to think about having you dragged here if need be. I knew once you started working on that blade that it would take more than the offer of a cup of wine to rip you away from it. We have been talking about you."

Varrus stood still, unaccountably hesitant to commit himself to taking the next step into the room. The four unknown men were staring at him expectantly and curiously, two of them nearly identical in appearance, and something in the atmosphere was making him feel distinctly uncomfortable and ill at ease.

"Why?"

"Hmm?" Ajax said, a tiny line between his brows. "Why what?"

"Why would you be talking about me before I arrived? You people are all old friends, are you not? You have a long, shared history, and I am no part of it in any sense. You have not seen each other for six years, so why would any of you want to talk about *me*?"

To his surprise, Ajax smiled and turned to the others. "Now do you believe what I was saying earlier? It must be a familial trait—speak out and be damned, even if you know not whom you're speaking to." Ajax addressed him as he moved to shut the door. "To begin with, you are wrong, though you cannot be expected to understand that yet, so all I can do is ask you to be patient. In the meantime, allow me to introduce my friends. From left to right as you look at them, their names are Thomas, Leon, Didymus, and Stratus. Thomas and Didymus are known as the Twins, for obvious reasons, although they are not related. I have known each of them for close to seventeen years. Fellow officers, I would like you to meet, and to welcome to our company, Quintus Publius Varrus, son of Marcus Varrus and grandson of Titanius Tertius Varrus."

Varrus was thunderstruck to hear Ajax speak his name—his true name—aloud to Roman military officers. But before he could say a word in protest the four men stepped forward as one, their hands outstretched to greet him, and one by one they looked him straight in the eye and smiled warmly as they shook with him, and stepped back to give place to the next in line. All of them said how great a pleasure it was to meet him, and he was left gaping open-mouthed at Ajax.

"You are wondering what's happening here, I know. Why I would expose you to strangers by using your real name while knowing you to be a fugitive from the Roman authorities in Londinium." He grinned. "Well, with these four knowing who you really are, you could not be better protected. So come and sit down and have some wine and we'll tell you about what's making you feel so foolish."

He moved to the wide work table that now held nothing but two jugs and six fine clay cups. One of the jugs held wine, Varrus knew. The other, he presumed, held water. The armourer pulled out a chair, waved Varrus down into it, then started pouring wine and adding water, and as he did so he spoke over his shoulder. "Tell him, Leon."

Leon dug his fists into the small of his back and stretched his spine before sitting down opposite Varrus. His friends arranged themselves on each side of him, leaving the chair on Varrus's left vacant for Ajax.

"Your name is safe with us, Magister Varrus," Leon said. "And remaining protective of it, and you, will be an honour. As soon as Ajax discovered we were here, he knew we would want to meet you." He picked up his wine cup and raised it in a silent toast to Varrus, and the others joined him.

Varrus stood up again instead, pushing his chair back from the table with his leg and frowning as he looked again from man to man, including Ajax.

"Why?" His tone was blunt. "How would Ignatius Ajax know such a thing—that you, four men closer to my father's age than to mine and utterly unknown to me, would wish to meet me? And what does that signify?"

"It signifies loyalty, Magister Varrus, and debts unpaid," the man called Stratus said. "And it entails an obligation, from us to you."

Varrus moved his head slightly to look at Ajax. "I am being patient, as you asked," he said, "but that patience is growing strained. So if you can make things clearer to me, I believe this would be the right time to do it."

"Oblige me, if you will, Magister Varrus. If you'll stop scowling like a condemned thief and sit down and drink your wine like a civilized man, I'll explain."

TWENTY-EIGHT

Quintus Varrus did not often find himself at a loss. Self-confident and assertive by nature and disposition, he had never found it necessary to learn how to dissemble, and so had grown accustomed to speaking out about whatever was in his mind. At that moment, though, there was nothing in his mind—or rather, there was nothing in his mind that he could understand at that moment. But he forced himself to sit again, and picked up his wine cup.

Ajax sank into his own chair and stared at Varrus. "I'm trying to find the best place to begin, Magister Varrus," he said slowly. "It's not easy, because everything I am about to tell you— No, everything *we* are about to tell you will run contrary to the disciplines by which we govern our lives. We spoke earlier today, you and I, about our former legate Placidus Pompey and the reasons for his removal. We finally broke the Ring. We—"

"We. Your secret military police, you mean. Your Mithraic Order."

Ajax cocked his head slightly sideways, his eyes swivelling to take in his four companions, none of whose faces betrayed a thing. "Magister Varrus, I am trying to explain. Believe me, it is more complicated than you could ever suspect. First of all, you misunderstood entirely what I said about the Mithraic Order being Diocletian's military police— No, wait, if you will!"

Varrus leaned back into his chair.

"The emperor formed a corps of military police to enforce military law among the legions. I am presuming, perhaps incorrectly, that you know there is a difference between martial law and civil law?"

Varrus nodded. "Martial law is far more stringent and rigorous than civil law, and it needs to be. I understand that."

Ajax nodded back. "There was nothing secret about the emperor's military police corps. It worked openly. Most infringements of military law involve corruption, and most of that is petty, small in scale and personal. Organized corruption, however, involving enormous volumes of theft and the mobilization of large numbers of men, is another matter entirely. Regular policing practices, open as they are required to be, are laughably inadequate against widespread conspiracy when the crimes involve wealthy and powerful men and senior officers with access to privileged information.

"Are you understanding me so far?" He peered directly at Varrus, who nodded wordlessly. "Good, then," he said. "Keep listening . . . If you are going to fight rot on a massive scale like that, with stakes as high as those I am describing, you need secrecy you can depend on. That is a *sine qua non* of being able to work against that kind of power. When you're dealing with the kind of organization we were facing— the Ring—*nothing* is more important than secrecy. And *that* is what brought about the inclusion of the Mithraic Order, a secret society with origins that are lost in the vaults of history, but which relies heavily on secrecy and silence in order to safeguard its mystic rites and sacred rituals.

"And so, under Diocletian, volunteers were sought among the Mithraic initiates. For the first time ever. Theoretically, that meant membership in the police corps was open to nearly every soldier in Rome's legions, since more than eighty of every hundred soldiers belong to the order. That meant, by extension, that very soon thereafter everyone in the world equated the order with the military police."

He scratched his cheek with one finger. "That was a lie, deliberately engineered and propagated."

Varrus offered no reaction of any kind to that, and Ajax continued.

"You were born with a defective knee, which meant you could never join the legions. That means you are not, and cannot be, a member of the Order of Mithras, because you lack the essential qualification of being a soldier. Let's sail around that inconvenience. Tell me, if you will, what do you know about the order?" He raised both hands, palms towards Varrus. "I promise you, that is not a trivial question."

Varrus shook his head slightly. "Not much at all. As you said, I'm disqualified."

"But surely you know something. You yourself said you come from a military family, so you must have picked up knowledge here and there throughout your life, even without being aware of it. So think about that now. What have you heard? Or what do you suspect? How many levels are there within the order, think you?"

Varrus ran a hand over his close-cropped scalp. "That much I know," he said. "There are three levels of initiation, all of which have to be earned, and qualification is necessarily difficult, requiring long hours of study and tuition from qualified sponsors who have already graduated. The demands of each level are more difficult and challenging than the one before it. Initiates spend months, sometimes years, absorbing and learning the ritual responses and liturgical requirements of each level before being rigorously examined and initiated into the fraternity."

"And the third level, what do you know of that?"

"It is the final one and the most difficult to attain. Once achieved, membership is lifelong and can never be taken away for any reason. Even if a third-level initiate of Mithras is impeached by fellow initiates, it requires a minimum of five voices to prefer charges against him, after which he may be considered to be disgraced, but he will nonetheless retain his membership in the third level."

"There, you see? You thought you knew nothing of our brother-hood, but you know sufficient to talk about it with some accuracy. You have a question?"

"Yes. What has this to do with the Ring? You said the military police were not capable of the kind of secrecy required to combat the corruption that was going on, so to what end were these Mithraic initiates being recruited? It makes no sense."

"It does, if you know what's involved. If you are going to fight corruption on a massive scale, and you need to ensure the secrecy and security of your planning and operations, how would you go about achieving that?"

"I . . . I have no idea."

Ajax blew his breath out forcefully and looked at his four friends. "This is difficult," he said to them. "I would not have believed how difficult it would be." He looked back then, hard, at Varrus. "Three levels," he said. "Three levels of initiation. Correct?"

"Correct," Varrus said, quirking one eyebrow slightly.

"Wrong. That is what the entire world believes, that there are three. In truth there are four levels. And the secrecy surrounding that fourth level and its membership is the most stringent possible. The brotherhood of the fourth level of the Mithraic Order is exceptional, sharing the highest ideals of citizenship, manhood, and loyalty imaginable, and an invitation to join its ranks is issued only after years of scrutiny by a panel of highly qualified brethren." He stopped talking then and the silence in the room was palpable; even the normal din of the surrounding armouries stilled for a fleeting space.

Varrus wanted to squirm in his seat but held himself still, betraying nothing. "I doubt you should be telling me this, Natius," he said quietly.

"I'm having great difficulty with it myself, but it is . . . necessary."

"I can't see why."

"You will. The force that crushed the Ring was drawn exclusively from the initiates of the fourth level of the Mithraic Order. Their commitment to secrecy and to maintaining unbreachable security was— and still is—absolute, bound by oaths and personal dedication to the ideals by which the brotherhood all live."

"You are . . . talking about yourselves."

"We are. All of us."

"Very well." Varrus looked from man to man, meeting each one's eye. "But I still don't see—"

"It wasn't always true," Ajax said, cutting him short. "In the early days, soon after Diocletian put his system in place, no one saw a need for such a force. But then, as thieves began to work the flaws and realized they could raid at random without fear of reprisal, things went rapidly downhill."

"Wait! Are you saying there was no force in place to fight these thieves from the outset?"

"No, there wasn't. Everyone was so happy that the armies were being properly supplied again that it simply didn't occur to anyone that thieves might steal from such a great achievement. We know now that such thinking was foolish, but after decades of abuse everyone was so glad to see the legions coming back to life that it was a natural error to expect that everyone would feel the same way about it. They didn't, of course."

He grimaced. "No one knows when the thieving began—though it probably started with the earliest deliveries, and was spur-of-the-moment opportunity most of the time. But once started, it grew. And then the first reports started coming in that supply trains were being targeted and the stolen supplies sold openly, because no one ever suspected that they might be army supplies. As the thieving increased, though, and the authorities began to react, the risks increased, too. It became unsafe to peddle the goods anywhere close to where they had been stolen, and so the thieves, who were growing organized by then, changed their methods.

"They started enlisting local chiefs and dignitaries to turn a blind eye to their thievery, paying them to let the stolen goods pass safely through their territories, and they were ruthless with anyone who wouldn't do what they wanted. The word soon went out that to defy them meant death—sometimes on a large scale, and always while the army was too far away to stop the bloodshed. By that time, these animals were *really* organized, and they had grown so rich that they had started buying people—legates like our Pompey and quaestors and lesser officials. People with ways and means of making sure the army never arrived in time to stop the raids.

"In the meantime, the organizers were raking in enormous quantities of wealth, and in doing so they had attracted some very powerful investors. The last thing those people wanted, though, was anarchy. So the organizers drew up a new set of ruthless rules, put them into place, and enforced them mercilessly. And after that, no one dared step out of line.

"By that time, our brotherhood had become involved and we were actively fighting them. And I suppose it was because of us that they became known as the Ring, because that's what we started calling them." He smiled, a bitter little rictus. "Ironic, that," he said. "That we should be the ones to name them. But that is the truth of it. Our organization was formed to fight theirs, and Diocletian entrusted the entire matter of the war against the Ring to a man he had trusted all his life."

He looked Varrus straight in the eye, holding his gaze. "That man was his closest and most loyal friend—your grandfather, Titanius Tertius Varrus."

Varrus found himself counting in the silence that followed those words. He hugged that silence to himself and counted, consciously, marking the pulse that thudded inside his head. He had reached fifteen before the man called Leon spoke into the stillness.

"None of us—the five of us here, I mean—ever met your grandfather, Magister Varrus, but we all knew who he was and we were in awe of his achievements, because all of us worked for him and admired him greatly. Titanius Tertius Varrus was the eminence to which, and to whom, we all looked up. He was the embodiment of all that we, and our brotherhood, stand for: integrity, probity, justice, honour, and the sanctity of goodwill, good faith, and openness in human dealings.

"Soon after we learned of the murder of him and his family—and by 'we' I mean our brotherhood—we launched an investigation that was intense and far-reaching, but we failed to discover who was responsible. And believe me, we tried. Hundreds of us tried, singly and in concert, and our search continued for a full year and for half of the one that followed. One of us, our friend Rufus, spent almost three years in Italia, leading a team of investigators who turned over everything looking for a culprit or a nest of culprits.

"We knew that Titanius Varrus had made powerful enemies throughout his life. How could he not, for he had held the reins of power over military law for almost forty years, and no man of his integrity could do such a thing without attracting enmity, and often open hatred, from people capable of harbouring great malice and undying lust for revenge. And so we examined every one of those whom we could identify. But our investigations turned up nothing. And so the brotherhood was forced to suspend our investigation because we could go no further."

He took a swig from his cup before resuming. "And then today, Natius told us about you, about how you were here and had knocked him on his arse by telling him your real name and your story. And once we heard that, we wanted to know more. You have made a favourable impression on our Natius, Quintus Varrus, and that means that you also impressed the four of us, because we all know, to our cost, what a stubborn, unappeasable, miserable whoreson he is. So if you can please him, we know we'll have no trouble with you.

"We understand that you are now a fugitive, believing yourself in danger because you and your uncle Marius are Titanius Tertius's last surviving relatives. When we heard that, we resolved to make sure of your safety from this time on."

He glanced around him, the gesture taking in his three companions, all of whom sat quietly, looking calmly at Varrus. "These three don't say much," he added. "But they have been known to speak from time to time. And as soldiers and brethren of the order, they leave nothing to be desired. So no matter what you might need from now on, you come to us and we'll make sure you get it. We'll be in Camulodunum for a while."

Varrus's throat had closed up while Leon was speaking, as he came to appreciate how genuinely these men had revered his grandfather.

He himself had always feared the old man; had seen him as a hectoring bully, constantly at odds with his two sons and contemptuous of any opinion that did not conform to his own. Now, though, with new and niggling awareness, he began to recognize that his early perspectives might have been flawed.

Titanius's quarrel with his younger son had been exactly what it appeared to be—a dispute between a headstrong son and a father who disapproved of that son's choice of career. Titanius had been legion born and bred, as had his family for centuries. He had no respect for, or tolerance of, the imperial navy, and he deplored Marius's commitment to it.

The eldest son, Marcus, had been another matter altogether. Marcus had joined the legions and had served his time in command roles, but as a career soldier, not a fighting one. His talents lay in other fields, and he had attached himself, early in his career, to the staff of the ambitious Constantine, the son of an equally ambitious father, Constantius Chlorus. When Constantius Chlorus became Augustus in the western empire, Constantine returned to join his father in Britain and took Marcus Varrus with him, promoting him to military tribune, and from that time onward, Marcus had become one of Constantine's close and trusted confidants, entrusted with diplomatic affairs that no plain-spoken fighting soldier could have handled. And therein, Varrus now saw, had lain the seeds of the constant confrontations between father and son: Titanius Varrus would have loathed politicians, with their glib, equivocatory compromises and self-serving ambiguities, and it must have galled him deeply to know that he had fathered one.

"I fear we've given our new friend too much to think about," the man called Stratus said. "Reminded him, perhaps, of painful matters . . ."

Varrus looked at the big man quickly and shook his head. "No, not so." He looked back at Leon. "You said none of you five ever met my grandsire. But someone must have—someone you knew and whose word you trusted. Were that not so, none of you would hold the esteem you have for him. Titanius Varrus lived most of his life in Italy and Dalmatia. He never came within a thousand miles of Britain, so how could you know him well enough to admire him as you do? Someone else must have told you about him."

"Well, that's true, someone did," Stratus said. "But it's not true, at the same time. Titanius did come here, about fifteen years ago, I think, and mayhap longer ago than that. Around the time Diocletian started talking about retiring. But it was Rufus who knew him. Rufus worked for him directly, for about a year, and came to know him well enough over that time to remain loyal to him for the rest of the old man's life."

"And where is Rufus now?"

It was one of the Twins, Thomas, who answered. "We think he's up north, either in Eboracum or Deva."

"But those are two legionary fortresses, are they not?"

"Aye. Deva's the Twentieth and Eboracum's the Sixth."

"Well surely he can't be in both legions."

"Ah," the Twin said. "I see what you mean. Rufus, you see, is one of us—or he was. That means he could go anywhere, belong to any unit, and show documents to prove it."

Didymus, the other Twin, spoke up. "That's one of the best parts o' belongin' to the brotherhood," he said. "We go where our work is, wherever we're needed. Always been that way, since your gramfer set things up. We go where we're needed and we go when we're sent, and there's always paperwork in place when we get there. Your gramfer was a clever man."

"So who's in charge now that he's dead?"

"He had a man set up to follow him. Trained him hisself, for years. He's in charge now and we've no complaints. Name's Numenicus."

"I know Numenicus. I met him"—he paused, remembering—"twice. He came to visit us in Dalmatia, in the year before the murders. I liked him."

"So did your gramfer."

"So what happened to your friend Rufus?"

"It's a long story," Ajax interrupted, "and we all tend to grow angry when we talk about it, so we'd better talk about something different for a while and calm down while we drink some wine in peace. Otherwise, we'll waste a lot of time in fretting over things that might have been, and none of us has time for that. Give me your cup."

TWENTY-NINE

Ajax meant what he said about changing the topic of their talk, and for the next half-hour the conversation ranged over a number of subjects. One of them was the merits of the new garrison legate, Gaius Cornelius Britannicus, where he had come from and how he had ended up in Camulodunum, and Varrus found himself listening closely, remembering how impressed he had been that the officer had ordered his men to draw aside, at great inconvenience to themselves, to permit a common funeral procession to pass by undisturbed. He had chosen to set privilege aside and had waited, patiently, even saluting the corpse as it passed by him. That, in Varrus's opinion, had set the man head and shoulders above his colleagues.

"Someone said—did I hear this correctly?—that he is a member of your brotherhood?"

"He is," Ajax answered. "Of long standing and senior rank."

"Forgive my curiosity, then, but then why is he here in Camulodunum? I mean, I understand that this is a strategically important fort, but it is second-level compared with Deva and the other two legionary fortresses. Why would your brotherhood send a senior officer to such a bywater?"

"Because it *is* a bywater," Leon answered, "and so it's seen as being less important than the legionary fortresses. On the other hand, it's also seen as involving less risk for people involved in thievery."

"You mean the Ring? But not an hour ago you were saying the Ring had been smashed."

"It was, Quintus," Ajax said. "But it hasn't yet been stamped out of existence. Not entirely. Not yet. Endor was a cunning, devious operator, and the structure he built is still standing in some places. Teetering on the edge of total collapse, but still standing. We believe this area was his home base—or at least an important centre of business for him, a kind of clearing house area—and so we're watching things around here very carefully. That's why Britannicus is here, and why he has cavalry with him. It will give him the ability to move far and fast when he needs to."

Quintus held up a hand to stop him. "Wait, slow down a little, please. Who is Endor?"

"Who *was* Endor. The son of a whore has been dead for a year now and the world is well rid of him."

"Then who *was* he?"

"He was the Ring's chief operative, the keystone of it all and the brains, we believed, that held it all together. Every part of it relied upon his influence and abilities, and both of those attributes were frightening. As long as he was alive, we could never inflict sufficient damage on the Ring to stop them, or even to make them falter. And Endor was absolutely evil. Easily the most evil man I've ever had to deal with. It's an easy term to use, but you don't often meet a truly evil person. It was a turning point when he was killed."

"And who killed him?"

"We like to think it was Rufus who got the bastard," Thomas said. "We can't know for certain, the way things worked out. But we like to think it was Rufus."

"I see," Varrus said, looking slowly from one to the other of the men surrounding him. "Rufus killed Endor, and brought about his own destruction by doing so. Is that what you are saying?"

"No." Didymus almost spat the word. "That's what Castor Lepodos tried to say, the stinking shit."

"Another name I have not heard before."

"And you'll never hear it again," Leon said quietly. "Unless we speak it here among ourselves. The name was never important. The function the whoreson fulfilled, on the other hand, was critical. Former commanding centurion, or pilus prior, of the Second Cohort, Second Legion Augusta. Dead now, of a serious accident last year. Apparently walked directly into the path of a flying arrow that hit him square in the temple and dashed his brains out. A shame. He was a by-the-book soldier. Killed a lot of people, they say . . . Mainly his own."

"That's enough," Ajax said. "We're back to the crux of things now, so let's get it out of the way once and for all. Leon, bring the jugs over here and top up our cups." He looked directly at Varrus. "I'll tell it, as I remember it, but I'm only going to give you the bare-bones version, so listen closely. This is the truth as far as I know it, after more than a few years of investigations and inquiries.

"Appius Endor—that was his full name—was a disciple, some say a first cousin, of Carausius. You know who he was, don't you?"

"Of course. The Pirate Emperor of Britain. Operated about thirty years ago."

"That's the man, bad luck to his memory. Held to the belief that everything a man does should be purely for his own benefit ahead of anyone else's. Endor worshipped Carausius and studied his methods— studied them hard, theft and warfare both—until Carausius was murdered by one of his own, another reptile called Allectus. Endor, who must have been about sixteen at that time, and a depraved young bastard, simply vanished for the next three years, until Allectus himself was killed, making it safe for him to come out again. *Benigne*," he said then, interrupting himself to thank Leon for the cup being offered him.

"We don't know where he went for those three years," he resumed, "but he was probably in the farthest parts of Cornua, perfecting his murderous ways among the peoples down there, for there's no Roman military presence there at all, and it's rife with pirates and savages. After

Allectus's death, though, he reappeared here, and we know he set about establishing himself as a clever and resourceful thief, using the methods of his hero Carausius. We also believe he set himself up as a murderer for hire. He certainly was one, but we believe he started operating openly around here in the beginning.

"That would have been . . ." He sucked air between his teeth as he threw his mind back, calculating the passage of years. "I'm going to say twenty-one or twenty-two years ago, just about the time Diocletian was settling his new supply system firmly into place. So the timing is perfect. Endor would have been one of the first to recognize an opportunity to grow fat off the wealth that was beginning to flow across the empire."

He sipped from his cup. "That's when he started shipping his stolen goods to Cornua, because he had contacts there, and safe shipping to Gaul and Eire, where he could sell his spoils far away from our attentions. And he prospered. By all the ancient gods, he prospered to the point where serious investors began to court him. You understand, these were people who believed they had sufficient money to grant them immunity from prosecution, and thought they could do anything they wanted to make more. And Endor took their money and increased the scope of what he did, endlessly—until he encountered us."

"But that makes no sense. Why would he take on partners when he already took all the profits?"

Ajax looked at him levelly. "Because selling part of the ownership, let's say ten percent to each of nine large investors, would have left him with ten percent for himself, but ten percent of an entity that was two or three times greater in size and scope. That meant that he doubled or tripled his income.

"I'd like to think we made his life harder when we started investigating him, but I doubt we did. He was too well entrenched by then and he laughed at us, because our efforts were laughable in those days. We grew better with experience, though, and our information about his operations became more and more substantial and perceptive all the time. We began coordinating information among what one twit of an officer called 'points of strategic power,' and that made a difference from the moment we started doing it.

"Rufus was the one thing the five of us here had in common. He brought us together in the first place, back at the outset of what would become the war against the Ring, and from there we all became friends simply by remaining together and sharing all the shit you have to share once you join the army. There were seven of us who ended up together, the five of us here, and Rufus and Ludo. Ludo's the one I told you about earlier. The one who died.

"There was one other fellow, a man called Alexander Strabo, who's important to this tale. He was our first commander when we all came together, and he married Rufus's sister Maria. Strabo was one of those officers destined for bigger, better things, you knew that on first meeting him, and he ended up as legionary legate of the Second Augusta, in Isca. But he was also one of us—one of the brotherhood."

"*Another* one? How many of you people are there?"

Ajax shrugged one shoulder. "Thousands. I told you, eighty out of every hundred soldiers in Rome's armies belong to the order. How many do you think that might be?" When Varrus made no attempt to answer him, he continued, "Thirty legions—that's the going number—stripped down to six thousand men in each legion, not counting auxiliaries. That's what? A hundred and eighty thousand men? And take one percent of that number as being the best, eligible for membership in our brotherhood. That's more than eighteen hundred already, and that's only being minimal. We have enough, believe me, and we have no attrition. We're never short of willing, qualified recruits."

He flung up a hand, dismissing the digression. "But that has nothing to do with this discussion, so what was I talking about? Strabo, and Isca. Yes . . . Eight years ago, or it might have been nine, when it became clear to us that the Ring's main area of activity had been moving more and more rapidly into Cornua, Strabo's command in Isca became strategically important—the single power base we had in the entire southwestern region."

"Wait," Varrus said, interrupting. "The *single* power base? Are there no other forts down there?"

"Of course there are. Fourteen of them, in varying sizes. But they all rely on Isca for everything, and they're all within a day's march of it. We have no presence at all in the wilds of the region, and it's a very large peninsula, with rocky, craggy, treacherous coastlines north and south. Isca's the end of the road down there. That is not simply a figure of speech. There are no roads south or west of there, so every step, every march, has to cross open country, and Rome's legions do not fare well in open country on long journeys, or even marches. That's why the empire is criss-crossed by roads."

"Could you not call upon the navy, for coastal patrols?"

"We could and we did, but the British fleet is not what it used to be, and patrolling the entire shoreline of the Cornua peninsula with four galleys—even if they were the largest, fastest, and strongest ships Rome has—was an exercise in futility. Any contact we ever had with any of the Ring's ships was completely accidental, because we never knew where they would sail from next."

"Of course. How could you? They could have been loaded anywhere. Forgive me. I talk too much at times. You were talking about Isca's importance to your campaign."

"Aye. So we reinforced its strength, and its information-gathering capabilities, and we began re-examining the written requisitions and shipping records of every base in Britain for the previous four years, looking for identifiable patterns that might lead to the instigators of the raids—the people within our own ranks who were feeding information to Endor's thieves about what was being shipped, from where, and precisely when. We had our quaestors and logistics clerks in Deva and Eboracum collecting the same material from their legionary outposts at the same time, and everything they gathered was shipped to Isca, where we eventually built up an army of clerical staff.

"But it was worthwhile, and soon we were able to start identifying the collaborators among our own people. We scooped up supposedly trustworthy citizens—career officers and long-serving functionaries—by the barrel-load. And don't think that didn't cause upheavals in the halls of power.

"That was how we were able to establish, finally, that Appius Endor was the main man behind everything the Ring did. Several of these people we picked up were more than happy to name him and some of his associates, in return for a lessening of their punishments. Mind you, the lessening did not amount to much. They cut back on the torture, but they were all imperial employees, guilty of treason, and they all faced court martial. They all died, too." He eyed Varrus. "That's where Castor Lepodos enters the picture."

"The fellow who walked into an arrow?"

"That's the one. He was second-in-command of the Second Cohort of Strabo's Second Legion at that time, and he was an ambitious, crawling snake of a creature. His men detested him. Called him Lepidus, after the third man in Julius Caesar's triumvirate—the nonentity. No one could ever explain how he attained the rank he held, because he was clearly unfit for it. But we know now. The word is nepotism. Anyway, he was based in an auxiliary fort called Isca Tertia, which lay about twenty miles from Isca itself, and he would not normally have had anything to do with any of this, but there was nothing normal here.

"We finally had some hard, factual information we could act on, and we were in what we believed to be the final stages of planning the destruction of the Ring, and with it, Appius Endor. Rufus was in Londinium when things came to a head, and couldn't break away from what he was doing in time to reach Isca for the final confrontation, but he knew what was going on. Dispatches had been flowing back and forth between provincial headquarters in Londinium and Strabo's headquarters in Isca for weeks. Everyone knew what his own part would be in the coming operation.

"What Rufus did not know—what none of us knew, and no one even suspected—was that this idiot centurion in Isca Tertia had an uncle in Londinium, in the provincial governor's department, who decided that his inept nephew Castor might find an opportunity to distinguish himself, were he in possession of sufficient information on what was about to happen. And so Uncle Andrew sent a private letter to his nephew, delivered incidentally by the official courier who carried the military dispatches, telling him, from the perspective of the governor's office, what was about to happen, and advising him to be on the alert for any opportunity he might find to distinguish himself in the service of the colony and its governor.

"The night before the attack, though, a man called Calvus, or Caldus—something like that—ate some bad mushrooms and poisoned himself. He died the following day. But he had been First Spear of the Second Cohort, and so his second-in-command, the very same Castor Lepodos, took over.

"Castor decided he knew better than Strabo or anyone else what needed to be done, and so he made up his mind to pre-empt everything by making a decisive move of his own. He committed his cohort to attack early, cutting off the enemy's escape route rather than leaving it open as he had been ordered. His troops were spotted as soon as they began to move, the trap was prematurely sprung, and Appius Endor, as always, managed to escape. It was a complete fiasco.

"And that was merely the start of the disaster. Appius Endor hadn't become the man he was by being unprepared for reversals, and he'd been planning just as carefully as Strabo and his crew had. He had people of his own inside Strabo's organization, and so he knew he was being watched, and he knew that Alexander Strabo, the imperial legate of Isca, was the man in charge of the campaign to destroy his organization in Cornua.

"No one ever discovered how the word was passed—though it must have been by a messenger pigeon—or who was responsible for what happened next, but that same afternoon, twenty miles away, a party of senior officers, escorting a finely appointed travelling carriage, entered the Isca fortress through the principal gate—their papers and permissions were flawless, perfect forgeries—and went directly to the legate's house, where they informed the legate's wife, Maria, that Legate Strabo had been forced to change his plans in reaction to an unexpected reversal that they were not permitted to discuss, and that he would be reconvening his court of inquiry in Camulodunum. They explained that they had been sent by the legate himself to bring her and her young son with them to join him there. And of course the lady went with them within the hour, accompanied by the boy, who was four years old and their only child, and her official equerry, a young subaltern.

"When questioned later, no one admitted to having recognized any of the officers in the escort party, and no one had thought to challenge them. They appeared to be precisely what they purported to be, an honour guard of tribunes and senior officers, and since it was common knowledge that the entire Second Legion was out there in the field, with no more than a skeleton force to hold the fortress, it appeared reasonable that the men in question should be unrecognizable, dressed as they were in full ceremonial armour with matching parade helmets that concealed their faces."

"You mean Endor *abducted* Strabo's wife and child?"

"Of course he did, and that's not all he took. Less than two weeks earlier, Strabo had issued a summons to all the senior officers in his command, throughout Britain, and they were all on their way south to Isca at the time of the abduction. The purpose of that assembly was to have been the presentation of damning evidence, collected over years of painstaking observation, of the complicity of several of this colony's most prominent figures—politicians, financiers, and merchant bankers—in financing the Ring's activities. When Strabo's wife and child were taken, those records were in the possession of Strabo's records-keeping staff, being held inside his personal quarters for additional safety. Four clerks were found dead in there and all the records had vanished, clearly taken out in one of the packing cases loaded into the carriage with Maria Strabo and her son."

"So do we know who these financiers were?"

Ajax ignored the question. "The next day, a young equerry presented himself in Strabo's camp and told the legate what needed to be done. He could barely speak, because his hands and his forearms had been crushed. Strabo was to meet with Endor, the messenger told him. Alone. To discuss terms. The lives of Strabo's wife and son were the price of his compliance."

Ajax fell silent, as though he no longer had the strength to talk. But Varrus would not let him leave it there.

"And? What happened then?"

Ajax sucked in a great, shaky breath. "What would you think happened? The equerry died, and Strabo went to meet Endor. Alone, as ordered. Threatened to court-martial anyone who sought to interfere . . . We found the bodies three days later, Strabo, Maria, and the boy, mutilated and burned on the open heath, and Endor was gone again, for three more years."

Varrus had been unaware that he was holding his breath, but now he exhaled noisily. "And the financiers? Do we know who they were?"

"Yes, damn it! Of course we know! But we have no *proof.* The records were stolen, so all we could do was point fingers but with no hope of proving anything. And when you are talking about people as powerful as those we were naming, pointing your fingers counts for nothing— other than bringing you unwelcome attention from people being well paid to notice you."

"So who were they?"

"Does the name Seneca mean anything to you?"

"Of course it does. My father's mother was a Seneca."

"That's the Roman branch. I'm talking about the offshoots here in Britain. The most powerful merchant bankers in the colony."

"In the whole empire, if you want to go that far and say what everyone knows anyway. The Seneca family has always been wealthy beyond most men's dreams. What of it?"

Ajax looked at him sardonically, one eyebrow raised. "Do you believe they grew that rich by being philanthropists?"

"What? No, of course not. But they're rich enough now to *be* philanthropists."

"Aye, perhaps . . . But we had evidence to prove that one of them at least—the eldest son, called Vassos, who operates from Londinium and Verulamium and should have been stifled at birth—was among the largest of Endor's financial backers, so make what you will of that. I'm not trying to denigrate your family, Magister Varrus. You asked me and I'm telling you what we knew to be the truth." He stopped, sounding disgusted, then added, "Oh, and that young equerry who died from having his arms destroyed? His name was Britannicus. He was our new legate's youngest brother, Cassio."

"I know Metellus Seneca," Varrus said. "The senior British Seneca. I met him years ago when he came to visit my grandmother. She was his aunt and he admired her. He is an old man now, and honourable, to the best of my knowledge."

"Aye, as you say, to the best of *your* knowledge. But he has five sons, and not one of them is worthy of spit when it comes to honour. They are parasites, every one of them. Leeches. And Vassos is the worst of them all. Rich as Croesus and absolute human filth."

"Well." Varrus shrugged. "I will accept your word on that. I know none of them, and I don't care about any of them. But what about this Lepodos fellow? Was he ever charged with anything?"

"Oh, there was a full inquest after the dust all died down, but nothing came of it. No one was ever blamed—not at that stage, anyway. The truth came out eventually, but not until much later, after Endor was dead."

"And Rufus killed Endor."

"Not quite. But it was certainly Rufus who brought about his death. He asked for and received a commission to find Endor, who by then had been tried and convicted *in absentia* for the torture and murder of Strabo and his family. Rufus became obsessed with the task. Nothing else in the world mattered to him. Strabo and his wife and son had been his closest family—his only family, really. His own wife and son had left him several years earlier and he hadn't seen them since. Didn't even know where they were . . . So he landed this new commission and vanished soon after that, for more than a year, without a word of his whereabouts to anyone.

"Within a few weeks a new legate took over at Isca. The investigations into the Ring continued, but their activities were almost non-existent by then, and from our viewpoint, nothing was ever the same again. We felt defeated and disheartened. But then, more than a year and a half later, Rufus appeared again, out of nowhere, and sent word to us that Endor had resurfaced north of the Thamis, near Londinium, and he was going after him. He was still under commission to find him and he had at least a couple of score of men with him, but he called on us to go with him if we could.

"We had all earned ample leave, and we all had it granted without a hitch. We had a month, we reckoned, and we set out to get the whore-son. And we did, near Londinium, in a place that we discovered he had owned for years, using a different name. I never did find out how Rufus had found him, but he had, and we moved in to take him. He was a condemned fugitive, so anyone finding him was expected to kill him. And this time, we did it."

Varrus sat forward in his seat. "How?"

"We attacked the house, as soon as we knew he was inside. It was a big place, a courtyard house with extras—well built, containing four large buildings—and it was surrounded by a high wall with only two doors, so we had to be careful. But we were watching, from a tower nearby, and we saw him on the second afternoon."

"And Endor didn't have the place sealed off, or occupied by his own men?"

"No. He thought he was safe-hidden, it seems."

"And how did you know it was him? Did you know him by sight?"

"We didn't need to. There was one thing about Appius Endor that always stood out. People laughed about it, though never to his face.

He wore a massive gold medallion on a chain of solid gold links, awarded to him as a boy by his hero Carausius, when he was emperor in Britain. Endor loved that thing and wore it all the time, so even in full armour he was unmistakable.

"We attacked as soon as we were ready. And discovered he had as many men hidden in there as we had hidden outside. We expected a quick, surprise victory. Instead we found ourselves besieging a fortified, garrisoned stronghold."

"So, how long did it take?"

"Oh, not long," the Twin called Thomas said. "Didymus was responsible for that . . . 'twas him who come up with the idea to smoke 'em all out. Three of the four buildings behind the wall was thatched and the upstairs sections was wooden, so we fired the roofs on the second day, and once the flames took 'old, 'twas but a matter o' time afore they tried to break out, both gates at once. We was ready for 'em, and no more than a handful of 'em got away. We took some prisoners, but not many. These was Endor's people, after all, so no one felt too fond of 'em."

Varrus turned back to Ajax. "And what about Endor? Who finished him? You said it wasn't Rufus."

"No, it was none of us—I mean none of our group of seven—but someone did, during the final stages of the fight. It had been chaos during the fighting, because the place was full of smoke, so most of us were fighting almost blind. But once the fighting was over and the fires were dying down, we turned the whole place inside out looking for him. We thought at first he must have managed to sneak away again. But then we found him. He had either been stabbed in the neck or chopped in the throat, and had died there in the fire, if he wasn't dead already. Some rafters had fallen on him and he was burnt almost beyond recognition, but it was him, all right. His bloody sword was still gripped in the clawed bones of his hand—it had his initials stamped into the blade—and he was still wearing that gold chain. The links had melted right into the black char of what had been his chest.

Rufus found him, and I still remember how furious he was at having been cheated of his right to kill the man himself."

"So who did?"

"We never found out. Nobody remembered killing him, so we decided it must have been one of the nine men we lost in the fighting. It might even have been Ludo, for he died right there in front of that same building."

"What happened then?"

"Rufus struck the head off the corpse and buried it, away from the rest of the body. He then ripped the sword out of the blackened claw and stuck it through the rib cage where the heart should have been, then threw what was left into an open pit and poured salt on it."

"What about his gold chain? Did no one claim it as a trophy?"

"Nah. It had melted right into his flesh in the fire and none of us wanted anything to do with it, so we left it as it was." He drained his cup. "It was what happened after that, though, that set the shit flying. As soon as the word went out that we had captured prisoners and killed Appius Endor, Lepodos the Idiot feared the story of his own stupidity might finally be exposed. It had been nearly two years since he'd triggered the fiasco, and not a word had yet been said about his criminal role. We know now that was because his uncle was able to cover up the truth, but anyway, the fool must have written to his uncle, and whatever he said, it set off a shit storm that cost both of them their lives." He stopped and raised his hands. "And I don't want to talk about this anymore. It makes me want to vomit. Leon, you tell the rest of it."

"I'll need some more wine, then. And less water." Leon rubbed his eyes with the heels of his hands. "The first we knew of anything strange going on after the debacle," he said to Varrus, "was when Rufus was arrested and charged with mutiny. He hadn't been anywhere or done anything, so that caught our attention, believe you me. But according to the official documents, Lepodos had refused to grant leave to six men of his cohort who had requested it—claimed he had not felt able to spare six men at that particular time. But the men had deserted anyway, he said, seduced from their sworn duties and led off on a hunting expedition with their mentor Rufus—that was the word he used, their mentor—which had resulted in the loss of nine legionaries, including the centurion known as Ludo Vicensius, in an unauthorized confrontation with criminal forces close to Londinium.

"Centurion Lepodos had therefore brought charges of sedition and mutiny against Marcus Licinius Cato, known as Rufus. The charges had been tendered through the office of the colonial governor, giving them additional weight and resonance. But they triggered a reaction that Lepodos could never have imagined. Rufus was respected, at every level of our force, and as soon as word of what was happening began to spread, the resources of the entire order came together in his defence. Lepodos was generally acknowledged to be an incompetent fool, but now his connection to the governor's office was exposed, his uncle's complicity was clearly indicated, and everyone saw quickly that incompetence was a Lepodos family trait.

"Every aspect of their uncle–nephew relationship was examined, and the story of the earlier betrayal was brought into the light in short order. Both men were dismissed in disgrace, and the uncle killed himself. The nephew didn't have the balls for that. He simply disappeared. Drifted into oblivion for months, then had his accident with the arrow."

"And what happened to Rufus?"

"All the charges were dropped and he was completely exonerated, but he had been devastated by the corrupt stink of the people he had been forced to deal with, and by his own failure to deliver Appius Endor to answer for his crimes in person. More than anything, though, he was gutted by the torture and murder of his sister, his best friend, and their four-year-old son."

Leon shook his head slowly. "And so he simply disappeared. Walked away from everything. Didn't even say goodbye to us. Packed up his gear and left in the middle of the night to slip out the gates as soon as they opened at dawn. We've no idea where he went, but he must be in either Deva or Eboracum, because he's still in the army and he wouldn't desert at this stage of his life. So we think he just went back to his home base in Eboracum and applied for a discharge, then settled down to wait for it to come . . . And now, as they say, you know everything there is to know about us and how we came to be here.

"But to round this whole thing out, and go back to where we began, Rufus was the one who worked with your grandsire in person, and your grandfather, in turn, is the reason for our wanting to meet you."

Varrus looked around them then, meeting each man's eye. "Well," he said, and then paused, searching for words. "I'm not quite sure what I can say to you, other than to offer you my thanks and assure you that I have no need of guardians nowadays. You have given me an entirely new insight into my grandfather, though, because I really never knew him. I mean, he was my *grandfather*—a rather ancient, frightening, distant figure, always looming in the background during my boyhood, and the two of us never came to know each other. It has never occurred to me that he might have done anything, in all his life, to earn the respect and loyalty of men like yourselves, and so for that insight, I am truly grateful to you."

"And that's the way it should be," Leon said. "He was a great man . . . And now Ajax tells us that you're about to be married, to a lass from Hibernia."

Varrus grinned for the first time since walking into the room, and he picked up his cup and drank the last of the warm wine it contained. "I am," he said. "But she believes she comes from a place called Eire. She refuses to believe there is a place called Hibernia, or that such a wintry-sounding place could ever be associated with her lush, green homeland. But yes, she is marrying me the day after tomorrow, and if you gentlemen would care to attend the wedding—Ajax is already invited—it will be our pleasure to have all of you witness our union."

The others all looked at Ajax, who simply smiled and said, "We'll be there."

THIRTY

"**I** hope you know that if you ever want to learn what it feels like to make love to another woman, you have until tomorrow night to find out."

It was a statement, not a question, and Varrus rolled towards her and pulled her against him, thinking incidentally that it had not taken them long to throw all restraint aside, once they had discovered how much they enjoyed sleeping together. Now, after only a few nights, it would never have crossed either of their minds to pretend to be less open with each other than they were.

"I already know that, woman," he said, inhaling her scent. "Tested it, found it vastly overrated, and discarded it as unsatisfactory long ago, before I ever met you, let alone before you ever came to Colcaster."

"Camulodunum." She slid one long leg over his thigh. "And what exactly was it you discarded? The issue itself, or the possibility of pursuing—"

"It's the lack of variety in variety, my love. It's remarkably unvaried and generally uninspiring in its sameness."

He stifled her with a kiss before she could say any more, and for a long time after that they said nothing at all, but when he lay back again eventually, with her head upon his chest and the softness of her breast filling his cupped hand, he said quietly, "Besides, I need you too much ever to run the risk of losing you that way." He tightened his arm at her waist, pulling her to him, hard. "And have you told Shanna yet about what we would like to do?"

He felt her body go tense for a moment, and then she said, in a different voice, "I started to, but Shanna had her own opinion . . . Are you very sleepy?"

"No, why, would you like to try that again?"

"In a while, perhaps, but not yet. The fire isn't dead yet, though, and we need to talk, you and I. So stay where you are and I'll rekindle the flames."

"No, here, I'll help you."

They scrambled out of bed together and went to the brazier in the chimney corner, where Lydia emptied out the contents of the tinderbox while Varrus crouched naked in front of the fire, blowing gently on the coals and stirring them cautiously until he had them glowing again. Then, as Lydia fed dried moss and twigs from the tinderbox to the coals to produce a flame, he fed the flame carefully with larger and larger twigs until those ignited with an audible puff and began to feed upon themselves. He stacked several more finger-thick twigs on top of those, then built a cone of fist-thick logs around them all. Then he took the shawl that Lydia offered him and wrapped it around himself before settling back onto the bed of cushions she had arranged at his back.

"There," he said. "We have fire. Now what is it that we need to talk about?"

"You think there is only one thing?" Her voice held laughter, but he could see in the strengthening firelight that she was serious. "I can think of three at least, on my side of the family, right at this moment."

"Three? Then you had better tell me about them. Start with the one that's bothering you most."

"That's Da."

"What's wrong with Dominic? Don't tell me he has changed his mind about us?"

"No. He wants to be married, too."

"He *what?*"

"He wants to be married. Says it came to him last night, when he was planning our second wedding in Londuin. He says we could make it a double celebration, father and daughter."

"Great limping Vulcan! Dominic wants to *marry*? That seems . . . outlandish. He's been widowed for what, twelve years or more? Who would he marry?" He straightened up suddenly, his eyes growing wide. "You can't mean he's thinking of marrying Shanna?"

"No, of course not. He barely knows her, and I'm not even sure he likes her much. And it's been much more than twelve years. My mother died when I was two. That's eighteen years ago. He wants to marry Camilla."

"Camilla. The friend who was with you when I first saw you in the marketplace in Londinium? The woman from Gaul with the white streak in her hair? She was your mother's friend."

"That's the one."

"And? Do you object?"

"How could I object? They are perfectly matched and they are very close. No, I think their marriage will be wonderful."

"Then why are you upset?"

She reached out a finger to hook a stray lock of hair off her face, then laid the backs of his fingers against her cheek. "I'm not upset," she said, though she clearly was. "At least, not about the match . . ." She hung there, looking for words, then added, "I think I'm most upset that he has waited all this time to tell me how he felt about Camilla. It's as though he was afraid to trust me earlier—as if he didn't trust me to accept how he felt about her."

"Perhaps he didn't want you to feel slighted, or unwelcome." Varrus hitched a shoulder, expressing doubt. "He might have been afraid of hurting you for some strange reason. We'll never know, I suppose. But now that you do know?"

"Well, I'm glad for them, of course."

"Then we should accept his offer of a joint celebration and enter into it willingly. Which reminds me of something."

"What?"

"Exactly. What? What am I going to wear on our wedding day? We'll be celebrating the day after tomorrow, and I should wear something other than my leather apron and thick boots."

"You should. And I have just the perfect thing for you," she said, and hitched herself closer to kiss him. The fire was blazing strongly by then, its heat washing over them, and he returned her kiss.

"I should have known you would," he said. "But how will you know if it fits?"

"It will fit. It was made for you. I want you to wear the white robe you wore that first day. I have it here."

"The robe that caused us all so much trouble? The robe that forced me to cut my hair and change its colour and take a different name? *That* robe? I fondly hope you are making fun of me, Lydia Mcuil."

She moved even closer, pushing the shawl off his bare shoulders and wrapping her arms around him, bringing his skin out in gooseflesh. "That was almost a year ago now, my dear Quintus, and it was in Londuin. Now we are in Camulodunum, and no one in the world, beyond our own little circle, knows who you really are. You will wear it for your wedding rites, and then never again if you don't want to. But be your beautiful self for that day. Will you indulge me?"

She was far too close to argue with, and her body much too compliant and smooth and soft to permit him to concentrate for long enough to answer, so he did not agree until some indeterminate time later, when they had both recovered their composure. And some time after that again, close to the point of drifting off, he murmured, "You said there were three immediate family problems. What are the other two?"

"Shamus, and Shanna."

He raised himself up on one elbow, looking down on her. "I'll talk to Shamus tomorrow and get that dealt with one way or the other. I've already worked something out with the man who runs the cooperage at the fort, and if Shamus decides to participate in the plan, then that will

take care of the Shanna situation . . . or will it? You said she has opinions of her own. Tell me about them."

She shifted lazily beside him, stretching to adjust to his own outline, and then she spoke into his shoulder. "She wants to leave here—
leave the house to us—and go home to Eire. She says she has the money
to do that."

"What? Why? That is ridiculous, Lydia. I don't care how much
money she has put by. What use is money going to be to her over there
anyway? From what I've heard, nobody uses money in Eire. They barter
for everything."

Lydia turned on to her back and looked up at him. "They may not
use money there, but she can buy livestock here before she goes and
have them moved in."

"Moved in how? There are no roads in Eire. No roads! Have you
any idea what that must mean to the people who live there, Lydia?
What it would mean to *you*? Where do you go, to escape, if there's no
road? And how do you even get there in the first place? She's an old
woman, and she's lived here all her married life—thirty years. She's
going to end up all alone in some godless, isolated place where she
knows no one and has nothing to live for. How is she going to survive?"

Lydia reached up and laid her hand against his face. "Shh, my love!
Shanna's no older than Da is, and he's getting married again. But she
has already buried two husbands and has no wish to find a third. Don't
think of her as a worn-out old woman. She is far from being anything
of the kind. She wants to go home, and we should not stand in her way."

He pushed himself up to a sitting position and looked down at her.
"No," he said. "I disagree. I think you couldn't be more wrong. I believe
she merely wants to move *away* and I think we *have* to stand in her way.
Here's what I think. Are you listening?"

"I am."

He bent and kissed her briefly, then straightened up again, but
placed his hand gently on her bare breast, kneading the nipple softly.

"Shanna wants to go home to Eire, she says. I doubt that's true. I think it's far more likely that she simply wants to clear out from under our feet. She has her pride, and she doesn't want to be a burden. She might have some coins saved somewhere, for Liam was thrifty, but she knows nothing about the money I received. So let us assume we paid her well, in gold, for this place, and I arranged to convert some gold into livestock and had the cattle shipped to Eire. But what then? What happens after that? Can you tell me?"

"She would be at home, where she wants to be."

"No, my love, she would not. She would be in the place she has always *thought* of as home, but she would be stuck there, unable to come back if things go wrong. Everyone she knew over there is probably dead, or they've moved away like her. And the folk who are there might take everything she has, leaving her with nothing. She would be completely alone and unsupported." He shook his head and squeezed her breast, as though to emphasize something only he could see. "No, we simply cannot let her go off on her own like that." He paused then, and waited until he saw the whites of her eyes looking up at him in the dim light. "What we *could* do easily, though, might be a wonderful idea for all of us, if you agree with the notion."

"I agree with it already, if you believe in it. Tell me."

"Well, what if we were to furnish Shanna with a farm of her own to live on here? A small farm that she could work herself, with a little help from time to time. We could buy one very close to town and set her up in comfort, and she could keep us provided with fresh eggs and butter, milk, and even bread once she started raising crops. And if it were close enough, she could even pasture our horses for us, leaving us with more space for our children, when they come. Do you think that might appeal to her?"

He had been watching her eyes growing excited in the firelight as he spoke, and now she smiled at him, radiantly. "I think it might suit her perfectly, my love. I know it appeals to me. I'll talk to her about it in the morning and I won't take no for an answer."

———

The following morning, Varrus found Shamus in the forge, working the bellows half-heartedly.

"You're looking chirpy for a man about to lose his freedom," Shamus growled. "Not goin' up to the fort today?"

"No, not today. Tomorrow I'm being married. Today I'm being lazy, contemplating my good fortune. What about you?"

"I have no good fortune."

"That's what your sister tells me. But you could have, I believe, if you cared to work for some."

"Work?" Shamus threw him a jaundiced look. "You mean *here*, if I face up to a life of slavery working at *your* forge?"

"Nup. I was talking about coming to grips with this matter of the Cornish girl you claim to care so much about. Lydia says you're not having much success there. Why do you sneak away with her at every opportunity, hiding and sidling and eyeing her shiftily all the time as though she was something to be drooled over? Why do you follow her around like a prowling animal? Why don't you step up and act like a man? Talk to her father and be open with her brothers about what you want to do for their sister?"

"Because I can't!" Shamus shouted. "I can't! They would laugh at me, and then they'd beat me half to death and throw me into the street. I have *nothing!* Nothing worthwhile to offer, and no prospects of ever having anything. It needs no brilliant mind to see me for what I am."

"What if you could be a barrel maker?"

"But I'm not a barrel maker," he snapped, "and I never will be."

"Why not? What are you lacking?"

The look Shamus turned on him then was one of pure disbelief. "Can you *hear* yourself, man? What am I *lacking?* Well, let me see. There's about fifteen years of learning the craft that I should have had before now. That's lacking. Then there's a suitable place to work from, with the right equipment—and the means to buy or even rent it. Then, just to make things better, there's the necessary cash to open up the doors and start making barrels, and to pay employees, because though you might never have thought about it, Quintus Varrus, it's not easy to build a barrel by yourself. You need extra hands."

He stopped suddenly, and straightened up slowly to his full height. "Why are you taunting me like this, Quintus? Did I make you angry?"

Varrus spun away, and kept turning, completing a full revolution and then raising a finger in the air. "I have a proposition for you, Shamus. You might find it interesting. We each have a problem, but we can help each other out if we work together. You need something in order to approach Eylin's family with any hope of success. I can provide you with that. And I need to keep working at the armouries, learning new elements of my own craft. You can help me do that. But we will both need two full years to do it. Wait, let me finish.

"There's a cooperage in the fort, run by a man called Mamercus. He's from Sicilia and he knows his craft. He's willing to take you under his wing for two years and teach you the basics of that craft. Sufficient to allow you to buy your own cooperage afterwards and operate it knowledgeably. You wouldn't be a cooper, not at first, but you would be an owner, able to run a business employing people who were fully trained and capable."

Shamus was wide-eyed, and for a moment Varrus saw hope dawning in his eyes, but then the young smith's face fell.

"I believe you could do that, Quintus—with the Sicilian fellow, I mean—and I thank you for that. But I could never raise the money for that last part. It would cost too much."

"Then I'll buy a cooperage and you can run it. We'll be partners." He saw the disbelief in the other man's eyes and spoke again, quickly. "Do you remember the box that came for me, just before Liam died?"

Shamus nodded. "I heard about it."

"It contained money, Shamus. Money from the sale of some of my grandfather's estates."

"Isn't that grand." It was a statement, not a question, but there was no malice in the younger man's voice. "Are you rich now, then?"

"I have enough for what I spoke about. I meant every word I said to you, Shamus. We can do this together."

Shamus stood staring at him. "What is it you think we can do?"

"You spend two years learning the barrel-making craft, and I'll buy us a barrel-making manufactory and stock it with everything you'll need. We'll hire master coopers to work in it and train apprentices, and you will run it, and we'll share the profits as partners."

Shamus stared back at him, the slightest frown ticking between his brows. "So," he said, "that would take care of one side of the partnership, but you said we would be helping each other. What do you want of me, then?"

"I want you—no, I *need* you—to keep doing what you've been doing here. Run the smithy in the mornings while I'm at the armouries, and then you'll go to the cooperage in the afternoons, just as I go to the armouries each morning. If you'll do that for two years, we will both benefit, and you will be able to hold your head up when you approach Eylin's family. You will have money to show them, as well as a business and a future. She will have you, will she not?"

"Aye." Shamus was very subdued. "She would have me now, with nothing." He narrowed his eyes to slits. "You would do this, for me? Why?"

"Why not? I told you, I need your help. Besides, I'm marrying your sister. We'll be brothers come tomorrow. Who better to have as a partner than a brother?"

"What about my da?"

"What about him? He'll dance at your wedding. So, are we agreed?"

Shamus nodded, a single, decisive bob of the head, already looking like a different man.

THIRTY-ONE

Varrus had one brilliant, all-effacing memory of his wedding that persisted for the remainder of his life. It was of the moment when he turned around, prompted by a sudden upsurge of noise at his back, and saw Lydia Mcuil enter the main room of the house, where all the guests—they had ended up with seventeen—had assembled to witness the ceremony. She was dressed in a magnificent shimmering robe of translucent yellow fabric that draped her to her feet in rippling, scalloped waves of shifting shades of yellow and gold. She was surely the most breathtaking woman ever to be seen in the town of Camulodunum since its founding in the days of the long-dead emperor Claudius. Varrus grinned like an idiot boy.

She came to him with a radiant smile, and from that point on he lost all coherent memory of the day, though he was aware, from time to time, of significant moments in the course of the wedding ceremony itself. For example, after holding up their joined hands and tying them together with a bright blue ribbon, Lydia held him tightly while others among the guests came forward and added ribbons of their own, joining the pair of them unmistakably in a gesture that needed no translation.

And he remembered one other event that occurred that day. After Lydia had withdrawn for a short time with the women, Varrus and Ajax drifted over to the smithy while talking idly on some trivial matter. As Varrus passed through the door, the anomalous little object that Liam had called Ler's Skull caught his eye, lodged in front of the smithy door to hold it open. Without interrupting what his companion was saying, Varrus crouched down smoothly and scooped the thing up, marvelling again at the unexpectedness of its weight. He turned to Natius Ajax.

"Here," he said, and when Natius reached out for the thing, Varrus dropped it into his palm, smiling as the weight of it forced the armourer to lurch forward and snatch at it with both hands before it could fall.

"What d'you make of that?" he asked. "Heavy little thing, is it not?"

"I'll grant you that," the armourer said, holding it up closer to examine it. "It's dense. What is it?"

"Liam called it Ler's Skull—see that domed bit, and those two holes that could be eye sockets? Ler is one of the old Erse gods, the kind they sometimes call the wee folk. As for what it's made of, I don't know. I think it's metal mixed with stone, but it's not any kind of ore that I've ever seen. And it's harder than anything I've ever known, too. Liam told me he tried to smelt it several times, but failed every time."

"Hmm. Where did it come from, did he say?"

"Said some fisherman dredged it up in his nets, but he couldn't say where, or even what sea it came from."

Ajax was holding the thing right up to his eyes, peering at it from less than a foot away. "Strange," he murmured. "It almost looks as though it might have started to melt at one time."

"That's what Liam thought, too. But that's not possible, is it?"

"That depends on how you define possible. I would never wager on the difference." He was still peering down, but his eyes had drifted away now, gazing off into the distance. "That's strange, though . . . Twice now, in a matter of weeks."

Varrus cocked his head. "What are you talking about?"

The armourer shook his head dismissively. "Nothing, really. A coincidence, that's all." He set the strange stone back in place. "I had another one of these things brought to me less than a month ago—a bit bigger than that one, but with the same kind of glazed effect on part of its surface. Strange-looking thing, but I wasn't too impressed. The fellow who brought it to me was a madman. Said it fell from the sky and was hot when he first found it."

"Hot? From the sky?"

"I know. That's what I thought, too. But that's what he claimed. Said he and his wife had been awakened one night by an unholy noise— a screaming whistle followed by a mighty crash that left them huddled awake all night long, too afraid to get out of bed and look to see what had happened. Next day though, when they went outside, they found their oak tree smashed to burning splinters and half buried in a great hole in the ground that was still smoking. Said it took him three days to grow brave enough to approach the place, even after the fire was out. As I said, a madman. I took the thing off his hands, as a curiosity, and gave him a few sesterces for it because the finish on it intrigued me. Thought I might try smelting it in the new furnace one of these days."

"We might try to smelt this one at the same time."

"Good idea, why not?"

They left it there, but for the remainder of the day Varrus found his thoughts returning to their conversation at odd times and always with discomfort, and he found it disquieting that he could not identify why that should trouble him.

Towards the middle of the afternoon, when the fine wine Dominic had lavishly provided was being freely consumed and the womenfolk were engaged in the kitchens preparing the nuptial meal, Demetrius Hanno beckoned him aside.

"Where do you . . . you hide things here when you need to?"

Varrus stiffened, thinking immediately of his newly hidden hoard of golden coins. But then he relaxed again, admonishing himself with a silent smile, for it was plain that Hanno had already consumed a few draughts of wine, and from the bleary way his eyes were flitting from side to side, evidently attempting to assess every conceivable hiding place in the room, it was clear that whatever was troubling the big smith had nothing to do with money.

"I've no idea what you're talking about, Demetrius," he said. "What do you need?"

"Need a hiding place," the giant said. "Ajax and I—" He paused solemnly and hiccuped. "We have a gift for Lydia, Ajax and me. But can't bring it in yet, so we have to hide it for a while."

"Then that's easy. Where is it?"

"At the fort. But I have a boy wait . . . waiting to go an' fetch it."

"Send him to get it now, then, and we'll hide it in the stables. May I ask what it is?"

"'S a mirror," Hanno said, then weaved away in the direction of the outer yard.

When he judged that enough time had passed, Varrus rounded up Ajax to witness the arrival of his gift, and the pair of them strolled out into the yard to join Hanno and wait with him by the smithy gates. The afternoon shadows had already lengthened sufficiently to throw the area into darkness, and so they moved on, through the gates and out into the street. There they saw two young men coming into view in the distance, manhandling an ungainly, shrouded burden between them.

"Here they come now," Varrus said. "That thing looks bulky. No wonder you need a hiding place for it."

As he said the words, he heard heavy footsteps at their back, and then someone behind them cleared his throat, bringing all three men swinging around. Ajax and Hanno immediately drew themselves up into a militarily erect and respectful stance, staring straight ahead. Varrus thought the man's face familiar, though he could not quite place it at first, and in the next instant he saw that it must be the new garrison legate, Britannicus, because the trio of men behind him were all in full dress uniform, adding emphasis to the unmilitary but aristocratic clothing the man himself wore.

"Centurion Ajax, is it not?" Britannicus's voice was deep and rich, precise yet friendly, and his eyes seemed to Varrus to contain a hint of amusement as he looked at the armourer and then beyond him to where Hanno stood straight as a spear. "I don't know you, though, do I?"

Hanno appeared to answer without moving his mouth. "Demetrius Hanno, Legate. I work in the armouries, as a smith."

Britannicus recognized him with a courteous dip of his head and then turned to look at Varrus, scanning him from head to toe and taking in the white richness of the Roman robe.

"A beautiful day, sir," he said cordially, extending a hand. "Too fine to spend cooped up inside. My name is Britannicus, newly appointed legate of the garrison." He paused, and his eyes narrowed. "Did we not see each other the day I arrived? There was a funeral procession, I remember. Were you not at the head of the mourners?"

Varrus nodded. "I was, sir. We were burying a friend, the local smith, Liam Mcuil."

The legate's eyes returned to Varrus's sumptuous white robe. "You are dressed differently today, though—more celebrant than mourner, I think."

"That is true, sir. I am newly wed today."

"Aha!" The legate's face broke into a wide smile. "Then you have my best wishes for this day and for your future. May I ask your name?"

Ajax and Hanno had not moved a muscle since they first caught sight of the legate and snapped to attention, but now Ajax's eyes widened as he saw the trap threatening his friend. Before Ajax could speak, though, Varrus relieved him of the need.

"My name is Varrus, Commander. Quintus Varrus."

"Well then, Magister Varrus, I will bid you good day and leave you to get on with your celebrations. Centurion, you may continue." He nodded cordially again to Varrus and Hanno, and moved away unhurriedly, followed by his three subordinates, all of whom had been staring at Varrus with varying degrees of curiosity.

Ajax let out his breath in a long hiss.

"Well, that was interesting," Varrus said, watching the quartet walk away. "I never expected to meet him in the town streets."

"Limping Vulcan," Ajax said. "That almost scared me sober . . . But you now have some idea of the kind of man he is. Nothing pretentious or demeaning in him, no matter who he's talking to." He barked a sudden laugh. "He must have wondered, though. You hardly look like the kind of citizen they might expect to find in the cobbled streets of a provincial town. Interesting that he didn't react to your name, though. It's common enough as a name, I suppose, but I would have expected more of a reaction from one of our brotherhood to hearing it used here. Unless, of course, he already knew you were here . . . Over here, lads." He beckoned to the two young porters and then led them into the stables, where Varrus showed them where he wanted them to lay their burden. Varrus thanked them both and insisted on giving each of them a few double denarii—coins that could be readily exchanged in a wine shop or taverns—and when they had left he turned back to Ajax.

"So, when will you present her with the mirror?"

"At dinner. There are other people here who have brought gifts. So when everyone has finished eating, and before the tables are cleared."

"So be it," Varrus said. "Give me a nod when you think the time is right, and I'll give a little speech, giving you time to bring it in."

When they returned to the house, there was music being played—two fiddlers and a piper playing lively, melodic Eirish tunes, and for a long, pleasant time, the newly wed couple circulated among their guests, laughing and talking with all of them until dinner was announced and everyone sat down to marvel over the delights that had been prepared in the kitchen. They dined on fresh vegetables—turnips, parsnips, and fresh asparagus—lentils served in several ways, both sweet and spicy, yearling venison, a roasted suckling pig with an apple in its mouth, and broiled salmon caught the previous day in the local river, and fresh-baked bread aplenty. At the latter part of the meal, the truly festive part, the women served honey-sweetened oatcakes and chewy sweetmeats made from pounded nuts and thickened with finely diced precious dates from Africa and chopped dried plums, accompanied by a hot, delicious sauce of whipped eggs and milk flavoured with nutmeg from Asia.

It was a sumptuous and protracted meal, and when it was over, leaving little to be cleared away, Dominic, as father of the bride, began the process of presenting the newly wed couple with the surprising profusion of gifts their guests had managed to provide despite the lack of time they had all had to prepare.

The gift provided by Ajax and Demetrius Hanno was easily the one that captured everyone's admiration. The mirror was unlike any seen before in Camulodunum. It was oval, measuring perhaps three feet in height and slightly less than half of that in width, and it was mounted in an ornate, free-standing frame with swivels mounted on either side, permitting it to be angled up or down. The mirror surface was of purest, unblemished, liquid-seeming silver, burnished and polished to a brightness that was almost supernatural. Few of the guests had ever seen their own reflections, as any mirror surface was precious, and the most common were of polished bronze or brass, or even copper. The liquid purity of silver brought gasps of amazement from everyone who looked into it.

The celebration that followed was enjoyable in the way that most such celebrations are, in that few of the participants would be able to remember much about the evening that was clear-edged, yet each would have his or her own memories of specific moments or events that stayed with them long afterwards. Shanna's ale was in great demand the entire evening, and fortunately there was no shortage of it, though it would take a long time for her stock to recover from the depredations of the thirsty guests that night. And as their enjoyment of the brew grew greater and sweeter, the innate love that the Celtic people have for song and story sprang free and flourished, with even the shyest, most self-effacing among the non-Roman guests stepping forward willingly to offer his or her own contributions to the spirit of the festivities.

The bride and groom stood together in their doorway and watched until the last of the guests vanished through the gate into the street outside, and then Varrus stooped and kissed the crown of his wife's head, enjoying the tightness of her arms around his waist as she nestled into the hollow beneath his shoulder. "Well, wife," he murmured. "I think that went well." He tightened his arm, squeezing her against him. "How does it make you feel, now that you are no longer simply Lydia Mcuil?"

She pivoted gently, turning him away from the door and back towards the interior of the house, which had now fallen completely silent. "I think it makes me feel exactly as I've wanted to feel for a long time now— happy and looking forward to a life of fulfillment and self-satisfied smugness."

He closed the outer door before facing her again, when he bent and scooped her up effortlessly, his right arm behind her knees. "And you'll have that, milady," he growled, his throat suddenly swollen with tenderness. "As long as I'm alive, I'll work to keep you smug and satisfied. And as soon as I can get you free of that yellow robe, I'll show you how I intend to do it . . ."

THIRTY-TWO

When he first became aware of it, in the days and weeks that followed his wedding day, Varrus was not particularly surprised that his grandfather should be in his thoughts much of the time, no matter what he found himself doing. He had been shown that his grandsire had in fact been the very antithesis of all he had believed him to be.

Small wonder, then, he thought, that he should now be shamed by the utter wrongness of his failure to see beyond the outward appearance to the inner truth of his grandfather's behaviour. As the days passed by and the image of the old man remained in his mind, sharp-edged and unfading, Varrus found himself growing preoccupied with one single recollection. In it, Titanius stood, as he so often had in young Quintus's boyhood, at the enormous table in the formal dining room of his villa in Salona. His right hand was raised in a sweeping, imperious gesture familiar to the boy, and he wore his favourite quilted, bright green dalmatic tunic, the one with the wide sleeves and shoulders and narrow but elaborately decorated vertical stripes of hand-worked gold wire, one of those much-loved garments that men regard as trusted, loyal friends but that wives frequently, and vainly, attempt to wrest from their husbands' possession, seeing them as shabby reminders of things long past. Titanius was surrounded by his family. His son Marcus stood in front of him and three other people sat at the table, looking up at Titanius as he spoke: his wife, Alexia Seneca; Marcus's wife, Maris, Quintus's mother; and his younger son Marius, wearing the blue-and-white civilian tunic of a naval officer on furlough.

Something about the look of his uncle Marius in that image bothered Varrus, but try as he would he could not grasp what it was, and each time he felt he was on the point of identifying what it was the recognition slipped from his grasp again, so that eventually he simply gritted his teeth when the vision came to him and resisted any temptation to waste more time fretting over it.

A few weeks later, early on a perfect afternoon, Varrus returned from the armoury to discover that Shamus had finished all that they were working on, leaving him some unexpected time, and so he took Lydia for a walk along the summer-clad banks of the River Colne on the outskirts of the town. They strolled aimlessly along the riverbank towards the sea a few miles ahead of them, enjoying the novelty of being out of the smithy and alone together on a lovely afternoon, and then they swung away inland, following the course of a meandering brook that had cut them off from walking any farther by spilling itself across their path and into the river. The brook itself was neither broad nor deep, but it presented a threat to Lydia's daintily slippered feet, and so rather than risk damaging her footwear, the young couple merely angled their way back towards the town, following the brook's path through an area of small farms.

Varrus was surprised to discover that the area was far more pleasant and attractive than he had expected, and that in turn set him thinking about the task he and Lydia had undertaken to find a suitable small farm for Shanna. He had stopped to admire one tidy, prosperous-looking little farm on the other side of the brook, knowing from the mere appearance of the clean, attractive buildings that it was highly unlikely to be available for sale, when Lydia drew his attention to something ahead of them, on their side of the brook. It was a mature oak, he guessed, but as he and Lydia neared it he could see that it was one of a pair, the second of which was riven and splintered, its glaring wounds new and shockingly raw, while its shattered branches yet held green foliage.

As soon as he saw it, Varrus knew he was looking at the tree Ajax had told him about, the one hit by the stone that had supposedly fallen from the sky, and suddenly he was breathing hard, squeezing Lydia's hand tightly enough to make her wince as he pulled her forward with him. When he told her what had happened to the tree, though, she threw back her head and laughed at him, convinced he was teasing her, and that gave him pause, because his own initial reaction to the story had been precisely the same scornful dismissal. A stone, falling from the sky, without being thrown up there by someone nearby? The idea of that alone was ludicrous. But when you suggested that the stone had fallen on a massive oak tree and hit it hard enough to shatter the tree and destroy it, well, considered objectively, it sounded truly insane.

"Something bothers me here," Varrus admitted at length. "And it is bothering me deeply . . . but I don't know how I can talk about it in any way that would make sense to you, my love, because it makes nonsense of all I've ever been taught about the natural world we live in."

"The natural world we live in . . ." She stared at him, no trace of teasing in her attitude now. "That sounds more than slightly ominous, husband. But I think I need to hear you tell me about it, nonetheless. What is it that bothers you?"

He waved his hand towards the ruined tree and the upturned, shattered ground surrounding it. "The people whose land this is were wakened in the middle of the night, not long ago, by a terrifying noise and an earth-shaking explosion. When they grew brave enough to go and look at what had happened, they found this oak tree destroyed— just as you see it now—and all the earth around it torn up around that huge hole from which smoke was still rising.

"I heard it took some days for the farmer to gather up the courage to look closer—and who could blame him for that? But when he did, he found a stone, a stone that was still hot, almost buried at the bottom of the hole. Once he grew convinced no more unnatural events would follow the first, he dug the thing out. I am not sure exactly how or why, but the farmer ended up bringing that stone to Natius, who thought he was mad, with his tale about stones falling out of the sky, but then Natius himself grew intrigued by the metallic sheen of the thing's surface, and so he bought it off the fellow.

"Now, here's where matters get even stranger. Liam has something similar in his smithy, a metallic-looking stone he calls Ler's Skull." He hesitated. "You know who Ler is, don't you?" Lydia nodded, and he continued. "Well, that stone was dredged up by some fisherman a long time earlier, and Liam kept it because he was curious about it—from the look of it, he thought it might have started to melt at some time. He never could heat it enough to smelt it further, though—his bellows were just not strong enough to blow sufficient air into the furnace fast enough, and simply ended up using it as a doorstop in the smithy . . ."

His voice trailed away, and Lydia made no attempt to draw him out of his reveries. She was the daughter in a household of smiths and was more than familiar with the ways in which something as inanimate and inert as raw metal could dominate the thinking of grown men, and so she waited, knowing that Quintus would resume when he was ready to say more.

Sure enough, he cleared his throat and started speaking again. "Anyway," he said, though more quietly than before, "Natius told me the story of this falling stone, and what I found really odd was that, once the novelty of what he had told me wore off and I had adjusted to the strangeness of the suggestion that the thing had fallen from the sky, I really had no difficulty in accepting that it might be true—that this other stone might have fallen from the sky more recently and landed here . . . But that was before I saw this." He nodded towards the hole in the ground. "Now I can see how impossible it was."

"Why impossible, Quintus? What's impossible?"

He pointed at the ruined tree. "That is, Lydia. That is impossible . . . This was a mature, healthy oak tree, and now look at it. Look at the thickness of that trunk. A month or two ago, it would have taken three grown men to encircle that bole with outstretched arms, and yet it's smashed to kindling. And look at those main branches. Those grew horizontally, thirty feet in length and thicker around than my chest—and again, look at them, smashed into splinters—lengthwise! I haven't seen the stone that supposedly caused all this, but I know Ajax has held it in his hands, so it can't be too big . . . heavy, certainly, but not too heavy to lift. Yet look at what it's supposed to have done to this tree, and to the ground beneath it . . . I can't begin to imagine the speed and force it must have had when it came down, to do all that damage. One small stone?"

He fell silent again, shaking his head in disbelief, then seemed to freeze for long moments, his eyes wide and once again unfocused, gazing outwards in astonishment at something Lydia instantly turned to look for. But there was nothing there to see other than the flat, empty expanse of the meadow and the winding brook.

"Quintus?" Her voice was uncertain. "What are you looking at?"

"My grandfather."

She felt a single, sudden thump of apprehension, and glanced towards the meadow, and then willed herself to do and say nothing, knowing he would explain when he was ready.

He stood silent again for several moments, then turned his head to look at her. "That's it," he said—speaking to her but looking through her, she thought. "That's the vision of my grandfather I've been seeing recently. I knew there was something strange about what Marius was wearing."

She waited again, still not moving, until she was sure he would say nothing more, and then she said, "Quintus?" He did not react, and she spoke again, more insistently this time. "Quintus? Look at me!" She waved her hand in front of his eyes, and she saw the change in his eyes as he rejoined her.

"What?"

"Where were you? I don't know where your mind went there, but you left me behind for a little while. You said something about seeing your grandfather."

"Oh!" His brow cleared instantly and he smiled at her, and she could see excitement dancing in his eyes. "I did. See him. But I've been seeing him for days and I couldn't understand why. This time, though, I saw it clearly."

"You said something about your uncle . . . about what he was wearing."

"Yes. He was wearing a tunic he shouldn't have been wearing—in my vision, I mean. That's one of the things I couldn't understand."

She reached out and pressed one hand flat against his sternum. "Stop," she said, "because I didn't understand a word you said there. Now kiss me, please, before you say anything else, then start again and tell me all about it, leaving nothing out."

"I'll tell you," he said. "But you still might not understand what I'm saying. There's nothing wrong, though, nothing for you to be concerned about."

"It has something to do with this place, this tree and this hole in the ground. Is that correct?"

"Yes."

"Hmm." She looked all around again, then pointed to where someone had dragged an ancient log to provide seating near where the bed of the brook widened to form a wide, deep hole. It had obviously been sitting there for decades, because the surface had been polished smooth by generations of use. "Let's rest over there and you can tell me what you are talking about."

A short time later, when she was snuggled against his side on the log with his arm around her shoulders, she looked up at him again. "Start by telling me about your uncle's tunic. What was so strange about it?"

He grinned again. "Nothing, really . . . other than the timing. He was wearing a distinctive blue-and-white tunic, the tunic of a trierarch. I had forgotten all about that."

She looked at him, unimpressed. "A trierarch. And what is a trierarch?"

"A ship's captain, the commander of a trireme. But at the time I'm talking of—the time of this memory of my grandfather—my uncle Marius was already a navarch, commanding a squadron of ships, and I remember him wearing that white uniform with the blue border in honour of one of his captains who had died in a battle during his last campaign, just before he came home on furlough . . . And that was the night when Grandfather Titanius told us all about the fireball that wiped out more than half his force in Dacia."

He hesitated, and Lydia shifted away from him slightly, peering up at him, and asked, "Where is Dacia? And whose force was wiped out? Your uncle's?"

Varrus smiled at her. "No, my love. My grandfather's. Or more accurately a group under my grandfather's command, led by a man called Provo. And I was not supposed to hear any of it. I was ten years old at the time, too young to be at table with the grown-ups, so I was hiding in a sideboard, listening to them in secret. I did that often when I was bored and had nothing else to do." He pulled her back close to him and kissed her, then held her in his arms while he related the story, which he now remembered vividly, that his grandfather had told the family that evening, about the falling of the great fireball in Dacia, decades before Quintus had been born. When he had finished, Lydia continued to cling closely to him for a long time, making no attempt to speak. When she let go and looked up into his eyes, her face was stamped by incomprehension.

"Quintus, that is an awful story," she said. "No wonder he refused to talk about it for so long. But I don't understand what it has to do with this, this oak tree, here and now."

"Degree, and perception. It's all a matter of how we perceive things, and how deeply we trust in what's before our eyes. Just minutes ago I was shaking my head at the power it would take for one falling stone to do as much damage as this one did here. And then I remembered my grandfather's story of what he saw with his own eyes—a ball of fire so large, and moving so quickly, that it streaked over the heads of his entire army, plunging the world into darkness and blinding and deafening hundreds of his men merely in passing. And when it hit the ground it destroyed a thousand fighting men and levelled miles and miles of standing forest as easily as a strong wind can flatten a field of grain. A ball of fire, Lydia. Think about that . . .

"And then remember what the farmer said. When he approached the hole days later, and found the stone at the bottom, it was still smoking, as though it had been cooling ever since it fell from the sky. That makes me wonder, Lydia. What if my grandfather's fireball was but a stone—a burning stone? The Greeks spoke of their gods throwing thunderbolts from Mount Olympus—great, flaming balls of fire that destroyed everything they struck. Is that what we had here, in Camulodunum? A thunderbolt? A small, barely significant thunderbolt? Could such a thing even be conceivable?"

"Of course it could," Lydia said, her voice barely audible. "You are talking about it, Quintus. That means you already consider it possible. And now I believe you need to talk about it with someone else, someone more able to talk sensibly about such things than I am."

The following morning, having listened to everything Varrus had said to him since bursting into his workplace almost a full hour earlier, Ajax sat back, wiping the corners of his mouth absently with a thumb and index finger.

"So," he said, cautiously, "what do you expect me to say, after that? Because, if I'm being honest, Quintus, it sounds mad."

"Believe me, Natius, I know how mad it sounds, because I've gone over it in my mind a hundred times since yesterday. But having been through it that hundred times, I now believe, absolutely, that my grandfather and all his people saw a giant thunderbolt fall to earth. None of them knew what it was, though. Their only explanation was that the gods had gone mad. But it was enormous beyond credence or description, and it fell from the sky. I believe that."

"I can see you do. But what comes next, then?"

"I need to see the stone that farmer brought you."

"Why?"

"Because it fell, too."

"Out of the sky, you mean."

"Yes."

"But that's mad, Quintus. From where in the sky? Everything that falls has to fall from somewhere. Do you think there are shelves up there above the clouds, laden with stones and thunderbolts waiting to fall off?"

Varrus faced his friend squarely. "I know it sounds insane, Natius, but it can't be. This was my grandfather's testimony—Titanius Varrus's own words. Would he fabricate such a tale? And if so, why? And besides, I think Ler's Skull is another of these things—except that it fell into the sea. I know I can't prove any of this. All I'm asking is that we ignore the madness of it all and simply try to smelt them in the new oven. Will you work with me to do that?"

Instead of answering directly, Ajax rose and went to the door, where he leaned out and shouted for an apprentice, then sent the lad scuttling off to fetch Demetrius Hanno. "Hanno's the man you have to talk to," he said, turning back and closing the door. "He's the one you'll have to work with. So you're going to have to go through the whole thing again, risk his ridicule, too."

Demetrius Hanno listened as attentively as Ajax had, but to Varrus's surprise he appeared completely unfazed by what the younger man described, and merely shrugged when he heard Varrus request permission to proceed.

"This skull you describe. Where is it?"

"It's here, in my knapsack."

Varrus dug it out and passed it over for the giant's inspection, and Hanno hefted it and shrugged again. "We'll need the full power of the bellows . . . and even that might not be enough. This metal looks *hard*. It might not want to melt—not with the kind of heat we can generate, anyway. But we won't know until we try." He set the skull aside and turned back to Varrus. "How is your wife this morning?"

Varrus grinned. "Enjoying married life. I left her preening herself in front of her new mirror. She might still be there when I get home. I know I would be, were I as beautiful as she is."

Hanno glanced over at Ajax sardonically. "Newlyweds," he growled. "Is love not wonderful?"

BOOK FOUR

Eboracum to Colcaster, A.D. 318

THIRTY-THREE

The young woman who brought Cato's ale thought he was smiling at her as she approached his table, and she smiled back at him and winked in a tacit commitment to come to know him a little better if he wished. Her face fell, though, when he ignored her and shifted his body to look beyond her, and she swished away with an indignant toss of her head that, like her smiling wink, went completely unnoticed. Marcus Licinius Cato was oblivious to anything other than what was happening at the only other occupied table, across the floor from where he sat alone. He was close to invisible against a dark, windowless wall, almost entirely obscured by the dimness that enveloped him despite the feeble, guttering light of the single smoky lamp on his small table.

Four men sat around a much wider table against the wall farthest from him, lit from above and behind by the daylight streaming in through a long, low window from the street outside. Cato had arrived mere moments ahead of them, going directly and instinctively to the dark side of the tavern, where he dropped his pack against the wall and slouched into a chair just in time to appear motionless when they came in. The serving girl had come to take his order—a simple mug of ale that he would test and perhaps consume later—but the other men had sent the girl away brusquely when she approached them. Now it was obvious, from the way they sat fidgeting, that the four were waiting for someone else to join them.

Cato already knew that, though, just as he knew the man for whom they were waiting. He had seen them in the street outside, a short time earlier, when he had stopped to adjust his heavy regimental backpack. He had removed the thing—it was damnably heavy and one of its buckles had been digging into his shoulder and causing him grief—and was in the process of heaving it back up onto his shoulders when he noticed the group ahead of him, huddled beneath an overhanging eave in the hamlet's single, narrow street, all four of them listening intently to a fifth man, the one they were now waiting for. Cato's reaction to seeing them might have seemed amusing, had anyone else been watching to see it, for in the act of swinging the heavy leather pack up over his shoulder, he had stopped short, almost allowing the weight of the thing to throw him off balance, so that he ended up snatching at it and clutching it to his chest with both hands as he stared, wide-eyed.

What stopped him in his tracks was his instant recognition of the man to whom the other four were listening avidly. The mere sight of him, and the certainty of who he was, filled Cato with leaping anxiety and made him look around in panic for some place to hide, to give himself time to think. Until that moment, Cato had believed the man in front of him to be dead, having seen with his own eyes, a year earlier, what he had believed to be the fellow's charred remains. And in that instant of recognition, laying eyes on the dead man, he accepted the sickening truth: he had been duped. Appius Endor was very much alive.

Cato had hesitated there in the open for a space of heartbeats, clutching his leather knapsack to his chest with both arms like a witless, gape-mouthed yokel and utterly incapable of moving, caught flat-footed between the urges to flee and to fight as he waited for the other man to turn and recognize him.

When Endor did glance in his direction, though, from a distance of five or six paces, Cato saw no flare of recognition in his eyes, and only then, on the very edge of starting away guiltily, did it occur to him that he had never met the man. Cato had known him and detested him and pursued him for years, had come to know aspects of the man's personality more intimately and in more ways than he cared to think about, but their paths had never actually crossed. Cato had known his quarry solely from the reports and observations of others who had been set to watch him closely, day and night. That realization almost overwhelmed Cato with a vast relief as he realized that he was nowhere near as vulnerable as he had first feared.

Appius Endor. The Basilisk. Now, watching the four hard-looking men across the room, Cato wondered idly who had first applied the nickname, for it was both accurate and appropriate. The basilisk was a mythical monster, an impossible creature born of a paradox: a reptile hatched from a cockerel's egg by a nursing snake, its mere gaze lethal, as was its poisonous breath. The man these four were now waiting for dealt in lethality as his daily commerce, with a cold-blooded lack of humanity that Cato knew to be genuinely reptilian.

The door from the street swung wide and Endor himself stepped into the tavern, his eyes sweeping the room as he entered, registering Cato's presence by the wall even as he dismissed him and moved to join his waiting hirelings. Cato had to resist an urge to pull his hood forward to shield his face. He did raise his hand to his face, but instead of tugging at the hood's cowl he brushed the tips of his fingers along his upper lip, feeling the alien smoothness there.

His beard had been gone for weeks already, but he had yet to grow accustomed to its absence and he doubted that he ever would. The single view he had had of his own face during those weeks, in the reflective surface of a smoothly polished platter on a silversmith's market stall in a town far north of where he was now, had shocked him deeply. He had barely recognized himself, but the startled, pale green eyes glaring back at him from that shockingly bare, pallid face had been his own, and the admission had depressed him for days afterwards. He had worn a full beard, trimmed to legionary specifications, for twenty years by then, almost from the day he joined the army as its newest recruit, and he had had the garrison barber shave him clean on the day he left the fort at Eboracum for the last time.

No longer a soldier, and profoundly unsure of what he might become, he had decided to embrace civilian life as quickly and whole-heartedly as he could, and shaving off the military beard had been an important part of that transition, a deliberate step into the unknown, relinquishing the reddish-brown beard that had won him the nickname of Rufus among his friends and messmates.

As soon as the Basilisk sat down, his four satellites closed ranks around him, leaning inwards as they listened to whatever he was telling them, and Cato knew he would hear or see nothing else until Endor's information had been delivered. He leaned back in his chair then and allowed himself to relax slightly, content to wait until the huddlers moved apart and began to speak normally again.

His ale was untouched on the table in front of him and now he picked it up and sipped at it tentatively, looking around the huge common room until his gaze arrived naturally at the counter against the end wall, where the landlord and the serving girl stood talking quietly to each other.

The place was a typical roadside mansio, one of many thousands built over the years throughout the empire, established in the distant past as collection and distribution points for the imperial post, and furnished and appointed for the comfort and convenience of imperial couriers, commercial messengers, and wealthy travellers. Rome's great network of roads had been built as individual units, each the shortest marching route between two points. Their sole purpose had been to facilitate the movement of Rome's conquering armies from one place to the next in the shortest possible time. Centuries later, those same roads facilitated the flow of commerce that was the life's blood of the sprawling empire. Mansios, some great, some smaller, lined each route, set at a distance of about twenty miles apart, a normal day's journey.

Cato had noticed that the adjoining stables, once extensive and spacious, were largely boarded up and derelict. Rundown and evil-smelling, they now housed no more than a few ill-fed, sway-backed nags, with the notable exception of a pair of fine, strong-looking horses that were stabled apart and obviously owned by some wealthy traveller. The once fine, spacious common room where he now sat was dingy, a slatternly tavern, carelessly swept and visibly in need of a thorough cleansing. The rushes on the floor had been left there for too long and smelled more than a little stale, and the tabletops that he could see looked as though they had not been wiped, let alone washed, since they had last been used.

His train of thought was interrupted by a movement at the edge of his vision, and he moved his head slightly to see one of Endor's men coming directly towards him, swaying truculently from side to side as he plodded heavily across the floor, his nail-studded boot soles dragging through the rushes that lay thick in some low-lying spots.

Cato sighed quietly. He had been expecting this. He set his ale down and raised his right foot to the cross-member of the chair opposite where he sat, and then he waited. When the fellow was within two steps of him, Cato straightened his leg and kicked the other chair out and away, not knocking it over but propelling it with exactly the right amount of velocity to reach the newcomer and stop in front of him. It was a precise move, interpretable in either of two ways: it might have been an invitation to stop and sit down; equally, it might have been a deliberate provocation for the fellow to stand still and state whatever he had to say. Either way, it stopped him in his tracks, and Cato took the initiative.

"I'm guessing you've come to tell me something, friend. What can I do for you?"

The civilly phrased comment, followed by the friendly question, left the newcomer nonplussed, and he stood frowning, but then his surliness asserted itself.

"Out," he said. "We need this table."

"Out," Cato repeated flatly. He looked all around the large room, slowly, then sniffed. "There's tables everywhere, Plodder," he said. "Why d'you need this one?"

"'Cause we want it. 'S all you need to know."

"No, that's not good enough."

Cato stood up smoothly, the move fluid and effortless, bringing him completely erect with no hint of imbalance, his straightening right leg knocking his chair backwards and over as he rose. His expression was calm and confident, challenging the other man to try and interfere with him. For the smallest fraction of a moment the fellow looked as though he might make an attempt, but by then Cato was already up and the opportunity, if it had ever been there, had passed. The Plodder merely stood glowering, fists clenched, and Cato grinned at him.

"Let's go ask your magister why you need it." He stepped around the table, brushing past the Plodder, and crossed the room directly to where Endor and the other three sat watching him.

"Do you know me," he asked, "or should I know you? Have we met somewhere before? I'm asking because your half-tame halfwit here told me I have to move on out of here, but I'm here for a purpose that has nothing to do with you and I'm not moving on before I'm ready. So let me ask you again. Do we know each other?"

Cato was watching Endor's eyes as the Basilisk evaluated his words, but simultaneously he was waiting for the Plodder's delayed reaction behind him, visualizing the thought process involved in the man's belated realization that he had been defamed and insulted. Then, knowing the Plodder's type as well as he did, he timed the man's move with exact precision. Without breaking his gaze from Endor's, he swayed slightly left as he cupped his fist into his other palm, braced his weight on one foot, and twisted his upper body hard and fast, driving his elbow up and back into the bridge of the charging Plodder's nose, shattering bone and cartilage and dropping the man to his knees like a head-spiked bull.

Endor's eyes never wavered, never acknowledged the Plodder's presence, let alone his fall. His three companions all started to rise, but he quelled them with one wordless gesture and they sank back like well-trained dogs.

"Why would you think we might know each other?" the man asked as though nothing at all had happened since Cato spoke, the question casual, almost disinterested.

"I don't," Cato said. "Not for a moment. I know I don't know you. Never set eyes on you before and I don't care who you are. But you might know me from somewhere, and I don't like that, don't like not knowing people who might think they might know me, and so I came to ask. And plainly you are the man to ask." He jerked his head, indicating the others at the table. "These three—four—were nothing more than lumps until you walked in. But you got them moving. That makes you the magister, the boss. So, one more time. Do you know me?"

There was a lengthy, thoughtful silence before Endor responded, but when he did his voice was placid. "No," he said. "I don't know who you are. But I know *what* you are . . . and where you came from."

"Oh, really? And where would that have been?"

Endor smiled a lazy, half-amused smile to match the one Cato had used in asking the question. "It might have been any one of a half score of places, but they all have 'legion' etched into them. You and I are of a kind and we both know it. Legion bred and legion trained. Long-service and hard-core, though I suspect you're out now. Are you?"

"Aye, three months ago."

"Which legion?"

"Twentieth Valeria. Legionary headquarters, Deva."

"Hmm. Rank?"

Cato narrowed his eyes, clearly deliberating whether he should answer, but then he shrugged, apologizing silently to the dead man whose face was in his mind at that moment.

"Pilus prior," he said. "Second Cohort. Ten years. Name's Blixus."

Gaius Blixus, his boyhood friend of more than twenty years, had been senior centurion of the Second of the Twentieth for the last ten years of his military career and had retired a half year earlier after twenty-five years of distinguished service. He had died at his family home near Londinium two months later, of what the medics called an apoplexy—a sudden, inexplicable convulsion. Cato had been one of the four old comrades, friends of long standing, in attendance at his funeral service. Blixus's service record was impeccable, but his death had been private, unpublicized and largely unnoticed. Cato knew Blixus would be glad to have his name used to confound Appius Endor, who had been as well known and loathed by him as he was by Cato.

Endor was already nodding as the name left Cato's mouth, accepting it completely for the moment, because of how easy it would be to verify. The man facing him would be a fool to lie about such a thing. He waved a finger towards the oaf Cato had felled, who had regained his senses and was now attempting to sit up with the help of one of his companions who was pressing a blood-soaked rag to his ruined nose and mouth.

"I sent Spero to tell you to leave because I have matters to conduct here that are not for strangers' ears." He paused. "Obviously, though, you chose not to go. Why would you refuse, faced with five of us?"

Cato faced him evenly, allowing nothing of what he was really feeling to show on his face. "Because I learned long ago never to back down if I see a chance of beating the odds, and your bully boys didn't look like much. If I let these clowns of yours get away with anything, even for a moment, then I might as well just lie down and die. So I'd rather go down fighting. Besides, I made arrangements to meet my contact here, and I have no intention of clucking around outside like a broody hen cut off from her clutch. I won't carry out my business in the street like a huckster to prevent offending *you*."

He glanced at the other three men, who were gaping at him, and then he folded the ends of his cloak back over his shoulders, exposing the matched pair of weapons, dagger and military short sword, that hung from the thick, well-used legionary belt at his waist. He looked back at Endor.

"So? Shall we get on with it, me against you and your three louts here, or will you suffer me to go back to my table and leave me to drink my ale in peace?"

One side of Endor's mouth twitched slightly upwards. "Things are different now," he said quietly. "You are no longer nameless, or faceless. With that in mind, I see no difficulty in your staying here . . . Other than the obvious."

"The obvious . . ." Cato thought about that for a moment and then decided he was being foolish and that he might as well ask outright. "And what is it that's so obvious?"

"Your table is too close, for one thing. If you would consider moving to another—say to that one over in the farthest corner there—then this whole quarrel would be unnecessary."

Cato looked at the table Endor had indicated. It was as far from where he stood as anything in the large room could be, and in the darkest corner.

"That's easy," he said, turning back. "I'll move, so be it they give me a brighter flame against the darkness. I've no interest in your guests or your business and I'll be able to conduct my own affairs without over-hearing or being overheard by you and your people."

He turned then to look at the remaining trio at the table. "You fellows might think about offering a bit more help to poor old Spero here. Clean him up a bit, see to that nose of his. One day it might be you on your arse in the rushes somewhere, needing all the help you can get, and Spero won't offer you his hand if he has no memory of yours reaching out to him."

He nodded curtly at Endor, then made his way to the counter, where the landlord and the serving maid had been watching tensely, no doubt worried about what might happen next. He was aware of a soreness in his hands, the result of having held them clenched into fists for too long, and so, with his back to the Basilisk's table, he unclenched them very deliberately, flexing his fingers and stretching them wide as he tried, uselessly, to make himself relax. He could feel his shoulders juddering with tension and repressed anger, but he knew that, so far, nothing was visible to anyone else. He also knew, from hard experience, that his tight control was temporary, and that he would soon start to shake in earnest unless he found some solitude. He asked the innkeeper for a new mug of ale and a freshly filled oil lamp, and as the pair at the counter moved to fill his requests, he returned to where he had been sitting earlier, collected his kit bag, and carried it to the distant corner table to await their arrival.

THIRTY-FOUR

By the time he reached his new table and set down his pack in the darkened corner, the trembling Cato had anticipated had begun, and he sat down quickly with his back to the room, tucking his hands beneath his crossed arms and clamping them tightly as he lowered his chin, afraid to relax in case the men at the distant table might see him shaking, even in the gloom that surrounded him. He willed himself to breathe steadily and evenly and regain his composure, and after a short while he felt himself beginning to uncoil. He continued the deep, exaggerated breathing for a while longer, though, allowing his heartbeat to settle down naturally, and uncrossed his arms just as the serving woman set down a tray holding a freshly lit lamp and a new mug of ale.

He smiled at her this time, and thanked her, but she offered no return acknowledgment, and as soon as she turned away his mind returned to his confrontation with Endor, still reeling at how suddenly life can switch from pleasantness to utter terror and the threat of imminent death. He picked up the mug of ale and drank almost a third of it before he set it down again. A lifetime of soldiering had taught him that the difference between life and death often depends on the length of time that passes between recognizing danger and reacting. He knew he should not have come out of that encounter as cleanly as he had. His reaction had been far too slow and he had been saved solely by the fact that the Basilisk had never seen his face.

He knew that his terror had been justifiable, nonetheless.

Until the moment of coming face to face with Endor less than half an hour earlier, Cato had believed that the man was dead, stabbed through the neck and burned in a fire that had partially consumed him, then eaten by worms in the unmarked, salt-filled grave into which he, Marcus Licinius Cato, had personally rolled him. Dead men did not come back to life, and any man who could effectively contrive to falsify his own death under the close scrutiny of judgmental officialdom was someone around whom a wise man should tread carefully.

Now Cato wondered about the true identity of the man he had buried that day—for he had buried a charred, disfigured corpse. Somewhere, he thought, someone else, some innocent, would long since have lost hope of ever finding a man, perhaps a well-loved man, who had simply vanished from existence that day.

He had sat down with his back to the room because he had been afraid that someone at Endor's table might see him shaking. Now, though, he wished he had not done that. He needed to watch the group at the other table. He stood up and moved to the chair across from where he had been sitting, noting as he turned that the man called Spero appeared to have recovered and was now seated with the others. None of them seemed to be paying attention to Cato, and he thought his change of seats might have gone unnoticed. He took another long pull at his mug of ale and then slid down in his seat, his eyes narrowing as he focused on the bright table beneath the window on the street wall and wondered what would happen next.

He was not waiting for anyone to join him. He had lied about that, realizing that without a guest to wait for he would have had no reason to remain here, and by that time he had no slightest desire to leave. The Basilisk, miraculously returned to life, had filled Cato's life with hard-edged purpose again after long months of boredom, and this dark, dingy room, stinking of stale beer and cheap wine, and traces of old sweat and urine, was its sole focus.

Cato had been making his way slowly south from Eboracum for

months, honourably discharged from military duty after twenty-five years of compulsory service, according to the official diploma of dismissal given him by a grateful empire. That was not quite true, though. He had served for only twenty years, and the additional five years were awarded, with pension, in tacit recognition of the extraordinary nature of his services, which had been known only to a limited number of highly placed superiors. And so at thirty-five years old he had changed everything, leaving behind the great stone fortress of Eboracum that had, at least according to official documents, been his home for almost two whole decades.

To his surprise, once out and free he had been reluctant to move away too quickly, and so his southward progress had been slow, and sometimes he went nowhere for days on end. It had taken him more than a month to travel the first eighty-odd miles between Eboracum and Danum, simply because he was enjoying the novelty of moving at his own pace, without urgency. And so he simply drifted, following the great south road but moving parallel to it, through forested countryside, making a solitary camp each night and sometimes staying in a spot with good fishing or other attractions for as long as a week at a time.

He could easily have ridden, for the accumulated back pay in his heavy moneybelt meant he was far from penniless, but he had never really liked horses and preferred to go afoot like the infantryman he was. And so he walked, taking his time and considering what he might do in the months and years ahead. He had no training for anything other than soldiering, but he was not concerned about that. He had sufficient money to set himself up in an alehouse or even a roadhouse, if he wanted that kind of life, and he knew that there were always billets available for well-qualified veterans who needed private work as bodyguards and household retainers on the larger villas.

He also had a wife out there somewhere, and an eleven-year-old son about whom he had found himself thinking a lot recently, ever since his decision to quit the army.

Rhea had been a decent woman, but ill suited to being a soldier's wife, and certainly not capable of coping with the demands of Cato's life, which was unusually active and complex for a senior centurion, even in garrison. She had tried doggedly for six years, but when Cato had been almost killed, inexplicably far from home, by one of his own men, a chronic malcontent with an uncontrollable temper and a grudge against all officers, she had had enough. She had forced Cato to choose between her and the army. It was no choice at all, and she had been gone within the month.

That had been six years earlier, and the last he had heard, from someone who had seen her there, was that she was living in Londinium. He didn't know whether she was still there, but the thought of heading down in that direction had been in his mind for several months now, and he found himself anticipating seeing his son, Nicodemo, after such a long time.

In the meantime, he'd reached the town of Danum and continued southward towards Lindum without stopping, following the great road that would lead him eventually to Londinium, two hundred miles farther south. He had picked up his pace after leaving Danum, making better time, and was three days south of Lindum when he was caught in a torrential downpour that gave him no time to erect a tent or find any kind of shelter. It had been a short-lived but brutally violent storm, and the steep-sided little gully in which he had sought shelter, barely more than a deep, shrub-choked ditch, had suddenly become a fast-flowing water chute that swept him off his feet and downstream for several hundred paces. When the spate passed, leaving him chilled and soaked through, he discovered that the water had penetrated his waxed leather kit bag and his rations were ruined, which meant he would have to stop at the next inhabited place he found, be it village or army post, in hopes of replenishing his supplies.

He had walked for another eight or nine miles after that, and had found this place. A mere posting station, between forty and fifty miles south of Lindum, it contained two principal features: a minor marching camp with a small, fifty-man garrison commanded by a junior centurion with the rank of optio, or deputy commander, and the former imperial posting inn in which he now sat. Since the mansio had seemed, from his first casual inspection, to be badly neglected, Cato had passed it by without a thought, going directly to the garrison quartermaster's store, where he had shown his discharge papers and received immediate attention to his needs. A welcome addition was a cup of wine that he drank with the decanus in charge of the commissary, in recognition of the demands of professional courtesy that made Rome's legions function as efficiently as they did at the centuriate level throughout the empire.

It was only after leaving the post, making his way slowly along the hamlet's single short street, that he had blundered into the knot of men blocking the sidewalk.

Everything was now unexpectedly at hazard, thrown open to chance in the crosswind of the instant, and his sole objective now was to stay close to Endor and wait for an opportunity to kill the man. Appius Endor had been tried and condemned *in absentia* by an imperial tribunal, sentenced to death for crimes against the empire and the military administration of Britain. Among those crimes had been one that was very personal to Cato: the murder of his friend Alexander Strabo and Strabo's wife Maria, Cato's own sister. And Endor had never been punished.

Nothing protects a human predator as well as wealth and power do.

And now the deception stood revealed, and Marcus Licinius Cato had no idea what to do next.

He had been too long on the road to be able to react effectively, too far from anywhere familiar to know where to look for resources. His former team disbanded, he had lost touch already with those who would have run to help him. Instead he was alone here, unprepared, unready, off balance. Had he had a day of warning, he thought, or even a few hours, he might have come up with something, some plan of attack, some strategy, no matter how wild and unrealistic it might have been.

The thought of leaving to find help and then coming back was ludicrous: he had no idea where Endor had come from, why he was here, or where the man might go to next. Once out of sight of the hamlet, he and his men might strike off in any direction and become untraceable once again. And Cato had already demonstrated to the decanus at the garrison stores that he was inactive, his legionary career legally finished. He cursed himself for blind carelessness there. Had he not gushed so loudly about being out after so long, he might now have gone to the officer in charge of the garrison and bluffed his way into winning some kind of assistance, but that cup of wine shared so talkatively with the friendly decanus had killed that chance. Knowing who and what he was, or who he had been, the authorities would almost certainly have taken his information and used it to go after Endor, but they would have locked Cato up rather than allow him to participate in an official military operation. Besides, the lessons he had learned in dealing with the authorities by the book were still too raw. Cato would never again trust anyone he did not know personally with information about Appius Endor, and that certainty was emphasized by his determination to be the man wielding the sword that took vengeance for the slaughtered Strabo family and all the multitude of others who had died to satisfy Endor's appetites.

Now, hearing a burst of laughter from the other table, Cato slumped even lower, flexing his shoulders and pressing his fingers into fists again, seething. He had to keep Endor within sight and within reach. But he could see no way to do that. Exposed as he now was, they would be rightfully suspicious if they saw him close to them again. Questions would be asked.

The only weapons he had were his short sword—the Hispanic gladius with its waisted twenty-three-inch blade—and its matching dagger. Both were formidable tools, designed solely for killing, and he had spent a lifetime mastering their use, but they were weapons designed to be used by men fighting in formations. They had severe limitations when used by a man alone. Endor and his four men were all heavily armed, and three of them presented a real threat in the kind of fight Cato would be facing: two carried long-handled war hammers of the kind used by the Germanic tribes along the Rhine, and a third was armed with an enormous twin-bladed axe of a kind Cato had never seen before. Any of those three could finish him from a distance before he ever came close enough to use his short sword. And then, of course, there was the Basilisk himself, who had allegedly killed more people with his own hands than any other single person. There was not the slightest doubt in Cato's mind that Endor, by himself, was at least as dangerous in a fight as all four of his men combined.

Almost audibly, the thought came to Cato that he would die there, in a rundown mansio in a nameless hamlet somewhere south of Lindum in the forests of Britannia. After an apparently successful career spent fighting military corruption, his life would be ended and all his work undone by the reappearance of Appius Endor, the single most notorious, treasonous criminal he had ever had to deal with. He had been seen to bring Endor down and had been lauded and rewarded for doing it, only to have the man spring back to life again and trap him here where no one knew him or would ever search for him. The Basilisk would win on all fronts now and might live to grow old and die naturally, his real identity a secret.

As that final irony registered in Cato's mind, Endor rose up from his seat and stood staring at him from across the room.

He recognizes me now. He knows who I am. The words rang in Cato's mind instantly and he accepted them without demur, but they were followed by another, more incongruous thought. *I never really realized how big he is.*

Even across the distance separating them, the Basilisk was massive, his shoulders immensely strong and broad, their width and the depth of his chest emphasized by the way his cloak was rucked back to hang down behind him. Cato saw his face clearly for a few moments but was not sure what he had seen in it, because Endor had moved sideways as he stood up, changing the angle of the light streaming through the window at his back, so that it brightened his outline but threw his face into shadow. The look on his face when he first stood up might have been an angry one, Cato thought, but it might equally have been puzzlement. Either way, he knew he was about to find out because Endor was now coming towards him, waving his own people down when two of them moved to rise.

Cato forced himself to sit still, shifting his right hand slowly and unobtrusively to the hilt of the sword at his waist, where he hooked his thumb comfortably behind it in a gesture of lifelong familiarity.

"Your friend appears to be late," Endor said when he arrived, standing above him.

"Who's to say what late means in a place like this and at this time of the year? He might have been caught in a storm." Cato pushed a chair towards him with one foot. "Sit down. Drink with me. The ale's remarkably good." He raised a hand and crooked a finger towards the serving girl, who had been watching from behind the counter, then spread two upraised fingers before turning back to face the other man.

"I saw you look at me before you came over. An odd look, I thought. Is there something you want from me?"

Endor picked up the heavy chair in one hand as though it were weightless and, in a silent, emotionless display of enormous strength and muscular control, spun it slowly, one-handed, in a complete revolution before replacing it precisely where it had been. "No," he said slowly, lowering himself into the chair. "I have something to offer you. If you are interested."

Cato did not react at all for several moments, but then he quirked an eyebrow. "Can't know if I will be or not until you tell me what it is."

He saw the tavern girl coming with their two fresh mugs and raised a warning finger to the man across from him, keeping an eye on the approaching girl. She arrived, set down their mugs, and left again without a word, and both men picked up and drank, paying close attention to the ale, its flavour and texture.

Cato set down his mug. "What would you offer me?"

"Work . . . to suit your capabilities. This ale *is* very good, considering the place is a pigsty."

A twitch of the mouth that might have been the start of a smile from Cato. "Which capabilities are you talking about?"

"All of them. Three months out of service, you say?" Endor drank again from his mug, then rested the butt of it against the arm folded across his chest. "They'll all still be sharp."

"You already have men working for you," Cato said. "Dragging their knuckles all around you. You want me to be one of those?"

Endor did smile then, a cold, humourless acknowledgment. "In your case, I was thinking more about your working *with* me. There's no limit to the pool of people willing to work *for* me. I throw coins at them and they do anything I want them to. But from time to time I need to be able to rely on people—associates—who can think . . . Think for themselves, and on my behalf."

"And why do you assume I could be one of those?"

"You commanded a cohort. You're a pilus prior, and I've never known one of those to be stupid or incompetent."

Cato inclined his head slightly, watching the man across from him through narrowed eyes, trying to read his mind through his expression, but Endor was at least as good at this as he was, and simply sat staring back at him, betraying nothing.

Finally Cato nodded. "So be it, then. Tell me who you are and what you do, and what kind of work you have at your disposal that needs the kind of man you describe." He paused, then added, "And tell me, too, while you're at it, what makes you think I might be interested in working for anyone, so soon after getting out of harness."

"Hmm." The grunt might have been one of amusement. "Last first," Endor said. "Same answer as last time. Because of who and what you were. You've been out three months. Probably have enough money to remove you from any need to work. But after three months of doing nothing useful, having nothing you really need to do and no objectives to achieve, I believe you might have had your fill of being bored, and so might find a challenge appealing."

Cato was feeling better with every moment that passed. Fate had provided its own solution, and all he had to do now was agree to go along with Endor's proposal and then wait for a suitable time to kill the man. He began to nod in agreement, then realized he had no need. The Basilisk, convinced that his own belief was all-powerful and that Cato's agreement could therefore be taken for granted, had already moved on without waiting for a response.

"My name is Janus Drusus Carbo. I'm a procurator." He pronounced the word in the formal, Latin manner, and Cato jumped on it, hard.

"A procurator?" His tone was skeptical. "Are you telling me you're an imperial official?"

Not even Endor had the gall to attempt that kind of effrontery. He shook his head. "No," he said. "A private procurator. For" —he hesitated— "powerful interests."

"You mean you procure things for private citizens who pay you well."

It was not a question, and Endor merely nodded. "Something of that nature."

Cato sniffed and kept his tone casual, mildly and naturally curious, sensing it might be dangerous to show no reaction at all to such information. "Am I likely to know any of these people?"

"I doubt it, but you might," came the answer. "How long have you been in the north, in Eboracum?"

Cato shrugged. "Most of my life, since I was sixteen. Twenty-five years." That was a lie. He had been granted five years' remission, which meant he was thirty-five not forty-one, but the Basilisk had no way of knowing that.

"And have you travelled much in that time, to the south?"

"Hardly at all."

"Then it's unlikely you'd know of these people or even their names. Most of them, my best clients, live in the south, by Glevum and Aquae Sulis, in the villa country there."

"I've heard of it," Cato said, knowing the area was home to the wealthiest Romans in Britannia. "Never been there, though." He took a drink of his ale. "So what do you procure for these people, then? And what would you expect me to do for them?"

"For them, nothing. You would work for me. For me and with me, for a monthly stipend augmented with whatever additional money you might need for costs incurred in doing your work."

"I see. And what kinds of things would I be required to do, working for and with you?"

"Whatever I need you to do in order to meet the needs of my clients."

"And that would be what?" Cato shrugged, seeing the other man's face harden at his persistence, and held up his hands placatingly. "Look, Master Carbo, I don't want to offend you, but I really need to know what this involves. You and I have never met before, and yet here you are offering to employ me, with no knowledge of who I am and absolutely no way of knowing whether or not I have lied to you. That makes me wonder what I might be agreeing to, if I accept. I am not saying no, but until I understand your offer, I'm not rushing to accept it. I'm not opposed to being a mercenary, if that's what you need, but you've said nothing about soldiering, and for all I know you might be hiring me to do things I have no wish to do. You might want me to be a thief, or to kill or torture people, or to supervise other people doing that kind of thing. If that's even close to being true, I'm not interested. I've lived this long without debasing myself, and I'm quite happy to continue the same way."

Endor picked up his mug and drank slowly, gazing into the middle distance with a thoughtful scowl on his face. He then replaced the vessel on the tabletop and looked Cato straight in the eye.

"I won't ask you to do anything like that," he said, and though Cato knew him to be a consummate liar, he found himself believing the man. "What I said to you at first is absolutely true," Endor continued. "I need a trustworthy associate. Someone I can rely on completely to do what I tell him to do and who will know when and how to do anything unforeseen that needs to be done when I am not around. I had such a man, for years, but he died last year and I have found no one yet who could replace him."

"What was his name?" Cato knew exactly who the other meant. Melchior Ritka had been Endor's most faithful follower for as long as Cato's people had been keeping records on the Basilisk, and his death from a lingering illness had been cause for celebration. Now he was curious to know how truthful Endor might be.

A tiny frown appeared between the other man's brows. "His name was Ritka, but why would you ask me that?"

Cato shrugged, flapped a hand. "I've no idea," he said. "It simply came into my head and I asked. How did he die?"

Endor grunted, and for a moment his attention went elsewhere, losing its sharpness as he looked absently into space. "Some kind of sickness took him," he said eventually. "The medics said he was eaten from inside. They had a name for what it was but I can't remember it. He simply grew sick and died, that's all I know. One day he was as he had always been, and then he started to lose weight and he was dead within months, shrunken to skin and bones."

Cato said nothing, simply twisting his mouth into a grimace of rueful understanding, but he was surprised by the evident sincerity of Endor's regret over the loss of his man. Endor and Ritka had been together for many years, but they had been very much master and man, legate and legionary.

"I never saw anything like it," Endor said, shaking his head with that empty, unfocused look still in his eyes. "And like you, with years in the legions, I've seen a lot of men die. But this was—different—starting so slowly and then moving so quickly once it began."

Cato nodded. "I know," he said. "My old man died like that. It's frightening to watch, seeing a person you know well simply fading away from day to day. We talk a lot about death in battle, but that's another thing altogether. That's a quick death even if it's sometimes messy and painful. But even a septic belly wound will take you out in days. To die in bed of sickness, though, and in agony, over months and years, that is truly terrifying . . . You say your man died a year ago?"

Endor nodded.

"Were you there? When he died?"

The other man cleared his throat. "No. But I'd seen him three days before. Barely knew him."

"Did he know you?"

"Don't know. He wasn't conscious at the time."

"And you had no one who could take over what he did?"

"I haven't found anyone yet, no."

Cato had been long enough with the legions to have grown aware of all the proclivities, sexual and otherwise, of the gamut of men he dealt with every day, and had long since become adept at picking up indications of homosexual behaviour and activities. He felt none of those here.

"Why do you think I could replace him?"

"You strike me as being . . . capable." Endor sniffed, and used the back of his hand to wipe a drop of moisture, probably ale, from the tip of his nose. "Can you read and write?"

"Of course."

"And count? Keep records?"

"Yes, but I loathe that kind of thing. It's why the gods made scribes. One of the first things I learned after being promoted into having a tent of my own was how to use functionaries like that—records keepers and accountants."

The other man nodded. "Good. That's the kind of thing I need more than anything else—someone to keep things in order. Once you have that set up, I'll expect you to travel, too. Do you own a horse?"

"No."

"You'll need one. In fact you'll need two."

"I don't like horses. I'd rather walk."

Endor quirked an eyebrow. "Really? Can you ride, or is that why you don't like horses?"

"I can ride, but I think horses are a pain in the arse, in all ways. They're expensive, inconvenient, and stupid. They need constant care in too many ways to count and they cause more trouble than they're worth."

"None of which matters in the slightest and there are grooms to take care of them, just as there are scribes to take care of numbers. I'll need you to travel fast and far at times, and that means riding. So buy yourself a pair of good mounts. I'll give you the money."

Now it was Cato who raised his eyebrows. "So we've begun already? I haven't agreed yet."

"No, we haven't begun. But we might have made a beginning."

"And you expect total obedience."

Again came that expression that might almost have been a smile. "No more than you would owe to any employer. I do expect total, complete loyalty, though, and I won't accept anything less." He paused, then said, "When I leave here I'll be returning to my home base in Camulodunum. Do you know it?"

"I've heard of it. Colonia Victricensis."

"That's the place. It's where I live most of the time, and it's where you'll live from now on if you accept the position. I'll pay you double what you made as a pilus prior, and I'll reimburse you for anything you have to spend in looking after my affairs. Is that acceptable?"

"Aye, it is. So . . . what now, then?" he asked his new employer. "What do you want me to do first?"

In response Endor sat up straighter and loosened the drawstring of the soft, roomy-looking leather pouch that hung from his waist. He reached right inside it and brought out three much smaller bags, made of either chamois or kidskin. He hefted all three and replaced one in his pouch, then passed the other two across the table. As he did so, the door from the street swung open and a newcomer stepped into the room, where he was greeted loudly by Endor's other men. The leader twisted in his seat to see what was happening, then turned back to Cato.

"That's my man," he said. "The one I've been waiting for. As soon as I'm done with him, I'm leaving for wherever he indicates I should be looking next. I don't know where that will be, or when I'll get back to Camulodunum, but when I do, I'll expect to find you there waiting for me. I have a house there, close outside the main city gate on the southern approach, so you'll have no trouble finding me. Just ask for the Carbo house, and when you find it, speak to the major-domo. His name is Albus. Tell him who you are and that I said he is to show you to Ritka's quarters. Once you're there, wait for me. I shouldn't be far behind you."

Cato nodded, wishing there was some way to ask the man where he might be going next or what he was looking for, then picked up the two surprisingly heavy little leather bags and weighed them in his palm. "And what is this for?"

"Expenses. As I said, you'll need two good mounts, and sooner rather than later, for you won't be walking much, working for me. You'll need decent reins and harness as well, but I doubt you'll find anything suitable here, so you'll probably have to go to Lindum to buy them . . . Back the way you came, straight up the road out there."

Cato nodded. "I know where it is."

"There's a good livestock market there. I bought some horses there myself about eight years ago, and it won't have changed much since then. You'll find everything you need there—saddle bags, bridles, blankets, tents, ropes, and some decent weaponry. That sword you have is lethal, but you'll need something with a greater reach against war hammers and long-shafted axes." He nodded at the two small bags. "You should have more than you need there, by long odds. Don't stint on gear. Buy the best you can find, of everything. I'll see you in Camulodunum." He stood up. "And don't worry about having nothing to do if you have to wait for me after you arrive. By the time I get back I'll have enough work to keep you busy for at least a year."

He stretched his arm out across the table and Cato shook with him, forearm to forearm, mildly pleased and completely astonished that he should be able to do so without showing any sign of the seething hatred of the man that bubbled in his breast.

THIRTY-FIVE

A snuffling grunt and a rattle of harness in the stalls behind him announced that the horses were awake, but Marcus Cato paid no attention. He was staring across at the villa on the other side of the road, watching for signs of life. He had arrived in Camulodunum the previous evening, just in time to find the Carbo estate before it grew dark. He had been looking for a house, but the place turned out to be much more than that, an isolated villa, set back from the road outside the town walls. He could see, through the still-open gates in the gathering dusk, that the main residence was a substantial villa built in the classical Roman style. The enclosure surrounding it, bounded by a high stone wall, contained three large outbuildings, and everything appeared to be built of what he presumed to be local sandstone, since equally solid buildings on nearby properties were built from the same material. He had not been able to see much more without risking exposing himself, and he had no wish to announce his presence before he was ready to, so he had remained hidden in the gathering murk until he was sure he could move away without being seen. It had been threatening to rain heavily by the time he found the building he was now in—an empty but well-stocked and serviceable stable in a field facing the main gate to the Carbo place—and he had moved in quickly, avoiding being drenched when the heavens opened soon after.

He had wakened in darkness a short time earlier when a sudden silence warned him that the rain had stopped. He had lain awake for a time, listening to the dripping of water and the rustling of mice in the thatching of the roof above his head, before his swollen bladder drove him outside to seek relief, and when he returned he had taken up the post he now occupied, leaning against the wall by an open window, watching the gates of the Carbo place emerge from the receding darkness. He broke his fast there, still watching, with a handful of road rations from the pouch at his waist, a chopped-up mixture of hazelnuts, walnuts, roasted grains, and dried fruits, mainly apples, figs, grapes, and apricots.

He saw the first signs of activity at daybreak, and moved back slightly, away from the window's brightness, as the gate swung open and three men emerged. They were on foot, muffled in foul-weather cloaks despite the increasing stretches of blue in the sky. Cato recognized them instantly as mercenaries: former soldiers, with that unmistakable air of competence and self-confident arrogance that set them apart from ordinary men. They were neither armoured nor obviously armed, but they reeked of aggression nonetheless. They closed the gate behind them and walked away in the direction of the city gates, half a mile along the road.

The man he was looking for was Endor's steward, Albus, who might or might not believe he was employed by a man named Janus Drusus Carbo. It was well past mid-morning by the time he emerged, and Cato knew it was him by the large empty basket he carried in the crook of his arm and the long black robe that covered him from neck to ankles. Endor was due to return at any time now, and so Albus, like any conscientious household steward, would be going to the weekly market to lay in a fresh supply of food for his master and his friends. He watched until the steward, too, vanished in the direction of the town, then he checked to make sure his horses had water and hay, made his way slowly across the road, and let himself in through the gates of the Carbo villa, where he paused, humming tunelessly to himself and looking around him.

The compound appeared to be deserted, as he'd hoped; the buildings even *felt* empty, he thought, and so he moved directly to the main house, crossing the forecourt quickly and stepping noiselessly into the central atrium and through to the open reception area beyond that. From there he made his way through the house methodically. It was a typical villa, with the formal reception rooms located centrally on the ground floor and connected by a corridor at the back, and a pair of matching wings extending forward towards the gates fronting the property. The household baths and sleeping quarters were located in the wing to his left as he looked back towards the main entrance, the family's on the upper floor, and the servants' quarters directly underneath. The wing on his right held the workaday buildings of the house's staff, beginning with the stables and livestock pens, farthest from the house, and progressing from there to dairies, dry-storage buildings, workshops of varying kinds and sizes, then narrow, white-washed cold-storage rooms, laundry rooms, ovens and roasting pit facilities, and kitchens coming last, closest to the dining rooms. He found nothing unusual anywhere.

The first of the outhouses, though, around the western corner of the house, contained an anomaly, though not a mysterious one. The building was not large, a single space approximately eight paces deep by twelve wide, and had the appearance of a jailhouse. A wall facing him as he stepped inside was pierced by two solid, heavy-looking doors, each of which stood open, showing the darkened interiors of windowless cells beyond. Three cots were ranged along the wall to his right, behind the entrance door, and he glanced idly at them, wondering briefly why the three mercenaries should all be sleeping side by side in one corner when there was nothing else in the room but a heavy wooden table with a stained, deeply scarred top. The fireplace was on the same side of the room as the cots, though, and that in itself might have been sufficient reason. The nights were, occasionally, still cold. He wasted no time speculating, though, and took no more than a few moments to glance into each of the remaining outhouses. He retraced his steps quickly, pulled the main gate closed behind him, collected his riding horse from the stable across the road, and rode into the city.

An hour later, as he was sitting at a curbside stall, eating a bowl of chicken stew flavoured with powerful, tangy garum and mopping up the delicious juice with fresh-baked bread, he saw Endor's tall, black-clad steward walk by, tilted now against the weight of his laden basket, and he watched him moving towards the outer gates until he was lost to view. He finished his meal, returned the earthen bowl to the stall-holder with a nod of thanks and appreciation, and asked where he might find a decent mug of ale. Then he untied his horse from the post by which he had been sitting and made his way to the sign of the Bull, where the ale turned out to be as fine as promised.

Two hours after that, in the middle of the afternoon, he returned to the Villa Carbo and introduced himself, using his alias of Gaius Blixus, to the man called Albus, explaining his encounter at the mansio with Master Carbo and the request that he present himself at the villa to assume his responsibilities. Albus agreed, albeit with a hint of wary skepticism, to provide a tour of the premises.

The steward was aloof and disdainful, but his disdain seemed born of naivety rather than cynicism. His sole function, he said, was to exercise stewardship over his master's home: to maintain the house and hire staff as was necessary from time to time in order to accommodate his employer's needs whenever he came to town, which was not often—perhaps three times in any given year, and seldom for more than ten days at a stretch.

Passing the outhouse that he knew held the three beds, Cato asked what its purpose was. Magister Carbo, Albus told him, was a prominent merchant, and as such he frequently had need of certain types of retainers—bodyguards and such—to protect him in his dealings with certain of his more unsavoury customers. Whenever he did have a need for such men, he brought them in and lodged them in the outhouse.

There they remained until their work was done, and Albus had no contact with them, or they with him.

Not even to feed them? Cato had asked, and had earned himself a scandalized glare of disapproval. They fed themselves, the steward inferred, at hostelries in the town whenever they were hungry. Such things were none of his business, he claimed, and Magister Carbo had made that very clear when Albus had come to work for him, eight years before. He was expressly forbidden to have anything to do with any of the outhouses—he called them warehouses—or with any of the activities being conducted therein, or to communicate in any way with the occasional hirelings brought in by Carbo or his agents. They, in turn, were forbidden access to the main house.

Cato concluded that the major-domo had to be either blind or stupid not to have guessed, after eight years, that his master might be less than the upright merchant he believed him to be. And yet, in fairness, Appius Endor had kept his identity and the scope of his activities concealed from Rome's finest investigative resources for more than a decade. Small wonder, then, that he could deceive an aging housekeeper obsessed with pleasing his master and retaining a highly lucrative position in which he had to please no one but himself for much of the year.

Albus showed him to the dead Ritka's quarters and left him there, and Cato unpacked his kit with the ease of long practice and stowed his few belongings on the shelves above the bed before stuffing the bag itself into the footlocker at the bed's end. Soon afterwards he heard a noise from the courtyard. He moved quickly to the passageway that ran in front of the sleeping rooms on the upper floor, where he stopped and leaned backwards, careful not to be seen. The three mercenaries were back, two of them pulling a long, narrow handcart as they crossed the cobbled forecourt towards their quarters. Taking care not to reveal himself, he crouched and moved cautiously along the passageway to keep them in sight between the railings of the walkway. They stopped in front of the entrance to the outhouse, peered about them suspiciously, then one of them raised the pole at the front of the cart and held it tilted while his two companions pulled the cloth-shrouded body of a man out of it. One glance at the shrouded form had convinced Cato that the man in the cart was dead, but as he was being pulled out of the cart bed the heavily muffled man convulsed and kicked out several times before he was hammered into unconsciousness by one of his captors. The man who had hit him then stooped and took the body over his shoulder, straightened up with a heave, and carried the inert shape inside. His two companions followed him in and closed the door.

Returning to the main house, Cato found Albus in a tiny cubiculum that he assumed to be the steward's official workplace. It was set off to one side of the formal dining room, reinforcing his impression that it was the steward's personal domain.

"Albus," he said, leaning into the tiny room and ignoring the man's petulant frown. "Magister Carbo told me to wait for him here, but he couldn't say when he would arrive. We were near Lindum at the time and he was due to meet with another merchant there. I have a reason for being curious. My brother lives fifteen miles south of here, and I have not seen him in years. I would like to visit him if I have time. The magister himself told me I'll have little free time once he returns—not for another year at least, he said—so I would like to take a day or two now, if that is possible. So would you know when he is due to arrive?"

"Yes, yes, yes," Albus said, contriving somehow to look annoyed and pleased to be asked at the same time. He turned away, nodding and muttering to himself, then straightened again, brandishing a flattened scroll with something of a flourish. "I had been expecting him later today or by tomorrow at the latest. When I returned from the market this afternoon, though, I found a mounted courier waiting for me, bearing this." He wiggled the missive again. "The magister has had to change his plans and was to leave Londinium on Mercury's Day, the day the courier left to come here. He would then travel west to Pontes, where he would remain for one more day—which means he would have left there yesterday—and would return here directly from there, passing through Londinium again. So I expect him to return sometime tomorrow, or failing that, the day after."

Cato nodded, solemn-faced. "My thanks, Albus. That means, I'm afraid, that my visit to my brother will have to wait. I have no wish to miss the magister's homecoming. Not after having come such a long way to meet him." He began to turn away, then hesitated. "I'm going to have to eat tonight, and I presume you must know the local hostelries. Is any one better than the others?"

The steward stared at him speculatively for a few moments, then said slowly, "I have to eat, too, Magister Blixus, but I cook for myself, here. You are welcome to join me."

Cato smiled, hiding his surprise. "I would be glad to do that, Magister Albus, but not tonight. Not without advance warning. That would be too much of an imposition on your goodwill. Besides, I have to visit the garrison commander's office in the town, to deliver something I promised to send to an old friend in my former cohort. If I might, though, I'll be glad to join you tomorrow night."

Albus grimaced a little and dipped his head to one side. "The master might be back tomorrow night, in which case, who knows what might happen?"

"Of course, but I'll gladly take whatever comes."

The steward nodded. "So be it, then. We'll take what comes."

That night after dark, Cato sat alone again in the passageway outside his room, watching the dim outline of the building housing the three mercenaries and their prisoner. When he saw the door swing open, spilling light into the forecourt, he followed the two men who emerged. They strolled towards the gates and then took the road into town. He stayed well behind them, enveloped in the blackness of the night, and when they entered the Bull tavern, he gave them time to settle themselves before he followed them inside. He seated himself at one of the three common tables and ordered a jug of ale and a hot pasty from the woman who came to serve him.

He had no way of knowing whether the place was unusually busy or not, but it was half-full, with bodies coming and going constantly, and no one paid him any attention as he sat quietly and enjoyed his meal. He sat facing the rear wall, because he remembered from his first visit that the common privy, a foul hole in the ground protected by a rotted, waist-high enclosure, lay at the back of the premises, beyond the rear door that had no other purpose than to offer access to the midden. He finished his pasty appreciatively, carefully sweeping the leftover flakes of pastry into his palm before scooping them up with his tongue, then sat minding his own business, nursing his ale and sucking at a stray piece of meat lodged between two teeth until the two mercenaries stood up and prepared to leave, neither of them apparently having a need to use the privy himself.

They did, though, as soon as they were outside and clear of the town walls, and Cato stood nearby, in the shadows, and listened to them piss. They returned to the villa after that, and he waited again, this time at the gateway, fingering the weapon that hung over his shoulder beneath his jerkin, until the third man, relieved of his guard duty, came out to go and find his own meal.

Cato's weapon was a supple, well-oiled, and slightly flattened tube of thick black leather, almost the length of his arm and divided into five sections that were filled with a mixture of sand and lead pellets. It was flexible, versatile, and lethal, and it hit the third man behind the ear as he walked past, dropping him instantly to his knees, before he folded at the waist and toppled sideways, unconscious. Cato dragged him out of sight, then trussed him expertly with arm's-length pieces of thin, strong rope that he had brought with him, folded over the belt at his waist. He gagged him with a small wad of cloth, then tied the wad in place with another piece of rope, and left the mercenary lying there against the wall while he went swiftly in the other direction, crossing the road to the stable. He led the packhorse back to where the bound man lay, then manhandled the inert figure with sheer brute strength until he had it draped across the animal's back. After pausing only briefly to let his breathing return to normal, he led the beast back to its stable, where he unloaded the still-unconscious mercenary, checked his bonds, added a few more for safety's sake, and made sure the gag was still securely in place. He then covered his prisoner with a horse blanket, covered that with hay, and made his way back to the villa, where he slept soundly for the next six hours.

THIRTY-SIX

Cato was astir again long before dawn, knowing that the two remaining mercenaries might not have slept well once they realized their companion had not returned, and so he was watching again when one of them let himself out of the building soon after dawn and set out on the road, presumably to look for the delinquent. He waited until he was sure the fellow had really gone, then made his way to their outbuilding. Now, at the door to the stone jailhouse, he paused with his hand hovering over the hilt of the sword on his right side, then changed his mind and pulled out the lead-weighted weapon he had used the night before. He held it dangling by his right leg, then pushed the door open smoothly with his left hand and stepped quickly inside.

The man directly inside, at the table, was asleep, cradling a shorthandled blacksmith's hammer. Whatever his purpose might have been for sitting there nursing the tool, though, the fellow had forgotten it, nodding off in his chair. He startled awake as he heard the door opening, but Cato gave him no opportunity to gather his wits. He lunged forward, swinging his heavy bludgeon in a round-armed swipe that sent the guard and his chair sprawling into the corner.

Even as he was bending into the swing, though, Cato sensed another, unexpected presence behind him and threw himself forward instinctively, following the man he had hit, and he heard the hissing strike of a hard-swung sword close to his head. Cursing himself for carelessness, he hurled himself down and sideways, dropping the leather flail and using his hand to push himself off the heavy tabletop in a tumbling roll towards the other corner, spinning as he moved and whipping the shorter of his two swords from its sheath as his knee struck the floor.

The attacker was coming at him again, his gladius held low and angled slightly upwards for the classic disembowelling short-sword slash. But Cato was already below his strike line, on the floor, and by the time the man had changed his grip Cato was rising again, the corner at his back and a sword in each hand. He heard the man he had hit whimpering in the other corner, so he knew there was no danger yet from that direction, and he gave all his attention to the fellow facing him. The two faced off briefly, crouching warily, each taking the measure of the other, aware of the lack of space surrounding them. Then they both lunged again and it was over. Cato caught the other man's incoming blade on the shorter sword in his left hand, hammering it aside with a vicious backhanded chop, and killed him at the same instant with the longer blade, thrusting the razor-sharp edge of the Hispanic steel through his ribs with the full, lunging strength of his blow. He stood there for a moment, watching the life drain from the wide, surprised eyes mere inches from his own, then pushed the body backwards, jerking his blade free as the dead weight fell away from him.

He held a deep breath for a count of five, then exhaled slowly and let the tension flow out of him before he looked at the fallen man in the corner, who was curled in a ball, moaning quietly and cradling his injured shoulder. Cato crossed to him in two steps and seized him by the wrist, straightening the arm and drawing a howl of protest. He squeezed the arm, testing it, then wiped his bloodied blade on the fellow's sleeve and released him, watching as he clutched the injured limb again in his free hand without looking up.

Cato sheathed his two swords and retrieved his leather club from the floor, then took away the downed fourth man's sword and threw it against the far wall. He stepped back to the injured fellow, grasped the long hair of his single, greasy forelock, and jerked his head up until he was looking into his eyes.

"Be quiet," he growled, and pulled him to his feet. The man moved unwillingly, but once he was up Cato spun him around and hauled his injured arm up behind his back, making him howl like a kicked dog, and used the leverage to propel him through the open cell door. The room was pitch-dark, but enough light spilled through the open door to show that it was bare except for a single wooden chair, and so Cato simply smacked the fellow at the base of the skull with the lead-filled sap and let him fall to the floor.

He replaced the overturned chair and then picked up the smith's hammer from the floor and laid it almost absent-mindedly on the tabletop before he turned to look at the body on the floor, aware that his miscalculation there had been inexcusable. He had accepted, without verifying, that there were only three mercenaries in the villa, just as he had accepted, without verifying, that the corpse he had seen a year earlier had been Endor's. He had been wrong on both occasions and had had no one but himself to blame. The unsuspected presence of the fourth man had come close to costing him his life, and that he had survived was a matter of nothing more than luck. When he was younger it would have been inconceivable for him to commit such a lax, fundamental error, and now he had done it twice.

The body had fallen beside a pair of buckets that stood against the wall close to the pleasantly burning fire in the grate. Attracted by the odour they gave off, he looked more closely at them and saw that one of them held four rag torches soaking in liquid pitch that was kept slightly warm by its proximity to the fire. The other was nearly full of drinking water, and he scooped up the attached ladle, filled it, and drank deeply, voraciously thirsty the moment he had seen it.

He dropped the ladle back into the pail, then squatted down, unfastened the sword belt around the dead man's waist, and pulled it free. He took hold of the body by the shoulders, straightened up with a grunt and a heave of his thighs, and dragged it into the cell with the other man, where he dropped it against the wall behind the door. Then he went back out and secured the door with a thick plank that slotted into brackets on either side of the frame.

He looked at the blood on the floor where the dead man had fallen and was surprised to see how little there was. But then, he thought, the fellow had died quickly—close to instantly—and dead men, unlike dying men, don't bleed much. The small puddle that remained was already sinking into the earth floor, and he knew that by the following morning it would be black, virtually invisible in the darkness of the floor itself. He didn't really care about it anyway, for he doubted that many people would be visiting the Villa Carbo in the days to come. He then picked up the dead man's sword from where he had thrown it by the door, sheathed it in the belt he had taken from the body, then threw it on one of the cots.

He looked around one last time, preparing to leave, then sighed, almost groaned, when he heard a sound from the other cell, the one holding the prisoner he had seen being brought in the day before. He had known the man was there when he came in, of course. He had simply not wanted to become involved with him or his problems, considering that he had more than enough of his own to deal with. Now, though, Cato cursed under his breath, then removed the locking bar and pulled the cell door open.

It was pitch-dark in there, so at first he could see nothing, but then he began to discern the outline of a man in a chair. Remembering the bucket in the room behind him, he went out and returned moments later with a blazing torch, to stand in front of a fair-haired man who had been tied into the chair that held him. It was a large chair, with solid arms and legs of dense-grained, heavy wood that looked like oak, and it was discoloured with age and thickly layered stains of what Cato took to be blood. The prisoner, Cato could see, was disoriented, blinking and grimacing against the brightness of the flickering torchlight. Cato took in the dried blood and livid swelling around his mouth, nose, and eyes, and thought he might have merely undergone a preliminary session—a loosening-up in preparation for the serious business of interrogation once Endor arrived.

"I'm going to cut you loose," he said. "But you might not be able to walk when I free you, so here's what we're going to do. I'll help you to stand up, and then I'll carry you into the other room. There's a cot in there, and a fire. Believe me, it's a lot more welcoming in there than here." He looked around until he saw a bracket on the wall, and dropped the flaming torch into it. Then he drew the shorter of his two swords and crouched quickly to cut the ropes binding the prisoner's limbs and torso to the chair.

"There," he said, straightening up and sheathing his blade. "Now stand up and bend forward over my shoulder."

The prisoner did as he was told, and Cato carried him into the other room and lowered him to one of the cots with barely more than a grunt of effort. By the time he laid him down on the thin mattress, though, the prisoner was beginning to twitch and moan, and Cato nodded as he stood up.

"Aye," he said, "those ropes were tight. That's going to hurt for a while, until your blood starts flowing normally again. Nothing I can do about that, so you're going to have to bite down and bear it." He paused, then added, "I don't know who you are and I don't care, but you were probably taken off the street in broad daylight, and I'm willing to wager there are people out there looking for you, worried about what's happened to you. Is that true?"

"Yes." The voice was weak, the word a mere whisper.

"Then stay here and let them worry. They'll be all the more relieved when you turn up alive and well. And you will, as long as you don't try to leave here alone. I have a task to finish here, and it involves putting an end to the man who had you snatched up. When I'm done with him, he'll be no further danger to anyone and you'll be free to go home. Now, did you see any of the people who took you?"

"No."

"Do you know why they took you?"

"No."

"Hmm. Those are bad answers, friend. Can you think of a reason why anyone would even want to—? What? What's the matter?"

The prisoner had gone rigid, peering directly up at him in sudden alarm, and Cato looked behind him, to see what had caused the reaction, but there was nothing there except the bright beam of light slanting down from the high window and dazzling him as he looked straight into it.

"Damn it," he said, ducking his head and looking back at the man in the cot, blinking against the sudden blindness that had hit him. "What's the matter?"

The prisoner pushed himself up onto one elbow, squinting with concentration as he peered at Cato's face. "I know you," he said, wonderingly. "I've met you before."

"Nah, you're wrong," Cato said. "I've never seen you before and I'm good with faces."

"No, we've met. We shared a camp together once, about a year ago. My friend and I were fishing, on the way here, to Camulodunum, and you were on your way from Londinium."

Cato frowned. "I remember that, but I don't remember you. I stayed that night with two Eirish smiths—"

"Called Mcuil," the prisoner said. "Fingael and Shamus Mcuil. I invited you to join us, called you out of the woods, remember?"

"I remember that, too. But that wasn't you." Cato's frown had deepened. "That man had dark hair, almost black, and dark skin. I remember him. Your hair's yellow."

"Almost yellow. And yours is red. The stubble on your chin is red. Your name is Rufus." The prisoner sat up sharply, as though stung. "Limping Vulcan! You're *Rufus* . . . Marcus Cato! I remember now. No wonder the name sounded familiar when I heard it."

Cato was thunderstruck, but the man on the cot gave him no time to absorb what he had said. He pushed himself up onto his knees, peering closely at the unshaven stubble on the other's face, which glowed ruddy gold in the light from the window overhead. "I'm right, am I not? You're Marcus Cato, and your friends all call you Rufus? That's *you!*"

Cato's mouth snapped shut and he spun away, frowning. He could not afford to have anyone recognize him or know who he really was. He took two steps away from the man and then swung back to face him again, raising a pointing, peremptory finger only to discover that he didn't know what to say. He simply stood there, his hand raised, his finger pointing and his mouth clamped shut. And then he dropped his arm to his side, suddenly acknowledging that this man was not an enemy.

"Who told you my name?"

The prisoner stood up off the bed and stood swaying slightly, testing his balance. "They all did." The answer, as obscure as everything else he had said, made Cato frown again, but the prisoner kept talking. "It was mostly Ajax, though. He talked about you more than any of the others."

"Ajax . . . *Ignatius* Ajax?"

"Yes." The stranger nodded. "His friends call him Natius, though."

"What friends?"

"The others. Thomas, Dido, Stratus, Leon, and Demetrius."

Cato nodded, accepting the revelations numbly. "Who is Demetrius?"

"Demetrius Hanno. He's the senior smith at the armouries. Works for Natius. He's my trainer."

"The armouries. You mean here, in Camulodunum? The others are *here*? Leon and Stratus and the Twins are in Camulodunum?"

"Yes." The prisoner blinked. "Did you not know that?"

"No, I didn't. Wait . . . I need a moment to think." Cato lowered his head and placed the heels of his hands on his temples, staring down at the floor as the prisoner watched in silence. Then he looked up again and shook his head. "You know," he said, "not a single word that you have said since I cut you loose has been anything like what I expected to hear. Plainly, though, we have the same friends, and that changes everything. How do we find them quickly, Natius and the others?"

"They're at the fort, right here in town."

"We're not in the town. We're outside the walls, in a private house. They brought you here after they snatched you. What's your name?"

"Varrus. Quintus Varrus. You knew my grandsire, I think. Titanius Varrus. We always called him Tertius."

Cato's eyes widened, and the expression on his face sharpened. "Tertius was your *grand*father? Then you must be Marcus's son. I thought you dead."

"You and everyone else, but yes, I'm Quintus, the one with the famous Varrus knee, and the last one left alive. Well, except for my uncle Marius."

Cato looked as though he was about to ask a question, but at that moment they heard a noise in the yard, and he whipped up a hand, demanding silence, then swung towards the door, listening intently. The noise was not repeated, but the sound of it had underlined the urgency of their situation.

"Listen," he said. "We need to reach the others, right now, but we need to be very careful, too. There were four men in the gang that took you. I've dealt with three of them, but the fourth one is still out there somewhere and he might come back at any moment. There's another man coming in, too, the ringleader of an entire group, and he's the one I'm waiting for. Trouble is, I don't know when he's coming—only that he's due sometime today. And he might not be alone—my guess is he'll have had an escort on the road."

Varrus nodded. "What do you want me to do, then?"

"I want you to get out of here and fetch the others, as fast as you can move. I'll stay here and wait. But don't waste any time. I'd like to be alive and well when you come back. Just tell Ajax I'm at the Villa Carbo, near the south gate, and I need help, then bring them back, quick as you can. And make sure they come fully armed."

"Done." Varrus picked up the sword belt Cato had thrown onto the cot. He loosened the blade in its sheath, then strapped the belt around his waist. "Why don't we both go?"

"Because I have to stay here, in case the man I'm waiting for arrives."

"And what if he does, and he has company with him? Your friends will be glad to see you, though not if you're dead when we arrive. Who is he, this mysterious man?"

"There's nothing mysterious about him. He's a condemned felon and a murderer and I'm here to kill him. You'll thank me for that, eventually, because he's the man who killed your family. There's no more mystery than—" He broke off suddenly, as the unmistakable clatter of shod hooves rang out in the yard. "Shit," he said. "He's here, and he's not alone. We'll have to take what the gods serve us on this one. Quick, back into the cell and sit on the chair. Take off that belt, but keep the blade in your hand, behind your back. Quick now." He led the way, and pulled the burning torch from the bracket where he had left it. "Sit," he said. "Hands behind you, head down, and straight-backed, as though you're tightly bound. Hold on to the sword and be ready to move quickly. Have you ever fought before?"

"Yes."

"Ever killed anyone?"

"Yes."

"Good, then be ready. Here goes."

He went out, carrying the torch.

THIRTY-SEVEN

Varrus half listened to Cato's footsteps receding in the direction of the outer door, but he was still hearing the words he had said moments earlier: *He's the man who killed your family . . . The man who killed your family.* He couldn't believe it. Cato must be wrong. The massacre had taken place in Dalmatia, so it seemed completely unlikely to Quintus that the murderer, whoever he had been, might now be in Britain. But then he remembered his own situation and the extent of his own travels since the murders, and saw the short-sightedness of his own expectations. He was still thinking about that when he heard the sound of the outside door being opened, followed by Cato's raised voice.

"Ah! I thought I heard horses. Who are you people?"

"Never mind who we are. Who are you, and what're you doing here?" The voice was rough and coarse, sounding as though it belonged to a big man.

"Gaius Blixus. My new employer, Janus Carbo, told me to come here and wait for him. So I'm here, waiting. What's going on?"

Varrus was listening intently now, trying to determine how many men were out there in the other room, but it was impossible, and on an impulse he rose to his feet and moved back cautiously, farther into the darkness at the back of the cell, to where he could see past the edge of the slightly open door into the other room with little risk of being seen himself. He could see three men there, one in the doorway and two others moving into the room, on either side of the door, all three

479

glowering at Cato, who stood facing them with his back to the cell and the sputtering torch still flaring in his hand.

The spokesman flicked a hand towards the man on his left, pointing backwards with his thumb. "Fetch the boss," he said. "Bring 'im here."

The fellow turned and left, slamming the door behind him, and the other two moved farther apart, one on each side of Cato, and neither bothered to hide his suspicion.

"What?" Cato asked. "What are you doing? Wha—?"

Both men lunged simultaneously, but Cato was more than ready for them and skipped nimbly back, swinging his flaming torch round-armed and hitting the leading man square in the mouth. Only then did Varrus see that the torch he had swung was not the one he had taken from the bracket in the cell. This was a new firebrand, still dripping with fresh pitch, and it soaked into the man's beard immediately, igniting it with a whooshing sound, turning his head instantly into a ball of fire and sending him away screaming, clawing at the roaring flames that suddenly engulfed his head. His companion hesitated in stunned surprise just long enough to allow Cato to whip out some kind of weighted leather club from beneath his tunic and swing it hard, crushing the fellow's skull before he knew what was happening. Cato had leaned fully into the swing, pivoting on one foot, and now he continued to spin, completing a full circle, his arms fully extended, to strike the burning man at the base of his skull, no doubt killing him instantly.

Varrus had not yet had time to move, and he stood motionless, stunned by having seen two men struck dead in the space of a few moments, and smelling the stink of burning human hair.

Cato threw the remnant of the burning torch into the fire basket with the other and slipped his weighted sap back into its place on his shoulder before drawing both his swords and turning back to Varrus. Before he could speak, though, the door flew open again and three more men burst in, all armed, one of them the fellow who had been sent to fetch Carbo.

The man in the middle was clearly the leader. Varrus saw that immediately, even though he had never set eyes on him before.

"You snake," Cato said to him, raising his swords. "I have you, you son of a whore."

Like a snake indeed, the man in the middle reared back. Varrus had never seen anyone react to anything so quickly before. Carbo leapt back instantly, sweeping the men on each side of him forward with both hands at the same time, and then he vanished through the open door more quickly than Varrus could believe.

Cato leapt forward after him but was tackled immediately by one of the two remaining mercenaries. The man threw an arm around Cato's neck, raising the sword in his other hand to finish him, but Cato's feet were already off the floor and his dead weight pulled his assailant down with him, leaving the third man hopping, looking for an opening that would allow him to finish Cato without stabbing his friend. Seeing the ridiculous little dance the fellow was performing snapped Varrus out of his trance-like state. He ran forward, unseen as he broke from the darkened room, and sank his short sword deep into the capering man's armpit, then twisted it, hard, and jerked it straight back out again. The stabbed man turned towards him, his eyes wide and his mouth gaping, then coughed up blood and dropped to his knees, his eyes already glazing over.

"Varrus! Get the whoreson. It's Endor! Don't let him escape."

Endor!

Everything he had heard about Appius Endor came together in Varrus's mind at the same instant, and he felt panic well up. The man was gone, again! He looked down at the sword in his hand and saw how useless it was for what he needed to do, but then he saw, too, the heavy smith's hammer with its columnar steel head, and he snatched it up from the table and ran for the door, ignoring Cato's struggles with the last man on the floor. He raced out the door and into the cobbled courtyard, where he stood reeling for a moment, trying to make sense of what he was seeing.

Something was moving, far off to his right, something strange, and at first he could not make out what it was, until his angle of vision changed and everything clicked into place. There were horses in the yard, four or five at least, and one of them was rearing and bucking wildly, resisting the efforts of Appius Endor on its far side as he tried to mount it. He was on the beast's right side, for one thing, the wrong side from which to approach an unfamiliar horse, and the animal had no saddle. Even as he saw that, though, Endor managed to haul himself up onto the horse's back and lean forward over its neck to seize the reins. He captured them and dug in his heels, but still the terrified animal fought him, galloping away from the gate and towards the farthest corner of the yard.

As the fugitive struggled to dominate the horse, Varrus realized that he was closer to the gate than Endor was. He began to run with his limping gait, pushing himself harder now than he ever had before, but even so, he knew he would not reach the gate in time, for Endor had finally gained control over his mount and was riding hard, straight towards the gate.

He's the man who killed your family. The words rang loud in Varrus's mind and he stopped running abruptly, teetering on the verge of losing his balance and fighting to control his breathing, watching as Appius Endor drew level with him and then forged past. Then he closed his eyes and stood up straight, hefting the blacksmith's hammer in his hand. He visualized what he needed to do, then opened his eyes and gauged Endor's speed and distance. And when the moment came he threw, hard and true, using every ounce of strength and conditioning his years of smithing had engendered.

The hammer turned over slowly in the air once, then twice, and struck the fleeing man square in the side of the head with a sound like one of the horse's flying hooves striking the cobblestones. Varrus almost *felt* the sound, so unexpected and loud was it. And then everything appeared to him to slow down and go silent as the fleeing man threw up his arms, letting the reins fly free, and was flung sideways, off the horse's back and down to land heavily on the cobblestones. He bounced once and rolled over several times, throwing bright, strong jets of blood into the air to spread and spray and fall, like a fine mist, to coat the stones around him.

"By Vulcan's bulbous balls, I have never seen anyone throw anything like that."

Cato had spoken from directly behind him.

Varrus could not take his eyes off the fallen man. "I stopped him, didn't I?"

"Stopped him?" Marcus Licinius Cato laughed grimly. "Oh yes, you stopped him. You stopped him dead." He was silent for a space, then added, quietly, "Your grandfather would be proud of you."

THIRTY-EIGHT

I t had been more than a week, and closer to two, since the events at the Carbo villa, and though Quintus Varrus—he could now call himself that openly—had taken care to thank the apprentice boy Aquino for his good work in summoning help as quickly as he had when he saw the abduction, Varrus had not yet had the opportunity to spend any time talking to the lad. He remembered that on his way back from the armoury that particular afternoon, and so he swung into the stables and paused in the doorway, inhaling the warm, dusty stable smells as he looked around for the boy. There was no sign of the apprentice, though, and it was only as he turned to walk away that Varrus caught sight of him, spread-eagled, belly down, and soundly asleep on the broad, glossy back of the big workhorse with whom he shared the stable. The horse, a large, heavy-headed, six-year-old chestnut gelding, had never had a name until the boy came along, but the lad had taken to calling him Tom from the day of his arrival, grooming the huge animal constantly and talking to him, so that now the enormous beast's coat shone with a rich gloss, and the animal went to him obediently when summoned by name.

Varrus stood grinning at the spectacle of horse and boy, listening to the soft crunching sounds as Tom contentedly pulled mouthfuls of hay from a newly split bale that had been hoisted right up into his high feeding crib, chewing placidly while doing nothing to disturb the boy sprawled across his back. Eventually, Varrus started to edge away, unwilling to rouse the sleeping boy, who had been up before dawn, awakening and refreshing the fires in the forge and preparing the smithy for the daily routine. Something alerted the boy to his presence, though, and he sat up with a jerk, blinking at his employer in surprise.

Varrus held up a hand in greeting, a half smile on his lips. "Pardon me, Aquino," he said. "I didn't want to waken you."

The boy merely shook his head, and Varrus continued. "Do you often sleep up there like that, on the horse's back?" The boy blinked again and nodded, then raised his right hand, which had been hidden on the horse's other side, to rub at his eye with the back of his wrist, and Varrus's smile grew broader when he saw the thin-nosed pliers clutched in his fist.

"You know," he said, "you could have asked me a hundred times to guess what you were holding in your hand there and I would have guessed wrongly every time. Can I ask why you are holding pliers while you sleep? Even if you pinched them tightly on Tom's mane, they wouldn't be strong enough to hold you in place up there if you fell sideways."

The boy looked down at the pliers, twisting them from side to side, then answered in his surprisingly deep voice. "Tom had a stone lodged in his foot—in his hoof," he said. "I took it out for him and then had nowhere to put the pliers without going back to the forge. So I stuck them in my belt. And when I climbed up here they hurt my belly, so I held them in my hand. Is it very painful for horses when stones get caught in their hooves?"

"I imagine it must be," Varrus said. "It makes them lame, so it must be painful. Horses are like people in that regard. They wouldn't limp if it didn't hurt. Do you really like them?"

The boy looked confused. "Like what? Horses?" He saw Varrus's nod and thought about the question for a moment. "I love horses," he said then. "Someday I'm going to work with horses, looking after them." He swung his right leg over the horse's back and slid easily to the ground to stand in front of Varrus.

"Did you put that up there, for Tom?" Varrus was pointing at the bale of hay in the horse's high manger.

"Yes," the boy said, suddenly sounding apprehensive. "Am I not allowed to do that?"

"No, no. Of course you are allowed to feed the horse. I was simply wondering how you raised it up so high."

The boy looked surprised by the question. "I lifted it up and tipped it in."

"Ah! Yes, of course . . . Obviously you must have. But still, I would have thought that bale might be too heavy. It's quite green, I see. That means it still contains moisture, and that would make it heavier than a dry bale of the same size."

"It was, a bit," came the reply. "But not too much. I was able to hoist it, once I got it off the ground."

"Why didn't you set it in the lower crib? That way you wouldn't have had to heave it all the way up there."

"Yes, but then Tom would have had to stoop too far all the time. He's a big horse."

"Of course . . . And he is big, isn't he? Do you like being here, Aquino, working in the smithy?"

"Ye-ess!" the boy whooped.

"And you love horses." Varrus paused, thinking, then smiled and said, "D'you know, I think I might have found a name for you." He watched the wide, intelligent eyes narrow and focus on him intently. "Your name is Simeon. Simeon of Aquino. Is that right?"

"Yes."

"I suspect you don't like the Simeon part much. Is that right, too?"

"Yes. It's strange."

"No, it's not strange, it's merely different. If other people around here used it, it wouldn't sound strange at all. What about your other name, Aquino? Do you like that one?"

"Not much."

"For the same reason?"

"Yes."

"Well, what about this. You love horses. You want to work with horses someday. You live here in the stable, for now at least. You're as strong as a horse, for your age—you're what, twelve?"

"Yes."

"I thought so. And your name, Aquino, sounds like equine, which means horsey. So what I thought was, why don't we take things one step further and call you Equus? It's a fine, strong name, straightforward and honest and full of character, and as you grow bigger and stronger, it will become better and better suited to you. Now, what do you think of that?"

"Equus," the boy said, as though testing the word for flavour and texture. "Equus . . . That would be my name?"

He did not sound displeased, so Varrus shrugged. "From this day on, if you like it," he said. "But only if *you* want it to be your name. No one else has any right to say who you can or cannot be. I've always thought a man should have the right to choose a name for himself, but most of us never have the opportunity." He grinned again. "You *can* choose, though. And I like Equus. I like the sound of it. It sounds a lot more Roman than Simeon."

"Equus . . . Equus!" The boy grinned then, a long, slow blossoming, and raised his hands above his head. "I am Equus!" he shouted, turning towards the horse. "Tom, my name is Equus!"

Varrus held out his hand. "So be it, then. Now give me those pliers and I'll take them back to the smithy. I have to get to work."

He left the newly named young man communing with his friend Tom and made his way into the empty smithy, which still smelled of the work Shamus had done that morning, and as he replaced the errant pliers on their rack he caught sight of the edge of the ill-placed, rusty little oven inside which his hoard of golden coins lay hidden. Two things crossed his mind as he looked at it: all it required was for one inquisitive person to take an idle look into what lay there for his vast wealth to be revealed; and even if such an inquisitive person were to find the hoard, he could not possibly steal all of the gold and run away with it.

He knew, nevertheless, that sooner or later he was going to have to find a really clever hiding place for all those coins, and that when he did, that place would have to be spacious enough to hold the entire hoard. Having thought deeply about that ever since taking delivery of the box from his uncle Marius, he now found himself naturally distrustful of the notion of splitting the coins into smaller collections. It raised too much potential for loss and inconvenience. Still, though, he had not the vaguest idea where he might begin to start looking for such a hiding place, and he was clever enough to know that there was little point in fretting over it when there was no need. One of these days, though . . . He walked away and forgot all about the golden coins as soon as he heard his wife's laughter coming from the open door to the house at the rear of the smithy.

"Quintus, there you are! Tribune Marcellus here came by to tell us that Legate Britannicus will be returning with the rest of our friends within the next few days, and I was about to offer him a cup of wine. Would you like one?"

Varrus went and put an arm about her and kissed her on the cheek before nodding in greeting to Marcellus, whose tunic with its broad purple edging marked him as a *tribunus laticlavius*. A broad-banded tribune was a political appointee rather than a military one, a privileged aristocrat who served time in the armies as a senior officer, usually second-in-command of a legion, as part of his education before moving on to higher things.

"Damian," he said. "You look well. When, exactly, do you expect them home from Londinium?"

Damian Marcellus smiled. "You know better than to ask me that, Quintus," he drawled. "Like every other traveller alive, they're hostages to the weather. I would guess they'll return tomorrow or the following day. Is it important, which day?"

"Not at all. I'm simply missing them all. We have much to talk about."

"How so?"

"Well, my life changed radically last time I saw them all—for the better, certainly—but I still don't know quite as much as I would like to about everything we talked about. I have a few questions about the whole situation with Endor."

"Ah! Well, I'm sure you must have, but were I you, I would be prepared for disappointment. The army loves to keep its secrets, especially from . . . non-military citizens. And your friends have, after all, been attending a military board of inquiry for the past week. You might find they've been warned to say nothing to anyone. It is all rather sensitive, I think you'll agree."

"Sensitive?" Varrus was about to say more, but Lydia approached at that moment carrying a tray from the heavy sideboard where Liam Mcuil had always kept his hospitality store of decanted wine, cups, and jugs. He glanced at the tray and counted three cups. "Thank you, my love," he said. "I see you are joining us, so we must have broached a new amphora of the Germanica, am I right?"

"You are, of course." She raised her cup in a salute to both of them, but spoke to the tribune. "I love this wine. It's tarter than most of the others, almost tangy, and I like the way it lingers after you've swallowed. It's very hard to come by, though, and we have to hoard it, so you were lucky in your choice of a visiting day, Tribune Marcellus. Now, what were you telling my husband he can't have?"

Marcellus lifted his cup in a silent dedication and sipped at it cautiously. "I can see why you treasure it," he said after a moment, his eyebrows raised in approval. He took a larger sip and savoured it, then lowered his cup and wrinkled his nose. "But you misunderstood me. I was not refusing Quintus anything. I was merely saying he ought not to expect openness from the army."

"He was saying the information on Endor is sensitive," Varrus said. "Which makes me wonder: to whom? Endor's dead, so he doesn't care what might be said about him. But are there others who might?" He turned to the tribune, all wide-eyed innocence, save that his eyes were dancing. "The people who accepted his premature death and claimed credit for it, perhaps?" He waved a hand. "But hey, I care for none of that, I promise you. What the army and the imperial authorities choose to do with their secrets and arcane knowledge is the last thing I care about."

Marcellus nodded, then drained his cup and set it back on the tray that Lydia had laid on a nearby table. "I believe you," he said. "Nonetheless, be prepared for them to tell you they have been forbidden to discuss the matter." He turned to Lydia and bowed smartly. "My thanks for the delicious refreshment, Mistress Varrus. I had best be getting back to my duties now. I wish you both well."

When he was gone, Lydia looked up at her husband with slitted eyes. "You look very sober, Magister Varrus. What are you thinking?"

"That I like Marcellus. I've met a number of his ilk that I detested on sight, but for an effete aristocrat, he'll be acceptable at my table. Speaking of which, we should have everyone here for dinner when they all come back."

"Very well. We'll have them all on the second night after they return. And I'll hire the baker and his wife to cook the meal." She pushed him away. "And now, have you no work to do in your forge? Go and do it, then, or I'll inveigle you into bed and we'll have no supper this night."

He remained where he stood, gazing at her until, slightly exasperated, she asked him what he was looking at.

"At your beauty," he said. "But I was wondering, too . . . Why the *second* night after they come back? Is there a reason for that?"

"Of course there's a reason," she said. "Several reasons, in fact. First of all, so they'll be road weary and saddle-sore when they return, infantrymen that they are, and they won't want to go far or do anything on their first night back in barracks. By the third night, they'll all have different things to do. So the second night is the only time we can expect them all to be available and willing. And were that not sufficient reason, we two are leaving within days after that for Londuin and our triumphant wedding with my father and his new bride, and we will be gone for at least a month, I believe, and by the time we return every one of those friends of yours could have been transferred to other parts and we might never see any of them again. So it's the second night or nothing. It's a simple thought process, my love."

"It is," he agreed. "And now I'll leave you to your preparations."

THIRTY-NINE

The travellers returned within the week, though without Cato, whom none of them had seen since the day after they arrived in Londinium, when he had disappeared in search of his lost family, and the dinner was duly arranged for the second night after their arrival. At noon on that second day, though, when Varrus returned from the armoury, he was much surprised to find Cato himself, looking both sober and subdued, waiting for him in the smithy. He took him into his little records cubicle, where he asked him straightforwardly what had happened.

Cato shrugged. "I found them," he said. "They're safe and doing well, and they seemed happy."

"Were they glad to see you?"

"They didn't see me. Rhea married another man, a wheelwright, two years ago. He treats her like an empress, he adopted the boy, and they both look happy. He's good to them. You can be sure I asked more than one person about that. The fellow is highly thought of, and so are they, Rhea and Nicodemo. So I decided to stay away from them. They don't need me fouling up their lives anymore . . . Now I'm back here, looking for information."

"About what?"

"A couple of things. For starters, where did that steward go, that Albus fellow? Do you know?"

"No. I didn't want to know. We agreed on that, remember? We

helped him to leave, and technically he was a felon, so the less we knew about his whereabouts after that, the better."

Varrus frowned slightly, remembering how appalled the steward had been at hearing the dark truth about the man for whom he had worked for years. But his horror had quickly turned to fear as soon as he realized that, as a trusted employee of a condemned felon, he himself would be considered complicit in his employer's criminality. Feeling certain Albus was utterly innocent of anything blameworthy, Varrus had persuaded Cato to help him send the man away safely, before any investigators arrived. There had been two workhorses in the stable, and a heavy, well-made wagon with iron tires and a tented cover, and Cato had suggested that those, plus an amount of fodder for the beasts, should be part of Albus's settlement, along with any coins or valuables the steward felt, in good conscience, were owed to him. By the time the investigators came to the villa the next morning, there was no sign that there had ever been a steward there.

"What has changed since that night?" Varrus asked. "Something must have, to make you wonder where Albus went."

Cato shrugged. "I'm simply trying to tidy up some loose ends that have been bothering me." He looked around the tiny room. "Is it safe to talk in here?"

"Safe? I think so. It's my house and we are the only ones here. Lydia's over at her friend's house, preparing food for tonight. I suppose, though, it depends on what you want to talk about. Some things are never safe to discuss."

"Oh, it's nothing like that." Cato shook his head apologetically. "I've been doing what I do for too long, I suppose. I always feel threatened when I feel exposed—and I feel exposed when I'm outside my own realm." He glanced around again, searching. "Do you have any wine?"

"Yes, but I also have a dinner to attend tonight, to celebrate the end of all this nonsense and to drink, finally, to Endor's damnation. You'll be welcome there, too—if you're still sober."

Cato dipped his head. "Fine, then. I'll be there."

"Good. I'll tell Lydia."

"In the meantime, can I have watered wine? I've been travelling for days and haven't had a drop."

Varrus left, returning a short time later with two cups and a jug of watered wine. He poured for both of them, then set the jug down on the window ledge and sipped his own, nodding in appreciation. He sat across from Cato and raised his cup in salute. "Welcome back, my friend. It's good to see you again."

"You, too." Cato returned the gesture. "Now, do you still have that labarum you were waving about in Londinium a few years ago?"

Varrus froze, his cup halfway to his mouth.

"Well? Do you? Or were you clever enough to get rid of it?"

Varrus settled back slowly into his chair, shaking his head in disbelief. "I cannot believe . . . How did you ever find out about that? I haven't spoken about it to anyone since I came here."

"It wasn't difficult." Cato's voice was level, unhurried. "You were snatched off the street in *Camulodunum*, Quintus! Hardly a centre of commerce or even of clandestine activities. Why? Why you? You're an apprentice smith, a devotee of Vulcan, black with smoke and ashes. Who, in the name of all the ancient gods, would want to abduct a blacksmith?

"And then I remembered you were Eirish when I met you, that time we ate fish together. Black-haired. Calling yourself Mcuil. And when you were snatched, you were golden-haired and Roman. So that made me wonder where you had been coming from when we met that first day."

He emptied his cup and look at Varrus with one eye closed, as though measuring him for something. "So I started asking questions, casually, among my brothers in the order, wondering if anyone had heard of anything unusual concerning a young Roman aristocrat who might have disappeared from Londinium a year ago. And I'm sure you can guess what I found.

"By sheer coincidence, the first man I asked had a vague memory of something he had heard around the time I was asking about. He was an old, trusted friend, and he said he had heard some outlandish tale about a rich but unknown young Roman with unusually long, gold-coloured hair who appeared in Londinium one day dressed like an ancient senator, in a full, white toga the like of which hadn't been seen outside of Rome in two hundred years, and took issue with some fool of a garrison patrolman in a squabble over a woman. Apparently the woman's brothers tried to interfere, and then this unknown Roman pulled out an imperial letter of authority and used it to quash the patrol leader's behaviour and to let the woman and her brothers go free. And then the stranger vanished and was never seen again.

"I won't insult you by asking you if that sounds familiar. But that would have been around the time—within a day or two of the time, even—when I first met you on the road, with your short, dark hair, when you were calling yourself an Eirish smith. Yet by the time you were snatched up, you had been transformed into a golden-haired Roman.

"I remember thinking, after I found you in the cell and you reminded me about that first meeting, that there had to be something outlandishly *wrong* in what had happened back in Londinium. It didn't fully sink home to me until much later, once I had time to chew it over, but it became obvious that whatever it was that had resulted in your being snatched up, it must have taken place in the weeks, perhaps even the days, before you changed your appearance, your name, and your racial origin and fled from Londinium. And the sole, memorable thing you had done there was to brandish a document bearing the imperial signature, with the personal power of the emperor attached to it, and then vanish.

"One question remained. What had you done with the document?" He eyed Varrus shrewdly. "The only logical answer was that you must have taken it with you, because if you hadn't, if you had surrendered it, or if it had been taken or impounded—in fact, if anyone at all, anywhere, had known what happened to it—there would have been no reason to go after you. You would have caused a minor stir, but you would have been unimportant to the men of power.

"As things stood, with both you and the document vanished without a trace, those men of power grew anxious. Each of them, probably all of them, would have paid gladly and grandly to possess that thing, and now it was in the hands of some unknown Roman fugitive, hiding who knew where." He stopped suddenly, and his expression changed to one of dubious surprise. "You do realize, I hope, why that is so important."

"Yes. I think so. That document represents the emperor's power to achieve things."

"Oh, no. No, Quintus, it does not." He drank some of his wine, then set the cup down carefully before shifting his backside around to a more comfortable position. "That *thing*—that labarum—gives *godly* powers to whoever possesses it. No, don't shrug off what I'm saying to you, Quintus. You think I'm exaggerating, but I am not. It would be impossible to exaggerate the potency of that thing. It gives unlimited power to whoever holds it. There is nothing—no crime, no sin, no imaginable transgression in the world—that cannot be disavowed by simply waving that document in the air and claiming the authority of the emperor whose signature it bears. It is a licence to do anything. Probably the most powerful document in all of Britain today." He paused again, then asked, "When did you last look closely at it, can you remember?"

Varrus pouted, thinking. "No, but it was a long time ago. I haven't looked at it since that afternoon in Londinium."

"Hmm. Can you remember anything about it?"

"Of course. I remember what it looks like, and what's written in it."

"You can remember what is written in it?"

"Do you want me to say no? It was very short. One line. Simply, 'This man acts in my name.' And it was signed C. A., for Constantinus Augustus. But it can't still be all *that* powerful, Cato. I mean, it's almost as old as I am. My uncle Marius found it when he was a navarch in the Euxine Sea, and that's more than eighteen years ago."

Cato shook his head dismissively. "Those things do not grow old until the emperor whose name they bear dies, and at that moment they all die, worse than worthless. When last I asked, Constantine was alive and well and apparently planning to remove the imperial court to someplace on the edge of nowhere that he intends to name after himself."

"Byzantium, on the Hellespont. I heard about that. Apparently it will be known henceforth as Constantinople. So the fact that Constantine is still alive means that the writ is still potent?"

"Hah! Beyond your wildest dreams, my friend. That's what got you snatched. Someone—someone powerful enough to act on his suspicions—kept up a search for you for an entire year. He never stopped looking for you from that day forth.

"So my next question then became, who, in Britain, has that much power and influence, let alone the wealth, to sustain a province-wide manhunt for all that time? And who, among those who have such resources, might be willing to expend so much time and resources to keep up the hunt for the emperor's licence, keeping teams of people on constant watch for one particular but nameless man who might have fled Britannia a full year earlier?" He shrugged, and made a self-deprecating face. "Mind you, those are the kinds of questions I enjoy. Because daunting though they may seem, they're usually easy to answer. Very few people are that wealthy or that powerful, and most of those who qualify for either status enjoy both. We are talking about men who move in very exclusive circles." His look reminded Varrus of a wolf's snarl as he added, "The kind of circles within which several prominent and senior members of our brotherhood revolve. And so I asked pointed questions and paid heed to what I was told."

"And did you find out who it was?"

"First I had to find out how they discovered where you were."

"How did you do that?"

"I already knew. Do you remember telling me about meeting Legate Britannicus in the street on your wedding day, when you were wearing your white robe that looked like a toga? You said there were three of his uniformed staff there, and that you talked about your wedding and your life."

"Of course I remember. That was the only time I have ever spoken with the man. What about it?"

"Well, someone there was paying very close attention to everything you said, because a report went straight from there to Londinium detailing every word."

"What?" Varrus sat straighter and set his cup down with exaggerated slowness. "Are you telling me that the new legate reported me to someone?"

"No. Absolutely not. He's one of us, one of the brotherhood. But one of his three attendants that day reported you. The word went from here to Londinium and straight out to Endor, with instructions to pick you up and relieve you of the labarum by whatever means necessary."

"Which man was it?"

"The only one who went back to Londinium that week. I could tell you his name but it would mean nothing to you. Suffice to say he has since been arrested and is facing accusations of divulging military secrets to enemies of the state." He shrugged. "Again, nothing miraculous involved. Questions, and then answers, and the wit to put them together. So what exactly happened to you that day you were snatched?"

Varrus shook his head. "I have no idea. One minute I was walking along the street, watching where I was stepping because some farmer had gone through ahead of me with a herd of cows and the cobblestones were ankle-deep in shit, and the next thing I knew, I was tied to a chair in that cell where you found me."

"So where is the labarum now?"

"At home. It's hanging in a closet with my foul-weather gear."

"At home. In a closet . . . I see. Safe among all your other precious documents, you mean. Am I correct in thinking you have no planned use for it?"

Varrus was smiling. "Why would you even ask me that?"

Cato shrugged a little. "Because I was hoping that, if you weren't planning to use it, you might give it to me."

"And why would I do that, now that I know how powerful and dangerous it is?"

"Because I *have* a use for it. An appropriate one, worthy of its solemnity."

"And what could that possibly be, to induce me to part with—what did you call it? The most powerful document in all of Britain today. Why would I part with that? What would you do with it, were I to give it to you?"

Cato sat staring into space for a while, then shook his head. "Same thing I would have done with it before," he said quietly. "I'd use it to get me close to a man I need to kill."

He stood up abruptly and began to pace the floor, his wine forgotten now. "I know the ringleader, Quintus, the man whose money and monumental greed made all this happen. The man responsible for the deaths of Strabo and my sister and their son, and so many hundreds of others. The man who has been the head of the snake from the very beginnings of the Ring, when Endor realized he would need willing and hungry help to turn his plans into reality. I know now who the bastard is and what he is—the leech who took over the Ring in the first place, and Endor with it. He's been the puppet master from the very start, and now I have him. And I know what has driven him, all along. It all came together in Londinium, when I asked one question and got an answer I had not expected.

"I had been moving forward, like everyone else involved since these investigations started, on the presumption that everything—all our investigations—revolved around the central fact that someone had devised a means of outwitting the imperial system of military logistics. Someone had discovered how to steal the empire's munitions and supplies with complete impunity. But then one evening, unexpectedly, when I was doing no more than making small talk with an influential member of the highest circle of our brotherhood, he made a couple of comments that struck me like blows from an armoured fist, for though I had heard both of them before, I had never thought of them in tandem.

"In the first place, he spoke of the earliest beginnings of the Ring, and how it had been Endor, inspired by his cousin Carausius's depraved, piratical audacity, who had dreamed up the concept of stealing from Diocletian's new system. But then he also said that, had it not been for a sudden and enormous injection of financial resources from some nameless sources, the Ring's existence would have been snuffed out years earlier by its own weaknesses and excesses. It was a massive, sustained injection of capital, over a period of several years, he said, that had enabled the organization to diversify its interests to the point where constant thievery on the roads and trade routes had become almost an incidental source of income.

"That 'incidental' imputation seemed outrageous to me and I couldn't let it go by, so I questioned him on it, and without blinking an eye, he quoted me facts and figures to demonstrate that the raids, albeit more successful than ever before, have been diminishing steadily in number and scope for several years.

"Why, and how could that be, were my next questions, and he shrugged his shoulders in a way that made me think I ought to know such things. With the profits made from those original investments of years ago bolstering the Ring's activities, he said, the organization's largest investors no longer needed the income from the thievery. They were still raking it in, of course. But they didn't need it. They already had so much, my friend said, that the Ring had outlived its usefulness.

"And that was when I knew what we had been missing all along. We had been underestimating what was happening, even as we allowed ourselves to believe we were overestimating it in the interests of defeating it. In an instant, I could see all of it—including the reasons why we hadn't been able to make headway before. We thought we had uncovered something huge, and we had, but the Ring itself was incomprehensibly bigger than we had imagined. We thought we had smashed it, but we were too small to realize how wrong we were. The Ring's still there, Quintus. It still exists, and the master puppeteer is merely waiting to restart it and take it in a different direction."

He stopped, and frowned, then raised a hand as though to point something out. "I thought I had saved your life, and Lydia's, but I was wrong there, too. You are both in great danger. He knows you are still alive and that you live in Camulodunum. He knows who you are and who your wife is, and he knows you have the labarum. And that labarum has become the thing he most desires in all the world. There are no restrictions on the power it controls. With that thing in his hands, he will be literally untouchable. As things stand today, he believes he is still safe in being who and what he is because we can't even *accuse* him of anything, not even with the full resources of the brotherhood of Mithras at our backs. We can't bring him down, without proof. We can't arrest him or stop him or even interfere with him because he's too damned powerful. He owns everyone who can be bought in Britain, and probably throughout the rest of the empire as well, and if he doesn't own them personally, he will be able to coerce someone who does. He's proved himself stronger than all of us, almost as secure as Constantine himself, and if he ever gains possession of that labarum of yours he will become completely monstrous and literally unassailable."

Varrus was beginning to believe his friend was falling apart, and it frightened him. "Then use your sources inside your brotherhood to denounce him directly to the Emperor himself."

Cato threw him a look that was almost pitying. "Do you think I haven't considered that? It can't be done, Quintus. That's what I've been saying. I don't know who to trust. Though I hate to say the words, I'm beginning to wonder how secure the brotherhood itself is these days. No, there are too many ways to die along the road to Rome. It appears that this man is inviolable. From where I stand, the only possible way to stop him is for me to kill him, and to be able to do that, I need to be able to reach him. And to do that, I need the labarum."

"Who is this man? Would I know him?"

"He's a relative of yours, you told Ajax, a cousin of some kind through your father's mother. He's one of the Seneca clan—the senior Seneca in Britain and Gaul since his father died a few months ago. His name is Vassos Seneca and he is the most repulsive, disgusting excuse for a human being that I've ever seen, known, or heard of. There is no shortage of depravity in the world, but Vassos Seneca takes even depravity to new depths. But somehow, through his immense wealth and the corruption his family and their connections have fostered throughout the empire, he seems to have achieved a distinction that cannot be challenged. He lives apart from common men, in indescribable luxury and isolation. And he is unapproachable to all but a small number of his peers—and that, again, is no exaggeration. Few people even know he exists. He has no public life, no public persona. Apart from those few peers I spoke of, everyone else—and I mean, quite literally, everyone else—must deal with him through intermediaries."

"But you would kill him."

"Within a heartbeat. Without a thought."

"How would you get close to him?"

"I said he's unapproachable, not immortal. I'd find a way. There's little that can stop a single, determined man, providing he cares nothing for the risk he takes. And I intend to kill this slug, to end this my way and give a purpose to my useless, wasted life, if only in death. But I thought that if I had that labarum of yours, it might provide me with some extra leverage in view of the size of the difficulty facing me."

He paused, his head cocked as thought recalling something once well known, then grinned, hard-eyed. "I remember what that old Greek Pythagoras is supposed to have said. Give me a place to stand, and with a lever I shall move the world."

"It was Archimedes who said that, Cato, not Pythagoras."

"Ah! And where was he from?"

"From Greece."

"There, you see? One Greek is much like another. So you'll give me the labarum?"

"On one condition."

"Name it."

"You told me, that day I killed Appius Endor, that he had killed my family. That was what made me angry enough to throw that hammer." He paused, and now it was his turn to stand with unfocused eyes, making mental connections, before he cocked his head to one side and asked, "So are you now telling me it was *Vassos Seneca* who was responsible, as head of the Ring?"

"Mmm." Cato moved his head from side to side, neither confirming nor denying the allegation. "That's complicated," he said. "The answer is both yes and no."

"Uncomplicate it for me, and give me one or the other."

"Ach, I can't exactly . . ." Cato's budding protest died unspoken as he looked into Varrus's eyes and recognized the expression there. "It really is complicated," he repeated. "But I'll try."

FORTY

Quintus Varrus sat silent as he waited for Cato to decide on whatever he was debating with himself about. He forced himself to be patient, knowing that there were certain things connected to his former work about which Cato could not and would not speak, because men's lives depended upon his silence. Varrus had once scoffed at that idea, but Ajax and his companions had not been amused by his attitude, and he had fallen silent as they described, using graphic examples, some of what they themselves had done from time to time and the risks to which they were often exposed. He had never since doubted either their need for secrecy or the dangers they faced every day, dangers that were routine and unexceptional to them but undreamed of by the ordinary grunt soldiers who worked beside them.

"*Benigne*, Quintus, for giving me time to think things through." Cato poured himself more wine from the jug on the window ledge.

When he sat down again, still having said nothing, Varrus, whose patience was at last wearing thin, decided to prompt him. "I didn't expect to hear what you said about Vassos Seneca," he said. "You told me originally that Endor killed my family, and I was prepared to believe that. But I had also been told earlier that no one knew who had killed them because there had been no evidence to indicate what had happened that night, and no trace of a connection to anyone identifiable."

Cato frowned quickly. "Who told you that nonsense?"

"Your own friends—Ajax and the others. They said the brotherhood of Mithras investigated the deaths and could find no evidence."

Cato looked bewildered. "Ajax told you that? And the others backed him up?"

"Yes."

"When did they tell you this?"

"Several weeks ago, before you first showed up here, and I believed every word they told me."

"Shit!" Cato threw both his hands in the air, spilling his drink. "That makes no sense at all, man." He pulled out a kerchief and began dabbing at the hem of his tunic. "And how would they have known, anyway? They were all here in Britain when the murders took place, but I was in Italy, chasing Endor. I did establish that he was there, and I did it officially, with records of witnessed testimony confirming that he had assembled a crew of killers for the raid on the Varrus villa on the night the massacre took place. We could always capture idiots and underlings, but most of those barely knew their own names and they had nothing worthwhile to tell us, even when we broke them. But on that occasion we actually found some participants who could talk. And with a little persuasion, they talked loudly and believably.

"So, Endor bears a great deal of responsibility, unquestionably, for that raid. While it was happening, though, he was far away, as usual. I began to think he must be able to smell me, for it seemed as though every time I came within spitting distance of him he would vanish again, reappearing a hundred miles away within mere days. But the truth, though we could never have suspected it at the time, was that he was being fed a constant stream of information on everything we were doing. And that was years ago. *Years* ago! I only found out the truth by sheerest accident, a few days ago, as I told you, when I understood what my senior brother had enabled me to see!"

He shook his head in disgust, apparently at his own stupidity, and drained the last drops from his cup. "I'm surprised the lads would tell you that, though. That it didn't happen as it did." He hesitated. "What, exactly, did Ajax say?"

"He said the entire resources of the brotherhood had been brought to bear upon solving the murders. They went through all the records of everyone my grandfather ever crossed and condemned or offended in the line of duty and examined each of them minutely—most particularly those who were still alive. They were looking for grudges and resentments powerful enough to create a motive for vengeance. But after a year and a half they had been unable to expose the slightest hint of a plot or a . . ." He stopped, because a deep frown had been growing on Cato's face and he had finally thrown up a hand to interrupt what Varrus was saying.

"Wait," he said. "They couldn't find the slightest hint of a plot against whom?"

"My grandfather. Titanius."

"*Titanius*? What in Hades has Titanius to do with any of this? He was inactive by then. He never even entered into this mess, unless it was as an advisor. Of course they couldn't find a plot against him, because there *was* none! Your grandfather had nothing to *do* with what happened at the villa that night. For the first time in his entire life, he must have been an innocent bystander, caught up in events he couldn't influence."

"What—?"

Varrus slumped in his seat, gaping at Cato, who stared back at him, bristling with indignation, and too disgusted with his friends to be articulate and logical. Neither of them spoke for some time after that.

Varrus was the first to speak again, holding up a hand, palm outwards, in a tacit request for time and consideration. "So . . ." he began. "My family was not murdered out of revenge for something my grandfather did years earlier. That is what you're saying, is it not?"

Cato nodded. "Yes. That's what I'm saying. What happened that night had nothing to do with your grandfather. Nothing at all."

Quintus Varrus seemed to crumple visibly, withdrawing into himself, and even his voice diminished to a whisper. "So it was random? It was all meaningless?"

Cato nodded again. "That's how it was supposed to look, yes."

Varrus's head came up immediately. "What d'you mean, *it was supposed to look?*"

Cato looked slightly confused. "What I said. It was supposed to look like a random, savage raid in order to deflect suspicion."

"Deflect suspicion from *whom*? You said there was no plot."

"No, I didn't." The indignation was back in Cato's voice, too. "What I said was that it had nothing to do with Titanius Varrus."

"Well then, who else was there?"

"Your father. He was the one they wanted dead!"

"That's ridiculous! My father was a—"

Varrus cut himself short, on the point of disparaging his father.

"Your father was a highly regarded personal advisor to the Emperor Constantine," Cato said quietly. "He was a diplomat of the highest imperial standing, entrusted with highly secretive negotiations on the Emperor's personal behalf. Extremely important, influential, far-advanced but essentially incomplete negotiations. I learned that later. *He*, Marcus Varrus, was the one the killers came looking for that night. Their task was to make sure those negotiations remained unresolved." He shrugged his shoulders regretfully. "They succeeded, but in order to complete the required illusion of brutal mindlessness, everyone there, every potential witness, had to die."

Quintus Varrus looked aimlessly around the tiny room as he wrestled with this new knowledge, and then turned to face the centurion, narrow-eyed and accusatory. "And you think Vassos Seneca was, at the highest level, responsible."

Cato shrugged. "Again, that's a yes-and-no response. I know approximately where the orders originated, but I don't know who actually issued them. There's a number of possibilities, and I can't entirely rule out the others."

"But? I can hear a 'but' in there, Cato."

"I know you can, because it's there. But the orders were issued authoritatively, and the word went out to find a special man to handle a special, highly delicate assignment. The price involved was enormous, because the task itself was huge and the need for secrecy even greater."

"And it went to Appius Endor."

"Yes. Conveniently, he was in Italy at the time, a fugitive, running from me. Not from me personally, of course, but I was the man charged with finding him and bringing him down."

"And why him? Was he that well known outside Britain?"

"No, but the forces using him weren't confined to Britain. They were empire-wide, connected at all levels. Endor had proved trustworthy, and he was ruthless and cruelly efficient, *ergo* when the need arose for a reliable specialist, his name was put forward. The broker's fee for that would have been substantial."

"And . . . you are saying Vassos Seneca was the broker."

"Seneca was the broker. He supplied the killer and he claimed the broker's fee. Endor was his prized possession, loyal and completely trustworthy."

"And the person who did the hiring? Tell me."

"It wasn't a person. It was a group. An entity. Remember what your father's work entailed."

"Negotiations." Varrus had barely had to think. "Dealing with one party on behalf of another. Who had he been negotiating with?"

"With the leaders of the Christian Church, on behalf of the Emperor Constantine."

Varrus's eyes slowly went wide with disbelief. "Are you saying the *Christians* were responsible?"

"No, not at all, though if the stakes were different I might not discount the possibility. *Someone* was responsible, though, and whoever they were, they made sure that no hint of any connection to them could be found afterwards, no matter how thoroughly we searched. It wasn't the Christians, and it certainly wasn't the Emperor. But those were the two stakeholders at the table—the principals in the negotiations—so if it wasn't them, who else could it have been?"

Varrus sat glowering, his brows knitted as he considered the question. "Someone who stood to lose heavily if the negotiations were successful, obviously. But I don't know who that could have been. Who do you think it was?"

"I don't need to think. I *know* who it was. What I need now is for you to see it, too, without help from me, so think a little harder. Constantine and the Christians are the principals in the negotiation, both focused tightly on their common interests. Who would stand to lose from their negotiations? It's not difficult."

Varrus thought for a moment longer, then shrugged. "It is, if you don't know what they were negotiating."

"You can't mean that!" Cato looked as though he had been slapped.

"Can't mean what? That I don't know what they were negotiating? How could I? I didn't even know they were talking to each other."

"But this is your *father* we're talking about! You must have heard something, formed *some* idea of what was happening."

"In my father's affairs? I doubt the man spoke ten words to me in fifteen years. He spent my entire life avoiding me. We might have slept under the same roof from time to time, but he barely acknowledged me and we were never friends. So no, I heard nothing and I cared even less."

"Oh . . ." Cato looked slightly deflated. "I didn't know that." He sat stock-still for a moment, eyeing the younger man, then nodded abruptly. "So be it. They were negotiating the terms under which Christianity would become respectable."

"Christianity *is* respectable. Has been for years. Constantine gave it official status long ago, when he became Emperor."

"Nah." Cato shook his head. "That made it official, but nowhere near respectable . . ." He paused, then sighed. "How much do you know about Christianity, really? Are you a Christian?"

"No, but my mother was, and my wife is."

"Was your mother devout?"

"Perhaps. I think so, but I don't really know."

"What about your wife?"

"She's Christian, but not really devout—at least I don't think she is. Her mother was Christian, too. Killed during the early anti-Christian riots in Diocletian's day."

"Galerius was the one behind that killing spree. Diocletian gets the blame, because he set things in motion, but it was Galerius who launched the real persecutions."

"Why would he do that?"

Cato quirked an eyebrow. "You really don't know, do you."

"About what? What don't I know, apart from almost everything? I grew up in Italy, but because I was a cripple who offended my father's sight, I spent most of my boyhood in Dalmatia. We didn't hear much about Christianity there, or about anything else, come to think of it. I was wild, as a boy. I never learned anything about religion."

Cato blew out air noisily, shaking his head and grimacing. "Well, then, you had better listen carefully to what I'm about to tell you. You're a clever fellow, I know that, but you have some gaping holes in your knowledge of the world you live in."

He narrowed his eyes, squinting into some place only he could see, then started talking. "Galerius was afraid of the Christians. Everyone in Rome was, and with good reason. They came out of Judea, after all, and that has always been the most dangerous wasp's nest in the whole damn empire, full of strife and rebellion and hate-spitting defiance. And once out, into the rest of the world, they spread like a contagion."

"What d'you mean, a contagion? They're peaceful people."

"I know, turning the other cheek and forgiving their enemies." The look Cato gave Varrus then was one of pure cynicism. "They came out of *Judea*, Quintus, and within decades the authorities had started to grow afraid of them because they were ungovernable. They refused to conform, and no one in authority could make them behave the way Rome wanted them to. They worshipped an all-powerful, all-seeing, all-forgiving god who they claimed was the sole god in existence, save for his son, who was the same god but with a different persona, and there was a third one, too, in case you weren't paying attention to the other two in one. Don't get me started on *that*. Anyway, the Christians weren't even afraid to die, because their Jesus god had died—crucified by us Romans, no less—and had come back to life again, so they knew they'd be reborn after death. That meant, in essence, that we—us, Rome—couldn't control them. Couldn't discipline them or punish them effectively, because they'd simply turn the other cheek and forgive the soldiers flogging them. And even if we crucified or slaughtered them, they died happily, going to the arms of their Jesus god in his Heaven. They didn't care about working to grow rich, either. They were happy being poor, so they paid no taxes, contributing nothing to the state except their refusal to be governed.

"Galerius saw that. He couldn't avoid seeing it, and no one else could, either. But the real trouble began because their creed spread like a fire in hillside grass, with its promises of happiness in a life to come and a better, blissful existence in some imaginary world free of pain and sickness and grief and taxes. Within a few years of first appearing in Rome itself, they were threatening the empire, diverting people away from the state temples and religions and undermining the traditions and ancient customs and colleges and cults that had built Rome into what it is today.

"That's what prompted Diocletian to try to bring them to heel—he was trying to protect Roman traditions and customs, and he thought he could do it by shutting down Christian houses of worship and forbidding them to worship any but the ancient Roman gods. Well, he couldn't. It was Galerius, though, who decided to stamp them out of existence. And *he* couldn't do *that*, either. They had to lift the suppression orders eventually, but they hadn't even come close to solving the problem.

"By the time Constantine came along, the Christians were the biggest headache the empire had, and everyone was more than happy to leave him to deal with it. He had made himself sole Emperor, they said, so they accorded him full responsibility for what happened during his reign."

"But Constantine was already well disposed towards the Christians, was he not?" Varrus felt vaguely uncomfortable with all he was being told here, and felt a need to defend the Emperor, though from what, he could not have said. "Wasn't his mother a Christian?"

"Helena?" Cato's grin was wolfish. "That depends on who you're talking to. She was a tavern whore, some say, when his father took up with her."

Varrus winced. "I hadn't heard that. But what I did hear—along with everyone else—was that the Christian god gave Constantine a sign before the battle at the Milvian Bridge that won him his crown as Augustus—the labarum symbol. He became a Christian right after that."

Cato grinned again, his expression sardonic. "Aye," he said softly. "But before your bubbling zeal makes you foam at the mouth, remember that Constantine had been a politician for long years before that. He's the son of Constantius Chlorus, one of the most successful politicians of our times, Caesar in the west for seven years, then Augustus after that until his death. No one achieves that kind of success without great intellect and great abilities, and his son studied his methods and techniques throughout his life.

"A wise man should never lose sight of the fact that in government of any kind, nothing is more important than politics. Politics and perceptions, my old commander in the brotherhood used to say, are the legs on which a ruler stands or falls. Perceptions, properly manipulated, instruct the people how to believe and what to think. Politics, properly executed, convinces them how to behave. And in both instances, direct interventions by the gods on behalf of a chosen one have an astounding amount of potency when it comes to swaying the common herd.

"Did you know, incidentally, that years before his miraculous experience with the Christian god, Constantine had had an equally famous visitation from Apollo, as god of the sun? It's true—depending, again, who you talk to. Apollo appeared to young Constantine in a dream and awarded him laurel wreaths with promises of great health and a long reign as Emperor, and Constantine wasted no time letting the entire world know of his divine blessings."

Varrus was looking at him strangely, and now he said, "You're sounding very cynical about our Emperor, Cato. Should I believe you or not? Or are you simply testing me? All I really know is that Constantine granted the Christians official status as soon as he was crowned. That sounds to me as though he had been predisposed to treat them well, long before he took the crown."

Cato grunted, then dipped his head in wry acknowledgment. "Aye, well, perhaps he was. Who knows what emperors think about when no one else is around? One thing is certain, though, and you should bear it in mind at all times when you are talking about our beloved Emperor. Constantine is a politician before all else. He never stops scheming, never stops weighing and assessing all the possibilities ahead of him. And he's good at it. According to the best brains in our brotherhood, there has been no one like him since Marcus Aurelius, and he died nigh on a hundred and a half years ago. So our Constantine is a clever lad. You can rely on that. The Christian problem landed in his lap as soon as he began to think about becoming our Augustus, which was probably around the time of his tenth birthday, and he hasn't spent a moment since then without thinking deeply on what to do about it."

"Problem? What Christian problem?"

"The problem caused by their existence! They're revolutionaries, Quintus. Everything they stand for opposes the Roman way of doing things. Their poisonous doctrine, taught to them by priests who call themselves bishops, is one of love and tolerance, forgiveness and compassion. They deal in hope, and in the belief that there is another, better world beyond this one. Suffer here, they say, to win eternal happiness in the next life. And that is truly revolutionary in a way that we hard-headed Romans cannot counter. There has never been a religion like this before now, and how is any government supposed to deal with it? Short of killing them all for simply being simple and loving their enemies, how does one punish them for being so different? You can't fine them or con-fiscate their goods, for they have nothing. You can't threaten them with death, because they'll welcome it. And you can't flog them because they exult in pain and suffering, in preparation for the next, eternal life. Do you understand?"

"I do."

"And do you still maintain you can't understand what 'problem' I am talking about?"

"No, I'm starting to appreciate it. So how does Constantine intend to resolve the matter?"

"By being a politician. He is relying heavily upon the fact that they are men, and therefore human."

"I assume you mean the priests, these bishops?"

"Correct."

"And what will their humanity provide to him, as Emperor?"

"Opportunity. He recognized their religion . . . when?" He paused, brows wrinkled. "Five years ago, it was. The year after he assumed supreme command. And since then he has been working—working very hard—on winning them over to his way of seeing the world. And until the day of his death, Marcus Varrus was his closest associate in that task. Your father was Constantine's field commander in the cam-paign against the Christians."

"So it's a war? I see. And how did that work?"

"Slowly and steadily, predicated upon the time-worn old truth that every man has a price at which he can be bought." He pursed his lips, eyeing the younger man. "Have you ever met a Christian bishop? No? Trust me, you would remember if you had. Your nostrils would not allow you to forget. Their notions of hygiene are . . . different. Anyway, each bishop has a territory for which he is responsible, and the most senior of them meet in a high council, guided by an elected president they call the Papa—the Father—and it dictates the policies governing their religion, policies that are constantly becoming more and more elaborate. But the most important thing the council is called upon to do is to elect a new Papa from among themselves whenever the ruling one dies.

"When Constantine first summoned this council to meet with him in person, they were all overawed. I know that because an old friend of mine was officer of the day that day and told me about it. He remembered how cowed they all were by where they were. And who wouldn't be cowed, to be summoned in person to attend upon the Emperor and talk to him about your life?

"So they met with the Emperor in all his glory, and they listened, spellbound, as he told them about his desires not only to recognize their religion personally, but to promote their divine inspiration and work together with them to spread their message. He's very good at that kind of thing.

"And of course he also told them about the difficulties he was having with the College of Pontiffs—the assembly of priests of the old religion that would like to see the Christians condemned as enemies of the state. These were impressive enemies, he pointed out, the proponents and followers of the gods and goddesses of the ancient Roman pantheon. The Pontifex Maximus, supreme priest of all of Rome's religions. The Flamen Dialis, high priest of the Temple of Jupiter. The Flamen Martialis, high priest of Mars. And of course the Vestal Virgins, the ancient, most sacred priestesses of Vesta, the goddess of the hearth and of the Roman ethos. He was attempting to deal with them, he told the Christians, but he was facing down more than fifteen hundred years of tradition and entrenched beliefs and rituals, and it was an enormous, time-consuming task. So while he was attending to that, he told the bishops, he would provide a personal envoy to act as interlocutor between himself and them, and he introduced them to your father."

He paused again, to empty his cup and set it down on the floor by his feet, then continued in a different tone of voice. "Now here's the interesting thing about that—and again, I heard about it from my friend who was officer of the day. He said he had never seen your father looking more splendid. What he actually said was, 'You should have seen Marcus Varrus that day, all dressed in golden clothes. But they were Constantine's clothes, and Constantine himself was wearing even richer ones—colours and clothing I had never seen before.' What d'you think of that?"

"I don't know what to think," Varrus answered slowly. "It makes no sense at all. My father was wearing the Emperor's clothing? I can't believe that."

"Believe it. He was, and it was deliberate. Those bishops looked and felt like starving crows in the imperial palace, barefoot and dressed in black rags tied up with rope belts. It was all part of Constantine's plan."

"His plan to do what?"

"To seduce them all . . . the Christian bishops. That first meeting was only the opening gambit in a long campaign that lasted for years, and your father was the manager, if you like—the spectacle director, the arranger—for as long as he lived. His main task, in the beginning, was to make those men aware of the splendour of everything surrounding them when they visited the Emperor, and of their own shabbiness. But it was subtle. He never shamed them, never belittled them. He simply showed them, constantly and with great care and attention to detail, how civilized imperial officials lived and dressed and functioned. Much later, once they had been lulled into the proper state of mind, he pointed out, gently, that the Emperor himself was being ridiculed for 'consorting with crows'—not that the Emperor really minded, he said, but it might be taken as a mark of great respect if, in return for the understanding and imperial courtesy being extended to them, the bishops themselves were to dress—at least for their sessions with the imperial dignitaries and the Emperor himself—in a style more befitting the palatial surroundings. Merely a selection of more courtly vestments just for those special occasions. If they so wished, a team of imperial tailors could be placed at their disposal to help them with such things. And by the end of three years, the bishops were attending their council meetings dressed in imperial finery, and enjoying it."

"So . . . what happened then?"

Cato shrugged. "Nothing. After each meeting, they had to return to their individual homes and conduct the rest of their work in their ordinary conditions. They were achieving miraculous amounts of work when meeting with the imperial officials in brightly lit surroundings with access to all the services they might ever need. But the contrast between that and what they were able to achieve at other times, when they had to work in their own, widely separated quarters far from the palace, grew steadily more noticeable."

"Until . . . ?" Varrus was leaning forward, one elbow resting on his thigh. "You're leading me on, aren't you? You have to be . . . This is a tomfoolery of some kind, because I can sense something coming, but I can't quite see what it is."

"Until . . ." Cato repeated solemnly. "One day, in a casual conversation with some of the assembled bishops, your father mentioned that he had overheard some of them talking about the difficulties the council was facing whenever it had to deal with matters outside the palace—difficulties with procedures that ought to be straightforward but were complicated by the inconveniences of having to communicate in primitive ways and over long distances. Of course he commiserated with them.

"When he met with them next time, he told them he had mentioned their dilemma to the Emperor, and Constantine himself had come up with a possible solution that might work to everyone's advantage. There was an imperial palace sitting empty in the city, the Emperor had said, and he could think of no better use for it than in the service of the

Christian God. Formerly known as the Domus Faustae, or the house of Fausta, his second wife, he had rebuilt it and renamed it the Lateran Palace, after its original owners, the Laterani family. He would be more than glad, he said, to lend it nominally, as a centre of church activity, to the senior bishop on the council, the Bishop of Rome. It was an official imperial palace, so the costs of maintenance would be entirely covered by the imperial treasury, and the crowning advantage would be that everything to do with church business could be conducted there, in one central place that was convenient and accessible to everyone. It was a wonderful idea, everyone agreed, and divinely inspired. The Lateran Palace became the official residence of the bishop of Rome nearly five years ago."

"I don't believe you!"

"Oh, you can believe it, because it is now a minor, almost insignificant point. Far more important than that is the reality that the Emperor himself is now a Christian bishop! The College of Pontiffs, the priests of the old religion, has been rendered voiceless. Who now is going to dare cry out for persecution or condemnation or discrimination against Christians anywhere?"

Cato picked up his empty cup and peered into it, but Varrus was already standing up.

"But . . . but that's . . ."

"What? Pathetic? Monstrous? Unbelievable, astounding, unacceptable? It's brilliant, Quintus, that's what it is! Politically brilliant. Perhaps the greatest reversal of its kind in history, and all of it due to the political astuteness of one man. One man, Quintus, who single-handedly drew the fangs of the most dangerous revolutionary movement ever to threaten the empire."

"No! How can you say that? The Christians are still out there, increasing in numbers every day."

"Aye, but their leadership has joined the empire! Their bishops are now courtly figures. Think about what that means, man. The ragged, ill-fed, leaderless rabble still turn the other cheek and preach tolerance and love, but the world can live with that. And their own leaders will hold them in restraint, now that they themselves are eating well and regularly, every day their God permits them to remain alive. And trust me, their voices will grow steadily less and less strident in demanding revolution as they grow more accustomed to luxury and wealth. And so the voices of dissent within the empire have been choked." He glanced down at his empty cup again and said quietly, almost musingly, "I think we're done here, though if I had more wine I'd drink to Constantine and his genius."

"No, we're not quite done, not yet."

Cato frowned. "What more is there to say? Have you something to tell me more impressive than what I have just finished telling you?"

"No, I don't, but I still have some unanswered questions. One main one, anyway."

"Fine, then. But not another word until I have a fresh drink in my hand."

FORTY-ONE

"Thirsty business this talking, isn't it?" Cato raised his cup in solemn salute and drank slowly. "Fortunate that you insisted on adding the water at the outset, my friend, and even so, I can feel the wine. It's very good. So, what's your question?"

"The obvious one, I think," said Varrus. "Who was responsible for killing my family?"

"I told you already."

"No, Cato, you did not. You told me your suspicions, but you never came out and said who you thought was behind the plot. Who was it?"

"We don't know, Quintus. And I did tell you that already. We never could find out who gave the orders for the killing. But it was one of the college guilds. That much we were sure of. We simply couldn't take it any further. All the doors leading out from that conclusion were closed and barred."

"The college guilds. You mean the College of Pontiffs? The priests of the old Roman religions?"

"Collectively, yes. When I asked you who else might benefit from the breakdown of your father's negotiations, you immediately said that it must be whoever stood to lose most if they were successfully concluded. Well, the College of Pontiffs stood to lose everything. That is no exaggeration. Their entire world was being threatened—their pantheon of gods and all the structures and embellishments that sustained it. If this upstart Christian sect acquired the validity and respectability it appeared to be winning, then their religions, all of them, would be declared *in*valid—their very lives would be destroyed, their worshippers would disappear, and they themselves would eventually be reduced to destitution."

He paused, squinting at Varrus, gauging his reaction. "I know that sounds dramatic, but think about it from the point of view of those priests and priestesses. Your father was negotiating with the Christians, to install them in the Lateran Palace and to have them accept the Emperor into the upper levels of governance of their church. The Emperor of Rome was considering becoming a ruler of a church that denied the ancient Roman gods that keep them fed and clothed."

"It's not the gods that keep them fed and clothed," Varrus said.

"Precisely. It isn't. That's exactly the point I want you to understand. It's the *worshippers* of the gods, the sacrifices they offer up and the donations they make, that keep priests fed and clothed. If you take away the ancient gods and abolish their worship, you disinherit legions of priests. *Legions* of them. Have you any idea how many priests are in Rome alone, how many are members of the College of Pontiffs?" He didn't wait for an answer. "There are thousands. Thousands, all dependent upon the existence of their particular gods, whether they be called Diana, Vulcan, Jupiter, Mars, or Venus, or even Baal, Aten, Ra, or Ptah. There is no shortage of gods, Quintus. Every people has a surfeit of them, and every one of them has priests or priestesses. But your father was negotiating to put an end to all of them."

"That seems a bit harsh," Varrus said, diffident in spite of what he had just heard. "They can't all be bad."

"I'm not saying they're bad. All I am saying is they're *there*, and they're *always* there, and they have always *been* there, since the beginning of time, being clad and fed by worshippers." He raised a hand dramatically, one finger pointing upwards. "Believe me, on the very first day that the very first man made the very first sacrifice to the very first god, the very first priest stepped out from behind a bush and said, 'The god can't be here to thank you for your offering in person, but he has appointed me to collect it from you on his behalf.'"

Cato nodded. "It was one of them, one of the colleges, believe me— but as for which one, your guess is as good as anyone else's."

"You mean . . . Are you saying that my family was destroyed by a college of Roman *priests*? You don't really believe that, do you?"

The slightest hint of a scowl marred Cato's forehead for an instant. "I said so, did I not? It might have been the Jupiter crew, the Flamen Dialis's gang, but it might just as easily have been the Mars worshippers. For that matter it might even have been the Vestals. You know what they say about vengeful women, and I doubt that Vestal Virgins are any different from their more carnal sisters." He shrugged. "Left to my own devices, I'd vote for the Vestals as the motivating force behind the entire debacle, but that's no more than my personal prejudices making themselves felt. I can't be sure, one way or the other. But to answer your question, yes, I really do believe that."

"No," Varrus said, shaking his head. "It's not that I disbelieve you, Marcus. But I'm having difficulty believing that a guild of priests would even think of such a thing, let alone organize it, hire a killer, and pay for the murders. It seems inconceivable to—" He stopped. "You think I'm being stupid," he said quietly. "I can see it in your face."

"No, Quintus, you are not being stupid," Cato said in a surprisingly gentle voice. "I can think of several other words that you might use to describe what you are. Young would be apt, and so would naive, and unworldly, and innocent in its true sense. You have not yet lived long enough to know what cynicism is or what starts it growing in men's hearts, and that ignorance is a wonderful thing that you should cherish. Or let Lydia cherish it, for I'm sure she knows it's there inside you."

He smiled and drank a little more. "In a way it's encouraging, even refreshing, that you should believe priests are incapable of murder, but it's not true. Priests and priestesses are men and women, Quintus. Human in all respects, which means they are as venal as anyone else. And I know people who will swear them to be worse."

"But how could they murder an innocent family? What could justify that?"

"Nothing could. But they were beyond justifications. They were looking to their own interests—to money and to power, and to their own survival."

His eyes narrowed as he gazed at the young smith. "You have your truth, Quintus, so accept it. Your family, through your father, fell afoul of a determined and desperate group of people with an enormous amount to lose if Marcus Varrus succeeded in what he set out to do. Unfortunately, because they were desperate and blinded by their own ambitions and beliefs, they failed to see that their enemy was not Marcus Varrus. He was no more than an intermediary, a man who was handling dangerous negotiations. Their principal antagonist was the Emperor—a possibility that must have been unutterably alien to them—and his motivations were purely political. The negotiations they were trying so desperately to annul were being fuelled and driven by Constantine himself.

"I'm not suggesting that Constantine bears any responsibility for the murder of your family, though. That's simply not true. He was doing what he had to do, as Emperor, and your father was doing what he had to do in turn, as a loyal servitor. The tragedy was that the aggrieved party sought to hire outside sources to resolve their difficulties for them, and they happened to find the most venal, lethal people available— Vassos Seneca and Appius Endor. Endor was the means to the end, the weapon that achieved their aims for them, but it was Vassos Seneca who provided all the impetus that made the murders possible. His was the power that brought the end about. He saw the profit to be made and he set out in cold blood to grasp it. He contracted and supplied the manpower, in the person of his most accomplished killer, Appius Endor, and he brokered and managed the entire operation, uncaring who died in the doing of it. And so your father perished, along with his family, for doing no more than his duty . . . I know that is difficult for you to accept. No man would find it easy. But your answer is there, nonetheless. Vassos Seneca was the malignant entity that made it all possible and deliberately brought it about. And though it might be small consolation, he failed, overall, because most of what your father was working to achieve has come to pass in the years since his death.

"In his own way, Marcus Varrus was as admirable as his father had been. Like Titanius, he helped his Emperor subdue a massive threat to the empire—perhaps the most dangerous and revolutionary threat it had ever encountered—converting it to a force that will eventually embrace and enhance all of Rome. That is an admirable legacy to have inherited. I envy you."

Varrus grunted, deep in his chest. "So be it," he said. "Wait here. I'll be right back."

When he returned, he was carrying a long tube of thick, highly polished bull's hide. "Here," he said, tossing it to Cato. "I hope it's as helpful as you think it might be."

Slowly, almost reverentially, Cato undid the fastenings on one end of the device and slid the tightly rolled scroll of the labarum out into his cupped hand. He set the tube aside then, and with great caution compressed the scroll in his hand and slid the ivory retaining ring off the end, placing it beside the carrying tube. Then, moving with excruciating slowness, he removed the protective linen sleeve and gently unrolled the parchment itself. It was magnificent, the colours vibrant and rich, the execution of the imperial crest impeccable. He held it out at arm's length, simply staring at it for a long time, then brought it closer to his eyes and read the one-line inscription aloud.

"This man acts in my name. Constantinus Augustus." He shivered involuntarily and looked at Varrus. "You are giving it to me, really?"

"It's yours. What will you do now?"

Cato looked back down at the scroll in his hand, his eyes returning to the single line of script along the bottom, and then, carefully, he released the tension, allowing the cylinder to close itself again for as far as it could. He tightened it with both hands before sliding it back into its linen envelope and securing it with the ivory ring.

"I'm going to show it to a fat slug," he said.

"When?"

"At the first opportunity I have." Cato's voice was distant. He straightened his shoulders and reached for the leather carrying case. "But I don't think I will dine with you tonight, Quintus. Too much to do, and too little time to do it. What hour of day is it?" He crossed to the door and looked outside. "It's barely mid-afternoon. There's six or seven hours of daylight left. I can be halfway to Londinium by this time tomorrow."

"Is that where you expect to find Vassos Seneca?"

"I've no idea where I'll find him, but Londinium's the place I'll start. The answers to where he's to be found are all there. All I have to do is ask the right questions, then pay attention to what people tell me. I do know, though, that I will find the whoreson, and when I do, the Ring will finally crumble."

"Then I still don't understand something. You would do that anyway, even had I destroyed the labarum as you thought I might have. So why do you need it now? You said you need it to enable you to get close to Seneca, but it doesn't sound to me as though you do. So why do you need it? . . . What are you smiling at?"

"At your short memory, my friend," Cato said. "Godlike powers, we said, in talking of this thing, remember? He who possesses the labarum possesses godly powers. And that's what I need it for. I want to stand over that obscene slug as he lies dying, holding up a parchment in my hand that says to all the world that I have done this with the full knowledge and the complete support of the Emperor of Rome. And after that, having avenged my friends, my brotherhood, my family—and yours—I want to walk away, my passage uncontested, my health unthreatened, and my vengeance-wearied bones alive and well."

He stepped forward suddenly, unexpectedly, and embraced Varrus closely, holding him tightly for a space of heartbeats before stepping back. "Thank you, my friend," he said. "*Benigne*, for your hospitality, your loyalty, and your friendship. I know not if we'll ever meet again, but you will travel with me in my heart from this day on. Be happy, give my best wishes to your wife, and live a long and satisfying life. And say goodbye to those army idiots for me. Farewell."

And suddenly he was gone, and Varrus was staring at the door that had not quite swung shut behind him. There should have been much more to say, he thought, and yet he felt, somehow, complete. He sighed, then collected the empty jug and the two cups they had used, and made his way back through the rear of the smithy and into the house.

EPILOGUE

A.D. 322

"That be a fine-looking barrel, but be there summat wrong wi' it?"

The rich, broad-vowelled voice came from behind him, and Varrus smiled, knowing who was there. "No, Master Yarrow, there's nothing wrong with it. It is an excellent barrel, sound and well made. Why would you think otherwise?"

The man called Yarrow, who was barrel-shaped himself, his massive belly swathed in a heavy leather apron that was crested with brick dust and dried mortar, shook his head. "I dunno," he said. "But ever' mornin', when I gets 'ere, I sees you standin' starin' at it like you was waitin' for it to split apart."

Varrus laughed aloud, realizing he had not even known he had formed a new habit. "No, but it is a very special barrel. You'll notice it sits up high off the ground, on the frame that was made for it. That allows me to check its bottom, every day, for signs of leakage. It has been there for a full year and I now believe it will never leak." He saw the uncomprehending look in the workman's eyes and laughed again. "My wife's brother made it, Master Yarrow. The first one ever to be made in his new manufactory, last year. I still have difficulty in believing it's a reality, but after a year of waiting, I have no choice left but to believe it is. How is my oven progressing?"

"Oh, we've no s'prises there. 'Er'll be done on time, well afore winter."

"Excellent. Then walk with me and show me what you have achieved till now."

The oven site was at the rear of the smithy, taking up most of a large enclosure Varrus had bought several months earlier to house it. The location had been ideal, abutting his property, the premises formerly owned by a furniture maker and sold after his death, and because of the merchant's need to keep his stocked wood dry and well aired, the buildings on the property were all solidly built and well ventilated. It had taken no more than three days to demolish part of the high wall between the two yards and install a strong, securely mounted connecting gate. The oven being built in the yard there now was modelled closely on the one Ajax had built years earlier for the armouries, but it was larger in all respects: wider, stronger, and six feet taller, creating a much longer chimney for the molten metal to fall down through the ashes of the furnace fuel to the collection tray in the base.

Hanno, Ajax, and Varrus himself, were all convinced after extensive study that, setting aside the truth that none of them remotely understood how it was achieved, one of the key elements in their production of harder, more malleable steel involved the distance that the melting ore fell between the smelting platform at the top of the furnace and the collection pan at the base. Varrus believed that the large amount of wood and charcoal ashes in the falling zone—the name he gave to the long chimney in the oven's interior—contributed somehow to the mutation of the molten ore, but he had no basis for that, other than intuition, and Ajax and Hanno merely clucked their tongues and looked at each other pityingly whenever he mentioned it.

Now Varrus walked quietly behind the master builder, as the man explained what was being done in the construction and showed him how the concrete elements of the furnace walls reinforced and enhanced the firebrick-lined interior of the kiln, enabling greater pressure to be built up in the bellows chamber in order to raise the temperature in the combustion chamber. It was all highly technical, but Varrus knew enough about ovens and kilns by then to be able to make sense of most of what he was told, and he nodded in satisfaction when he had seen everything, clapping the builder on the shoulder and leaving him and his men to their work. He made his way directly back into the yard behind the smithy proper then, where he smiled at the sound of a voice and braced himself as the small, sturdy boy ran directly at him, head lowered.

"Dada!" Thirty pounds of compact, bustling, three-year-old muscle hit him at knee level, his weakest point, and tried, almost successfully, to bowl him over, but he whooped and swooped, bracing his malformed leg with the ease of long years of practice as he caught the child's solid little body beneath the shoulders and whipped him up into the air, tossing and spinning him to catch him at the top of his flight and bring him down to sit on his shoulder, where he anchored him by clutching both chubby ankles in one hand, then let him fall again, secure in his father's firm grasp, to hang upside down less than a foot above the ground, shrieking and gurgling with delight. Grinning widely at Lydia, who was approaching him from the house, he bent his arm and lifted the boy higher, then swung him to where he could catch his upper body with his other hand, and held him out horizontally towards his mother.

"Is this yours, woman?"

Unimpressed, she approached until she was close enough to reach up and pull his head down to where she could kiss him, and he made no move to lower the boy to the ground until their kiss was finished. He set the child down then, holding him against his knee with a hand on his shoulder while he looked his wife up and down, missing no detail of her dress or appearance.

"You look very elegant, my lady. Are you going out?"

She batted her long lashes at him. "I am," she purred. "Can you guess who I am going to meet?"

"I could name half the men in Colcaster, my love, but I would likely be wrong, so surprise me. Who *are* you going to meet?"

"Eylin, of course. Who else is there?"

Eylin was finally with child and suffering daily because of it, and Lydia, who had carried young Marcus to term three years earlier without a single day of sickness or distress, found it hard to imagine what her brother's wife was going through.

Now Varrus cocked his head and squinted at her, looking into her eyes curiously as he stirred his fingers in his son's long, soft hair. "Are you feeling well?"

"Of course I am," she said. "Why would you ask me that?"

He half-shrugged. "Merely curious." He dropped his eyes to his son's head. "Are you taking this fellow with you?"

"I think so. You have things to do this morning."

"I do indeed. I have nails to make. That must be the most boring chore a smith can have, other than making bronze rings for armoured shirts." He sighed, looking sorry for himself. "Nail-making is a task sadly lacking in variety, my love." He grinned, the quick, mischievous flash of eyes and teeth that she loved. "But at least it stops people from wondering where we find enough money to feed ourselves. So that's what I'll be doing while you console poor Eylin. Give me a kiss now and stop distracting me."

He kissed her lingeringly, then crouched and turned his son towards him, holding him by the shoulders. "And you, young Varrus. Look after your mother while she's away from home. Guard her well, out there in the savage world, and bring her home safely to me. Will you do that?"

The boy nodded, wide-eyed, his adoration of his father shining on his face as he gazed up at him.

"Wonderful! Be off, then, the pair of you!" He watched them cross the yard and disappear, and then he went inside the smithy.

Equus, now a hulking, good-natured, and quick-witted young giant close to sixteen, had the furnace prepared perfectly and all the nail-making materials laid out to hand. They chatted amiably for a few moments, more like father and son than master and apprentice, and then, by mutual consent, they buckled down to the tedious task of cutting and shaping nails from thinly hammered sheets of metal, and quickly became lost in the repetitive monotony of endless duplication.

Sometime towards the middle of the day Varrus called a halt and they went into the body of the house to eat the lunch that Lydia had left for them in the scullery—two finger-thick slices of cold roasted pork from a young shoat that Varrus had taken in payment for a job of work, sprinkled with salt and laid between slabs of freshly baked bread, washed down with wine that was heavily diluted by cold water from the house's deep well. And as they were finishing, preparing to go back to work, Ajax walked in.

Surprised and happy to see his friend, who had been off on military business in Londinium for almost an entire month, Varrus immediately offered him a cup of wine, but Ajax waved the offer aside as young Equus let himself out discreetly, leaving the two men alone together.

"I'm on my way to meet with Damian Marcellus. I'm late as it is, but I wanted to tell you I ran into Leon and the Twins down there in Londuin, and they'll be back here soon—probably within the month— because Britannicus asked for them to be posted back to his command. So that's good news and I thought you might be glad to hear it. I know I was."

"I am. *Benigne*, for telling me. I've missed all you people recently. The town seems empty without your ugly faces darkening every corner. But when did you start calling Londinium *Londuin*?"

"While I was there this time. That's what everyone's calling it now."

"Hmm. I wonder how the high command will warm to that. And what about Cato? Any word of him?"

Ajax's face fell and he shook his head, mute. No one had heard a word from or about Cato since he had left, four years earlier. They had put out the word among their many contacts and acquaintances to keep eyes and ears open for any mention of a Marcus Licinius Cato, or a Rufus Cato or even a Rufus, but the silence had been profound. They had tried to cheer themselves up by reflecting that no news is usually good news

and that ill news travels fast, but the total lack of information surrounding Cato's disappearance had upset them all more than any of them
would ever admit, and over the course of the progressing months and
years they had gradually stopped talking about him altogether.

"Idiot probably got himself killed," Ajax blurted suddenly. "Whole
damned world is full of worthless fools, and he was one of the few
worthwhile ones. But he got himself killed anyway, no doubt trying to
do something stupid and noble—honourable. Shit!" He straightened up
to his full height, blinking eyes that had suddenly teared over, and Varrus
felt something move deep within himself. "Shit!" he barked again. "I
have to go."

"Hang on," Varrus said. "I'll come out with you. I'm finished here."
He set his cup aside, by the stone kitchen sink, then walked back into
the smithy side by side with Ajax, who stopped by the forge and looked
all around him.

"This place is really yours now, isn't it? Can't see a single trace of old
Liam left in here. It's all Quintus Varrus, which is as it should be. I'll see
you later, when I'm done with Marcellus." He started to turn away, then
stopped and reached into the scrip hanging from his belt. "I nearly
forgot. I bought you a gift in Londuin." He flicked his hand and Varrus
had to move quickly to catch the flying object thrown at him. He held
it up, looking at it quizzically. It was a narrow, heavy, hexagonal steel
cylinder the width of his ring finger, with one end tapered to a narrow
point. It looked almost like a chisel, but was too small to be a useful tool.

"What is it?"

"What does it look like? It's a stamp. Here." He reached down and
unsheathed the Hispanic sword hanging by his left side. "I knew you didn't
own one yet, and my damn blade's unfinished, so you can fix it now."

He laid the blade flat on the anvil, and as soon as he saw the sword
bared, Varrus recognized it for one of his own. Only then did he realize
what Ajax had given him. He raised the cylinder again, bringing it close
to his eyes this time, and looked at the tapered point, seeing the tooled

"V" on the end of it. "V" for Varrus, the mark he would stamp from that time on into every blade he made. He felt his throat close up, and would have been at a loss for words had Ajax not growled, "Come on, Quintus, I told you I'm late. Stamp your mark on the damned blade and let me get out of here." And Quintus Varrus, vainly trying to blink away the tears that flooded his eyes, bent over his anvil and with great precision, placing the tool in the exact centre of the blade directly below the boss of the hilt, stamped his first "V" into a blade he had made with his own hands.

"*Benigne*," Ajax said. "This one has a place on my wall. I'll come back later, once I'm free." He started to turn away and stopped yet again. "What's that?" he asked.

Varrus knew what he had seen and picked it up, holding it out to Ajax. "Another old sword, the latest from Dominic," he said. "It came in the last shipment of ingots while you were away. It's Cretan, I think. That's what it's supposed to be anyway, according to the fellow Dominic bought it from."

It was a sword, of sorts, with a heavy, leaf-styled blade that was obviously ancient, and a long tang that showed no signs of ever having anchored a hilt.

"Ugly old thing, isn't it?" Ajax said, peering closely at its rust-pitted blade. "Not pretty enough to hang on my wall, anyway." His mouth flickered in the beginnings of a smile and he laid the old sword down gently. "You must be getting quite a collection by now, with that collection of Liam's you bought and all the old junk Dom sends you, and the other stuff you buy yourself."

"I am," Varrus said. "When you come back I'll show you the notes I keep on every item as I acquire it, some detailed, others sketchy and mostly guesswork. But you'd better run. Tribunes don't enjoy being kept waiting."

"Right. I'm gone."

Equus returned as soon as Ajax had left, and without another word the two smiths went back to work, hammering and filing and tapping, shaping nails and counting them painstakingly into small wooden boxes, allocating one, two, or three score each to differently sized boxes.

Some time after Ajax's departure—it might have been an hour, possibly even two—Varrus looked up again, distracted by a movement at the edge of his vision. He half-expected it to be Ajax, and so he was surprised to see not one but two men in the doorway of the smithy, silhouetted against the afternoon brightness at their backs. He was even more surprised to see the tall, ornately crested helmet worn by the taller of the two men, and at first he thought it must be the adjutant, Damian Marcellus. As soon as he began to move towards the newcomers, though, he saw that the taller man was the legate Gaius Cornelius Britannicus, the garrison commander.

Setting down his hammer and signalling to Equus to make himself scarce, he moved quickly to greet the elegant, black-clad cavalryman, wiping his hands on a rag as he went.

"Legate Britannicus," he said cordially. "Be welcome, and forgive the way you find me. I was not expecting company."

Britannicus smiled gently and turned to his companion with a wave of his hand, at which the fellow snapped to attention, spun on his heel, and marched smartly away, presumably to mount guard at the smithy door. Varrus watched him go, then glanced at his visitor. "Impressive," he murmured, not quite smiling. "Smart, crisp, efficient. I hope he doesn't try to keep my wife out if she comes home while he's there."

Britannicus laughed and reached up to unfasten the clasp beneath his chin. "May I?" He removed the elaborate headpiece and scrubbed at his bared scalp like every other man who had ever worn a helmet. "These things are brutally heavy."

"Of course they are," Varrus said. "They have to be. Set it on the bench there, if you like. As I was saying, it's gritty, but I was not expecting company."

"Nor should you be apologizing. You are a working man practising his occupation. It's only in the army that we seek to make a virtue out of cleanliness while working, and it is seldom effective. Forgive my unexpected arrival, but I was passing by and remembered the first time we met—or was it the second time? It was your wedding day, anyway. Four years ago, is that correct?"

"It is." He hesitated, then asked, "Could I offer you a cup of watered wine?"

The legate smiled. "*Benigne*," he said. "I would enjoy that."

"Excellent, then come into the house, if you will, and I'll pour us some."

As Varrus busied himself preparing drinks, Britannicus said, "We returned yesterday from Londinium, as you probably already know. It's difficult to disguise such comings and goings in a military town, and I know Ignatius Ajax is a friend of yours, as was his former colleague Marcus Licinius Cato."

He said no more, but he watched the deliberate manner in which the smith picked up the cups of wine and carried them to the table where he sat. He took the cup that Varrus proffered and nodded graciously, then sipped the wine appreciatively and set it down. "Delicious," he said. "Rhenish? Definitely Germanic? I thought so." He sat silent for a space of heartbeats, before saying, "I acquired some information in Londinium that I think might be of interest to you, Magister Varrus."

He spoke quietly, articulating his words slowly and precisely. "It was . . . unusual information, and it came to me through channels best described as unofficial, and I must underline the fanciful, even conjectural nature of what was nevertheless relayed to me as unassailable truth. And those muddy waters are roiled even further by the fact that, when my informant attempted to verify the information, he—they—met with no success. None at all. They found no evidence to attest to the accuracy of the information, or even to its authenticity."

He sipped at his wine again, somehow managing to convey an air of assertive, competent fastidiousness in the mere act of drinking. Varrus, meanwhile, sat watching him narrow-lidded. He had no slightest idea of what to expect from this man.

"Are you by chance familiar with what is said to be happening on the Hellespont?"

The question snapped Varrus into full, wary attentiveness. "Byzantium, you mean?" He waited for confirmation, then nodded. "Yes, I've heard about the Emperor's plans for it. He has decided that it would be far better and more appropriate as the seat of the imperial government than Rome. It dominates the central hub of the world's trading routes. The town is to be rebuilt as a city and renamed Constantinopolis, and they have been working on the rebuilding and refurbishing for several years already, with a view to declaring it a new and open city in a few years' time."

Britannicus grunted appreciatively. "Well done, Magister Varrus. Forgive me, but I must admit I had not expected you to know so much about the topic. Knowing you are that well informed, I can continue with my tale unobstructed.

"Some time ago, according to my sources, in an isolated region of southeastern Gaul, in the province of Narbonensis and within three days' ride of the port of Massilia, the word began to spread, no more than a few years ago, of an unnamed but evil and malignant presence that appeared to have sprung up and was flourishing in one specific but uncharted area. Large numbers of people were disappearing, never to be seen or heard from again, and dreadful rites and rituals were allegedly being conducted on heavily guarded private lands in vast, wealthy estates amid great secrecy. Of course, nothing about any of those rumours could be proved, rumours being what they are, and no living person came forward with complaints or concerns specific enough to trigger an official investigation, and so the matter never came, officially, to anyone's attention. Eventually it lapsed into oblivion and was discussed no further, officially, though the rumours persisted. Eventually, too, after several years of nothing having happened, what little fuss there had been earlier died away completely. Until a new uproar broke out."

He sipped again at his wine. "Now here is where this grows most interesting, because it is at this point that the conjectural element comes into prominence. The commander of the garrison in Massilia, whose name was Talus, received a written communication, hand-delivered to his quarters by a military courier whom no one could identify afterwards." He paused. "Think about that, Magister Varrus. A military courier who had no military identity. No recognizable distinctions on his uniform, no recognizable or memorable insignia, no unit badges or identifiable regalia. Nothing. He was a soldier, yet a cypher—armoured, equipped, mounted, and invisible. He vanished as soon as he had delivered his dispatch, which of course no one noticed, until the legate sent for him afterwards to question him.

"The letter this man delivered caused quite a stir. It was addressed to Legate Talus in Massilia, by name, and it alleged that a notorious enemy of the state was about to be slain on his private estate, a three-day ride from Massilia. It listed detailed instructions on how to find the place. It also warned that the estate lands housed a private, disciplined army of six hundred mercenaries—a full, legionary cohort—superbly equipped and trained, and sworn to destroy anyone who sought to trespass on the estate. It also spoke of mass graves on the estate grounds, and extensive prison buildings with elaborate torture chambers attached. All in all, a document designed effectively to penetrate the shell of lethargy that had previously prevented much reaction to the earlier reports of strange goings-on in those parts.

"Talus, as was his duty, summoned reinforcements from all his auxiliary camps and outposts in the Massilia region, and marched with a full thousand-strong cohort to investigate."

Varrus was sitting wide-eyed, scarcely believing what he was hearing. "Did they find the place?"

"They did. And they engaged the mercenaries and defeated them. That is the only part of the report that is verifiable, but even that has been obscured, altered somehow to a report of an armed excursion against a strong party of seaborne raiders who had landed nearby. Be that as it may, the lines delineating what took place are blurred beyond recognition after that encounter with the mercenaries. Officially, no one knows what happened at the villa, other than that a prominent citizen—a very successful merchant banker—seems to have been hauled from his bed by raiding bandits who penetrated his estate's defences and dragged him down into a cellar, where they tortured him and killed him.

"The unofficial, speculative reports cite something radically different. Apparently the searchers found a man awaiting them when they arrived at the villa in question. He was standing in full view, unarmed and dressed completely in white, and when the lead party arrived he raised his hand, in which he held a scroll of some kind, and asked permission to approach the commanding legate. Given the appropriate permission, he handed the scroll to Talus, who examined it with great care, several times, and then nodded, formally accepting it. The waiting man then led the searchers down into the bowels of the villa, where they found the naked body of a grotesquely fat man. He had been castrated and his throat was cut so deeply that his head was almost completely severed.

"Then Talus, for reasons unknown at the time, instructed a squad of men to escort the unknown man, whoever he might have been, off the premises and deliver him safely to the nearest seaport."

The legate finished his wine and set down the cup, then stared into it for several moments. "That's my little tale," he said. "Short and mystifying as it is. And now I have to go. I hope I have not bored you, and I trust I have given you some food for thought, if only about the speculative aspects of rumour-mongering and the dissemination of truth."

"You have, and I thank you," Varrus said. "But may I ask you, why did you decide to tell this tale to me?"

Britannicus smiled. "Because it intrigued me when I heard it and, after thinking about it for several days, there is really no one else to whom I could tell it. It's hardly the kind of thing an imperial legate could discuss with his subordinates, is it? I find myself intrigued most of all, though, that the man whom they found waiting in the villa, so important to the exposure of all that followed, simply vanished—as had the courier. Were they one and the same?" He shrugged. "Perhaps no one will ever know the truth of that.

"As for the document he was holding, it was supposedly signed by the Emperor Constantine himself, if you can bring yourself to believe that. And it, too, has disappeared, lost somehow, with no blame assigned to anyone.

"Unofficially, though, and speculatively again, Talus's closest subordinate supposedly asked him afterwards what had transpired between him and the stranger, and was told that the fellow was leaving Gaul to make his way across the world, to Byzantium."

He smiled and stood up.

"And now I really must go, so let me thank you for your hospitality and for giving me the opportunity to spend a short time talking like a normal human being. Give my best wishes to your friend Marcus Licinius Cato, by the way, if ever you run into him again. I greatly enjoyed his company in the short time I spent with him. Farewell, Magister Varrus."

Acknowledgments

They say it is always unwise to deal in generalities, but I know that what I want to say here, general though it might be, is sound and true, because I've lived through it.

I've been lucky for years in having been able to dance lightly when this section of my novels came around, because I've largely been dealing—particularly in the post-Roman British books—with pretty obscure, sixteen-hundred-year-old material that generally lacks specific attribution and is forever open to interpretation, permitting me to put my own personal slant on whatever I've wanted to.

This time, though, I've decided it's time to step forward and acknowledge those people who, over the past quarter-century and more, have consistently influenced both my writing and my storytelling skills and, coincidental though it might seem, there is nothing accidental about the preponderance of Penguin Canada personnel in the list—Viking Press/Penguin Books has been my sole Canadian publisher and my major publisher throughout my career, though its name and influence have changed radically from time to time in recent years. That truth is reflected in what follows here.

The drafts of all my earliest efforts (I started writing my first novel, *The Skystone*, back around 1975 or '76,) fell categorically into what is now the virtually extinct genre of "Men's Books," in that they were invariably written with a predominantly male readership in mind. It was taken for granted by almost everyone then that women had no interest in spending their valuable time reading sweeping works of non-academic but exhaustively researched historical fiction that featured (mostly) male protagonists.

And so I wrote Men's Books, because that is the background that existed then: I had learned to do things in what I saw then as the "right," traditional way, and that's how I proceeded: I wrote for my own amusement and satisfaction, fully aware of the challenges and the competitive standards involved, and I did so to the best of my ability, struggling to put together a well-crafted story that was different to anything ever written before on my chosen topic.

So I wrote alone and in private for close to fifteen years, and I guarded my work jealously, allowing less than a handful of close friends to see even glimpses of my scribblings during all that time.

But even then, that long ago, I was beholden to several women for shaping my progress.

Sword At Sunset was a novel published in the USA in 1963 by a writer called Rosemary Sutcliffe, and it was the first novel, ever, that physically shook me awake to the possibilities of the Arthurian tales I had always loved; it stimulated me to understand that there might be other, more subtle and therefore more effective ways of telling a story, eschewing the tried and true formulae of the "great" authors of historical fiction. Many of those, including such giants as Taylor Caldwell and George Eliot, had no other choice than to publish as "men" in order to see their work in print. But even then, a sprinkling of other women like Mary Stewart and Marion Zimmer Bradley had begun to make an impact on the market for Historical Fiction.

I was greatly honoured, therefore, when, I was invited by the editorial staff at Chicago Review Press to write a Foreword to their reprint of *Sword At Sunset*, published in 2008 to mark the 45th Anniversary of the book's original publication.

As long ago as 1990, at the insistence of my long-time friend Alma Lee, who ran the Vancouver Writers Festival for years, I attended my first Master Class for Writers, taught by the inimitable and irreplace-able Ursula K. Le Guin, who insisted, logically it seemed to me, that attendance at a Master Class should entail some kind of mastery over one's craft and its stock in trade, which was the manipulation and bewitchingly simple presentation of good old plain, highly-polished English. Ms Le Guin insisted, therefore, that her classes should be competitive, and attendance at them should essentially be something in the nature of a prize. I never forgot that, and my own work to this day is predicated upon what she taught me.

Brad Martin and Doug Gibson, two of the brightest male luminar-ies of Canadian publishing at that time, stood shoulder to shoulder with me initially in finding a suitable and appropriate publisher (no simple thing, since I was a totally unknown and unproven entity with a com-plex, bulky series of novels that essentially rewrote the entire Arthurian legend, without magic) but soon after that, I found myself surrounded by a sea of enormously competent, delightfully self-confident women editors, the most current of whom is Lara Hinchberger.

Cynthia Good was my original publisher at Penguin Books Canada, and under her leadership I soon came to know a legion of female edi-tors who set out collectively to civilize me, change my deplorable atti-tudes, and reshape my entire mindset on the matter of writing to, about, and for women. They included Catherine Marjoribanks, the substan-tive editor with whom I have now worked for twenty-six years, and her US counterpart at Tor Books in New York, Claire Eddy.

I remember Martin Gould, too, for being the artist—at that time he was Art Director of Penguin Canada—who first brought my per-sonal graphic designs and ideas to life, showing me how important my input was and is. What a joy it is to discern an idea for a template or a piece of cover art, and then see afterwards the influence it can generate in the hands of a professional illustrator/designer. I have not had the pleasure of working with Martin in more than a decade now, but I understand that he is a thriving, independent designer of books in

Ontario, and despite the highly-touted benefits of modern living, communications, and travel, I just don't get around much any more ... especially east of Winnipeg.

I have enjoyed working with a number of top-flight agents through the years, too, starting with Perry Knowlton of Curtis Brown Limited of New York, who died almost two decades ago, and including my current representatives, Russ Galen of CGG Literary Agency and Danny Baror of Baror International Inc., who handles my off-shore publishers. It was Russ Galen who who made it clear to me, years ago, that my livelihood consisted in deconstructing legends, not in building them ...

And finally, my personal thanks to the friends and colleagues I have garnered over a quarter-century of involvement with the Surrey International Writers Conference: Diana Gabaldon; Anne Perry; Ian Rankin; Guy Gavriel Kay; Hallie Ephron; Roberst McCammon; Michael Slade, AKA Jay Clark; Robert Dugoni; and a host of others. I feel honoured and privileged to have worked with each and every one of you.